MEDUSA
AND
THE DOOMED OASIS

Also by Hammond Innes

FICTION

Wreckers Must Breathe
The Trojan Horse
Attack Alarm
Dead and Alive
The Lonely Skier
Maddon's Rock
Killer Mine
The Blue Ice
The White South
The Angry Mountain
Air Bridge
Campbell's Kingdom
The Strange Land
The Wreck of the Mary Deare
The Land God Gave to Cain
Altlantic Fury
The Strode Venturer

Levkas Man
Golden Soak
North Star
The Big Footprints
The Last Voyage
Solomon's Seal
The Black Tide
High Stand
Medusa
Isvik
Target Antarctica

TRAVEL

Harvest of Journeys
Sea and Islands

HISTORY

The Conquistadors

HAMMOND INNES

Hammond Innes was born in Sussex in 1913. He has now written thirty international bestsellers, all being reissued by Pan. He has also written a superb history of the Conquistadors, two books of his world travels and sailing, and an evocative illustrated book on East Anglia. It was in the early fifties, with books like *The Lonely Skier, Campbell's Kingdom, The White South* and *The Wreck of the Mary Deare*, all of them filmed, that he achieved international fame.

HAMMOND INNES

MEDUSA

AND

THE DOOMED OASIS

PAN BOOKS

Medusa first published 1988 by William Collins & Co. Ltd.
First published in paperback by Pan Books 1996.
The Doomed Oasis first published 1960 by William Collins & Co. Ltd.
First published in paperback by Pan Books 1998.

This omnibus edition published 2003 by Pan Books
an imprint of Pan Macmillan Ltd
Pan Macmillan, 20 New Wharf Road, London N1 9RR
Basingstoke and Oxford
Associated companies throughout the world
www.panmacmillan.com

ISBN 0 330 43677 5

1 3 5 7 9 8 6 4 2

A CIP catalogue record for this book is available from
the British Library.

Printed and bound in Great Britain by
Mackays of Chatham plc, Chatham, Kent

MEDUSA

To
My wife's cousins,
the John Langs, father and son,
who, when in command, have done so
much over the years to involve
me in the work of the
Royal Navy.

CONTENTS

MENORCA

Ciudadela

Ferrerias

Cap d'Artrutx

Atlantic Sea

FRANCE

SPAIN

YUGOSLAVIA

Barcelona

ITALY

IBIZA

MALLORCA

MENORCA

CORSICA

Rome

Gibraltar

Balearic Isles

SARDINIA

Malaga

Algiers

NORTH AFRICA

SICILY

Mediterranean Sea

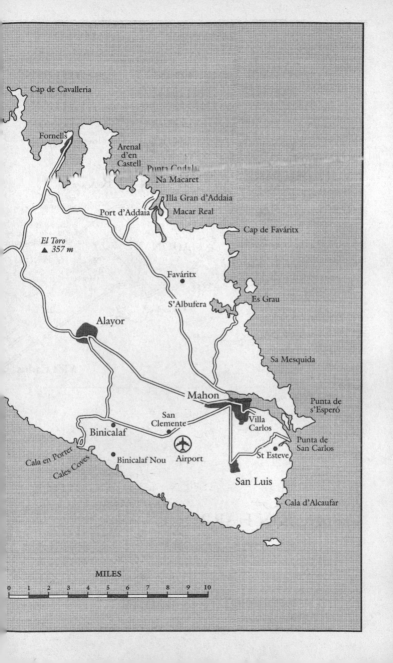

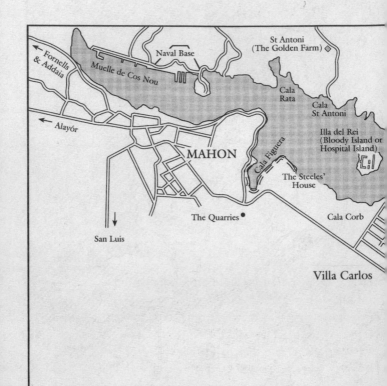

MAHON HARBOUR

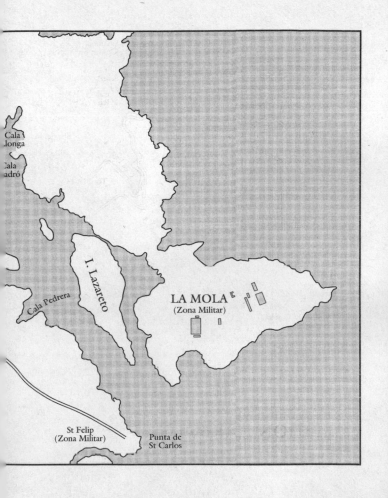

PART ONE

THUNDERFLASH

CHAPTER ONE

I was at the office window, looking out over the still waters of the harbour and watching a small boat break the reflection of Bloody Island's hospital ruins, when he drove up. It was our first real spring morning, the air fresh and clear, red roofs shining in the sun of the promontory opposite and the sounds of the port coming with great clarity across the water. He was driving one of those small Italian cars hired out to tourists and I watched idly as he backed it into the raw parking lot we had recently bulldozed out where the roadway stopped abruptly at the water's edge.

The local people had thought us mad to set up shop in this cul-de-sac on the east side of the Cala Figuera. It was so far from the main waterfront highway and almost overhung by the cliffs on which the small town of Villa Carlos was built. But we were close to the Atlante, one of the best restaurants in Mahon, and we had found that people liked an excuse to come to this rather wild little spot that gave them a totally different view of the harbour.

I glanced at my watch, looking down at him, still idly, as he got out of the car and stood there in the sunshine, gazing out to the small motor boat now clear of Bloody Island and cutting a broad arrow as it headed towards Cala Rata on the far side of the harbour. It was not yet eight, early for anybody to visit us on business, and at that hour you don't expect the arrival of somebody destined to shatter your whole life. Nevertheless, there was something about him, his hesitation perhaps, or the way he held himself – I couldn't take my eyes off the man.

He seemed to brace himself, closing the car door and turning abruptly. But instead of crossing the roadway, he stood there, still hesitant, his hair gleaming black in the sun. He had the sturdy compactness of a climber, or a man who played games, and he was good-looking; neatly dressed too, in blue trousers, white short-sleeved shirt open at the neck, and his bare arms had the paleness of somebody who had spent the winter in the north. He glanced up at the open window where I was standing. It was a big bay window we had built out over the roadway to give us more room in the tiny office. He could not help seeing me and he began to cross the road.

But then he checked, stood staring for a moment at the chandlery, then turned quickly and strode back to the car.

The door below me slammed shut and Carp came out, walking across the road to his motor bike, which was parked as usual against one of the old bollards. He was dressed in overalls with a thick cardigan over the top, the bald patch at the back of his head catching the sun.

Carp was the only Englishman we employed. He was an East Coast man, and that cardigan, or some form of woollen pullover, was never discarded until it was hot enough to melt the tar on the Martires Atlante opposite. He looked after our boats. His full name, of course, was Carpenter and he always left for the naval quay about this time of the morning. But instead of starting off immediately, he paused after jerking the bike off its stand, turning to look back at the driver of the Fiat.

For a moment the two of them were quite still, facing each other. Then the visitor reached out and opened the door of his car, ducking his head inside, searching for something, while Carp began to prop the bike up on its stand again. I thought he was going to speak to the man, but he seemed to think better of it. He shook his head slightly, half-shrugging as he kick-started the engine.

As soon as he was gone the visitor came out from the car's interior and shut the door again, standing quite still, watching until the motor bike disappeared round the bend by the restaurant. He was frowning, his rather square, clean-cut features suddenly creased with lines. He turned slowly, facing towards me, but not looking up, and he just stood there, still frowning, as though unable to make up his mind. Finally, almost reluctantly it seemed, he started across the road.

Our premises were the only buildings there, so I called down to him and asked if he wanted something from the chandlery.

He checked abruptly, head back, looking straight up at me. 'Am I too early?' He said it as though he would have been glad of an excuse to postpone his visit.

'The door's not locked,' I said.

He nodded, still standing there. Only a few years separate us in age, but at that first meeting he seemed very young.

'What is it you want?'

'Just a chart.' He said it quickly. 'Of Mahon and Fornells. And one of the island as a whole if you have it. Admiralty Charts 1466 and 1703.' He rattled the numbers off, then added, all in a rush, 'Are you Michael Steele?'

I nodded, looking beyond him to the sharp-cut shadows of the old hospital, the peace of the harbour, resenting his intrusion. It was such a lovely morning and I wanted to get out on the water.

'I think you know a Mr Philip Turner.' He said it hesitantly.

'Phil Turner?'

'Yes, owns a yacht called *Fizzabout*. If I could have a word with you . . .' His voice trailed away.

'All right, I'll come down.' Two years back I had skippered *Fizzabout* in the Middle Sea Race and Phil had laid up with us the following winter.

It was dark on the stairs after the sunlight. The bell over the door rang as he entered the chandlery and Soo called out to me from the kitchen to check that I was answering it. Ramón usually looked after this side of the business, but I had sent him over to Binicalaf Nou with the materials for a villa we were repainting. 'So you're a friend of Phil's,' I said as I reached the trestle table that did service as a counter.

There was a long pause, then he muttered, 'No, not exactly.' He was standing just inside the door, his back to the light and his face in shadow. 'It was Graham Wade suggested I contact you. He and Turner, they both belong to the Cruising Association. Have you met Wade?'

'I don't think so.'

Another long pause. 'No, I thought not.' And he just stood there as though he didn't know how to proceed.

'You wanted some charts,' I reminded him. 'The large scale chart of Port Mahon and Fornells also gives details of the passage between Ibiza and Formentera.' I knew the details of it because there was a regular demand for that particular sheet. I produced it for him, also Chart 1703 which covers the whole of the Balearics. 'Where's your boat?' I asked him. 'At the Club Maritimo?'

He shook his head, and when I asked him where he was berthed, he said, 'I haven't got a boat.'

'You on a package tour then?'

'Not exactly.' He produced a wad of peseta notes and paid for the charts, but he didn't leave. 'Wade said you'd been living here quite a few years. He thought you'd be the best person to contact – to find out about the island.'

'What do you want to know?' I was curious then, wondering why he wanted charts when he hadn't got a boat.

He didn't give me a direct answer. 'Your wife, she's half Maltese, isn't she?' He said it awkwardly, and without waiting for a reply stumbled quickly on – 'I mean, you must know Malta pretty well.'

'I was born there,' I told him.

He nodded and I had the feeling he already knew that part of my background.

'Why? Do you know it?' I enquired.

'I've just come from there.' He glanced out of the window, his face catching the light and reminding me suddenly of Michelangelo's David in Florence, the same straight brows, broad forehead and the wavy, slightly curling hair. It was an attractive face, the classic mould only broken by the lines developing at the corners of mouth and eyes. 'Grand Harbour,' he said. 'It's not so big as Mahon.' His voice, still hesitant, had an undercurrent of accent I couldn't place.

'No. This is one of the biggest harbours in the Mediterranean. That's why Nelson was here.' I still thought he was connected with sailing in some way. 'It's not as big as Pylos on the west coast of the Peloponnese, of course, but more sheltered. The best of the lot I'd say.'

His eyes, glancing round the chandlery, returned to me. 'You've done a lot of sailing, have you? I mean, you know the Mediterranean?'

'Pretty well.'

He didn't pursue that. 'Wade said you rented out villas.'

'Depends when you want to rent. Our main business, apart from boats, is villa maintenance. We only own two villas ourselves and they're fairly well booked. I'll get my wife down if you like. She looks after the renting of them.'

But he was shaking his head. 'No, sorry – I'm not wanting to rent.'

'Then what do you want?' I asked, glancing rather pointedly at the clock on the wall.

'Nothing. Just the charts.' I had rolled them up for him and he reached out, but then changed his mind, pushing his hand into his hip pocket and coming up with a photograph. 'Have you met this man – on the island here?' He handed me the photograph. It was a full-face picture, head and shoulders, of a big, bearded man wearing a seaman's peaked cap, a scarf round his neck and what looked like an anorak or some sort of dark jacket.

'What makes you think I might have met him?' I asked.

'Wade thought, if he was here, perhaps he'd have chartered a yacht from you, or he might have come to you about renting a villa.'

'We haven't any yachts for charter, only an old converted fishing boat,' I told him. 'As for villas, there are thousands here, and a lot of people doing what we do – care and maintenance.' The man in the photograph looked as though he had seen a lot of life, a very strong face with big teeth showing through the beard, eyes deeply wrinkled at the corners and lines across the forehead. There was something about the eyes. They were wide and staring, so that they seemed to be looking out at the world with hostility. 'What's his name?' I asked.

He didn't reply for a moment, then he gave a little shrug. 'Evans. Patrick Evans. Or Jones. Sometimes Jones – it varies. I thought he might be in Malta.' He shook his head. 'Wade said if he wasn't in Malta I'd probably find him here.'

'He's Welsh, is he?' I was still looking down at the photograph, puzzled by something in that hard stare that seemed vaguely familiar. Then, because of the silence, I looked up. 'A friend of yours?'

He seemed to have some difficulty answering that, his eyes slipping away from me. 'I've met him,' he muttered vaguely, picking up the charts and tucking the roll under his arm. 'Let me know, will you, if he turns up.' And he added, 'You can keep the photograph.'

I asked him where I could get in touch with him and he scribbled his address on a sheet of paper I tore out of our receipts book. It was in Fornells, a private address, not a hotel. And he had written his name – Gareth Lloyd Jones. 'Perhaps we could have a drink together sometime,' he suggested. Then he was walking out with an easy, almost casual wave of the hand, all the hesitancy gone as though relieved to get away from me and out into the sunshine.

I watched him drive off and then my gaze returned

to the photograph. Soo called down that coffee was ready. Weekdays coffee was all we had in the morning. Sunday was the only day we treated ourselves to an English breakfast. I went back upstairs, and when I showed her the photograph, she said without a moment's hesitation, 'I'm sure he didn't have a beard.'

I took it to the window, looking at it in the clear sunlight, trying to visualise the man clean-shaven. 'The eyes were different, too,' she said, joining me at the window, the bulge of her pregnancy showing through the looseness of her dressing gown.

'Who is he?'

'Es Grau, don't you remember?' And she added, 'You're not concentrating.'

'How the hell can I?' I gave her bottom a smack, caught hold of one buttock and pulled her close so that her stomach was hard against me. 'Any kicks yet?'

She thrust herself clear, turning quickly and pouring the coffee. 'He was in that little bar-restaurant where they haul the boats up. It was raining and we had a cup of coffee and a Quinta there after we'd looked at that villa out near S'Albufera. Now do you remember? He was with two or three Menorquins.'

She poured me my coffee and I stood sipping it, staring down at the photograph. I remembered the man now, but only vaguely. I had been more interested in the other two. One was Ismail Fuxá. I had never met him, but I had recognised him instantly from pictures in the local press. He was a member of the *Partido Socialista*, on the extreme left of the party and very active politically. My attention, however, had been focused on the little man sitting with his back to the window. I was almost certain he was the fellow I had chased one evening out near Binicalaf Nou. It had been dusk and I had stopped off to check one of the two villas we had under care in that neighbourhood. As I let myself in through the front door he had jumped out of a side window. He had had to run right past me and I had had a brief glimpse of his face looking scared. I went after him of course, but he had a motor bike parked down the dirt road and he'd got away from me.

When I returned to the villa and went into the big downstairs room I found he had sprayed *URBANIZAR ES DESTRUIER* right across one wall, and below that the letters *SALV* . . . I knew the rest of it by heart, so many villas had been sprayed with it – *SALVEMO MENORCA*. 'Yes,' I said. 'I remember now. But it was months ago, last autumn.' I was thinking of all that had happened since, the orchestrated build-up of hostility by the separatists. 'That was the first,' I added, gazing out at the limpid harbour water where a cruise ship showed white against the far shore.

'The first what?' Her back was turned as she filled her cup.

'The first of our villas to be daubed.'

'They've only sprayed two of them, and they're not ours anyway. We only look after them.' She turned, cup in hand, pushing her dog out of the way with a bare foot. It was a basenji so we called it Benjie and it slept on her bed, a pleasant little fellow all dressed in *café-au-lait* with a long, serious head, a perpetual frown, spindly legs and a curlycue of a tail. It was barkless and I could never understand the purpose of a dog that was a virtual mute. 'I've got something in mind,' she said. 'I want to talk to you about it.'

I knew what was coming then and turned my back on her, gazing out of the window again. 'Just look at it!'

'Look at what? You haven't been listening.'

'The morning,' I said. 'The sun on the water, everything crystal bright.' And I began to sing, *'Oh, what a bootiful mornin', Oh, what a bootiful day ...* Remember that moonlit evening in the courtyard of your mother's house, the old gramophone?' I tried to grab her, thinking to take her mind off her obsession with property. But she evaded me, eyes gone black and suddenly wide, hands across her belly. 'Go on,' she said. 'Finish it, why don't you?'

'I got a bootiful feelin', Everything's goin' ma way.'

She came back to the window then, gazing out, but not seeing the sunshine or the golden gleam of the water. 'That's the feeling I've got,' she said, and she was looking straight at me. 'Miguel rang last night.' I could see it in her eyes. For weeks she had been on at me to take advantage of the rash of villas that had recently come on to the market. She put her cup down, then turned to face me again. 'It was just before you came in. I didn't tell you because we were already late for the Rawlings', and afterwards ... Well, it wasn't the moment, was it?'

'What did Miguel want?' Miguel Gallardo was the contractor we used when there was maintenance work we couldn't handle ourselves. He was now building a villa out on Punta Codolar, a bare, bleak headland in the north of the island that was crisscrossed with the half-completed roads of a new *urbanización*.

'He needs help,' she said.

'Money?'

She nodded. 'It's all this build-up of trouble in the Med, of course – Libya in particular. The American he's building for has suddenly got cold feet and wants out. He's offering Miguel the whole place in lieu of what he owes him.' She reached out, her fingers gripping my arm as though she had hold of the villa already. 'I had a look at it with Petra when you were delivering that boat to Ajaccio, and now he says we can have it, as it stands, at cost. We pay Miguel's account, and that's that – it's ours.' She gave me the figure then, adding, 'It's a chance in a million, Mike.'

'Miguel to complete, of course.'

'Well, that's only fair.'

'It's barely half-completed, remember.' But it wasn't the cost of completion I was thinking about. It was the political tension building up locally. 'There's been windows broken, one villa set on fire, another smashed down by a runaway road roller . . .'

'That's just a passing phase.' I shook my head, but she went on quickly: 'It won't last, and when the panic is over, a lot of people will be cursing themselves for putting their villas on the market at knockdown prices. I'm thinking of the future.' The cups and plaques on the shelves behind her glimmered bright with memories of days gone. What future? She kept them so well polished I sometimes felt it was the crack shot, the Olympic sailor, the image she had of me, not myself, not the essential lazy, mediocre, ill-educated – oh hell, what deadly blows life deals to a man's self-confidence! Maybe she was right, polish the mirror-bright image, retain the front intact and forget the human freight behind. And now she wasn't thinking of us, only of the child. She had less than two months to go, and if this was another boy, and he lived . . . I hesitated, looking out to the bay. She had a good head for business and a highly developed sense for property, but politically – she was a fool politically. 'It's too lovely a day to argue,' I said, thinking of the smell of cut grass on the Bisley Ranges, the whiff of cordite in the hot air, gun oil and the targets shimmering.

'You're going sailing, is that it?' Her tone had sharpened.

A bit of a breeze was coming in, ruffling the water so that the surface of the harbour had darkened. She had always resented the sailing side of my life, my sudden absences. 'I'll take the dinghy, and if the wind holds I'll sail across to Bloody Island, see how the dig's going. You coming?' She enjoyed day sailing, for picnics and when the weather was fine.

'Petra's not there,' she said.

The phone rang and she answered it, speaking swiftly in Spanish. A long silence as she listened. Then she turned to me, her hand over the mouthpiece. 'It's Miguel. He's had a firm offer.'

The bell sounded from below and a voice called to me urgently from the chandlery. 'Tell him to take it then,' I said as I went down the stairs to find Ramón standing at the back of the workshop by the storeroom door, his teeth showing long and pointed as he smiled nervously. He had picked up Lennie, the Australian who did most of our repainting, but when they had arrived at the villa near Binicalaf Nou they had found the patio door ajar. It had been forced open and one of the bedrooms had been occupied. Both beds had been used, sheets and blankets grubby with dirt, a filthy pile of discarded clothes lying in a corner, and in the bathroom a tap left running, the basin overflowing, the floor awash. He had left Lennie clearing up the mess and had come back to pick up lime, cement and sand, all the materials they would need to replaster the kitchen ceiling immediately below.

We went through into the store, which was virtually a cave hacked out of the cliff that formed the back wall of the building. I don't know what it had been originally, probably a fisherman's boathouse, but it was bone dry and very secure, almost like having a private vault. As we went in Ramón said, 'No good, these people, señor. They make much dirt.' And he added, 'I not like.' His long face was tight-lipped and uneasy.

If only I had gone for a sail earlier . . . But it would probably have made no difference. There are days in one's life, moments even, when a whole series of small happenings come together in such a way that in retrospect one can say, that was the start of it. But only in retrospect. At the time I was just angry at the way Soo had acted. Instead of telling Miguel to take the offer, she had called out to me as she put the phone down, 'I've told him we'll match it.' She came halfway down the stairs then, clutching at the guard rope, her eyes bright, her mouth set in that funny way of hers that produced holes like dimples at the corners of her mouth, adding breathlessly, 'I'm sure we'll get it now. I'm sure we will.'

I was on my way out to the car with a cardboard box of the things Lennie would need and I stood there, staring up at her flushed, excited face, thinking how quickly one's life can be caught up in a web of material responsibilities so that there is no time left for the things one really wants to do. But it was no use arguing with her in that mood, her big, very white teeth almost clenched with determination, and in the end I went out, kicking the door to behind me.

My anger drained away as I headed out of Mahon on the San Clemente road, the sun a welcome change after weeks of cloud and blustery outbreaks of rain. The sudden warmth had brought the wild flowers out, the green of the fields a chequerboard of colour, yellow mainly, but here and there white splashes of narcissi. And there were kites hanging in the blue of the sky.

I passed the talayots by Binicalaf, my spirits lifting as they always did approaching this area of concentrated megalithic remains, the stone beehive-like mounds standing sharply outlined. The place where Lennie was working was on a track to the west of Cales Coves. It was about the nicest of the fifty or so villas we looked after. From the main bedroom you could just see the first of the coves, the cliffs beyond showing the gaping holes of several caves. He had cleared up most of the mess by the time I arrived, the sodden plaster stripped from the kitchen ceiling. It could have been worse, but it was unfortunate the squatters had picked on this particular villa, the owner being a man who argued over almost every item on his account. 'Where are the clothes they left behind?' I asked, wondering whether it was worth bringing the *Guardia* into it.

Lennie showed me a dirt-encrusted bundle of discarded clothing. He had been over it carefully, but had found nothing to indicate who the men were. 'Looks like they been digging. Two of them, I reck'n.' He thought perhaps the rains had flushed them out of one of the caves. Some of the old cave dwellings were still used and in summer there were women as well as men in them, kids too, often as not the whole family wandering about stark naked. 'It's like snakes out in the bush,' he muttered, holding up a filthy remnant of patched jeans. 'Always discarding their old skin. There's usually bits and pieces of worn-out rag below the cave entrances.'

In the circumstances there didn't seem much point in notifying the authorities. Lennie agreed. 'What the hell can they do? Anyway, look at it from their point of view, why should they bother? It's another foreign villa broken into, that's all. Who cares?' And then, as I was leaving, he suddenly said, 'That girl you're so keen on, mate—' and he grinned at me slyly. 'The archy-logical piece wot's digging over by the old hospital . . .' He paused there, his pale eyes narrowed, watching for my reaction.

He was referring to Petra, of course. The huge, hulking ruins of the old hospital were what had given Illa del Rei the nickname of Bloody Island. 'Well, go on,' I said. 'What about her?'

'Workmen up the road say they've seen her several times. I was asking them about these two bastards.' He tossed the bundle of rags into the back of my estate car. 'They couldn't tell me a damned thing, only that a girl in a Der Chevoh had been going into one of the caves. And this morning, just after Ramón and I got here, she come skidding to a halt wanting to know where she could find you. She was bright-eyed as a cricket, all steamed up about something.'

'Did she say what?'

He shook his head, the leathery skin of his face stretched in a grin. 'You want to watch it, mate. You go wandering around in them caves alone with a sheila like that and you'll get yourself thrown out of the house – straight into the drink, I wouldn't wonder.'

'Soo wouldn't even notice.' I couldn't help it, my voice suddenly giving vent to my anger. 'She's just bought a villa and now I've got to go over there and sort out the details.'

'Don't push your luck,' he said, suddenly serious. He looked then, as he often did, like an elderly tortoise. 'You go taking that girl on your next delivery run . . . Yeah, you thought I didn't hear, but I was right there in the back of the shop when she asked you. You do that and Soo'd notice all right.'

I caught hold of his shoulder then, shaking him. 'You let your sense of humour run away with you sometimes. This isn't the moment to have Soo getting upset.'

'Okay then, mum's the word.' And he gave that high-pitched, cackling laugh of his. Christ! I could have hit the man, he was so damned aggravating at times, and I was on a short fuse anyway. I had been going through a bad patch with Soo ever since she'd found she was pregnant again. She was worried, of course, and knowing how I felt about having a kid around the place, a boy I could teach to sail . . .

I was thinking about that as I drove north across the island to Punta Codolar, about Lennie, too, how tiresome he could be. Australian – born of Irish parents, claiming his name was McKay and with a passport to prove it, we knew no more of his background than when he had landed from the Barcelona ferry almost two years ago with nothing but the clothes he stood up in and an elderly squeezebox wrapped in a piece of sacking. I had found him playing for his supper at one of the quayside restaurants, a small terrier of a man with something appealing about him, and when I said I needed an extra hand scrubbing the bottoms of the boats we were fitting out, he had simply said, 'Okay, mate.' And that was that. He had been with us ever since, and because he was a trained scuba diver he was soon indispensable, being able to handle yachts with underwater problems without their having to be lifted out of the water. It was just after Soo had lost the child and she had taken to him as she would have to any stray, regarding him virtually as one of the family.

While the distance between Port Mahon in the east and the old capital of Ciudadela in the west is at least fifty kilometres, driving across the island from south to north it is only about twenty. Even so it always seems longer, for the road is narrow and winding and you have to go through Alayór, which is the third largest town and the central hub of the island. I toyed with the idea of dropping off at the Flórez garage to see if I could get him to increase his offer for the *Santa Maria*. Juan Flórez, besides being *alcalde*, or mayor of the town, ran the largest garage outside of Mahon and was a very sharp dealer in almost anything anybody cared to sell that was worth a good percentage in commission. For the past few months he had been trying to persuade me to part with the old fishing boat I let out on charter. But the sun was shining, so I drove straight across the main Ciudadela–Mahon road and up through the old town to the Fornells road.

Here the country changes very noticeably, the earth suddenly becoming a dark red, and away to the left, Monte Toro, the highest point on Menorca, the only 'mountain' in fact, with its rocky peak capped by the white of the Sanctuary buildings and the army communications mast dominating the whole countryside, red soil giving way to gravel after a few kilometres, cultivated fields to pines and maquis, the scent of resin and rosemary filling the car.

It is the constant variety of the scene in such a small island that had attracted us in the first place, particularly Soo after living most of her life on an island that is about the same size, but solidly limestone with very little variation. Just short of Macaret, and in sight of the sea again, I turned left on to the road to Arenal d'en Castell, a beautiful almost perfectly horseshoe-shaped bay of sand totally ruined by three concrete block hotels. Beyond the bay, on the eastern side, a rocky cape that had once been hard walking was now crisscrossed with half-finished roads so that one could drive over most of it. The few villas that had been built so far looked very lost in the wild expanse of heath and bare, jagged rock.

The villa Miguel Gallardo was now building stood right on the point, a little south and east of one he had completed two years before. There was a turning place nearby, but instead of swinging round it, I edged the car into the cul-de-sac beyond where it dipped steeply to the cliff edge. A tramontana was beginning to blow and even before I had switched the engine off I could hear the break of the waves two hundred feet or so below. I sat there for a moment, looking out towards the coast of France, remembering how it had been two years ago when I had taken a boat over to Genoa and a tramontana had caught us, a full gale, straight off the Alps and as cold as hell. We had been lucky to get away with it, the boat leaking and one of the spreaders broken so that we could only sail on the port tack.

I put the handbrake hard on, turned the wheels into the rubble of rock at the roadside and got out of the car, the breeze ruffling my hair, the salt air filling my lungs. God! It felt good, and I stretched my arms. There were little puffs of cloud on the horizon, the scene very different from the quiet of the southern coast, no protection at all. The *urbanización*, when it was built, would be facing the open sea and the full brunt of the north winds, so why the hell buy a villa here? I tried to see it in summer, all white stucco and red tiles, cacti on the retaining wall, passion flowers and bougainvillaea, with trailers of morning-glory over a Moroccan-style façade. It would be cool in summer and a breathtaking view, the dreadful hotels of Arenal d'en Castell hidden by the headland and the rock coast stretching east all the way to the lighthouse of Faváritx on the dragon-toothed finger of land after which it was named.

The engine of Miguel's cement mixer started into life and I climbed back up the slope, making for the gaunt skeletal structure of the half-completed villa. He was waiting for me at the foot of a ladder lashed to the wooden scaffolding. '*Buenos dias*. You come to inspect, eh?' He was a thickset man with a long, doleful face and a big hooked nose. He was from Granada, from the Arab district of Albacein, and claimed kinship with both Moors and Jews, his family going back five centuries to Ferdinand and Isabella and the Inquisition that followed their conquest of the last Moorish stronghold in Europe. 'Iss your property now.' He said it hesitantly, seeking confirmation, the inflexion of his voice making it a question rather than a statement.

'Let's have a look at it,' I said.

I saw the sudden doubt in his eyes, his dark,

unshaven features solemn and uneasy. 'Okay, señor.'
The formality was a measure of his unease. He normally called me by my Christian name. 'But you have
seen it before, also the plans.'

'I didn't know I was buying it then.'

'And now you are?' Again the question in his voice,
the dark eyes watching me, his broad forehead creased
in a frown.

'Let's have a look at it,' I said again. 'Starting at
the top.'

He shrugged, motioning me to go ahead of him.
The scaffolding shook as we climbed to the first storey,
the heat-dried wooden poles lashed with ropes. Everything – boards, scaffolding, ladders – was coated with
a dusting of cement that only half-concealed the age-
old layers of splashed paint. A younger brother,
Antoni, and a cousin whose name I could not remember, were rendering the southern face of the building.

'It will be a very beautiful villa,' Miguel said tentatively. 'When we have finished it, you will see, it will
look – pretty good, eh?' He prided himself on his
English.

We climbed to the top, and he stood there looking
about him. He was one of a family of thirteen. Back
in Granada his father had a tiny little jewellery shop in
one of those alleys behind the Capila Real, mostly
second-hand stuff, the window full of watches with
paper tags on them. I think his real business was
money-lending, the contents of the shop largely personal items that had been pawned. '*Buena vista*, eh?'
And Miguel added, 'You can have a garden here. The

roof is flat, you see. And the lookout . . . all that sea.'
His tone had brightened, knowing I was a sailor.

'There is also a fine view of the water tanks on the
top of those bloody hotels at Arenal d'en Castell.'

'You grow some vines, you never see them.'

'In tubs and trained over a trellis? Come off it,
Miguel. The first puff of wind out of the north . . .'

He looked away uncomfortably, knowing how
exposed the position was. 'It will be nice and cool in
summer. It was good here when we make foundations.'

We worked our way down to the ground floor,
which was almost finished. He was using one of the
rooms as an office and we went over the costings. I
suggested certain adjustments, chiefly to the lighting,
cut out the air-conditioning and one or two other
luxuries I considered unnecessary, agreed a price for
completion, and we shook hands on it.

There was never any need to have Miguel put anything into writing. His family had been small traders
on the banks of the Darro and in the Plaza Bib-Rambla
for generations. I had first met him when he was filling
in as a guide to the Alhambra Palace and the General-
ife. Then a few days later I had found him working
on repairs to a building near his home, which was in
the Cuesta Yesqueros, a stepped alley running steeply
up the hillside opposite the old Puerta Monaita. I was
staying at the Alhambra Palace Hotel at the time,
waiting for an Italian to turn up who owed me quite
a lot of money, and to this day I have no idea whether
I was the cause of Miguel shifting to Menorca or

not. He had never mentioned it, but I think it highly probable.

'Who was it made you the offer my wife agreed to match?' I asked him as he accompanied me back to the car. 'Or did you make that up?'

'No, of course I don't make up.' He glared at me angrily. 'You know me too long to think I play games like that.'

'Well then, who was it?'

'Somebody I don't trust so much.'

I got it out of him in the end. It was Flórez. And then, as I was settling myself behind the wheel, he leaned forward, peering over my shoulder at the back seat, his eyes narrowed and a frown on his face. 'A friend of yours?'

I turned to find I had tossed the photograph Lloyd Jones had left with me into the back and it was lying there face-up. 'You know him, do you?' I asked.

He shook his head, the frown deepening.

'It was probably taken some time ago,' I told him. 'He may not have a beard now.'

'No beard, eh?' I saw the dawn of recognition in his eyes and he nodded. '*Si. No barba.*' He looked at me then. 'Who is, plees?'

'You've seen him, have you?'

He glanced at the picture again, then nodded emphatically.

'When?'

'A month ago, maybe more. He come here and look over the work. Say he knows the owner and he want to see the progress we make in the construction of the villa as he is thinking he will make Señor Wilkins an offer.'

'Did he say how much he was prepared to offer?'

'No, he don't say.'

'What was his name? Do you remember?'

But he shook his head. He had been into Macaret that day to phone his suppliers and he had come back to find the man standing on the scaffold's upper staging staring eastward, out towards Faváritx. It was only when he had asked him what he was doing there that the man said anything about making an offer.

'And he didn't give his name?'

'No. I ask him, but he don't answer me. Instead, he speak of making Señor Wilkins an offer. I have not seen him since that day.'

He couldn't tell me anything else and I drove off after confirming that I'd get my lawyer to draw up something we could both sign. A bank of cloud was spreading across the sky, and as I approached the main Mahon–Fornells road the sun went in. The still beauty of the morning was gone and I gave up any thought of sailing. Instead, I headed westward through the pines to Fornells.

Ever since Lloyd Jones had given me the address where he was staying I had been puzzled as to why he had chosen the place. Fornells is a little fishing port almost halfway along the north coast. It has the second largest inlet, five of the best fish restaurants on the island and is the Menorquins' favourite place for Sunday lunch. Who had told him about it? I wondered. Since he wasn't staying at a hotel, and had clearly

never been to Menorca before, Phil or Wade, somebody, must have told him about the private lodgings
where he was staying in the Calle des Moli.

I kept to the main street through Fornells and asked
my way of a waiter I knew who was leaning against
the door of the restaurant that stands back from the
harbour. The Calle des Moli proved to be a narrow
little back street leading nowhere, except to the
remains of a windmill and a bare hill topped by one
of those stone round towers that dominate several of
the island's headlands. The houses were small and
stood shoulder-to-shoulder, their doors opening
straight on to the street.

I left my car in the Plaza de Pedro M. Cardona.
The address he had given me was near the top end,
the door standing open and a little girl sitting on the
step nursing a rag doll. The woman who answered my
knock was big and florid. '*El señor Inglés?*' She shook
her head. I had just missed him. He had been out all
morning, had returned about half an hour ago and
had then gone out again almost immediately, leaving
his car parked in the street. She indicated the small
red Fiat parked a few doors up.

I glanced at my watch and was surprised to find
the morning had gone. It was already past noon and
since she said she didn't provide meals for her visitors,
and he had left his car, I presumed he was lunching at
one of the restaurants in the port. I asked her how
long he had been staying at her house and she said he
had arrived the previous afternoon about five-thirty.

No, he hadn't booked in advance. There was no necessity since it was early in the year for visitors.

I produced the photograph then, but she shook her head. She had never seen the man, and she didn't know how long her visitor would be staying, so I left her and drove back to the harbour where I found him at a table outside the better of the two waterfront restaurants. He was alone, bent over one of the charts I had sold him, which was neatly folded and propped against the carafe of wine in front of him. He looked up quickly at my greeting, then half rose to his feet. I pulled up a chair and sat down, enquiring whether he had had a rewarding morning.

He nodded vaguely, telling me that since I had last seen him he had driven round Villa Carlos, then on to the little inlet of St Esteve immediately to the south, had had a look at the tunnelled redoubt known as Marlborough's Fort, and finally, before coming back to Fornells for lunch, he had been all round the small fishing port of Es Grau to the north of Mahon. He spoke quickly, giving me a very precise inventory of his morning's tour as though he were making a report, and all the time he was staring past me, out towards the light at the end of the eastern arm of the harbour. There was a girl in a wet suit board-sailing across the entrance, a glistening, statuesque figure, the orange sail bright in the sun. But I don't think he saw her. I had a strange feeling he was talking for the sake of talking, as though he sensed what I had come to tell him and was putting it off.

The waiter appeared with a plate of four large

mussels cooked with herbs and garlic. 'Will you join me?' The clouds were gone now and it was quite warm again sitting there in the sun, the town and the hill behind it sheltering us from the wind. I nodded and he said, '*Dos*,' holding up two fingers in case he had not made his meaning clear. After that he didn't say anything, the silence hanging heavy in the air as the waiter filled a glass for me. When he was gone I produced the photograph. 'When was that taken?' I asked him.

He shook his head. 'Several years ago, I imagine.'

'Is he a seaman? He certainly looks like one with that peaked cap.'

He didn't say anything.

'What's he do for a living then?'

He gave a little shrug, his head turned towards the harbour entrance again.

'But you do know him?'

'Of course.' He hesitated, then he added, 'We were at school together, you see.'

'You know him quite well then?'

'Well enough.' The words seemed forced out of him. 'He saved my life – not once, but twice.' His eyes were blank, his mind turned inwards.

'He hasn't got a beard now,' I said.

He turned his head then, a quick movement, his eyes staring straight at me, hard now and grey in the sunshine. 'You've seen him.' It wasn't a question. He knew, and suddenly he seemed a different man, no longer hesitant, his voice sharper, a note of authority in it. 'When? Recently? Within the last few days?'

'No. Several months ago.' And I told him about the three men Soo and I had seen that filthy wet day when we had gone into the bar-restaurant at Es Grau, and how Miguel had seen him more recently.

'Where?'

'On Punta Codolar.' And I told him about the villa Miguel was working on.

'Punta Codolar. Where's that? Show me.' He turned the chart towards me, but I pushed it away.

'It's only a few miles from here, the next headland to the east.'

'And he was at this villa. How long ago, did your builder friend say?'

'About a month.'

'He made an offer for it, for a half-finished villa?'

'So Miguel said.'

He opened the chart up, his stubby finger stabbing at the irregular shape of Punta Codolar. 'Why? Did he say why?' He didn't wait for me to answer, shaking his head – 'No. No of course not, he wouldn't tell you that. But the headland there is the western arm of Macaret and Port D'Addaia.' After that he didn't say anything. He seemed quite stunned, his eyes staring past me, seeing nothing.

'Better eat those while they're hot,' I said, indicating the *mejillones* in the little dish in front of him. 'They're very good, but it's important they should be piping hot.'

He nodded, picking up the small spoon and digging a mussel out of its shell, the movement quite automatic, his mind still far away. 'And you haven't seen him since the autumn?'

'No.'

'But the builder fellow saw him about a month ago. Has he seen him at all since then?'

'I don't think so. Miguel would have said if he had.'

'A month ago.' He repeated it slowly, chewing over a mussel, his eyes screwed up against the sun. 'And he was clean-shaven.' He gave a long sigh as though I had saddled him with some impossible burden. 'And when you and your wife saw him in that bar, who were the two men he was with – you said something about their being politically motivated. What exactly did you mean?'

I explained then about Ismail Fuxá, that he was supposed to be one of the leaders of the separatist movement.

'An activist?'

'I think so. But he keeps in the background.'

'And the other man?'

'I can't be certain,' I said, 'but he looked very much like a man I had surprised paint-spraying a slogan on the living-room wall of a villa we look after.' I started to explain how I'd only caught a glimpse of him, but he interrupted me.

'Where was this? Where's the villa he daubed?'

'Between Binicalaf and Binicalaf Nou.'

'Those names mean nothing to me.' He opened the chart out. 'Could you show me please.' I pointed to the position of the villa and he said, 'That's on the south side of the island, the opposite coast to Macaret. There's an inlet there.' He turned the map sideways so that he could read the name. 'Cales Coves. Do you know it?'

'Of course,' I said. 'I've sailed in there quite a few times. There are two inlets in fact, that's why Cales is plural. Coves refers to the caves.'

'I suppose you know just about all the inlets round Menorca.'

'Well, not quite all. There are over a hundred and fifty of them and not all are suitable for a deep-draught boat.' He enquired what sort of boat I had and when I said it was an old fishing boat, he asked me whether I hired it out to visitors.

'In the summer, yes,' I told him. 'The *Santa Maria* is not the ideal craft for charter work, but the sort of yacht I need to make that part of the business pay calls for far more money than we can afford. It's a risky game, a lot of competition.' He seemed more relaxed now, as though he had got used to the idea that the man he was trying to catch up with had been seen on the island. More mussels arrived and another carafe of wine, and he began asking me about other inlets to the south, particularly those closest to Mahon. Except for St Esteve he had only looked at the inlets to the north.

'How long have you been here?'

'Two days.'

The first day he had spent taking over his hire car and having a look at the peninsula that forms the northern arm of Port Mahon, the land that provided the view from our office window.

'What about the megalithic remains,' I asked him – 'the taulas, talayots and navetas?'

But he hadn't seen any of that, and I don't think he took it in when I told him the whole of Menorca was more or less an open-air archaeological museum. All he wanted me to talk about was the little ports and coves. For a man who hadn't got a boat, and who wasn't involved in sailing, it struck me as odd. I got to my feet, telling him I was going to phone my wife. 'I'll join you for lunch if I may, it's too late to go back home.'

When I got through to Soo she said she had Petra with her. 'She's waiting for the boat, and Mike – she wants to take you into a cave over by Cales Coves.'

'I know,' I said. 'Lennie told me. Said she was very excited about something. Has she told you what it is?'

'No. She can't explain it, you've got to see it, she says.'

I offered to return to Binicalaf and meet her there after lunch, but she said Petra had to get back to camp to get herself organised for the evening. 'You haven't forgotten we asked her to the Red Cross do tonight, have you?' There was the sound of muffled voices, then Soo added, 'She says she'll try and explain it to us this evening.' And then she was asking me about my meeting with Miguel.

When I got back to the table Lloyd Jones had refilled my glass and was sitting with his head in his hands staring fixedly out to sea. He didn't look up as

I sat down. The girl was still balanced on her sailboard, gliding effortlessly in towards the steps. Even then he didn't see her, while I was thinking how nice it would have been to have had her as a pupil when I was running my sailboard courses. 'Have you ordered?' I asked. The *mejillones* were merely an appetiser.

He shook his head. 'You know the place. Whatever you advise.' He didn't seem to care what he had, his mind far away, lost in his own thoughts.

I ordered *zarzuela* for us both, and because he didn't seem inclined to conversation, I began telling him a little about the megalithic remains and the hypostilic chamber Petra Callis was excavating by the fallen dolmen on Bloody Island.

The food arrived almost immediately, and because *zarzuela* is roughly a stew of mixed fish in a piquant sauce, we were too busy dealing with the bones to do much talking. He wasn't interested in Bronze Age remains anyway, and as soon as he had finished he pushed his plate aside and spread the chart out again. He thought he would have a look at the other side of the island after lunch. Somebody had told him about the Xorai caves above Cala en Porter.

'They're strictly for the tourists,' I told him. 'Anyway, they're not open at this time of year. If you want to see caves, you'd much better look into Cales Coves.' And because the track down to the first inlet isn't easy to find I gave him instructions how to get there.

He thought about that, concentrating on the chart. And then suddenly he asked me which of all the inlets on Menorca I would choose if I had to land something secretly from a boat, something to be delivered to Mahon.

It was so unexpected that I stared at him, wondering what the hell he had in mind. 'Are we talking about contraband?'

He hesitated. 'Yes, I suppose we are.' And he added, 'If you were going to land something secretly – ' His eyes were looking directly at me then. 'You ever run anything like that?'

I didn't say anything, suddenly wary. It was a long time ago, before I was married.

'If you had, I mean,' he said quickly, 'where would you have landed the stuff?' The tone of his voice had sharpened, so that it crossed my mind he could be a customs man attached to Interpol or something like that, his manner so abruptly changed to one of alertness, those grey eyes of his catching the sun again as hard as glass as they stared into mine. 'Well, where? I need to know.'

'Why?'

'That man you saw at Es Grau—' He stopped there. 'Well, where would you land it?'

By then I'd decided this was getting a little dangerous and I kept my mouth shut.

'I'm talking hypothetically, of course,' he went on. 'Let's say it's TV sets, something like that – something fairly heavy, fairly bulky . . . What about Cales Coves? You mentioned cave dwellings.'

I shook my head. 'Those caves are in the cliffs, at least all those that look directly out on to the water, so you'd have to haul everything up. And then you wouldn't be able to get the stuff ashore – I don't think any of them have a landward entrance. They're just holes in the cliff face or up in the sides of the ravine that leads down into the twin coves.'

'So where would you land it?'

He went on questioning me like that, claiming it was all hypothetical and the motivation nothing but his curiosity. At least it made for conversation. He no longer sat in silence brooding over whatever it was that filled his mind, and as he questioned me about the sparsely inhabited north coast to the west of Fornells, he made entries on the chart against each of the coves I mentioned, his writing small and very neat. In the end he shook his head. 'It would have to be closer to Mahon, wouldn't it – a short drive on a good road.' His pen shifted eastward across the great headland opposite where we were sitting. 'What about Arenal d'en Castell?' And when I told him it was overlooked by three large hotels, he asked about the two big bays south of Faváritx.

'Too rocky,' I told him. 'But Addaia – you go in there, almost to the end, and there's a new quay not yet finished, the place still quite wild and more or less deserted.'

'Not overlooked?'

'Two or three fishermen's houses converted to summer homes, that's all.'

'I don't see any quay shown on the chart.' I marked the position of it for him and he stared at it, finally nodding his head. 'I'll have a look at that after I've

seen those cliff caves.' He called for the bill and got
to his feet. 'That boat of yours. Has it got an echo-
sounder?'

'Of course. VHF, too, a big chart table, bunks for
six . . .'

'How much if I want to charter it – for a day, say?'

I told him it depended whether it was a bareboat
charter or fully stocked and crewed.

'Just you and me.' And then he seemed to change
his mind. 'Forget it. Just an idea.' He settled the bill,
insisting I was his guest, and on the spur of the
moment, as we were walking to the cars, I asked him
whether he would care to join us at the Red Cross
party that evening. 'It's run by a Menorquin friend of
ours, Manuela Renato,' I told him. 'Usually it's at a
dance hall and restaurant beyond Villa Carlos, but this
year she's organised it in the Quarries just above where
we live. Should be quite fun – barbecue, bonfire, dancing, fireworks, all in a huge great rock chamber that
looks like something hacked out for the tomb of a
pharaoh.'

Why I should have asked him, God knows. Curiosity, I suppose. The man was under pressure, I could
see it in his eyes, something hanging over him. And
the photograph. I tried to recall the scene in that bar,
but Soo and I had been discussing the villa we had
just looked over, and it was only when the three of
them were putting on their coats and going out into
the rain that I really took any notice of them.

We had reached my car and I stood there waiting
for his answer, trying to figure out from the hard jut

of his chin, the shape of that short neck and the solid head, the lines at the corners of his eyes and mouth, what sort of a man he really was. What did he do for a living? Above all, why was he here?

'All right,' he said finally. 'I'll come.' He didn't thank me, his acceptance almost grudging, as though he felt he shouldn't be wasting his time on such frivolities.

'Good,' I said. 'That's settled then. Eight-thirty at our place.' And I got into my car, never dreaming that my casual invitation would be the catalyst to something that would get completely out of hand.

He wasn't looking at me as I backed away from the water's edge and drove off. He had turned his head towards the harbour entrance again and was standing there, quite still, staring towards the horizon with an intensity that left me with the odd feeling that he was expecting some visitation from the sea.

The road from Fornells enters the outskirts of Mahon at the opposite end to where we live, and instead of heading straight along the waterfront, past the *Aduana*, the Customs House, and the commercial wharf, I turned left and drove out on to the naval quay where the boats we had laid up out of the water were parked. I drove straight up to the elderly Hillyard we were working on and called up to Carp. The Danish owner, who had picked the boat up cheap in Palma the previous autumn, had phoned me just before Christmas and I had promised to have it ready in time for him to leave for a family cruise in the Greek islands at Easter. We had left it a little late, particularly as there was a new engine to be installed.

I called again as I started up the ladder and Carp's tonsured head popped out of the wheelhouse. He was his usual gloomy self as he showed me another frame with its fastenings gone, also at least three deck beams that needed replacement. 'Won't ever finish in time, will we?' he grumbled as he indicated one of the knees rotted where water had been seeping from the deck above. 'And the engine still to be fiddled in, all the rigging. I'll 'ave to take Rod off of the American boat for that.'

I told him that was impossible. He already had Luis varnishing the brightwork. With Rodriguez, that would make two of our locals, as well as himself, working on the one boat. 'Well,' he said, looking me straight in the face, 'd'you want 'er finished on time, or don't you?' And he added, 'Up to you. I didn't promise nothing.'

In the end I agreed, as he knew I would. And all the time we were talking I had the feeling there was something else on his mind. It wasn't until I was leaving that he suddenly blurted it out – 'That man outside the shop this morning – did you see him? A little red car. He was there just as I left. Did he come into the shop?'

I was on the ladder then, beginning to climb down, my face almost level with the deck. 'Yes. I sold him a couple of charts.'

'Did he say who he was?' I told him the man's name and he nodded. 'Thort so. He must have recognised me, but he didn't want to know me, did he, so I thort I was mistaken.' He leaned out towards me. 'If it wasn't for me that man would've died of cold. Well, not just me. There was four of us in the pilot boat, see, but it was me wot cut him down off the Wood-bridge Haven buoy. Did he give you any sort of rank?'

'No,' I said, curious now and climbing back up the ladder.

'Mebbe he hasn't got one now. There was a lot of talk at the time.'

'About what?'

'Well, it was an arms run, wasn't it, and he was a Navy lieutenant.' And then he was telling me the whole story, how the Deben pilot at Felixstowe Ferry had seen something odd fixed to the Haven buoy and the four of them had gone out in the dawn to find a man fully clothed and tied to the side of the buoy with a mooring line. 'Poor bastard. We thort he was dead. Cold as buggery off the bar it was, the wind out of the north and beginning to whip up quite a sea. Then later, when he's out of hospital, he comes and buys us all a pint or two in the Ferryboat, so he knows bloody well I was one of those that rescued him. Funny!' he said. 'I mean, you'd think he'd come and say hullo, wouldn't you? I'd seen 'im before, too. When he were a little runt of a fella living with a no-good couple and their son on an old 'ouseboat in a mud creek back of the Ferryboat, an' I wasn't the only one that recognised him. That's what started tongues wagging.'

'How do you mean?'

'Well, you bin there, when you were looking for a

boat that spring. You know wot it's like there, an' a couple of kids, no proper man to control them. They broke into a yacht moored back of the Horse Sand and got at the drink locker. No harm done, but later they had a go at the RAF mess over at Bawdsey – for a lark they said. People remember that sort of thing.'

I didn't see what he was getting at. 'What's that got to do with arms-running?' I asked. 'You said something about arms-running.'

'That's right. But we didn't know about that at the time, did we? There was just a lot of rumours flying about on account of strangers poking around in the mud at the entrance to the King's Fleet. Then, after those terrorist attacks on police stations at Liverpool and Glasgow, and on that court in Clerkenwell, the papers were full of it. This Lieutenant Jones, he makes a statement, about how he'd been bird-watching an' had seen them unloading the arms at the King's Fleet, about half a mile inside the Deben mouth. It was an IRA gun run, you see, and they caught him watching 'em from the high bank of the river as they landed the stuff. That's how he come to be on the buoy. Didn't shoot him; instead, they threw him overboard out beyond the Deben bar, so he'd drown and it would look like an accident.'

He shook his head slightly, muttering to himself: 'Funny that – him not wanting to talk to me.' And then he brightened. 'Mebbe they sacked 'im. That'd account for it. There was a swarm of investorigaty journalists digging into his background, and some of the stories they ran . . .' He gave a little shrug and turned away, 'Well, better get on if we're ever goin' ter finish this job.' And without another word he went back to the wheelhouse and disappeared below.

Was that it? Was he now into some smuggling racket, having been forced to resign his commission? All those questions about coves and inlets . . . I was wondering about him as I drove home along the waterfront, wondering whether I would be able to get anything out of him during the evening.

CHAPTER TWO

He was punctual, of course, the bell of the chandlery sounding virtually on the dot of 20.30. I called down to him to come up, and introducing him to Soo, I said, 'Is it Mr Lloyd Jones or do you have anything in the way of a rank?'

'Gareth Lloyd Jones will do,' he said, smiling and taking Soo's outstretched hand. Some sort of a spark must have passed between them even then, her cheeks suddenly flushed and a bright flash of excitement in those dark eyes of hers as she said, 'I think you'll enjoy this evening. Manuela and her friends have done a great job of the preparations.' But I didn't take note of it at the time, still thinking about the way he had parried my question. If my suspicions were correct I wasn't at all sure I wanted to be seen entertaining a man who might land himself in trouble.

Petra was usually late and that evening was no exception. She was a large-boned girl with a freckled face and wide mouth that always seemed to be full of teeth. But her real attraction was her vitality. She came thundering up the stairs, that broad grin on her face and breathless with apologies. 'Sorry. Found I'd ripped my pants dancing the other evening and had to change.' She saw Lloyd Jones and stopped. 'I'm Petra Callis.' She held out her hand.

'Gareth Lloyd Jones.' And then, as I was getting her a drink, I heard her say, 'Soo will have told you what I'm up to, digging about in megalithic holes. I live out there on Bloody Island, a leaky tent among the ruins.' She jerked her head towards the window. Then she asked with blatant curiosity, 'What's your line of country? Yachts, I suppose, or are you a villa man?'

'No, neither.'

But Petra wasn't the sort of girl to be put off like that. She opened her mouth wide and laughed. 'Well, come on – what do you do? Or is it something mysterious that we don't talk about?'

I glanced back over my shoulder to see Lloyd Jones staring at her, a shut look on his face, mouth half-open and his eyes wide as though in a state of shock at the blatantness of her curiosity. Then he smiled, a surprisingly charming smile as he forced himself to relax. 'Nothing mysterious about it. I'm a Navy officer.'

As I passed Petra her gin and tonic Soo was asking him what branch of the Navy. 'Exec,' he replied, and she picked that up immediately. 'So was my father. Came up through the lower deck.' A moment later I heard the word Ganges mentioned.

'HMS *Ganges*?' I asked. 'On Shotley Point just north of Harwich. Is that the school you were referring to this morning, the one you and Evans were at?' And when he nodded, I said, 'It's called Eurosport Village now, or was when I was last there. I know it quite well. There's a commercial range and I used to practise there before going on to Bisley for the Meeting.'

'These cups, they're for shooting then, are they?' He couldn't help noticing them. He was standing right next to the pinewood cabinet I had purchased to house them and Gloria, our help, was a determined silver polisher. We talked about Shotley for a moment, then Soo butted in again, asking him how it had been when he was being trained there. From that they progressed to Malta. It was her mother who was Maltese. Her father had been a naval officer posted to Malta back in the days when there was a C-in-C Med and an old frigate fitted out as the Commander-in-Chief's yacht for showing the flag and entertaining. He had been the Navigating Officer on board and though she had been far too young to remember anything about it, she was always ready to talk of the parties he had described on the open lamplit deck.

It was past nine before we finally left, and though it was barely a mile away, by the time we had found a place to park the car and had walked through the quarry, somebody had already lit the bonfire. The effect was magic, the flames lighting the great square stone buttresses, flickering over the lofty limestone roof, shadows dancing on the moonlit cliffs, so that the whole effect was like some wild biblical scene.

In the great rectangular cavern itself the dirt base of it had been levelled off to provide a makeshift dance floor round which chairs had been placed and trestle tables bright with cloths and cutlery and bottles of wine.

The band began to play just as we found our table. Manuela came over, and, while Soo was introducing Lloyd Jones, Petra and I were momentarily on our own. 'You wanted to talk to me,' I said.

'Did I?' Her eyes were on the movement of people towards the dance floor, her foot tapping, her body moving to the beat of the music.

'Now, what have you discovered?' I asked her. 'Another of those hypostilic chambers or is it an underground temple to the Earth Mother like that place in Malta?'

'The Hypogeum?' She shook her head. 'No, nothing like that. Just a charcoal drawing. But it could be a lot older. I've only seen part of it. I don't know whether it represents a deer, a horse, a bison or a mammoth. I don't know what it is. A woolly rhinoceros perhaps.' She gripped hold of my arm. 'Come on, let's dance. I'll settle for a woolly rhinoceros and tell you the rest while we're dancing.'

But she couldn't tell me much. 'You'll have to see it for yourself. I think it's early man – cave-dwelling man – but of course I don't know. Not yet.'

'Then why consult me? I don't know the difference between the drawings of early man and a potholer's graffiti.'

She hesitated, then said, 'Well, it's not just that I've

unearthed what looked like a sea cave painting, it's the fact that people have been digging in that cave.'

'Archaeologists, you mean?'

'No, no. People who haven't the slightest idea they've uncovered anything. And if they did know, I imagine they couldn't care less. The charcoal drawing was only uncovered because they had been clearing a roof fall, and part of the drawing has already been sliced away when they were shovelling the rubble clear. They've dug out a hole I think I could have wriggled through, but I wasn't going to risk that on my own, it looked too unsafe.' And she added, 'I could hear water slopping around, Mike, and there was a draught of air. I think they've opened up a way through to the sea. But why?' She stared up at me, her body close against mine. 'Do you think that's what they were up to, cutting a way through to the sea?'

'How do I know?' I said. 'I'd have to see it . . .'

'Exactly. That's why I want you to come over there with me. Now. Before they have time to block it up, or do whatever it is they plan to do with it. They may be working on it this minute, so if we went now . . .'

'What – right in the middle of the party? I can't leave Soo, and anyway—'

'Well, afterwards. As soon as the party is over.'

I shook my head. 'It's quite out of the question.' And I told her the sensible thing would be to wait for daylight and then go back in with the curator from the museum or somebody from the Mayor's Office, one of the planning officials. It crossed my mind that this might have some connection with the squatters who had been sleeping in the villa Lennie was repairing, but I didn't tell her that. 'Wait till the morning,' I said again, 'and take one of the local authority officials in with you.'

'No.' She stopped abruptly, standing back from me in the middle of the dancing throng staring me in the face. 'Tonight. Please.' And then in a rush: 'You know how things work here, or rather don't – not always. It could be days before any official bothered to come out. They're not interested in caves and digs. A few people are, Father Pepito for instance, but none of the officials I know, not really, and I want somebody to see it now, before the charcoal outline of that figure is totally destroyed or the roof collapses again. Please, Mike. It's important to me.'

'I'll think about it,' I said, and we went on dancing, which was a mistake with Soo in her condition. She had been watching us and she was furious, telling me I had humiliated her in front of everybody. That was after I had returned to our table and Lloyd Jones had taken Petra off to dance. It made no difference that we had only been dancing together because Petra had wanted to get me to visit the cave and see what it was she'd discovered.

'So you're going with her. When?'

'Oh, don't be so silly,' I said. 'She just wants to show me a bit of a charcoal wall painting, that's all. It won't take long.'

'When?' she repeated, and there was a hot flush on her cheeks.

'Tonight,' I told her. 'She wants me to go tonight.'

'I see.' Her tone was icy, and after that she wouldn't speak to me. In the end I went over to the bar and got myself a large Soberano to chase down the wine I had been drinking. A hand gripped my elbow and I turned to find Manuela's husband, Gonzalez, beside me. 'You come to our table for a moment if you please. The Alcalde wish to speak with you about the opening of the new *urbanización* near the lake at Albufera next month. Jorge has been asked to make the opening and he wish you to take part in it, okay?'

I was not altogether surprised that Jorge Martinez should ask me to take part in the official opening of a new *urbanización*. I was one of the founder members of an unofficial association of resident English businessmen and I had on occasions acted as spokesman when the bureaucrats in the *ayuntiamento* had proved to be more than usually difficult over a planning application so that I knew Jorge in his official capacity as Mayor at the Mahon town hall as well as socially. In any case, since I was involved in property it was important for me to keep in with him.

In the post-Franco era, the political structure of what had become a monarchical democracy had steadily developed. The Baleares islands became one of the seventeen autonomous regions with its own elected parliament. The centre of this local government was at Palma, Mallorca. Foreign policy, finance and defence was, of course, still administered from Madrid through a Provincial Governor appointed by the ruling party. There was also a Military Governor. But Palma was over a hundred sea miles from Mahon and the comparatively recent introduction of this regional democratic autonomy had increased the importance of the local town halls and their councils, and in particular the power of the mayors who were elected by those councils. At least that's how it seemed to me, and I mention it here because I cannot help thinking that this dissemination of power may have had a bearing on what happened later.

Jorge Martinez was a lawyer, a slim man with sharp features and a way of holding his long, narrow head that suggested a cobra about to strike. He was, in fact, a very formidable little man and quite a prominent member of the ruling party, the *Partido Socialista Obrero Español* or PSOE. He had only been Alcalde in Mahon a short time but already he had his hands firmly on the local power reins, his political sense acute. He got up as I reached the table, shook me by the hand, holding my elbow at the same time, and waved me to an empty seat opposite him. His wife was there, a dark-eyed, vivacious woman, also another lawyer and Colonel Jiménez of the *Guardia Civil*. Gonzalez topped up my glass with more brandy.

The Alcalde not only wanted me to attend the opening, but would I make a speech? 'Five, ten minutes, what you like, Mr Steele.' And he smiled, his use of the English address rather than the Spanish *señor* quite deliberate. 'You are very much known in your community and you will comprehend that here in Menorca we have problems – political problems arising from all the villa people. Not those who come to end their lifes here, but the summer migration. It is a question of the environment. So you speak about that, hah?'

He stopped there, waiting for some acknowledgement, and when I made no comment he said brusquely, 'You speak about the regulations the developers are agreeing to. Also you say this *urbanización* is a good developing; it is small, villas not too close, the environment of Albufera acknowledged, and it is good for our island. It brings work, it brings money, some foreign currency. Okay? You speak first in Spanish, then in English, so very short speaking, but the political point made very clear.' And he added, 'I am informed you always have good co-operation with my officials at the *ayuntiamento*. So you agree, hah?'

He had that explosive way of asking a question and insisting on agreement at the same time. In any case, when you have had a few drinks, and the commitment is over two weeks away, it is easier to say yes than to think up some convincing excuse on the spur of the moment. '*Bueno, bueno.*' He smiled, a glint of gold teeth. 'So nice to talk with you, señor.' I was dismissed, and I left the table with the feeling that if I had declined his invitation he would have seen to it that next time I needed a permit for something from the Mahon town hall it would not be forthcoming. But a speech in Spanish – or did he mean the local Catalan, which is very different? In any case, my Spanish was a hybrid of the two, having been picked up quite haphazardly as occasion demanded.

Somebody had thrown a pile of furze on the fire, the band half-drowned in the crackle of the flames.

Flórez passed, light on his feet, the young woman in his arms glittering with tinsel, the button eyes in his round face fixed on the table I had just left as though watching for an opportunity to ingratiate himself. I went back to the bar and stood there watching the shadows of the dancers moving against the limestone roofing and far recesses of the great cavern. The dancers themselves were a flicker of fire-red images, the whole scene so lurid and theatrical that it seemed almost grotesque, the band thumping out a brazen cacophony of sound that ricocheted off the stone walls, the beat so magnified it almost split one's ears.

'Manuela has a good idea, no?' a voice shouted in my ear. It was the Commander of the Naval Base. 'Why does nobody think to use this place before? It is magnificent, eh?'

The music stopped abruptly, the dancers coming to a halt. Floodlights either side of the cavern entrance were switched on, spotlighting white-capped cooks and the charcoal fires with their steaming pans of soup and steaks sizzling and flaming on the coals. Lloyd Jones had stopped quite near us and I hailed him over. 'I'd like you to meet Fernando Perez,' I said. 'He's *Jefe* of the Navy here.' I introduced him as Lieutenant Lloyd Jones of the Royal Navy, adding, 'That's right, isn't it?'

I sensed a moment's hesitation. 'In fact, I'm now a Lieutenant Commander.' He laughed, a little embarrassed. 'I've just been promoted.'

We offered him our congratulations and Perez asked him what he was doing in Menorca. 'You are on leave per'aps?' He had a good command of English, particularly sea terminology, having had a short exchange posting to an RN carrier, though quite why they sent him to an aircraft carrier when he was a gunnery officer I don't know.

'Yes, on leave,' Lloyd Jones said.

'You have a ship, or are you posting ashore, like me?' And Fernando Perez gave a deprecatory little smile.

'No, I'm very lucky,' Lloyd Jones replied. 'With the promotion I've been offered a ship.'

'And where is that?'

'I'll be joining at Gibraltar as soon as my leave is up.'

Fernando turned down the corners of his mouth. 'You are indeed fortunate. Except for the Americans, who have so many ships, like the Russians, all our navies are in the same boat, eh?' He smiled, looking pleased at having achieved a touch of humour in a foreign language. 'Myself, I do not have a ship since five, no six years now. Already I have been 'ere three, stuck on a little island where nothing ever happen.'

'But at least you have the biggest guns in the Mediterranean,' I said.

'That is true. But what use are they, those big guns? They belong to another age and we have so few ammunition . . . Well, you know yourself. We fire them once a year and everybody complain because windows are shaken all over Mahon, some broken.'

'Are these the guns out on the northern arm of the Mahon entrance?' Lloyd Jones asked.

'On La Mola, yes. If you wish I take you to look

at them. It is a *Zona Militar*, a prohibited area, but there is nothing secret about those guns, they 'ave been there too long. Everybody know about them.'

They started talking then about the problems of island defence and after a while I left them to see that the girls were being looked after, Soo in particular. I didn't want her standing in the queue and maybe getting jostled. In any case, she was becoming a little self-conscious about her figure, I think because all our friends knew very well she had lost the first. But she was no longer at our table. She was at Manuela's. Petra, too, and they had already finished their soup and were tucking into steak and mashed potato, Gonzalez Renato sitting between them and everybody at the table flushed with wine and talking animatedly.

I went to get myself some food then and Miguel joined me in the line-up for the barbecue. He had his cousin with him, both of them in dark suits, their hair oiled and their faces so scrubbed and clean I hardly recognised them. They hadn't booked a table so I took them to mine. They had their wives with them, Miguel's a large, very vivacious woman with beautiful skin and eyes, Antoni's a small, youngish girl with plump breasts and enormous dark eyes that seemed to watch me all the time. I think she was nervous. I danced with her once. She moved most beautifully, very light on her feet, but she never said a word.

It was as I took her back to the table that I saw Soo dancing with Lloyd Jones. She shouldn't really have been dancing at all, but by then I'd had a lot to drink and I didn't care. Petra joined me and we danced together for the rest of the evening, and whenever I saw Soo she was with the Navy, looking flushed and happy, and talking hard.

At midnight the band stopped playing and Manuela lit the train that set the fireworks crackling. It was a short display and afterwards everybody began to drift off home. That was when Petra announced that I was going to drive her over to Cales Coves.

I should have refused, but the moon was high, the night so beautiful, and I was curious. I did make some effort to discourage her. 'It's almost midnight,' I said. 'Too late to go messing around in those caves in the dark. And you're not dressed for it.'

'That's soon remedied,' she said. 'Oh, come on. You promised.'

'I did no such thing,' I told her, but she had already turned to Soo, who was standing there with Lloyd Jones close beside her. 'Why don't you come, too – both of you?' And she added, 'It'll be fun, going there now. The moon's almost full. It'll be quite light. Anyway, it won't matter in the cave itself. If it were broad daylight we'd still need torches.'

I thought Soo would be furious, but instead, she seemed to accept it. Maybe the two of them had already talked about it when they had gone off together to the girls' latrine at the end of the meal. At any rate, she didn't say anything. She had hold of Lloyd Jones's arm and seemed in a much happier frame of mind, humming to herself as we walked down the grass-grown track to the road where I'd left the car.

There was no wind, the sky clear and the moon a

white eye high in the sky as I turned the car off the Villa Carlos road on to the steep descent to Cala Figuera. 'Have you ever seen anything so beautiful!' Petra exclaimed. 'I love it when it's still, like this, nothing stirring on the water, and Mahon a white sprawl above it. Sometimes I wake up in the night and pull back the tent flap. It looks like an Arab town then, so white, and everything reflected in the water. It's so beautiful.'

'Malta is better,' Soo cut in. 'What do you think, Gareth? You've just come from there.' She was sitting in the back with him. 'The buildings are so much more impressive, so solid. You haven't seen Malta, have you, Petra? Compared with Valetta and Grand Harbour – well, you can't compare them, can you, Gareth? Mahon is just a little provincial port.'

'But still beautiful,' Petra's tone, though insistent, was quite relaxed. 'And from Bloody Island I can see the whole sweep of it.'

'I don't think beautiful is the right word for a port,' Lloyd Jones said. 'Not for Malta anyway.' Out of the corner of my eye I saw him turn to Soo. 'Impressive now. I think impressive is the word. Those old strongholds, the great castles of the Knights that withstood the Turks and the German bombs.' And he added, 'But Gozo – Gozo is different somehow. I took a boat out to Gozo. That really is beautiful.'

I looked at them in the mirror. They were sitting very close together and she nodded, smiling happily. I think it was her smile that prompted him to say, 'I've been thinking, you know, about this visit to Cales Coves.' He leant forward suddenly, speaking to Petra and myself. 'I saw the inlets this afternoon, but I was only there a short while. It would be nice to see them by moonlight. And it's not far off my way back to Fornells, so I'll join you if I may.'

We had reached the end of the road and I turned the car on to the raw gravel of our new car park. We were facing the water then, close beside his little Fiat, and there was a yacht coming in under motor, her mains'l a white triangle in the moonlight as she moved steadily across the crouched outline of the hospital ruins.

'If Gareth is going,' Soo said suddenly, 'then I'm going too.'

'It's your bedtime,' I told her. 'Remember what the doctor said. You shouldn't have been dancing really.'

'Well, I'm not gong to be left behind on my own, that's definite.' And then, as Lloyd Jones helped her out, she was asking Petra whether she could lend her anything. But she had come ashore with all the clothes she needed. 'You never know,' she said as she retrieved her holdall from under the trestle table in the chandlery. 'It can blow up pretty fast here and you only get caught out at a party once with a full gale blowing and nothing to change into. I've never forgotten it. I got soaked to the skin and so cold . . .' She went with Soo up the stairs and into the bedroom.

Lloyd Jones followed them with his eyes, and when the door was shut he seemed suddenly ill-at-ease, as though unhappy at being left alone with me. 'I'll get you something more suitable to wear,' I said and went into the back premises, where I found him a spare sweater of mine and an old pair of working pants.

We made a quick change right there in the chandlery. 'You knew I was a Naval officer.' He was staring at me. 'The moment I arrived here, you knew. Do you have a rank? you asked.' I didn't say anything, an awkward silence growing between us. Then he went on, 'When I arrived here this morning – yesterday morning now – there was a man here, a short man in overalls and sweater. He was coming out of the door there.'

'Carp,' I said. 'His name's Carpenter.'

'An employee of yours? English, isn't he?'

'Yes.'

'Where from?'

'A little place on the East Coast. Felixstowe Ferry.'

He nodded. 'Thought I recognised him.' He was standing quite still, staring at me. 'So you know the whole stupid story?'

'About your being found clinging to a buoy off the Deben entrance? Yes.' And I asked him why he had ducked his head inside his car to avoid speaking to Carp. 'He was one of the men who rescued you, wasn't he? In fact, he says it was he who cut you down.'

'Yes.' There was a long pause, and then he said, 'It sounds silly, you know, but it's not something I'm very proud of – Navy officer found half frozen to death and roped to a buoy off a North Sea estuary. The media had a lot of fun at my expense, and seeing the man coming out of your door – it was a hell of a shock. I just didn't want to be reminded of the episode.'

Soo's voice called to ask if we were ready. 'Well, take Benjie out for a pee, will you, and Petra says to remind you about torches.'

I slipped a sweater over my head. 'I see your point,' I told him, 'but it's no excuse for not even saying hullo. He was very hurt.'

He shrugged. 'I'm sorry.'

The little dog had been shut in the store where he had a box to sleep in when we were out, and after I had taken him down the road to do his stuff, I went into the store with him and searched out the spare torches I kept with our boat gear. By the time I had found them, and some spare batteries, Soo and the other two were waiting for me out on the road. 'You take Petra,' she said as I locked the door. 'I'll show Gareth the way. We'll meet you on the track down into the cove. Okay?' And she took hold of Lloyd Jones's arm, steering him across to his Fiat, as though afraid I might object.

'Well, she seems quite happy about it, now we're all going,' Petra said as we got into the car. 'But you'd better tell Gareth to stay with her while we're in the cave. It's one of those entrances that are halfway up the side of the ravine and the last part is a bit of a climb.'

It was just past twelve-thirty by the dashboard clock as I took the old Jag through San Clemente and out on the four-kilometre straight to the Binicalaf turn-off, the moon so bright we could see the talayot to the left of the road very clearly, a huge cairn of interlocking stone blocks. Shortly after that I turned left, past the

Biniadris development and another talayot, Petra talking all the time about the cave drawings she had seen when studying in France. The one we were going to see now reminded her of Font-de-Gaume in the Dordogne, the entrance to it similarly placed, halfway up a cliff.

'When they'd opened up Font-de-Gaume they found a series of chambers with pictures of animals on the walls, chiefly reindeer and mammoth. And there was another cave, Rouffignac, much longer, and older I think. The drawings there were of rhinoceros and bison as well as mammoths, and the floor was pockmarked with the pits of hibernating bears, like small craters.' She laughed at the recollection and then, suddenly urgent again: 'Most of those drawings were from way back in time, Mike, at least 17,000 years ago, and if the little bit of a drawing I'm going to show you is really that of a woolly rhinoceros, then it'll be at least as old as those Dordogne paintings.'

I remember the way she said that, the intensity, the excitement in her voice. She really did believe she had found something important. And then we were at the start of the track that wound down the cliff-edged ravine to the first cove.

'You turn left in about a hundred yards,' Petra said. 'After that we walk.'

I stopped at the turn-off, waiting for the others, and after that we were on sand and gravel – not a road, nor even a track, just a piece of cliff-top country, a sort of maquis. Judging by the litter and the worn patches of thyme people came here to picnic, fornicate, or simply park their cars and sleep in the sun. It was tired, worn-looking country, but as I pushed on, driving carefully round the worst of the potholes, I realised that we had moved on to some sort of a track. A sharp turning to the right, a cave entrance marked by a sprinkling of tattered rags, then we were dropping down very steeply. 'You'll be able to park at the bottom,' Petra assured me. 'There's just room to turn there. Do you know this place?'

'Once or twice I've stopped at the top,' I said. 'But only for a bite to eat or to relieve myself before going down to the cove.'

She nodded. 'If you'd got out and walked around you'd have found quite a few cave entrances. There's one that looks almost like a house. It's got a painted front door, a couple of windows, a stove pipe stuck out of the side and a vine trained over an arbour of wooden posts. I'm told the man it belongs to visits it regularly right through the winter.'

We reached the bottom, the narrow gravel track petering out into what looked like a watercourse. There was only just room to turn the two cars and park them with their back ends in the shrubbery. I thought we had reached the bottom of the ravine then, but Petra said no, we still had a hundred yards or so to go, then there was a soft patch, almost a stretch of bog to cross before climbing up to the cave entrance. 'It will take us about ten minutes.'

By then we were out of the cars, all four of us standing in a patch of moonlight. The bushes were higher here, their shadows very black, and no sign of the cliffs that edged the ravine. 'How did you find it?' Soo asked her.

'I don't know really – some sixth sense, I think. The first time I came to Cales Coves was about six months ago. I've always been fascinated by natural caves. Most of them are in limestone and water-worn like these. And after I had explored several of them, I made enquiries and managed to locate a fisherman who uses a cave down by the water, just by the rock ledge that leads round into the other cove. He keeps his nets and gear there and it was he who told me there were several caves about here on the far side of the ravine. He thought it probable that very few people knew about them. The cave openings are mostly hidden by vegetation. At any rate, he hadn't heard of anybody visiting them, and though he thought I was mad, he very kindly came with me that first time. There are about half a dozen of them up there at the base of the cliffs. I came here several times after that, and then yesterday I found somebody had been digging in one of them. That's where the wall drawing is.' She started to move off. 'Come on. I'll lead the way.'

But Soo wasn't at all happy at being left on her own, and it was only when Lloyd Jones agreed to stay with her that she accepted the situation. I hesitated, suddenly uneasy at leaving her there. But Petra had already bounded off into the bushes. 'I'll tell you about it on the way home,' I said and followed her along what seemed to be the ghost of a path. The ground became damper, the light of my torch showing the imprint of soft-soled shoes.

We came to water, a shallow flow over gravel, the bright green of aquatic plants, and at that point we could see the moon shining on the cliffs above us, a grey, very broken curtain of rock splattered with the black of cave entrances. Almost immediately the ground began to rise and we lost sight of them. We were moving across the steep side of the ravine, still following traces of a path. It reached a point where we could see the waters of the cove entrance black in shadow, then it doubled back on itself, steeper now as we moved out on to the detritus caused by weathering of the cliff face above. Once Petra stopped to point the torch I had lent her at skid marks on the surface of the scree. 'Looks as though a bed or a crate, something heavy, has been hauled up here. Did you notice the imprint of feet down in the bottom?'

She scrambled up the steep bend, following the path across loose stone until it reached the base of the cliff where there were bushes growing, the entrance to the cave above screened by a dense thicket. Again there were indications of recent use, twigs snapped, small branches bent back, and in the black hole of the entrance itself the dry dust of the floor was scuffed by feet. 'That's not me,' she said, flashing her torch. 'I've only been into this cave once.' Again there were skid marks as though a box had been dragged along the ground. 'Watch the roof.' She went on ahead of me, the height of the cave gradually lessening until I had to stoop. The sides of it were very smooth. 'I'm not sure,' her voice echoed back at me, 'whether this has been scooped out by surface water making its way to the sea or by the sea itself.'

There were any number of caves around the coast, most of them well below sea level, some reached only by water-filled sumps or chimneys. Looking back at the moonlit half-circle of the entrance, I realised we were striking into the cliff at an oblique angle. We were also moving downwards. 'You've got to remember,' I said, 'that when the ice-caps and the glaciers melted at the end of the last ice age the level of the sea rose very considerably.'

'I know. The best of the caves are thirty to sixty feet down.'

'Is that what your diving friend says?'

'Bill Tanner? Yes. He says there's a marvellous one by Arenal d'en Castell, a sort of blue grotto, enormous. He's promised to take me down, sometime when I'm not fossicking around, as he calls it.'

I switched off my torch, looking back up the slope. The entrance was no longer visible, only the glimmer of moonlight on stone showing a ghostly pale. The roof was getting very low, though at that point the walls had pulled back as though this were some sort of expansion chamber. Like the other caves in the Cales Coves area, the walls here were water-worn and the upper entrance high above sea level. It must have been formed at some period when the island's rainfall was very much greater than it was now. The pounding of the sea so far below could never have done it by air pressure alone.

'Here's the roof fall.' Petra's voice came to me

distorted and booming. 'I'm just about there. But mind your head.' And then I heard her swear.

'What is it? Have you hurt yourself?' I snapped my torch on, swinging it to send the beam lancing ahead down the tunnel.

'No. Nothing like that.' She was crouched down, her torch on the left-hand wall. In front of her the cave appeared to have collapsed, loose rock piled almost to the roof, rubble everywhere.

'What is it then?' I scrambled down the slope.

'Look! It's gone. The bastards have put their bloody shovels right across it. They've scraped it clean away. Why did they have to enlarge the hole?' She was leaning forward, brushing at the rock face with her fingers, the fine limestone dust sifting on to the stone below and almost white in the torchlight. She sat back on her haunches, cursing softly under her breath. 'If only I'd sent you a message and come straight back here and waited. When do you think they did it?'

She turned her torch on the fallen rock and the gap that showed between the broken rock and the rubble below was about three feet wide and not more than two feet at the highest point. There was air coming through it. I could feel it cool on my face and there was a smell of the sea. 'I should have come back,' she said again. 'Knowing somebody had been working on this fall, I should have stayed here to explain to them how important that drawing was.'

I tried to tell her not to worry about it too much. 'This is quite an extensive roof fall. Get this rubble shifted and you may find more drawings as you expose the rest of the cave walls.' It wasn't the cave drawing that interested me, though I realised the loss of it meant a lot to her, it was the fact that a passage had been cleared through the roof fall. It wasn't only that I could smell salt water, I could hear it, the slop of wavelets on the rocks in the cove or against the base of the cliffs. 'I'm going through,' I said.

'No.' Her hand gripped my arm. 'It's dangerous.'

'Don't you want to know what's the other side, why they've been digging away at this roof fall?'

'Well, of course I do.' We were crouched together in what was clearly another expansion chamber, and as I circled it with my torch I saw that all the rubble they had cleared from the fall had been piled around the walls. Petra was straining at a large chunk of rock. 'Give me a hand, will you?' But when we pulled it away, and she had cleared the rubble and dust that was piled behind it, exposing another foot or so of the limestone wall, there was nothing there, the surface completely bare. Her frustration and anger was something tangible. I could feel it as she shifted her body into the gap, kneeling now and working away at the rubble, dust rising in a cloud as she scooped the loose fragments of rock up in her hands and thrust them behind her.

'Leave it till tomorrow,' I said.

'No. I must know what's here.'

'In the morning you can come back again with the proper tools.'

'I must know,' she repeated, her voice urgent. 'If there are more drawings, then I'll have to stay here, make certain they don't start shovelling out more of this debris. If they come here again in the morning and begin enlarging the passage through this roof fall—'

'Listen'

'What?'

'Just stay still for a moment.' She had been working so furiously, making such a clatter in the confined space, that I couldn't be certain I had really heard it. 'Listen!' I said again and she sat back on her haunches. Dust blew up into our faces, and in the sudden silence the slap of waves breaking seemed preternaturally loud.

'The wind's getting up,' she whispered. 'That's all.' And then, when I didn't say anything, all my senses concentrated on listening for that sound again, she asked, 'Did you hear something besides the wind and the sea?'

I nodded.

'What?'

'A voice. I thought I heard a voice.'

'Are you sure?'

'No. Of course I'm not sure.'

We stayed frozen for a while, listening. 'There's nothing,' she said. 'Just the wind. I can feel it on my face, much stronger now.'

I could feel it, too. It was as though a door had been opened and was letting in a draught. She bent forward again, working at a rock up-ended against the side of the cave. My torch, probing the hole through the roof fall, picked out a grey sliver of what proved to be bone. But when I showed it to her she brushed it aside. 'There are several bits of bone lying around. A sheep, or a goat maybe. Probably got trapped in here, or came seeking a dark den in which to die. It's drawings of animals, not their bones I'm looking for.' And when I again suggested that she leave it till it was daylight, she turned on me quite fiercely. 'Can't you understand? I must be sure there are no more drawings in danger of being destroyed.'

Five minutes later she was uncovering a mark on the wall that looked like discoloration. It was very faint, a faded ochre line sweeping upwards and stopping abruptly where the roof had fallen away. 'Could be the back of some animal.' Her voice was breathless with excitement. 'What do you think it is, Mike? The arch of the neck perhaps? A bull? At Lascaux there's a great bull right across the roof of the cave, and there are deer being hunted and plunging to their deaths over a cliff.'

She went on working at it, exposing more and more of the faded ochre line where it disappeared into the rubble. I was holding the torch for her and she was working so hard I could smell the warmth of her, dust clinging to her damp skin, her face a pale mask. Then I heard it again and I gripped her arm to silence her. 'Somebody called,' I said.

She turned, the piece of rock she had just prised loose still in her hand, her head on one side. Even her hair was covered with a grey film. 'I don't hear anything.' She brushed my hand away, thrusting the chunk of stone behind her.

'I'm going through,' I said.

She didn't seem to hear me, leaning forward again, brushing gently with her fingers at the section of wall she had just exposed.

I pushed her out of the way and crawled foward over the rubble, turning on my side. I was just starting to wriggle into the gap feet-first when, back up the slope of the cave, I saw a glimmer of light. It grew rapidly brighter, hardening into the beam of a torch, and a moment later Gareth Lloyd Jones was crouched beside us.

'Where's Soo?' I asked him. 'You said you'd stay with her.'

'Waiting in the car.' He was breathing hard. 'I came up to tell you.' He was kneeling now, his face close to mine as I lay with only my head and shoulders protruding from the hole. 'How far does it go, right through to the cliff face?' He thought I had already explored the continuation.

'I don't know,' I told him. 'I'm just going to find out.'

'But you've been here for a quarter of an hour or more.' Petra and I started to explain about the mark on the wall of the cave, both of us speaking at once, but he brushed our explanation aside. 'Have you heard something? Anybody moving about?'

'I thought I heard somebody call out,' I said. 'And before that there was something like the murmur of voices. It could have been the sea. Or it could have been squatters.' And I started to tell him about the villa near Binicalaf Nou.

'Voices,' he said. 'That's what you heard. There's

somebody in there. I came up to warn you.' Instead of waiting in the bush-shadowed dark of that track, he and Soo had decided to drive down to the cove. They had left the car and were walking down through the loose sand of the beach toward the sea when they had seen a light on the cliff face away to the left. 'We were just at the point where somebody had made a little trough in the rock and put up a notice to say the water in it was from a spring and good to drink. You know where I mean?'

'Yes, of course. But where exactly was the light? In one of the cave entrances?'

'Yes, and it wasn't there long. It wasn't very bright either, more like a hurricane lamp, or even a candle. A slightly yellowish light, and low down, only a little above the sea.'

I asked him whether it could have been the riding light of a ship, or perhaps the masthead light of a sailing boat, but he said definitely not. With the moon so bright it would have been impossible for them not to have seen a vessel if there had been one there. 'Even with the cliff face in shadow, the dark hole where we saw the light was plainly visible. And then suddenly it wasn't there any more.' He didn't know whether it had been snuffed out, switched off, or whether somebody had moved it away from the aperture. 'I was looking seaward at the time, so was Soo. We both thought somebody must be signalling a boat in through the entrance. But there was nothing coming into the cove. Then, when I looked back at the cave, it was gone. That's when I decided to come up here and warn you. They're in one of the caves, but whether it's this one . . .'

'Only one way to find out.' I started wriggling through again, using my elbows, but he stopped me.

'No. If they knew we were here . . .' I could see his face in the diffused light of our torches. It was shining with sweat and his mouth was moving uncontrollably.

'What's the matter?'

'Nothing. It's just . . .' He reached out, gripping hold of my shoulder. 'Leave it till morning, man. Please. Then we can come back – with one or two of your employees, or the police. If you go in now – ' He shook his head, his voice trembling.

Christ! The man was scared. 'They're only squatters,' I told him. 'Nothing to worry about. And if this is the cave they're in, then they'll have heard us. I'm going in,' I said again. 'Soon find out if there's anyone here or not.'

'What about your wife? And Petra here? If they know you're in the cave . . .' He stopped there, the rest of his words bitten back and his face set. 'All right,' he said. 'I'll come with you.'

'You don't have to.'

'Yes, I do. I'll come with you,' he said again, his voice quite obstinate now. He seemed suddenly to have made up his mind, and when I suggested he go back to the car and wait with Soo, he shook his head. 'If you're going to try and reach the cliff entrance, then I'm coming with you. It's my duty.' It seemed an odd way of putting it, but I didn't think about it then. I was already working my way in over the roof fall and he was coming after me headfirst.

The fall was only about ten metres through and then we were crouched low and moving down a steep incline, the breeze quite strong on our faces and our torches showing a low arched tunnel swinging away to the right. As soon as we rounded the bend we could see the cliff-face entrance, a pale rectangle of moonlight, and we could stand upright, for here, at the sea-worn end, the cave was much larger. There were camp beds ranged against the walls, four of them with sleeping bags, wooden packing cases for tables and seats and a paraffin stove that looked as though it had come out of some derelict fishing boat. The stove was for heating as well as cooking, and there were dishcloths, a couple of shirts too, hung on a line above the pipe that carried the fumes out to the cliff face. The whole place was equipped for living in, quite comfortably equipped, and propped against the wall was a heavy timber frame covered with plywood that had been tailored to fit the entrance. It had a little window and great iron bolts that slotted into sockets drilled in the rock so that even in a sou'westerly gale the place would be quite snug.

The noise of the sea was loud now, the dishcloths swaying in the wind. I went over to the entrance and leaned out. The cliff was sheer, a drop of about twenty feet or so to a narrow rock ledge that formed a sort of natural quay with deep water beyond, and the cave's entrance had been beautifully worked into scrolled pillars either side supporting a rather Greek-style portico. Inside, ledges had been carved out of both walls, a place for ornaments or household crockery. Whoever had originally fashioned the cave as a home must have been a real craftsman, a stonemason probably, everything so professionally done. 'All you need is a rope ladder,' Lloyd Jones said, peering down to the narrow ledge of rock below.

'And a yacht,' I added. 'Champagne cooling in the further recesses of the cave and a beautiful girl sunbathing down there in a bikini.' Or perhaps not in a bikini, just lying there on that ledge, nude in the moonlight.

He didn't laugh, and nor did I, for I found myself thinking of Petra, how well she would fit the picture in my mind. 'Nobody here,' I said.

'No.' He sounded relieved. 'But they've been here.' He had moved back from the entrance, his voice puzzled as he probed with his torch.

I was puzzled, too, the cave showing every sign of recent occupation and nobody there. The broken remains of an old cupboard full of cans of food. There were biscuits and cornflakes in a rusty cake tin, flour, rice, dried fruit, plastic containers with water, and those dishcloths and shirts hung up to dry.

'Where are the heads?' he asked.

'The heads?'

'It's all right throwing the slops out into the cove. But if I want to shit, where do I do it?' He swung his torch back up the way we had come. That was how we found the offshoot cave. It was quite narrow, the entrance draped with an old piece of sacking so covered with dust it was virtually the same colour as the surrounding wall, and when we pulled it aside, there it was, a chemical loo.

We were both of us standing there, peering down the narrow passage that continued on beyond the old oil drum with its wooden lid, when suddenly there was a cry and Petra was calling my name, her voice high and urgent, reverberating down the cave shaft – 'Mi-i-ke!' I was running then, crouched low. There was the sound of rocks dislodged, a man's voice cursing, and as I rounded the bend, the beam of my torch showed the soles of his canvas shoes disappearing over the rubble of the roof fall.

I must have been close behind him as I flung myself on to my belly, but by the time I had squirmed half through the gap, the tunnel beyond was empty. 'Two of them,' Petra said, her voice breathless. She was crouched against the wall. 'I thought it was you and Gareth, then my torch was knocked out of my hand and I was flung back, one of them cursing at me as they pushed past.'

'English or Spanish?' I was cursing too by then, my hands lacerated as I dragged my legs clear.

'I'm not sure.' She was on her knees, groping for her torch.

I glanced over my shoulder, struggling to my feet. 'Hurry!' He was right behind me and I was thinking of Soo, alone in the car. Damn the man! Why hadn't he stayed with her? I ran, bent low, the beam of my torch following the curve of the cave until the gap of the entrance showed a pale oval. A moment later I was out into the cool of the night air, thrusting through the bushes to stand in the moonlight staring down the path where it ran steeply towards the cove.

There was nothing there.

I searched the hillside. Nothing moved. Then a car's engine started, down below, where we had parked, and a few moments later I saw it burst out on to the track where it crossed open country just before joining the road, its engine screaming. It was the red Fiat.

'My God!' Lloyd Jones, beside me now, had recognised it, too.

We went straight down the hillside then, moving as fast as we could in the tricky light, jumping from rock outcrop to rock outcrop, splashing through the water at the bottom. My car was still there, but no sign of Soo. Frantically I began searching the bushes, calling her name.

'They couldn't have taken her with them, surely.' He was standing there, staring helplessly about him.

'Well, she's not here. Nor is your car. Why the hell didn't you stay with her?'

'I'm sorry, but you were so long . . . She asked me to go – ' He turned his head. 'What was that?'

It came again, high up the alley side from under the cliffs, and suddenly I knew what it was. 'Petra,' I said. 'It's Petra, and she's found her.'

We climbed back up the hillside, retracing our steps. 'Here,' she called, standing suddenly upright beside a patch of scrub. 'It's Soo. She's had a fall.'

I could hear her then, moaning with pain. Her

body was lying twisted in a heap in the middle of a low clump of bushes, Petra bending down to her again, cradling her head as we reached the spot. 'I think she must have followed the path right up to the cave entrance, then lost her balance when they pushed past her.'

'Anything broken?' My torch showed her face badly bruised and shining with sweat. Her breath came in great gasps and she was moaning all the time.

'I've moved her limbs. They seem all right. But internally . . .'

'It's the baby then. If she's going to have it now . . .' I turned on Lloyd Jones. 'Why the bloody hell didn't you stay with her, man? If she loses the child—'

Petra silenced me, gripping my arm, as Soo murmured quite coherently, 'It's not – Gareth's – fault. I asked him . . .' Her voice trailed away, her right hand moving to her swollen belly, a bubble of saliva at her mouth as she cried out with pain. Then she passed out.

'We've got to get her to hospital.' Petra's voice was sharp. 'As soon as possible.'

Soo only screamed once as we carried her down the slope to the car. I think she was unconscious most of the time. And she didn't cry out all the time I was driving back to Mahon. I drove like a maniac, Petra said afterwards, my face set and anger taking hold. Anger at Lloyd Jones for being the cause of her leaving the car and climbing the path to the cave alone, above all, anger at those two bastards who had brushed her from their path as they rushed down the hillside to drive off in that hire car.

I took her straight to the Residencia Sanitaria, which is just up from the Port Mahon Hotel. This is the emergency hospital, and the night Petra and I spent there is not one either of us is ever likely to forget. Fortunately they did have a bed available in the maternity ward. Two women were in labour at the time and the place was something of a mad house. There were nurses rushing about, a nun in attendance, no sign of a doctor. They got Soo to bed and I left Petra with her and phoned the *Guardia Civil*.

It was while I was telling them what had happened that Petra came down to say Soo was in labour. 'They've found a doctor. A very young man. I think he's scared. He's already lost one baby tonight. That's what one of the nurses told me.'

The time was 03.17, the words coming in a breathless rush. 'I'll go back now . . . No, don't come with me. There's nothing you can do. I'll let you know as soon as it comes.'

'It's not due for more than a month.' I remember I said that, standing there, helpless.

'What's it matter when it's due? She's having it now. I just hope to God . . .' She turned abruptly, not finishing the sentence, and hurried back up the stairs.

I remember getting rid of Gareth Lloyd Jones and then I was going over it all for the benefit of a young sergeant of the *Guardia*. Since it had happened in the country, not in Mahon, it was their responsibility. He made some notes, then offered his sympathies and said he would make a report. Perhaps it was a matter for the *Aduana*. At my insistence he agreed to inform Inspector Molina of the national police. I knew him slightly and I thought it might be something the plain-clothes boys should know about.

After the sergeant was gone I was alone there in that cold little reception area. Sometimes I paced up and down. Nobody came and time passed slowly. Dawn began to break in the street outside. Then suddenly Petra was there, her face very pale under the freckles, her eyes dark-edged with weariness and worry. 'She's conscious.' The words seemed dragged out of her. 'The doctor thinks it's just that she's badly bruised inside. She'll be okay. That's what he hopes – when she's had some rest.'

'And the child?' I asked.

'For God's sake, Mike, what did you expect? She must have fallen right on top of it. It was a breech, didn't you know that from the scan? Round the wrong way, the poor little thing's head was right against the wall of the stomach. It hadn't a chance.'

'What was it, a boy or a girl?'

'A boy.'

I went up to her then, feeling tired and very depressed, wanting a drink and not knowing what the hell I was going to say to her. She was lying on her back, her eyes closed, the olive skin of her face looking sallow, a deathly pallor against the tumbled black of her hair. They had cleaned her up, of course, but her hair and skin were still damp, her features so drained that I thought for a moment she was dead.

I don't think I said anything, but she must have sensed my presence for her eyes opened. They stared straight up at me, great brown pools in a white face. Her lips moved. 'I'm – sorry.' The words came faintly, then she was gone, the eyelids closing down, consciousness slipping away.

I bent and kissed her. Her skin was hot as though she was in a fever, her breathing so shallow it was hardly noticeable. Petra touched my arm, motioning me with her head to leave. The nun was hovering and a sister had arrived and was talking to her. 'She'll sleep now. They've given her an injection.' Petra led me out.

I don't remember driving home. We drank the remains of a bottle of brandy as the sun came up, both of us sitting in the office, and all I could think about was Soo's eyes staring up at me, huge brown pools of sorrow in the whiteness of her face, her hair still dank where it lay unkempt on the pillow, and her words, those sad words of apology for a miscarriage she couldn't help.

And after that I fell asleep, my head on Petra's shoulder.

CHAPTER THREE

When I next saw Soo she had been moved to a smaller room and her face was to the wall. I don't know whether she was asleep or not, but when it happened on both the visits I made the following day, it was clear she didn't want to talk to me. Apart from the bruising, she was in a state of shock. Even so, the doctor, as well as the nurses, said she was making quite good progress and should be home in a few days.

By then the *Guardia* had recovered the stolen hire car. It had been found abandoned in Alayór, in one of the streets winding down from the church. They had also examined the cave, but had not been disposed to take the matter very seriously. Petra had been with them and she said they considered the two men who had been flushed out by our unexpected arrival to be cave squatters, and then, when they bumped into her at the roof fall and Soo outside, they had panicked and taken the car as a handy means of making their escape.

After the police had gone she had walked round to the second cove, past the sea-level caves. There was a small cottage at the far end, its cabbage patch clinging to the side of a steep ravine. The family there knew nothing about the two men. They hadn't even known the cave had been occupied. Remembering the light Lloyd Jones had seen, she had asked them if they had noticed any vessel entering the cove during the previous two nights. There had been one, they said, and they wouldn't have seen it but for the moonlight, for the boat was all dark, not a light anywhere, and it had looked like two ships rafted together. There had been an onshore breeze, quite strong at times, so the two vessels couldn't anchor and had left immediately. The only other boats they had seen during the past few days had been local fishing boats, mostly from Cala en Porter, which was the next cove to the west and one of the better tourist resorts with a big hotel and some plush villas.

This she told me when she came ashore the following day, hauling her inflatable out and parking it in our car park. She was on her way to Cales Coves, hoping to uncover some more of that cave drawing, and we were walking along the waterfront to where the Martires Atlante runs out past the Club Maritimo to the old fort that marks the entrance proper to Mahon harbour.

The sun was shining again, an easterly funnelling up the harbour, rattling the halyards of the yachts moored at the Club pontoon, and Petra, looking wildly attractive with her auburn hair blowing about her face, suddenly said, 'That Navy man, have you seen any more of him?' She was wearing faded denims, an orange shirt open almost to the navel, no bra and her feet were bare.

'No, not since that night,' I told her.

'Did you know he'd been seeing Soo? He's been to the hospital several times.'

I didn't say anything, sullen in the knowledge of what she was trying to tell me. Her face was in profile, a strong face, the nose fine-boned and straight, the teeth white in a mouth that wore no lipstick. 'Did Soo tell you that?'

'No. Gareth told me.' She stopped then and turned to me. 'He's in love with her, you know that?'

I half shook my head, shrugging it off. What do you say to a statement like that? And coming from a girl you're half in love with yourself. What the hell do you say? 'How do you know he's in love with her? How the bloody hell do you know?'

Soo, of course. Soo must have confided in her. Hurt and lonely, it seemed reasonable, two young women together in the carbolic atmosphere of a hospital ward. But no – 'He told me himself.' And she added, 'You haven't seen him, have you? He hasn't tracked you down – to say he's sorry, offer his condolences, anything like that?'

'No.'

She nodded. 'Well, that's why. You don't go looking for a man when you've fallen head-over-heels in love with his wife. At least, I wouldn't think that's how they do it in the Navy. Cuckolding a fellow, if only in thought – well, not quite the thing, eh?' She gave me that wide grin of hers and began to walk on again. 'No need to worry about it, he says his leave will soon be over.'

'What about Soo?' I asked. 'How does she feel?'

She gave a little shrug. 'She likes him. I don't know how much more she feels.' She glanced at me quickly, a flash of something in her eyes and smiling now, quietly to herself. 'I'm not exactly in her confidence.'

I caught hold of her arm. 'Let's go for a sail.'

'No.' And she added, still with that little smile, 'That's your answer to every problem, isn't it? Let's go for a sail.'

'When did you see him?'

'This morning.'

'Where?'

'Bloody Island. At the dig.' She nodded towards the grey sprawl of the hospital ruins looking quite distant now that the harbour was full of whitecaps. 'He hired a boat and came over to see me.'

'To say goodbye?'

She shook her head.

'Then why?'

'I think because he wanted you to know. He also said he was sorry.'

'For leaving Soo on her own that night, or for falling in love with her?'

'Both, I imagine.'

We had stopped again and I was staring seaward,

out beyond the fortress of St Felip to where the horizon lay, a dark line in a blue sea flecked with white. So his leave would soon be up and he'd be off to Gib to take command of his ship. A Navy man, newly promoted and on his way up the service ladder. No wonder she found him attractive, feeling as she did about her father. I thought of the wretched little house, one of a line of Victorian dwellings in a back street in Southsea. It was all her father had to show for almost forty years in the Navy, his pay mostly spent on good living, and what savings he had achieved thrown away on speculative investments that had never produced the fortune they promised him. That lovely little courtyard full of music from the old record player, the mellow limestone house overlooking the sea between Sliema and St George's Bay, it had all seemed a long way away when we had last visited her parents. That was just after the loss of her first child, which I had thought might be some weakness inherited from her mother. But after that visit I was convinced that if it was an inherited weakness then it had to be from her father.

Still thinking about that, I glanced at Petra, standing Junoesque in the sunshine, the curve of a breast showing in the V of her orange shirt, the skin tawny brown with wind and salt, the patched denims filmed with the dust of the dig she was working on. No weakness there, and if she were to let up on the pill and have a child, she'd probably deliver it herself, no trouble at all, and get right on with the dig next day.

She turned her head and caught my gaze, the flicker of a smile back at the corners of her mouth. Something in her eyes made me wonder if she could read my thoughts. Were we that close already, and nothing said, just an acceptance that there were moments when the satisfaction of our needs . . .? 'You go for that sail. It'll do you good. I've got things to do.' She turned away then, a wave of the hand as she called over her shoulder, 'And don't fall in. It's blowing quite hard out there.'

I watched her as she crossed the road and disappeared up the stone staircase leading to the upper road where she always parked her battered little Citroën. She moved with the grace of an athlete, taking the steps at a run, her hair catching the sun like a burnished helmet of bronze. She must have known I was watching her, but she didn't look back, and when she reached the top she didn't look down or wave, though I caught the flash of that helmet of hair for a moment above the ornate balustrade.

She was right about the wind. It would have been fine if she had come with me, but single-handed the Flying Dutchman I had picked up in lieu of an unpaid bill was quite a handful, more like board-sailing than cruising. I reefed, of course, before slipping from our pontoon and sailing out of the shelter of Cala Figuera, but the wind was funnelling down the length of the harbour approaches, and not much shelter to be had in the lee of the islands. It was very wet as I beat past Villa Carlos and out as far as the big island called Lazareto, and when I went about and freed the main for the run back, we were planing on the break of the waves and every now and then that powerful little dinghy took the bit between her teeth and tried to broach-to.

I was wet and tired by the time I got in. Instead of providing me with the opportunity of thinking things through, it had taken all my concentration just to keep the dinghy upright and avoid capsizing. Ramón was sitting waiting for me with a whole string of queries, mostly about matters that Soo would normally have dealt with, and there was the mail. I hadn't dealt with the day's mail yet and I loathed typing letters. 'There is a telephone call.' He was hovering over me as I stripped and towelled myself down. 'About the *Santa Maria*.'

'You deal with it,' I said. 'You know the charter terms.'

'He don't want a charter.'

'You mean he wants to buy her . . .' I had been trying to sell the *Santa Maria* for over a year now.

But Ramón shook his head. 'He already have a boat.'

I paused in the act of stepping into a dry pair of trousers. 'Then what the hell does he want? Who is he?'

'Señor Flórez. He want you to phone him.'

Apparently Flórez was acting for the owner of a catamaran lying at the commercial dock, in the area reserved for larger yachts and those on passage. 'He want to make some sort of exchange,' Ramón added.

A big cat had come in that morning. I had seen it running in under jib alone when I was talking to Petra, dark blue hulls with the paint flaking and a bad scrape along the port side. But she had still looked beautiful and very purposeful, a real thoroughbred.

I zipped up my trousers, pulled on a light sweater, Ramón still standing there and my mind in a whirl. The fishing boat wasn't worth much, not here in Menorca, and running it for charter was a lot of work with very little in it for us. It had never really paid its way. 'How big is this cat?'

Ramón shrugged. 'You phone Señor Flórez, then he tell you everything you want to know.'

But when I rang Flórez, all he said was, 'Come and see it for yourself.' He and the owner would be on board that evening. 'Then we talk about it, eh? I have a very good deal for you, Mr Steele.' And he had put the phone down, leaving me with all my questions unanswered and the deal not specified.

I would like to have driven over to the commercial dock right away. Looking through the yachting magazines, I had often thought what a perfect charter vehicle a big cat would be, and now I was being offered one, right here in Mahon. But the phone began ringing and I couldn't get away. There were two calls from England, as well as letters. Spring was in the air and people suddenly anxious to be sure their boats or their villas would be ready for the holidays.

I worked right through lunch, sending Ramón out to the restaurant at the corner for the fish-and-rice dish they often put up for us when Soo was too busy to cook anything for herself. It was shellfish this time, *arroz de marisco*, with *calamares* tentacles finely chopped to give it body. All the time I was eating, and afterwards, I kept thinking about that catamaran, wondering what it would be like, what condition it would be in, what accommodation it would have, the navigation equipment and the state of the sails, excitement building though I knew bloody well the Mediterranean was a graveyard of shattered dreams.

It was late afternoon before I finally caught up with the office work and then it was time to visit the hospital again. I didn't mention the catamaran to Soo, even though I found her sitting up in bed reading a Spanish novel she had been lent. She looked much better, the dark patches under her eyes almost gone, some of the old sparkle back and her face more animated. The doctor had said she would be fit to leave the following day. 'Eleven o'clock. Will that be all right? Can you come for me then?'

I said, 'Of course', and then she talked for a bit, about the friends who had been to visit her, the gossip they had passed on, and particularly about the Renatos' Red Cross party in the Quarries. 'What will you say when you speak at the opening of that Albufera development? You never told me the Alcalde had asked you. Am I invited?'

'I imagine so.'

'But he didn't ask me, did he?'

'I'm sure he will. When they send out the official invitations.'

She was silent then and I feared she was going into one of her sulky moods. But after a moment she brightened and began asking questions about the business – how Lennie was getting on with the villa out at Binicalaf, whether the equipment for the extra bathroom in another of the villas in our care had been flown in yet, had I remembered about completing the forms for customs clearance, and the accounts to settle with two of our suppliers. 'You know, I'm really looking forward to being back. Lying here with nothing to do but read and listen to the radio and think.' And she added darkly, 'I've had all the time in the world to think these past few days.' And almost without a pause: 'Did Gareth come and see you before he left? No, of course – I remember. He said it was bad enough seeing me, feeling it was his fault I'd lost the child, and though I told him I might have lost it anyway, he still said he couldn't face you. You told him it was his fault. I have a distinct memory of that. *Why the hell didn't you stay with her?* you shouted at him, and accusing him like that . . .'

Her voice trailed away. Then suddenly she said, 'Did you know, he came up through the lower deck – *Ganges*, Dartmouth, the Fleet Board. Just like Papa. It makes a difference, doesn't it? You're more vulnerable then. Everything that bit harder. No admiral ever came up through the lower deck that I can remember. And it wasn't his fault. It wasn't anybody's fault.' Tears welled. I went to comfort her, but she pushed me away. 'I know what you think. And you're probably right. I'll never have a child now.'

I didn't know what to say. Life doesn't make sense. There was Petra who didn't want a child, but would almost certainly have no difficulty if she did find herself with a bun in the oven. And Soo's mother, she had

had five, one every two years, regular as clockwork. Then, being a devout Catholic, she must have gone on strike. That was probably why Soo and her father had been so close.

It was almost dark by the time I left the hospital and cut down the little hairpinned gut that led to the waterfront. I could see the catamaran before I had even parked the car, a broad cabin top spanning the whole width of the twin hulls, her single mast standing very tall and overtopping the dock sheds. She was moored outside of a big yawl, and when I asked permission to cross over to the catamaran, an American in a blue jersey, half-glasses perched on his nose, poked his head out of the doghouse. 'Sure. But there's nobody on board. They're over at the café-bar across the road.'

I asked him where he was from and he said, 'Newport, Rhode Island, via Gibraltar and Ibiza.'

I swung my leg over his guardrails, crossed the foredeck to stand by the shrouds looking down on the long, slim line of the two hulls, their bows poking out from the broad foredeck platform, a safety net slung between them.

'Good trip,' he went on. 'We made it across the ditch in just over sixteen days, almost all of it under sail.'

A woman's head appeared in the hatch, grey-haired like the man. 'That cat belong to you?' she asked.

'I wish it did.' I jumped on to the cabin top, moving aft across the top of it to drop down into the cockpit. There was a swivel chair for the helmsman immediately aft of the wheel and a console full of dials – engine revs, speed through the water, true and apparent wind speeds, just about everything anybody could want, and though the door was locked, I could see through the glass panel that the whole arrangement was repeated in the saloon, which was broad and spacious, running across the ship with a semi-circular settle, a big folding table and steps leading down into the hulls on each side. Compared with the old *Santa Maria* the accommodation was so grand it was more like a house, and around the chart table, on the starb'd side, there was everything a navigator could wish for, radar, sat-nav and Decca, ship-to-shore radio telephone . . .

'Quite a machine, eh?' the American said.

I nodded, laughing ruefully. To own this sort of a vessel I'd have to sell both our villas. They were in our joint names, and even if Soo agreed and we succeeded in selling them on the present market, it would probably not be enough. The ship needed painting, of course, and the scrape along the outer curve of the port hull was deeper than I had thought. It looked as though some frames might be broken. But otherwise she seemed in remarkably good shape. There was even a big semi-inflatable moored alongside with wheel steering, spray screen and remote controls to the outboard engine.

I hauled myself back on to the American's deck. 'You came through Gib, you say. Did you see a Royal Navy frigate in the harbour there?'

'Not that I recall. It's a big place, all those high stone quays, and anyway we were round in the marina.' And he added, 'We saw some US Navy ships though. They were powering through the Straits as we came in from Cape St Vincent. Destroyers by the look of them. More watchdogs for the Sixth Fleet's carriers, I guess.'

I was back on the dock then, wondering why anyone should want an old fishing boat like the *Santa Maria* in place of that cat. I could see her name now. It was on the flat, sloping stern of each hull – *Thunderflash*. If I owned a machine like that . . . I turned back to the American. 'What made you think I was the owner?'

He smiled and gave a quick shrug. 'Something in the way you were moving about her. Thought maybe it was a delivery job.' There had been four of them on board, he told me, when they came in that morning. One he took to be the skipper, two were obviously crew, and there had also been a short, dark man dressed in a suit who looked and behaved like a passenger. They had had to clear immigration, as well as health and customs, so he presumed the boat had come from France or Italy, which could of course mean Corsica or Sardinia. The passenger had gone ashore immediately afterwards, the skipper about an hour later, while the others just sat around drinking wine and listening to the radio. The skipper had returned about half an hour before I had arrived with a man who was obviously Flórez and the four of them had then gone across to Anton's for a drink.

The café–bar was almost opposite the Estación Maritima, just back of the Customs House. Above it loomed the older part of Mahon, clouds scudding over a moon-dark sky. As always at this time of night, the bar was dark and very crowded. They were at a table at the far end, heads close together, coffee cups and glasses at their elbows, a bottle in the centre. They were talking in English and as I approached I heard one of them say, 'Fifteen minutes, and that's not driving fast.'

Flórez saw me then, and as he switched on a smile and got to his feet, the man sitting with his back to me raised his hand as though for silence. 'You want a drink with your coffee, Mr Steele?' Flórez called the order to the barman and pulled up a chair. 'Later we go over to the ship.' He didn't introduce me to any of the others, merely saying I was the man he had been talking about.

There was a short, awkward silence after I had sat down. I was between Flórez and the man I took to be the skipper. He wore an old reefer and his neck stuck out of the collar of it like a column running straight up into the long, narrow head. His face, what little I could see of it in that light, was weathered to a dark brown, a strong, flamboyantly handsome face with a powerful jaw line and a nose that hung straight and sharp over a narrow, tight-lipped mouth. It was an almost Gallic face, the eyes very bright, the brilliance of the whites under the thick head of black hair giving them a wide-eyed look that was almost a stare. A little black moustache, turned down over the corners of the mouth, seemed to split his features in two, dividing the jaw and the mouth from the sharp, pointed nose and staring eyes. If it hadn't been for the moustache, I think I might have recognised him at once.

'That fishing boat of yours . . .' he said. 'Señor Flórez took me to see it this morning. Just what I and my two friends here are looking for.' His two friends, seated across the table from me, nodded. One of them was small and sharp-featured, the other much larger, a big barrel of a chest, broad shoulders, his crumpled features reminding me of a boxer from Dublin I had picked up one time in Gib and delivered to Tangier. 'We got to earn a living.' He smiled an engaging, friendly smile. 'Nice place, Mahon. Fishing good, too.' There was a softness in his voice, the accent faintly Irish.

'What he means is we're just about broke,' the man beside me went on. 'We need a fishing boat and somewhere ashore where we can live and store our gear. You happen to have what we want. I saw that villa you're building this afternoon. I also had a look at Port d'Addaia. If we had the villa we'd keep the boat there. Nice and handy. Well sheltered, too.' He wasn't looking at me now, his eyes on his coffee as though talking to himself and his hands flat on the table. They were big, fine-boned, very capable-looking hands. 'Now tell me something about this fishing boat of yours – speed, range, charts on board, sails, etc. I've read the details, of course, and one of your men showed me over her, but I'd like to hear about her from you, okay?'

My coffee came as I began to run through the inventory and the performance, and all the time I was thinking of that catamaran and trying to build up the value of the *Santa Maria*, knowing that the exchange was heavily weighted in my favour. To build a cat like that at the present time – good God, it would cost a fortune.

A glass had come with my coffee. He reached for the bottle and filled it for me. '*Salud*!' We drank, raising our glasses as though the deal was already completed.

'I saw you come in this morning,' I said. 'Where were you from?'

He stared at me, and there was something about the eyes . . . but then he had turned away. 'Fishing,' he said. 'We'd been fishing.'

'You had a passenger on board, so I naturally thought . . .'

'I tell you, we'd been fishing.' He looked at me again, his eyes coldly hostile. 'There was a friend of mine with us. We enjoy fishing. All of us.' He stared at me hard for a moment. 'Don't we?' he said to the other two, and they nodded. 'Okay.' He knocked back the rest of his drink and got almost violently to his feet. 'If you're interested in the deal, then we'll go over to *Thunderflash* and you can poke around down below. But—' and he leaned suddenly over me, prodding my chest with a hard index finger, 'don't go asking stupid questions, see. One of the reasons we're all here is because Flórez said you were discreet – when it was to your advantage. Right?'

I didn't say anything. Looking up at him and seeing those eyes staring down at me, I suddenly realised who he was. This was the man Gareth Lloyd Jones had been looking for. Evans. Patrick Evans. Slowly I got to my feet, the others too, and we all went out and across the road to the dock. The American was below as we clambered across his boat and dropped on to the deck of the catamaran. Evans unlocked the door, ushering me below in a way that left me in no doubt that he was the owner, and the moment I stepped down into that great saloon, with its breadth and comfort and the fabulous view for'ard, I was hooked. I had never been in this type of craft before. Even at the Boat Show in London, the last time I had been there, I hadn't seen anything like this, so immaculately designed, so perfectly suited to cruising in the Mediterranean.

He showed me round himself, double beds in each of the hulls with washbasin, loo and shower for'ard, hanging lockers aft and two single berths, the steps down from the saloon built over the port and starb'd engines, and all the time my mind racing, thinking what I could do with it, a different charter clientele entirely – San Tropez, Monte Carlo, Capri, the Aegean. We went back to the saloon and he produced a bottle of whisky. 'Well?' He was smiling. He knew from my comments, from the look on my face, that he'd be able to get what he wanted. And I? – with luck I would get what I wanted, what I'd always wanted – oh my God yes. We drank, smiling at each other, and then I nearly ruined it. 'I don't think I got your name.'

'Lloyd,' he said.

Not Evans or Jones, but the first part of Gareth's

surname – Lloyd. 'Do you know a man named Gareth Lloyd Jones?' His eyes snapped wide, suddenly wary, his face gone hard again and quite expressionless. 'He was here on leave,' I said, floundering slightly as I explained. 'He was looking for somebody – somebody rather like you. And I thought I saw you – in Es Grau, a bar there, three, four months ago. Were you here then?'

He glanced at Flórez, half rising to his feet, those powerful hands of his clenched so tight the knuckles showed white. But then he smiled at me and sat down again, forcing himself to relax. 'Yes,' he said. 'That's when I decided on Menorca. I was looking for somewhere to settle, you see.' He picked up his whisky, swallowed some of it, staring at me all the time, hostility gradually giving way to curiosity. 'How well do you know Gareth?' he asked me. And when I explained how we had met, he leaned back against the cushions of the settle. 'He's still here, is he?' he asked.

'No,' I said. 'He left yesterday.'

'How long was he here?'

'About five days, I think.'

'Did you see much of him?'

I shook my head. 'We had lunch together at Fornells, that's about all, and that same evening he came to the Red Cross barbecue with us. I think my wife saw more of him than I did.'

He sat there for a moment, quite still and apparently lost in thought, his eyes fixed on a shelf full of bottles at the end of the bar. 'That night,' he said slowly. 'He was with you, wasn't he? Flórez says there was some trouble. You flushed a couple of squatters out of a cave and they pinched his car. Right?'

I nodded, wondering at his interest.

'Did you see them? Would you be able to recognise them?' And he added quickly, 'I'm sorry about your wife. I believe she was hurt.'

'No, we didn't see them,' I said. And I told him briefly what had happened. But he didn't seem interested in the details, only in the fact that Gareth Lloyd Jones had been there. 'You say he was looking for me?' he interrupted. 'Did he say why?'

'He said you were at school together, that you saved his life.' And because I wanted to get back to the business in hand and clarify the ownership details, I said, 'He also told me your name was Evans.'

I saw him hesitate. But it was only momentary. 'Lloyd Evans. It's a double name, see, like Gareth's.' And he added, 'Said we were at school together, did he?' He was smiling now, seemingly at ease again. 'HMS *Ganges*. That's what he was referring to.' He gave a little laugh. 'Yes, I suppose you could call it a school. It was a training establishment for naval ratings. It had a flagpole. Still there, I believe – a bloody great pole about a mile high, and some stupid sod of a PO makes him go up to the top almost his first day. A punishment, he called it, but it was straight bloody sadism. Christ! the poor little bastard had only just arrived, raw as a cucumber and scared out of his wits. I had to go up and talk him down. Practically carried him.'

He nodded his head, still smiling to himself. 'Got

plenty of spunk, I'll say that for him. He was a town boy, East End of London, mother owned a green-grocer's, something like that. Don't reck'n he'd ever been up a mast before in his life. I remember watching, a squad of ten nozzers we were, and that bastard of a PO orders him over the futtock shrouds, wot we called the Devil's Elbow. It was all of a hundred feet up. Somehow he made it, and up the rope ladder. After that it was bare pole and he'd been told to touch the button at the top.' He looked at me quickly. 'Difficult for you to imagine what it's like. Most people never seen a mast that high except in the distance on one of the Tall Ships.'

I nodded, the picture of it clear in my mind. 'I've seen that mast,' I said. 'You don't have to tell me about the height of it.'

'Seen it?' He looked surprised, and when I explained, he nodded. 'I heard it was turned into a sports centre. Best thing for it with all those messes and officers' quarters with polished wooden decks. And the ranges, of course. So you're into competition shooting, are you?' He was looking at me hard as though that somehow made a difference. 'Bisley?'

'Yes,' I said. 'Until a few years back.'

He nodded. 'I know somebody who practises at Shotley on the old ranges we used as kids. That's how I know about the commercial range facilities.'

'Who was that?' I asked him, but he was already back to the story of Gareth Lloyd Jones climbing that mast. 'Poor little bugger, he got himself to the top of the ladder and it was at that point he made the mistake of looking down. I know what it feels like, looking down from that height, because I was the cadet chosen to stand point, right on top of that fucking button. There's a lightning conductor there and that's all you've got to hang on to, standing to attention with the others manning the yard and some bloody admiral inspecting the school.' He leaned back, his eyes half-closed, and still that smile. 'Hadn't thought about it till now, but yes, I suppose he'd feel I'd saved his life.'

The way he had told it, such relish in the recollection, and now going on to explain how he had got Gareth down, talking to him all the time. 'You get pretty close to a boy when you've been through an experience like that together. It wasn't easy for either of us.' There was a flamboyance about the man. It was as though he had an urgent need for self-dramatis-ation. I think this is often the case with men who are preternaturally handsome, perhaps because their looks make things appear so easy at first, and then suddenly they begin to realise looks are not enough. 'Still in the Navy, is he?' And when I told him Lloyd Jones had just been promoted and had left Menorca to take com-mand of a frigate waiting for him in Gibraltar, he nodded. 'Of course. He was cut out for it, real Navy material. But Lieutenant Commander, and a frigate of his own . . .' He swirled the whisky round in his glass. 'You sure he didn't say anything about why he was looking for me?' He raised his eyes, staring at me.

'I don't think I asked him,' I said. 'I presumed, when he said you were at school together, that you were close friends, is that right?'

'Yes, I suppose so. We're certainly close.' And he smiled as though at some private joke. He smiled a lot during that meeting on *Thunderflash*, but the smile never reached his eyes, and his face wasn't a smiling face. When he smiled it was a conscious stretching of the mouth that revealed teeth so white and even they might have been false. And it wasn't only his face that was hard. His body was hard, too. Even then I was conscious that he was a very fit, very tough man.

'You saved his life twice,' I said. But he wasn't to be drawn on that, his mind already back to the subject of the *Santa Maria* and the villa up on Punta Codolar. He wanted to start fishing right away. And he added with a thin, rather wry smile, 'Silly, isn't it? Here I am with this boat that's worth a small fortune, and I'm short of money and nowhere to live.' He wanted to make the exchange right away. 'Tomorrow. I'd like us to be free to shift our gear on to the fishing boat tomorrow. You're not using her for anything. I've looked her over and she's ready to go. So's *Thunder-flash*. A quick clean round the ship after we've gone and you could have a charter party on board by the weekend. What do you say?'

What I said, of course, was that I'd have to talk it over with Soo and she wouldn't be out of hospital until next morning. 'Exchanging boats is one thing,' I told him. 'But that villa was my wife's idea. I don't know whether she'll agree.' For a moment I toyed with the thought that I might force through an exchange on a boat-for-boat basis, perhaps with a small cash addition, but he wasn't that much of a fool.

In the end he agreed to leave it over until I had had a chance to talk to Soo. 'Ring Señor Flórez here. He'll know where to find me. But I want that fishing boat by Saturday at the latest, tanked up with fuel and ready to go. That gives you two days, okay?' He got to his feet then, and when I asked him whether he needed anybody local to show him the best fishing grounds, he looked at me sharply and said, 'Don't bother. I know where I'm going.'

'What about charts then?'

'Not your problem. I got all the charts.' And he added, 'You ring Flórez, eh? Tomorrow, right after you pick up your wife from the hospital.'

I told him that might not be long enough to talk her into the deal, but in fact Soo proved much easier to persuade than I had expected. She was more interested in the man's friendship with Gareth Lloyd Jones at *Ganges* than in the future of the villa she had so recklessly acquired the day before she lost the child. 'But didn't you ask him?' she demanded almost angrily when I told her I had no idea what the relationship of the two men had been after the flagpole episode. 'I'm certain there was something between them, an intimacy – I don't think it was sexual. You don't think Gareth's in any sense gay, do you? I mean, he doesn't behave like one.'

'No,' I said. 'I don't think he is.' In fact, I hadn't given it a thought.

'Hero worship?' She was sprawled on the old couch we had picked up in Barcelona, her head turned to the window, staring at the sea. 'Was that why he was looking for this man?' Her smooth, darkish forehead was slightly puckered, her eyes half-closed, her body slim again, no lovely curve to her belly and the madonna look quite gone from her face so that it was now pinched, even a little haggard.

I think she was quite glad not to have to cope with the problems of overseeing the completion of that villa. At any rate, she accepted the situation. But later, much later, she was to insist that if I hadn't been so obsessed with my 'new toy' I would have known what was going on. She was, of course, much closer to the people of the island than I was. She had a lot of friends, not only in Mahon and Ciudadela, but out in the country among the farms, and she did pass on to me some of the talk she picked up about the growing popularity of the separatist movement. It was backed by the two communist parties, the *Partido Communista de España*, or PCE, and the *Partido Communista de los Pueblos de España*, or PCPE, and appeared to be gaining ground. *Menorca*, the *Diario Insular* or local paper, and even *La Ultima Hora* of Palma in Mallorca had carried the occasional article on the subject. But now I had no time any more to read the local newspapers. I was fully stretched getting *Thunderflash* ready for sea.

Once I had agreed the deal with Patrick Evans and checked the share ownership certificate, which showed him to be the sole owner, with sixty-four-sixty-fourths of the shares, I had pictures taken of the catamaran, some with the sails up, others of the saloon with the table laid, a vase of wild flowers and a large Balearic crayfish as the centrepiece. These I mailed off to a dozen of the most up-market agencies specialising in Mediterranean travel, together with a plan of the layout and full details. Three of them I actually phoned, and within a week two of these had expressed interest, and one of them, representing an American agency, had their representative fly in from Mallorca to inspect the boat and cable a report direct to Miami. Two days later I received a cable offering a two-week charter if I could pick up a party of eight Americans at Grand Harbour, Malta, on May 2. There was no quibble about the price, which would mean that in just one fortnight *Thunderflash* would earn more than the *Santa Maria* had made the whole of the previous season.

Moments like this make one feel on top of the world. I didn't stop to wonder why Evans had gone fishing instead of chartering the cat himself. I simply cabled acceptance, asking for twenty per cent deposit, and when this came through by return, I hardly thought of anything else, my energies concentrated on getting *Thunderflash* repainted and in perfect condition, the hulls white, not blue, and the boat in tip-top condition.

We finished her just three days before I was due to speak at the opening of the Albufera *urbanización*, and when I got back that night Soo was almost starry-eyed, not because *Thunderflash* was back in the water and moored right outside, but because she had received a note from Gareth Lloyd Jones in Gibraltar. 'He says he was piped aboard at fifteen thirty-two on Wednesday afternoon.' And she added, the letter clutched in her hand, 'It's there in the log – Captain piped on board HMS *Medusa*.' She looked up at me then. '*Medusa* was one of Nelson's ships, wasn't she?'

'Ask Carp,' I said. 'There's a *Medusa* buoy off Harwich. I sailed past it once on a navigational course.'

'But you were Army.'

'The outfit I was in, they expected you to be able to find your way at sea.'

'*It made me feel good* – that's all he says.' She folded the letter up. 'What a wonderfully exciting moment it must have been for him – the piercing whistle of the bo's'n's pipes, his salute to the quarter-deck, and thinking all the time that he'd made it, from *Ganges* and the lower deck right up to the command of a frigate.'

I went through to the office and checked the mail. Another charter – that made two lined up for the summer. Things were beginning to look real good. At least the boating fraternity weren't to be put off by the threat of bombs following the Libyan raid, or the fall in the dollar. Not even the information that another of our villas had been paint-sprayed could dampen my spirits. It was the usual slogan – URBANIZAR ES DESTRUIER SALVEMO MENORCA, and Miguel had written me a long letter of complaint in Spanish. I told Soo to deal with it, my mind still on *Thunderflash*.

The weather was set fair for the moment and next morning, standing at the open window in the blazing sun, drinking my coffee, I could hardly believe it, the twin hulls so beautiful, such a thoroughbred, lying there to her reflection, no wind that early in the morning, the surface of Mahon harbour absolutely still.

I called Soo to come and look at her. 'We'll take her out under engines as far as La Mola, wait for the wind there.' But she had promised to pick up one of the Renato girls at their vineyard farm beyond St Luis and picnic on the limestone rock ledges of Cala d'Alcaufar. Carp appeared with the semi-inflatable from the direction of the naval quay, the aluminium bows half-lifted out of the water as the big outboard thrust the tender close past the Club Maritimo, the metal masts of the yachts alongside the pontoon winking in the sun as they bobbed and swayed to the sharp-cut wake.

East Coasters tend to keep their emotions under control, but though he didn't show it, I sensed Carp's excitement as the two of us scrambled aboard and got the engines started and the anchor up. He had never skippered anything like this before and the fact that I had put him in charge of the boat had done wonders for his ego. He had bought himself one of those baseball-type hats with a long America's Cup peak and he couldn't stop talking as we motored out past Bloody Island, rounding the northern end of it, bare earth showing where Petra had trenched beyond the great stone capping slabs of the hypostilic chamber she had been excavating. The water was so still we could have nosed in for her to jump on board.

She would have loved it, but two days after Soo

had left hospital I had had the unpleasant task of taking a telex out to her camp with the news that her father had been badly injured in a car crash. A vacant seat on a charter flight had enabled her to leave that same afternoon. We had not heard from her since, and now, sitting there at the wheel, driving the big catamaran close-hauled past the La Mola fortifications, I missed her. It was such a perfect day for trials, the wind coming in from the south-east and building up through the afternoon, so that the B and G instruments showed us touching fifteen knots as we ran back into the harbour under full main and spinnaker, the spray flying, the sun shining, the wind hard on the side of my face. And the boat behaved perfectly. Nothing more to do to her, except a few replacements to the rigging, a little fine tuning.

'I've talked to Miguel on the phone,' was Soo's greeting as I came in, tired and elated. 'He'll have a word with you on Monday, after the Albufera ceremony.'

'What's his problem?' I asked, pouring myself the Balearic version of a horse's neck. 'We've paid him for the work to date.' I was thinking of the speech I had promised Jorge Martinez I would make. In the excitement of getting *Thunderflash* ready I had forgotten all about it.

'It isn't the money,' Soo said.

'What is it then?'

'It's the work. He's short of work.'

'What does he expect?' With the vandalism that

was going on, builders were finding life difficult. 'He's lucky to have a villa to complete.'

'That's the trouble. Evans has told him to stop work. He and his two mates have moved into the ground floor and Miguel's been told to clear the site. Anything still to be done they'll do themselves. The agreement, you remember, was that we'd employ him to finish the building.'

'You may have told him that. I didn't.' I went over to the window, propping myself on the desk top and enjoying the ice-cold fizz of the brandy and ginger ale, my mouth still dry with salt. The lights were coming on, the old town showing white above the steps leading up to the Port Mahon Hotel and the Avenida Giron. 'He's got no claim on us at all.'

'He thinks he has.' And Soo added, 'A matter of honour, he said.'

'Oh, bugger that,' I told her. 'There's nothing in writing. I saw the lawyers early last week.' But in the end I agreed I would have a talk with him. 'It's not far from Albufera to Codolar Point. We could easily run over there either before or after the ceremony and see what Evans has to say about it, if he's in residence. Do you know if he is?'

'Miguel says not. He moved in with his two mates, did a quick do-it-yourself job making the lower half habitable, then brought the *Santa Maria* round into the bay at Arenal d'en Castell and the following morning they were gone.'

'When was that?'

'Last week. Friday, I think.'

'Then they should be back by now. Nobody stays out fishing off Menorca two weekends at a stretch.'

But they did. At any rate, there was no sign of them on the Monday morning when I drove out to the point just before the opening ceremony. This was due to start at twelve-thirty followed by a buffet lunch in the hospitality pavilion on the Addaia–Arenal approach road. The villa was deserted, some of the windows covered with sheets of plastic, the scaffolding still there and the whole place a mess of builders' rubble. People I spoke to on the approach road to the development said they had seen no sign of anybody there for more than a week.

The site for the ceremony was a newly completed villa standing on a rise a little back from the road and close to the entrance to the Albufera development. A white tape had been stretched across this road and a little crowd was already gathered on the villa's terraces and by the shrubbery that covered the hillside. The sun was shining and there was a magnificent view across Arenal to the Fornells peninsula. There was a guard of honour provided by the military, also a band, which began to play just after Soo and I had taken our seats. The Renatos were there and several other friends, the atmosphere that of a provincial function almost anywhere, except for that view and the ever-present Menorcan wind.

The Mayor arrived, only eight minutes late, accompanied by a *Guardia* motor-cycle escort. His car drove straight up to the tape and Jorge Martinez jumped out. Waving and smiling, he came running up the steps, his body slim in a sky-blue suit, his face dark in shadow and full of vitality. 'You speak after Señor Alvarez,' he said to me as he shook hands. Mario Alvarez was the construction engineer for the project. 'First in English, then in Spanish – just a few words. Okay? I speak last.'

I nodded and he took his place, sitting quickly down and signalling for the band to stop. In the sudden silence the voices of the children playing hide-and-seek among the shrubs seemed startlingly loud, and I could hear the gulls calling as they planed above the cliffs.

Alvarez spoke for perhaps five minutes, a very flowery speech, both in his reference to the project and to the Alcalde, who looked pleased. So did the workmen, who were also complimented, the faces of all those present wreathed in smiles suitable to the occasion. Then it was my turn, and since I made a point of referring to the activities of the separatists, the smiles disappeared. Jorge Martinez understood English better than he spoke it. He was not amused, but a reference to the involvement of the PCE and PCPE had him nodding his head vigorously. He was a right-wing socialist and detested the communists. And when, after I had repeated my remarks in Spanish, I sat down, he was smiling again and nodding as he clapped his hands, and everybody did the same, apparently happy at what I had said.

Abruptly, he jumped to his feet, and just as abruptly, the clapping ceased and everybody fell silent, except the children. As always, he spoke very fast, not reading his speech, but talking as though straight from the heart. His line was that Menorca was a small island with few natural resources. But it had the sea and it was warm. Tourism and the foreigners who purchased villas such as this one, bringing much-needed foreign currency – hard currency so that the life of the people could be improved and made less hard . . .

It was as he was saying this, his arms outflung as though embracing the island and all its people, his face lit by that broad political smile of his and his voice carrying conviction across the little gathering to the rock outcrops of the cliff line beyond, it was then that a sound cracked like a whip over the proceedings. His head jerked forward, the smile still there, a rictus in a spreading welter of blood and grey matter, his whole body toppling forward, a staggering, headlong fall that took him down the flight of six steps that led from the upper terrace where he had been standing.

I remember my eyes recording with a sort of instant paralysis of horror the neat round hole in the back of his head as he fell sprawling forward. Then his body hit the lower terrace and rolled over, the eyes seeming to hang loose in that dreadful, bloody mash-up of a face. Manuela let out a stifled cry, Soo was retching, her face white and her eyes closed. From shocked silence, the little crowd was suddenly in an uproar of noise, women, and some men, screaming, soldiers moving forward as their officer shouted an order, the *Guardia* abandoning their motor bikes, drawing their pistols and looking about them in bewilderment.

Somebody shouted for a doctor. But there was no doctor, no need of one anyway. Jorge Martinez was patently very dead, killed instantly by a single bullet, and no sign of the killer who must have been an expert marksman. The soldiers were running now, up over the terraces and round the back of the villa, sealing it off. But though the shot had obviously come from behind us, perhaps from one of the villa windows, the gunman could equally have fired from the shrubbery on the hill above.

The minutes passed in a seemingly aimless search, the official guests and the little crowd of local people all beginning to talk as the initial shock wore off. A small boy was brought to the *Guardia* corporal, his little face white and creased with tears, his mouth hanging loose, his eyes large. Word spread in a sea of whispering – the child had seen the gunman as he went into the bushes behind the villa. No, he wasn't playing with his friend. We could hear the child's voice now, high and very frightened. He had gone to have a pee and had found the man lying there with a gun. The kid had been right there when he had fired, only feet away, and then the killer had scrambled to his feet and disappeared up the slope.

Soldiers and bandsmen fanned out, climbing the slope behind us, and Alvarez in a shaken voice asked us all to go down to the pavilion where there would be some wine and something to eat. Would we go now please, then the authorities could take any statements they might need. He glanced down at the body of the Mayor. A soldier was covering it with a plastic sheet encrusted with cement. Alvarez made the sign of the cross and turned abruptly, walking stiffly erect down to the road. I watched Gonzalez Renato stand for a moment, head bowed over the body, then go to his car. Most of the guests did the same, and watching them pay their respects to the inert bundle that only a moment before had been so full of vitality, I had the feeling they were not thinking about Jorge Martinez, but about themselves, and wondering what would happen now. Politically he was the nearest to a strong man the island had known since the end of the French occupation in 1802. Now he was dead and nobody to replace him, nobody who had the charisma and the public appeal to guide a volatile, insular and basically peasant people into an increasingly uncertain future.

We were held in the hospitality pavilion most of the afternoon. Plain-clothes police arrived, noting down names and addresses, interviewing those nearest to the murdered man and anyone who might have had a glimpse of the gunman. The food disappeared almost at a gulp, the wine too, the babble of voices on a high pitch as speculation reached the verge of hysteria. Who had done it – the extreme right, the extreme left, Eta? Or was it a delayed reaction to events in Africa? *Salvemo Menorca*. For myself, and the scattering of other ex-pats attending the ceremony, it was not a pleasant experience. We might not be directly responsible, but you could see it in their eyes – we were to blame.

There was something quite primitive in the way some of them looked at us, as though we had the Evil Eye. And the *Guardia* in particular reacted in a similar manner, their manner of questioning increasingly hostile. It was almost as though they had convinced themselves that one of us, one of the *extranjeros*, must know who had done it and be connected with it in some way. You could see it from their point of view. This was an island. To kill like that, in cold blood, it had to be somebody from outside – a terrorist, some representative of a foreign organisation, not one of their own people. It was a gut reaction. They were looking for a scapegoat, but the fact remained that all of us who were being questioned, all except the children and a mother who had gone looking for her little boy, we were all of us gathered there in full view, so that in the end they had to let us go.

Soo and I didn't talk much on the drive back. It was late afternoon, the air full of the clean smell of pines and everywhere the fields massed with colour, the predominantly golden carpet of flowers patched with the startling white of wild narcissi, the sun blazing out of a blue sky. What a lovely day for a killing! What the hell was wrong with Man that he couldn't enjoy the beauty of the world around him? Politics. Always politics. I felt almost physically sick. There was so much here in Menorca that I loved – the sea, the sun, the peace. And now it was shattered. Martinez had been much more than just the Alcalde of Mahon. He had been a power throughout the island.

That evening several of us met in a restaurant near the square in Villa Carlos. But though we talked late into the night we achieved nothing except a fragile sense of solidarity. There were men there who had been in the island many years, but though they tried to kid themselves they were now Menorquins, they knew in their heart of hearts they were still foreigners. We were all of us *extranjeros*.

I was not in a happy frame of mind when I finally returned home. Soo, thank God, was already in bed and asleep. I undressed in the dark, a breeze blowing the curtains. Lying there, eyes closed, my mind went over and over the events of the day, the talk at that crowded restaurant table. Too much brandy, too much coffee. And then the phone rang.

I thought it might be America. Sometimes Americans forget the time difference. I rolled over, reaching blindly for the receiver, but Soo was before me. 'Yes?' She switched on the light. And then, after a moment: 'For you.' She passed it across to me and turned over, away from the light, as a man's voice spoke in my ear: 'Wade here. We've just got the news. You were there, I gather.'

I came awake then, wondering who the hell he was. 'Who is it? Who's speaking?'

'Wade,' he repeated. 'Commander Wade.'

I remembered then. 'Where are you speaking from?'

'London,' he said. 'Where did you think?' He had a quiet, crisp, well-educated voice. 'Did you see him?'

'Who?'

'The man who shot Martinez, of course. Did you recognise him?'

'I didn't see him. How should I? Nobody saw him, not to recognise him.' And I asked him, 'What's it got to do with you, anyway?'

But he ignored that. 'We have a picture here. It's

just come in. It shows you seated right beside the Mayor. You must have seen what happened.'

'Of course I did. But the shot came from the villa behind and I was looking at Jorge Martinez, we all were, watching him as he pitched forward down the steps on to the terrace below. The police have full information, they took statements—'

'Yes, yes, we've got a telex copy of your statement here.'

'Then why the hell are you phoning me? It's after one in the morning.'

'I'm well aware of the time.' His tone was slightly weary and I guessed he had been at some Navy office most of the evening.

'What are you, Intelligence?' I asked. But all he said was, 'This is an open line, so let's keep to the point. I'm phoning you because Lloyd Jones reported you'd been very helpful in locating a *friend* of his.' His emphasis on the word friend made it clear he didn't want the man's name mentioned. 'I understand you have now exchanged an unfinished villa and an old fishing boat for his catamaran. Where is he, do you know?' And when I said I had no idea, that he was away fishing somewhere, he asked when I had last seen him.

'Almost two weeks ago.' And I added, 'What business is it of yours? Anyway, you have my statement. You've just said so.'

'Yes, but there's nothing in it about your dealings with this friend of Lloyd Jones. We need to know where he is now, and where he was at the time the

Mayor was shot . . . Hullo, hullo! Are you still there?'
His voice had sharpened.

'Yes, I'm still here.'

'You didn't answer.'

'Why should I?' I was fully awake now and wondering what his real purpose was. 'I've no intention of acting for your organisation.'

'What organisation?'

'Intelligence,' I said. 'I want no part of it and I'm going to hang up now.'

'No. Don't do that. Not for the moment.' He said it as though he were giving an order on his own quarterdeck.

'I'm sorry,' I said. 'Goodbye.'

'Ahmed Bey. Remember? And the Mattarella brothers.'

'What do you mean?' The receiver was back at my ear, a quite involuntary movement.

'Kenitra,' he said. 'On the coast of Morocco.' And he added, 'You see, I've had a few enquiries made about you. I don't think I need say any more. Now answer my questions please.' There was a coldness in his voice that hadn't been there before, a certainty that I would do what he asked. 'Have you seen our friend since you handed the *Santa Maria* over to him ten days ago?'

'No,' I said.

'Have you asked the police where he is?'

'Why should I? A man out fishing . . .'

'You think he's fishing?' He didn't wait for an

answer. 'So you don't know where he is now or where he's been?'

'No.'

'Well, kindly find out.'

'I'm busy,' I said. 'I have clients . . .'

'Just find out for me. Understand? I'll ring you tomorrow night.'

I opened my mouth to tell him I wouldn't be in, that there was no point, but instead I heard myself say, 'When?'

'Eighteen hundred hours.'

I started to say I would be out then, but the line went suddenly dead.

I lay back, my eyes closed. Ahmed Bey! Jesus! that was more than ten years back. The Jedida–Marseilles run.

'What did he want?' Soo was propped up on one elbow, her large, dark eyes staring at me. 'Who was he?'

'A client, talking about boats.'

'At this time of night?'

'Go to sleep,' I said. I needed to think.

'He said his name was Commander something or other. Was it about Gareth?'

God almighty! She was still thinking of Lloyd Jones. 'No, of course not.' But I could see she didn't believe me.

'Why did he ring then? It's almost half past one. Was it about this man who persuaded you to part with the villa? You shouldn't have done it, Mike. A lovely villa like that, the *Santa Maria* too, and all you've got for it is that bloody catamaran. What did he say? What did he want?' She was leaning forward, fingers gripped urgently on my arm. 'Is it to do with – what happened today?'

'Yesterday,' I said. Already it was yesterday and Wade in London, the man who had told Lloyd Jones to contact me ... No, ordered more likely. Ordered him to check with me in the hope of discovering Evans's whereabouts ... Wade was concerned enough about what had happened here in Menorca to ring me in the middle of the night.

'Patrick. That's what Gareth called him.' She let go of my arm, slumping back on the pillow. 'What's he been up to now?'

'Now?' My mind shifted from my talk with Wade to Lloyd Jones sitting across from me at that table on the Fornells waterfront. Had he told her more than he had told me?' 'What do you know about Patrick Evans?' She shook her head quickly, her eyes sliding away from me. 'What did he tell you?' I was leaning over, shaking her, but all she did was stare at me blankly. 'Nothing – only that he'd saved his life.'

'I know that. Anything else?'

She hesitated, and then she said, 'They're related.'

'In what way?'

'Just related, that's all. He was explaining why he was so anxious to find the man. A message, I think it was the man's mother. She had asked Gareth to take a message.'

She didn't know what the message was. She thought it might be something to do with a cottage they owned in a place called Gwenogle. 'I remember the name because it sounded so odd, and yet the way Gareth said it . . .' She was smiling to herself. 'I think maybe he was born in that little Welsh hill village.'

'Who – Gareth or Patrick Evans?'

'Patrick. They're both of them Welsh, of course.' She reached out and switched off the bedside light. I closed my eyes and in the silent darkness I saw Ahmed Bey's face as I had seen it that last time, the bullets slamming his thickset body backwards into the wake of the Italian boat ranging alongside. That was the last trip. They dumped us in an inflatable, no food, no water, the west coast of Africa more than twenty miles away and all desert when we reached it. We were lucky to get out of it alive.

How the hell did Wade know about that? We'd never been caught by the authorities. Was there some sort of a file on me at Naval Intelligence? And then I began thinking about Patrick Evans. There had to be some connection – first Lloyd Jones searching for him with out-of-date pictures, then the man himself, and now Wade.

It was in the very middle of the night, still half awake, my mind drowsily running over the possibilities, my imagination working overtime, that I suddenly had an ugly thought. If Wade knew what I'd been up to as a kid, there might be others, Evans, for instance. In which case . . .

The feeling was so strong, so frightening, I nearly got up there and then in the middle of the night. I didn't sleep after that, waiting for the dawn, certain now that Evans would have retained a key to the catamaran.

At first light I slid out of bed and dressed in the office across the stairhead. I was just searching my pockets for the car keys when Soo emerged, a pale shadow in her cream nightdress, her face still flushed with sleep. She didn't ask me what I was up to or where I was going. She simply said, 'I'll make you some coffee.'

I could have hugged her then, all the love we'd felt for each other surging back in that moment. She knew. That intuitive sense between those who have shared several years of their lives, the sense that at times is pure telepathy, had communicated my fears to her. She knew where I was going, and why. The terrible thought that was in my mind was in hers.

She brought me my coffee, then stood by the window to drink her own. She didn't say anything. There was no need. The sun shining through the thin nightie limned the dark outline of her body, her face, her breasts, the long legs, all in silhouette. She looked infinitely desirable.

I drank the coffee quickly, urgent to be gone, to set my mind at rest, alternatively to . . . But the alternative didn't bear thinking about. If a search of the boat confirmed my fear, what would I do about it – where would I take it? Out to sea? Come back with it here and take the dinghy?

I put down the cup and walked over to her. I didn't put my arms round her, and she just lifted her face to me, our kiss without passion, gentle and understanding. After all, we had both been there, we had both heard the crack of the gun, no silencer, had seen the poor devil's face explode in a red mash as he had fallen. 'I may be some time,' I said, and she nodded, still not saying anything, but I knew she would be here, waiting for me when I returned.

CHAPTER FOUR

The sun was just rising as I drove round the end of Cala Figuera and on to the Levante, the harbour water still as glass, not a breath of wind, and as yet hardly anyone about. At the harbour end I turned right, then right again on to the approach road to the naval barracks. The naval quay is a large open space used occasionally as a parade ground. Yachts are allowed to be lifted out and laid up there, and there was still quite a line of them not yet in the water. The cat was lying stern-on just next to an old wooden yawl, the paint of her starb'd hull a-glint with the sun's reflected light as the wash of a harbour tug brought ripples slapping against the concrete walls. Beyond her, the city shone red and warm against a blue sky.

The tug hooted as I jumped on board. Aft, by the wheel with its swivel chair, I stood for a moment looking the vessel over, trying to sense whether anybody had been on board during the night. No footmarks and the lock on the saloon door had not been tampered with. But that didn't mean anything. He had given me two ignition keys, but only one for the saloon door. Some fool had dropped the other overboard, he had said.

I must have stood there for several minutes, thinking it over, trying to put myself in his shoes. But then the trouble was I was jumping to too many conclusions, and in the end I said to hell with it, opened the boat up and went below into that big saloon with its repeat bank of instruments, large chart area and semi-circular banquette behind the table on the port side. There were some overalls bundled up on the ledge below the low sweep of windows. They hadn't been there last time I had been on board, nor the long-peaked cap. That would be Carp's, probably the overalls, too. There was a cardboard box full of paint tins and brushes, and the steps to the left that normally led down into the port hull had been folded back so that he could get at the engine. A steel tool box stood open on the floor nearby.

I had brought a couple of torches with me, for this was a bilge-and-hidden-cranny search. A rummage, in fact, and however long it took, I had to be sure the ship was clean.

I started on the starb'd hull, cupboards, lockers, drawers, mattresses, then finally the bilges, remembering the one time I had experienced a customs rummage. It was in Juan-les-Pins where I had run for shelter, six *officiers de douane* turning the whole ship inside out, body searching myself and my crew. I think they would have liked to beat us up, but I was

Morocco-registered, flying the Moroccan flag, and there were political reasons why, having found nothing, they should respect that flag.

It took me a good half-hour to go through that one hull, despite the floor being well supplied with inspection covers, each with a brass ring for ease of lifting. All I found in the bilges was a pair of glasses in a slipcase, some dirty overalls and a couple of bottles of Mistra, a Maltese wine, that looked as though they had been there some time.

The saloon didn't take long. If he had hidden it somewhere it was unlikely he would have chosen such an obvious place, unless of course he was willing to take his time and unscrew the panels housing the electrics. And the port hull was as clean as the other, odds and ends of equipment, a half-empty bottle of Gordon's in the bilges, nothing else, and both engine compartments I could see at a glance were clear.

I returned to the saloon, sat on the helmsman's swivel chair and tried to think what I would have done in his place. He had had the boat for some time, that much had been clear at our meeting. If I had known the boat as well as that, where would I have hidden it? Fuel or freshwater tanks were the obvious places for small packets, but there was no way he could have introduced such a large object into any of the tanks without dismantling them. Sails? But I had checked the sail bags. They were in the bows, in lockers for'ard of the loos on both sides that held chain, anchors, rope, paint. My eyes, roving round the saloon, fastened on the up-ended steps of the port hull, the exposed top of the port diesel engine. Engines! It was always engines that caused trouble.

I went over to it, bending down again and directing my torch below the shock-absorbent bedding bolts and after along the line of the drive shaft to the propeller, sure that he or his engineer would have known every detail of the compartment. There was an area below the prop shaft that the beam of my torch could not reach. There was nothing for it but to strip down and wriggle in there. I got thoroughly dirty, of course, and it proved to be wasted effort, though the slope of the bilge underneath the shaft was fully long enough and deep enough. I came out of that painful exercise cursing, the room for manoeuvre in that restricted space so limited that I damn nearly got myself stuck. Nobody, I was certain, would have attempted to hide anything in such an awkward place, not if he were in a hurry.

I stood there, naked except for my pants that were now streaked black with oil. I was staring at the steps down into the starb'd hull that concealed the other engine. And then there was the panelling. I was already scratched and bleeding in a couple of places, but I knew if I didn't check out the other cavity I would never be really certain. I lifted the steps. The compartment was exactly the same as the other, just room for me to wriggle my way headfirst between the outboard side of the hull and the cold metal of the engine. The torch was dimming, but rather than go back for the other, I squirmed further in, feeling down below the shaft with my outstretched hand.

That's how I found it – a hard, chunky package wrapped in plastic.

It took some ingenuity and some juggling to extract it from the confined space, working my way backwards at the same time. But when I was finally out, standing in the sunlight streaming through the saloon windows, and the thing in my hand, there was no doubt what it was. The only question was the type and where it had come from.

I turned quickly to the open cockpit door, feeling suddenly furtive as I slammed it shut and bolted it. Christ almighty! If somebody saw me holding this . . . My hands were trembling as I unwrapped the package. It had been zipped into one of those plastic travelling cases for suits, rolled into a tight bundle, then taped. I had to get a carving knife from the gallery to rip it open.

By then I hadn't much doubt, the shape of the telescope and the folding butt apparent through the stiff red plastic. It was the most common of guns, a 7.62 mm Kalashnikov. But not the ordinary assault rifle. What I unwrapped from the plastic was the sniper's version of the AK-47. In addition to telescopic sights it had a double strut folding metal butt. The struts were in the folded position. Automatically, almost without thinking, I unfolded them, bringing the rifle to my shoulder and sighting through the for'ard window of the saloon at a gull on a mooring buoy out by the naval jetty. It felt snug and workmanlike, and I could imagine how it had been to the killer, the back of Jorge's head there in the magnified field of vision, dead-centred on the cross wires.

I glanced at the maker's stamp on the side of it, Czechoslovakian, not Russian. Then I checked the firing mechanism. The safety catch was on and it was set at single shot. I sniffed the muzzle. It still smelt faintly of gun smoke, so did the inside of the plastic, and when I took the magazine off I found one round was missing.

My worst fears confirmed I stood there in a sort of daze, appalled at the evil of the man. To kill for political reasons, yes, maybe that could be justified by somebody deeply committed to a cause – that was a matter between him and whatever god he accepted. But Evans could have no possible commitment to a Menorquin, or even a Spanish political faction. To kill in cold blood as a mercenary, and then to plant the weapon on somebody else, on a man he didn't know, had only just met . . .!

I felt the chill of it in my guts. Man might be a rogue species; Petra certainly thought so and had discussed it with me in one of her more serious moments. But this – this was quite abnormal, quite outside of my experience. Once, and once only, I had undertaken an arms run. Explosives, detonators, some land mines, Kalashnikovs and Birettas – we had landed them in a deserted cove just south of Finisterre, handing the whole cargo over to Basque separatists. At least the Eta boys who took delivery had had a cause. But this . . .

I sat down in one of the chairs that stood by the

saloon table, wondering what to do now. Go to
the *Guardia*? Tell the plain-clothes detectives of the
national police who had been put on to the case? But
I could see the expression of disbelief on the face of
the *Inspector Jefe*. I had met him once, a small, very
dark man with eyes too close together and a sharp,
suspicious face. They would be looking for somebody
they could pin the atrocity on and I had a feeling I
would do just as well as anyone else, so long as it was
a foreigner and local politics not involved. The fact
that I had been standing beside Martinez didn't mean
I couldn't have organised the whole thing. And now,
with the killer's weapon in my hands, what the hell
was I to do with it? Dump it at sea, I suppose. Take it
out in the dinghy and dump it, somewhere out beyond
Bloody Island, and hope nobody would have their
binoculars trained on me at the time.

Carp arrived just as I put the kettle on. I heard his
motor bike splutter to a stop on the quay and I called
out to him to ask if he would like a cup of tea. By
then I had cleaned myself up and dressed, everything
more or less normal, except for the rolled-up bedding
on the settle by the cockpit door. I told him I had
spilled some oil on it and was taking it ashore to be
cleaned.

He wasn't surprised to find me on board at that
hour. The boat was due to leave for Malta in a few
days' time and everything was in the last-minute-rush
stage. We sat around for ten minutes or so, drinking
our tea and talking over all the things that still had to
be done.

It was when I was in the car and actually driving back along the waterfront, the gun in the back, that the idea came to me. I eased up on the accelerator, my mind racing as I glanced in the rear mirror. It was such a neat counter-thrust, but was I sure? Was I absolutely certain it was Evans who had planted that thing on board? But who else? And even if it was one of the others, then it didn't make any difference. I eased into the parking space just past the commercial wharf, swung the wheel over, making a U-turn that headed me back, past the turning to Cala Rata and Mesquida, past the connecting road to the main Mahon–Ciudad-ela Highway and out along the Fornells road. A quarter of an hour later I had reached the crossroads and had turned right on to the side road heading to Port d'Addaia and Arenal d'en Castell, the sun higher now and the air warm as it blew in through the open sun-shine roof.

The headland running out to Punta Codolar was brown against the blue of sea and sky. It was just after nine and everything bright and fresh. Bougainvillaea flashed purple on the wall of a villa. A beautiful morn-ing, one of those days it was good to be alive. I should have been singing at the top of my voice. Instead, all I could think about was that bloody rifle and whether I would find Evans back from his voyage in the *Santa Maria*. What the hell did I do if he, or one of his mates, was in residence?

The villa rose slowly above the flat, scrub-clad rock of the headland like the rusty hulk of a ship coming up over the horizon. There were still vestiges of Miguel's scaffolding clinging to the breeze-block sides and as I drove up to it I thought how ugly it looked in its half-finished state, its upper windows gaping squares that looked like the gun embrasures of a coastal defence blockhouse.

I parked the car and got out, standing for a moment, staring up at it, thinking about what I would say if there was somebody there. I could have left something behind. Any excuse would do. But there was no vehicle anywhere around and it looked empty enough. I went up to the door and hammered on it. Nobody answered. I tried it, but it was locked, or more probably bolted from the inside, for when I went round to the back, I found a hasp had been screwed on to the rear door frame and there was a brand new padlock to secure it.

The villa, isolated there on the very point of the headland, was several hundred metres from any other building. Looking round, I counted seven villas within sight, all of them only just visible, and all of them apparently deserted, no sign of any movement of either people or vehicles. The garage window was the one I finally chose, bunching an old dinghy sail I had in the car against one of the four panes and slamming my elbow into it until the glass cracked. Only one piece fell on the floor and that I cleared up later; the rest I was able to pull out by hand, leaving a neat empty square through which it was easy to reach the latch. There was always a chance that the absence of that one pane might go unnoticed for a time.

It took me several minutes to find what I wanted,

a loose section of flooring where the electrician had been at work. It was in the kitchen and I prised it up with two of the knives lying among a pile of unwashed plates in the sink. Underneath, between the concrete base and the wood floor, grey plastic-coated wires followed the copper piping that carried water to the kitchen taps and the water heater above the draining board. I took the wrapping off the gun, wiped it over carefully with my handkerchief, then thrust it as far into the cavity as I could and hammered the shortened section of floorboard back into place with my feet.

Looking at it, I felt a certain sense of satisfaction. There was nothing to indicate that it had been tampered with, but police officers searching the building would certainly want to see underneath. I left by the way I had come, gathering up the little pile of broken glass and latching the window after me. It was only when I was driving back to Mahon that I began to wonder where Evans and his two men were now, how long it would be before they returned to the villa.

Back at Cala Figuera I found two plain-clothes detectives waiting for me, their car parked outside the chandlery. They were in the office, an inspector and his assistant, both of them drinking coffee while Soo, her dressing gown over her nightie, sat across the desk from them, looking pale and angry. 'I keep telling them where we were sitting we couldn't possibly have had anything to do with it. They came just after you left. They wanted to talk to you, but I didn't know where you'd gone, how to get in touch with you, so they started asking me questions, then this man –' she jerked her head at the inspector – 'said they must search the house and they have been over everywhere, including the store.' All this she said in a rush, the words tumbling over themselves. 'Now they're waiting for you, so I gave them some coffee.' And she added, 'They want to search the boat, too. They seem to think we're hiding something.'

By then they were on their feet, their behaviour very correct. 'Some questions please. Then we go to this catamaran you have acquired.' The inspector was the taller of the two, a dark, hook-nosed man, his Spanish markedly Catalan. 'You have been down to this catamaran this morning?'

'*Si.*' And I told him why. 'It is due in Malta shortly to pick up some American tourists.'

'So you are getting it ready.' He nodded. 'You go with it, or you stay here – which?'

I hesitated. It hadn't occurred to me until then. 'I'm not sure,' I said. 'Señor Carpenter may take her with just one other man, but if the weather is bad –' I left it at that and he began questioning me about where I had been, what I had done after we had been allowed to leave the Albufera hospitality pavilion the previous afternoon.

'I've already told him,' Soo said.

He understood English, even if he did not speak it, for he said, '*Si, si,* but, señor, I wish to hear it from you.'

So we went over it all again, an interrogation that took about quarter of an hour. Then suddenly he seemed to get bored with it. 'Now we go and inspect your ship please.' He called it a *barco*, so avoiding the word catamaran. 'You want to come, señora?' He turned politely to Soo.

She smiled. 'Not unless you insist.'

'No, of course not. I do not insist.' He bowed politely as she took her cue and left the office. 'May I use your telephone please?' He lifted the receiver and when he got through he spoke to somebody who was obviously his superior, reporting that he had discovered nothing new and telling him that they were on their way now to search the boat. '*Si, Jefe*. Señor Steele will be accompanying us.'

It took them a good hour to search the boat, and when they had finished, having failed to find what they were looking for, they settled themselves at the saloon table, the inspector taking out a notebook and beginning to scribble a report. Knowing from the phone call he had made in the office that they would stay here until their chief, an *inspector jefe*, arrived, I asked them whether they would like a drink. The inspector hesitated, then declined somewhat reluctantly. I told him I had work to do and would he excuse me, but he shook his head, becoming suddenly quite excited and making it very clear that I was to stay here on board.

'For how long?' I asked him.

'As long as is necessary.'

'And if I go ashore now?'

'I shall be forced to stop you.' He used the word *detención*.

I went up on deck then and gave Carp a hand. He

needed to go up the mast to reeve a new spinnaker halyard and wanted somebody else beside Luis on the winch. It was while we were hoisting him up in the bo's'n's chair that the *Inspector Jefe* arrived. As soon as Carp was at the top, we made the hoist fast and I went aft to welcome him.

'Garcia Menendez.' He gave a little bow as we shook hands, his manner polite, but at the same time assertive, his sharp eyes, almost black in the sunlight, staring at me full of alert curiosity. 'Inspector Molina, is he still here? . . . Good. Then we go inside where there are no distractions.' He made a gesture with his hand that seemed to embrace the sunshine, the water, all the movement of Mahon harbour at noon on a fine spring day. He had an engineer with him. He did not introduce him to me, but he did ask my permission before telling him to go ahead with a search of the engine compartments.

We went below and I offered him a drink. He shook his head, taking the inspector's place on the banquette and waving me to a position opposite him. The engineer was already slipping into a pair of white overalls. I watched him as he folded back the steps to the starb'd hull accommodation and probed the interior of the engine compartment with his torch. I felt slightly sick, knowing that somebody must have told them where to look. 'Some questions please,' the *Jefe* said. 'Matters that have arisen in the course of our investigation. First, the ownership of this yacht which arrive here from Marseilles. There is a passenger on board. You know him?'

'No.' And I explained about the deal Evans and I had agreed on, all the time conscious of the engineer working his way into the afterpart of the engine compartment. Like so many engineers he was not a small man and I could hear him grunting with the effort of squeezing his way to a point where he could check the whole length of the prop shaft and the bilge cavity below it. There was no doubt about it – they had been told exactly where to look. If I hadn't got there before them ... 'I would like to see the documents please.' Menendez's words, sharp and official, cut across my thoughts. 'The documents of exchange,' he added. 'You have exchanged a fishing boat and an uncompleted villa on Punta Codolar, you say, for this big catamaran yacht. Who is your lawyer?'

'Martin Lopez.'

'Ah *si*. And he has the documents I suppose?'

'He is drawing them up,' I told him. 'It was all done in rather a hurry.'

'The ship's papers then. I would like to see the Certificate of Registry. Or are they also being prepared by your lawyer?'

That was when I realised how complete the trap had been, how cleverly prepared, for I couldn't produce the ship's papers and all I could tell him was that I had seen them, but Evans had told me he had had to lodge them with the Banca Espagñol as security for a small overdraft he had requested after opening an account with them. 'He is arranging for a copy to be sent to my lawyer.'

'I have already spoken to Señor Lopez and he does

not have it. He has sent it to England for the boat to be registered in your name.'

The engineer had emerged from the engine compartment, his overalls no longer white. He was breathing heavily and reported he had found nothing. 'Then it is in the *other* engine,' Menendez said. The engineer nodded and crossed to the port side of the saloon beyond the chart table and lifted the steps that covered that engine. Menendez watched me, waiting for some sign of panic. 'Also,' he said, speaking slowly, 'there is some problem about the exchange document.'

'What problem?' I asked him. It was the first I'd heard that there was any difficulty over the paperwork and from what he was saying it was obvious he had known every detail of the arrangements between Evans and myself before coming on board and asking me questions. But then in a place like Mahon, where everyone of importance knew everyone else, I suppose it is inevitable, particularly as I was an *extranjero*. 'That's the first I've heard that there's any difficulty over the papers,' I told him. 'Did you gather what the trouble was?'

'Only that Señor Lopez was unable to contact this man Evans.'

'He is always fishing. That's why he wanted the *Santa Maria* in a hurry, so that he could earn some money fishing.'

The *Jefe* nodded. 'Of course. He is a *pescador*.' And then looking straight at me – 'Do you think he is a good one?' The thick lips under the hooked nose gave me a little crooked smile.

'I've no idea.'

'But you let him go off with your boat, the *Santa Maria*, and with no proper security. You are a business-man, Señor Steele. Does it surprise you that I find that a little strange?' He stared at me a moment, then switched his gaze to the torch-lit cavity of the open engine compartment, waiting for his engineer to report that he had found what they were looking for. 'It is a question of dates,' he added, his eyes still fixed on the starb'd side, the fingers of his right hand tapping impatiently at the table top. 'The precise date when you take over this boat.'

I sat there, feeling numb, the trap springing shut, and seeing the way they had planned it, the devilish simplicity of it. He was watching me again now, pulling out a packet of cigarettes. He offered me one, and when I said I only smoked a pipe, he laughed, and then in the act of lighting his own, quite casually, he said, 'The *Cruz Rojo*. You remember? And after, when the fireworks are over, where do you go then?' And when I didn't say anything, wondering what his question was leading up to, he went on, 'It was the night of the gala Manuela Renato arrange in the Quarries above Figuera. We were both there. Remember?'

I nodded wondering what Petra had said, or Soo, talking to the sisters, babbling under anaesthetic? Had they dreamed up a scenario in which I was involved in running contraband into the island?

'No,' he said. 'You don't forget because in the early hours of the morning your wife gives birth prematurely and your baby is dead.'

'Have you found the men?' I asked him. 'The two men who pushed her down the slope in their haste to get out of that cave?'

He shook his head. 'No. I don't think we ever will. They are not Menorquin and we think they almost certainly leave the island very soon after.' And he added, 'Unless they go to the mainland of Spain, it is very difficult for us to trace their movements. Even in Barcelona, if they take the ferry, it is simple for them to disappear across the French border. No,' he said again, 'we do not know anything about them. What we do know, however, is that the night before there is a boat in Cales Coves and it is tied up against the rocks below the cave you were in that night. We have a description of that boat, a description that is indicative of a single mast and two hulls. We have checked with the harbour authorities and there is no boat of such description in either Mahon or Ciudadela, not in Fornells either — only this one.'

'So,' I said. 'What is the significance of that?' But I knew bloody well what was in his mind.

He was smiling now. 'Did you know there is a landward exit from that cave?' And when I explained we had been solely concerned with the two men who had rushed out from that passage, he nodded. 'Of course. And it is unfortunate about the father of Señorita Callis, that she is not here to answer some questions.'

'You're checking, I suppose, that her father really does exist, that this car accident did happen?'

'Of course. It takes time, and meanwhile you are

here to answer all our questions. Let us suppose,' he said, his eyes almost closed. 'It is just a thought, eh? Suppose it is this yacht that is in Cales Coves the night before she takes you to that cave. What do you think it might be doing there?'

'Sheltering, I suppose.'

'Why? Why Cales Coves and not Mahon or Ciudadela?'

'If they'd had a longish passage, from Mallorca or Corsica—'

'Or Tunis,' he said softly. 'Somewhere along the shores of North Africa.'

'If there'd been a passage like that,' I told him, 'with poor weather conditions you can get awfully tired, even in a stable boat like this. Then you just put in to the first shelter you find, head down and lights out.'

He nodded, still with that little smile. 'Of course. I understand. But no navigation lights when coming in. Also there is a light in that cave mouth for a full hour before the boat appear. That is what attracted the attention of this witness we interview.' He paused, watching me. 'The boat has no lights all the time it was tied up under the cliffs, and there is no light any longer in the cave mouth. But there is the occasional flash of torches. There was a moon, you see, and some cloud in the sky.' He sat back, suddenly relaxed. 'Well now, you are a businessman, Señor Steele, you have a position in Menorca, Spanish friends. But it was not always like that, eh? Before you come to Menorca, before your marriage. So, what does the description I have given you of what our witness saw suggest to you?'

If I said it suggested smuggling, he would think I was involved. If I said it didn't suggest a damn thing, he'd know I was lying and be even more suspicious.

'You don't say anything?'

I shrugged, stretching my face into a smile. 'Your guess is as good as mine.'

'You have been to Bisley?' The question took me by surprise. But of course, somebody would have told him about the cups. The inspector might have taken a note of them and reported. 'You are a good shot I think.' He was smiling again, the eyes bright like a bird that has seen a particularly succulent snail.

I nodded. 'Why? What's that got to do with it?'

He sat there, smiling still, and not answering, everything so quiet I could hear the distant chime of the cathedral clock. 'Look, for God's sake! I was there, right beside Jorge Martinez, sitting in front of a whole crowd of people. However good a shot I was at Bisley, there's no way I could have done it.'

'No. But there is somebody else. Antonio Barriago. You know him? A Spaniard who live in Algiers.'

Barriago! We stared at each other. Had he been the passenger that American yachtsman had said was on *Thunderflash* when she arrived in Mahon? Had Evans sailed the boat from a North African port, merely calling in at Marseilles on the way? 'What about him?' I asked. Barriago had been in the final shoot-off for the Oporto Cup, which was almost the last event I had taken part in.

'You don't know him?' It was put subtly, an invitation to deny all knowledge.

'No, I don't *know* him,' I said. 'I've shot against him. That was three years ago and I haven't seen him since. Why?' And when he didn't say anything, just sat there staring at me, I asked him why he was searching the boat.

For a moment I thought he wasn't going to tell me that, but in the end he gave a little shrug and said, 'Suppose it is Barriago who kill the Alcalde. And suppose – just suppose, Señor Steele – he has been on board this boat—'

But I stopped him there. 'I tell you, I haven't seen the man for three years.'

'All right then. Suppose he is on board when Señor Evans is the owner of it.' He nodded at the engineer's protruding feet. 'That is why we are searching your boat. It has been in your possession since more than two weeks before the Alcalde is killed and we have been advised where is the most safe place for him to have hidden it.'

'Who advised you?' I asked him.

But he had turned away, watching the engineer again as he began to wriggle backwards. 'Now I think we know whether you are involved or not. *Bueno?*' he asked.

The engineer grunted something unintelligible, and when he finally emerged, switching off his torch and standing there, wiping his hands and face on a bit of cotton waste, Menendez repeated his question, his voice sharp and urgent – '*Bueno y bueno, qué has encontrado?*'

'*Nada.*' The engineer pulled up the steps, slamming the engine compartment shut. It was clear he had had enough of clambering round in the confined space of the yacht's engines.

Menendez turned to the inspector, checking the details of their earlier search. Then he gave a little shrug. '*Eh bueno*, it seems this boat is now clean.' He was staring at me, a hard look in his eyes as he emphasised the word *now*.

'Barriago,' I said. 'Why do you think he killed Jorge Martinez?'

'You do not know?' Still that hard stare as he waited for an answer. 'A man answering his description, but with a different name, took an Aviaco flight out of here for Mallorca less than two hours after the shooting. At Palma he changed planes and flew on to Tunisia. The police in Tunis are endeavouring to trace him for us.'

I told him I didn't see what this had to do with me, but all he said was, 'He is a crack shot – ' He used the words *tirador experto* – 'and you knew him. That is all. Nothing more.' He reached for an ashtray and stubbed out his cigarette. '*Eh bueno*,' he said again and got to his feet, the others following him. 'When you wish to make a statement . . .' Those sharp little eyes were fixed on mine. 'A full statement, then you come to my office. Okay?' He was suddenly smiling again.

'You really think I had something to do with Martinez's death?'

He shrugged. 'That is between you and your conscience. When you are ready to talk . . .' He said this over his shoulder as he went up the steps to the cockpit, his two officers behind him. 'The truth, that is all I am interested in.' He was standing like a cut-out against the blueness of the sky, his hair very black in the sunlight.

'I wonder you don't ask for my passport?' It was a silly thing to say, but he could have arrested me if he had been sure enough to charge me with anything.

He turned as he reached the quay. 'I already have your passport,' he said. 'It was the main reason I sent my officers to search your premises. In fact, your wife was kind enough to give it to them.' He raised his hand, a little gesture of farewell. '*Adiós.*' His driver was holding the car door open and he stepped in and was driven off. The other two lingered for a moment, staring at the boat as though trying to remember everything about her. Then they, too, drove away and I was left alone with Carp, his craggy features more puckered than usual. He didn't speak Spanish, but he understood enough to know I was in trouble. 'Come the next few days reck'n you'll find out who your real friends are,' he said, his Suffolk accent broader than ever. That was all and he turned away. 'That spi rope's rove, but Luis an' I gotter coil down the port anchor warp. Be for'ard if you want me.' And then, as he crossed the coachroof, heading for the port bow, he said over his shoulder, 'I'll be ready whenever you say – just in case you're coming too.'

I went back into the saloon then, standing there alone and trying to think things out. Antonio Barriago. That was three years back, the thousand-yard range and the two of us lying side by side shooting it out, a crowd gathered behind us, the smell of gun oil and cordite hanging on the still air and the targets shimmering in the haze. And afterwards, in one of the messes – I couldn't remember which – the two of us professing our friendship and promising to meet again. We never had, and the next I heard of him he was a mercenary captured by SWAPO on the Zaire border.

That was all I knew about him. He might well be Basque and a member of Eta, but why risk a terrorist attack so far from the political centre of Spain? In any case, a mercenary was hardly likely to be a committed political activist.

Either his departure from Menorca so soon after the shooting was purely coincidental, or else, if he really had killed Martinez, then he had been hired to do the job. In which case, hired by whom, and for what purpose? Did the Chief Inspector really think I had hired him? In that case, he must think I had a reason. What? What possible reason could I have for wanting Jorge Martinez killed? And Wade, where did he fit in? Or Lloyd Jones, or Evans? If the police were tapping my phone . . .

I got myself a glass of iced coffee from the ship's fridge and sat there thinking about it, conscious all the time of Carp and Luis moving about the deck. I should be up there with them, helping prepare the boat for sea, not sitting alone at the saloon table wondering what the hell to do. Ring the lawyer, check about the exchange documents, contact some of the people who might know where Evans was. But what I was really thinking about was Soo giving them my passport. She might at least have told me. And Wade phoning me again this evening.

I finished my coffee, then drove back to the office. Soo was out. She had left a note to say she would be back around four. I phoned Martin Lopez, catching him just as he was going to lunch. He confirmed that the catamaran's certificate of registration had been sent to England for alteration. And yes, there had been a little problem with the exchange contract, nothing serious, just a matter of dating it. Evans had signed it all right, but he had dated it the previous month. Intentionally? No, just a mistake, it happened quite often.

Like hell it did! Not if you knew the purpose behind it. For a moment I was tempted to take him into my confidence, tell him about the Kalashnikov. But that meant telling him what I had done with it, and anyway a lawyer who handled the affairs of some of the most prominent people in Menorca would hardly relish the thought that he might be acting for a foreigner who had got himself involved in the murder of a politician so universally popular as Jorge Martinez. I kept my mouth shut, and in doing so made myself not only accessory to an act of terrorism, but also to all that followed.

How was I, yachtsman, charterer, small-time businessman, an escapee if you like into the lotus life of the Mediterranean, to know, or even to understand, the machinations of those far removed from the little Balearic island of Menorca? There was Wade, of course, and Gareth Lloyd Jones, Patrick Evans with his two toughies and a lovely catamaran with which to tempt me. I should have known. At any rate, I should have guessed. But that is hindsight. God almighty! I couldn't possibly have known, not then, sitting at my desk with a gin and tonic and staring out of the open window, not a breath of air stirring, the water mirror-calm and the shimmering hulk of the hospital riding to its upside-down reflection like one of those great floating batteries the French and Spanish navies had used against Gibraltar at the end of the eighteenth century.

If only Petra were still here. I could have talked it over with her – practical, matter-of-fact, and that bouncing, vital body of hers. I had a sudden picture of her lying naked on top of me, that last time, the day after Soo had lost the baby. If only she'd been out there in that tent on the far side of the island. No breeze at all and the air outside almost as hot as midsummer.

I got suddenly to my feet, finished my drink and drove round to a little restaurant I often used near the Club Maritimo. I had *gazpacho* and *gambas plancha* with half a bottle of Camp Viejo, sitting there in the darkened interior, shocked to find myself eating alone as though I were some sort of pariah. In the old days

I'd done that quite often. I'd had to. But since I had come to Menorca . . . since then, of course, there'd always been Soo and the host of friends we had made – people we knew, anyway. Never the need to be alone.

Back in the office I began ringing round to discover whether Evans had put in anywhere. I think if I had phoned Flórez he might have told me right away. But Flórez was the last person I wanted to contact in the circumstances. It took me three calls before I thought of Félipe Lopescado who ran a little *taberna* on the Ciudadela waterfront. '*La* Santa Maria? *Si – un señor Inglés*.' He even knew the name. 'Pat Eevanz.' The boat had come in to the *puerto* at Ciudadela late the night before last. There had been three men on board and they had come ashore for a drink about ten-thirty. '*Si*, at the Taberna Félipe.'

'Is the boat still there?' I asked him.

'*Si*.'

'Was it there yesterday?'

'*Si*, all day.' And he assured me the men were still on board, all three of them.

'Do you know where they were at midday yester-day?' I had to ask him straight out like that, there was no alternative.

'They were here in the *taberna*.'

'For how long?'

'About three hours. You have eat here, señor. You and the señora. You know how long it takes.'

'They had lunch at your place then, all three of them?'

'*Si*. They have *mejillones*. The mussels are fresh in

that morning, very good, very beeg. Then the *capitán* have *rabo de toro* and there is one *pollo* and one *escalope*. Also my *taberna* Rioja and some Quinta with the coffee.'

'And the captain's name?'

'I tell you, he is Pat Eevanz.'

I had him describe the man then, but it was Patrick Evans all right, and after leaving the *taberna*, Evans, with one of the others, had taken a taxi into the *centro*, while the third man returned on board. Félipe couldn't tell me when Evans had returned but he assured me the man had been there this morning, because he'd seen him talking to the harbour master on the quay, and the *Santa Maria* was still anchored in the same position. He thought it likely that their catch had been off-loaded at some other port. Certainly, no fish had been landed from the vessel in Ciudadela.

I was left wondering when Evans had planted that gun in the starb'd engine compartment, even whether he had.

I cleared my desk, then drove out to the airport just south of the San Clemente road. I thought Alejándro Suárez, the assistant manager and one of the few islanders who really enjoyed sailing, might be able to produce somebody on the airport staff, or at the Aviaco desk, who had actually spoken to Tony Barriago, somebody who could give me an idea of the man's state of mind. It would have taken him no more than half an hour at the outside to clock in at the airport, which would mean perhaps half an hour of waiting before actually boarding the plane. Plenty of time for his nerves to become ragged.

But Alex said the police had already interrogated everyone who might have spoken to him and the only person who had been able to recall him was the Aviaco woman who had dealt with his ticket. She remembered him because he had come back afterwards to enquire whether the plane had arrived yet, and when she said it was due in almost immediately, he had thanked her and turned away, apparently quite satisfied. He had appeared relaxed, not in the least nervous or upset. 'Do they think he is the killer of Don Martinez?'

'Possibly.' We were standing in the airport lounge, which was packed with people. The PA system suddenly broke into life, the hubbub rising to a crescendo as friends and relatives said their goodbyes to passengers on a Barcelona flight.

'Pardon. I have to go now. If there is anything else . . .' Alex smiled at me apologetically and went through into the departure area where, in addition to immigration and customs officials, security officers were screening the passengers before embarkation. Would Tony Barriago have been sweating as he went through the last stage before boarding the plane? But the security officer on duty now might not be the same as yesterday, and anyway, it was such an obvious line of enquiry that the police would have covered it already.

The crowd in the main lounge had thinned to a few people sitting at tables drinking coffee or wine and waiting for another flight. I wandered out into the long passageway that led to the arrivals area. This was what Tony would have done, mingled with the crowd from an incoming flight, even taken a stroll outside, anything rather than sit in the main lounge, boxed in and too conspicuous until it had filled up. I had a word with Maria at the stand that sold magazines and postcards, and then it occurred to me that he might have had a taxi waiting for him outside, just in case.

I went out and began checking with the drivers. A British charter flight was due in and there was quite a line of taxis waiting. It was about the ninth or tenth I spoke to, a fat man with a Panama hat perched on his head, who said he'd been there the previous afternoon when the *Guardia* drove up to the airport, and yes, he had seen a taxi waiting in the car park opposite. He had noticed it because normally taxis waited in a line. They did not park with the private cars. And when the police arrived, a short, hook-nosed man, who had presumably hired the taxi, went across and spoke with the driver. He had stayed there talking to him for several minutes, right up until the time his flight was called. Then he had hurried back into the airport.

'And the taxi?' I asked him.

'He come out of the car park and join us in the taxi line.'

'He had paid him off then?'

'Yes, the man pay him before going back into the airport.'

'Did the taxi leave the car park immediately?'

'No, he wait there until the plane take off. Then he join us.'

I asked him the driver's name then and he said 'Gonzalez.' He did not know his other name, but he thought he came from Villa Carlos.

I thanked him and went back to my car, convinced now that Menendez had been right. The description fitted and Tony Barriago had got away with it. At the time he flew out to Palma, and then on to Tunis, the police had had no idea who they were looking for.

Soo had returned by the time I got back. She had been to see Manuela Renato's sister, Maria, who was married to Hernando Pons, the most successful of the local property developers. 'They're very worried,' she said. 'Jorge's death leaves a vacuum and they're now getting together with their friends to fill it. The problem is they don't have any one man in mind, so that already there is a danger they'll split up into factions, each advancing their own candidate. The effect may well be that a man nobody wants will be elected.'

'Who?' I asked.

'Maria couldn't say. Flórez perhaps since he has a garage in Mahon as well as in Alayór, and of course business friends in both towns. Even Ismail Fuxá's name was mentioned. Those were the two worst possibilities, of course, but it shows what a problem this thing has created, and what she was saying to me was that it was time to be out of property in Menorca, at least until things have settled down. I saw Carmen, too. She was in one of her tense moods, a little scared I thought, and she had that wicked little woman, Mercedes, with her. Mercedes said we should leave now, go back to England, or wherever it was we came from, that it was all our fault – Thatcher, Reagan, bombs, new development . . . She was quite rude.' And Soo added, as though it were all part of the gossip she'd picked up, 'They took your passport, by the way.'

'Menendez said you gave it to them.'

'They asked where it was, so I told them.' And she added, a little defensively, 'They'd have found it anyway.'

'Possibly.'

She flared up at that. 'Not possibly – inevitably. You can't pin the loss of your passport on me. They'd have turned the whole place inside out if I hadn't told them.'

I went through into the kitchen, got some ice and mixed a strong dry martini. Damned if I was going to have a row with her over it, but just to give it to them without argument or even any sort of protest . . . 'Do you want one?' I asked her.

She nodded, standing by the window with Benjie in her arms.

I took down two glasses, and when I had poured the drinks, we stood there, not saying anything, just drinking in silence. And all the time I was conscious of her staring at me, her dark eyes big and round, the question she dared not ask on the tip of her tongue. In the end all she said was, 'Your passport wouldn't be any use; they'll be watching the airport, the ferry terminal—'

'They know who did it,' I told her.

'Who?'

'A Spaniard. He left immediately afterwards – by plane.'

'Then why—'

'I knew him, at Bisley.'

She turned to glance at the cups, then gulped down the rest of her martini, her eyes very wide and fixed on me. 'The weapon then? Where is it?' Her face had a pallid, frightened look.

I gave a little shrug. The closeness that had once been between us was gone now and I was no longer willing to share my thoughts and actions with her the way I had. It wasn't that I didn't trust her. It was just that the links that had bound us close were no longer strong enough, so that I felt instinctively it was best for her not to know what I had done with the gun, or even that I had found it hidden on board.

'So you'll be taking the boat yourself.' She was still staring at me, holding herself very stiff, her small body almost quivering with tension.

I hadn't made up my mind, and the way she said it I knew what she must be thinking. But I wouldn't be running away from anything, only giving myself time and room for manoeuvre. The boat was just about ready, and in Malta I could probably produce some reasonable excuse for being without a passport.

'I'm right, aren't I? You'll go with the boat to Malta.' She had put the dog down, holding her glass tight with both hands and gazing out across the water.

'Perhaps,' I murmured. I can remember the way I said it, flatly, without feeling, and looking back on it now, I realised it wasn't fear of arrest that was driving me to get away on my own for a time. Even if Menendez did decide to accuse me of smuggling arms, the knowledge that I was completely innocent made me certain Martin Lopez would be able to sort the whole thing out, given time. No, it was Soo. If she had slept with the man, had an affair with him, that was something I could have lived with. But love, a real passion – that is something that strikes at the heart of a man. It leaves him nothing – nothing to strive for, no purpose. Both pride and practicality dictated a break.

'Are any of the people you knew still there? Have you kept in touch?'

I shook my head. 'Mintoff and the new man will have made it impossible for them.'

'There's my mother's relatives.'

'Your mother hasn't been back since your father retired.' I took her glass and refilled it, then mixed some more and went back to the window. Flurries of an onshore breeze were darkening the water. This was the view I had looked out on ever since we had married and settled down to build a business on this island.

'Gareth might be useful.' She said it tentatively.

'How do you mean?'

'In addition to showing the flag in the Balearics and one or two of the Italian islands, he thought it possible Malta would be included in his orders. He asked if I had any messages.'

'Did he say when he was leaving Gib?'

'No. His letter was written the day after he went on board. There was no mention of his having received orders, only that he looked forward to seeing us again when *Medusa* visited Mahon.'

'Wade may know his movements.' I stood there, sipping my martini, staring out of the window and thinking about the future. Malta was over six hundred miles away and even if we averaged ten knots, which was just possible with a favourable wind, it would take us the better part of three days.

We didn't say much after that, our thoughts locked in on ourselves, and as the shadows lengthened and six o'clock approached, I asked her to leave me so that I could talk to Wade on my own. I remember I shut the door behind her and in doing so it seemed as though I was shutting myself out from the past.

Wade was late. Only a few minutes, but expecting him to come through prompt at 18.00, waiting, it seemed an age. The sound of the phone when it came was startlingly loud, his voice even more upper-class English, more clipped than when he had phoned me in the early hours. 'Wade here. Did you locate him?'

'Yes.' And I told him where Evans was and how he had been having a meal in the Taberna Félipe on the Ciudadela waterfront at the time of the shooting. 'He couldn't have done it,' I said.

'Of course not.' And he added, 'Yesterday the Spanish police asked Interpol to locate an Italian from Naples who was booked out of Menorca on two consecutive flights, the first to Mallorca, the second to Barcelona. The name on his passport, which was forged of course, was given as Alfredo Geronimo. In fact, they now discover he is Spanish and his real name is Antonio Barriago. I believe you know him.'

'I've met him,' I said cautiously. 'Three years ago.'

'You fired together in the finals for the Oporto Cup. Had you met him before that?'

'Once,' I said. 'When I was shooting in Spain.'

'He wasn't one of the men with you when Ahmed Bey was killed?'

'No.'

'Or on the Italian boat?'

'Not as far as I know.'

'The police in Mahon seem to think the connection is a lot closer than just competition shooting. They've asked both Interpol and the Yard people over here for all the information they have on you, a dossier in fact. You and Barriago.'

'And Evans?' I asked. 'What about Evans?'

'I don't think so.'

'He's involved,' I said. 'I'm sure of it.'

'Why? You say he was at Ciudadela.' His voice was sharper now. 'What makes you think he's involved?'

But I was already regretting my attempt to involve Evans so directly. 'I just feel it,' I answered rather lamely, wondering how my words would be interpreted when they searched the villa and found the gun. 'Lloyd Jones,' I said. 'Where does he fit in? He came out here with a picture of Evans in his pocket.' I was remembering what Carp had told me, that odd incident on the East Coast of England. 'He'd said he was on leave, a holiday before taking up his new appointment. But his sole object seemed to be to find

Evans. Why?' There was no answer. 'Are you still there?'

'Yes.' And then he said, 'They were at HMS *Ganges* together, almost the last batch of youngsters to go through before the school was closed.'

'I know that. But they are related in some way.'

'Who told you that?'

'My wife.' And I added, 'Is it true? Are they related?'

I thought he wasn't going to answer that, but then he said, 'They both have the same father. No reason you shouldn't know that.'

'But why send him to me?' I asked. 'He said it was at your suggestion he was contacting me.'

'Not my suggestion. Philip Turner's. He put us on to you.' And he added, with something near to a smile in his voice, 'When we checked your background, it was obvious you were just the man we were looking for. Malta, Menorca, Gibraltar, you know them all – all the Western Med, that is.'

He was covering himself. Phones are funny things, very revealing. You pick up nuances of expression, the hint of hidden meanings. I had the sudden sense of a void opening up, certain he had let something slip, that he hadn't meant to be so specific. 'I'll be in Malta a week from now,' I said.

'Malta. Why?' And when I told him I had a charter fixed for the catamaran, he said, 'I know that, but you can send somebody else. There are things I want to know and you're the man who can tell me. The new mayor, for instance. Who is it going to be? Who are they going to elect?'

'I've no idea.'

'Well, find out for me, will you?' And when I told him I wouldn't have time, that I needed to get away tomorrow night, he said, 'What's the hurry? Has something happened I don't know about?' I told him then how the police had searched the office and my home, then rummaged the boat. 'Are you under house arrest?'

'No, but they took my passport.'

'Under surveillance?'

'I don't think so.'

'But they suspect you?'

'How can they?' I said. 'I was sitting there in full view when it happened.'

'Yes, but the gun. I take it they haven't found it yet.' And he added, 'You see, they don't know how Barriago came by it. He couldn't have entered Menorca with the thing tucked under his arm. And what did he do with it afterwards? Do you know?'

'Of course not.'

He didn't say anything then, and I wondered whether he believed me.

'Has Lloyd Jones left Gib yet?' I asked him.

'I can't answer that.' And when I persisted, he said he was not privy to the detailed movements of ships. That was when I asked him what department of the Navy he was. He hesitated before answering. 'Planning. Forward Planning.'

'Then perhaps you can tell me if *Medusa* will be putting in to Malta.'

'I think she may.'

'Before or after she visits Mahon?'

'Before probably.' And then he asked me what my ETA Grand Harbour would be. 'You're leaving tomorrow, you say?'

'No, not tomorrow.' I couldn't do that. I couldn't just sail out of the port here and head straight for Malta. 'It'll have to be the early hours of the following day,' I said. Carp could motor the catamaran round to Es Grau or Port d'Addaia, one of the smaller inlets, then we could slip out when everyone was asleep.

'And your ETA?' he asked again.

'Five days from now,' I said. 'If we're lucky and the weather holds.'

'I see.' He seemed to be thinking something out. Then to my surprise he said, 'Well, good luck!' He said it in quite a cheerful, friendly voice, and with that he rang off.

PART TWO

MALTA INCIDENT

CHAPTER ONE

The weather, in fact, did not hold. Carp had the boat ready for sea well before noon, he and Luis motoring her across to the commercial quay where they took on fuel and water, cleared customs and immigration, and loaded the fresh stores Soo had ordered, also the last-minute purchases. They were away by 14.30. By then it was blowing force four from just north of east, the wind funnelling up the harbour so that they were motor-sailing with jib and main hard in.

I was there to see them off. I had spent most of the morning talking to people on the phone, chiefly the foreign element, those who had established themselves in business and were permanently resident. Some of them, of course, like myself, had not involved themselves in the political life of the island. But even they were beginning to get worried. Those with Spanish connections were more deeply concerned and Fuxá's name constantly cropped up. Others were mentioned, of course – one of the leading PSOE figures, in particular – but it was Ismail Fuxá who really scared them. Most regarded his separatist, anti-foreign movement as having grown alarmingly in recent months, some even thought he might have enough support in council to get himself elected as the new alcalde.

Only one of them was willing to talk about it openly and at length. That was Freddie McManus, a retired property developer who had once stood as Conservative candidate for some Scottish constituency. He pointed out to me that however the 1978 constitution might try to safeguard the powers of the central government, the establishment of the Balearics as one of the seventeen independent provinces meant in practice that the potential power of the locally elected alcaldes was greatly increased. 'It's a charter for the emergence of little Gauleiters. All that's required is a dominant personality. And if the man has a cause, then he's even more dangerous.' And he had gone on to point out to me that to islanders stuck out on the eastern fringe of a small group in the Western Mediterranean, Madrid was a long way away. Also, and he had emphasised this very strongly, the power of the alcalde was rooted in the history of Spain, when in 1485 Queen Isabella struck at the nobility through the *Ordenancas Reales* with a court of two alcaldes to administer justice in every town of thirty or more inhabitants. 'Given a weak governor in Palma,' he said, 'anything could happen if that man Fuxá became Jorge Martinez's successor.'

None of the others I talked to were as forthcoming

as that and quite a few were unwilling to discuss the political situation with me at all, some making it clear in the nicest possible way that they wanted to distance themselves from me, others quite blunt about it. There was, of course, an element of guilt involved. An island the size of Malta with a third of its wildest rock coast blanketed by villa and hotel development is not a pretty sight and most of us were getting our living from the *urbanizaciós* in one form or another. It wasn't as bad as Benidorm or Tenerife, but to those with a conservationist conscience it still left a nasty taste in the mouth, bearing in mind how unspoilt Menorca had been before.

I must have contacted between twenty and thirty people that morning, all men who had as much to lose as I had if the political stability of the island was destroyed, and by the time I drove round to the commercial quay to check that Carp was cleared and ready to sail, my mind was made up. Tongues were wagging, and if I stayed, I might well find myself the scapegoat for what had happened. I was lucky to be free at the moment. If I hadn't got up at first light the previous day and searched the ship I would undoubtedly be under interrogation at *Guardia* headquarters, perhaps even flown off to mainland Spain. I had talked it over with Carp late that night. He knew what to do and the deterioration in the weather would make it all the more convincing that he had to put back into the nearest shelter to clear a warp wrapped round one of the prop shafts or deal with some water in the fuel tank. The probability was that nobody would bother to report the cat in Addaia, but if they did, then he had any number of good excuses.

The *Policia Municipal* building looks right down on to the commercial quay, so that I was not surprised when a police car with two officers in it drew up on the quayside. We were just taking the last of the fresh stores on board and they parked there, watching us. If I had not come ashore when Luis uncleated the stern warp preparatory to letting go, they would have been on the radio immediately for a harbour launch, which would have stopped us before we had even reached Bloody Island.

I watched from the quay as Luis coiled down the stern warp, then ran for'ard to hoist the jib. The mains'l was already set and flapping on a loose sheet as the engines took her out into the open waters of the harbour and Carp turned her into the wind, heading east to clear the old grassed-over fort on Figuera Point at the entrance to the harbour proper. She looked a lovely sight once the sails had been hauled in tight, a rather hazy sun glinting on the new paint of the hull and transforming the twin bow waves into silver glitters of spray.

I turned then, thinking as I walked back to my car that I might catch up with them before they cleared the point. But then the police car cruised up alongside. 'You are not going with them?' It was Inspector Molina, and he was smiling at me. 'Such a nice boat. It must be very tempting. And Malta. Your wife comes from Malta.'

He was still smiling as I said, 'Yes, I would have enjoyed the trip. But you have my passport.'

'Ah *si*, and you are a law-abiding citizen of our island.' And he added, 'They can see your boat is preparing to sail from up there.' He nodded in the direction of the citadel with the slip road snaking up like a staircase with two hairpin bends in it. 'I just come to make sure.'

It was on the tip of my tongue then to tell him he would have been better employed searching the *Santa Maria* and the villa on Punta Codolar, but I checked myself. Sooner or later it was surely inevitable they would find the gun where I had hidden it. '*Adiós.*' They drove off and I went back to the office to ring Lopescado at the Taberna Félipe in Ciudadela. The *Santa Maria* had left.

'When?'

But he didn't know. Sometime during the night, he said, for it had been there the previous evening. In fact, all three of them had come ashore about eight o'clock. They had sat around outside and had a few drinks, then they had gone into the fish bar for a meal. They had left about ten-thirty and gone straight back to the ship.

'All of them?' I asked.

'Yes, all of them, and the boat is still there when I go to bed, with a light shining in the wheelhouse aft as well as a riding light at the forestay.'

'Did you gather where they were going? Did they clear customs, anything like that?'

'No, I never saw any official go on board, not then,

nor any time earlier during the evening. But then I was very busy last night, a beeg party from Banyos, a German party . . .' He hesitated, then said, 'Once, when I am serving the next table, I hear your name mentioned. It was something about the *policia*. They were arguing about why some information had not been acted on. The last I hear they think you will try to leave Mahon sometime today. No, you will *have* to leave. Those were his words.'

'Whose words?' I asked. 'Was it Evans who said that?'

'*Si*. The boss man with the Guevara moustache. Pat Eevanz.'

He couldn't tell me anything more and when I put the phone down I sat there at the desk for a moment, gazing out towards La Mola and the Mahon entrance four miles away and wondering where the *Santa Maria* was now, what Evans was up to. I could just see *Thunderflash*, her white hulls and sails outlined against the hazy shape of Lazareto Island. Once they were clear of Punta del Esperó, the easternmost tip of La Mola, they would have a beam wind and a fast run to Cape Faváritx, then only five miles and all downhill to Macaret at the entrance to Port d'Addaia. Perhaps I should have arranged for them to put into Es Grau, but the entrance was very narrow and overlooked by almost every house in the little fishing village. In any case, I hadn't known then that Evans had sailed, and even if he did intend to spend the night at the villa on Punta Codolar he would probably anchor the *Santa Maria* in Arenal d'en Castell. It would be very sheltered there in an easterly blow. A picture flashed through my mind then of him opening a can of beer, or sitting down to a quick meal, at the table in that kitchen with the gun he thought was still on board the catamaran right there under the floorboards at his feet.

Soo came in then with the news that the council had been in session at the *ayuntamiento* most of the day. Nothing had been decided and there was talk of a local election.

I finished my packing and took her to the Atlante, the restaurant a few doors away, for an early meal. Sitting there, drinking *vino verde* as an aperitif, we discussed the possible choices that a newly elected council would have. But even we, whose interests were identical, could not agree – I favoured Gonzalez Renato, while Soo wanted Antonio Alvarez to be the next alcalde, chiefly I think because he would support a progressive building and development policy.

It was just as the waiter was serving our marinated sardines that the door opened and a small man in a brightly coloured short-sleeved shirt, and wearing a red floppy hat pulled down over his ears, looked in. He said something to Manuel, the patron, glanced quickly across at us, nodded and then left. 'Who was that?' I asked the waiter, conscious suddenly that I had seen the man lounging against one of the bollards when I'd come back from seeing Carp and Luis off in *Thunderflash*.

The waiter hesitated, looking at Manuel and repeating the question. Manuel in his turn looked uneasy, as though reluctant to be drawn into giving me any information about the man. '*Vigilancia?*' I asked him, and after a moment's hesitation, he nodded. The *Cuerpo de Vigilancia* were plain-clothes security police and like the *Guardia Civil* they were paramilitary and came under the direct control of the Provincial Governor. The fact that they had me under surveillance was confirmation, if I needed any, that I should get out while the going was good. Also it suggested that the killing of Martinez was regarded by the authorities as something more than just an isolated terrorist incident.

I suppose I had fallen silent after the door had closed on the man and Manuel had confirmed he was one of the *Vigilancia*. Certainly my mind was concentrated on the future, on what life held in store for me – for both of us. 'Eat up,' Soo said, 'these sardines are delicious.' And then, almost in the same breath, 'What will you do when you get there? How long will you stay? Have you decided yet?'

It was a strange meal, both of us trying to look ahead, and at one stage, when we were sitting over our coffee and a large Soberano, I had the distinct impression that she was flying something close to a flag of seduction. Soo was odd that way, always had been. I think it was the Maltese in her. She was so volatile in her emotions, one minute cold as ice, the next minute . . . I remember we sat there like a couple of lovers, gazing into each other's eyes and actually holding hands across the table, clinking our brandy glasses.

God almighty! Why can't people be more sensible,

more consistent? And why the hell was I so set on a son? What would a son do for me? You change its nappies, see it through all those infantile diseases, watch it teething and grow up, and the next thing it's borrowing the parental bed to poke a girl or getting high on drugs, or worse still, standing for cap'n in place of Dad, waiting for the old sod to drop dead.

I ordered more coffee, and another brandy for us both, and we sat there, not saying anything, each alone with our own thoughts. I touched her hand again, the fingers answering to the pressure of mine, her grip almost urgent. Did she want me to stay? Was that the message she was trying to convey? And the slight flutter of her nerves. Was she scared? I hadn't thought about it until that moment, my mind so concentrated on my own predicament. Now I tried to see it from her point of view, alone here, her husband slipping away on a yacht bound for Malta and the police suspecting him of complicity in a political murder.

Political? It had to be political. Martinez had no other interests. He hadn't been in business, he hadn't fiddled his taxes. He hadn't slept with other men's wives. No breath of scandal had ever touched him. But political enemies – he had those all right, and of course decisions had been made that did affect the business community. 'It'll be all right,' I said, holding her hand tight. 'Once I'm away they'll forget all about me and concentrate on other leads. A week and they'll know for sure that I had nothing to do with it. They'll get the date when I took *Thunderflash* over and then they will begin to enquire into Evans's movements.'

Her hand tightened on mine as she slowly nodded her head. 'But suppose – ' she hesitated – 'suppose the police are in on it? Suppose it's political and they're covering up.'

'Then there'd be a single name emerging as the new alcalde.'

She sat there for a moment, her head still bent and not saying anything, the almost black hair gleaming in the lights, which had just been switched on. 'Fuxá,' she murmured. 'I keep hearing the name Fuxá. Ismail Fuxá.'

'He makes a lot of noise,' I said. 'But the separatist element is only a small minority. The people know very well an island like this could never make it on its own.'

We talked about it for a moment, then I paid the bill and we left, hand-in-hand, and the man in the red floppy hat watched us from his post by the bollard just a few yards from the Atlante. Maybe it was the brandy, but I felt warm and very close to Soo at that moment, and my mind, dreaming in the softness of the evening, the faint lap of wavelets the only sound, turned to thoughts of a ménage à trois, wondering whether I was macho enough to keep both a wife and mistress satisfied. Petra with child! Petra on Bloody Island, a kid running around the dig, our son, Soo here in the house with her basenji, running the office. She and Petra, they liked each other. They were so different it might work. Soo cared about marriage. The Navy and Malta, she'd been very conventionally brought up. But Petra – I had never discussed it with her, of course, but I was quite sure she didn't give a damn.

It might work, but as I climbed the stairs my mind returned to normal and I knew it was only a dream.

I got my holdall and my oilskins and dumped them in the boot of the car. 'What about your minder?' Soo said. 'The guy in the floppy hat.'

'You drive,' I said, still buoyed by the drink. 'I'll ride in the boot till we're clear of the town.' I crawled in, holding the lid of it slightly open. I had done it more or less as a lark, and Soo, who was always very quick to respond to a mood, was giggling as she said, 'You look like something out of *Alice* crouched in there.' She was still giggling to herself as she got in and started the engine.

We went about a hundred yards and then she slowed to a stop and I heard her say, 'Am I permitted to drive out to see my friends? I'm supposed to be playing bridge tonight.' And a male voice answered her in Spanish, 'Of course, señora. You do not take your husband?'

'No. He's looking after Benjie.'

'Benjie? I do not understand.'

'The dog – *el perro*.'

'*Ah si, el perro*.' And then they were both laughing as though Soo was out on a cuckolding run. I nearly burst out laughing myself, thinking of Gareth Lloyd Jones safely tucked away in a frigate under the massive bulk of the Rock.

She drove fast after that, following the curves of the waterfront, and I watched the road astern through the slit under the boot lid. Nothing followed us, the cars along the Levante all parked, their owners still occupied with whatever it was they had come to the harbour for. By the Aduana I glimpsed the lights of a vehicle snaking down the Abundancia from the centre of town, but when it reached the Customs House it turned away from us.

By then we had reached the point where the Andén de Poniente runs into the Passo de la Alameda and the road to Fornells. I banged on the lid and after a while Soo stopped. 'I thought perhaps you'd gone to sleep.' She was still in a giggly mood. 'You could have got out back by the Maritimo. There was nobody following us. I was watching in the mirror.' And she added, 'Are you sure you haven't got delusions of grandeur? I'm beginning to wonder if it's all an excuse to go for a sail in that damned cat.'

I didn't answer that, simply got in beside her and we drove on. Now that I was on my way and committed to leaving Spanish soil without clearance, I was in a more sombre mood.

'You're sure this journey of yours is absolutely necessary?' She said it lightly, still joking, but there was an undercurrent of concern in it that matched my own mood. I said nothing and we drove on in silence.

It was 22.57 when we turned north on to the Macaret road, 23.07 when we started down into Port d'Addaia. Soon we could see the water of the inlet, the islands at the entrance dark shapes, no moon, no stars. *Thunderflash* was already there, riding to her anchor just off the new quay, the semi-inflatable ready alongside. I flashed our lights, then switched them off and got my gear out of the boot.

The tender was on its way almost immediately, so there was only a brief moment of privacy to say good-bye. Perhaps that was as well. I don't know what Soo was thinking as I kissed her, but my own thoughts were already on the voyage ahead and what it would be like to be back in Malta, this time without a passport. She didn't cling to me. In fact, she showed remarkably little emotion. Perhaps she was thinking of Lloyd Jones, wondering if his frigate would put into Mahon while I was away.

It was Luis driving the tender and he cut the engine just right, sliding in to the concrete edge of the quay and throwing the painter to me as the little launch floated to a stop. 'Good trip?' I asked.

'*Si, bueno*. We take five hours, speed reach sixteen knots. No motor.' A flash of teeth in the dark face grinning up at me. He had enjoyed himself and I was glad. 'Beeg sea, but everything very steady.'

'What's the forecast?' I asked him.

'Do'know. Carp attending it now. But we have nearly twenty knots, a levanter from Mahon to this place.'

I tossed my gear into the stern, gave Soo a final hug and jumped in. It might be blowing force five outside, but here, at the upper end of the long Macaret inlet, all was quite, the water barely ruffled. By the time I got myself and my gear on board, Soo was already climbing the hill out of Addaia, the beam of the car's headlights altering as she took the sharp bends.

Carp came up out of the saloon. He looked pleased with himself. The ship had behaved itself – he called it a ship – and there had been no problems, the helm very easy on all points of sailing. 'We have a fast run to Malta – with luck.' He gave a gap-toothed smile. 'Wind twenty to twenty-five knots, backing north-east, possibly north, viz good.'

'A tramontana then?'

He nodded. 'But no rain. There's a high to the west of us moving south. Seas two to three metres, so it could be bouncy.'

I glanced back at the quay and the loom of the land behind it. It was quite dark now, no sign of Soo. So this was it – the moment of departure. We hauled the tender up on to the stern, fixed the lashings, then went below. 'Had any sleep on the way over?' It was unlikely for they would have been too busy in the rising wind and sea.

Carp shook his head. 'Would you like some coffee?' he asked. 'Something to eat?'

'No thanks. We'll get our heads down for a couple of hours. We need to be away about two, then we'll be well clear of the island and in international waters by first light.'

I had the double bed in the port hull and had just drifted off when I felt a shake of the shoulder and opened my eyes to see Carp's face leaning over me. 'We got company.'

'Coastal patrol?' I had come fully awake in a flash, the duvet thrown back and my feet already feeling for the locker top beside the bunk.

'No. Nothing official.'

'Who then?' I was thrusting my bare feet into my sea-boots.

But Carp was already climbing the steps that led up to the saloon. 'Come and see for yourself.'

He was standing in the open, beside the helmsman's seat, looking aft when I joined him, the rattle of a chain sounding loud in the quiet of the anchorage. No lights anywhere now, the houses all asleep, clouds low overhead. And there, a dim shape and barely fifty metres astern of us, was a fishing boat. 'The *Santa Maria*?' I asked him.

He nodded. 'Thought you'd want to know.' And he added, 'I was asleep on the settee just inside the saloon door when I was woken by the thump of a diesel close alongside. You reck'n they've come in for shelter?'

I didn't say anything and we stood there watching as the chain was stopped with a clunk and they began to lower the dinghy, the *Santa Maria* gradually swinging bows-to-wind so that we lost sight of all that side of the vessel. Luis started to come up just as the dinghy came out from under the *Santa Maria*'s stern and I told him to go back. 'Two of us,' I said. 'They must only see two of us.' Carp nodded, the night glasses trained on the dinghy, which had swung towards us, one man in the stern handling the outboard, the other amidships, his head tucked into his shoulders as the spray began to fly. 'Who is it?' I asked.

'The gaffer, I reck'n.' He passed me the glasses. 'You have a look. I only seen the fellow once.'

It was Evans all right. I recognised the strong, column-like neck, the way it held his head. 'I'll be in the port hull, right for'ard in the loo.' And I added, 'If he wants to know where I am, as far as you know I'm at home.'

Carp nodded. 'I'll see he doesn't bother you.' He gave me that gap-toothed smile. 'Reminds me of the days when we used to slip over to Holland and come back into the Deben, crossing the bar at night and dumping a couple of bags full of de Kuyper's Geneva bottles with a float attached like we were laying lobster pots.'

I nodded and ducked below, sending Luis up on deck while I went to the double bunk I'd been using on the port side to make certain there was nothing lying around to indicate I was on board. Soon I caught the sound of the outboard approaching, then a voice hailing us. The engine died with a splutter and after a moment I heard the sound of Evans's voice – 'Wrapped around the prop, eh? Which one?' Then feet on the steps down into the saloon and a voice much nearer. 'Well, it's fortunate I found you. When we swapped boats I discovered I was missing a packet containing a spare aerial and masthead bracket picked up with other radio gear duty-free in Gib on the way out. Stuffed it all in the bilges and conveniently forget about it. You know how it is.'

I heard a non-committal grunt from Carp and Evans's voice went on, 'Tell me, did customs, police, anybody search the ship before you left yesterday?'

'No, not yesterday,' Carp replied. 'Day before we

had an Inspector Mallyno on board with 'is sidekick. The Heffy too.'

'The Heffy?'

'Ah. The Chief Inspector of police. Inspector Heffy.' Carp invariably got awkward names or words slightly wrong. He'd call a transistor a transactor or a tachometer a taxmaster, and always that slight sibilance as the breath whistled through those two broken teeth of his. 'They was on board quite a while talking with the boss.'

'Mike Steele?'

'Ah, the boss.'

'What were they talking about?'

'Oh, this and that, I reck'n.'

A pause then. Finally Evans came right out with it. 'Well, did they search the ship or not?'

'How would I know?'

'You said you were there.'

'I was up the mast, wasn't I?'

'How the hell would I know you were up the mast? I wasn't there.' Evans's tone was one of exasperation at Carp's odd turn of phrase. I couldn't hear anything after that. He must have turned away. Then a moment later, his voice sounding much louder, as though he had moved to the entrance to the starb'd hull, 'And what about the starb'd engine compartment? Did they look in there, too?'

'They may have done. That where you hid it?' I heard the steps being folded back. 'Well, there you are, mate. You can see for yourself. There's nothing there.'

'Right at the back.'

There was the sound of movement, then Carp's voice again, much sharper. 'No you don't. You're not pushing in among those pipes an' leads.'

Evans started to argue, then the stepped lid slammed down and Carp said, 'You lost anything, you talk to the boss. I don't want that engine conking out again. Not halfway to Malta I don't. And anyways, if we find it, we'll know whose it is and see you get it back.'

A pause, then Evans said, 'Okay, so long as you don't show it to anybody. I don't want it to get around that I slipped anything in under the noses of the customs people, not when we're trying to set ourselves up in the fishing here. All right?' And then, his voice fading as he turned away, 'Where's your boss now? Do you know?'

I didn't hear the answer, the murmur of their voices lost as they went back into the saloon. I came out of the loo then and moved aft as far as the turn of the steps over the engine. I could hear Evans's voice then, sharp and hard as he said, 'Felixstowe Ferry! What the hell are you talking about?' And Carp answering, 'Well, ever since you came down to the Navy quay to take over the *Santa Maria* I bin wondering. Thort I recognised you, see. But red hair – that's wot fixed me.'

'Red hair? What do you mean?'

'Moira. That's wot I mean. Red Moira.' And Carp went on, his accent broader and talking fast: 'Just before you get to the Ferryboat there's a dyke runs off to the left alongside a little tidal creek full of old clung-bungs used as houseboats. There was one, I remember, belonged to some bit actor feller – was on TV once in a while, then he'd be full of drink an' happy as a lark for a week. After that, broke again and morose as if he'd had sight of Black Shuck himself. Used to wander alone along towards the King's Fleet. Same name as yours.'

'So what?' Evans's voice was harsh. 'It's a common enough name.'

'Well, he's dead now. Shacked up with this Irish broad. Red Moira she was known as all along the beach. Lived in an old boat called the *Betty-Ann* that lay there in the mud, with a rickety old bit of flotsam planking the only way of getting on board. They had a son. Used to call 'im Pat.'

'You've got me mixed up with somebody else.'

'Mebbe. But then this Navy fellow came looking for you, and the odd thing is that when he was a kid he was sent to stay with the Evanses. I'd see the two of you out swimming together, larking about, all over the place you were until you broke into a cabin cruiser, downed some drink and got pissed as farts. It was the other one fell into the 'oggin, I remember, and Billie had to go after 'im with the pilot boat, the tide fair sluicing and the poor little bugger carried right out towards the shingle banks.'

Evans said something about it being time they were in bed and the sound of their voices faded as the two of them went out into the night. Shortly afterwards the outboard started up, the sound of it gradually dying away as Carp called down to me that I could come out now. He was grinning. 'Couldn't get away fast enough, could he? I reck'n it was him all right.'

'The boy you knew as a kid?' He nodded, and I said, 'I thought you said he had red hair.'

'That's right. Real Tishan. But you can dye it, can't you? Dye it black and it alters the whole look of a man. And that funny moustache. That's why I couldn't be sure, not at first. But the way he said it was 'is bedtime . . . You know there was a moment when I thort he was going to call up his mate and have a go at searching that engine compartment without permission. That's why I started telling him about Felixstowe Ferry. Pat Evans. That was the boy's name. Same name, you see. And both of them sent off to *Ganges*. It was the nearest place, outside of the Borstal over by Hollesley, to instil some discipline into the young rascals.'

He rubbed his hands on his denims. 'Quite a dag up on deck, real wet, like a mist had come down. Care for some coffee?' And before I could reply, he went on, 'Had the nerve to ask me if we'd got any liquor on board. He'd run out, he said. What he was after, of course, was to start a drinking session, so as he'd get my tongue loosened up and mebbe learn something I wouldn't have told him otherwise. I said we needed what little we'd got on board for the voyage over.' He shook his head, rubbing his hands over the greying bristles of his chin. 'Don't ever change their spots, do they? Well, wot about you? Shall I brew some coffee?'

He didn't feel like turning in and nor did I. We'd lost a precious half hour's sleep and already it was

01.37. 'Coffee and a small glass of something warming,' I said. 'Then we'll get under way.'

'Didn't like my reminding him he'd been at Felixstowe Ferry when he was a kid, did he?' He grinned as he turned away towards the galley at the after end of the port hull. 'It'll be instant, I'm afraid.' I heard the clink of metal, the sound of water running, then the plop of the butane burner igniting. 'Funny about that hair of his,' he called out. 'Makes you wonder what goes on in a man's mind, don't it?'

'How d'you mean?' I asked.

'Well, how long's he had it dyed, that's what I mean. Can't be just to conceal his identity, otherwise he'd've changed his name, wouldn't he? You see, we didn't reck'n they were married – Tim Evans and Red Moira. She was just a living-in girlfriend on a houseboat, that was our reck'ning. Partic'ly as she was pretty free with her favours. Well, not free if you know wot I mean. She charged – when she felt like it, or when she was short of cash.'

The kettle began whistling and when he returned with the coffee, he said, 'They claimed they was married. Mr and Mrs Evans.' He laughed. 'But if they wasn't, then that makes son Patrick a bastard. Reck'n that's why he dyed his hair – not wanting to be tarred with his mother's red brush?' He was opening a locker beside the table. 'Soberano or a real genuine malt that Lennie scrounged from one of the yacht skippers at the Maritimo.'

He pulled out the bottle and poured two stubby glasses full of the golden liquor. It was Macallan twelve-year-old, a mellow dream after the sweeter, more fiery taste of Spanish brandy. 'Little better than a whore,' he went on. 'And a tongue on her that could lash an East Coast barge skipper into silence. An' she used it, too, whenever she was drunk, which was pretty often. No wonder the poor devil committed suicide. To be shacked up with a whore who's been sleeping around with other men is one thing, but a red-headed Irish bitch with a tongue as coarse as a barge-load of grit . . .' He shrugged. 'Ah well, he's dead now, so who cares?'

Knowing the area, even the little mud creek back of the Ferryboat Inn with the dyke-top path running north to join the Deben riverbank, remembering the old houseboats I had seen there that cold, bleak spring day, their slimy bottoms sunk deep in the tide-exposed mud, I could picture what it must have been like for a boy to grow up in a home and a family atmosphere like that. And the father committing suicide. 'How did he do it?' I asked.

'Drowned 'isself,' Carp answered. 'Wot else? It's easy enough to do at the Ferry with the shingle beach dropping almost sheer and a sluicing ebb tide that runs over five knots at springs. He was missing two days before anybody took Moira's whimpers seriously. He'd done it before, gone off on 'is own without her knowing where. Very unpredictable man. Once he slept out at Minsmere in the woods there two whole days. Bird-watching at the Reserve there is wot he said, but we all reck'ned it was because he'd 'ad enough of it. They found 'is body out by the Haven buoy . . . That's right,

the same buoy that young lieutenant was found clinging to. It was a yacht outward bound for Dutchland
wot found 'im. Hulluva way to start a cruise, fishing
a body out of the water that's been dead – well, it
must have been close on a week by then.'

A horn blared from the direction of the quay and
I poked my head out of the saloon door, thinking
perhaps Soo had come back for some reason. There
was a car parked there, its headlights at high beam
and directed straight at the *Santa Maria*. The wheelhouse light came on and a moment later the dinghy
slid away from her side, the outboard sounding as
harsh as a chainsaw in the stillness.

We watched from the doorway as the dinghy
swung alongside the quay where the driver was waiting
to receive the box or large carton that was handed
up to him. The car drove off and the dinghy returned
to the *Santa Maria*. The lights went out, everything
still again, only the wind moaning in the trees and
undergrowth of the protecting peninsula to the east of
us.

'Some more coffee?' Luis had emerged and was
holding the pot up in invitation. We had it with the
rest of our Macallan at the chart table, checking
the position at which we should finally turn on to our
course for Malta. It was a straight run on a course of
155° that passed some thirty miles south of Sardinia.
'Six hundred miles,' Carp said. 'We should make it
without motoring in a little over three days.'

'If the wind holds,' I said. 'Which it seldom does.'

It took us only a few minutes to get ready for sea,

then we hoisted the main, holding the cat head-to-wind and pulling the anchor warp in by hand until it was up and down. I didn't start the engines, not even one of them, sailing the anchor out and hauling in on the main sheet until, with the wind abeam, we were headed to pass east of the island that lay across the inlet's narrows like a cork in a bottle and separated Macaret harbour from the upper reaches of the inlet, which was Port d'Addaia. We passed within less than a cable's length of the *Santa Maria*, slipping through the water quite silently, only a slight chuckle at the bows. Nobody stirred, no lights came on, and in a moment the bulk of the island hid her from view.

Carp and Luis hoisted the jib, and as we hardened in on the sheet, *Thunderflash* picked up her skirts and began to move. Off Macaret itself we began to feel the weight of the wind, the speed indicator moving towards seven knots. There was movement, too, as we got the wind coming in through the entrance. 'Everything stowed?' I asked Luis, and when he nodded I told him to go below and check again. 'It will be rough when we come out of the lee of Illa Gran.'

Carp suddenly hailed me from for'ard. 'There's a boat coming in.'

'Where?'

But he was already pointing, his arm indicating a position straight over the bows. By then the speed indicator was flickering on ten and a second later I saw it, a dark shape, with no lights. It was only the white of her bow wave that had enabled Carp to pick it out. 'Bloody fool!' he said as he landed on the teak grid beside my swivel chair.

'What is it?' I asked him. 'Coastal patrol?'

'Don't reck'n so. Bugger's coming in without a single light showing. Could be Navy. An exercise. Otherwise . . .'

I was thinking of the *Santa Maria*, lying at the head of the inlet, and the car that had met Evans on the quay. I was certain it was Evans who had taken that box or case ashore. 'We'll know soon enough,' I said. Already we could hear the thump of her diesel, and at that moment she was picked out for an instant by the headlights of a car on a bend ashore. There were barely a dozen metres between us as she went thundering past, and caught like that in the sweep of the car's lights, the dark silhouette of three men showed in the wheelhouse. She was a motor yacht of the fifties vintage or even earlier. 'Saving her batteries,' Carp said. 'Either that or she's bringing in a nice little present for somebody on the quiet.'

I didn't say anything, certain now that this clandestine arrival had something to do with the presence of the *Santa Maria* in the inner anchorage. But I had no time to dwell on that, for almost immediately we opened up the gap between the promontory of Macar Real and Illa Gran, the starb'd hull beginning to lift as the wind, funnelling through the gap, hit us. I had my work cut out then to keep her on course for the entrance.

A few minutes more and we were out into the open, the sea short and very steep with a lot of white water. I was steering 040°, the speed risen to almost eighteen knots, and every wave that broke sent the spray flying, droplets of water that were hard as shot-gun pellets driven against my face by an apparent windspeed that must have been well over forty knots. I called to Carp to get his oilskins on and take the helm while I went below to get a fix on the Faváritx light.

It took us only twenty minutes or so to run our distance off Menorca, the bows smashing through the waves, spray bursting almost as high as the radar scanner at the cross-trees and the twin hulls slamming their way through the water at a speed that made it seem hard as concrete, the shocks of impact jarring every bone in our bodies. At 02.27 we went about on to the port tack, setting course for Malta, and with the wind tending to back in the gusts, the motion was easier, though we were still close-hauled. We changed down to the number two jib, took a couple of rolls in the main and went into two-hour watches.

From my bunk I had periodic glimpses of the moon through the perspex hatch and when dawn broke I went up into the saloon on the chance of getting a last sight of Menorca and so fix our position. But there was no sign of any land, the catamaran now on a broad reach, driving fast and comfortably across a wilderness of broken water.

It was a long day merging into night, intermittent sun and cloud. I was able to get a noon fix that was close to the sat-nav position and showed we had been clocking up an average of nine and a half miles per hour over the ground during the ten hours we had been at sea. The movement was very different to anything I had known before. A monohull does not dash into the seas, it accommodates itself to the rise and swoop of the waves. A multihull is much more uncompromising, and with no let-up in the wind, we were all of us very tired by the time night fell, the sun going down in a ball of fire and an odd-looking rainbow curling across a black rain cloud to the south.

We had two days of force five to seven from between NNE and NNW and there were times when I thought for a moment she was going to start flying a hull. On the third day, the wind backed into the west so that we were able to shake out our reefs and for almost four and a half hours we had a spinnaker run. After that the wind fell light and we started to motor. From white, breaking waves the sea smoothed out till it took on an oily, almost viscous surface, only the low swell from the north to remind us of the hard weather that had been pushing us south-eastward down the Med at such a spanking speed. A pod of dolphins joined us and we spent over two hours watching them as they cavorted round the bows. Carp tried to take a picture of their underwater shapes, lying flat on the safety net that stretched between the twin hulls at the bows. He came back aft soaking wet, one of the dolphins having slapped its tail on the surface and showered him with spray. 'I swear he did it o'purpose, because he rolled over on his side and looked me straight in the face, an' he was grinning! Not sure 'e didn't wink 'is eye at me. Talk about a sense of fun . . .'

As suddenly as they had arrived, the dolphins disappeared. The sun was shining out of a blue sky as they left us, the spray thrown up by their speed and the arching curve of their sleek bodies glittered silver in the bright light. A noon sight put us within fifty miles of Sicily and by evening we could see the mountains standing pale in the sunset, wisps of cloud clinging to their tops.

It had been a lazy day, hot and sleepy-making, a welcome contrast. I had spent part of it trying to explain to Carp how to calculate his position from sights taken with the sextant. He was a good inshore pilot, but he had never had occasion to learn navigation, had never handled a sextant before. We had sat-nav and Decca on board, everything as automatic as could be, which is fine so long as your batteries hold out and no electrical faults develop in the hardware. The joy of a sextant is that there's virtually nothing to go wrong, unless you're fool enough to drop the thing overboard or forget to bring your azimuth tables with you.

That day I also began to think about our landfall. If we went straight into Grand Harbour, then it was unlikely I'd get ashore without being observed. The alternative, which was to slip into one of the smaller bolt holes like Marsaxlokk in the south of the island, or even drop off at the smaller island of Gozo, involved a risk that Carp could be in real trouble with the authorities if I were picked up by the police for having no papers and entering Malta illegally. In any case, when it came to leaving the island, I would have to do it secretly.

I didn't discuss the matter with Carp. It was something I had to make up my own mind about and in the end I decided to brazen it out and tell the authorities I had inadvertently lost my passport overboard, a very easy thing to do at night if one was stupid enough to leave it in one's anorak.

By late afternoon a heat haze was developing and we took in the clothes and bedding we had hung out to air. At six Luis relieved Carp at the helm and for the first time in three days the two of us were able to relax over an evening drink before putting the stew back on the stove. Two questions had clarified in my mind during the night watches, both concerning Gareth Lloyd Jones. First and foremost was the exact relationship between him and Evans, but all Carp said was, 'If he's bringing his ship into Mahon, then you'll be able to ask 'im yourself.'

'How long were the two boys together on that houseboat?' I asked.

'Not more'n three weeks, a month or so. If it'd been longer reck'n they'd've bin in real trouble, they was getting that wild. And Tim Evans accusing that Moira of all sorts of unnatural practices, accusing her publicly, right in front of everybody in the Ferryboat.' He knocked back the rest of his whisky and poured himself another, staring down at his glass, lost in his recollections.

'What do you mean – unnatural practices?' I was intrigued by his extraordinary choice of words.

'Well, can't say I know exactly wot the women were clacking about, but the fact is that the boy Gareth was just about the age for it and he was there on the boat with Moira an' nobody else for – oh, I forget now, but Tim Evans was away quite a while. Filming was wot Moira said. But I heard later he was so desperate for money he shipped as cook on a deep-sea trawler sailing out of Yarmouth for that Russian place, Novy Zembla.'

'And he accused her of taking the boy into her bed – is that what you're saying?'

'Well, I was in the pub there, wasn't I? Heard 'im say it myself. Shoutin' at 'er, he was.'

'So what was the boy's position? Why was it unnatural?'

Carp shrugged. 'There was rumours, you see.'

I waited, and when he didn't say anything further, I asked him what sort of rumours.

'That they was half-brothers. That's wot some people said.' He gave a little shrug. 'Place like the Ferry, tongues wag, partic'larly over people as strange as Tim and Moira.'

'Which of them was supposed to be the common parent?' I asked.

'Oh, the bloke of course. Moira was much too fly to get caught more than once. Least that's my reck'ning. But that boy, he had hair as red as hers, an' freckles, too. He was her kid, no doubt o'that. An' older than Gareth. A year at least. The local paper gave their ages as thirteen and fourteen.' And he went on to say that as he remembered it Gareth was the son of a couple named Lloyd Jones who ran a newsagent's somewhere in the East End of London. Seems it happened when Tim Evans was working at a municipal theatre in the Mile End Road. It was then, at the theatre, that he met up with Moira. She was barmaid there, so rumour had it.'

'You mean Tim Evans was having it off with both women at the same time?'

'Oh, I don't know about that. Story was that this Lloyd Jones fellow had to go into hospital for an operation and his wife was left running the newsagent's on her own. By then Tim Evans was out of a job, so she got him into the shop to help her. That's how he paid for 'is lodgings.'

'By giving her a son?'

He grinned. 'All I said was he helped her in the shop. As far as we was concerned it was the red-haired lad as was illegit.'

Luis called down to us that he had just picked up the loom of a light almost dead over the bows. After about a quarter of an hour, when the white beam of it finally lifted above the horizon, we were able to identify it positively as the lighthouse on the highest point of the island of Gozo, which is 595 feet above sea level and has a range of twenty-four miles.

With no vessel in sight, I stopped both engines and we lay to, so that for the first time in three days we could have our drinks and our evening meal together in the saloon. By then I had finally made up my mind to go straight in at first light and clear health, customs and immigration in the normal way. Grand Harbour was no more than forty miles away, five hours' motoring at an economical eight knots, which meant three-hour watches for each of us, starting with Luis at 21.00.

It seemed an awful long time that I lay awake thinking about Malta. So much history, and the pale, honey-coloured limestone seeming to sprout churches, barracks, ramparts and fortresses everywhere, with hotels and every other type and period of building in such profusion that it hardly seemed possible there were farms scattered all over the island, secreted behind the endless stone walls. I had spent just over a year there, first training, then training others. Later I had gone back to stay with a Maltese family, one of those that are descended from the Knights, proud people whose forebears fought the Turks in the Great Siege of 1565. That was when I met Soo.

Now, with all the vast stone familiarity of the place a short night's sleep away, my mind kept going over and over the future and its problems, recollections merging with thoughts of Gareth Lloyd Jones, wondering whether his ship would be there, how much the island would have changed, what the attitude of Soo's relatives would be. Her mother's father was still alive I knew, and the younger brother, who had gone into the Church, was vicar of the big church in Birzebbuga when last heard from – the elder brother had emigrated to Australia and was running a cattle station up north in Queensland. Soo herself had a cousin, Victoria, who was married to a lawyer and living in Sliema; the male cousins had both got themselves jobs in the States. I had met the lawyer once, a man of about my own age, very conservative in outlook, but a good underwater swimmer and he liked sailing.

I heard the watch change and the muffled beat of the engines starting up, felt the change of movement. We were under way again and after that I slept until Carp gave me a shake just after 03.00. 'Gozo just coming abeam,' he reported, 'and I can now see the light on the St Elmo breakwater.'

It was a bright, starlit morning, the dark sprawl of Gozo clearly visible under the swinging beam of the lighthouse high up in the centre of the island. I was alone at the wheel then, virtually no wind and the engines purring us along at eight knots, dawn gradually filling in the details of the landscape on our starb'd hand. I could make out the hotel I had once stayed in at St Paul's Bay, which is the spot where the disciple is supposed to have been shipwrecked. So many places I remember, and when the sun came up in a ball of fire the honey-coloured buildings of Sliema and Valetta took on a rosy glow, the whole urban complex that surrounds the great harbour inlets of Marsamxett and Grand Harbour looking fresh as the phoenix still engulfed in flames.

I steered close under the old fortress of St Elmo, heading for Gallows Point, and when I turned into Grand Harbour itself, I called Luis and Carp to come up and see it, neither of them having been to Malta before. To come in like this, from the sea, is to see it as the Turks saw it in May 1565, as all one hundred and ninety of their ships passed slowly across the entrance to bring the greatest fighting force then in existence to attack the Knights of St John in the stronghold they had retired to after being driven out of Rhodes.

We hoisted the yellow Q flag, and heading up the harbour, there on the port hand was Kalkara Creek and the massive ramparts of St Angelo and Senglea either side of Dockyard Creek. And right in front of us, bang in the middle of Grand Harbour and looking as though it owned the place, was the solid grey armour of a cruiser flying a red ensign with hammer and sickle on it. How many British admirals, I wondered, had turned in their graves at the thought of all the other nations that now used *their* harbour? There was a Libyan freighter at the quay further in, a small Cuban warship moored off, and a gaggle of coastal patrol vessels among the ferryboats in the creek. And then I caught sight of a pale grey shape, awkwardly placed right behind the Libyan freighter and tucked in against the dockyard quay right under one of the cranes. It looked like a Royal Navy ship. A gaily painted *dghajsa* was being rowed across our bows, the man at the oars calling to ask us if we wished to be taken ashore. But by then one of the harbour launches was coming out to meet us.

CHAPTER TWO

Things had been difficult enough during the Mintoff era, which is why we had only been back twice since our marriage, but now the bureaucracy, as represented by the puffed-up little immigration officer who came out to us, seemed to have become even more rigid and uncooperative. No doubt he had his orders, for as soon as I said my name he demanded to see my passport, and when I told him I had lost it overboard, he nodded, smiling, as though that was what he had expected.

I had been hoping, of course, that by now Martin Lopez would have had time to straighten things out, but when he ordered us to move nearer the dockyard area, presumably so that they could keep a closer watch on us, and said that nobody was to land, it was obvious the Menorcan authorities had been in touch with them. I pointed out to him that we had been at sea for almost four days and must send somebody ashore for fresh food, but the brown eyes in the smooth dark face stared at me uncomprehendingly. In the end he told us to arrange with one of the *dghajsas* to supply our needs. 'If you go ashore before you have clearance,' he said, 'you will be arrested.'

I was too tired to argue with him and shortly after he had left a Harbour Police launch appeared and under their direction we shifted to the industrial part of the harbour, anchoring just north of the largest of the dry docks, which was occupied by a Panamanian-registered cruise ship. Our new anchorage was noisy and smelt strongly of oil and sewage, the water thick and dark, the viscidity of its surface gleaming with a bluebottle iridescence in the bright sunlight.

The RN ship was a frigate; we could see her quite clearly now, but not her name, only the number on her side prefixed F. She was berthed alongside a quay on the Senglea shore of French Creek at about the spot where the Turks had tried so desperately to tear down the improvised palisade the Knights had erected to protect their southern flank. Maltese swimmers, armed with knives and short swords, had driven them off, and then on July 15, in the full heat of summer, Mustapha Pasha had launched what was intended as a final crushing blow against the Knights of St John. I remember the date because it was the day Soo and I had been married. The Janissaries, the Spahis, the Iayalars, the Levies were all thrown in, the galleys as well that had been dragged overland from Marsamxett. Three thousand fanatical Muslims died that day.

How much had changed! Yet over the long gap of four centuries, the forts, ramparts and ravelins of the

Knights still stood massive in the sunshine – Senglea and St Michael, Birgu and St Angelo, and Fort St Elmo away to my left on the Valetta side of Grand Harbour. I had been reading up on the Great Siege when I first met Soo and it was she who had taken me to all sorts of places I would otherwise have missed. It was, in fact, the Great Siege that had brought us together, the beginning of our love, and seeing it again all bright on that cloudless morning brought a lump to my throat.

A sudden flurry of activity on the deck of the frigate brought my mind back from the past. The gangway staff had been alerted by the approach of a launch speeding across from Valetta. I watched as it came alongside the accommodation ladder, sailors with boathooks fore and aft and a naval officer stepping out and climbing quickly to the deck above. There was a twitter of bo's'n's pipes and I wondered if it was the Captain returning from a courtesy visit. Was it Lloyd Jones? Would he know about the Great Siege? Would that spark I had seen explode between them compensate for all the things Soo and I had shared? And then, more practically, I was looking at the frigate's superstructure, the tangle of radio and radar equipment. There, if the worst came to the worst, was the means of communicating with the outside world, if he would play.

That thought stayed in my mind all day. I needed to know what was happening back at Mahon, what my position was. I had been so convinced I would be in the clear by the time we reached Malta, and Evans? . . . surely they would have searched the villa by now?

Lying in the broad double bunk in the port hull my mind went over and over the stupidity of it all. To fall into such a heavily baited trap – me, with all the experience I had of sailing close to the wind – Christ! It was unbelievable.

And then, when I finally got off to sleep, there was the jar of a launch alongside, Maltese voices and the thump of feet on deck. It was the customs back again, this time with orders to search the boat, which they did from end to end, peering into all the bilges, prodding cushions and bedding and searching every locker, the engine compartments, too. Periodically I asked them what they were looking for, but each time the senior officer replied, 'A routine search. Nothing more. Just routine.'

They were on board the better part of two hours. When they left I was advised once again not to go ashore. 'And don't send any bags, laundry, anything like that ashore. You wait here until you are cleared, okay?'

Nothing is more demoralising than being confined on board a sailing boat in port and at anchor, nothing to do but wait, and so many things I could have been doing ashore. Carp retired philosophically to his bunk, but though I followed his example, I couldn't sleep. After lunch I got the inflatable into the water and the outboard fixed to its bracket in readiness. If I had been on my own I think I would have risked it, but I had Carp to consider and so I sat there in the helmsman's chair watching the world go by, the sun hot on my bare shoulders, a drink in my hand and the sounds of Malta at work all about me.

Nobody else came out to us and time passed slowly. The flamboyantly painted *dghajsas* and ferries full of tourists scurried to and fro across the water between Valetta and Kalkara or Vittoriosa, and there were launches and service craft constantly moving among the vessels at anchor. Just before five the launch lying alongside the frigate's gangway was manned again and an officer appeared on the deck above. I got the glasses, but I couldn't be sure it was Lloyd Jones, the peak of his cap casting a shadow across his face. He was taken across the harbour to land by the Customs House where a car was waiting for him. Inside of an hour he was back on board. By then the sun was sinking over the Marsa township and the honey-coloured limestone of the older buildings ashore began to glow with a warmth that turned rapidly from gold to a fiery red.

By then the shipyard noises had been briefly swamped by the engines and horns of the rush-hour traffic. Lights appeared in the streets and on the wharfs, the windows of buildings blazed like a myriad fireflies, and suddenly the frigate was lit from end to end, a circlet of electric light bulbs. I think it was this that finally made up my mind for me. I went below, changed into a decent pair of trousers, put on a shirt and tie, then asked Carp to run me over to the frigate.

He looked at me hard for a moment, then he nodded. 'Okay, if that's what you want. You can always say it doesn't count – as going ashore, I mean.'

It took us less than five minutes to cross the flat

calm strip of water that separated us from the frigate. The launch had been hoisted into its davits so that, once I had checked that Lloyd Jones was the frigate's Captain and the Quartermaster had satisfied himself I really did know him, we were able to go straight alongside the accommodation ladder. 'Want me to wait for you?' Carp asked as I seized one of the stanchions and swung myself up on the grating.

'No.' I didn't want it made that easy for them to get rid of me. 'Either they'll bring me back or I'll have them flash you up on their signal lamp.'

By the time I reached the frigate's deck Carp was already on his way back to the boat and a very young-looking officer was waiting for me. He confirmed that Lloyd Jones was the Captain and when I told him I was a friend, he asked me to wait while he phoned. He came back almost immediately with Gareth Lloyd Jones. He looked very smart in an open-necked shirt, immaculately white, black trousers and cummerbund, and the gold of his new rank bright on his shoulder boards, a smile on that pleasant open face of his. 'Mike. It's good to see you.' He held out his hand, seeming genuinely pleased. 'John, take Mr Steele up to my cabin,' he told the young officer, 'and have Petty Officer Jarvis get him a drink.' Then to me he said, 'You'll excuse me for a moment. There's a party going ashore for supper at the invitation of a Maltese wine company and I want to have a word with them before they leave.'

He left me then, climbing the ladder to the helicopter flight deck ahead of me and disappearing round the hangar on the port side. John Kent, a dark-haired, dark-browed young man, who proved to be one of the seamen officers, led the way for me, up to the flight deck, for'ard past the illuminated funnel and in through a watertight door to a passageway that led across to the curtained entrance to the Commanding Officer's day cabin. 'Make yourself at home, sir, while I find the Captain's steward.'

The cabin was a roomy one with a desk, two arm-chairs and a couch with a coffee table in front of it, and there was a small dining table by one of the two portholes with utilitarian upright chairs. The port-holes, which had grips for steel shuttering, gave me a view of the concrete wall at the back of the quay and the lit buildings behind it rising to the back of the Senglea peninsula. There was nobody on the wharf or at the end of the shore-side gangway, which I could see a short distance aft of where I was standing. The only sounds that penetrated the cabin were shipboard sounds of whirring machinery and air-conditioning.

On the wall by the desk there was a telephone communications system, also a microphone and loud-speaker, and on the desk itself there was a naval manual of some sort, a Folio Society edition of Fitzroy's *Voyage of HMS Beagle*, a paperback copy of one of Patrick O'Brian's sea stories, also a framed photograph of Soo sunbathing on a rock. It looked like a picture I had taken myself, at Cala d'Alcaufar when we had first come to Menorca. It was a shock to have this visual evidence of how much my wife now meant to this man living a monastic existence on one of Her Majesty's ships.

'What would you care to drink, sir?'

I turned with a start to find a round-faced young man in dark blue, almost black, Navy trousers, and white shirt gazing at me curiously from the doorway. I ordered a gin and tonic and moved back to the porthole. There was movement now, a steady stream of sailors, all in civvies, looking clean and smart with their hair well brushed, moving down the gangway on to the wharf. I counted twenty-seven of them as they walked briskly across the wharf, separating into little groups as they disappeared from view round the corner of a storage shed. A moment later Gareth Lloyd Jones came in. 'Nobody offered you a drink?'

'Yes, it's coming,' I said.

Now that I had a chance to examine him more closely I thought he looked tired and edgy, as though his new command was getting him down.

The steward came in with two large gins on ice and a bottle of tonic. 'Fifty-fifty, plenty of tonic?' Gareth gave me a quick grin, poured the tonic, then took a long pull at his own drink before subsiding on to the couch. 'Well, what brings you here? That's your catamaran over by the dry dock, isn't it?' He must have caught sight of Soo's photograph then, for he suddenly bounced up, went over to the desk, and under the pretext of looking at some papers, turned the picture face down.

Briefly I explained what had happened, finally asking him whether there was any way he could find out what the attitude of the authorities in Menorca was to me now. 'Have you anyone there you can contact by radio?'

He hesitated. 'Yes, but . . .' He got to his feet and went back to the desk, lifted the mike off its rest and press-buttoned a number. 'Captain. Is the Yeoman of Signals there? Ask him to have a word with me.' He put the mike back on its rest. 'Funny ship, this,' he said. 'It's an antique really, but after being moth-balled for several years and threatened with the knacker's yard twice, their lordships suddenly hauled it back into service, gave it a quick face-lift, and then fitted it out with the latest in communications systems so that to that extent we must be the envy of the Fleet. We also have sonar equipment that's on its last legs and an Ops Room that belongs to the Ark and is on the blink . . .' There was a tap at the door and he said, 'Come in, Yeo.' He turned to his desk, reached for a message pad and began to write as a thin man with a dark pointed beard pushed aside the curtain. When he had finished, he said, 'Have that sent and make it immediate. And they're to stand by for a reply. This is Mr Steele, incidentally. Petty Officer Gordon, my Yeoman of Signals.'

The beard and I smiled at each other, and as he left Gareth said, 'It may be a little time before we get a reply to that. Meanwhile, perhaps you'd join me for my evening meal.' And when I demurred, he said, 'No, of course not – no trouble at all. I'll be glad of your company anyway. Occasionally I mess in the ward-room, and I have messed with the Senior Rates once, but mostly I feed alone. It's the custom, you know. So as I say, I'll be glad of your company.' He called to the steward to bring us another drink. 'I never drink at sea, of course –' He spoke as though he had been in command for years – 'but now that we're tied up alongside . . .' He gave a little shrug, as though the fact of being tied up to a quay absolved him of some of the responsibility of command.

But as time passed I began to realise that his position weighed heavily on him, more heavily than it should, even for a man newly appointed to the command of a ship. It was as though he had something on his mind and the only clue he gave as to what it might be was when he suddenly said, apropos of nothing, 'You know, it's a strange thing, here I am flying the White Ensign, but tucked away against this filthy little quay, as though the Maltese didn't want to recognise the flag that's flown here for so many years. I'm out on a limb. Nobody wants to know us. Officially, that is. We're sort of pariahs. I've been here four days and not a day has passed but the authorities have dropped hints it's time we left. We have in fact flashed up the boilers so that we are ready to sail at short notice if we have to.'

He paused then, but two gins had loosened his tongue and he went on, talking fast: 'They don't want to make a thing of it, tell us outright to go, but they've made it very clear they don't want us here. You see, wherever we are, in this ship – any RN ship – we're a bit of the UK. That's what the Union flag is telling them, and they don't like it – not now, not any more.

Politically, here in Grand Harbour, we stick out like a sore thumb.' And he added with a wry smile, 'Our visit isn't a bit like it was for the last frigate that showed the flag here.'

'That was the first courtesy visit in seven years if I remember rightly,' I said.

'Well, not quite. The *Brazen* was the first ship to visit Malta after the British Forces finally left the island in 1979. She had the C-in-C Fleet embarked. Prince Charles came later with ninety thousand Maltese cheering and waving flags.' He made a face, shrugging his shoulders. 'That's what the papers said anyway. And look at us, tucked away in a corner where nobody can see us, and that bloody great Russian cruiser lording it in the centre of the harbour. That's why I had the lights rigged.'

'I don't think La Valette would have approved of their presence here,' I said.

He smiled, 'Ah, so you know what happened. More than four centuries ago and we still talk of St Elmo's fire.' He had read Ernle Bradford's book, knew the whole incredible story, the astonishing bravery of the Maltese when led by men like the Knights and motivated by religious faith and the fear of being captured and sent to the Turkish galleys. 'And now they are under the hand of another Muslim ruler.'

There was a knock at the door and a thickset, bull-headed Lieutenant Commander with greying hair entered, cap under his left arm, some papers gripped in his hand. He was a good deal older than his newly appointed captain. His name was Robin Makewate,

'MEO,' Gareth said, explaining that it meant Marine Engineer Officer. It was a state-of-the-engines routine visit, and when he had gone, Gareth said, 'He's forty-three, started as a stoker at the age of nineteen after studying engineering at night school. Volunteered for the job here, even though he knew he'd be serving under a much younger man.' He finished his drink, saying as he did so that it was odd being in command of a ship that was filled partly by volunteers, partly by throw-outs from the rest of the Fleet.

That wry smile again, his eyes not looking at me, not seeing anything but what was in his mind as he went on, speaking so quietly I could hardly hear him: 'I've a total complement of well over two hundred, and of those, fifty-seven are volunteers. Why? I don't know, and I'm the Captain. They don't know, and they're the ones who volunteered. Something dangerous, that's all some of them have been told. There's one or two I picked myself. The Appointers were generous in that respect – my Navigating Officer, Peter Craig. Also the SCO – that's my Communications Officer, Lieutenant Woburn – and Tony Draycott, my Weapons Engineer Officer. I've also got a CPO who was at *Ganges* when I was there. Most of the key people, they're volunteers, but there's others, fifty or sixty at least, who've been quietly wished on me by other ships' captains as though word had been put around that *Medusa* was a sort of personnel dustbin and I was a sucker on whom they could foist all the yobbos and troublemakers they wanted to be rid of. Oh, well . . .' Again the wry smile, the slight shrug.

'Let's have some food. I'm hungry. You must be, too, listening to me.'

He called for the steward, and over the avocado and shrimp cocktail we talked of Libya and the PLO, Beirut and the effect of the Gulf War. A daily signal from Fleet Headquarters at Northwood near London plus the World News of the BBC kept him very well informed. He needed to be, I thought, tied up here like a sitting duck in a little independent country that was set in the very centre of the Mediterranean like a stepping stone to the most volatile and unreliable country in Africa. And even as I was thinking about that, full of curiosity and wondering whether I could ask him about his plans, what orders he had received, and if he was headed for Menorca next, he was called on the intercom loudspeaker. It was the Officer of the Day reporting a little crowd beginning to gather on the quay.

I got to my feet then and looked out of the nearest porthole. It was almost dark on the concrete apron, only one small light still showing at the corner of the storage shed opposite. A dozen or so figures stood silent against the corrugated metal sheeting of the shed. It was like a stage set with others drifting in from the wings in ones and twos.

'Have you informed the First Lieutenant? They could be dockers waiting to unload. Is there a ship coming in?'

'Not that I can see, sir, and the First Lieutenant's trying to contact the port authorities to see if they can tell him what it's all about.'

'All right, tell him to report anything he finds out. And keep an eye on them. Let me know if their numbers noticeably increase.' He switched off, had a quick look through the other porthole, then returned to the table, muttering to himself, 'I don't like it.'

He didn't talk much after that. The main course was roast lamb and he ate it quickly, jumping up every few minutes to glance out of the porthole. Coffee came and we both stood at the window to drink it. The numbers had grown. It looked as though there were at least forty or fifty men down there lounging in the shadows. 'What the hell are they waiting for?' He turned at a knock on the entrance bulkhead. 'Well, what's the form?'

His First Lieutenant was a thin gangling man with what I suspected was a permanently worried expression. He had to duck his sharp-nosed halberd of a head to enter. He looked forty-fiveish, but perhaps he was less. His name was Randolph Mault, and his rank was the same as Gareth's. 'I don't know,' he said slowly. 'Looks like they're waiting for something to happen.'

'Trouble?'

'Could be a demonstration.'

'Against us?'

The executive officers hesitated. 'We know there's an anti-British – anti-West at any rate – element in Malta. We've been briefed on that. And it's supposed to be quite deliberately fostered and well organised.'

Gareth Lloyd Jones turned back to the porthole. 'Yes,' he said. 'That's probably why our people advised

us to anchor out in the middle of the harbour. I thought
at first it was because we'd be more conspicuous there,
something to counteract the presence of that Russian
cruiser, but it did cross my mind, when the Maltese
authorities insisted on our lying alongside in this Godforsaken spot, that besides making us as inconspicuous
as possible, it also made us more vulnerable to some
shore-based whipped-up anti-Western feeling. Pity we
didn't rig the lights right round the ship.' He stood for
a moment, gazing out at the darkened quay and the
figures grouped in the shadows.

The First Lieutenant had moved nearer so that he
could also see down on to the quay. 'What time is the
shore party due back, do you know?' he asked.

Gareth shook his head. 'No time was specified on
the invite.' He glanced at his watch. 'Soon, I would
think. And I told them to be sure they remained sober.
Do you think they'll be sober when they return?'

'It's not just a wine company, you know. It's also
a distillery. They produce a local brandy, also a sort
of gin. I found one of their brochures in the wardroom
bar. Apparently we've shipped some cases of their
wine, or maybe it was a present – I'm not sure.'

Gareth turned abruptly from the window. 'Very
well.' His voice was suddenly different, sharp and
incisive. 'Have young Kent go over to the company's
office – my apologies to the Director, but something
has cropped up and the shore party is to return to the
ship immediately.' He produced a key from his pocket
and passed it across. 'Tell him to take the car we hired
yesterday. It's parked behind the shed there. And he'd

better take somebody with him.' He glanced out of
the window. 'And tell him to get a hustle on. I have a
feeling all they're waiting for now is someone to give
them a lead.'

'Aye, aye, sir.' The First Lieutenant turned and
ducked quickly out.

'I'd better leave,' I said, but Gareth didn't seem to
hear me, standing very still at the porthole, watching.
'If you'd be good enough to have one of your people
signal to *Thunderflash* . . .'

He turned then. 'No, no. You wait here till we get
an answer from Menorca. Shouldn't be long now.' And
he added, 'I'm going up to the bridge – care to join
me?'

We went up a flight of steps just outside his cabin.
The bridge was dark and empty, only the glow of
various instruments and a solitary figure, a senior petty
officer, who came in from the head of the ladder leading down to the sidedeck. 'Lieutenant Kent's just leaving now, sir.'

'Who's he taking with him?'

''Fraid I don't know, sir.'

'Hastings.' It was the First Lieutenant. He had just
come on to the bridge. I recognised the rather high
voice.

'Good choice.' Gareth Lloyd Jones nodded and
turned to me with a quick smile. 'He's our PT instruc-
tor. Keeps us on our toes and the flab under control.
That's the theory of it, anyway.'

He went out through the bridge wing door on the
port side and I followed him. From the head of

the ladder we watched as the officer who had met me on arrival went quickly down the gangway, followed by a broad-shouldered, powerful-looking seaman. As they reached the quay there was movement among the shadows, voices sounding in the night, Maltese voices plainly audible above the continuous thrum of the ship. Suddenly a solitary voice was raised above the rest and the movement became purposeful, the shadowy figures coalescing into two groups and moving to block the way round the end of the storage shed.

'Have the ten-inch signal lamp manned and put out a call for the photographer.'

'Aye, aye, sir.' But before the petty officer could move Mault had reached for the bridge phone. He had been followed now by several other officers. 'I've closed the duty watch up, sir,' one of them reported.

'Good.' The acknowledgement was barely audible and Gareth didn't turn his head, his hands gripped on the rail, his body leaning intently forward as he watched the two figures advancing in step and without hesitation towards the group that now stood in a huddle blocking the exit at the eastern end of the shed. For a moment everything seemed to go quiet, the Maltese all standing very still, so that the only movement was the two uniformed figures advancing across the quay. I thought I could hear the sound of their marching feet, and then they had reached the group blocking the exit and were forced to stop. The young lieutenant might have made it. He was standing there, talking to them quietly, but whatever it was he was saying could not be heard by the group at the other end of the shed. They were starting to move, a little uncertainly, but their intention was clear. They were headed for the foot of the gangway to cut the two Navy men off.

'Shall I recall them?' It was the First Lieutenant and he had a microphone for the upper-deck broadcast system ready in his hand.

Lloyd Jones's hesitation was only fractional, but then one of the Maltese shouted something and in the instant the whole quay was in an uproar, the figures moving like a shadowy tide to engulf the dark blue uniforms. 'Lieutenant Kent to report back to the ship.' Mault's metallic, magnified voice seemed to fill the night. 'Both of you at the double.'

Lloyd Jones suddenly came to life, seizing the microphone from the First Lieutenant's hand, his voice booming out of it as he countermanded the order for the men to double and called for the signal lamp to be switched on to the quay. Instantly the whole concrete apron was flooded in a harsh light, the figures no longer shadowy, but leaping into focus, a sea of faces. They checked, and while they were held there, like a crowd scene under the glare of a film-set spotlight, Kent and the burly PO marched smartly back to the gangway. 'Where's the photographer?' Lloyd Jones's voice was crisp.

'Here, sir.' A man in a crumpled sweater with his equipment slung round his neck stepped out on to the wing of the bridge.

'I want pictures. Clear enough to identify individuals.' He raised the mike to his lips again. 'This is the Captain speaking. I don't know why you have gathered on the quay in front of my ship, but I would ask you all to disperse now and allow my officer to proceed. I should add that my photographer is now taking pictures so that if he is impeded going about his duty each of you will be identifiable when I raise the matter personally with the authorities here in Malta.'

I think he would have succeeded in getting them to disperse, for some of them, particularly those nearest the ship, had turned away their heads as soon as the signal lamp had been switched on and quite a number of them began to drift away at the threat of being photographed. But then a motor bike appeared round the corner of the shed and a man in black leather, like a Hell's Angel, thrust it on to its stand and began haranguing them in a voice that was almost as powerful as Gareth's had been with the use of the loudhailer.

It checked the backward flow, but by then Kent had reached the bottom of the gangway and was standing there staring up at us, white-faced in the hard light, waiting for orders. 'What do you think, Number One – can he make it?' Lloyd Jones was still leaning on the rail, still looking down on the scene, the bullroarer gripped tight in his right hand. 'Take a party to the foot of the gangway,' he ordered. 'See what a show of strength does.' He leaned over the rail, his voice quite calm as he ordered Kent to proceed. 'But you'll have to move fast when you get to the roadway, before that man whips them up into a mood of violence.'

Kent and the Leading Hand moved smartly back

across the quay, the Maltese watching them and the motor cyclist shouting at the top of his voice. They reached the corner of the shed, and then, as they disappeared from view, the crowd began to move, Gareth yelling at them through the megaphone to hold fast while men from the ship tumbled down the gangway to form up at the foot of it. The mob took no notice, all of them streaming out towards the roadway, to come to a sudden halt as the lights of a car went blazing past, the engine revving in low gear.

Standing as I was, right next to Gareth, I heard his breath come out in a sigh, saw him relax momentarily. But then he braced himself, turning slowly as he gave orders for the men on the searchlight to be ready. The quay was almost empty.

'You think they'll be back, sir?'

''Fraid so. This has been planned. It was planned before ever they allocated us a berth alongside this bloody quay.' He spoke quietly, more to himself than to his First Lieutenant. 'And have a full Damage Control Party closed up, fire hoses ready to be run out and full pressure on the pumps when we need it.'

'Internal Security platoon, sir?'

Gareth hesitated.

'A show of strength, as you said,' Mault added. 'It might do the trick.'

Gareth didn't answer, staring down at the quay. Already the crowd was drifting back, a group of them gathering round the motor cyclist. He was a barrel-chested, tough-looking man, his face almost square with a thick nose, and he had black curly hair that covered his head like a helmet. 'All right, have the arms issued. Say twenty men under the command of that Marine sergeant.'

'Simmonds?'

'Yes. Perhaps it's for this sort of thing he was posted to the ship.' Gareth's face creased in a grin. 'I did wonder.' And he added, 'But keep them out of sight. A parade of arms is the last thing we want.' And then, half to himself, he said, 'About time I sent a signal to CINCFLEET telling them what's going on.' He went back into the bridge to telephone, and after that it was a long wait. Finally we returned to his day cabin. 'No good my hanging around the bridge, looking anxious. They'd begin to get the jitters.'

'What about you?' I asked.

He laughed. 'Oh, I've got the jitters, of course I have.' His steward appeared and he ordered some more coffee. 'Care for a brandy with it? Or would you prefer Armagnac? The wardroom shipped some Armagnac at Gib, really first-rate stuff.' But he wasn't drinking now so I thanked him and said I was all right. We drank our coffee in silence, listening to the reports that began to come in over the loudspeakers: damage control first, then MEI confirming there would be full pressure on the hydrants, WRO to say the searchlight was manned. Finally the First Lieutenant's voice announcing that the IS platoon was at readiness and fully armed. 'God! I hope we don't have to resort to that.'

'You think it might come to that?' I asked him.

He shrugged and went to the window, standing

there looking out, his coffee gripped in his hand. 'That bunch isn't gathered out there for nothing.' There was a knock on the bulkhead by the curtained doorway and the Yeoman of Signals poked his bearded face in. 'Signal from CINCFLEET passing a telex from Menorca, sir.'

Gareth took it, read it through, then handed it on to me. 'Sorry about that. It looks as though you're still suspect.'

The telex was short and to the point: *Ref your query Michael Steele, his sudden departure confirmed authorities in their suspicions. Legal proceedings now being initiated for extradition Malta. For your information weapon used by Barriago still not found.* There was no signature, and when I asked him who had sent it, he shook his head. 'Everything on this ship that's connected with Communications is classified. But as far as I know the source is absolutely reliable.' He held out his hand for the signal. 'Too bad. I wish I could have provided you with better news.'

I thanked him and got to my feet. 'I'd best be going,' I said.

He shook his head. 'Not now.' He glanced at the clock on the bulkhead above the desk. 'Five minutes to get them off the company's premises, ten more for them to reach the quay here.' He finished his coffee and reached for his cap. 'Time to go up to the bridge. Coming?'

I followed him into the passage and up the ladder to the bridge. The scene had changed very little, except that the crowd seemed to have grown larger. We went out on to the wing. A big searchlight was mounted now and manned, and the damage control people were lowering hoses onto the quay. No sign of the boarding party, but a Marine sergeant was standing by the davits on the deck below. Gareth called him up to the bridge wing. 'I'll give you the order, Sergeant, when I want your men paraded on the quay. Once there you'll have to act as the situation demands. Your job is to see that all the ship's personnel get back on board unhurt. But just remember this, any action you take will have political repercussions and will ultimately be exposed to the full glare of publicity.'

The sergeant stared at him impassively. 'Aye, aye, sir.'

Silence then, just the thrumming of the ship's machinery, a slight trembling of the deck plates underfoot, and men everywhere around the deck waiting and watching, while down on the quay the excited, nervous babble of Maltese voices came up to us as an audible complement to the constantly shifting pattern of the waiting crowd. I could see the motor cyclist in his black leather talking and gesticulating to the little group gathered round him, and there were others, shadowy figures, among the various groups.

The Marine sergeant was back with his men on the deck below and Gareth was glancing at his watch for the third or fourth time. The brass nozzle of a fire hose hit the ship's side with a clang, then a sudden shout and a flurry of movement on the quay, the crowd pouring through the gap between the east wall of the shed and the neighbouring building. A horn blared, shouts and yells, and a small red car appeared in the gap, almost totally submerged in a flood of people. The noise increased, the sound of fists pounding on roof and bonnet, the horn now blaring continuously.

Gareth raised the megaphone. 'Searchlight.' The white glare of it was so brilliant and so sudden that all movement ceased abruptly. For an instant there was silence. Then the car's engine revved, nosing into the crowd, spearheading a path for the men following in its wake.

There was a shout, one word, not a Maltese word, but French – *Attaquez*, and on the instant the scene changed, a rush of movement, the car was picked up bodily from one side, the engine screaming as it was pitched on to its side and the wheels came free of the ground. Screams and shouts, and the two fire hoses, run out now across half the width of the quay, bulged, their nozzles hissing like snakes, water bursting out in a broad arc. But the car and the crowd were too far away. The jets of water barely reached them. I heard Mault's voice, but before he had even given the order, the Marine sergeant and his men, all in uniform and with bayonets fixed to their self-loading rifles, came thundering down the gangway.

If they had moved in before the shore party had reached the quay, if they had broken up the crowd, grabbed the ringleaders and the other agitators . . . But that would have meant taking the initiative with the Navy blamed for everything that followed. As it was, the men forming up in a compact body at the foot of the gangway and then advancing might still have been sufficient intimidation to get the sailors back on board. Instead, the sergeant ordered them to charge, and that was just the catalyst needed to turn an ugly little incident into a political bombshell.

The crowd round the car were already opening out. In a moment they would have run. But then it happened, a spurt of flame, the sound of a shot, and Lieutenant Kent, climbing out of the car, all of his torso reared up in the open window on the driver's side, threw up his hands and began to scream. And as he lost consciousness, his body sagging to lie crumpled across the side of the vehicle, I saw the man who had fired the shot drop his pistol, turn and slide away to the rear of the crowd.

I saw him, but I don't think the others did, for their attention had switched to the armed party. They had suddenly stopped, the sergeant's voice ringing out as he gave the order to fire over the heads of the crowd. The volley was ragged, but the noise of it and the sight of those men in blue with their rifles raised and the bayonets glinting in the glare of the searchlight was enough. The crowd broke and ran, melting away so quickly that for an instant the only figure left on the scene was the motor cyclist trying to kick-start his bike into life. Finally he threw it down and ran.

I think the enormity of what had happened was immediately apparent to Gareth, for he stood there on the bridge wing, his face white with shock, too stunned, it seemed, to take command. It was Mault who ordered the armed party back on board, sent for the medical orderly and a stretcher party to get the young lieutenant to the sick bay, and had the shore party drawn up at the foot of the gangway and checked against a list of names to make certain nobody was missing. They were coming back on board and the damage control men were rolling up their hoses before Gareth finally came out of his state of shock. 'Lieutenant Commander Mault.'

Mault turned, an interrogatory lift of his straight, very black eyebrows.

'Time we got out of here. Come to immediate notice for sea and go to harbour stations as soon as you're ready. We'll move out into the open harbour and anchor seaward of that Russian cruiser. After that we'll see.' He turned abruptly, going back into the bridge housing. 'Find Chief Petty Officer Gordon and tell him to have a word with me,' he said to one of the seamen. 'I'll be in my cabin.' And he disappeared hurriedly through the door at the back.

I realised that he had understood more than any of the officers around him, including his First Lieutenant, the full implications of what had happened – an armed party had landed from a Royal Navy ship and had opened fire on a crowd of Maltese. Never mind that they had fired in the air, that their action had been provoked and an officer had been shot, it had been done on Maltese soil. An invasive and hostile act, that's how it would be presented, to the Maltese and throughout the Third World and the non-aligned states. He had forgotten all about my presence on the ship, and I couldn't blame him.

The main broadcast suddenly blared out, Mault's

voice ordering the crew to harbour stations. I waited until he had finished his announcement, then suggested he signal *Thunderflash* to come and collect me, but he shook his head. 'Sorry. You'll have to wait until we're anchored.' He had hung up the mike and now had glasses trained on the main dock area where a crowd had gathered at the slip by Somerset Wharf. 'The whole place will soon be in an uproar.' He turned to the chart table, shaking his head. 'Bad business.'

He shouldn't have said that, not in front of me, and certainly not with the Navigating Officer standing beside him. And the way he said it, as though it were nothing to do with him – I knew then that he was trying to distance himself from his captain. At the time, of course, I put it down to the fact that he was older, a resentment at being passed over. Later I was to discover his grandfather had been an admiral in the First World War, his father killed at sea in the Second, and he himself had come up through the traditional officer education of the Navy, Pangbourne, Dartmouth, then service at sea. What had damaged his career was volunteering for submarines and then, when he was posted to HMS *Dolphin* for a submariners' course, finding he was subject to claustrophobia and unable to concentrate when submerged.

In the circumstances it was a bit hard to find himself serving under a man who had joined the Navy as a boy seaman at *Ganges* and been commissioned out of the lower deck, was several years his junior and newly promoted to Lieutenant Commander, a rank he had held more years than he cared to remember. Added to which, he had never had command of a ship in his life, and now this raw young Welshman was plunging him straight into a first-class Mediterranean balls-up. That was his choice of words, and he went on: 'There's Chinese in the dockyard here, one of the latest Russian cruisers anchored in Grand Harbour, and the Libyans barely two hundred miles away. We should never have come to the wharf here. We should never have agreed to tie up alongside.' He turned away, muttering something that sounded like, 'He should have had more sense.' Then he was giving orders for singling up and sailors were letting go all but the head and stern ropes and the springs.

The bridge had now filled up with the special sea duty men, the Navigator standing in the middle by the pelorus. Mault, watching from the bridge wing, finally told him to inform the Captain the ship was singled up and ready to proceed.

I was watching the quay, so I didn't see Mault's face as the Pilot put the phone down and told him the Captain was in the main communications office and he was to take the ship out to the new anchorage himself, but I did notice the sharpness in his tone as he gave the order to let go aft and, picking up the mike to the wheelhouse below, said, 'Port thirty, slow ahead port, slow ahead starb'd.'

I could feel the beat of the engines under my feet, saw the stern swing clear of the quay, then we were backing out past the rust-patched freighter moored at the Parlatorio Wharf. 'Harbour launch, sir, coming away from Gun Wharf, heading towards us.'

Mault nodded his acknowledgement of the look-out's report, the ship still going astern and turning. As soon as we were clear of the freighter and had sea room to complete the 180° turn, he went ahead, the long arm of the harbour opening up in front of us as we turned the end of Senglea Point with the massive fortress of St Angelo showing beyond it. The harbour was a broad lane of flat water ablaze with lights on either side and at the end of it the swinging beam of the St Elmo light flashing three every fifteen seconds, with the small light on the end of the breakwater winking steadily.

Mault moved to the chart table, calling to the Pilot to join him. 'Plan to anchor about there,' he said, pointing his finger to a position roughly south-west of what used to be Gallows Point but was now shown on the chart in Maltese as Il-Ponta Ta'Ricasoli.

'Right in the fairway?'

'Well no, a little in towards Bighi Bay.'

The Navigating Officer nodded. 'Nine Fathoms Bank. You'll have eighteen to nineteen metres. That do you?' He had the plot going and there was a PO on the radar. Through the sloping windows I could see the Russian cruiser looming large and brilliantly lit. 'Harbour launch on the port quarter, sir. About one hundred metres off. He's signalling us to stop.'

'Thank you, Stevens.'

There was a little group closed up around the capstan on the fo'c's'le and I could see men on the deck of the cruiser. She looked enormous as we ran close down her starb'd side and it crossed my mind that if the Russians became involved in any way it really would be an international incident. And then I saw a man with a rag in his hand waving from the open door of the helicopter hangar aft and the thought was suddenly absurd.

'Matey, isn't he?' The Pilot smiled at me. 'The way they behave sometimes you'd think they were our comrades-in-arms. And that's one of their *Kresta* class – very lethal!' He was a short man with a round face, a puggy blob of a nose and a twinkle in his eyes. 'My name's Craig, by the way. Peter Craig. I'm supposed to see my lords and masters here don't scrape their bottom along the seabed or hit a headland.' He waved at the chart. 'That's where we'll be anchoring.' He indicated a little cross he had pencilled in. 'Then we'll start explaining ourselves to the harbour master.' He glanced at his watch. 'Twenty-two minutes to go till the next news. Think they'll have it on the World Service?'

A sub-lieutenant, standing beside the chart table with his back to the bulkhead, said quietly, 'If the BBC includes it in the news, then the PM will be tearing the guts out of the C-in-C and we'll be in the shit good and deep. Thank your lucky stars, Pilot, you're just a common navigator. I wouldn't be in Taffy's shoes right now . . .' He stopped then, glancing at me apologetically. 'Sorry, sir, no disrespect, but all Welshmen are Taffy to the boys, just as anybody called Brown is Buster and anybody with a name like Randolph, our Chief, becomes Randy. No disrespect, you see.' Like the Pilot, he was a Scot, a Glaswegian by the sound of his voice. His name was Robinson and he was a seaman officer-under-training, one step up from midshipman. I thought he was probably not more than nineteen or twenty years old.

The Pilot was concentrating now on the approach to the anchorage and it was an older officer standing by the radar who answered him. 'You shoot your mouth off like that and it's you who'll be in the shit.' And he added, 'Right now nobody wants to be reminded what could happen following that little incident, so forget your old man's on the ITN news desk and keep your trap shut. Okay?'

There was a juddering under my feet and I turned to see the ship was slowing: 'Harbour launch close abeam, still signalling Stop.' Mault ignored the report. He came back to the chart table, took a quick glance at the position the Navigating Officer had pencilled in, then asked him to report how far before letting go the anchor as he moved to the port bridge wing and took up one of the microphones. Everyone was silent now, waiting, the ship slowing, small alterations of helm, the shore lights barely changing position. 'Let go!' I felt, rather than heard, the rumble of the chain, then the voice of the officer on the fo'c's'le was reporting how many shackles of cable had gone out.

'Well, that's that.' Craig checked the time, entered it on the chart against the fix he had taken as the anchor was let go. Behind him, the bridge began to empty. 'Care to join me for a drink in the wardroom, sir?'

I hesitated, then nodded. Lloyd Jones would be as

anxious to get rid of me as I was to go, so no point in making a nuisance of myself. Besides, I was interested to know what the officers thought of it all.

The wardroom was two decks down on the starb'd side. Half a dozen officers were already there and all of them silent, listening for Big Ben on the loudspeaker set high in the corner. It came just as Peter Craig handed me the horse's neck I had asked for, the solemn tones of the hour striking, then the announcer's voice giving the headlines. It was the third item and followed bomb blasts in Belfast and Lyons – 'A frigate of the Royal Navy on a courtesy visit to Malta was involved this evening in an incident in which a shore party had to be given protection. Shots were fired and one officer was injured.' That was all.

'Playing it down,' Craig said, sucking eagerly at his drink and turning to look around him. 'Where's young Robbie? Hey, Robinson – tell yer dad he'll have to do better than that. The people at home should know what really happened.' His words about summed up the view of the others. A put-up job, that was their verdict, and then Mault came in. 'Mr Steele. The Captain would like a word with you. He's in his cabin.'

I nodded, finishing my drink, but waiting for the news broadcaster to come to the end of the Lyons outrage and move on to the Malta incident. It was padded out, of course, nothing new, and nothing to upset the Maltese, no indication that it was they who had fired the first shot, or that the ship had been deliberately moored alongside Hamilton Wharf so that an anti-British mob could move in from the nearby Malta Dry Docks and threaten the lives of British sailors returning from a wine party that had almost certainly been organised solely for the purpose of luring them ashore.

I thanked Craig for the drink, excused myself and went up to the Captain's cabin. It was empty, a cup of black coffee untouched on the desk. I went to one of the portholes. We had swung to our anchor and were now bows-on to the harbour entrance so that I was looking straight across to the cathedral and the domes of Valetta with the signal flagstaff towering above them. The harbour launch had been joined by two police launches, all three of them keeping station opposite to the bridge on the port side. An officer on the leading police launch had a loudhailer to his mouth, the words coming muffled as they reached me through the shatterproof glass: 'You will plees to lower your gangway. I wish to come on to your ship and spik with the Captain.' And the reply, from somewhere above me – 'When you bring the British High Commissioner out we can discuss things. Okay?'

The steward put his head round the pantry door. 'Captain's apologies, sir, but he's been called to the MCO. Can I get you a drink?'

I shook my head. 'Another cup of coffee would be nice though.'

He nodded, retrieved the untouched cup from the desk and, as he was taking it back into the pantry, he hesitated. 'Excuse me asking, sir, but do you know the

Captain well? I mean, you're a friend of his, aren't you?'

I didn't know how to answer that, so I just gave a bit of a nod and waited.

The steward stood there with the cup in his hand as though trying to make up his mind. Finally he said, 'I can't tell him, sir, but perhaps you can. There's a lot of rumours going round the ship. In the seaman's messes, I mean. They say the Captain's –' again the hesitation – 'well, bad luck, if you get me. A sort of Jonah. And it's not just the Captain. It's the ship.'

'Any particular reason?' I asked.

He stood there awkwardly, feeling no doubt he had said too much already. 'There's quite a few – misfits on board, sir.'

'Troublemakers, do you mean?' I asked.

He gave a little shrug, shaking his head. 'Hard to say, sir. Toughies certainly. Real toughies. Some of the lads feel they've been landed with a load of shit – if you'll excuse me – men that other ships wanted to be rid of.' And he added, 'These are the comments of lads that volunteered, you understand, specialists most of them, real good lads who thought *Medusa* was intended for some sort of special service. That's why they volunteered.'

I took him up then on the use of the word 'specialists' and he said they had been on courses, some of them, that weren't the usual run of courses sailors got sent on – demolition, assault, urban guerrilla warfare. 'There's even men on board here who've been trained by the SAS.' And he added, 'They volunteered for something out of the ordinary. At least, that's what they thought, something that sounded to them like it was as near to active service as you could get in peace-time. Instead, they find themselves on a ship that's got a hardcore of throw-outs in the crew. Tell him, will you, sir? Privately. He should know the feeling.' He said that quickly, almost in a whisper, and as he turned to go into the pantry, the entrance curtain was swept aside and Gareth entered, his face white, his lips a hard, tight line, and he was scowling. 'Get me some coffee, Jarvis.' He had a sheet of paper in his hand and he went straight to his desk and sat there, staring at it. He seemed completely oblivious to my presence. The main broadcast began to sound through the ship, Mault's voice ordering special sea duty men and the cable party to close up. 'All action stations to be manned and gun crews closed up.'

I couldn't believe it. I stared at Lloyd Jones. He'd heard it, but he made no move to counteract the order. 'Can you drop me off now?' I asked him. 'The harbour launch . . .'

He was staring at me, his eyes wide, that shocked look on his face as though suddenly aware that he had a civilian witness to what was happening on board. He shook his head. 'Sorry.' He held up the sheet of paper. 'Orders. No contact with the shore and put to sea immediately. Resist any attempt to prevent departure. Ministry of Defence. Whitehall's orders.' He put his hand to his head, leaning forward. 'Downing Street by the sound of it. Christ!' And then he suddenly seemed to get a grip of himself. He smiled. 'Glad to have you aboard. My God I am!' The steward brought him his coffee and he gulped it down, then reached for his cap and jumped to his feet. 'Make yourself at home. I'm afraid you'll have to put up with us for some time now.' He stopped in the doorway, his face grim as he said very quietly, so that only I could hear him, '*Medusa* is to leave now – immediately.' He hesitated, then added, 'It's Menorca. Port Mahon. I'm sorry, but those are my orders.' He turned then, putting his hat on and dropping the curtain behind him. There were feet pounding the deck, the throb of engines again and a clanking for'ard, the chain coming in.

I went up to the bridge. Everyone was back at their stations and the officer on the fo'c's'le reporting the anchor up and down, the shorelights beginning to move as the ship got under way. The harbour and police launches were maintaining station on the port side and one of their officers shouting through a loud-hailer, his amplified voice clearly audible and nobody paying attention, the beat of the engines increasing, the ship gathering speed. Port Mahon! Why Mahon? Why was *Medusa* ordered to Menorca immediately? Regardless of the Maltese.

'Vessel putting out from Kalkara, sir. Looks like a patrol boat.'

It was Mault who acknowledged the lookout's report, the Captain merely raising his glasses to look at it.

'They're signalling, sir. An order to stop.'

Gareth nodded. 'Maximum revs as soon as you're clear of that ferry.'

I had tucked myself as inconspicuously as possible against the rear bulkhead, between the chart table and the echo-sounder, which was clicking away over my left shoulder. I saw the ferry emerge virtually from under our bows as we sliced into its wake, the rising hum of the engines almost swamped by the surge of the bow wave as Gareth pulled open the port-side door to look back at the launches.

'That's not a patrol boat.' Mault's voice sounded high and a little tense. 'It's that big customs launch.' He strode across the bridge to Gareth. 'What happens if they open fire?'

'They won't.' Gareth's voice was firm and absolutely calm.

'You mean they won't dare. Then what about that cruiser?'

Gareth spun round. 'Our orders are specific. Leave Malta immediately. Are you seriously suggesting the Russians would risk an international incident of such magnitude? To open fire on a British warship in a friendly harbour would amount to something very close to a declaration of war – against us, against Nato.' He had spoken with sudden heat, an outburst almost. It indicated the pressure he was now under, the nervous strain. I also realised that his words were spoken for the benefit of everybody on the bridge, and thus for the ship as a whole.

He turned to the open doorway again, his back and the raising of his glasses indicating that the subject was closed. Nobody spoke after that, except for essential orders and reports, the hum of machinery, the sound of water, the shuddering and clattering of loose items, everything building to a crescendo as the two double reduction geared turbines piled on full power and the ship's twin props reached maximum revs. We were out past Gallows Point, the end of the breakwater approaching fast and the light at the end of it swinging across us so that every five seconds we were caught in its beam. Nobody fired at us, nobody followed as we pounded past it and out to sea, where we turned to port and set course to clear Gozo and leave the volcanic island of Pantelleria to port.

Craig pulled out Chart 165, and looking over his shoulder as he pencilled in our final course past the southern tip of Sardinia, I saw on the extreme left of it the eastern half of Menorca. Six hundred miles, say thirty to thirty-four hours at full speed. Why the hurry? And what would my position be when we got there? Customs, health and immigration would come on board in the usual way when we arrived and it was very unlikely Gareth would attempt to conceal my presence.

'If you care to come with me, sir, I'll show you to your cabin.' It was Petty Officer Jarvis and he had a bag in his hand. 'I've looked out some clothes of the Captain's – shirt, sweater, pyjamas, socks, that sort of thing. He thought they'd fit all right, you being about his size.'

The cabin was two decks down, just aft of the room housing the gyro compass machinery. It had two berths, both unoccupied, and when I finally turned in, lying there, conscious of the movement of the ship and unable to sleep, I couldn't help thinking how odd it was to be wearing the pyjamas of a man who would probably cuckold me within the week, may indeed have already done so. But that hardly seemed so important now as I stared into the darkness, my mind going over and over the events of the day. I thought of Wade, that telephone conversation, the trouble he had taken to trace my background, that bastard Evans trying to implicate me, and now this ship, sent to Malta, then, just after a nasty little shooting incident, sent off on a wild dash to Mahon. Why? And we had actually left Grand Harbour at action stations with gun crews closed up. Turning it over in my mind it seemed so incredible that at length I couldn't think of anything else.

PART THREE

MERCENARY MAN

CHAPTER ONE

I must have slept, for the next thing I knew was the shrill note of the bo's'n's pipe echoing over the main broadcast followed by a metallic voice declaring the start of another day: 'Call the hands, call the hands, call the hands.' It was 06.30 and since the movement had become a jerky roll and an occasional shivering crash for'ard, I guessed we had now cleared the western tip of Sicily with the full fetch of the Tyrrhenian Sea on our starb'd beam. The cabin door lurched back and Petty Officer Jarvis entered balancing a cup with a saucer on top of it. 'Captain's compliments, sir, and would you join him for breakfast as soon as you're ready.'

The tea was dark, strong and very sweet. I drank it quickly, then staggered along the passageway to the heads. It took me some time to shave and dress because of the unpredictability of the ship's movement, so that by the time I reached the Captain's day cabin he had finished his meal and was seated at the desk reading through a clip-board of signals with the Yeoman standing by. 'Sleep well?' It was a perfunctory query, his mind concentrated on the sheets in his hand, his face drawn and tense, dark shadows under his eyes. After a while he said, 'Very good, Yeo. Better send it now. They'll need to have all the details.' And then he turned to me. 'The BBC had it on the six o'clock news and it was also referred to in the round-up of the day's papers. *The Times* called it The Malta Incident and one of the tabloids had the headline: NAVY SCUTTLES OUT OF GRAND HARBOUR.' He smiled, but without humour, and he didn't refer to it again, the routine of a ship taking over as the Marine Engineer Officer came in to report engine and fuel states, followed by other officers with reports and queries.

I had finished breakfast and was having a final cup of coffee when he suddenly stood up and reached for his cap. 'Care to come round the ship with me?'

I followed him out into the passageway and down the ladder. For that moment we were alone, the first opportunity I had to ask him if he knew why he'd been despatched to Mahon in such haste.

He looked at me, tight-lipped. 'I seem to remember I told you, last night. I shouldn't have done, but I did.' And he added, 'I wasn't quite myself, a bit tensed-up.'

'You told me you'd had orders to leave, and you mentioned 10 Downing Street. But nothing else.'

'That's it – orders.'

'But why?'

He stopped then. 'This is the Navy, Mike. Politicians make the decisions, we carry out the orders.'

'But you must have some idea of the reasons for those orders.'

'Some idea, yes.' He said it slowly, hesitantly. 'The rest I'm having to guess at.' He started down the next ladder to the deck below. It was then that I passed on to him what Jarvis had said about the mood on the mess decks. He turned to me. 'I know about that. It can't be helped.' And when I persisted, suggesting that some hint of the reason for the orders he had received would make his men, and myself, a good deal happier, he gripped hold of my arm and said angrily, 'Leave it at that, will you. I'm pleased to have you on board, but don't ask questions.'

He went on ahead then, down a long passageway to the sick bay, where he found Kent pale but cheerful, sitting up bare-chested and heavily bandaged. 'Pity we've no helicopter,' Gareth told him. 'But another twenty-four hours and we'll either have a Spanish surgeon here on board to get that bullet out or we'll fly you home.'

'I'd rather have it out on board, sir.' But as we left him there were beads of perspiration forming on his forehead, his skin very white. Gareth said to me quietly, 'Good man, that. He'll leave a gap I'll have great difficulty in filling.' And he added, 'If we'd had a helicopter, we could have flown him ashore from here.'

The tour of inspection took in three decks and lasted just over half an hour, and all the time Gareth was making an effort to imprint his personality on the officers and men he talked to and play down what had happened at the wharf in Malta. Finally we reached the flight deck, going through the hangar to look down on to the quarterdeck below where the white of our seething wake and the roar of water boiling up from the twin screws made it almost impossible to talk. 'What's wrong with the helicopter – out of service?' I shouted to him.

He shook his head. 'I haven't been allocated one.'

'So what do you keep in the hangar?' I was curious because the shut steel doors had seals on the locks.

He didn't answer that, looking at me sharply, then turning away. Later, talking to the Pilot on the bridge, I learned that those seals were inspected by the Captain or WEO personally mornings and evenings, that they each held a key to the doors and it required both of them present in person to unlock them.

But by then I was less interested in the sealed hangar than in the political repercussions of the Malta affair. It was, in fact, the main topic of conversation, not just on the bridge or among the officers, but throughout the ship. At first it was no more than a small item at the end of the early morning news. By 09.00 the BBC had slotted it in as a major news item immediately following the latest exchange of notes between the Kremlin and the White House, and it was clear from the way in which the incident was being presented that it was being blown up into a major political row. Later the World Service of the BBC announced that the British High Commissioner had been summoned to the office of the Maltese premier where he had been handed a note of protest to the

British Government for the 'high-handed, irresponsible and internationally outrageous behaviour of one of HM ships in opening fire on innocent people when on a courtesy visit'. Almost simultaneously the Maltese High Commissioner in London had been called to the Foreign Office. The Opposition spokesman on foreign affairs had put down a question for the Prime Minister to answer at Question Time in the House that afternoon and there was even some talk of an emergency cabinet meeting later in the day.

The repercussions of all this bore heavily on Gareth, who spent most of the day at his desk replying to the stream of signals that came in, one of them from 10 Downing Street itself demanding an immediate personal report of the affair direct to the Prime Minister's Office.

And on top of this, in the late afternoon, there was a sudden flurry on the bridge, messages flying around the ship and the Captain himself finally being called. We were then approaching Cape Spartivento at the southern end of Sardinia with the wind increasing from the north-east, the surface of the sea flecked with whitecaps and the sky so overcast it looked as though night was about to fall.

It was the Communications Officer who first alerted the officer of the watch. He was a flamboyant, cocky lieutenant with a round, smiling face. His name was Woburn, so everybody referred to him as The Smiler. But he wasn't smiling when he appeared on the bridge in the late afternoon, his face set as he and the Pilot searched the murk through the bridge glasses.

We were on collision course apparently with a section of the Sixth Fleet, which had left the Bay of Naples the previous day and was now spread out over quite a large area of sea.

Night had fallen before we sighted the aircraft carrier. It came up over the horizon like the gas flare of an oil rig, so bright and red was the masthead light, and then, as we closed in, two American destroyers powered towards us at full speed, swirling round and stationing themselves between us and the carrier like protecting sheepdogs. When we passed it we were so close that the side of it was like the blurred outline of a harbour wall, and always the destroyers tracking alongside us, close enough at one point for Gareth to slide open the starb'd bridge door and exchange greetings with one of their captains over loud-hailers. Then they peeled away and for the next half-hour we were threading through a litter of radar blips that only occasionally resolved themselves into fleeting glimpses of actual ships.

As a result our evening meal was later than usual. It was also a rather hurried one with Gareth hardly saying a word, his mind concentrated on the problems facing him. One of those problems was, of course, my presence on the ship. Due to the decrease in speed while crossing the track of the US ships, and the fact that we had to alter course to starb'd, our ETA at Mahon the next day had been delayed by about two hours to 08.45. It was hardly likely he would risk putting me ashore in daylight, and once we were tied up at the Naval Base . . . 'What are you going to do about me?' I asked him.

He looked at me vaguely. Then his eyes focused as though suddenly recalling my presence in the cabin. 'I haven't decided yet.' He got suddenly to his feet, hesitated, then crossed to his desk. 'This came in just after we cleared that carrier.'

Time of receipt of the message he passed to me was 21.13. It read: *Weapon that killed Jorge Martinez found in home of Michael Steele. Police statement just issued indicates Steele arrived Malta on twin-hulled yacht Thunderflash then disappeared. Recent owner of yacht name of Evans also wanted for questioning; thought to be on fishing expedition. Political situation here still tense. In view of what happened Malta suggest you anchor off Villa Carlos well clear of Mahon port area.*

I was still in a state of shock, reading again the first line of that message, when he said, 'You understand, I hope – the sooner you're off my ship the better.' I began to protest that I had had nothing to do with the Martinez killing, but he stopped me. 'Whether you were involved or not is immaterial. The gun was apparently found in your house and I've got troubles enough—'

'It wasn't in my house. It was in the starb'd engine compartment—'

'I don't care where it was,' he cut in. 'I want you off the ship and the sooner—'

'For God's sake, listen will you . . .'

'No, you listen.' His hand was up, an abrupt, imperative gesture. 'I'm sorry, but you must understand.

You're dynamite in my present circumstances.' He took the paper from me, staring down at it and muttering something about 'he was bound to be mixed up in it somewhere', then folding it and slipping it into his pocket with a bitter little laugh as he told me I was probably the least of his worries, everybody blaming him for the Malta Incident. 'And the PM insisting I act with more circumspection in Menorca. Circumspection! That'll be the Foreign Office putting their oar in.' The boyish smile flashed out, but it was only a glimmer, then he banged his cap on his head and was gone, hurrying down the ladder to the Communications Office.

I finished my coffee, my mind in turmoil. Finally I went back up to the bridge, preferring contact with the outside world to the confines of the cabin, where I had nothing to do but think about Soo and what the hell had been going on for that gun to have been found in the house.

The watch was just changing, and shortly afterwards young Davison, a fresh-faced, tow-headed officer-under-training appeared at my elbow to say the Captain had phoned to enquire if I would join him for a drink.

I found him sitting hunched over his desk, the reading light pulled down to spotlight the pad on which he had been making notes, his face, his whole body set rigid, and a cigarette smouldering in a scallop-shell ashtray. He looked up, his eyes blank.

'What is it?' I asked. And when he didn't reply, I said, 'You asked me down for a drink.'

'Oh yes.' His eyes blinked quickly and he seemed to pull himself together, jumping to his feet and waving me to a seat at the low table. He picked up the bottle standing there. 'Real cognac, or would you prefer brandy and ginger ale?' I opted for the cognac, and as he poured it the neck of the bottle rattled against the rim of the glass. That, and the awkward silence as he helped himself to a Coke and sat down opposite me, was an indication of how tensed-up he was.

'You're thinking about tomorrow,' I said.

He nodded, stubbing out the remains of his cigarette, lighting another, then leaning back, drawing the smoke into his lungs as though he were at high altitude sucking in oxygen. In the silence that followed I was conscious of the engines, the far-off sound of the bow wave surging along the frigate's side, the rattle of crockery in the steward's pantry.

'I was wondering . . .' But it's not easy to ask a favour of a man who's in love with your wife. 'Why don't you drop me off on one of the islands as you go into Mahon?' I asked him finally, very conscious of the hesitancy in my voice. He was the Captain of a Royal Navy ship on an official visit and my suggestion was tantamount to smuggling a wanted man back into Spain. And when he didn't say anything, I made the point that I hadn't asked to stay on his ship. 'You virtually kidnapped me.' And I added, 'Drop me off. Forget I was ever on board.'

'Yes, I've thought of that.' He nodded. 'But there's over two hundred men on this ship and most of them know you're here.' He got up, pacing back and forth behind me so nervously that I began to think it must be a more personal matter he wanted to discuss. He and Soo had probably been corresponding while he was in Malta, or before he had left Gibraltar. They might even have made up their minds already. But then he said, 'How well do you know Pat?'

'Evans?' I swung round in my chair.

'Yes.' He had stopped pacing. 'What do you know about him?'

'Not very much.' I paused. 'No more really than Carp has told me.'

He leaned down, staring at me. 'Tell me something.' His dark eyes fixed themselves on my face. 'The murder weapon – a rifle was it?'

'An AK-47,' I told him. 'The sniper version with folding butt.'

'So you've seen it?'

I didn't say anything. It had been such an easy trap and I had fallen for it.

'Where did you see it? Did that man Barriago give it to you?' He didn't wait for an answer. 'Was Pat involved?'

'Yes,' I said. 'I'm pretty certain he was and I was trying to tell you when you shut me up. I don't know whether he acquired the weapon for Barriago, but he certainly disposed of it.' He listened to me then as I told him what had happened, how I'd found the gun tucked away at the stern end of the starb'd engine compartment under the prop shaft, how I'd taken it up to the villa and concealed it under the floorboards in the kitchen.

'And now they've found it.'

'Apparently.'

Silence then and the sound of a door slamming, both of us thinking about that message from Menorca. Suddenly he laughed. 'So you paid him back in his own coin, and now he's fixed you again.' His laughter was without mirth. 'Par for the course,' he muttered. 'And now?' He stared at me as though expecting an answer, then shrugged and sat down opposite me. 'I gather that fellow Carpenter has told you about my being sent to live with Moira Evans at Felixstowe Ferry, and then Pat arriving?' He nodded. 'He would know, of course – all the gossip, all the things they said. Felixstowe Ferry! My God!' He was smiling and shaking his head. 'Lost my innocence there, found a no-good bastard of a half-brother – then, years later . . . But you know about that.'

'The Haven buoy?'

He nodded. 'That Haven buoy episode hangs round my neck like a millstone. It's the cause . . .' He put his head in his hands, rubbing the palms of them over his eyes. 'He crucified me. He didn't know it at the time. He thought he was saving my life, but he crucified me – and now the agony begins.'

'What agony?' I asked. His face had gone very pale, his eyes half-closed. 'You all right?' He looked as though he might pass out. His eyes flicked open then, his mind on something else. I asked him about his use of the word bastard. 'Did you mean that literally? Is Evans your father's illegitimate son?'

He didn't answer for a moment, then suddenly he

burst out laughing. 'Is that what Carpenter told you, man? If so, he's got it the wrong way round. Whatever else Pat is, he's legitimate.' And then, his mood changing again, he put his elbows on the table, his head thrust forward. 'Look now, I'm going to tell you something I haven't told anyone else. In confidence, mind you. You'll see why. You've heard part of it, so you may as well know it all. Especially as it's my belief you've now got the boat they brought the stuff ashore in.' He nodded towards the bottle. 'Help yourself. This may take a little time.' He leaned back, drawing on his cigarette. 'The King's Fleet mean anything to you?'

'By the entrance to the Deben River, isn't it?'

He nodded. 'I heard you visited Woodbridge and Felixstowe Ferry a while back when you were searching for a boat. The Fleet was used by the Vikings, and the Romans before them. Now it's cut off from the river by a high flood bank. But there's still a few stretches of water left. When I was about fourteen and living for a time at the Ferry, Pat and I used to bird-watch there. It was a great place for nesting swans, some of the rarer water birds, too.' And he added, 'It was only later I discovered Pat's real interest – he liked to smash the eggs with steel balls fired from a catapult, or try and put out a swan's eye with it.'

'Charming!' I murmured, but he picked me up on that.

'It wasn't viciousness, you understand. It was a question of marksmanship. Later he acquired an airgun. It was the challenge, you understand. He didn't think about the cruelty of it. He hasn't that sort of imagination.' He shook his head, staring vacantly at his empty glass, his mind back in the past. 'Perhaps he doesn't have any imagination at all. I'm not sure.'

'What happened?' I asked. 'You were going to tell me what happened there.'

'Oh yes.' He nodded. 'Over four years ago now. I was on leave, the first since my wife and I split up. I thought it would be fun to go back to Suffolk, stay at the Ferry, particularly as it was November, a good time for bird-watching.' He leaned back, his eyes half-closed again. 'The second night I was there, after the evening meal, I took some chocolate biscuits and a Thermos of coffee and rum and walked along the Deben bank to the King's Fleet. Half a mile or so in from the river there's a series of little Broads-type lakes. The farmer had parked a trailer there part-loaded with bags of fertiliser. It made an ideal hide and I hadn't been propped up there, my back against the bags, more than half an hour before I heard the beat of wings. They passed almost directly over my head, five dark shapes against the Milky Way, the beat fading, then strengthening again as the birds circled. Suddenly I had them in the glasses, coming in low, the wet glimmer of the Fleet shattered, a flurry of water as they breasted it, then only ripples and the five shapes gliding ghostly white. Five Brent, and if nothing else happened that night it would have been worth it just to see the way they touched down. It was magic.'

Recalling the pleasure of that night was, I think, a sort of displacement activity for him. It helped to relieve some of the tension, his eyes half-closed, his mind totally concentrated and the Welsh lilt in his voice suddenly quite pronounced, the words with a poetic touch: '. . . a slow, heavy beat, a single bird this time and quite invisible until the splash of its touchdown showed white on the black pewter surface of the Fleet. It was a swan, but it carried its neck stiff like a column, with none of the graceful curve of the ubiquitous mute. It looked like a Bewick, a juvenile, the feathers drab instead of white. And then I thought it might possibly be a whooper. It would be unusual, but by then it was past midnight and I felt anything could happen, having already had a very good night with the sighting of a goosander as well as three grebes among the coots.'

He was smiling to himself, reliving a night that was indelibly etched on his mind. 'I drank the last of my coffee and rum with the buildings of Felixstowe Ferry sharp-etched against the light of the rising moon, the dark line of the sea's horizon just visible. When the moon finally rose above the sea the patches of water close by me were full of shadow shapes, coots bobbing their white-blazed heads, mallard and pochards motionless, the swans gliding slowly; no zephyr of a breeze, everything frozen still, a light winking far away in the approaches to Harwich. I remember I started thinking about another night; when I had come out to the Fleet with Pat and his father; then suddenly my thoughts were interrupted by the sound of an engine.'

His eyes flicked open, dark pupils with the glazed look of jet. 'It came from beyond the hill where an old farmhouse stood among some trees, a low hill that marked the limit of what had once been the great marsh that was part of the vanished port of Goseford. I waited for the sound of it to fade away towards Kirton village and the main Felixstowe–Ipswich road, but instead it gradually increased, no lights and a shadow moving on the road down from the farm.'

Through his glasses he had seen it was a van, the engine quieter as it coasted without lights down the slope to the Fleet. Duck shooters was his first thought – poachers. There were two of them in the van and they had driven straight on, finally parking against the high grass bank that shut the Fleet off from its entrance into the Deben. 'I didn't worry about them after that, presuming they were fishermen. Now that the moon was clear of cloud I could see that what I had thought was a goosander, the pinkish breast showing pale and the down-turned bill just visible, was in fact a red-breasted merganser, a much more likely bird to see close by an East Coast estuary. I watched for another half-hour, and then a breeze sprang up, blowing in little gusts off the North Sea and bitterly cold. There was a dampness in the air, too, so that a rime of frost formed on my anorak. My fingers were numb by then and I got to my feet, climbing down off the trailer, and after picking up my knapsack with the Thermos flask in it, I headed down the track towards the Deben. Several times I stopped to watch the Fleet, my breath smoking and the birds mostly hidden now among the reeds, or still shadows fast asleep. It was just after one when I reached the grass-grown bank of the river.' He paused. 'That was when I heard the sound of voices and the clink of metal on metal, the clatter of a halyard flapping.'

He was staring straight at me, his eyes blacker than ever in the glare of the wall light. 'It was a little unnerving really. I was alone, you see, and yet I couldn't help it. I had to know what it was all about. So I clambered up the bank, and as soon as my head cleared the top of it, I stopped.' He paused again, and it was almost as though he did it for effect. Then he went on, his voice very quiet: 'Tide was at the full, and it was a spring tide, the river and the inlet of the King's Fleet almost brimming over with water, otherwise they would never have got it in there. I just stood there, gaping at the thing, it was such an incredible sight – a large catamaran, black-hulled, its single aluminium mast gleaming like silver in the moonlight. It was moored stern-on to the bank with an anchor out in the middle of the Fleet, and there were men passing cases up through a hatch in the starb'd hull to others on the bank.'

His hand was gripped on the edge of the table, the stub of his cigarette burning unheeded in the ashtray. 'The quick furtiveness of their movements, their faces covered by stocking masks, gave a weirdness to the scene, the moon bright now and everything very clear and sharp in the frost. I snuggled down in the whitened grasses. Smugglers! I wasn't sure, but clearly something was being run ashore at dead of night, and that meant contraband of some sort.' His eyes flicked up at me. 'What the hell do you do in a situation like that?' And he went on, softly as though talking to himself. 'I was alone, you see. I trained my glasses on them. There were three on deck, two ashore, and another passing the cases up. Six altogether, and one of them standing with his hand on his hip . . . I focused the glasses on the case being passed up over the stern, searched the growing pile on the bank. That's when I began to be really scared.'

He was silent for a moment, staring into space. 'It wasn't drink, you see, nor drugs. It was arms! I wasn't in any doubt. There were long cases that could only contain hand-held rocket-launchers, others that looked more like rifles, but it was the ammunition boxes – I'd seen too many of those not to recognise them instantly.'

He stopped then, stubbing out his cigarette, and in the silence I was conscious again of the ship's sounds, and of the movement, too. 'Maybe he caught the glint of my binocular lenses in the moonlight,' he went on slowly. 'Whatever it was, he was suddenly looking straight at me. Then he said something to the others and they froze, their stocking faces all turned towards me.' He shook his head. 'It was unbelievable. The coincidence of it. The two of us . . .' His voice faded into silence.

'You mean it was Evans?'

'Yes. Pat.' He nodded. 'And now – again. Out here. It's as though some devilish fate . . .' He left the sentence unfinished, and when I asked him what had happened, he shrugged. 'What you'd expect, considering the cargo they were running. They had a man in the outfield, hidden in the tall grasses by the sluice. I ran straight into him. Big fellow. Rose up right in front of me and knocked me out, cold. Next thing I knew I was lying on the wooden grating of the catamaran's steering platform with Pat bending over me.' And after a moment he said, 'Lucky for me. They'd have killed me if he hadn't been there.' He lit another cigarette, his eyes closed, his mind far away so that I had to get the rest of it out of him by question and answer.

When he had come round the catamaran was already under way. He could hear the winches clicking as the sails were hoisted and hardened in. Then the engines were cut and Evans whispered urgently to him to lie still. 'I could hear voices on the deck for'ard, Irish voices, and Pat with his mouth right against my ear telling me he'd slip me into the water as close to Woodbridge Haven buoy as possible. He told me they'd tied up to it on the way in, waiting for the tide to make over the bar. The warp hadn't been double-ended, so instead of slipping it, they had cut it.'

He stopped there, apparently lost in the memory of that night and what had happened after they'd crossed the bar.

'And that was the rope you used to lash yourself to the buoy,' I prompted.

He nodded slowly. 'He had me flung overboard up-tide of the buoy so that I pretty well drifted down on to it. They were Irish on board, not East Coasters, and they didn't understand. They wanted me dead, but not with a bullet in my guts. Found drowned ...' He smiled wryly. 'Nobody can ever be accused of murder if you're picked up out of the sea with your lungs full of water.'

'But why did he do it?' I asked. The blood relationship was all very well, but the man was running arms to the IRA in England . . .

'There was a condition, of course.' I hardly heard the words, they were spoken so softly.

'But you couldn't possibly keep quiet about it,' I said. Anyway, he hadn't attempted to conceal the fact that he had seen them landing arms at the King's Fleet. 'Or was it just his identity you promised not to reveal?'

He nodded. 'I swore I'd never tell anyone I'd recognised him. I wouldn't have done, anyway,' he murmured. 'He knew that. But he made me swear it all the same.'

'Then why have you told me?' I asked him.

He got up suddenly and began pacing back and forth again, his shoulders hunched, the new cigarette burning unheeded in his hand. When I repeated the question, he said, 'I'm not sure really.' He stopped just behind my chair. 'To show you the sort of man Pat is. That's one reason. A warning. And at the same time . . .' He went over to his desk and sat down, pulling the message slip out of his pocket and going through it again. 'God in heaven!' he murmured. 'Why doesn't he get the hell out? Now, while nobody knows he's involved.'

And then he turned to me. 'He's not all bad, you see. And to end up in prison. A life sentence. He's not the sort of man who could bear imprisonment. Freedom is everything to him. That's why he deserted from the Navy, why he couldn't stand any ordinary sort of job. It's against his nature, you understand.' He was pleading with me, trying to persuade me to keep quiet about where I had found that Russian gun. I remembered Soo's words then, wondering what exactly the relationship had been between this man, who was now the Captain of a Royal Navy frigate, and his half-brother, who was a gun-runner, what they had felt for each other when they were both youngsters at *Ganges* and Pat Evans had got him down from the top of that mast.

He looked up at me suddenly. 'How old's that catamaran you sailed to Malta?'

'It was built six years ago,' I said.

He nodded perfunctorily as though it was what he had expected. 'The hulls are painted white now, but underneath – any sign of black paint?'

'You'd have to ask Carp,' I told him. But neither of us were in any doubt it was the same boat.

He didn't say anything after that, sitting hunched at the desk the way he had been when I had come down from the bridge to have a drink with him, his mind closed to everything else but the signals lying there under his hands.

The loudspeaker burst into life, a muffled announcement about the deadline for posting letters home. He listened to it briefly, then returned to the papers.

'About tomorrow?' I reminded him.

He looked up, frowning. 'I'll think about it. Meanwhile, if you've finished your drink . . .' He returned to the papers, his withdrawn manner making it clear the period of intimacy was over. 'See you in the morning.' But then, as I was going out, he stopped me. 'Ever done any board-sailing?' And when I told him I had run sailboard courses when I first came to Menorca, he nodded. 'That might help.' And he added, 'I'll think about it. Let you know in the morning.'

I went up to the bridge then, standing inconspicuously by the radar, watching the knife-like bows rise and fall beyond the twin barrels of the 4.5-inch guns, the white glimmer of the bow wave either side, my body adapting to the pitch and roll as we drove northwestwards through breaking seas. The wind had backed into the north and was blowing about force five. Standing in the dark like that, conscious of the engines vibrating under my feet, the sound of them overlaid by the noise of the sea, and the watch on duty still like shadows all about me, there was an extraordinary sense of isolation, of time standing still. I was thinking of *Thunderflash* and the voyage to Malta, all the other occasions when I had been alone at the helm, just the sea and my thoughts for company. But now it was different. Now I had the feeling I had reached some sort of watershed.

Tomorrow! And my life slipping through my mind. Nothing achieved, never anything solid, all I had built in Menorca breaking in my hands, Soo, the business, everything, and now that bloody catamaran ... 'Care for some coffee, sir? Or there's kai if you prefer it.' One of the leading seamen was standing at my elbow with a tin tray full of mugs. I chose the chocolate and took it over to the chart table, where the Navigating

Officer was now checking our position against the plot. 'Do you know where we'll be anchoring?' I asked him as he completed the log entry.

For answer he pulled open the topmost drawer and extracted the chart that gave plans of Mahon and Fornells harbours, as well as two in Ibiza. 'About there, we reckon.' He indicated the Mahon plan, where he had pencilled a cross just south of Cala Llonga right opposite Villa Carlos. 'ETA is now 09.30 approx.' He looked at me curiously. 'You staying on board or is the Captain arranging to put you ashore?'

'I'm not certain,' I said.

He nodded, smiling at me. He understood the problem. 'It might interest you to know he's just rung me to say he wants one sailboard with wet suit and goggles ready on the flight deck by 09.00. I'm in charge of sailing, you see.' And he added, 'Sorry about the board, but it's the best we can do. No dinghies, I'm afraid.'

It was probably nervous exhaustion that finally got me off to sleep that night for I was dead to the world when Petty Officer Jarvis shook me into consciousness. He was earlier than usual. 'Lieutenant Craig would like you to select whichever one fits best.' He dumped three wet suits on the foot of the bunk. 'They're the only sizes we have on board.' And as he went out, he asked me to leave the two I didn't want and any borrowed clothing on the rack above my bunk.

By then the bo's'n's mate was rousing the ship, and shortly afterwards Gareth's voice announced: '*This is the Captain. Just to bring you up to date. We are now approaching Port Mahon, the main harbour and capital of Menorca, one of the Spanish Balearic islands. For obvious reasons we shall not be tying up alongside. Instead, I propose to anchor well clear of the town in the approaches opposite Villa Carlos. In the circumstances. I do not see any possibility of shore leave. I will let you know how long this courtesy visit is to last as soon as I can. That is all.'*

His cabin was empty by the time I arrived for breakfast. 'Captain's on the bridge,' Petty Officer Jarvis told me. 'And there's no choice this morning.' He placed a heaped plateful of bacon, sausages, eggs and fried bread in front of me. 'He thought you might appreciate it. Later in the day, that is.'

I was still working through it when Gareth appeared. 'We shall be abreast of St Carlos Point and La Mola in approximately fifteen minutes. Things will begin to hot up then. As soon as you've finished, I'd be glad if you'd return to your cabin and wait there until Petty Officer Jarvis comes to take you down to the flightdeck. Chief Petty Officer Clark will meet you there. He will have—'

The Sinbad loudspeaker interrupted him, a voice from the bridge reporting that revs were now being reduced. 'Also, there's a small vessel lying off Lazareto. Spanish Navy by the look of her sir. Could be coastal patrol, or one of those small minesweepers, can't tell yet.'

Gareth reached for the mike. 'Very good, Simon. I'll be up.' He turned to me again. 'That could complicate matters. I didn't expect an escort.'

'You've decided have you – to get me off the ship by sailboard?'

'Yes, didn't Peter Craig warn you last night?'

'All he told me was that you'd ordered him to have a board ready on the flight deck by 09.00. I didn't know you'd made up your mind till your steward brought me a choice of wet suits with my tea this morning.' I hesitated, but this looked like my last chance to question him. 'Has Wade been in touch with you?' I asked him.

'Commander Wade?'

I nodded, watching him closely as he said he couldn't discuss official contacts with me.

'Particularly Wade I suppose?'

He didn't answer. I think he had intended having a cup of coffee with me, but now he put his hat back on his head. 'I'll try and arrange it so that *Medusa* is between you and the escort when we drop you off. The engines will be stopped for that moment and I'll get as much of the way off the ship as I can. You've got a good breeze, so with luck you'll be on the board and sailing fast enough to remain hidden from the escort vessel as we gather way again. Okay?' He smiled then and held out his hand. 'Good luck, Mike!' And as we shook hands he had the gall to add, 'If you make it to Bloody Island you'll be able to hide up with that archaeological Amazon of yours.'

There is something about a Navy ship that instils a sense of something akin to discipline even in a civilian visitor like myself. I could have turned left, gone up to the bridge and watched our approach to Mahon.

Nobody would have stopped me. I could have got my things, found my way aft down to the flight deck and waited there. Instead, I did what Gareth had told me and went straight to my cabin. I wished I hadn't. Sitting on the bunk, staring at nothing except the opposite berth and the cabin fittings, time passed slowly. There was no porthole and even if I had had something to read, the ceiling light was too dim, so that I would have had to stretch out on the bunk with the little bulkhead light on.

Shortly after 08.40 I felt the engines slow, then Mault's voice called for the watch on deck to muster and put fenders out on the starb'd side. Somebody was coming aboard, presumably from the patrol boat. The engines stopped, feet pounding on the deck and orders shouted, then a slight bump as the other vessel came alongside. This was the moment they should have dropped me over the side, but nobody came and the beat of the engines started up again.

It was 08.55 when Petty Officer Jarvis knocked at the cabin door. 'Everything's ready, sir, if you'll bring the wet suit with you. And the Captain asked me to give you this.'

'What is it?' I asked as he handed me a nasty-looking bit of black fur in a plastic bag.

'A beard, sir. Compliments of our entertainments officer. The Captain thought it might help if somebody had their glasses on you.'

There was a CPO waiting for us on the flight deck. The sailboard was propped against the hangar doors, mast and sail rigged, and a thin line attached to the bows was coiled ready. To starb'd the cliffs of La Mola and the brown of the military casements came into view. 'We'll be approaching the narrows at the southern end of Lazareto Island in a few minutes,' the CPO said. 'Lieutenant Craig estimates the distance from the buoys marking the narrows to the spot where we'll be anchoring as roughly nine cables. He'll stop engines when we come abreast of the little island immediately beyond Lazareto. That will be the signal for you to go.'

I stripped off my clothes and he helped me into the wet suit, zipping me up and slipping a bum-bolster round my buttocks. ''Fraid the harness isn't exactly a speed seat. You'll have to adjust it as you go. And the board's just an ordinary production job for funboard sailing, so if you want air, you won't find it.' Looking at it, I could see it was no jump board, more a beginner's board, which suited me in the circumstances. 'Got any goggles?' I asked.

He reached into his pocket and produced a narrow, almost slit-eyed pair with black surround. I put them on and adjusted them to fit my head. 'Don't forget the beard, sir.' He was grinning. 'You look like you could play Mephistopheles in that. Nobody could possibly recognise you.'

By then the conical buoy with its flashing light marking the channel on the starb'd side was already bobbing in our wash, the sharp southern point of Lazareto, Punta de San Felipet, appearing at the same instant. The engines were slowing now, the speed dropping off. 'How long do you reckon?' I asked the CPO.

'Seven, eight minutes.'

The beard was close-fitting and warm, the sea goggles on the tight side. They wrapped up my clothes and taped them into a plastic bag, which they tied firmly to the base of the sailboard's mast in such a way that it did not restrict its pintle fitting. Petty Officer Jarvis excused himself. He had to attend to the needs of the Captain and his visitor, who was the Spanish Navy's *Jefe*, Captain Perez. The long brown line of Lazareto went slowly by. Peering out to port, I could see the buildings of Villa Carlos coming closer. Soon now, and I was wondering whether Petra would be back from burying her father, whether she would be on the island, and how the hell I was going to live with the police watching for me and no money. All I had in the pocket of my trousers, now screwed up in a plastic ball, was £235 in traveller's cheques which I couldn't cash because it meant going to a bank or a hotel.

Cala Pedrera. Punta de Medio. I could see Punta de Cala Fonts coming up, and beyond the point, the Villa Carlos promenade with its hotels and restaurants and the Cafayas light. 'Stand by, sir.' The engines were slowing, the sound of water slipping past the plates dying away. I caught a glimpse to starb'd of the Plana de Mahon light. 'Ready?' The CPO took one end of the sailboard, I took the other. A few steps, a heave, and it was overboard, the slim board surfing alongside as he held it by the line. 'Away you go, sir, and whatever you do, hang on to the beard. Entertainments want it back.' He was grinning as he clapped me on the shoulder. Not quite a shove, but it reminded me of the one occasion I had parachuted under instruction. I jumped, my head in my arms, my knees up in a foetal position. Wham! I hit the water, the ship still moving, its displacement dragging me under. And then I was up, the grey stern moving past, the board within yards, anchored by the sail which was lying flat on the surface.

It was over two years since I had been on a sailboard. The technique doesn't leave one, but, like skiing, the muscles lose their sharpness. I flipped on to it all right, but instead of getting myself and the sail up in virtually the same movement, it was all a bit of a scramble. The wind was funnelling down the harbour, a good breeze that had me away on the starb'd tack and going fast before I was visible to the escort vessel, which was on the far side of *Medusa* and lying a little ahead of her, one of the old minesweepers by the look of it.

There was a moment, of course, when I felt naked and unsure of myself, but as my arms and knees began to respond to the drive of the sail, confidence returned, and after I had snapped the harness on I began to enjoy myself, steering close to the wind, my weight a little further aft and the speed increasing, my exhilaration, too. I found I went better if I railed it down to leeward. Gradually, as I became more relaxed and let the harness take some of the strain off my arms, I was able to glance over my shoulder at the pale grey shape of the frigate with its bristling antennae. I was paralleling her course and going faster, so that I was soon abreast of her for'ard guns. There was a little group of men gathered on the fo'c's'le ready for anchoring and the four international code flags flying from the yardarm. Ahead of me, and beyond Villa Carlos, I could now see Bloody Island, with the old hospital buildings looking even more like a stranded steamer.

I swung round, passing the sail across as I went through the wind on to the other tack. I was heading directly towards the patrol boat now and there were other boats about – a launch, two motor cruisers and a sailing yacht, several rowing boats and a tug moving across to Cala Figuera to perform its regular job of taking the small supply tanker in tow. Without thinking I put my hand to my chin. I knew the beard was still there. I could feel it. But I still had to touch it, to be sure nobody could recognise me. By then I had worked the board up to about twelve knots and it was really skimming across the flat surface of the water. The tug hooted, and as though that were a signal, *Medusa*'s anchor splashed down, the clatter of the chain running out echoing back from the rocky shore, a cloud of seabirds rising from the small boat gut in the middle of Villa Carlos.

I turned again, driving the board hard on the wind through the gap between Bloody Island and the shore, heading straight for the north side of Cala Figuera until I could see the quay I'd built and the chandlery and my home tucked tight in against the cliffs. There were two boats moored stern-to by the quay, figures moving about their decks and the chandlery door wide open. So the business was still operating. I passed within two hundred metres of it. No sign of Soo, but the office balcony window was open. I was then heading straight for the Club Maritimo, and seeing a big inflatable coming out from the huddle of yachts moored at the pontoon, I swung away towards the other shore.

If I hadn't been distracted by a small freighter coming out of Mahon itself, I would have recognised that inflatable sooner. Or would I? The fact was that I was thoroughly enjoying myself now, the water and the sailboard having temporarily divorced me from reality, so that perhaps I had no desire to recognise it, subconsciously aware that reality and all the problems of the future were at the helm. I ploughed my way into the freighter's wake, swinging down-wind and surfing in the turbulence. And then, when I was almost back at Bloody Island and could see the inflatable heading straight for it, I knew, and in the instant I couldn't resist the joke of heading straight for it, just to see what she'd do, a bearded stranger sailboarding along side.

It was Petra all right. She smiled and waved, her features half-hidden by that ridiculous sombrero she sometimes wore. She held up the tail end of a rope, offering me a tow, and I felt a pang of jealousy, seeing her suddenly as a girl on her own making overtures to an unattached male. Or did she guess who it was? I swept round and chased her all the way to Bloody Island, running the sailboard in right behind her and flopping into the water alongside the inflatable. 'I thought we might have dinner together,' I suggested.

She was out on the rock that did service as a

quay, leaning down, her shirt gaping. Her eyes lit up. 'Where?' She was smiling that big-mouthed smile of hers, the lips open so that her strong features looked all teeth.

'Here,' I said. 'On the island. I'm told you have a tent . . .'

'That beard of yours.' She was squatting down on her hunkers, her eyes very wide and bright in her tanned face. 'It's crooked.' She began to giggle uncontrollably.

Reality closed in on me before I had even hauled the sailboard out of the water, words pouring out of her, a rush of information as she moored the inflatable and began unloading her stores. There had been several quite large political demonstrations ahead of next week's election and during the night a bomb had gone off in the little square in the centre of Villa Carlos. Two soldiers on sentry duty outside the military HQ and one of the *Guardia* had been injured, and it had affected the telephone exchange, all lines between Villa Carlos and St Félip being cut. 'Two-thirty in the morning. It woke me up. I thought one of the big guns on La Mola had gone off. And now I've just heard there was another bomb went off in that big new hotel at Santa Galdana and fires started at several of the most congested *urbanizaciós* – St Tomas in particular and St Jaimé. None of your properties are involved. At least, Lennie doesn't think so.' She asked me what I had been up to. 'You've been in Malta, I gather. Were you mixed up in that disturbance? I was picking up newsflashes about it as I waited at Gatwick for my plane.'

I told her a bit of what had happened as I helped her hump her shopping up to the camp, which was in the lee of one of the hospital's standing walls, close by the old burial ground and the dig. There was just the one big tent. Now that the hypostile was fully excavated she was using that as an office-cum-store-room, the big stone roofing slabs covered with vegetation providing protection from sun as well as wind and rain.

Her father was dead and she had only been back a few days, having stayed on after the funeral to help her mother move up to her sister's in Nottingham. 'I've traded in my car, by the way. The little CV2 had just about had it and that old rogue Flórez offered me a Beetle – very cheap!' I asked her if she had had time to see Soo since she had arrived back in Mahon and she said she had been talking to her only a few hours before.

'How is she?' I asked.

'Oh, she's fine, and very full of what her Lieutenant Commander has been up to, and now that he's right here . . .' She was grinning at me and I told her not to be bitchy, but she only laughed. 'You can't blame her when every time she looks out of the window now she can see his ship anchored there.' And then she switched to her work. 'You remember the drawing on the cave roof I took you to see?'

'The night of the Red Cross barbecue?' I stared at her angrily. 'I'm hardly likely to forget it.'

She ignored that, telling me how she had checked on it while she was in England. 'They don't think it can be anything important, probably done with a burnt stick in roughly the same period as the megalithic remains. Certainly no older, which is a pity because Lennie knows of some more drawings – drawings that are fully exposed, human figures as well as animals – in a passageway leading back into the headland above that big underwater cave Bill Tanner told me about at Arenal d'en Castell.'

By then she had disposed of the stores she had brought out and, still talking, she began to help me off with my wet suit. I asked her for more details about the night's bombings, whether she had picked up any gossip about the reaction of the authorities, but she had no official information, only what she had heard from Lennie when she had met him coming out of the chandlery. 'He said it's been panic stations since the early hours with the *policia* and the *Guardia* rushing around all the major foreign developments.' The violence had been directed exclusively against foreign-owned property. 'Except for the Villa Carlos bomb. It was in a parked car and they think it may have gone off by accident. There's talk, too, of disturbances in Alayór and Ciudadela, but nothing serious – just demonstrations, no bombs.'

'Well, that's something,' I murmured and asked her for the loan of a towel as she pulled the wet suit clear of my feet. But instead of handing it to me she insisted on towelling me down with the inevitable result that we finished up in each other's arms arguing hilariously as to how we should proceed, her camp bed being designed strictly for one person and the floor being bare earth and rock. We had just settled for a sleeping bag opened out and spread on the floor when we were interrupted by the sound of an outboard coming steadily nearer. 'Oh hell! I forgot.' Petra pulled herself away from me and glanced at her watch, which by then was the only thing she had on. 'Lennie! I told him to be here by ten.'

'Why?' I was annoyed and frustrated, suddenly suspicious. 'Lennie should be painting a villa over by Cala en Porter.'

'Well, he's not painting it today,' she said, struggling into her trousers. 'Or any other day.' God! She was a big, powerful girl. I watched her button up her shirt, no bra and her breasts big and round as melons, and suddenly a picture flashed into my mind of her wrestling with Lennie on that narrow bed of hers, the morning sun heating the canvas of the tent above them. And then she said, 'Lennie's old-fashioned, you know. Shot his mouth off to Soo about her playing around with a Navy officer when her husband was in trouble. Said it wasn't fair on you and she shouldn't have had Gareth up to the house when you were busy with that catamaran and under suspicion of being implicated in a political murder. Tore her off quite a strip. She didn't like it, so she fired him.' The engine note died. 'I told him he could come and work for me. This whole complex is opening out. Just before Daddy had that crash I found what I thought was the base of a fallen taula.'

She slipped her big feet into a pair of flip-flops, tied her scarf round her neck, and standing there, looking down at me, she said with that endearing giggle of hers, 'It's a foine upstanding figure of a man you are, Mike, lying there on the floor of my tent without a stitch on. But I think you'd better get dressed.' And then she was gone, and as I reached for my bundle of clothes, I heard her calling a welcome to Lennie, her voice powerful as a bullroarer.

Lennie was one of those men who seem to wear the same clothes year in, year out, who will doss down anywhere and have no interest in the ownership of anything. He had no car, not even a motor bike, and would go to endless pains to cadge a lift or avoid paying for a drink. He was one of the meanest men I had ever met, except where scuba diving was concerned. For that he treated himself to the very latest equipment, his diving boat a replica of one of those big inshore lifeboats that have an alloy hull with inflatable surround, the power of the outboard such that the sound of it was unmistakable and the boat packed with all the latest gadgets for locating objects on the seabed.

While he was fussing over the mooring of it, the battered remains of an Aussie-type hat jammed on his head and the tails of his khaki shirt flapping in the breeze, I walked over to the dig, which was on the north side of the island about fifty metres from the flashing beacon and facing across the narrows to the shore just west of Cala Llonga. The exposure of a flat stone surface about eight feet long was the only change since I had last seen the site over six weeks ago, except that it was now a riot of wild flowers, even the rock steps leading down into the hypostile half-hidden by a tangle of some blue rock creeper. The hypostile itself was an extraordinary place, a large chamber with walls of up-ended stone slabs and a stone slab roof supported by stone columns. There were rock couches, or perhaps sacrificial altars, around the walls, and the human bones that showed here and there between the roofing slabs were a grisly reminder of the wars that had filled the island's hospital. It was the result of reading a letter from a soldier to his girlfriend in England after he had had his arm amputated at the hospital that had started Petra digging on the burial site, and looking down into the stone chamber she had uncovered in the shadow of the hospital ruins, it was difficult to disassociate the two and see it as a megalithic religious complex.

I remember that moment very well, the hospital ruins dark against the sun, the entrance to the hypostile yawning open at my feet like some ancient burial vault, and my mind on what Petra had told me. The political implications of what had happened in the night were disturbing enough, particularly if the army were unable to stop a recurrence of the violence, but I was thinking of the haste with which we had left Malta. Remembering Gareth's tenseness, I wondered what information he had received that had despatched him so abruptly to Mahon. And now, in the sunlit morning, everything appeared so deceptively peaceful, the town white above the waterfront, the surface of the great harbour inlet barely ruffled by the breeze and the only sound the murmur of traffic moving between Villa Carlos and Mahon.

The rattle of tools made me turn. It was Lennie wheeling a barrow with an assortment of picks, spades and shovels. 'Looks like the prospect of two of us on the island with nothing better to do has gone to the lady's head.' He parked the barrow and shook my hand. 'Glad to see the Navy delivered you safe and sound. And the beard kinda suits you.' He looked me over, a gap-toothed grin lighting his craggy features. 'Stable door's wide open, mate. Better zip up before I jump to any conclusions.' He took a pick from the barrow and approached the exposed slab of pale stone, standing there waiting for me to fix my trousers. 'Petra says to work round it with care, like it was a piece of Ming porcelain. She's making some coffee for us.' He hesitated, looking across to where *Medusa*'s super-structure showed above the back of the island. 'Chris'-sakes, that's an old frigate. I was in the Navy once so whether they're Aussie or Pom, I don't much go for Navy ships, but by God I'm glad to see that one here. You heard what went on last night?

I nodded. 'Petra told me.'

'Okay. Well, while we're trying to clear a little more of the rubble round this stone she thinks is a taula, I'll tell you what happened to me last night. It concerns you in a way since it was your boat until a few weeks back.' He cocked his head at me sideways. 'I haven't told her this, so keep it to yourself. She thinks we're going to have a look at rock drawings.'

He began picking gently away at the weed growth along one side of the exposed stone as he told me how Miguel had taken him over to Arenal d'en Castell one evening to show him some plastering work he wanted done in one of the hotels. They had then driven back by way of the villa he had been building, on Punta Codolar. 'Up there, you know, you look across to that cave and the villa above it where I did a bit of work on the side.'

He grinned at me, leaning on his pick, waiting I think for me to complain that he had been working for two people at the same time. 'It was a funny sort of night, no wind and black as hell with the clouds hanging right on top of us. I wouldn't have seen it except that Miguel had to turn the car and on the slope there the beam of the headlights swept across it. Your boat.' He nodded. 'The old *Santa Maria*. No doubt about it. I had Miguel turn back and hold the headlights right on her for a moment.'

Apparently she had been lying close in, right opposite the mouth of the cave. He couldn't see whether she was anchored or not. What he did see was that there were men on deck lowering a case into the water. He paused there and I asked him what he thought they were up to. 'Well, I tell you this, mate, they weren't fishing.'

'So what did you do?'

'Had Miguel turn the car and drive off, double quick. You see something like that, you don't hang around.'

'No.' I was thinking of Gareth Lloyd Jones and the King's Fleet. 'So what are you planning to do tonight?'

'Go and look at rock drawings.' He gave that funny grin of his and turned back to picking at the weed growth round the stone slab. 'You want to come?' And he added, 'But don't let on to Petra what I've told you. She'd be thinking of what happened that night at Cales Coves.'

The paths leading one deeper and deeper into trouble can be very tenuous. If Lennie hadn't shot his mouth off to Soo on my behalf, if Petra hadn't heard he was out of a job and asked him to help out on Bloody Island, if his arrival there hadn't coincided . . . But there are so many ifs in life, and the threads that weave the pattern of our existence seem so haphazard that we are inclined to attribute to accident what older races of men put down to fate. At that moment, on Bloody Island, I thought I couldn't be more deeply involved than I was. And yet, standing there in the sunshine, with all of Mahon and Villa Carlos spread out before me, the Holden Farm of Nelson fame red-roofed across the water on the long peninsula that ran out to the military casements and the big gun positions of La Mola, and the stone of the hospital ruins dark in shadow, I was on the threshold of something that would make my present circumstances seem totally irrelevant.

But I wasn't thinking about that. I was watching the Spanish patrol boat steaming back to the naval quay and passing through the narrows so close I could have thrown a stone on to its deck if I'd been standing by the beacon. And there was movement on *Medusa* now, a launch manned by bluejackets coming out from under her stern and pointing its bows to pass the other side of Bloody Island. There was an officer standing in the stern and somehow I knew it was Gareth, knew where he was going. I climbed to a vantage point at the south end of the hospital ruins and watched as the launch powered past me, cutting an arrowhead wake that pointed straight at Cala Figuera. A few minutes and it was alongside the quay we had built, Gareth clambering out and going straight across the road and in through the open door of the chandlery.

He was only there a short time. No reason for me to feel hurt, but I did, and when I returned to the dig, neither Lennie nor Petra made any reference to my absence. They were drinking coffee, and when we had finished, the three of us got to work.

All through the day we were hard at it, picking and shovelling with care and carting the rubble away. At one point we were involved in the awkward removal of a complete skeleton, and then, after only a short break for lunch, we hit what I thought at first was the island's bedrock. Petra was back by then, and as we uncovered more of it, she became very excited, her conviction growing that what she was unearthing really was a fallen taula. She had reason to be excited, for if it was a taula it would confirm the site as a megalithic religious complex. The centrepiece of such sites was always a huge stone monument of two rectangular slabs, one slotted into the top of the other in the form of a T, the upper slab like a lofty table raised sometimes as much as twelve to fourteen feet above the ground. Occasionally two slabs supported the top.

Petra's excitement was infectious and my mind gradually became concentrated on the dig. Before her father's death she had been working largely on her own. Now in one day the three of us had exposed all one side of a fallen upright, also part of the jointing of the capping slab, which unfortunately was broken into three pieces. I knew of at least eight taulas in Menorca, some of them either raised up or still standing, but this was the first I had ever seen on one of the subsidiary islands.

We went on until just after sunset, when we went back to the tent, lit the pressure lamp and had a celebratory drink. There was no doubt then about what it was we had uncovered. 'A taula here on Bloody Island—' Her eyes were bright in the sizzling light. 'If only the professor I saw at the V and A about that cave drawing had been a little more enthusiastic, then with what I have discovered here I could have developed my theory on the growth of the Mediterranean culture to the point where I could have written a paper on it.'

CHAPTER TWO

We had a quick meal and left shortly after dark.
Petra wasn't all that keen. I think she had
accepted that any cave drawing she discovered on
Menorca would be what she would call recent. It was
Lennie who insisted on our taking a look at the water-
worn passageway he had discovered by accident below
the villa where he had been moonlighting. He was very
determined I should see it. It was all open country, he
said, and even if we were stopped the chances of my
being recognised were slight. Anyway, I wanted to
know what Evans had been doing with the *Santa
Maria* moored above that cave entrance.

Petra had a bag full of archaeological papers to
justify her journey in the unlikely event that we ran
into a roadblock, also she had fastened the beard more
securely to my chin with some adhesive tape. Having
forced myself to wear it all day, I had become quite
used to it and she assured me it was a great improve-

ment in my appearance. 'Very macho,' she whispered to me with a grin as she finally stuck it in place.

It was a clear night, no wind, and the stars very bright. We only passed two cars between the turn-off to the little fishing port of Es Grau and the crossroads where we turned right for Macaret and Punta Codolar. The warm air coming in through Petra's open window was full of the resin scent of pines and the more pungent smell of the maquis growth that blanketed much of the gravel country we were passing through.

The villa to which Lennie directed her was only a short distance from the half-completed one I had traded for *Thunderflash*, and as we swung down the western slope of the headland, I caught a glimpse of it, still with the scaffold up and what looked like a big removal van parked outside it, the box-like shape momentarily in silhouette against a naked light bulb shining from one of the downstairs windows. I wondered if it was Evans and how he would react if Petra dropped me off there and I walked in on him. But then we were on the eastern arm of Arenal d'en Castell's little horseshoe cove and Lennie was telling her to drive on past what he called the cave villa. 'We'll park down by one of the hotels.'

The villa was in darkness, one of those architect-designed summer homes built into the rocky slope on several layers, its garden stepped in terraces. The owner was apparently a German bank executive, and Miguel, who looked after it for him, had told Lennie he was not expected until the middle of June. We left the car at the first hotel, parked among a covey of hired Fiats, and climbed back up the hill, Petra with her bag of archaeological stuff slung over her shoulder, Lennie and I with the torches, pressure lamp, a bottle of wine and a coil of rope taken from his boat. The driveway swung off direct to the garage, which was built into the hillside at the bottom of the garden. 'We had to blast that out of solid rock.' Lennie had done the blasting. 'That was what he wanted me for.' He had worked at one time in one of the Kalgoorlie mines. He had been a prospector, too. 'It's limestone here, nice easy stuff. That's why there's caves and blowholes.' We climbed up the terraces and let ourselves in through the garden door, the house very dark inside and smelling faintly of paint and sea damp. 'Better not show a light.' Lennie closed the door and pocketed the key. 'Had it copied,' he said with a wink. 'You never know.' And he added, 'You two wait here while I locate the cellar door.'

The cellar itself was reached by a curving flight of half a dozen concrete steps. It had been blasted out of the solid rock, an area of about thirty square metres lined with wine racks. He swung his torch over the array of bottles that hid the naked rock of the walls. 'Got some good stuff here, certainly has. Haven't been in the cellar since he got it fully stocked.' He went over to the far corner where there was an olive-wood table and two seats made out of oak-staved barrels standing on a sheet of corrugated iron. When we had shifted the furniture and pulled the tin sheet aside, there was a jagged-edged hole dropping away into what looked like nothingness with the slop and gurgle of water faintly audible.

'Well, there it is,' he said to Petra. 'Down you go. Turn right at the bottom and you'll find the drawings on the roof about twenty yards away. If you get to the rock fall where I blasted out the blowhole to make the garage you've gone past it, okay?' He was fastening one end of the rope to the base of one of the bottle racks, then he put a couple of foot loops into it before passing the end of it down the hole. ''Bout ten feet, that's all, then you're into the blowhole.' He passed Petra one of the torches and held her while she got her foot into the first loop. She looked very strange, her body disappearing into the floor, shadows flickering on the walls and the bottles watching with a dusty glint.

We lit the pressure lamp and passed it down to her. Then we lowered ourselves into the cave-like passageway beside her. It was wider than I had expected, the walls very irregular, and quite different to the cellar, for the rock here had not been blasted, but was carved out by centuries of pressurised sea water as the waves of the tramontana crashed against the coast.

'We'll leave you for a moment,' Lennie told her.

'Why? Where are you going?'

Lennie nodded in the opposite direction. 'We'll head down the slope. I want Mike to see how the blowhole drops into the cave. Won't be long.' We left her then, moving quickly down the irregular passageway. At times we were almost crawling, then suddenly the passage would open out into an expansion chamber so that we could walk virtually upright. Here and there Lennie paused, the beam of his torch directed at the scuffed dust of the floor, and all the time the sound of the sea increasing as it slopped and gurgled in the cavern ahead. Round the first bend he paused. 'I wasn't telling Petra this. She's hooked on cave drawings and such. But this is what I came to check on.' His hand was on my arm, a tight grip as he pulled me down to take a closer look at the floor. 'A lot of stuff has been dragged along here. Heavy stuff in cases, I'd say. And here and there the imprint of a shoe. Look!' And he let go my arm, tracing a blurred imprint in the dust.

'Smuggling?' I was thinking of Gareth, all the questions he had asked over that lunch at Fornells – and that story of his about Evans in the King's Fleet. 'You say you saw the *Santa Maria* lying off here?'

'Sure did.' Lennie straightened up. 'Come on. And be careful now. It gets steeper. Then I'll show you how it's done.'

We continued on, another expansion chamber opening up, the sound of the sea suddenly very loud. At the far end the blowhole tunnel fell right away, an almost vertical drop, the nearside of which had been heavily scored as though by a large shovel or scraper. Rigged across the hole was a lattice of small scaffolding poles bolted together to hold a heavy metal pulley. We slithered down till we could clutch the scaffolding, then, leaning out over the abyss and probing downwards with our torches, we could see the surge of the waves in the cave mouth, the water in the cavern itself rising and falling against a steep little beach of dark sand and round, water-rolled stones that gleamed wetly.

There was also something else, a heavy old anchor, brown with rust and half-buried in the beach. A heavy-duty purchase of the type used in large yachts before the switch to winches was shackled to the eye of the stock, and nylon sheets or warps ran through the pulleys and out into the sea. 'That's what I came here for.' Lennie's voice was a whisper as though at any moment he expected one of the smugglers to rise like a genie out of the blowhole. 'To see how they did it.'

'So what do you think they were bringing ashore?' I asked him.

'Dunno, mate. I thought it would be just ordinary household things, TV sets, electric cookers, glassware, jewellery, anything that was taxable. But after last night . . .'

'What are you suggesting – arms?'

'Well, it certainly ain't drugs. The Menorquins haven't gone for that so far and the villa people . . .' He stopped abruptly as Petra slithered down to join us, the pressure lamp casting her shadow behind her, lighting up the latticework of steel tubing on which we leaned.

She was panting, her eyes wide and a little wild. 'Some silly bugger's been playing around with candles. They're not cave drawings at all.' She gulped for air. 'But it's not that. I thought I heard voices, the sound of an engine.'

'Where?' Lennie asked.

'Beyond the garage.' She took a deep breath, pulling herself together. 'There's no cave-in there, no rock fall. It's all been cleared away.'

'You mean you went inside the garage?'

'No.' She shook her head, the dust stirring in her shoulder-length hair. 'No, it was boarded up. A jagged hole stopped up with what looked like fresh match-boarding.'

Lennie didn't wait to hear any more. He pushed past her and started back up the slope, clawing his way up on all fours. I followed, dragging Petra after me. We were all together in a bunch as we ducked past the rope we had rigged from the cellar and came to the boarded-up hole into the garage. 'Look at it!' Petra held the pressure lamp up and her voice was an angry whisper as she rubbed at the blurred black outline of some four-legged animals on the roof. 'Candle-black.' She showed me the palm of her hand. It looked as though she had been handling a badly printed newspaper, and the head of the beast was smudged. 'The sort of thing a schoolboy would do, and I was fool enough to hope . . .'

Lennie's hand clamped suddenly over her mouth. 'Listen!' He opened the valve of the pressure lamp, his torch switched off, the hiss of the gas mantle dying away and in the darkness the scrape of a door sounding muffled and a voice, very faint from beyond the boarding, instructing somebody to back right up to the door. An engine revved, more directions, than a babble of whispering voices barely audible as the engine noise died away and was suddenly cut. A tailboard slammed and somebody said, 'Quiet! Keep everything quiet.' There was no more talking after that, only the sound of heavy boxes or crates being loaded.

'The cellar,' Lennie breathed. 'Follow me and keep hold.'

We felt our way back down the blowhole till we came to the rope again. Lennie went first, then Petra. My foot was in the first loop, ready to follow her, when the crash of breaking wood sounded hollow along the passageway. I froze, thinking for a moment they had heard us and were breaking through from the garage. Somebody swore, a muffled voice – 'That was my fucking foot, you bastard.' An answering voice, then the two of them arguing until somebody shouted at them to cool it. By then I was on to the second loop and reaching up to clutch hold of Lennie's hand. As soon as I was out of the hole he unhitched the end of the rope, coiling it and slinging it over his shoulder, then he swung the torch to show us the steps leading up to the cellar door. 'Just follow me.' Black darkness as he switched off the torch again and we felt our way up to the room above.

Back at the garden door we waited, listening. No sound now, only the door squeaking as he pulled it gently open. The garden was in three terraces, dropping away steeply to the garage driveway. Two cars were parked there, and where the garage itself disappeared into the hillside, the protruding section was merged with the body of a truck that looked like the one we had seen parked outside the Punta Codolar villa. A figure appeared out of the garage, heading for the nearest car, then turning towards us and slowing. Finally, beside the thin pencil point of a cypress, he stood quite still, feet apart, head thrown back, staring straight at us.

Could he see us in the starlight? Could he see that the door we were peering out of was half-open? We stood there, the three of us, absolutely still, waiting. The man bent his head, both hands to his front, as though holding a weapon. Then he turned and went back to the garage. 'Pissing.' Lennie breathed a sigh of relief, and Petra giggled under her breath as he added, 'It was his cock, not a gun. He was just relieving himself.' He closed the door and led us up through the villa's three levels, up into a large room that faced both ways.

From a circular porthole window we looked out on to the hilltop where barely twenty metres of shrubland separated us from the road. Here a low stone wall marked the limit of the property and a brick arch framed an elaborate wrought-iron gate. A gravel path flanked by stone urns planted with cacti led to the heavy cedarwood door beside us. Lennie eased the catch and pushed it gently open, leaning his head out through the gap. The stars were very bright. 'Looks clear enough.' His scrawny neck, the lined, leathery features, the way he cocked his eyes over the landscape – I had the sudden impression of a turkey checking that nobody was going to grab him for their Christmas dinner. My mind also registered a picture of Gareth being grabbed as he ran from the King's Fleet towards Felixstowe Ferry.

'Shut the door,' I hissed.

He turned, eyeing me curiously. 'Wot's up? Nobody there.'

'If it's Evans loading that truck, he'll have somebody hidden up this side of the villa, just in case.'

'Okay. So we wait.'

He was just shutting the window when we saw lights approaching, and heard the sound of an engine. It was a car, moving fast, and as it passed the villa's gate Lennie sucked in his breath. 'Jesus Christ!' he muttered and half leant out of the window as though to call to the driver. 'Why the hell does he come out here now?'

'Who?' I had only caught a glimpse of the car, a battered estate. I hadn't seen who was driving it.

'Miguel,' he said, still peering out of the window as the car slowed on the dip and turned into the villa's driveway. 'The poor stupid bloody bastard – to come here now, just when they're loading up.' The car's lights flickered through the shrubbery, then they were gone, snuffed out by the corner of the building. The engine note died abruptly.

We listened, but there was no sound – no shouts, no outcry or altercation. Just nothing.

We felt our way across to the other side of the room, standing at the window there, looking down across the flat-topped roofs of the villa's lower levels to the truck, the whole shadowy shape of it now visible as a sort of elongated extension of the garage. And beyond it, on the sweep of the drive, as well as the two cars they had come in, there was the estate car standing black and seemingly empty.

A hand gripped mine, Petra's voice in my ear whispering, 'What is it?' Her fingers tightened convulsively, but it wasn't fear. It was excitement. Her breath was warm on my cheek, her hair touched my ear. 'Is it to do with what happened last night?'

I couldn't answer that. I didn't know. In any case, I was wondering about Miguel. Was he one of them? Was that why he was here? Or had he walked right into it, unarmed and unprepared?

'It's arms, isn't it? It's an arms cache.' And when I still didn't say anything, she whispered urgently, 'If it's arms, then we have to notify somebody, warn the authorities.'

'Not yet – when they've gone . . .' And I added, 'Maybe we can follow them.'

She had moved her head slightly so that it was outlined against the window. I saw the shape of it nod against the stars, her hand still in mine, still the grip of excitement, so that I was reminded that between school and college she had done a VSO stint in the Andes, trekking alone on the borders of Chile, Peru and Bolivia looking for old Inca remains. I don't think she knew what fear was, otherwise she would never have been able to go it alone at such high altitude with only the Quechua Indians for company. 'What's the time?'

Lennie glanced at the luminous dial of his diving watch. 'Twenty after midnight.'

'Do you think it's arms?' she asked him.

'Yes, I do.'

'Then if they're going to use them tonight they'll have to get a move on.'

At that moment, as though the hoarse whisper of her voice had carried to the garage below, the dark shadow of a man came hurrying up through the garden, leaping the steps between the terraces and angling away to the right. Abreast of the upper part of the villa he put his hand to his mouth and gave a piercing whistle on two notes like the call of a bird. A figure rose out of a dark mass of shrubbery beside the road some two hundred yards away, glanced quickly round, then hurried to join the man below. The two of them went back down the terraces to the garage where half a dozen men were now heading for the parked cars. The slam of a door came to us faintly, then the truck's engine started up. The men got into the cars, all three of them, including Miguel's estate, and the little convoy moved off, slowly and without lights, then swung left at the driveway end and from the front of the villa we watched them pass along the road, dark shapes in silhouette against the stars heading for Punta Codolar.

'What do we do now – get the car and follow them?'

'Depends how good you are at driving without lights,' I told her.

She laughed. 'Won't be the first time.'

Lennie had the door open and we were out into the night, slamming it behind us and running to the road. It was all downhill to where Petra had parked the Beetle and took us barely two minutes. 'Where now?' she asked breathlessly as she started the engine. I hesitated. There was only one road out until the crossroads junction with the main Mahon–Fornells road, unless they were heading for the ports of either Macaret or Addaia. 'Back up the hill,' I said. 'It's just possible they'll stop at the Punta Codolar villa.' If Evans was involved and they were operating to an exact timetable, then I thought they might be using it as a rendezvous.

She drove fast, a lot faster than I would have cared to drive in that dim light, up past the villa where they had been loading the truck, over the shoulder of the cove's sheltering arm and out on to the bleak empty heathland beyond. There was more light here, cliffs all round us dropping to the sea which reflected the starlight, and against that milky glimmer the Punta Codolar villa stood out solitary and square like a concrete pillbox, and beside it, also outlined against the stars, was the black rectangular shape of the truck.

Petra slammed on the brakes and we rolled to a stop. 'Where now?'

We had just passed a service road under construction and some two hundred yards away to the right there was a road roller hull-down in the heathland. I told her to back up and park beside it. Close against the road roller, our front wheels hard into the rubble of an open trench where an electricity cable was being laid, the Beetle was almost indistinguishable from the heavy mass of the roller's iron.

For almost the first time since I'd known her Petra's obsession with the island's megalithic past was overlaid by more immediate concerns as we speculated about what they planned to do and when, the villa hull-down and indistinct on the heathland's horizon. I asked her whether she had any glasses in the car. She reached over to the back seat, grabbed the bag that contained her archaeological gear, and after rummaging around in it, produced a pair of those very small, high-magnification binoculars. I rolled the window down and with some difficulty managed to focus them on the villa. The field of vision was very small. 'I was only once involved in a political upheaval.' Petra's voice was low and intense as through she were afraid of being overheard. 'I was in the Cordillera Real just north of La Paz and a ragged bunch of them passed through my camp. Defeated revolutionaries are very unpredictable. South American revolutionaries, anyway, and I had found an Inca tamba that nobody had discovered before. All very exciting, worked stone blocks jigsawed together so that they wouldn't be toppled by earthquakes, and these exhausted men in fear of their lives flopping down in the undergrowth I'd cleared. There was a thick cloud mist, everything very damp and cold. They lit a fire, huddling round it.'

It was strange to be watching the villa through glasses. Last time I had seen it I had been breaking in by the garage window and there had been nobody there. Now it was just as dark, but the cars and the truck were clear proof that there were men inside it. They must be sitting there, waiting.

'What is it? Can you see something?'

I shook my head. All the glasses showed me was the Moorish front with its arched colonnade, the low wall that separated it from the road and the block-house shape of it against the night sky with the cars tucked in against the garage and the truck left out in the road.

'Go on, Petra.' Lennie leaned forward, his head between us. 'What happened? Did they mess you about?'

'If you mean what I think you mean, the answer is no, they were too bloody tired. But they did something worse. They ate up everything I had, all my stores, then went off with my tent, even my sleeping bag. I think they'd have had the clothes off my back if I'd been a man, they were that ragged and desperate. Only their guns looked in good condition.'

I thought I saw the glow of a cigarette. It was there for a second, then Lennie knocked against me and I lost it. It had come from the last arch of the villa's colonnaded front, and focusing on it, I thought I could just make out the darker outline of a figure standing there. I heard Petra say something about trekking more than twenty miles through snow and ice and a blazing midday sun before she managed to hitch a ride with some geologists into La Paz.

'And what happened to the men who pillaged your camp?' Lennie asked.

'Oh, the Army caught up with them in the end. About a dozen of them were gunned down from a helicopter, the rest were tracked down, tortured and hanged. The usual thing. There's no mercy in the Andes.'

'I never experienced anything like that,' Lennie said quietly. 'And I've been around. But nothing like that.' And he added, leaning his head further forward between us, 'You think there's going to be a revolution here?'

She didn't tell him not to be ridiculous. She didn't comment. She just sat there, not saying a word, and at that moment a bright star shot up from the sea to our right, blazing a vertical trail that burst into a blob of white so bright that even at that distance it lit up our faces. 'Bloody hell!' Lennie pushed his nose almost against the windscreen. 'What is it?'

'Pyrotechnic.' The pop of its burst came to us faintly as I jumped out of the car, steadying my elbow on the top of it and searching with the glasses for the ship that had fired it. A second stream of sparks flew up, a second burst, but this time green. I still couldn't pick out the shape of the vessel, so it was presumably close in below the line of the cliffs.

'That a distress signal?' Petra asked, but I think she knew it wasn't, because her head was turned towards the villa. Through the glasses I saw shadows moving, followed almost immediately by the sound of a car engine starting up. Doors slammed, the cars emerging on to the road. Then the truck's diesel roared into life and it began to move, one car in front, the other behind. The time was 01.32. Miguel's estate stayed parked against the wall.

'What now?' Petra had already started the engine.

'Go back,' I told her. 'Back down towards Arenal, then take the main development road and we'll wait for them just short of where it joins the Alayór highway.' Either they were meeting up with a ship at Macaret or else somewhere further up the long inlet that finished at the new quay just beyond Addaia.

'I don't get it, mate,' Lennie muttered in my ear as Petra felt her way along the dark strip of the road without lights. 'What do they want with a ship when their truck's already loaded? They can't be picking up more.' But I was thinking about Wade then, that first visit of Gareth's to Menorca, the questions he had asked me over that lunch. And on board *Medusa*, the suddenness with which we had left Malta, the way he had looked that evening when I went back down to his cabin from the bridge, his sudden decision to tell me about Evans.

We reached the crossroads and Petra pulled in to the verge. We sat there for perhaps five minutes, but there was no sound and nothing passed. I told her to drive straight across and head for the high point above the entrance to the Addaia inlet. From there we would have a clear view of Macaret itself and the seaward entrance to the harbour. We would also be able to look southwards down the length of the inlet to the two small islands that protected the final anchorage.

When we got there we were just in time to catch a glimpse of a small vessel heading down the pale ribbon of the inlet. 'Fishing boat by the look of it,' Lennie muttered.

Out of the car again, I was able to fix the glasses

on it. No doubt about it. The boat was the *Santa
Maria*. I jumped back into the passenger seat and told
Petra to turn the car, go back to the main road, then
take the cut-off down the steep little hill to Port d'Addaia itself. 'But go carefully,' I warned her as she swung
the Beetle round. 'They may have dropped somebody
off to keep watch. And stop near the top so that we
can check if they're there or not.'

When we reached Addaia she tucked herself into
a little parking bay where we had a clear view of the
quay across pantile roofs and the steep overgrown
slope of the hillside, and it wasn't just the truck from
Codolar that was waiting there. I counted no less than
five trucks, all parked in line along the concrete edge
of the quay and facing towards us. There were more
than a dozen cars, too, and a lot of men, most of them
gathered round the back of the last truck, where crates
were being dumped on the quay, prised open and the
weapons they contained handed out.

'Christ! See that, mate. They got rocket-launchers.
The hand-held type. What do the bastards want with
them?' Lennie had followed me out of the car and
across the road. From there we had a clear view of the
anchorage where I had joined Carp for the voyage to
Malta. And there, as though I were seeing it all again,
like on video but from a different angle, was the *Santa
Maria* motoring in through the narrows that separated
the humpbacked outline of the second island from the
muddy foreshore and the huddle of fishermen's dwellings. The boat was headed straight for the quay, and

as she slowed and swung her stern to lie alongside, I saw she had a stern light showing.

That was when we heard the rumble of engines coming from seaward, and a moment later we saw the dim shape of a flat box of a vessel. There were two of them, old LCTs dating from the days before they called them logistic landing craft. I recognised them immediately, one of them having dropped me off at Loch Boisdale on its way to St Kilda some years back. The *Santa Maria* had clearly been leading them in. Now she was alongside and a man had jumped ashore. I watched him through the glasses as the men on the quay gathered round him. Even in that dim light I was certain it was Evans. He was head and shoulders taller than most of them, standing there, hands on hips, issuing orders. He wore a kepi-like forage cap and camouflage jacket and trousers, and the way he stood, the arrogance and the air of command, I was suddenly reminded of early pictures of Castro.

A splash, and the first of the logistic vessels had dropped its stern anchor, the big drum winch on the afterdeck reeling out the hawser as the ship nosed into the quay. The bow doors opened, then with a clank and a crash, the ramp dropped on to the quay. By then the second vessel was coming in alongside it and a moment later the vehicles inside the two slab-sided hulls, their engines already running, began to trundle out. They were half-tracks, each of them mounting what looked like a heavy Bofors gun, and as they came off the ramps they were joined by small detachments of the men on shore.

Behind the half-tracks came men, dozens of them, dressed in some drab uniform and loaded down with equipment, each of them pausing for a moment as they stepped on to the terra firma of the quay's concrete edge. It was as though they needed to find their feet. Some, as they stood there, arched their backs and stretched. A babble of human voices reached up to us. It was the natural reaction of men who had been cooped up in a confined space for some considerable time and for a moment the scene below us was one of disorder, almost chaos. Then somebody shouted. I think it was Evans, and the men standing around the parked trucks began splitting up and moving to join the new arrivals, the mêlée gradually sorting itself out as they formed up into units and marched off to embark in the waiting trucks or climb on to the backs of the half-tracks.

It was less than ten minutes from the time the LCTs had put their ramps down to the moment when the local vehicles were all loaded and the whole convoy beginning to move off, and by then I was convinced that what we were witnessing was the start of an armed usurpation of the political power in the island. Who the men were that had landed from the two LCTs, where they had come from – that was of no importance for the moment. What was important was to alert somebody in Mahon to the danger. I saw it all in a mental flash, dissident elements, gathered from the various towns, meeting here to be given arms and then to be distributed amongst the newly arrived mercenaries, or whatever they were, to guide them to objectives that had already been decided on.

It seemed ridiculous on the face of it. There couldn't be more than a hundred and fifty to two hundred men down there on the quay and the military garrison of the island I knew to be somewhere around 15,000. But if what Petra had told me was correct, the effect of the previous night's violence had been a redeployment of the available forces, so that the towns, and particularly the *urbanizacións* inhabited by foreign visitors, were fully protected. As a result, the men below me had not only the advantage of surprise – essential in an operation of this sort – but also the certainty that the island's defences were thinly spread and the targets they would be aiming at that much more vulnerable. In such circumstances anything was possible.

All this passed through my mind in a flash as the vehicles moved out on to the steep road up from the port and Lennie and I flung ourselves back across the road and into the car. 'Mahon,' I told Petra. 'Lights on and drive like hell.'

She didn't hesitate. She had seen the ships, the mustering men. She swung out on to the Alayór road, her foot hard down and the elderly Beetle shaking and swaying at the rear. 'Who are they?' She was taking a bend fast, pines rushing at us. 'What are you going to do?' And when I said I had to get to the frigate, she started to argue, asking why I didn't stop off somewhere and phone the nearest *Guardia Civil* post or Military Headquarters in Mahon.

'For God's sake! Who would believe me?' I started to remind her then that I was suspected of complicity in the Martinez murder. 'Anyway,' I added, 'they'll almost certainly have cut the telephone wires.'

'Alayór then. Alayór is nearer than Mahon.'

'No, Mahon,' I told her. It was Gareth I needed. He had all the means of communication there on board, the whole world at call. And then I was briefing her what to tell Soo after she had dropped us off at the Maritimo pontoon, who to telephone, very conscious that it would be the early hours of the morning, everybody asleep and in no mood to believe that danger was imminent.

'You'll have to come with me,' she argued. 'Even if I can get through to somebody in authority . . .'

'No,' I said. 'I've got to make contact with Gareth.'

But the frigate was something too remote for her to grasp, and anyway she did not want the responsibility of alerting people locally. 'You know what they are. They won't believe a woman. I'll never get it across to them.' And even when I told her she was one of the few people outside of government they would believe, that as an English archaeologist she had the standing of a scientist and therefore would be regarded as a reliable witness, she went on arguing until the crossroads came up in the headlights and I put my hand on her knee and told her to turn left for Mahon or I'd switch the engine off, drive the car myself and leave her at the side of the road.

An angry silence filled the car after she had made the turn, the road snaking through a forest of pine, with the scent of resin all-pervading, then straightening out with no sign of lights anywhere. Something flapped across the beam of our headlights, a kite probably. We reached the turn-off to Faváritx, and still nothing on the road. In fact, we did not see another vehicle until we were running into the outskirts of Mahon. Where the road curved down the hill from the main Ciudadela highway we had to wait for a small convoy of three army trucks which swung into the road in front of us, then turned off to the left, almost certainly bound for the Zona Militar barracks out on La Mola.

'Why not try the Naval Base?' Petra said. 'Fernando likes you. He would believe what you told him.'

I had already thought of that. It was very tempting, the Naval Base so close we were almost at the entrance to it. But how long would it take me to get through to Perez? 'No,' I said. 'Gareth is a safer bet.' I was watching the tail-lights of the convoy climbing up the hill beside the Base, the white beam of their heads shining on the heathland scrub with its pillboxes and old stone fortifications built to stand against Napoleon. Another ten minutes, maybe quarter of an hour, and other vehicles would be rolling up that road on to the long peninsula that formed the northern arm of the finest deep-water natural port in the Western Mediterranean, and at the end of that peninsula was La Mola with its barracks and casements and those huge guns. I had absolutely no doubt that this would be one of the main objectives, La Mola being little more than an island, the neck joining it to the main arm of the land so narrow it could readily be sealed with mines, the whole garrison then cut off. 'Keep going,' I told her. 'I haven't time to argue with the Navy guard at the entrance. And Perez might be in Ciudadela, anywhere.'

We passed the turning to the Base and over my left shoulder there were lights on a freighter lying alongside the new quay, and beyond it, lights flashing green on the naval jetty. Then we were under the mass of Mahon itself, hammering along the waterfront past the commercial quay. There was a ferry lying there and out beyond Bloody Island I could see the dim shape of *Medusa* lying broadside to the town. A minute later we had rounded Punta Maritimo and Petra was bringing the car to a halt at the pontoon. I remember telling her to say something nice to Soo for me as I flung open the door and leapt out, the black, limpid water of the harbour washing lazily at the concrete of the roadway, the wooden boards of the pontoon moving under my feet. 'You reck'n they'll go for La Mola?' Lennie asked as he cord-whipped the outboard into life and we nosed out past the mooring lines of a big French sloop, the bows lifting as he increased the revs, heading to pass just north of Bloody Island where the frigate's bows were pointing towards Nelson's Golden Farm.

I nodded, the noise too great for conversation.

'They could just concentrate on the town, you know,' he yelled in my ear. 'Seize the town hall, take a crack at Military HQ and occupy the radio station. Wouldn't that be enough?'

I shrugged, unable to answer him, thinking ahead

to my meeting with Gareth. I could imagine him asking me just those questions and what the hell would I say? We passed the quick-flashing red beacon close to the dig, Lennie cutting it so fine I could see the wheelbarrows still full of the rubble we had been shifting, and then the businesslike outline of *Medusa* was looming nearer. 'Which side?' he shouted in my ear.

'Starb'd,' I said, and he swung in a tight arc, passing so close under the bows I thought he would smash into the anchor cable. The engine slowed, then died with a cough as he brought the inflatable alongside where the accommodation ladder had been lifted clear of the water. By then I had Petra's big torch beamed on the bridge, flicking the switch on and off – three dots, three dashes, three dots – hoping that whoever was on watch would realise the SOS was to signify urgency, not just some drunk from the shore playing silly buggers. I could hear the hum of the ship's machinery now, sense the power of the organisation that was in her. 'Ahoy there, *Medusa!*' I was shouting for the Officer of the Day, the Captain, anyone, my voice raised high, desperate with the need to be got on board quickly. A face under a sailor's hat leaned out above me. 'Wot you want?'

'The Captain,' I shouted up to him. 'Tell the Captain it's Mike Steele and it's urgent. Every minute counts.' A door slammed and a beam of light was directed straight at me, my eyes blinded, and a voice said, 'Good evening, sir. You come to return that beard we lent you?' It was young Davison, the officer-under-training, and he was grinning. 'The Captain!' I yelled at him again.

'The Captain's asleep, sir.'

'Well, wake him up. And get me on board. I have information for him that must be transmitted to London immediately.'

He stood there for a moment, mouth agape, gazing down at me. I could see his brain working, trying to decide whether this was a joke or something deadly serious. Fortunately the beard was in my pocket, where it had been for some time now, otherwise he might have thought I was fooling. 'Hurry, man! For God's sake hurry!'

He nodded, suddenly seeming to pull himself together as he ordered a sailor to lower the ladder, then turned and ran to the bridge. He was back by the time I had scrambled up to the deck. 'This way, sir. Captain says to take you to his cabin.'

Gareth was in his dressing gown as I was shown in, his face pale, his hair tousled. 'Thank you, Davison. That'll do.' He turned to me. 'Now, what's this all about?'

I made it as short as possible, but before I had finished he had reached for the phone, flicking a switch. 'Captain. Call all hands. Lieutenant Commander Mault to my cabin immediately.' He had pulled out a notebook and was flicking through the pages. 'Anchored out here we're not on a land line, so we have to slot in to the telephone system through ship-to-shore. However, I can contact the Naval Base on UHF.' He was reaching for the phone again when

Davison's voice broke in on the loudspeaker – 'Captain, sir. This is the bridge.' He sounded a bit nervous, very excited. 'There's what sounds like shots coming from the direction of La Mola – and, sir, we're just picking up bursts of machine-gun fire from the town now.'

'Very good, I'll be up.' Gareth turned to glance at the wall clock, picking up a comb and smoothing his hair. The second hand flicked to the vertical. It was exactly 03.31. 'From what you've told me, looks like the time of attack on all objectives was zero-three-thirty.' And he added, 'I've been expecting something like this.' He slipped out of his dressing gown and began pulling on trousers and white polo-necked sweater over his pyjamas. 'But not those logistic craft.' He had me describe in detail the scene on the quay at Addaia. 'You're certain it was Pat? He was on that fishing boat of yours and led them in?'

'Yes,' I said. 'And he was organising them ashore.'

'The whole thing – I mean, the men who came ashore from those LCTs as well as the locals? You're sure?'

'I think so.' It was obvious he didn't want to believe that the man was totally involved, but when I told him it was bright starlight and I had ten-magnification glasses on him, he sighed and said, 'I suppose I should have expected that.' He was buttoning up his jacket. 'Well, no good trying to alert Capitán Perez now. His boys can hear the shooting just as well as we can here. Let's go up to the bridge.'

Outside the cabin all was bustle as the ship came

to readiness, men in various stages of dress hurrying to their posts, the bridge itself beginning to fill up. As soon as we reached it, we could hear the firing out on La Mola, for they had both wing doors open. We went out on to the starb'd wing and stood there looking at the black outline of the peninsula sprawled against the stars. 'When do you reckon first light, Pilot?'

'With the sky as clear as this, sir, there should be a glimmer in the east within the hour.'

'An hour's darkness.' Gareth nodded, then turned to me. 'Nice timing, the whole thing highly organised.' And he added, 'That will be Pat. He's had a lot of experience – Angola chiefly, Mozambique, with the Polisario, and Wade says they thought he had done a spell with the Contras, so he's had the benefit of American as well as South African training.'

Mault appeared at his elbow. 'I was ordered to report to your cabin, but you weren't there.'

'No, I'm here.' Gareth's voice was sharp. 'Have the launch brought alongside and go across to the Base. Try and see Capitán Perez personally. Offer him any assistance he needs. Oh, and tell him the entire force at the disposal of the insurgents at this moment in time is not more than two hundred. They are supported by professional troops landed from two small logistics craft at Addaia. I have an eye-witness of the landing here on board *Medusa*.'

Mault hesitated, glancing at me. 'Wouldn't it be better if I took Mr Steele with me?'

'No.' Gareth's voice was even sharper. 'Tell the *Jefe* he can interview him here on board if he wants to.'

And he added, 'Now hurry, man. Things are happening, and happening fast. Perez needs to know that the whole thing can be controlled and suppressed if he acts quickly enough.' He turned to Davison. 'Is somebody looking after that inflatable and the man who was with Mr Steele?'

'Yes, sir. He's been taken to the petty officers' mess for some coffee.'

'Good.' He turned back into the body of the bridge as the Yeoman of Signals appeared at his side with a piece of paper in his hand. 'A sit-rep, sir. The Communications Office were alerting the radar unit on top of the Toro rock when the radio contact suddenly went dead, there's a small foreign outfit in Alayór, nobody knows yet what nationality but Arab by the look of them, and there's a ham of sorts broadcasting Independence Day messages from Ciudadela.'

Gareth glanced through the paper, nodded, dealt with the little queue of officers waiting to be briefed, then went over to the nearest mike, his voice stilling all conversation as it blared out over the ship's main broadcast: '*This is the Captain speaking. We have a situation ashore that was not wholly unexpected and is to some extent our reason for being here in Port Mahon . . .*' And then he was outlining briefly what the firing was all about. He also indicated that there had been outside intervention . . . '*Whether by political sympathisers, mercenaries or some foreign power is not yet clear. I will keep you informed.*' Just as he said that there was a flash, followed immediately by the rumble of a heavy explosion, the rumbling muffled as though it were underground, and suddenly the highest point of La Mola was lit by a pyrotechnic display that was so colourful and went on for so long it was more like fireworks than the destruction of a military target. 'Looks like they've got the garrison's ammunition dump.' Gareth had a pair of the bridge binoculars fixed on La Mola. Davison said something to him and he lowered the glasses, frowning. 'Funny! I should have thought he would have been glad of a coffee, even a drink . . .' He turned to me. 'That Australian of yours. Seems he was worried about something, so he's pushed off. Said he'd be at the dig when you wanted him. Yes, Yeo?'

The Yeoman of Signals was at his elbow again. 'Looks as though they've taken the radio station, sir. They're playing local music interspersed with announcements of this sort.' He handed Gareth a slip of paper.

'Ismail Fuxá – ' Gareth was reading it aloud – 'I imagine you pronounce it Fusha, the X is sh, isn't it? He's described here as leader of the Independent Movement and it says he'll be broadcasting an Independence Day message to the Menorquin people at 06.00. Apparently the speech will be repeated every hour on the hour throughout the rest of the day. What do you think?' He glanced up at me. 'The speech taped in advance?' And he added, 'Must have been. Which suggests a degree of organisation . . .'

The Navigating Officer interrupted him. 'Message from the Naval Base, sir. No answer from the garrison command post on La Mola. And the *Jefe* would like a word with you on UHF.'

The ultra high frequency set used by Nato service units was on the far side of the bridge. He picked up the headset with its boom-mike and though I couldn't hear what was said I saw the lines of strain on his face ease. He was talking for barely a minute and then he said, 'Well, thank God for that. They haven't got the Naval Base.' He said it loud enough for all on the bridge to hear, knowing I suppose that it would spread from there right through the ship.

'Launch coming back now, sir.'

He nodded, watching it come out from behind Bloody Island, making an arrowed arc as it swung to pass under the bows and come alongside the ladder. To seaward the first glimmer of the dawn was etching black the outline of Lazareto Island with the bulk of La Mola reared up behind it.

Mault, when he reached the bridge, reported that he had been received very formally. He had the impression that his visit was not welcomed and that the Spanish Navy *Jefe* was wanting to distance himself from the British naval presence in the harbour.

'You saw Perez himself, did you?' Gareth asked him.

'In the end, yes.'

'Would you say his coolness was dictated by higher authority?'

'Yes. He asked me to thank you for your offer of assistance, but to tell you it would not be necessary.'

'He's in touch with Madrid then?'

Mault nodded. 'I think so. But locally I had the feeling he was cut off. I was with him when the explosion occurred on La Mola. That was when he told me his Communications people could no longer talk to the garrison there. He seemed very dejected. In the circumstances the sensible thing would seem to be for us to withdraw to Gibraltar.'

Gareth looked at him, gave a short bark of a laugh and said, 'The sensible thing!' His voice was full of irony. 'Oh yes, Lieutenant Commander – that would undoubtedly be the sensible thing. Unfortunately, our orders are quite the opposite. We stay here.' And he turned on his heel, striding quickly up and down the bridge several times, his face tight-drawn, an expression almost of anguish on his face. He seemed to be struggling to make up his mind about something. Finally, he turned to me. 'Wait for me in my cabin.' He was moving towards the door and when I started to say something about it being time I was off his ship he turned on me angrily. 'Just do as I tell you. Wait in my cabin. I may need you if I manage to contact any of Soo's friends.'

He went below then and shortly afterwards the Navigator advised me to do as he said. His hand was on my arm, steering me to the door. On the stairs outside he suddenly stopped. 'He needs you, sir. You know the island and the people here, and you're not a part of the ship. That's important.' And he added, speaking quite urgently now, 'There's one or two of the officers here trying to dismiss him as a jumped-up little Welshman from the lower deck promoted too quickly and not big enough for the job. They don't know what the job is, of course, and nor do I, but I can tell you this – he's carrying a burden hardly anybody on board yet realises, a burden I can only guess at from hints dropped by Phil Woburn, our Communications Officer. I admire him.' He gave a quick embarrassed grin. 'So do as he says, will you? He needs you.'

It was on the tip of my tongue to tell him to keep the man away from my wife. But instead I nodded and went down to his cabin, wondering again why he had been given this particular command and what the hell the ship was supposed to do here.

I was there on my own for a good half-hour and for most of that time I was standing by the porthole which looked out past Bloody Island to the port and the Naval Base. Once one of the naval patrol boats put out heading for Cala Figuera, but a few minutes after disappearing behind Bloody Island it emerged again and returned to base. Otherwise, there was virtually nothing moving in that section of the harbour and the waterfront was too far away for me to identify the few vehicles that were on the road.

To pass the time I had a look at the books on the shelf above the desk. They were most of them reference books, including the Admiralty Pilot for the Mediterranean Volumes I and II, also, surprisingly, Kemp's encyclopaedic work, *Ships and the Sea*, and beside that was Conrad's *The Secret Agent* and a rather battered copy of a collection of Kipling's verse. Opening it at a marker, I found he had underlined a passage from 'How Fear Came' – '*When ye fight with a Wolf of the*

Pack, ye must fight him alone and afar, Lest others take part in the quarrel, and the Pack be diminished by war.' And earlier there was a ticket to the Shakespeare Theatre, Stratford-upon-Avon, marking 'The English Flag'. '*And what should they know of England who only England know.*' I felt the wrench of that second line, thinking of spring and blossom, chestnuts bursting. Then Petty Officer Jarvis came in to say he would be serving breakfast as soon as the Captain arrived, meanwhile could he offer me a cup of coffee? By then it was 06.09 and I wondered what Ismail Fuxá had said in his Independence Day message.

Gareth had listened to it on the radio, of course. But when he came in some ten minutes later he couldn't tell me what the man had said, apart from the fact that it was a declaration of the island's independence, but he seemed to have got a very vivid impression of Fuxá himself. 'A little like listening to a re-run of the German Führer speaking at one of the big Nazi rallies in the thirties – very emotional, the voice rising in pitch to the point of screaming, then suddenly falling away so that it seemed to be whispering in one's ear.' He slumped down on the settle, passing a hand over his eyes as though to rub out the weariness that showed there. 'Quite an exercise. Very compelling, almost hypnotic. I think we're in trouble.' He said it so softly I could hardly catch the words. 'They seem to have taken all the key points except the Naval Base, which suggests there were sympathisers among some of the military.'

He had contacted several of our English-speaking

friends, but none of them, not even the Renatos, were willing to talk about what was happening ashore. 'In the absence of any effective opposition they're not prepared to stick their necks out.' Jarvis had brought him a tray of coffee and he sat drinking it and staring vacantly at the clock on the wall. 'It's up to the politicians now. Everybody's been informed – Madrid, London, Washington, and Moscow, of course. They'll have a finger in it somewhere, I suppose. That cruiser we saw in Grand Harbour sailed yesterday evening and a flotilla of Soviet ships has just passed through the Straits of Bonifacio. Elements of the Sixth Fleet, the ships we passed through yesterday evening, have put about and are headed back into the Western Mediterranean at full speed.' He poured himself some more coffee, drank it quickly and went out. 'Won't be long, then we'll have breakfast.'

This time he was gone the better part of an hour, and when he came back his face looked grim. 'The BBC News led off with it at seven o'clock. There was a short statement from Madrid to the effect that the Spanish Government was greatly concerned and would be watching events closely.' He was standing at the window looking out towards the town, the white of the buildings touched with gold as the sun rose above the northern arm of the harbour. It was one of those still mornings, the water glassy calm, a molten look that was a sure sign of heat to come. 'In other words, they're not sure of themselves and are waiting upon developments locally. No suggestion at the moment that they are prepared to take any positive and determined action.' He turned to me. 'How left is this man Fuxá, would you say?'

'We always thought of him as more of an anarchist than a communist,' I said.

'My information is that he has spent some time in the Soviet Union and is probably Russian trained.' He gave a little shrug, went over to his desk and sat down, staring vacantly at the litter of signals that covered it. 'Oh well, we'll know soon enough. If that's correct, then he'll almost certainly request recognition from Moscow, even perhaps some assistance if the going gets rough.'

He seemed to be using me as a sounding board, for he went on talking about how the situation might develop, the political repercussions outside of Menorca. At the back of his mind, of course, was the American bombing of Libya. 'Do you think they're involved?' He was staring at me, but I don't think he was seeing me at all, only what was in his mind, the question purely rhetorical. 'Russian warships, the American Sixth Fleet, and those big guns out on La Mola. If they know how to fire them, somebody's got to take them out before any naval ships hostile to this new regime can enter Port Mahon. There are Spanish Navy ships in Barcelona, but they haven't moved. Perhaps that's why.'

'Surely they could knock them out,' I suggested. 'An air strike . . .'

But he was shaking his head. 'The situation is too confused for them to do that. They don't know who they'd be attacking. Their own people perhaps.'

'What does Palma say?' I asked him.

'The Civil Governor has called for calm throughout the Province and appealed for the maintenance of democratic government. Usual sort of thing.'

'And the Military Governor?'

'Nothing so far from him. Not that we've been able to pick up, and nothing on the BBC News or even the World Service. Madrid seems to be keeping a low profile.' He banged his fist against the arm of his chair. 'Time is passing, and every minute counts. They don't seem to realise—'

'Nor do you,' I said.

He stared at me. 'How do you mean?'

'It's obvious, isn't it – they're afraid of aggravating the situation. If you'd lived in the islands you'd understand something of their history and how recent and how delicate is the matter of provincial autonomy.'

'I know that. But they're dithering and they haven't time for that.' His voice had risen almost to a note of shrillness. 'They haven't time,' he repeated more quietly, gazing into space. 'God almighty!' It was an invocation that seemed forced out of him by his lone position at the centre of events that were beyond his control. 'Better get some breakfast now.' He got up from the desk and led me over to the table under the portholes, calling for Petty Officer Jarvis.

'Your people knew something like this was going to happen,' I said as we sat down. 'That's why you were ordered out of Malta in such haste.' He didn't answer, his mind locked in on itself. 'Well, wasn't it?

And wasn't that why you came to Menorca in the first place, before you took command of this ship?'

That got through to him, his eyes coming into focus and staring at me across the table. 'I suppose so.' Jarvis appeared with two plates loaded with bacon, sausage and fried egg.

'So what are you supposed to do? A British Navy ship, you can't take any part in a coup d'état like this.'

'No, of course not.'

'So, what's the point?'

'Toast?' He pushed the rack towards me, concentrating now on his food.

'You can't do any good here,' I told him.

He nodded, the broad forehead under the black curly hair creased in a frown. 'Jesus! Do you think I don't know that?'

'So why were you sent here?' I asked him.

'Why?' He looked surprised. 'For the same reason Nelson was here. And poor Byng – executed because he wouldn't face the French.' And he added, 'These people, they have this one priceless asset – the finest deep-water harbour in the Western Med. That's what it's all about. That's why I'm here.' He gave a hollow laugh. 'If there had been any opposition, if Madrid had reacted to the situation—'

He stopped there, the loudspeaker breaking in on his thoughts: 'Bridge here, sir. There's a launch approaching. Harbour launch by the look of it.'

Gareth finished his breakfast quickly and a few minutes later the same voice announced that it was the harbour master himself wanting to speak to the

Captain. Gareth asked for the man's name, then turned
to me. 'Francisco Romacho. Is that right?'

'No,' I said. 'It should be Juan Terron.'

He nodded. 'They haven't wasted any time. A key
appointment and he's in position already.' Then into
the intercom: 'Does he speak English? No, well get
hold of Sykes, then send the two of them up.' He
suggested I conceal myself in the steward's pantry. 'See
if you recognise him.'

The man who entered was short and very dark
with an aquiline face. I had never seen him before. He
was dressed in khaki trousers and camouflage tunic.
He came straight to the point. 'Señor Fuxá – *el Presidente* – feels that, in the circumstances, he cannot accept
the presence of a foreign warship in the port of
Mahon.' Watching through a crack in the serving
hatch, Victor Sykes came into my line of vision. He was
another of the young officers-under-training, probably
posted to the ship for his knowledge of Spanish. He
looked a little scared, his voice low as he interpreted.
The three of them were seated at the coffee table,
Gareth pointing out that what went on ashore was not
his concern, he was simply in Mahon on a courtesy
visit and if there had been some change in the government of the island, he was sure the new regime would
extend the same welcome to one of Her Majesty's ships
as the old.

The interview went on like that for some time,
Romacho insisting that *Medusa* leave Mahon, Gareth
pointing out that his orders came from London and
he had no authority to leave without new instructions.

At one point he said, 'This is a matter for the Spanish and British governments.' And Romacho answered quickly, 'I don't think so. We are now an independent state.'

'Then I suggest your president takes the question up directly with the Foreign Office in London.'

'He cannot do that until we have recognition. In the meantime, he insists that you leave Mahon.'

'I have explained that my orders—'

'Your orders are to leave. Immediately.' Romacho had jumped to his feet. 'This is our water. Our port. You have no right to be here when we don't invite you. You will leave immediately please.'

Gareth had risen to his feet. 'Unfortunately we have a problem.' And he went on to explain that the high-pressure boilers delivering steam to the turbines had sprung some leaks and his Marine Engineer Officer had taken the opportunity to close the boilers down for maintenance work on the condenser pipes.

It was obvious that Romacho didn't believe him, but he couldn't very well demand to inspect the engine room. Instead, he said, 'In that case, we will have to arrange a tow for you. Fortunately the tanker that keeps the Cala Figuera depot supplied has just finished off-loading and we have our own harbour tug. I will arrange for the two of them to tow you to Palma in Mallorca.'

'That will not be necessary,' Gareth said.

'You will leave then under your own steam?'

'When I have orders to leave I will leave. Not before.'

'So! You are not going to leave?'

'No.'

'Very well, *Capitán*. I also have orders. *El Presidente* instructs me to say that you have until noon. If you are not away from Mahon by midday he will be forced to regard your continued presence here as a hostile act. You understand?' He gave a formal little bow, and without waiting for Gareth's reply, turned quickly and made for the door. His last words as he went out were, 'You have until midday.'

PART FOUR

BLOODY ISLAND

CHAPTER ONE

I remember standing by the taula on Bloody Island watching as the minute hand of my watch crept towards the vertical. Clouds were forming to the south over St Félip, the day already hot and airless, as I had known it would be, and the frigate lay to her reflection in the oily water, nothing moving on her deck, everything very still and silent. I was alone, and had been since *Medusa*'s launch returned me to the island shortly after eight that morning. Gareth had accompanied me to the head of the ship's ladder. 'You'll be going ashore, will you?' By that he had meant, of course, going across to Mahon. 'Give my love to Soo.' He smiled then, a funny, crooked little smile, and then he had said, 'Pray for me, both of you.' A perfunctory salute and he had turned on his heel and disappeared back up to the bridge.

It wasn't until after I had landed and the launch was on its way back to *Medusa* that the full import of what he had said began to sink in. By then I had discovered, not only that Petra's inflatable wasn't at the landing place, but there was also no sign of Lennie's semi-rigid diving boat. I was on my own and plenty of time to think about it. Also, I had no means of knowing what was going on ashore.

The odd thing was that everything seemed normal enough, the usual volume of traffic along the waterfront, so shops and businesses must be opening as usual. But on the water itself virtually nothing moved. As for the outside world, now that I was off the frigate all I had was Petra's little portable radio, and listening to the news bulletins I got the impression the media was deliberately playing down events in Mahon. The unilateral declaration of independence was referred to, but only briefly, and even the Overseas Service relegated it to a late spot in the World News. This could, of course, be the result of a local clampdown. It could equally be political pressure at home.

Sitting there in the sun, stripped to the waist as the day advanced, there was something quite uncanny about the brooding ruins of the hospital, the sense of isolation, and that lonely British warship riding there so peacefully to her reflection. She looked puny against the shimmering sprawl of La Mola and it was hard to realise that inside the battered plates of that grey hull the Communications Room must be humming with messages bounced off satellites as the well-known names of international politics, roused from their beds at an unaccustomed hour or called to their offices unexpectedly, endeavoured to grapple with the possible repercussions of Fuxá's seizure of power on a small island in the Western Mediterranean. Was Gareth right when he had said it was all because of this four and a half miles of deep, sheltered water that stretched away on either side of me?

Shortly after eleven a single mobile gun took up a position in the garden of a villa above Cala Llonga. Now, as I waited by the beacon beyond the dig, periodically checking my watch as the seconds ticked away to noon, I wondered whether it would actually open fire, whether there were other guns ranged on the frigate. La Mola had been very quiet since that early morning explosion.

Noon. And nothing happened. The sun blazed down, everything very still, the frigate's anchor chain hanging slack, the water flat like polished brass. Fearing the worst it was almost an anti-climax. Away to the south a plane rose from the airport. It looked like a military plane, but it flew west towards Ciudadela.

I stayed there, watching, and shortly after twelve-thirty a launch moved out from the commercial quay heading straight for Bloody Island. It was the same launch that had brought the new harbour master out to *Medusa*. I turned the glasses on to the naval quay. Still the same three ships there – a fast patrol boat, one of the big fishery protection launches and the old minesweeper that had escorted *Medusa* in. The launch came through the narrows, making for the frigate, and as it passed I could see a little group of three men in the stern of it. One was Romacho. He was now wearing an official cap and beside him was a man in uniform, an Army officer by the look of it. The third man was in civilian clothes and I wondered who it was. He had his back to me and it wasn't until he turned to speak to Romacho that I realised it was Fuxá himself.

So the RN presence was that important. The launch swung alongside the frigate's accommodation ladder where they were met by one of the officers, Mault I think, certainly not Gareth, and all three of them went on board.

I stayed there by the beacon, watching through the glasses, waiting to see what would happen now. They were on board exactly seventeen and a half minutes by my watch and it was Gareth himself who escorted Fuxá and his two companions to the head of the ladder, saluting perfunctorily, then turning away. The Army officer did not salute and there were no handshakes, the three of them hurrying down the ladder to the waiting launch without looking back.

I watched them all the time through the glasses, and all the way through the narrows they stood silent and grim-faced, none of them saying a word.

Nothing happened after the launch had returned to the inner harbour. Nobody else came out to the frigate, so I presumed the deadline had been extended. It was siesta time anyway. The day dragged on, no sign of Petra or Lennie, with the result that I was marooned in the midst of what now seemed something of a non-event, everything so quiet, so peaceful it was almost unbelievable, and only the absence of any movement in or out of the harbour to convince me of the reality of it.

I had time then to think about myself – my own

life and how sailing, and a fascination for the precision of target shooting, had given me the means to live by my wits in a world that seemed to be getting everlastingly richer as more and more successful businessmen decided to make the Mediterranean their playpen. It had seemed so easy. Exciting too. Then I had met Soo and the urge to build something solid, a business of my own, a family, had brought me here.

And now?

I went over it all in my mind, sitting in the blazing sun beside the half-cleared outline of that fallen taula – the night of that Red Cross barbecue in the Quarries, the cave and the loss of the child, the murder of Jorge Martinez, that big beautiful catamaran and the blind stupidity of my desire to own it.

And Soo. My mind kept coming back to Soo. The only sheet anchor I had ever had. And I had lost her. *Give my love to Soo*, he had said with that funny little smile. And he was there, on that frigate, and she could see the ship from her bedroom window. *Pray for me*, he had said.

Hell! It was I who needed praying for, sitting alone beside a religious monument fashioned by Bronze Age men some three thousand years ago, and wanted by the police.

Shortly after four, with Mahon active again after the three-hour break, a convoy of over half a dozen yachts left. There was activity in the port area now. But still no sign of either Petra or Lennie, and no means of crossing the water to Mahon. The narrows on the north side of Bloody Island are barely three hundred metres wide and I was greatly tempted to swim across, but it would undoubtedly be under observation, and apart from the Naval Base, I was certain the whole peninsula that formed the northern arm of the harbour was in the hands of the new regime. How much of Menorca they held, outside of the Mahon area, I had no means of knowing. Not all of it probably. Several times I thought I heard firing away to the south-west, in the direction of the airport. Then suddenly there was the sound of engines, a distant rumble from the far end of the port, by the new cargo quay.

It was the Libyan freighter getting under way, the harbour tug pulling her bows clear and swinging them round, so that they were pointed straight towards me. At the same time, the harbour master's launch left the Estación Maritima, accompanied by two other launches. I was standing by the red-flashing beacon again when they passed through the narrows, but I couldn't see who was on board the harbour launch. It was flanked by what looked like a harbour police launch and a customs launch. Only the harbour master's launch went alongside *Medusa*'s ladder, and though somebody attempted to go on board, his way was blocked by a burly petty officer standing immovably halfway up it.

The little tableau remained motionless for some time, the man on the grating gesticulating very energetically and an officer, Sykes probably, on the deck above. I watched them arguing through the glasses until my attention was distracted by the increasing rumble of ships' engines. The freighter, with the tug leading it, was approaching the narrows. It was low in the water, not yet unloaded, so it could hardly be intending to leave port. And behind me, just visible beyond the rocks above Petra's landing place, I could see the bows of the small oil tanker lying in Cala Figuera beginning to swing as she fetched her anchor.

The tug was through the narrows by then and headed direct for *Medusa*. The beat of the freighter's engines slowed as she passed so close to me I could see that the Arabic letters of her name had been painted over some earlier name, the outline of which suggested that she had originally been Greek, possibly Russian, for the faint lettering appeared to be Cyrillic. The rusty plates slid by, the bridge housing at the stern seeming to tower over me.

In the distance I could just hear the tug exchanging words with the harbour launch over loudhailers, and at the same time Gareth appeared on the frigate's bridge wing. He had his hand to his mouth, holding a mike I think, because even at that distance I could hear his voice quite clearly, it was so powerfully amplified. He spoke in English, very simply: *'I have to warn you that any ship coming within two hundred metres of my anchorage will be regarded as having committed a hostile act.'*

He turned then and I think he must have given an order, for as Lieutenant Sykes hurried to his side and began repeating what he had said in Spanish, the turret of the two 4.5-inch guns slowly swivelled, the barrels no longer aimed at the heights above Cala Llonga, but being lowered, slowly and menacingly, to point directly at the freighter.

It flashed through my mind then what a chance he was taking – or was he bluffing? For a British warship to open fire on the ship of a country we were not at war with, however unfriendly that country might be, and to do it while anchored in the harbour of a Nato ally . . . It didn't bear thinking about and I almost held my breath as I waited to see what the freighter would do, wondering whether Gareth was acting on his own initiative or whether he was covered by explicit orders. I hoped, for his sake, that it was the latter.

Everything now was in slow motion. The launch had pulled away from *Medusa*'s side to join the others, the three of them in a close huddle as though the vessels themselves were discussing the situation. The frigate's guns stayed implacably levelled at the approaching super-structure of the freighter, which was now barely moving. A sudden swirl of water at her stern and she was stationary, everything held motionless as in a still picture.

The sun had begun to set, a lovely golden glow lighting up the grey slab-plated side of the frigate. Time passed, nothing happening, but the tension seeming steadily to increase as the sunset glow deepened to red so that the villas above Cala Llonga and Cala Lladró were all aflame, the bare scrubland above taking fire.

The police launch was the first to break away, ploughing back through the narrows at full speed. At the same time the harbour launch went alongside the tug. It was there for several minutes, then it made across to the freighter, going alongside on the port hand where I couldn't see it. Meanwhile, the customs launch had passed astern of *Medusa* and disappeared in the direction of Cala Llonga, or perhaps further along the peninsula, by Lazareto Island. I couldn't follow its movements because it was hidden from me by the frigate.

By now lights had begun to appear along the Mahon waterfront and in the town above. The clouds had thickened, darkness closing in early. I could still just see the harbour launch. It paused briefly to turn and run parallel with the tanker, which was already approaching the narrows. Then, when it had resumed course for the Estación Maritima, the tanker changed direction to pass out of my sight to the south of Bloody Island. At that moment *Medusa* leapt suddenly into fairy-like outline, her deck, upperworks and mast all picked out by strings of light bulbs – Gareth Lloyd Jones cocking a snook at the waiting ships and the shore. It was as if he was saying, 'Here I am, still anchored here and my guns ready. What are you going to do about it?'

After that I didn't stay much longer by the beacon. There was no point. It was already too dark to see what was going on ashore. The tug and the freighter had been joined by the tanker, all three of them anchored astern of the frigate and well beyond the two-hundred-metre protection zone Gareth had declared for himself. Stiff and tired, I went back to the camp, where I lit the pressure lamp, raided Petra's drink cupboard for a glass of brandy, and got the paraffin stove going to heat up one of her packets of instant food.

The sound of an engine sent me tumbling back to my lookout point by the red-flashing beacon. It was the harbour launch, back again, and I watched as the dim shape of it passed through the narrows, making straight for *Medusa*. The frigate had swung with the slight movement of the tide, so that through the glasses I had an even clearer view of the launch as it went alongside the ladder. One man only got off and was escorted to the bridge. It wasn't Romacho, and it certainly wasn't Fuxá. This was a much taller man wearing a seaman's cap and dark jersey.

A stone clinked behind me and I swung round as a voice spoke out of the darkness – 'Your grub's boiling over, mate.'

It was Lennie. He had rowed across in a borrowed dinghy from the little gut in the cliffs below Villa Carlos known as Cala Corb. 'I turned the stove off. Better eat it now, then if you want to go ashore I'll take yer.' He was staggering off towards the dark bulk of the hospital ruins. 'They've kicked most of the prisoners out of the jail and locked up half a dozen senior officers of the *Guardia* and the national police instead, including your friends Menendez and Molina. You'll be safe enough.' His voice was slurred and he moved with care for he had spent most of the day in the waterfront café-bars. No, he didn't know where Petra was, and he hadn't been near the chandlery nor seen anything of Soo. 'Wouldn't go near 'er, mate. I told

yer. She fired me. Just like that. She can go to hell.'
He was very drunk, holding himself stiff and erect.

His news, gathered at second hand in the waterfront café-bars, was that as yet the new regime controlled barely half the island. But they had the key
points – La Mola and Punta de Santo Carlos to the
south of the Mahon entrance, both airports, the radio
and radar station on El Toro, also the town of Alayór.
But in the country south and west of Alayór there
were rumours of fighting between local factions. 'They
say the Russians are coming.' But he admitted that
was just bar talk. 'They're full of talk over in the port,
wild talk.'

He waved away my suggestion that he joined me
and get some food into himself. 'Don't wan'
food – 'nuther drink.' He had found the cupboard with
the Soberano in it. 'Their own bloody fault, yer know.
Didn't think it through.'

'How do you mean?'

But his mind had switched to something else. 'Pinched my boat.' He slopped the brandy into the glass,
the bottle clinking on the rim, then slumped into a
chair. 'Left it at the Club pontoon, only gone an hour
– well, mebbe two. Bloody bastards!' His eyes focused
on me with difficulty. 'What was that you asked? Oh
yes. Didn't cotton on, the fools – all that bombing.
Two nights ago. An' next day, orders of the Military
Governor over in Palma they say, all them raw young
conscripts spread around the island to protect the
urbanizacións and foreign property. Clever! Did the
job, yer see. One night's bombing and it got them La

Mola. Hardly any military left in the barracks there.'
And he added after a moment's thought, 'But there's
talk of some regulars over at Ciudadela that could act
as a rally – a rallying point. Talk, talk, talk . . . In one
bar – yer know, the one by the commercial quay –
there was a trucker came in said he'd seen military
vehicles moving towards Alayór, told us Fuxá wouldn't
be able to hold the airport for long. Then some silly
bastard starts talking about the Russians. Snow on
their boots!' He snickered. 'That was a long time ago.'
His voice trailed away, the hiss of the pressure lamp
making him sleepy. 'Didn't think it through,' he said
again. 'All part of the plan an' they fell for it. Clever!'
His head was lolling. 'An' now that Navy ship, boxed
in with a Libby bloody freighter sitting on 'er tail.'

He didn't seem to have anything more to tell me,
so I asked him why he had slipped away from the petty
officers' mess that morning. 'You left me stranded.'

He nodded, mumbling something about, 'It's all
right for you'.

'You should have checked the chandlery, had a
word with my wife and made certain Petra was all
right.' His head was sinking into his arms. I reached
out across the table and shook him. 'It wasn't the
Australian Navy you deserted from, was it? It was
the Royal Navy.'

'Wot if it was?'

'And that's why you got pissed.'

'Well, wouldn't you, mate?' There was a note of
belligerence in his voice now. 'I do'n want ter think

back to them days. And those petty officers – Chris'-sakes! They could've picked me up jus' like that.'

I told him he was a bloody fool. All those years ago . . . But he was fast asleep, his head fallen sideways on to his arm. I finished my meal, then put what clothes I had on, turned the pressure lamp off and went down to the landing point. It was a plastic dinghy, and though he had been drunk, he had still hauled it out on to the rocks, stowed the oars neatly and made fast the painter.

The water looked inky black as I floated it off and stepped in, Mahon a blaze of light as though nothing had happened and it was just a normal evening. Fortu-nately there was no wind, for the boat was no better than a plastic skimming dish. Clear of Bloody Island the brightly lit shape of the frigate blazed like a jewel, the tug and the freighter in black silhouette, the tanker barely visible and no sign of the launches. I made straight for Cala Figuera and our own quay. My car was there, but nothing else, no sign of Petra's Beetle. No lights on in the windows of the house either and when I crossed the road I found the door to the chandlery standing half-open.

I think I knew by then there was nobody there. I called, but there was no answer, the only sound a sort of scratching as though a net curtain was flapping in the breeze from an open window. It came from above and as I climbed the stairs I had an unpleasant feeling there was something in the house, something alive.

I reached the landing and stopped. The scratching sound came from the bedroom, and suddenly I knew.

The dog! 'All right, Benjie.' The poor little beast couldn't bark and as I pushed open the door I could smell it, a mixture of urine and excreta. He flung himself at me, making that extraordinary singing noise in the head. I switched on the light. He was shivering uncontrollably. Apart from the messes and the smell, the bedroom looked much as usual. I got a bowl of water from the kitchen and he drank it straight off, lapping with desperate urgency. Clearly he had been shut in that room for some considerable time and Soo would never have done that. She doted on the animal.

I went through into the front room then, and as soon as I switched on the light my heart sank – a chair tipped over, Soo's typewriter on the floor, its cable ripped out as though somebody had tripped over it, a jug of flowers lying in a litter of papers, a damp patch on the Bokhara rug and an occasional table on its side with one leg smashed. There had been a struggle and I stood, staring helplessly at the evidence of it, asking myself why – why for God's sake should anybody want to attack Soo, and what had they done with her?

Anger, a feeling of desperation, of inadequacy almost, came over me, not knowing where she was or what to do. I got some food for the dog. He was hungry as well as thirsty. The fact that he hadn't been able to contain himself might be partly nerves, but clearly he'd been shut up for some time, so whatever had happened to Soo had happened quite a few hours back. I cleared up the mess in the bedroom, moving about in a daze, wondering all the time where she was, what had happened. I found myself back in the front room, in the office, staring out at the dark glimmer of the water. The dog was pawing at my trousers.

I took it down the stairs and out into the road, where it did what it had to while I stared across the water to the lit outline of the frigate. A bell sounded above the cliffs in Villa Carlos. I glanced at my watch, scooped up the dog and ran back up the stairs. The news was already being read as I switched on the radio, the announcer in the middle of saying that the self-styled President of Menorca had called upon Moscow to recognise the new island republic and provide immediate assistance in dealing with dissident elements endeavouring to impose what was described as 'a reactionary fascist regime centred on the old capital, Ciudadela'.

I switched to the World Service where it was now the lead story, the announcer listing a whole series of countries who had been asked to recognise the island republic. So far only Libya and Albania had complied. Madrid had still not taken any positive action, but there was clearly intense activity on the political front. The Spanish ambassador had been to the Kremlin and it was reported that the Government had called upon all EEC countries to assist in maintaining Spanish sovereignty over the Balearic Islands. More practically, Spanish Navy ships in Barcelona had been put on alert and parachutists were standing by.

But, listening to that news, it was clear everybody was waiting upon Moscow, and Moscow was saying nothing, for the moment. Towards the end there was a reference to a British frigate being on a courtesy visit to the island, and the Foreign Secretary, in answer to a question in the House, had made a statement to the effect that if the ship was molested in any way the Captain would be fully entitled to take any action he felt appropriate. In other words, the responsibility for anything which might happen was Gareth's. No wonder the poor devil had asked us to pray for him!

Comments followed from BBC reporters in various capitals, but by then I was on the phone, enquiring about Soo. The Renatos first, but they were out and the others I contacted knew nothing. In desperation I tried the hospital, but the line was either engaged or out of order. I went down the stairs again. The store was locked and no sign of Ramón. But he had been there that morning for he had signed out paint, varnish and anti-fouling to Rodriguez who was the only one left working on the boats. Life went on, it seemed.

I returned to the office, put the typewriter back on the desk and sat there staring out of the window to the lit frigate, wondering what the hell had happened here, where they had taken her, and why – why, for God's sake? Until I knew that . . . A door slammed, feet on the stairs, and before she burst in I knew who it was. 'Thank God you're here,' she cried. 'I've been searching everywhere. Have you found her?'

'No. When did you discover she had gone?'

'This afternoon. Some time around four.' And she added, speaking breathlessly, 'Soo was all right this morning. We had breakfast together.' She had come straight here, she said, after leaving Lennie and myself at the pontoon and had phoned, first the Military HQ, then the Naval Base. 'I don't think it did any good. It took so long to get hold of anybody in authority.' She sank into the armchair by the window. 'God! I'm tired now. What do you think happened? The typewriter was on the floor, that chair broken, everything a mess. She'd put up a fight before they could drag her away. Who were they? Have you any idea?' Her eyes bulged as she stared at me. 'No, of course you haven't.'

'Did you go into the bedroom?' I asked.

'Yes, of course. I searched the whole house.'

'You didn't see the dog?'

'No.'

So the poor little beast had been so scared at what had happened it must have hidden itself under the bed. 'And there was no mess?' She shook her head. 'Then it looks as though they came for her late morning, around lunchtime.'

'Yes, but who?' She was slumped there, staring miserably at the water below, her big capable hands folded in her lap. One of the side zippers of her jeans had slipped to show a little bulge of brown flesh. She was as swarthy as an Indian. 'The police or these new people? Do they know you're back, here in Mahon? There must be a reason. There's always a reason.'

'We'll know in due course.' A note of resignation had crept into my voice.

'I'll make some tea.' She bounced to her feet, her face suddenly alive again, the relief of something positive revitalising her. 'Or would you prefer a drink?'

'No,' I said. 'Tea will do fine.' I didn't care what I had.

When she came back I was still sitting there. 'Noon,' I said.

'You think that's when it happened?' She poured a cup and passed it to me.

'No, he was given till noon.' I told her about the new harbour master, his visit to *Medusa* and how, after the deadline was up, Fuxá himself had gone out to see Gareth. 'But he hasn't moved. He's still there and lit up like a Christmas tree.'

'What are those ships doing there?' She had poured herself a cup and was sitting down again, lying half back in the chair.

'Waiting to tow him out,' I said.

'Well, why don't they?' She was staring out of the window towards the fairy outline of the frigate bright against the dark bulk of the peninsula behind. 'Oh, I see. They're anchored.' She turned and looked at me. 'Why?'

'Because he's threatened to blow them out of the water if they come any nearer.' And as I told her what I thought the purpose of his presence here in Mahon was I could see the same thought was in both our minds.

'What are you suggesting? That they've taken Soo because ... Oh no, surely not. How would they know?' She was leaning forward now, staring at me, her eyes wide and appalled. We both knew what she meant.

'There was gossip,' I said. 'There must have been gossip.'

'Oh yes, there was plenty of that – after she lost

the baby. In a place like this, a tight little circle, tongues wag all the time. Gareth here, a British naval officer – they would have had their eyes on him anyway, but after what happened . . . And there was you and me. Our friends made a meal of it.' And she added, frowning, 'But are you really suggesting Soo could be used as a hostage in that way, to force Gareth to take his ship out of Mahon?'

'I don't know. They might think it a possibility.' I shook my head, the warmth of the tea comforting. 'Anyway, it's the only motive that occurs to me.'

'So who do we contact?'

There was only one person I could think of. 'Evans.' But how to reach him? 'Where's Fuxá established himself, do you know?'

'Esmerelda said he'd taken over the Military Government Headquarters block on Isabel II.'

'That makes sense. I'll phone there.' I drank the rest of my tea and was just getting to my feet when Petra leaned forward, peering intently through the window.

'Wait a minute. There's a boat coming in.'

As it came alongside our quay I saw it was *Medusa*'s launch. A young midshipman jumped ashore. It was a boy named Masterton. He glanced quickly left and right as though to make certain he wasn't going to be challenged, then scuttled quickly across the road. The bell sounded and I went down. 'Good evening, sir. Captain's compliments and would you be good enough to join him on board. He says it's important.' And he handed me a note.

It was very short and had clearly been dashed off in a hurry: *I am sending the launch for you. Something has occurred that you should know about. It concerns Soo. Hurry, it's urgent. Gareth.*

Petra was at my elbow and I passed it on to her. 'It's what we feared.' I grabbed my anorak. 'Look after the dog, will you? Take it round to the restaurant if you're not spending the night here. They look after it sometimes.' I found a key for her, checked that I had my own, and then I was across the road and into the launch. 'Is there somebody with the Captain?' I asked the youngster as we swung away from the quay and headed for the lit outline of the frigate.

'Not at the moment, sir. But I think he's expecting someone.'

'Who? Do you know?'

But he couldn't tell me that. 'There's been quite a bit of coming and going. First of all it was the President's personal aide in a speedboat out of Cala Llonga, then it was the President himself. That was just after midday.' There had apparently been other visitors, but they had come out from Cala Llonga, which was why I had not seen them. None of them, except Fuxá, had been allowed on board. 'The Captain says that's because we don't recognise the new government here.'

'What about the three launches that came out from Port Mahon just as it was getting dark?' I asked him. 'One man was allowed on board. Do you know who he was?'

'No, sir. A seaman of some sort.'

'Is he still there?'

'No. He went off towards Cala Llonga in the harbour launch. I heard him say he was going to fetch somebody. The other boats have gone, but we've still got three ships anchored near. They wanted to tow us out, but our Captain wasn't having that.' And he added, 'What's it like ashore, sir? It all looks very normal from where we're anchored, though we can hear firing sometimes away to the south, towards the airport.'

Excited to be caught up in an event that was world news, he chatted on like that all the way out to the green-flashing beacon on the south side of Bloody Island. It slid past us very close, the bulk of the hospital a solid backdrop, the tower outlined against the stars, and I was wondering what Gareth intended to do, how I could persuade him that Soo's life was more important than his career. I was leaning against the canopy, the beat of the engine pulsing through my body and the launch already swinging in a wide arc to come alongside, the lit outline of the frigate growing larger.

There was no other reason that I could see for what had happened. If somebody had told them the commander of the British frigate was in love with my wife . . . But did they really believe the man would take his ship to sea without specific orders? Thinking it over, it seemed barely possible, but then men who live by violence often find it difficult to accept that others are governed by a code of social behaviour and operate within the framework of a disciplined order. I had seen something of that myself. The idea that every man has his price is mirrored in the belief that violence is totally effective in changing people's minds. Why else use torture?

It was that thought that was in my mind as we slid alongside the frigate's accommodation ladder and I stepped out on to the wooden grating. The sudden rush to leave Malta, the way Gareth had dropped his anchor in about the most conspicuous position in the whole long inlet, the blazing lights above my head – the ship was there for a purpose, and that purpose could only be to act as a block to any power thinking of supporting a rebel regime unopposed. If I was right, then Soo's life was of total unimportance as compared with the job Lieutenant Commander Lloyd Jones RN had been sent here to do. Her death, even her torture, could make no difference, and knowing that, I felt sick with fear as I climbed the gangway.

I was met at the top by one of the officers, I can't remember who. He took me to the Captain's day cabin where we had breakfasted – was it only that morning? I barely heard him tell me the Captain would be with me shortly as I tried to marshal my arguments, my mind perversely concentrated on all the forms of torture I had heard and read about, a picture there as vivid as the day I had seen it – on a beach in Mali, a palm-frond hut, and lying there in his own excreta with the flies crawling, the only man I have ever seen tortured to death. His face – I could see his face still, the lips chewed to ribbons, the teeth protruding white and the eyes starting from his head. And then I was thinking of Soo as I had last seen her, laughing as she had left me on the quay at Addaia.

I went over to the settee and sat down, suddenly tired, the two images merging, so that in my mind's eye I saw them as one, the Arab's tortured features superimposed on Soo's. I don't remember how long I sat there, numbed at the vision of what might happen to her if Gareth didn't take his ship out of Mahon. This wasn't just a matter of Ismail Fuxá and his personal ambitions. It was bigger than that, much bigger, Fuxá just a pawn in a game being played far away from Menorca behind closed doors. Political figures with hot lines and satellites at their disposal. A young woman, held as a hostage – that was nothing. A unit of flesh. Disposable. Just as this ship was disposable, the men I had lived with on the hurried run from Malta . . .

'Glad we were able to contact you.' His voice was flat. It seemed tired, and he didn't smile as he crossed the cabin, pulled up a chair and sat down facing me. 'I don't know how long we've got. Not long.' He sounded resigned, his face grey as though he hadn't slept for a long time. I thought he had aged since I had seen him that morning, the broad forehead puckered deeper, the lines at the corners of eyes and mouth more pronounced, and he just sat there staring at me dumbly.

'Where is she?' I asked.

He gave a little shrug. But he didn't say anything. It was as though he didn't know how to begin.

'They've contacted you, have they?'

He nodded.

'So where is she? Where is she being held?'

'Then you know.' He seemed relieved, the knowledge that he hadn't got to break the news to me releasing his tongue. 'I sent across to Bloody Island for you as soon as it was dark, but you weren't there. Then we saw lights in your place at Cala Figuera, so I took a chance and sent young Leslie Masterton in to see if you were there. I'm glad you were.' His eyes were fixed on me. 'What happened? Do you know?'

I told him briefly of the scene that had greeted me, and then, unable to restrain myself, I burst out, 'It wouldn't have happened if you hadn't pushed your way into our lives. It's your bloody fault. All your fault.' And seeing that image again in my mind's eye, I leaned forward and grabbed hold of him. 'Who was it came for her? Who were they that grabbed her so brutally? Benjie – that little dog of ours – was shit scared. He's always so clean, and a brave little beast normally. Those bastards must have been rough with her.'

'All right, all right.' He was holding up his hand, pleading with me. 'You've told me how they took her, and you're right, it's because of me. I'm sorry. It's my fault.' And then, his voice suddenly stronger, 'But it's happened. You have to accept that. We both do.' His tone took on a note of authority. 'The question now is how we handle the situation. They started piling on the pressure for me to take the ship out shortly after two o'clock local time, an emissary from some sort of military commander. He came out in a speedboat from

Cala Llonga. I wouldn't allow him on board, of course, and I told him my position was unchanged – I could only put to sea when I had orders to do so. The same thing I had told that man Fuxá. Until then I would remain here. He came out once more, threatening to open fire on me, and I warned him that if he did so I had the authority of the British Government to take what action I considered necessary to defend my ship. In short, I asked him to tell his general not to be a bloody fool and push me that hard.'

'Soo,' I said. 'What about Soo?' My voice was too high and I tried to get a grip on myself. 'All you've talked about so far is your problem. I'm not interested. It's my wife I'm concerned about.'

'Do you think I'm not concerned? What the hell do you take me for?' He straightened his shoulders, his hands clasped tightly. 'I'm sorry.' The anger was gone from his voice. 'My problems are my own. I agree. But they do concern you.'

'No, you,' I said. 'Not me. My concern—'

He suddenly banged the coffee table between us. 'Will you listen for God's sake. I've told you. We haven't much time. And my position, as Captain of one of HM ships, is very relevant to what has happened to Soo. I have my orders, and the fact that she's a hostage—' He was interrupted by a knock and his eyes flicked to the doorway. 'Come in, Leading Seaman Stanway.' He was always very punctilious about rank and I had to sit silent while he went through a whole sheaf of messages.

'We may be an old ship,' he said, as he dismissed

the young seaman, 'but they've fitted us out with a pretty sophisticated communications set-up so I'm getting a steady stream of messages, news briefs, and of course we're picking up secret naval information and orders. Besides Victor Sykes, who is not only fluent in Spanish, but also speaks French, German and Italian, I have a man on loan from one of the oil companies who speaks a number of the Arab languages, also a PO who has recently completed a Russian language course.' He was still looking down at the messages in his hand. 'That Russian cruiser was sighted visually just south of Spartivento at 16.03. She was steaming at thirty knots plus. The course and speed of the other ships I mentioned suggest that they will rendezvous with her fourteen miles east of La Mola shortly after midnight. So it's like I said, we haven't much time.'

'Time for what?' I was losing patience with him. 'It's Soo I'm worried about. I want to know where she is, whether she's all right, and I want her back – safe.'

He didn't say anything, his hands clasped tight on the wadge of papers, his shoulders stooping forward. God! he looked tired, as though the weight of the world was on his shoulders and it was too much for him. 'There's a signal here says a D-20 class destroyer, two frigates and some fast attack craft have just left Barcelona. They'll be joined by a couple of subs.' Even his voice sounded tired. 'There's some French warships about to sail from Toulon. They're too far away, of course, and they're not members of Nato. The Italians are even further. The earliest any of those ships can be off the entrance here is 03.00. That'll be at least two hours too late.'

'Why are you telling me this?' But I knew why. I had been right about his role. 'You're going to stay here. Is that what you're saying?'

He shrugged, an almost Gallic gesture, the palms of his hands spread.

Silence then, both of us thinking our own thoughts. He got slowly to his feet and began pacing up and down. Could I still persuade him? 'If you could pretend to leave. A gesture. Enough at least to get them to return her . . .'

He turned on me then, his voice rising on a note of anger as he said, 'Don't be a fool, man. You're not dealing with amateurs.' And he added, 'You don't know Pat. I do. He's cold-blooded, ruthless. That's his nature, and all his adult life he's lived in the cold-blooded, ruthless world of violence and terrorism.'

'But he let you go,' I said. 'That's what you told me, sitting right here at your desk. You said he dropped you overboard up-tide of the buoy, so you'd drift down on it. And you promised you wouldn't tell anyone who he was.'

He nodded, standing in the centre of the cabin, a silhouette against the light, so that I couldn't see the expression on his face. 'Yes.' His voice was toneless. 'He gave me my life, and I made a promise.'

'Why? The blood tie? The fact that you share the same father. Is that why he saved your life?'

'No.' And after a moment he went on slowly, 'No, I don't think it was that, more a matter of putting me in his debt. I've never been a part of Pat's world, so I can't be sure, but I have an idea that, besides the ruthlessness, there's a primitive sense of loyalty. You do somebody a good turn, then you're in credit with him and some day you can make a claim on him.' He glanced at his watch. 'I'll find out about that soon enough. Won't be long now.'

'You're expecting him?'

'Yes.'

'So what are you going to do?'

He sat down opposite me again and I thought for a moment he had reached a decision. But all he said was, 'Have you any idea of the average age of this ship's company?' He was interrupted again. More messages. He flicked through them, nodded briefly to Stanway, turning back to me and saying, 'Well, have you? The average age.' He slapped his hand on the table. 'You won't believe this, but it's not quite twenty-three and a half. That's the *average* age of everybody, officers, senior rates, the lot. They're kids, most of them, with mothers and fathers, girlfriends, quite a few of them married, and I'm responsible. Not just for them, for their lives, but to all those people I've never met.'

'All right,' I said. 'So what *are* you going to do?'

'What can I do?' He got suddenly to his feet. 'You don't seem to realise – this potty little island is the centre of the world. Just for the moment. For the next few hours.' He started to pace up and down. 'There are warships converging on it, the whole apparatus of military confrontation beginning to be put in motion.

The heads of half a dozen of the world's most powerful countries will be consulting their advisers, despatching envoys with cautionary notes, even talking to each other direct, and all because of a little jumped-up peasant farmer called Ismail Fuxá, a bunch of disaffected locals and a couple of hundred highly trained professional soldiers, commandos probably, and almost certainly from an Arab country. In these circumstances, speed and ruthlessness, a willingness to take chances – hit the other fellow before he knows what's happening. God! I've had plenty of instruction on this. If you strike fast enough and hard enough you can change the face of the world. And you're asking me . . .'

The loudspeaker interrupted him. 'There's a boat coming out from Cala Llonga, sir. The speedboat again, I think.'

He picked up the mike. 'Very well. It should be a man named Evans. Have him met at the ladder and if it is bring him straight to my cabin.'

'Very good, sir.'

He turned back to me. 'You're worried about your wife, and so am I. But just try to get this clear in your mind – you, me, Soo, all the boys on this ship, we're just pawns in a game that is being played on a world board.' He turned away, staring out to the lights of the waterfront. 'It will all depend now on whether I can persuade Pat.' He gave a little shrug. 'Frankly I doubt it. This must surely be the biggest thing he's ever been involved in.' He looked at his watch. 'Cape Spartivento is about two-forty miles from here – eight hours' steaming, something like that, and it's nearly nine already. Five hours gone. By midnight a whole fleet of ships could be gathering off the entrance here. An hour after that they could be steaming in past Villa Carlos, and if they were able to do that unopposed . . . Then it would be a case of possession being nine-tenths of the law. International law, that is, and Fuxá has appealed to Moscow for help. Belatedly Spain has called upon her EEC partners to assist in maintaining her sovereignty here.'

He was running over it again for his own benefit, not mine. 'And on our side – ' He was at the port hole. '*Mahonnaise!* That's what Richelieu's chef called his version of the local *allioli*. You know what that was for?' He was talking for the sake of talking. 'For the banquet. The French were holding a banquet here at Mahon after their victory over Byng. We'd held the islands for almost fifty years, from 1708 till 1756. *Mahonnaise!*' he said again. 'Poor Byng!' His voice had dropped to a whisper. 'We were here for another nineteen years, from 1763, and then yet again for four very important years during the Napoleonic Wars. That was when Nelson was supposed to have stayed up there at Golden Farm.'

He turned back to me, smiling sardonically. 'You see, I've been well briefed on the naval background. Grand Harbour, Mahon, Gibraltar, a string of naval strongholds stretching across the Western Mediterranean. We've held them all, and I wouldn't be surprised if there aren't quite a number of people back home, people who are in a position to influence events, who still hanker after them. So you see – ' He hesitated. 'What I'm trying to make you understand, Mike, is that we're all just pawns – all of us who are here on the spot where it's happening. Pat included. I don't know what he gets out of it, but there's nothing you or I could offer him – ' He swung round at the sound of the loudspeaker again. 'Yes?'

'It *is* Mr Evans, sir. I'll send him up, shall I?'

'Is he on his own?' Gareth's voice sounded suddenly nervous.

'There's three of them altogether, but he's the only one who's come aboard and he's asking to see you personally.'

'Then have him sent up right away.'

'Very good, sir.'

The loudspeaker clicked off, Gareth standing by his desk fiddling with a ruler. Was he scared of the man? The spate of words he had been pouring out to me was in itself a sign of nerves. 'Better let me do the talking.' He was on edge and I wondered how much of a hold this half-brother of his had on him. The years of *Ganges*, then on that houseboat in the mud gut at Felixstowe Ferry. And Evans – he must be very sure of himself, to come on board this ship.

The knock came sooner than I had expected. Gareth sat himself down abruptly at his desk. 'Come in.'

It was Davison. 'Mr Evans, sir.'

'Show him in. Then draw the curtain and wait outside.'

He seemed taller, the face more craggy, and the

neck solid as a stone column. He wore no hat, his dark hair rumpled, and his shirt and the camouflage jacket were open at the neck. He was smiling, but no warmth in it, just an indication that he was prepared to be reasonable – or was he nervous, too, was there a certain insecurity under that tough exterior?

'Come in, Pat.' Gareth had risen to his feet. 'Sit down.' He waved him to a chair. 'Mike Steele you know.'

'Yeah, we've met before.' He sat down, smiling at me, his voice low key. 'How's the boat behaving?' But he didn't expect an answer for he turned to Gareth, the smile gone from his face. 'Well, when do you leave?' And he added, 'It better be soon. Very soon.'

Gareth sat down opposite him. 'Didn't they tell you about the engines?'

'Don't give me that crap.'

'We have condenser trouble.'

'I said, don't give me that crap.' The voice had hardened. 'The oldest gimmick there is – can't move because the engines don't work.' He laughed, his voice a sneering mockery. 'Considering why you're here, it's hardly likely their fucking Lordships would have let you to sea with engines that were on the blink. So you get your fancy marine engineer on the blower and tell him to start up.'

'Unfortunately, you're wrong about the engines.' The trembling of his lower lip somehow made the statement unconvincing. 'You should know how mean things can be in the Royal Navy. This is an old ship and she was fitted out in a hurry.'

'So that you, and the rest of them on board, could be blown to hell. You always were a soft option, boy. You sit here for another two or three hours . . . Look, the bastards who give the orders, they aren't going to be here to hold your hand when Fuxá gets the support he's asked for and all hell breaks loose.' He leaned suddenly forward, his voice softer, more urgent. 'Don't be a sucker. You're expendable, the whole lot of you. Nobody cares about you. So be sensible. And if you want to stick to that fiction about the engines, then there's a tug and two other ships waiting out there to give you a tow.'

'If I go at all I'll go under my own steam. Not under tow. And what I do depends on my orders.'

There was a long silence after that, the two of them staring at each other, and in that silence I heard my own voice, sounding like a stranger, as I said, 'And what about my wife?'

There was no answer, both of them apparently locked in their own thoughts.

'Where is she?'

Evans turned slowly and looked at me. 'Not far away.' He said it so reasonably, as though kidnapping a woman was the most ordinary thing in the world. 'I'll come to her in a moment.' He glanced at his watch. 'It's nine forty-seven. I'll give you until ten p.m. to sort your engines out and get under way. Fifteen minutes. Okay?' He had risen to his feet.

'And if I don't?' Gareth hadn't moved from his chair and the silence stretched between them as they stared at each other like a pair of gladiators.

'It's been a long time,' Evans said. 'Must be four years now.'

'Just on five.'

'Yeah. Well, you would remember, wouldn't you. Moira wrote me you'd been picked up. Sent me a copy of the *East Anglian* with a picture of you tied to the buoy.' His mouth stretched to something close to a grin, the teeth bared. 'And now they've landed you with something that looks to me like a bloody suicide mission.' He leaned forward again. 'Look, boy, you owe it to yourself, to the men you've got cooped up in this tin can they've given you – get out now, before it's too late.'

Gareth stared at him as though hypnotised.

'Well, say something, for Christ's sake. What's it to be? Stay here and get pulverised to nothing, or up your hook and get to hell out before it's too late?'

A funny little half-smile showed on Gareth's face. He shook his head. 'Come off it, Pat. You're not here just to try and save my life again. You're here because you know damn well the presence of one of HM ships in Mahon harbour makes the whole thing impossible. Your plan of operations depends on two things for success – surprise and unimpeded access to the harbour here. The first you've achieved. In fact, your people exploited the element of surprise so well that you were able to seize control of all the key positions at this end of the island. What you didn't expect was that there would be a Nato warship anchored in Port Mahon. Your coup now needs the backing of a major power and I doubt very much whether you'll get it as long as this tin can, as you call it, remains anchored here. At least that's my reading of all the flurry of signals my Communications Office is picking up.'

His voice had become stronger, more authoritative as he developed his argument. Now he leaned forward, both elbows on the desk, his eyes fixed on his half-brother. 'My advice to you – it's the same advice as you've just been giving me – get out now, while you can.' Abruptly his right hand came up, jabbing a finger. 'Time is against you, man. You know it. I know it.'

'You'll be smashed to hell, boy.'

'Maybe. But I don't think so.' Somehow his voice managed to carry conviction. 'By dawn you'll be faced with crack Spanish troops and the arrival of the first of their naval units.'

'And how will they get into Mahon? We'll blast them out of the water with those big guns on La Mola. As for troops – what troops? They can't land . . .'

'Paratroops,' Gareth said quietly. 'I've just heard they'll be taking off about an hour before dawn.'

'Thank you. I'll pass the information on. But I think Madrid may have second thoughts. Landing paratroops anywhere on Menorca would amount to invasion of the new republic's territory, and with the powerful support we shall then have—'

'That's provided you can get *Medusa* out of the way,' Gareth cut in. 'That's why you're here, isn't it?' And he repeated his previous argument: 'Because you know damn well that support won't be forthcoming so long as there's a Nato presence in Port Mahon.'

'So you won't listen to reason.' The line of the

man's mouth had hardened, so had his voice. There was anger in it now as he said, 'Then I'll have to use another form of persuasion. The woman. We're holding her hostage for your departure.' He turned to me. 'Your wife, Steele. You haven't said much so far, but I'm telling you now, if you don't want her death on your hands, you'd better start persuading young Gareth here to get the hell out of Mahon.'

'Where is she?' I asked.

'I told you, not far from here.'

'Was it you who broke into the house and took her?'

He shook his head. 'Not me. Two of my crew. You met them the day you agreed to swap *Thunderflash* for that fishing boat of yours. They say she fought like an alley cat.'

'Is she all right? Is she hurt?'

'They had to tie her down, that's all.' He was looking straight at me. 'No, she's not hurt. Not yet.' He turned back again to Gareth and added, 'But she will be if you don't get out of here fast.'

'I have my orders.'

'Then get some new ones. Tell them there's a woman hostage and you're in love with her. You *are* in love with her, aren't you?' Gareth's eyes flicked in my direction and he passed his tongue over his lips. Evans was grinning, knowing now that his information was correct. 'You can have her back the instant you're clear of Port Mahon. I'll hand her over to Steele here. That suit you?'

Gareth half shook his head, his hands locked, the

fingers moving. I thought I detected a new mood, one of indecision. Evans saw it, too, and it was then that I heard him say, 'Look, Gareth, the people I'm with aren't squeamish, you know. Nor am I. But *they're* real hard. You know what I mean?'

Gareth half shook his head again, his eyes slitted as though wincing in advance of what he seemed to know was coming.

'Good. I think you do.' Evans swung round on me. 'But for your benefit I'll spell it out. If your wife's lover –' the words were spoken quite viciously, so that it was obvious he got a vicarious pleasure out of his shock use of them – 'doesn't shift his ship out of here within quarter of an hour, you could be getting her back in bits and pieces. Okay?' He got to his feet.

I had an instant ghastly picture in my mind of Soo laid out on a wooden slab while a man stood over her with an axe, her arms stretched out and pinioned ready for the blow. I felt sickened, and glancing across at Gareth I saw his face was ashen. What must have been going on in his mind at that moment I cannot think, Soo's life balanced against those years of being trained to carry out the orders of his naval superiors, and all the time the knowledge that forces beyond his control were moving inexorably to a point of crisis. And if he gave in to Evans's demands I had the feeling he would be doing so on the basis that, whatever he did, he and his men were doomed to extinction.

Evans glanced at the clock on the wall, then at his watch. 'Okay, so you're on local time. It's now 21.53. If you're not fetching your anchor by 22.10—'

'I can't do it. Not to an exact deadline.' Once again he was arguing that the state of the ship's engines made an immediate move impossible. I don't know when he decided to do what he finally did, but it must have been at about this point, and he must have been something of a natural actor – maybe that was the Celt in him – but he did manage eventually to convince Evans there was a problem with the engines. I think what finally did it was an open discussion over the telephone with Robin Makewate, his Marine Engineer Officer, which ended with him saying, 'Half an hour then. I'll have them standing by the anchor at 22.15. I want power on that one engine by 22.15 at the latest. Without fail, Robin . . . Yes, that's an order. Do it how you like, but get one of them going by then or we're in trouble.'

He put the phone down and turned to Evans. 'That's the best I can do. I presume you didn't come on board without making some provision against my detaining you here?'

'Correct. VHF contact.' He patted the sagging pocket of his camouflage jacket. 'If I don't report in on the hour . . .' He gave a little shrug. 'But don't worry, I'll be on to them in a minute. Meantime, you want to know how we hand the woman back. Since you've got Steele here, and she's his wife, it better be to him.'

They discussed it between themselves, no reference to me and Soo treated as though she was some sort of parcel that was proving difficult to deliver. In the end it was agreed that Evans and I should be landed on

Bloody Island to await the frigate's departure. As soon
as it was out past the island of Lazareto, Evans would
radio his base contact and Soo would be delivered to
me in exchange for Evans. 'I'll have the Sergeant of
Marines issue you with a gun,' Gareth said to me.
'You'll have to sign for it, of course, and somehow it
will have to be returned.' He turned back to Evans. 'I
take it you're not armed.'

Evans laughed. 'Not much point, one man against
a whole ship's company.'

Gareth nodded and dabbed a number on the intercom system. 'Have Sergeant Simmonds report to my
cabin and tell the First Lieutenant I want a word with
him.' He went to the curtain and pulled it back. 'Escort
Mr Evans to the head of the ladder,' he told Davison.
'He'll be sending his boat back to Cala Llonga. And
have our own launch stand by to take both these
gentlemen across to Bloody Island. After that have it
brought on board and stowed.' He turned to Evans.
'Whilst you're out in the open I suggest you take the
opportunity to report in to your base that you're okay.'

Evans stood there for a moment, frowning, his eyes
fixed on Gareth who had already turned back at the
sound of a voice calling him over the intercom. It was
Mault and he told him, 'I want the ship closed up
ready for sea, Number One. We'll be getting under
way as soon as MEO can give us the necessary power.'

'We've received new orders, have we?' Mault's
voice was a mixture of curiosity and doubt.

'You've just received *my* orders, Number One, so
get on with it.' There was a crisp finality in the way

he said it that even the thickest-skinned could not fail to understand. 'We'll be out of here by 22.15 at the latest.' He switched off before his second-in-command could ask any more awkward questions and turned back to Evans. 'When you report in, tell your people to bring Mrs Steele down to Cala Llonga ready to take her out to Bloody Island. I don't know how far away she is, but I'd like her down on the beach there before we sail.'

Evans nodded. 'No problem. We'll have her waiting for you there. Then you can see her and identify her through your glasses. Okay?' And he added. 'There's some countries I been in where death is a way of life, as you might say. So don't fool around with me, either of you, see.' He turned on his heel then and left the cabin just as Sergeant Simmonds arrived.

Gareth told him to take me down to the armoury and issue me with whatever weapon he thought most suitable for holding a dangerous man hostage for half an hour or so. He was quite close to me when he said that and he gripped hold of my arm. 'Don't let him jump you. Just keep your distance and the gun on him the whole time.' His fingers were digging into me, his hand trembling. God help me, I thought, he was scared of the man. 'Just keep your distance,' he said again. 'All the time you're alone with him on the island. Particularly at the moment of exchange. If it gets to that, if they actually bring her out to the island, then he'll have those two thugs of his to back him up, so don't let your eyes stray. He'll be waiting for that, the moment when Soo moves towards you.' And he added, 'Both of you held as hostage would complicate things.'

His hand relaxed his grip on my arm. He turned and picked up his cap. 'I'm going up to the bridge now. When you're armed, you can join Pat at the gangway. By then the launch will be waiting to run you over to the island. And remember – watch him, every moment.'

CHAPTER TWO

'**Z**ulu One Zero, this is Zulu One. Come in, Zulu One Zero. Over . . . Yes, I've been put ashore as agreed on the island. You can bring the woman down as soon as the frigate starts to fetch its anchor . . . Yes, of course they did. It's the husband. That fellow Steele . . . Sure he's got a gun, one of those Stirling sub-machine pistols, but I don't know how good he is with it . . .' He glanced across at me, his teeth gleaming in the light of my torch. 'That's right, wait till you see the frigate's stern light disappear beyond Lazareto, then put her in the speedboat. You can come out for me soon as the Colonel reports he is locked on. Okay? . . . Good. Out.'

He turned to me, his teeth still showing white in that strange smile of his. 'Relax, for Chris'sake. Another half-hour and with any luck you'll have your wife back and I'll be gone.' He slipped the radiophone back into the pocket of his jacket and came down from the ruined wall on which he had been standing.

I backed away, watching him, and he laughed as he came towards me. 'Think I'm going to jump you? No way. I've seen the silverware in that room of yours above the chandlery.' He walked right past me, out into the open where he had a clear view of the frigate. The launch was just going alongside and at the same moment all the upper-deck lights that gave the outline of the ship such a fairy look went suddenly out.

He walked past the dig, out to the northern end of the hospital's long seaward-facing block. From there the frigate was no more than three cables away and we could hear the voices of the men on the fo'c's'le as they waited for the order to weigh anchor. Evans lit a cigarette, his features picked out in the flare of the match. 'Suppose Gareth boy takes his tin can out and you don't get your wife back – what then, eh?' He blew out a stream of smoke, watching me.

I didn't say anything. The man was built like a tank, all hard bone and muscle. How many shots would it take to kill him? I had never fired a machine pistol before and I tried to remember what I'd been told. Was it high they fired, or low?

'Well?' He was grinning at me, but his eyes were cold and calculating in the torchlight, as though he were trying to make up his mind whether I was capable of shooting him down in cold blood.

A searchlight stabbed out from somewhere by the radio mast on the high point of La Mola, the beam blinding me. He could have rushed me then, but he had turned his head away and was staring out towards the frigate, now a black shape in silhouette. The clank of the anchor cable sounded loud in the stillness as they shortened in. The clanking stopped and in the searchlight's brilliant beam I could see the chain itself hanging straight up and down from the bows. Shortly after that the hum of machinery told us they had got one of the two turbines going again.

'Any minute now,' I said, my voice sounding strained. I only said it to relieve the tension.

Evans was still staring intently at the ship and I heard him mutter, 'It's against all his training . . .' He swung round on me. 'You reck'n he'll take her out, or is he up to something?' He started towards me. 'If you and he . . .'

I told him to stay where he was, my finger back on the trigger. 'Don't make me fire this thing.'

I don't think he heard me, for he had turned and was staring out again across the dark water. 'Like I said, it's against all his training. And if he thinks he's going to lie off the entrance till you've got your wife back—'

'You've been over all that,' I said. 'Once those guns can be brought to bear . . .'

'The guns – yes.' He nodded. 'A direct hit and he'd be blown out of the water.' He shook his head, standing very still. 'To throw it all away for that woman.' He glanced round at me, the teeth showing white again. 'No offence, but Christ! I don't understand.'

'Then you've never been in love,' I said.

He laughed. It was more like a guffaw. 'A four-letter word or a three-letter word, what the hell? It's sex, isn't it, and my mother taught him about that on board the *Betty Ann*. Didn't he tell you?' The clank of the anchor chain started up again. 'In a mud berth.' He seemed to find that funny, laughing still as he watched the ship. 'Quite a girl, my mother. But to throw away his whole career, everything he's worked for . . . Or is he scared? Is that why he's getting his anchor up, scared of being blown to hell if he stays?'

He looked at me for a moment, then his gaze switched back again to the black shape of the ship, his body quite still, almost tense. The navigation lights were on now, the anchor just coming clear of the water. The frigate was beginning to move. 'Poor little bugger!' I heard him murmur. Then he turned on me suddenly. 'Suppose I don't let her go? You going to gun me down?' The searchlight was switched off and I heard him laugh, everything suddenly very dark. I stepped back, expecting him to rush me, and tripped over a stone.

'He's going astern,' Evans said.

I switched on my torch again. He hadn't moved, but now his head was turned back, his gaze fixed on the dim shape out there on the water. The frigate's bows were swinging, the stern coming towards us. The sound of the engines suddenly increased. Or was it just one engine? The sound died abruptly as the ship lost way. Was there really something wrong with her machinery after all? The sound increased again, the bows swinging. It was as though they were having difficulty with the steering. I could see the stern light, the ship again coming straight towards us and growing steadily larger.

Several times she started to go ahead, but each time she veered to port, finally entering the narrows on the north side of Bloody Island stern-first. It wasn't exactly the most direct route if he was making out to sea, but it seemed it was only at slow astern they could steer a reasonably straight course.

Evans followed them back along the north shore of the island as far as the dig. I kept about twenty paces behind him. By this time the frigate was so close I was looking straight into the bridge, and in the brief moments I dared take my eyes off him, I could actually identify individual officers. Gareth was there and I saw him slip out of the captain's chair and move to the front of the bridge. Mault followed him.

The next time I glanced at the bridge the two of them seemed to be arguing, and they had been joined by Peter Craig. Evans had now crossed the dig and was standing by the beacon, staring at the frigate, which was then level with us, the slightly waved metal side of her gliding past within biscuit-toss. I stopped, and as the bridge came level with me I saw Robin Makewate had joined the other three. At that moment Mault turned and walked off the bridge.

I caught a movement out of the corner of my eye and half turned. Evans had shifted his position and was looking behind him, towards Cala Figuera. I heard it then, the buzz-saw sound of an outboard coming nearer. At the same time *Medusa*'s stern came clear of the narrows and began to swing towards us. There was a great threshing under the counter and she checked just in time, moving slowly ahead, her bows swinging all the time to port.

Evans left his post by the beacon and came towards me. 'I should have stayed on board.'

I motioned him to keep his distance, the gun pointed at his stomach. 'Why?'

'Then I'd have some idea what the hell's going on.'

The sound of the outboard died, but I was barely conscious of it, my eyes half on Evans, half on the frigate, which was now going astern again and swinging more sharply. In this way it turned itself completely round until it was lying just off the landing place with its bows pointing almost directly at the big hotel above our house. 'Has he really got engine trouble?'

I didn't say anything, wondering about that glimpse I had had of Mault arguing with Gareth on the bridge.

The frigate was beginning to go ahead again. I thought she was endeavouring to round the island and head seaward through the wider southern passage, but the bows started to swing again so that it looked as though the whole grey bulk of her would land up stern-first in the hospital ruins.

Evans was hurrying now as he skirted the dig, took the path to the landing place, then turned off on the track that circled the old hospital building. It was brighter here, the frigate outlined against the lights of Villa Carlos. Water swirled at her stern, small waves rushing against the rocks. Evans had stopped. I think, like me, he was too astonished to do anything but stare at the dark shape coming closer, the bows swinging clear, but the low flat stern, with its flight deck and hangar, closing on the rocks just south of our boat landing. She was coming towards us with no check, the hum of the one engine, the suck of the prop, the waves beating at the shore, all getting louder.

The grinding crunch of her grounding on the rocks was a rising cacophony of sound that seemed to go on and on, the stern rising till it was so close it looked from where I stood as though Evans could step across on to the deck itself. Then suddenly everything was still, a quietness gradually descending over the scene, the propeller bedded against rock, the water subsiding to the stillness of a balmy Mediterranean night. 'The silly bloody idiot!' The anger of Evans's voice was tinged with something else. Resignation? I wasn't sure. And there were other voices now, from on board the frigate. Men tumbling up from below, out on to the deck to see what had happened, and Gareth standing there in the open wing door of the bridge on the port side, standing still as stone as though shocked into immobility.

It was like that for a moment, a blurred picture of disaster recorded by the eye's retina and made strange by the darkness and the lights beyond, the ruined hospital standing over it all like the mirror image of the stranding. Then Gareth moved, the upper-deck broadcast system blaring orders. The lights came on again, the ship's outline illuminated for all the world to see that she was ashore, her stern smashed into the rocks. God! What he must be feeling!

I knew who it was running up from the landing

point before she reached me. I heard her panting and at the same time Evans had whipped out his radio-phone and was talking into it, passing the word that the frigate was aground.

'He did it on purpose.' She caught hold of my arm. 'I saw it, Mike. I was right there in the boat. Christ! I thought he was going to drive her straight over me.' Her mouth was wide, her teeth white in the frigate's lights and those big eyes of hers almost starting out of her head. 'Why? Why did he do it?'

'Where have you been?' I asked her.

'Looking for Soo. But why for God's sake?' She was staring at me. 'I didn't find her. I don't know where they've taken her. Nobody seems to know.' And she said urgently, 'What will happen to him? It's a court martial, isn't it – running your ship aground? The Navy won't stand for that.'

'Probably not,' I said. The ship's decks were alive with men now and Gareth was down at the hangar doors, Mault with him. The sense of activity and purpose was fascinating to watch as the hangar door was slid back to reveal the dark interior of it stacked with wooden cases and all sorts of weapons, some that looked like rocket-launchers.

That was when he grabbed her. Fool that I was, I hadn't registered the fact that he should have been standing in dark silhouette against the light. But instead of being in full view, he suddenly appeared out of the shadows to my right. I heard Petra gasp, and as I turned and flashed my torch, the blade of a knife flicked in the beam, a steely glint pointing straight at her throat, his face, hard as rock, right beside hers as she opened her mouth wide and began to scream, her left arm twisted up behind her as he frogmarched her slowly backwards.

He didn't bother to tell me to drop the gun. He knew I wouldn't shoot as long as he was holding her as a shield. 'Don't move.' The order was hissed at me through those big teeth. 'Stay where you are and she'll be all right.' He was backing on to the path leading to the landing. 'And tell your wife's lover, he's just signed his death warrant. Hers too.'

He kept Petra between himself and me all the way back to the track that ran past the tent and down to the landing place. I didn't dare move. I had a feeling he was a desperate man now and capable of anything, even cold-blooded murder if it served his purpose. And then the incredible happened. The flap of the tent was pushed aside and Lennie appeared.

He stood there, stretching and yawning. I don't know whether he was still drunk, or just half-asleep, but it took a moment for the scene to register with him. Then his eyes were suddenly wide with shock as he saw, first the ship, then Petra in the grip of Evans as he backed down the path.

He was like that for an instant, his eyes wide. Then they narrowed, and in the same instant he moved, an instinctive, almost reflex action, moved with extraordinary speed, so that Evans was quite unprepared, Lennie's fist slamming into his face, knocking him backwards. 'Out of the way, girl!' He was moving after Evans and she just stood there in a daze, blocking his path.

It almost cost him his life. She moved, but too late, Evans pulling himself to his feet again and brushing past her in a crouching run. The knife flashed as Lennie lashed out at him, and the next thing I saw was the Australian staggering backwards, clutching at his face and blood spurting between his fingers.

The knife slashed again and he went down, a strangled screaming like a trapped rabbit. Then Evans turned and ran, dropping out of sight almost immediately as he made for the landing place. I didn't shout. I didn't go after him. My concern was for Lennie. I couldn't tell whether he was alive or dead. He just lay there on a bed of wild flowers at the edge of the path, blood spurting from the loose flap of his cheek, where the knife had slashed it open, and a dark patch beginning to spread over his shirt as blood welled up from somewhere not far from his heart.

Petra moved to my side, her eyes wild as she grabbed at my arm. She was sobbing. But then she was suddenly silent, squatting down, her bare knee bent against a rock, still as a statue, horror-struck as she stared at the blood on Lennie's face, the ghastly cheek flap. 'Oh, my God!' He was no longer screaming, his body quite still. 'Is he dead?'

I shook my head. Blood was welling out over his shirt and I thought I could detect a slight movement of his chest. 'You look after him,' I said. 'I'll see if the ship will take him.'

It was then, as I rose to my feet, that I heard the

outboard start, the sound of it rising as Petra's inflatable shot into view, hugging the rocks. I glimpsed it briefly as Evans skidded it round the north-western bulge of the island. Then it was lost to view as he ran it under the beacon and into the narrows. I turned back to the ship then, and as I hurried up the path under the hospital walls, I met two naval ratings lugging a case of rockets. Others passed me as I ran to the frigate's stern, shouting for the Captain.

Nobody took any notice of me for a moment. They had rigged a gangway from the stern to the top of a flat rock close by the path, the scene chaotic as almost the whole crew swarmed like ants from ship to shore, humping equipment from the hangar, listening gear and telephones, as well as rocket-launchers and ammunition. Orders were being shouted, arms issued, cases ripped open and ammunition got ready.

In the end it was Peter Craig who answered my call for help and, after some delay, he managed to find the medical orderly who finally got Lennie on to a stretcher and carried him on board. I wasn't allowed to go with him. Craig was adamant about that. And when I asked for Gareth, he told me the Captain was in the Communications Office and there was absolutely no chance of my seeing him until the situation had clarified itself.

'They'll do what they can for him,' he assured me. 'We've no doctor on board. You know that, I think, but those two did a good job on John Kent. Looked after him until we could get ashore. They'll do the same for your man, and we'll get him ashore and into the military hospital as soon as possible. That is,' he added, 'if any of us are alive by morning.'

He smiled at me a little uncertainly. 'Remember what I said to you on the bridge that night, about the Captain carrying a weight of responsibility few of the officers realised. Well, now they do. We're in the thick of it, and if you or I are around in the morning, then by God I'll stand you a drink.' He tried to smile again, to make a joke of it, but it didn't work. Instead, he clapped me on the back before hurrying off up the gangway to continue supervising the unloading.

Back at the camp I found Petra busy preparing a meal. I think she was doing it more to distract herself from what was happening than from any want of food. 'Is he all right?'

'He's alive,' I said. 'They'll get him ashore when things have sorted themselves out. Some time tomorrow presumably. Meanwhile, I imagine they'll stitch him up as best they can.'

She poured me some wine. It was a good dark Rioja, the colour of blood. I drank it down at a gulp. 'They're a bit preoccupied right now,' I told her, and at that moment, as though to emphasise the point, the lights that lit the outline of the frigate went suddenly out, everything dark again.

She nodded. All around us we could hear voices, the clink of metal on metal, the tramp of feet. 'They've started to dig in,' she said.

I nodded and poured myself some more wine. I was suddenly very tired. Tension probably. I had never really contemplated death before. At other times, when

I had been in danger, it had all happened too fast. Even that time Ahmed Bey had been killed, it had been very sudden, the Italian boat coming at us out of the darkness, and later, the days at sea and the heat, the trek along the African shore, getting weaker and weaker, it hadn't been the same at all.

Now I had been given virtually the exact time of death, the rendezvous approximately midnight fourteen miles off the coast. Fourteen miles. Just over half an hour at full speed. Say another half-hour while they argued it out over radio. I was remembering suddenly that Gareth had said he had a civilian on board who was fluent in Russian. Probable time of engagement, therefore, would be around 01.00. And my watch showed it was already almost midnight.

An hour to live! Perhaps a little more. But not another dawn.

If the decision had been taken to occupy Mahon harbour, then the opposition of a puny and obsolete RN frigate would be brushed aside in a holocaust of missiles. The whole of Bloody Island would be blasted to hell. Evans was right. His half-brother and the crew of his ship were doomed to extinction. So was I. So was Petra.

I looked across at her, wondering if she understood. 'Have you got any more brandy?' I asked her. 'Lennie finished that bottle of Soberano.'

She stared at me dully, her mouth turned slightly down at the corners, the big capable hands gripped on the edge of the table. I think she knew all right, for after a moment she nodded and got to her feet, opening the lid of a store box and rummaging around inside. She came up with a bottle, looked at the label, and said, 'No Soberano. It's Fundador. Will that do?' She was suddenly smiling. She knew damn well anything would do. 'You going to get drunk?' She handed me the bottle.

I shrugged as I screwed the cap off. 'Possibly.'

She sat down again, finished her wine and pushed the glass across to me. 'How long have we got?'

'Long enough.' I wasn't going to tell her how long it would be. 'In any case, a lot can happen . . .' I poured us both a good measure. '*Salud!*' And I added under my breath, 'Here's to the dawn!'

We were on our second brandy, and I was wondering in a vague sort of way whether it would be better to die in a drunken stupor or whether the two of us should lie together and die naked with the warmth of our bodies to give us comfort at the moment of impacting oblivion, when there was the sound of footsteps outside the tent and a voice said, 'Mr Steele?'

'Yes?' I went to the flap and pulled it back. Petty Officer Jarvis was standing there. 'Captain says if you and the lady would care to go ashore, he'll have the launch sent round to the landing point.'

I looked at my watch. It was now well past midnight – 00.37. The Russian ships could already be off La Mola, approaching the entrance to Port Mahon. Any moment things would start happening and he was giving Petra and myself a way out. And yet I stood there, feeling as though I'd been struck dumb. It was a lifeline he was offering us and I hesitated. Having braced myself for what was about to happen, having come to terms, or something very near to it, with the fact that I was about to die and would not live to see the sun rise, the offered reprieve seemed an affront to my manhood. Perversely, I found myself on the point of refusing. It was as though I would be running away, revealing myself to be a coward. It was only the thought of Petra that stopped me. Or was it? Was I really a coward seeking justification, an excuse for acceptance?

'Please thank him,' I told Jarvis. My mouth felt dry. 'Tell him I accept his offer. I have to find my wife. Tell him that. And Miss Callis should undoubtedly be got off the island.' And I added, 'Is there any chance I can have a word with him before we leave?'

'I doubt it, sir. He's in the Ops room. At least that's where he phoned me from. And I gathered from his manner things were a bit hectic. A lot going on, if you understand my meaning, sir.'

'Yes, of course,' I said. 'Only to be expected.'

'Five minutes, sir. The launch will be there in five minutes, probably less. Okay?' He didn't wait to see my nod, but hurried off back to the ship.

Petra was already searching around frantically for her archaeological material, scrabbling up notebooks, rolls of film, dumping them in a holdall. I grabbed a sweater and told her to hurry. 'We've no time to lose.'

'My thesis,' she said. 'There's a draft of my thesis somewhere. I must have it.' And then she stopped. 'Oh, my God! It's in the hypostile. I left it there. Won't be a minute.'

She was ducking out of the tent when I seized hold of her arm. 'Forget it,' I told her. 'They'll hit this island any minute now. Alive, you can redraft it. Dead, it won't matter anyway.'

She was trying to wrench herself free, but at my words she stopped struggling and stared at me, appalled. 'D'you mean that? D'you mean it's – now?'

'Any minute,' I said. 'There's a Russian cruiser, several other warships. They should be off the entrance now.'

She came with me then, pulling on a loose cardigan as we hurried down to the landing point. The launch was already there, two sailors holding it alongside the rock with boathooks, Leslie Masterton in the stern, the engine ticking over. He took Petra's holdall, helped her in, and as I followed her, he gave the order to push the launch clear.

'What's the latest news?' I asked him as we pulled away from the rocks.

'I don't know, sir. Everybody's at action stations—' He rolled the words off his tongue as though savouring them with excited anticipation. For a moment he concentrated on swinging the launch under the frigate's bows. Then, when we were headed for Cala Figuera, he added, 'But the Captain hasn't said anything. There's been no announcement. So I don't know anything really, nobody does. All we've been told is to stay on maximum alert until we're ordered otherwise. A lot of the boys are off the ship and among the ruins of that hospital. But you know that. Seems the Captain's expecting some sort of an attack.' He was strung up, the words pouring out of him. 'I've been allocated the launch.' He grinned. 'Didn't expect the opportunity of a run ashore.'

I glanced at Petra and she smiled. I think we were both wondering whether Gareth had done it purposely, an excuse for getting this pleasant kid out of the firing line. I pulled back the sleeve of my sweater and looked at my watch. It was already 01.11. Eleven minutes after the time I thought they might be steaming in through the entrance.

It was then that one of the sailors said quietly, 'Ship on the port bow, sir. Close inshore.' He pointed and I could see it then, a dim shape under the Villa Carlos cliff line momentarily outlined by the double red flash of the light on the point. It was a small vessel, moving slowly and very low in the water. 'Looks like that customs launch,' Masterton said and throttled back until we were barely moving. Even so, the vessel, heading in towards Mahon itself, would cut right across our bows. We lay there without lights, waiting. And when I suggested that we make a dash for it, the young midshipman said, without even hesitating to consider the possibility, 'Sorry, but my orders are to take no chances and return immediately if challenged.'

We could see the launch quite clearly now each time the Villa Carlos light flashed red. She was low in the water because she was crowded with people. Soon we could hear the sound of the engine. She would cross our bows at a distance of about two hundred metres, and lying quite still, with no lights behind us, there was just a chance we would remain unseen.

But then, as the launch was approaching the point where she would cross our bows and we could see that the pack of men standing on the deck were most of them armed, a string of lights appeared behind us on the road above Cala Lladró. We were suddenly in silhouette against them. Somebody on the customs launch shouted, several of them were pointing at us, and then there was the flash and crack of a rifle fired. I didn't hear the bullet whistle past. It was lost in the roar of our engine as Masterton gunned it and swung the wheel, turning the launch round and heading back towards Bloody Island. I caught a glimpse of some sort of struggle on the deck of the customs launch. There was the crackle of small-arms fire, spurts of flame, splinters flying off the woodwork of our stern, a glass window shattered, and little geysers bouncing past us as bullets slapped the water close alongside.

The moment of shock passed, the customs launch receding into the distance until it was finally lost in the dark of Mahon's harbour. There seemed no reason then why we shouldn't resume our course for Cala Figuera, but when I suggested this to Masterton I found myself faced, not by a kid, but by Midshipman Masterton, a budding officer to whom orders were orders. He had been told to take no chances and return if he was challenged. He had been challenged. Not only that, he'd been fired on, and though I argued that the customs launch was now out of sight and no danger, he said, 'I don't know who they were on that launch, but they were armed and they opened fire. Before we can make your quay at Cala Figuera they could be ashore and somebody on the phone to the military.'

Nothing I or Petra could say would change his mind. The nice cheerful face had suddenly become obstinate, his manner indicating the implacability of naval training. I think he was quite capable of initiative, but not when he had been given specific orders. 'I'll have to report back.' He said that twice. 'Then, if I'm instructed to proceed . . .'

But he received no such instructions. We ran straight alongside *Medusa* and it was the First Lieutenant, looking down on us from the bridge wing, who received his report. 'Are you sure it was the customs launch?'

'I think so, sir.'

'And crowded with men. How many would you say?'

'Can't be sure, sir.' Masterton's voice was pitched a little higher now that he was being de-briefed by his senior officer. 'Fifty. Sixty. Quite a lot, sir.'

Mault asked me then. 'What do you say, Mr Steele?'

'No idea,' I replied. 'It was too dark. But she was low in the water so I should think Mr Masterton's estimate is about right.'

'Good.' He seemed pleased, but when I suggested that we could proceed to Cala Figuera, he shook his head. 'Sorry. No time now. We may need our launch.' And he ordered Masterton to land us, then return and tie up alongside pending further orders. I tried to argue with him, but he turned on me and said, 'If you're so urgent to get away from here . . .' He checked himself, then leaned out and said, 'Has it occurred to you, Mr Steele, that if it weren't for you and that wife of yours we wouldn't be in the mess we are?' He stared down at me, then turned abruptly and disappeared inside the bridge, leaving me wondering how he knew about Soo. Had Gareth let it slip out, arguing with the man as he backed the frigate through the narrows, or later when he'd put her on the rocks?

I was thinking about that as the sailors pushed off and we manœuvred round the rocks and into the loading point. Five minutes later we were back at the tent and as I held the flap back for Petra, I noticed the lights of at least half a dozen vehicles moving west along the main road from Villa Carlos. They were evenly spaced and looked like a military convoy. I thought perhaps they were reinforcements for the defence of the airport, or perhaps for a dawn offensive towards Ciudadela. Their real significance never occurred to me.

In the dim interior of the tent it was as though we had never left it, the chairs, the table, the unwashed plates, the glasses and the bottle of Fundador. 'Damn that bastard Mault.' I reached for my glass, which still had some brandy in it. I was angry and frustrated, and when Petra said, 'It's not his fault, everybody must be very tense by now,' I told her to go to hell, downed the rest of my drink and walked out. I wasn't only angry with Mault, I was angry with myself. I should have handled it better. I should have insisted on seeing Gareth. I had the chance then, whilst we'd been tied up alongside, but I'd been so shattered by Mault's words, his obvious hostility, that I hadn't thought of it. And there was an element of truth in what he had said. That's what made it so hard to swallow. Putting his ship aground had been the one action Gareth could take that would effectively make Soo totally ineffective as a hostage, the one way he could save her life and at the same time carry out his orders to stay in Mahon under all circumstances. The only other thing he could have done was to put to sea, and that was out of the question.

Thinking about it, I almost fell into a newly dug slit trench. A Scots voice cursed me for a clumsy bastard, a hand gripping hold of my ankle. 'Luke where ye're fuckin' goin', laddie. There's some of us doon here that are still alive, ye noo.'

I was in the graveyard area and there were four of them sprawled on the ground with a couple of hand-held rocket-launchers. From where they lay they could see into the steep-sided little bay draped with the pale glimmer of villas that was Cala Llonga. I asked them if any vessel had put out in the last half-hour. But they had seen nothing, so clearly the customs launch had come either from Lazareto Island or from the La Mola peninsula itself. Perhaps even from Cala Pedrera on the other side of the Mahon entrance.

I squatted there talking to them for several minutes. Two of them were leading seamen whom I had met on the bridge during the trip out from Malta, one of them had brought me kai that night. But they couldn't tell me anything I didn't already know. They had had a word with the Captain, they said, just after midnight. Apparently Gareth had made a tour of all the positions established round the island and in the hospital ruins, but it had been more of a morale booster. He hadn't told them anything very much, only warned them that if they were attacked, it would all happen very quickly. He had also said jokingly that if they weren't attacked, they'd probably be stuck out there all night. 'I asked him straight oot,' the Scots lad said, 'wha' are we expectin' then, but he was no' verra communicative. He just said, if it comes, make cairtin ye've said yer prayers. An' he wasna jokin'. He was daid sairious.'

The time was then ten minutes short of two o'clock and still nothing had happened. I started back towards the tent, but just before I reached it, I saw a little group coming down the gangway from *Medusa*'s stern. With no lights, I couldn't see who they were, but they headed towards me along the path under the hospital walls, so I waited. It was Gareth, setting out on a second tour of inspection. Mault was with him, and Sergeant Simmonds. I don't think he saw me at first. He was walking with his head bent, not saying anything to his companions, as though lost in his own thoughts, and when I spoke his head came up with a startled jerk and he looked at me, tight-lipped and very tense. 'Sorry you didn't make it ashore,' he said.

I asked him what was going on in the outside world and he just shook his head. He would let me know, he said, as soon as he had any definite news.

And he added that, until he knew for certain what the situation was, there was no question of his risking the launch in another attempt to take us into Cala Figuera. And when I pressed him, saying that something had to be done about Soo, he just looked at me and said in a voice that was dead and without emotion, 'Your wife is only one of many factors I have to take into consideration.' And he added, in that same dead tone, as though he were talking about something quite remote and impersonal, 'In the overall scale of things I'm afraid she ranks very low, however important she may be to you, and to me.' He muttered something about being in a hurry – 'A lot on my plate at the moment.' And he nodded briefly, brushing past me.

I went back to the tent then. Nothing else I could do. With no boat, Petra and I were marooned on the island, and we just sat there, waiting. It was long past the time when the warships that were supposed to be supporting Fuxá's coup d'état should have been entering Mahon harbour, and though I fiddled around with Petra's little radio, all I could get was dance music. God knows what was going on in the world outside of Bloody Island.

All around us there were the sounds of men settling in for the night in improvised trenches or in the stone walls of the hospital itself. And though I went out and talked to some of them, I couldn't find anyone who knew any more than we did. In fact, I suppose the only people who could have told us what was going on in the outside world were Gareth and his communications team. I learned afterwards that, apart from those two quick tours of the island's makeshift defences, he spent the whole night there, sifting endlessly through the mass of reports, signals, newsflashes, and speculative comment from all around the world picked up by the ship's antennae.

Back in the tent again I found Petra sitting there, not drinking, not doing anything, just sitting there with a shut look on her face. I said something to her. I don't remember what. But she didn't answer. She had withdrawn into some secret world of her own. And then, suddenly, she got to her feet, a quick, decisive movement. 'I'm tired,' she said. 'God! I'm tired. No point sitting here waiting for something to happen. I'm going to bed.'

I was desperately tired myself, my mind seemingly no longer capable of constructive thought. The picture of that room, the little dog, and Evans – the way he had talked about sending her to Gareth in bits and pieces. Christ! What a hell of a mess! All I could think of was the poor girl out there somewhere in the hands of those bastards.

In the end I found a spare sleeping bag and followed Petra's example. But before curling myself up in it, I went outside again. It was quite chill now, a whisper of a breeze coming down from the high ground above the harbour, the scent of wild flowers on the air, and as I stood there, relieving myself, I was conscious of the bodies all around me. It was very strange, hearing nothing, but knowing they were there, like the ghosts of all those buried dead.

But then the glow of a cigarette, showing for an

instant under the hospital wall, brought my mind back to reality. Away to the right I could just make out the dim shape of a sailor standing in silhouette against the stars, and when I climbed to the top of a rock there was the outline of the frigate, stern-on and not a light showing. Somebody coughed, a hastily suppressed sound, and as I went back into the tent I heard a clink of metal on stone somewhere out beyond the dig.

It was almost four. Another hour and dawn would be starting to break. Perhaps it was the coffee, or perhaps I was just too damned tired, but I couldn't seem to sleep, my mind going round in circles, worrying about Soo, about the future, about what it would be like if she were killed.

Then suddenly I was being shaken violently and Petra's voice was saying, 'Wake up! Wake up, Mike! It's all over.'

'What the devil are you talking about? What's all over?' I sat up so abruptly my head caught her on the chin. The flap of the tent was drawn back, the sun blazing in. Blinking in the glare of it, I asked her what time it was.

'Just after ten and there's three Spanish warships steaming past us.'

I wriggled out of the sleeping bag, slipped my shoes on and went outside. They made a brave sight, two destroyers and what looked like some sort of a logistic ship, the sun blazing full on them, outsize Spanish flags streaming from the ensign staffs on the ships' sterns and the water of the harbour mirror-calm ahead of them, Mahon blindingly white above. The tanker was back in Cala Figuera, moving in to the fuel depot with the tug in attendance.

It really did look as though Petra was right and it was all over. But the Navy was clearly taking no chances, the frigate lying there against the rocks, silent and watchful, no movement on deck and only the hum of machinery to show that the inside of it was alive with men. No movement on the island either, only the occasional whisper of a voice to indicate that there were sailors there, standing to their weapons and waiting.

I clambered up on to the ruined wall above the dig, where I had an uninterrupted view eastwards towards La Mola. No sign of the Libyan freighter, the water flat calm and empty of anything except a small boat trawling for fish. The slit trench with the Scots leading seaman I had talked to in the night was quite close, but all they could tell me was that they had heard the freighter fetching its anchor sometime around three-thirty, just after they had seen the lights of a dozen or more vehicles moving away from La Mola along the road above Cala Llonga. They couldn't tell me whether the freighter had headed seaward or gone back to Mahon.

They were far more relaxed than when I had talked to them in the early hours. *Medusa*'s galleys had pro-duced a hot breakfast for them at the usual time, the ground still strewn with mess tins and eating irons. They thought it wouldn't be long now before they were allowed to stand down.

I was still in my underpants and I went back to the tent to get myself dressed. Petra was cooking us some breakfast. I remember that very distinctly, the smell of bacon and eggs, and sitting there in the sunshine, neither of us talking. I don't know how many men there were around us, but the sense of hushed expectancy was almost overpowering.

Then suddenly the frigate's broadcast system was blaring out *Rule Britannia*, men erupting on to the deck, the island around us coming alive as word was passed to stand down, everybody talking at once, a roar of voices mingled with the high quick laughter that comes of nervous relief.

I joined a party lugging equipment and the debris of a meal down to the stern of the ship. There was an officer there, a man I hadn't seen before. He refused to let me on board and I was forced to scribble a note to Gareth on a message pad. But even as a seaman went for'ard to deliver it, I saw Gareth, dressed in what looked like his best uniform, scrambling down a rope ladder and jumping into the launch, which then headed for the harbour where the Spanish warships were anchored close off the Naval Base. I would now have to wait until he had paid his respects to the Spanish naval commander, and even then he might not feel able to send me ashore.

Shortly after that I walked out to the dig and stood by the red-flashing beacon, staring across the narrow strip of water to the steep rise of the land beyond with villas perched white on the slopes. Where would they have taken her? Pulling out suddenly like that, what for Christ's sake would they have done with her? They would hardly have taken her in that convoy of vehicles that had left from La Mola in the dark of night. Or would they?

I sat down on a rock, my mind going round and round, gnawing at the problem. And in the sunshine, with wild flowers in every crevice, I saw her as she had been back in Malta when I had first met her. A picnic on Gozo, her body lying on a rock all golden warm like the limestone of the buildings on the hill above caught in the slanting rays of a glorious sunset. And in that little trellis garden of her mother's, bougainvillaea and morning-glory, and the two of us dancing to that old portable gramophone, our bodies close and the moon full above the curved roof tiles. A world apart, the two of us hopelessly in love in the moonlight, not another thought in our heads, not a care in the world, our bodies tingling to the touch of our fingers, the ache for each other growing.

God in heaven! What had happened to us? To me? What had changed it?

Questions, questions, the result emotional torment and my heart reaching out to her. Surely to God two people who had been as close to each other as we had been then could make contact across the distance that now separated us. If I thought hard enough, if I could concentrate my mind sufficiently, surely I could evoke some response from her, some telepathic indication of where she was.

I was there by that beacon for a long time, alone with my thoughts, and right above me the Golden

Farm to remind me of two other lovers. And then Petra came to say the launch had finally returned.

'Any message from the ship?' I asked her.

She shook her head and I stared at that narrow strip of water, wondering whether I could make it, picturing him back in his day cabin, his desk piled with urgent messages. In the circumstances, my note would hardly seem of great importance. Soo would either be dead or abandoned somewhere. Whichever it was, he had every reason to think a few more hours would make little difference.

I was in the tent, stripped to my underpants and stuffing my clothes, pipe, matches, keys, money, everything I might need ashore, into a plastic bag, when the flap was pulled back and I looked up to find Petty Officer Jarvis standing there. 'Captain's compliments, sir, and the launch is waiting to take you ashore.'

I shall always bless him for that. In the midst of all his problems he had read my note and understood my urgency, the depth of my feeling. I didn't attempt to see him. I just scribbled a note of thanks and handed it to Jarvis as he led me up the gangway on to the stern and for'ard to where the rope ladder was rigged. The same midshipman was in charge of the launch, and as we swung away from the frigate's side, I asked him what the news was. He looked at me, wide grey eyes in a serious face. 'News, sir? You haven't heard?' And when I told him it had been a long night and I had slept late, he grinned at me and said, 'They miffed off. The revolutionaries and those mercenaries who put that Fuschia chap in. The fleet, too – the fleet that was going to support the new government. It just faded off the radar screen. And all because of *Medusa*.'

'A Russian fleet, do you mean?'

'Yes, the Russians. The American Sixth Fleet is shadowing them.'

'Is that official?' I asked him. 'About the Russian and American fleets?' We had swung away from the ship's side and were heading for Cala Figuera, the note of the engine making it difficult to talk. 'Did you hear it on the news?'

He shook his head. 'I haven't had a chance to listen to the BBC, but that's what they're saying – saw them off all on our own, long before those Spanish ships arrived.' And he added, 'Now that he's back from seeing the Spanish admiral, I've no doubt the Captain will be making an announcement. I'd like to have heard that.' He gave an order to the helm, then turned back to me. 'You know him well, don't you, sir?' It was more a statement than a question and he didn't wait for me to answer. 'He's a super man. Never batted an eye all night, going the rounds, chatting and joking with everybody and all of us expecting to be blown out of the water any minute. Then, when it's all over, he has a thanksgiving in the wardroom.'

'When was that?'

'It was early, about 04.30. Just those on the ship. A few prayers, a hymn or two. All he told us then was that the situation had improved and we should give thanks to God.' The boy was smiling to himself, remembering the scene. '*Lead kindly light* ... I can still hear him singing it in that fine voice of his. He's

Welsh, you see.' And he grinned apologetically, embarrassed at being carried away and forgetting I would have known that. And when I asked him how the ship had come to land up on Bloody Island, he looked at me uncertainly, suddenly hesitant. But the excitement of events and his admiration for his Captain got the better of him. 'The buzz is he put her aground himself,' he said brightly.

'Deliberately?'

'I couldn't say, sir. I wasn't on the bridge. But that's what they're saying – so that there was no way they could shift us. We were committed then, you see, a Nato ship stuck there and prepared to fire at anything that didn't support the legitimate Spanish government and the Spanish King.'

I nodded. He wouldn't know about Soo, of course. None of them would, except Mault. At least I hoped he was the only one. For the time being anyway. The midshipman saw it solely in terms of naval tactics, the sort of move Nelson or Cochrane might have made, not realising that what Gareth had done was to take the one positive action that could nullify absolutely his half-brother's threats. God knows what it had cost him in mental anguish to take such a gamble, not just with Soo's life, but with his own, and with the lives of all his men. He had called Evans's bluff and he had won, and I was hearing it from this kid of a midshipman, who was standing there, starry-eyed and bubbling with excitement, as he told me how he had spent the first half of the night in charge of half a dozen seamen on the hospital tower, acting as lookouts and armed with hand-held rocket-launchers.

It was hot as the launch slowed to run alongside our quay, the sun blazing out of a blue sky, the surface of the water oily-calm, and traffic moving on the steep road from the Martires Atlante to the Carrero Blanco. Everything looked so normal it was hard to believe that there had been several hours during the night when the future of Menorca had hung in the balance, the threat of hostilities looming.

And then I was ashore, the chandlery door open and Ramón coming out of the store in answer to my call. No, he had no news of the señora. I raced up the stairs. Somebody had cleared the place up, the maid I suppose. The telephone was still working. I sat down at the table by the window and rang the Renatos, but Manuela had no information about her. She suggested I ring the *Gobierno Militar*. Gonzalez had been there since early morning and might have heard something. But her husband was no longer there, and when I finally tracked him down at the *ayuntamiento*, he had heard nothing. I tried the *policia*, the *Guardia Civil*, finally in desperation I rang the Residencia Sanitaria. They had quite a few casualties in, but they were all men, including an Australian who had just been brought in from the English warship. When I asked how serious his injuries were, they said he had not yet been fully examined. If I liked to enquire a little later ...

I said I would ring back in an hour's time, and then as a last resort tried to get through to Perez at the Naval Base, but the phone was engaged and when I finally did manage to reach his office, he was out and the officer who answered the phone had no idea when he would be back. I rang the Army then, out at La Mola, and to my surprise I was connected immediately with some sort of duty officer. He put me through to somebody in one of the casements, who said a woman had been seen with a group of the '*soldadi del revolución*', but where they had taken her he did not know. Needless to say he was not prepared to discuss what had happened the previous day nor even where she had been held.

All this took time and it was late afternoon before I had exhausted all possible sources of information and was forced to the conclusion that I would have to go out to Addaia, or wherever it was they had embarked, in the hope of finding somebody who had actually witnessed their departure. But first I needed a car. Mine had disappeared. I tried to borrow one, but everybody I rang was either out or their car was in use, and I couldn't hire one because my driving licence was in the pocket of my own car. In the end I persuaded the people who provided cars for tourists staying at the Port Mahon Hotel to let me have one of their little Fiats on the understanding that I applied immediately for a copy of my licence.

I tried the hospital again while I was waiting for one of their drivers to bring it round. After some time I was able to speak to one of the sisters, who told me Lennie's cheek had been stitched up and the knife wound in the chest, which had narrowly missed the heart, had pierced the lung. He was under sedation at the moment, so no point in my trying to see him. She advised me to ring again in the morning.

As I put the phone down Ramón called to me from below. I thought it was to say the car had arrived, but he shouted up to me that it was Miguel Gallardo's wife, asking to see me.

She was waiting for me in the chandlery, her large, comfortable-looking body seeming to fill the place, but all the vivacity gone out of her, a worried look on the round, olive-complexioned face, her large eyes wide below the black hair cut in a fringe. She had been trying to phone me, she said. About Miguel. She was speaking in a rush and obviously in a very emotional state. He hadn't been home for two nights and she wondered whether I had seen him or had any idea where he might be. She had been to the *Guardia*, of course, and the hospitals, but everything was so confused following all the happenings of the last two days ... And I just stood there, listening to her, a sickening feeling inside me, remembering how her husband had driven up to that villa in his battered estate car. Christ! I'd forgotten all about it until that moment.

What the hell could I tell her? That Miguel, innocent and unsuspecting, had driven straight into a bunch of men loading arms and ammunitions from an underground cache and on the brink of a desperate coup? And then, as I stood there, speechless and unable to give her a word of encouragement, it hit me. That cellar, that hole in the floor. An oubliette. Oh God!

I told her he might have had business somewhere,

and in the circumstances he might not have been able to let her know he was delayed in some other part of the island. She nodded, drinking in my words, clutching at hope – and my own heart thumping. Would I know – if she were alive, or if she were dead? Would Miguel's wife, her hands folded and on the verge of tears, know if *he* were alive?

The car arrived and thankfully I escaped into the routine of taking it over. 'I've got to go now,' I told her. 'But I'll keep an eye open and if I see him . . .' I left it at that, the sickening feeling with me again as I offered her a lift. But she was all right. Her daughter had a shoe shop just by the Club Maritimo. She would take her home. Her hands were warm and pudgy as she clasped mine, thanking me profusely, her lips trembling. 'You will telephone me plees.' She was very near to tears now. 'If you hear anything. Plees, you promise.'

I promised, escaping quickly out to the car, close to tears myself as I thought of what might have happened. Evans wouldn't have taken any chances. He wouldn't have left her body lying about. And the villa of that absent German businessman was barely four miles from Addaia, ten minutes by car. Less if the *Santa Maria* had been shifted to the seaward end of the inlet and had been waiting for him at Macaret. The villa wasn't two miles from Macaret, and I had been so busy trying to find somebody in Mahon who might have seen her or know where she was that I hadn't thought of it.

I dropped the driver off at his garage on the Villa

Carlos road, then took the shortest route to the waterfront, cutting down the General Sanjurjo to the Plaza
España. It was getting dark already, the lights on in
the shops and the narrow streets thronged with people,
most of whom seemed there just to meet their friends
and express their pleasure at the return to normality.
And when I finally reached the waterfront even the
Passo de la Alameda was full of people come to look
at the Spanish warships anchored off.

There was considerable activity at the three Naval
Base jetties, a coastal minesweeper coming alongside
with what looked like a fishing boat in tow and a
fishery protection launch pulling out. Standing off was
a fierce little warship that I knew, the Barcelo-class
fast attack patrol boat that Fernando Perez had taken
me over one hot September day the previous year. All
this, and the destroyers, with the *Manuel Soto*, the big
white ferry from Barcelona, towering over the Muelle
Commercial, was enough to give the Menorquins back
their confidence. There was a lot of drinking going on
in the port, an air of gaiety, and at the bottom of the
Abundancia I had threaded my way through a crowd
of about a hundred dancing in the street to a guitar.

Past the turning off to the right that led to the
Naval Base and La Mola, I was suddenly on my own,
the road ahead empty. Nothing now to distract my
mind as I put my foot down, pushing the little car fast
towards the crossroads and the turning to Macaret
and Arenal d'en Castell. There is a garage on the
right going towards Fornells. Its lights were on and I
stopped there briefly to obtain confirmation from

Señora Garcia that a convoy of vehicles had in fact passed along this road in the early hours of the morning. She had been woken up by several very noisy motor bikes ridden flat out and was actually standing at her window looking out when the line of vehicles passed. She had counted them – nineteen Army trucks and over thirty private cars, all heading towards Fornells. The *Guardia Civil* and the Army had already questioned her about the numbers and she had told them that all the vehicles had been crowded with men. I asked her if she had seen a woman in any of them, but she said no, it had been too dark.

Back in the car it seemed an age before I reached the crossroads. The scent of pines filled the night air. I passed the turning down to Addaia, swung left into a world of gravel and heath littered with the desolate dirt tracks of the tentative *urbanización*, and then, suddenly, there was the half-finished villa that Miguel had built and I had bartered for that catamaran. It stood four-square like a blockhouse on the cliff edge, the desolate heathland dropping away below it to the sea.

It was there for an instant in my headlights, the window openings of the upper storey still boarded up, a forlorn sense of emptiness about it. I didn't stop. He wouldn't have left her there. I was already on the slope of the dirt road we had driven down to leave Petra's Beetle at the Arenal d'en Castell hotel. The villa where we had watched them arming up was so crouched into the slope that I was almost past it before I glimpsed the wrought-iron gate in the low wall.

I slammed on the brakes, then backed. But when I got out of the car, I didn't go straight in. I just stood there, too scared to move. The windows, opaque in the starlight, were like blank eyes in a stucco skull and I was scared of what I'd find. The blackness of the heath, the sound of the sea snarling at the rocks, and the villa silent as the grave. What would they have done to her? For Christ's sake . . .

I braced myself and reached for the latch of the gate. Only one way to find out. But God help me, what *would* I find? I tried to still the thumping of my blood, blot out my too-imaginative fears. I was never in any doubt, you see, that she was there. The house, with just its upper floor peering over the rim of the slope, its silence, its air of watchfulness – it seemed to be telling me something.

I jabbed my elbow against the largest window, the crash of glass loud in the night, the stillness afterwards more pronounced. I put my hand in, feeling for the catch. The window swung open. I had to go back to the car then for the torch I had left on the passenger seat. After that I moved quickly down through the villa's three levels and on down the steps into the cellar. I stopped there, the beam of my torch directed at the rack of bottles and the metal sheet on which it stood. Was that how we had left it? I couldn't be sure.

The rack was almost too heavy for me on my own, but emptying the bottles out of it would have taken time and by now I was desperate to know what waited for me in that rock passage below. The air in the cellar was still and very humid. I was sweating by the time

I had managed to shift the rack clear and I stood there for a moment, gasping for breath and staring down at that metal sheet. I thought I could smell something. The dank air maybe. I took a deep breath, stooped down and pulled the corrugated iron clear of the hole.

I was certain then. It was the sweet, nauseous smell of decay. I called, but there was no answer.

I bent down, my head thrust into the hole, and shouted her name, the echo of it coming back to me with the soft slop of the sea. No answer, and the passage below empty for as far as the torch would reach. It was ten feet or more to the floor of it and no way of climbing out if I made the jump. I tried to remember what Lennie had done with the rope we had used. I was certain he hadn't had it with him when we had left the villa to run back to the car.

In the end I found it up in the top level, lying under a chest. He must have kicked it there just before we left. I grabbed it up and ran back with it down the stairs, back into that cellar, fastening it to the bottle rack as we had done before. In a moment my foot was in the first of Lennie's loops and I had dropped through the hole and was in the water-worn rock passage below shouting her name again. And when there was no reply, I followed my nose, the blood pounding in my veins as I turned a bend, the blowhole passageway narrowing to finish abruptly in the pale yellow of the matchboarding where we had heard the sound of their voices and the truck's engine as it backed up to the garage doors.

One of the lengths of boarding was splintered now.

It had clearly been prised off and then nailed roughly back into place. But it wasn't the splintered boarding that held my gaze. It was Miguel's body.

He was lying just as he had fallen after being stuffed through the hole in the boarding, his eyes open and staring and the back of his head smashed in. There was blood mingled with the rock dust of the floor, smears of it on the fresh wood of the boarding, and his eyes reflected dully the light of my torch. The sight of him, and the smell . . . I turned away, feeling suddenly sick. And then I was hurrying back along the blowhole passage, doubt mingled with dread, wondering what they would have done with her. If they had killed her, then no point in bringing the body here. A weight tied to the feet, then overboard and the Balearic lobsters would do the rest.

I ducked past the rope and when I reached the second expansion chamber and could see the water-worn passage falling away and the scaffold poles rigged over the blowhole, I stopped. There was nobody there. I was shouting her name again, but it was a futile gesture, only sepulchral echoes answering me and the slop of the sea loud in my ears.

I was turning away when I thought I heard something. It was a high sound, like the scream of a gull. I stood there for a moment, listening. But all I heard was the sea, and nobody would go down into the cave itself without diving gear, for the entrance to it was deep under water and in a gale . . . And then it came again, high and quavering.

I flung myself down the slope, slamming into the

scaffold poles and gripping tight as I leaned out over the hole, the beam of my torch almost lost in the expanse of water that flooded the cavern below. The tide seemed higher than when Lennie and I looked down at it, the beach no more than a narrow strip and only the upper fluke of the rusty anchor above water. I didn't see her at first. She had retreated to the far end of the beach, her body pressed back against the rock wall of the cavern, so that all I could see of her was a vague shadow in the yellowing beam.

'Soo! Is that you?'

She was too far away and she had her hands up to her face. I couldn't be sure. I called again, but she shrank back, scared that one of the men who had held her captive had returned. It wasn't until I called my own name several times that she finally moved. She came across the beach very slowly, her face growing clearer and whiter as she approached, her black hair turned almost grey with rock dust, her eyes large and wild-looking. She wouldn't believe it was really me till I shone the torch on my face, and then she suddenly collapsed.

There was nothing for it but to go down to her. Fortunately the rope on the pulley was a long one, so that I was able to fasten one end of it round my body and use the other part to lower myself to the beach. She had passed out completely, her body limp, her eyes closed. There was a nasty bruise on her cheek and a gash on the back of her right wrist that had left the whole hand tacky with half-congealed blood. I bathed her face in sea water, the hand too, but it only caused the bleeding to start again.

The sting of it must have brought her round, for when I had scooped up some more water in my cupped hands, I came back to find her staring up at me. 'Who are you?' The words were barely audible, her body stiff and trembling uncontrollably.

'It's Mike,' I said and reached out for the torch, shining it on my face again.

'Oh, my God!' She reached out, gripping hold of me, her fingers digging into my flesh so violently they hurt.

I don't know how long I sat there on that wet uncomfortable beach holding her in my arms, trying to comfort her. Not long I suppose, but long enough for my mind to try to grapple with the future and what this meant to us. 'I love you.' She said that twice, like an incantation, her voice very quiet as though the words meant a great deal to her, and holding her tight, I thought, well, maybe we could try again.

I got her up and put her foot in the looped end of the rope, passing it round her body under the arms. I was just pressing her hands on to the standing part of it, imploring her to hold tight while I was hoisting her up to the scaffolding above, when she began to giggle. 'The barrel . . .' she murmured.

'Barrel?' I had been on the point of putting my weight on the tail end of the rope, but now I hesitated, letting go of it and shining the torch on her face. Her eyes looked enormous, the whites catching the light, and her mouth was open, bubbling with uncontrollable laughter.

It was reaction, of course. Not hysteria, just reaction from the strain of all she had been through in the last thirty-six hours or so. 'Don't you remember? That record. *And then the barrel . . .*' She had deepened her voice, tears welling in her eyes, tears of laughter.

And suddenly I remembered. 'Hoffnung. Gerard Hoffnung.' The silly saga of that barrel full of bricks.

'*And then I met the barrel coming down.*' Her laughter became a giggle again. 'For a moment I thought I was the barrel. If I pulled you off your feet . . . We could be yo-yoing up and down . . .' She put her hand to her mouth, stilling her giggles. And after that she gripped the rope again. 'When I get to the top, don't let go, please.' She smiled at me, both of us remembering what had happened when the bricky had hoisted the barrel back up to the top of the chimney.

I hesitated, not sure whether I could trust her to reach for the scaffolding and haul herself out. But she seemed to have steadied herself. 'Okay,' I said. 'You're the barrel and you're going up.'

She was more of a weight than I had realised, and when her legs finally disappeared into the blowhole I began to wonder if I could hold her. Then suddenly I was on the floor, the rope slack in my hands. 'You all right, Mike?' Her voice, remote and strangely hollow, seemed to come from the roof of the cavern.

'Yes, I'm all right.' I got to my feet and stood there

for a moment, letting the rope end down and getting my breath back. The height I had to hoist myself looked further than I had reckoned and if I couldn't make it . . . I swept the beam of my torch over the rock roof of the cavern where it came down to meet the water. Not a nice place to spend hours waiting for rescue, plagued by the thought that a gale might spring up from the north-west and the sea level rise. I knew then what it had been like for Soo, and she had lowered herself down on to the beach with no torch and no certainty that anybody would ever find her there.

I tied the end of the rope round my chest, put my foot in the loop and hauled down on the other end of it. For a moment I didn't think I would ever get off the ground, then suddenly I was swinging free, and after that it was a little easier. I didn't realise it at the time, but Soo was hauling too and it was her weight that made the difference.

It was when we were back in the first expansion chamber that she said, 'You know about Miguel?' The whisper of her voice trembled on the dank air.

'Yes.'

'You saw him?'

It wasn't something I wanted her to dwell on, so I didn't answer.

'I only had matches. Book matches from the Figuera Restaurant. I used five of them. Poor Miguel. He looked terrible. After that I had barely half a dozen left. I used the last after I'd lowered myself into the cave. I think if you hadn't come . . . It was so dark and damp, and the sound of the water . . . I think a few hours more and I would have gone for a swim. I couldn't have stood it much longer.' Her words came in a rush, her body trembling again. The smell was there in our nostrils and I think it was that more than anything that had brought back her fears.

We had reached the rope hanging from the hole in the cellar floor and when I had hauled her up the trembling had stopped. I took her back the way I had come and out through the door in the villa's top level. She stopped there, staring up at the stars, breathing deeply. I shall never forget that moment, the ecstatic smile on her face, the tears in her eyes. 'My God!' she whispered, her hand gripping my arm. 'I never realised what life meant before, not really. Freedom and the smell of plants growing, the stars, being able to see. And you,' she added, looking up at me, wide-eyed. 'Oh, God, Mike!' And she was in my arms and I was kissing her. 'Let's go somewhere,' she said. 'Not home. I'd have to cook something. I'm hungry. My God! I'm hungry. Let's pretend we've only just met. Lets go out somewhere and celebrate. Just the two of us.'

I knew she couldn't settle now, she was too keyed up, so I drove her to Fornells, to a favourite restaurant of ours that stood back from the waterfront. We knew the people there and she was able to clean herself up, telling them we had been exploring a cave and she had fallen down a hole.

It was past midnight when we left Fornells and she was asleep before we reached the old salt pans and the end of the shallow inlet. We had shared a bottle of Rioja *tinto* over the meal and she had had a large La Ina before it and two brandies with the coffee. She had every reason to sleep, but as soon as I turned the car on to the quay she was awake. Petra's inflatable was lying alongside and she saw it before I could switch the lights off. 'What's Petra doing here?'

I thought I detected a note of hostility in her voice, so I said nothing. Somebody must have recovered the boat from Cala Llonga, or wherever Evans had beached it, somebody from *Medusa* presumably. The lights were on in our flat upstairs, the chandlery door ajar, and as we went in Petra appeared at the top of the stairs. 'You found her.' She was looking down at Soo. 'Thank God for that. We've been waiting here – hours it seems, waiting and wondering. You all right, Soo?'

'Yes. I'm all right.' Her voice shook slightly.

'Who's with you?' I asked. 'You said *we*.'

I think I knew the answer, but when she said 'Gareth', Soo gave a little gasp and I cursed under my breath. It wasn't the moment. 'What the hell's he want?'

'You'd better come up,' Petra said. 'It's been a long couple of hours, and not knowing didn't help.' Her voice was a little slurred.

I told her to get Soo to bed and pushed past her, taking the stairs two at a time. I wanted to get shot of him, to save Soo the emotional strain of meeting him face-to-face. I didn't know what the effect on her would be.

He was in the front room, sitting in the wing chair I normally used with a glass in his hand and a bottle of brandy open on the table beside him. He was dressed in a white open-necked shirt and grey flannels, his face gleaming with perspiration, and his eyes had difficulty in focusing on me. 'Ah, M-Mike.' He hauled himself to his feet, clutching the back of the chair. He was very, very tight. He started to say something, but then he stopped, his eyes narrowing as he stared past me.

I turned to find Soo in the doorway, her eyes wide and fixed on Gareth as he tried to pull himself together. 'Y'rorlright-th'n,' he mumbled.

She nodded and they stood there, the two of them, gazing at each other. Then abruptly Soo turned away, walking blindly into Petra, who had been standing just behind her in the doorway. 'Get her to bed,' I told her again, and she took Soo's arm and led her off to the bedroom. But she was back almost immediately. 'She's asking for Benjie.'

I'd forgotten about the dog. 'Tell her I'll get it for her.'

Gareth had subsided back into my chair, his arms slack, his eyes closing. 'Where did you find her?' he asked. And when I told him, he muttered, 'That's like Pat. Leave it to the sea, anything so long as he doesn't have to do it himself.' He hesitated. 'Impersonal,' he went on reflectively. 'Couldn't stand close contact, y'know. Didn't like to touch people, women especially.' And he added, 'Strange sort of man.'

Those last words were mumbled so softly I could

barely hear them, and when I told him how he had seized hold of Petra and held a knife at her throat, he didn't seem to take it in, muttering something about he'd been thinking, his eyes half-closed.

I picked up the bottle and poured myself a drink. As I put it back on the side table, he reached out for it. 'B'n thinking,' he said again, leaning forward and staring down at his glass, which was half-full. 'Abou' what they did to poor ol' Byng.' He shook his head, picking up his glass. He stared at it for a moment, then put it down again, carefully. 'Had enough, eh?' He collapsed back in his chair. 'Byng. And now me. Know what they'll do to me?' He was leaning back, his black hair limp against the wing of the chair, deep furrows creasing his forehead, and his dark eyes staring into space. 'I b'n wress-wrestling all afternoon with a bloody form, man. S two three t-two – report on collision and grounding. I grounded my ship, y'see.' The eyes fixed suddenly on me. 'How the hell do I explain that?' And then, leaning suddenly forward, 'Bu' I di'n run.' He was peering up at me. 'I di'n run like poor ol' Byng. Shot him,' he added. 'On the quarterdeck of the ol' *Monarch* – in Portsmouth Harbour with the whole Fleet gawping at it.' And then he quoted, speaking slowly, groping for the words: '*Il est bon de tuer de temps en temps un amiral pour encrug-encourager les autres* – that's what Voltaire said. F-fortunately I'm not an admiral. *Tuer non, mais . . .*'

He paused, staring at me sombrely. 'You ever b'n at a court martial?' He didn't wait for me to shake my head, but went straight on: 'That's what'll happen to me, y'know. They'll fly me to Portsmouth, an' just inside the main gate, ther'shpeshul room for poor buggers like me who've run their ships aground, an' you go back in with the prisoner's friend an' there's your sword with the b-blade pointing at you.' He shook his head angrily. 'An' all because I can't tell them the truth about why I ran *Medusa* ashore. All because of that devil Pat . . .' His voice trailed away. 'If Pat hadn't got hold of her . . . I can't tell them that, can I? So I'll be shot – figuratively, you un'erstand. They'd never . . .' His head was nodding. 'Never admit personal reason as legit-gitimate defence.' He reached out his hand to the side table, groping for his glass.

'That's the second bottle.' Petra had come back and was standing looking at him. 'I've given her something to make her sleep. She'll be all right now.' She nodded towards Gareth. 'After they'd recovered the inflatable he insisted on coming ashore with me. Said he wanted to see you. But I think it was Soo really. He wanted to make certain she was all right.' And she added, 'He's been here ever since – waiting. What are we going to do with him? He can't go back to his ship in this state. And he's worried sick about the future.' She touched my arm. 'Why did he do it, Mike? I was there. I saw it. He ran his ship aground – deliberately. Why?'

That was the question the Board of Enquiry was to ask him four days later. Not because Mrs Suzanne Steele was being held as hostage, they didn't know about that at the outset. Their primary concern was whether he could have achieved his purpose of holding fast in the approaches to Mahon without the need to ground his ship. But that was before they called Lieutenant Commander Mault to give evidence.

PART FIVE

BOARD OF ENQUIRY

CHAPTER ONE

It **never** occurred to me that I would be involved. A Naval Board of Enquiry, Gareth explained as I took him down the stairs and out into the bright sunlight next morning, is much like that for any commercial shipping incident, except that the resulting report often includes a recommendation for court martial proceedings to be taken against those thought to be responsible. 'I shall, of course, be held solely responsible. And rightly.'

He stood there for a moment on the quay, looking out to the frigate half-merged in the shadowed bulk of the hospital ruins. 'I'll be relieved of my command and sent back for trial.' He said it slowly, a note of resignation in his voice. He looked dreadful in that dazzlingly crisp light, dark rings under his eyes, a worried look and his mouth compressed to a hard line. Then he suddenly smiled and his face lit up. 'Must be one of the shortest and most fraught commands anybody has ever had.' He shook his head, still smiling, and with a careful jauntiness walked across the quay to the waiting launch.

His last words to me before jumping in were, 'Tell her to forget all about me. I shan't attempt to see her again.' He thanked me then for putting him up for the night, gave me a quick, perfunctory salute, and seated himself in the stern.

It was Masterton who was in charge again. He looked up at me, waiting for me to follow. 'Well, don't let's hang around, Midshipman Masterton,' Gareth snapped at him. 'Get going.'

'Yes, sir. Sorry, sir.' The boy gave the order to cast off. 'My regards to Miss Callis please,' he called out to me brightly. Then he swung the launch away from the quay and headed out to the grounded frigate, where the port tug was already standing by to try to tow her off on the top of the tide.

That was Saturday and by mid-morning, with the help of one of the Spanish destroyers, *Medusa* was off the rocks and lying to her anchor some three cables off the Club Maritimo, not far from where the oil tanker usually anchored. Apart from the fact that her pumps had to be kept going and that extra pumps brought in from the Naval Base were gushing water over the side, she looked perfectly all right. However, divers were down most of the day examining the stern, and that evening I heard that both propellers were damaged and it was thought the port prop shaft had been forced out of alignment. She was expected to be towed to Barcelona for repairs within the week.

Wade phoned me from London on Sunday morning

to ask if I had any news of Evans. His voice sounded relaxed, even friendly. And when I told him I hadn't the slightest idea where the man was, he laughed and said, 'No, I didn't expect you would. But did you gather any idea what his future plans were? You had a meeting with him on *Medusa*.'

'How do you know that?'

He ignored my question. 'I imagine the main point of that meeting was to use your wife as a lever to get Lloyd Jones to take his frigate out of Mahon. I'm not asking you for details of that meeting,' he added quickly. 'That will be a matter for Captain Wheatcroft. What I want to know is, did Evans at any time during that meeting, or when you were on the island together, give any indication of what his plans were?'

'Of course not,' I said. 'Until the frigate went aground he was fully committed to the new government of Ismail Fuxá and to ensuring that the powerful aid it had asked for would not be hindered from entering the port.'

'Yes, but afterwards – after *Medusa* had gone aground?'

'The grounding and Miss Callis's arrival were almost simultaneous. You know about what happened after that, do you?' I asked him.

'Yes. But I'm not interested in that, only in whether he gave you any indication of what he might do next, where he would go?'

'There wasn't time.'

'All right, but earlier, when you and he were with Lloyd Jones in his cabin on *Medusa*.'

Again I told him there was no reason for Evans to even think about where he might go next. 'The discussion was about my wife and getting Lloyd Jones to take his frigate out of Mahon. He'd no reason then to think beyond the next few hours.'

'I see.' He was silent then, and the silence lasted so long I began to think we had been disconnected. Suddenly he said, 'You don't think he's still on Menorca then?'

'It hadn't occurred to me,' I said. 'Why?'

'That fishing boat you let him have – did you know it was sighted abandoned and on fire just outside Spanish territorial waters?' Another silence, and then he said, 'Oh well, doubtless he's pushed off with the rest of them.' And he added, 'Now if you'd been able to tell me he was hiding up somewhere on the island . . .' I could almost hear his shrug over the line as he went on, 'Pity! Looks as though somebody will have to start picking up the trail all over again.' And without another word he rang off.

Captain Wheatcroft, the officer sent out to head the Board of Enquiry, arrived that afternoon. With him on the same plane were his two Board Members, a Commander Lovelock from Naval Plans, a marine engineering commander, and a smart little snub-nosed Wren Writer with black hair and rather bulging eyes. All four stayed at the Port Mahon Hotel, which had rooms to spare, some of their American guests having decided to get out. Also on the plane was a Commander Firth. Gareth had apparently served under him and having recently relinquished command of another frigate, he had been flown out to help and advise Gareth during the Enquiry – a sort of prisoner's friend. The Board began their sittings the following day, on board *Medusa*.

The morning was taken up with questions arising from her Captain's report of the grounding and the reasons for it, the afternoon with the evidence of one or two of the other officers, Lieutenant Commander Mault in particular. He was questioned by the Board for well over an hour.

I only heard about this, of course, later, after it was all over. I knew nothing about it at the time, but after Wade's phone call I was not altogether surprised when a midshipman, not Masterton, delivered a note from the Chairman of the Board calling me as a witness and requesting that I attend on board HMS *Medusa* at 10.00 hours the next morning. There would be a launch sent for me at 09.30.

Soo's immediate reaction when I told her was, 'Do they know about me?' and she added quickly, 'About my being held as a hostage?'

'Of course.' My own desperate enquiries had made that inevitable, and Miguel's body being found where she had been left to die had ensured maximum publicity.

'I know what they'll try and do. They'll try and prove he grounded his ship because of me. That's why you're being called.' Her large, dark eyes had a wild look. 'Can't you say he barely knew me, that when you were on board with Gareth and that wretched half-brother of his, he was making use of me just as

423

he would any other hostage? I mean, so long as they don't know he was seeing me, then they'll have to accept that he put his ship aground because it was the only way he could be sure he wouldn't be towed out . . .' The words had been pouring out of her she was so tensed up, but I was shaking my head and slowly her voice died.

In the end I told her quite bluntly that what had happened was common knowledge. 'Things happen. That's life. And once they've happened they can't be undone.'

She nodded slowly, biting her lip. And then suddenly she began to cry. I tried to say I would do what I could. 'I've no desire to ruin his career, but if they bring it up I'm not going to pretend I'm a fool and didn't know.' And I added, 'A lot will depend on the sort of man Captain Wheatcroft turns out to be, how understanding he is of the emotional needs of naval officers, particularly somebody like Gareth.' But she wasn't listening. She had turned away, shaking her head, and with her hand to her mouth she ran to the bedroom and shut the door.

The Board of Enquiry had taken over the Captain's day cabin, the three members seated at a folding table that had been brought up from the wardroom, their blue uniforms with the gold bands on cuffs and shoulder straps solidly impressive. I was shown to a chair set facing them and after the preliminaries the Chairman went out of his way to put me at my ease by saying, 'This is not in any sense a court, Mr Steele, but you will understand, I am sure, that an expensive and valuable Navy ship has been set aground and we have to enquire into the circumstances of that grounding. For instance, was it accidental grounding or was it deliberate? If the latter, then what were the reasons for the decision to set the ship aground?'

He was leaning a little forward, a long, fine-boned face with sharply pointed nose and high-domed forehead largely devoid of hair. 'I want you to understand – whatever your personal feelings – that the purpose of this Board is to resolve those two questions and report our findings. You will appreciate, of course, that the circumstances were very unusual – almost, I might say, unprecedented. And the odd thing is that you, a civilian, were on board, and to some extent involved, at several of the most crucial moments.'

Captain Wheatcroft had considerable charm, his manner friendly and altogether disarming, except that, as the questions developed, his voice, which was what I would call very establishment Navy, became more aloof and inquisitorial. He had me describe the frigate's movements from the time she raised her anchor to the time she grounded, and here I was able to avoid any reference to the glimpse I had had of an altercation between Gareth and his First Lieutenant. 'So you're suggesting the ship was out of control?'

'It looked like it,' I replied.

'Because he went stern-first through the narrows?' He didn't wait for me to agree, but added, 'He'd no reason to go through the narrows. He had far more sea room to the east of Bloody Island.' And then he said, 'I think I should tell you the evidence we have already heard makes it clear that there was nothing wrong with the engines. That was a put-up job to justify the Captain's refusal to move his ship when he had been ordered to leave by the port authorities, and indeed by the self-styled president of the new regime himself. You know about that, I think?' And when I nodded, he smiled as though he had established a point he had been trying to make. 'You realise, of course, what follows from that?'

I nodded.

'So can I have a direct answer from you on the first question we are having to resolve – in your opinion was the grounding of the frigate *Medusa* deliberate? Yes or no, please.'

'Yes,' I said.

'Good. Now to the second question, Mr Steele, and this I think you may find some difficulty in answering. What in your opinion was the overriding reason for Lieutenant Commander Lloyd Jones's action in deliberately grounding his ship? And let me say here we already know that you were on board and here in this very cabin when a man named Evans arrived from Cala Llonga and was brought up to see him.' He glanced hurriedly through his notes. 'The three of you were together here, with nobody else present, for approximately ten minutes, perhaps a little longer. Now, would you kindly tell us exactly what was said? Evans was holding your wife hostage, correct?'

'Yes.'

'Any particular reason why they should have seized your wife rather than somebody else's wife?'

I told him that perhaps it was because Lloyd Jones had personally met her. She wasn't a stranger to him. And I added, 'The circumstances were somewhat unusual and I was sure Evans would have heard about it.' I knew I was treading on thin ice here, and to avoid saying too much, I told him exactly what had happened the night of the barbecue.

'And you think, if Evans knew about that, it would be sufficient to make him single her out from all the wives in Mahon?' And he went straight on, 'You know, of course, that Evans is Lieutenant Commander Lloyd Jones's half-brother. Moreover, Evans had saved his life. That would surely be enough without bringing a woman into it?'

I didn't answer that. The man had been too well briefed, by Wade probably. He smiled and leaned back in his chair. 'Well go on, Mr Steele. You were going to tell us what exactly took place in this cabin when the Captain, you and Evans were closeted here together for over ten minutes.'

I gave him a brief account of what had been said, without referring to the vicious way Evans had tried to needle us both. But it wasn't Wade who had briefed him. It was somebody local, or else one of the officers, Mault probably, had leapt to conclusions, for he didn't wait for me to finish before saying, 'I'm afraid I must now ask a delicate and very personal question. I am sure you will understand why it is absolutely essential you give me a frank answer. What was the exact nature of the relationship between Lieutenant Commander Lloyd Jones and your wife?'

'I don't follow you,' I said.

'I think you do.'

'Are you suggesting there was something wrong with the relationship? They met for the first time at that Red Cross barbecue. I told you that. Within a fortnight Gareth Lloyd Jones left for Gibraltar to take command of this ship. If you're suggesting what I think you are, then they knew each other for much too short a time.'

He looked at me quizzically. 'No offence, Mr Steele, but it doesn't take long, and it would explain, you see, why Evans would think that by seizing hold of your wife and threatening her life—'

'That's enough,' I said, pushing back my chair and getting to my feet. 'You've no right to make allegations like that on hearsay.' I don't know why, but I was angry, for Gareth as well as Soo. I felt he had been through quite enough without having this thrown in his face. And why should Soo's name be dragged into it, just because they were both human and had reacted quite spontaneously to something they couldn't help?

Standing there, I told Wheatcroft what I thought of him. 'You post a man to the command of a ship that's half volunteers, half throw-outs, tell him to do the impossible, and then when he does it, you come here chairing an enquiry that will send him to court martial, and you have the effrontery to suggest, as a means of destroying him, that he was having an affair with my wife.'

He smiled, oddly enough quite a warm smile. 'You say he wasn't having an affair, that there is no truth—'

'Of course I do.' And I added, 'I would hardly have gone on board his ship in Malta if I had suspected anything like that, would I?' I made it a question in the hope that he would believe me.

'So, if there was a court martial, you would categorically deny that there was any truth in the allegation?'

'Certainly.'

'You would be under oath remember.'

I nodded. I didn't trust myself to say any more.

'And that suggestion was never made by Evans when he was alone here with the two of you trying to persuade Lloyd Jones to leave Mahon?'

'It was made,' I said. 'As a try-on. Having grabbed my wife, he was probing on the off-chance he could use her more effectively.'

'And it didn't work?'

'No.'

'It had no connection with the subsequent grounding?'

'Why should it if it wasn't true? In any case, Gareth – ' and I used his Christian name then for the first time – 'was fixing it so that there was no way they could get him to leave port. Soo didn't come into it.'

'And your testimony as regards that will stand at the court martial?'

'If he's court-martialled, and I'm called to give evidence, then that's what I shall say.'

He stared at me a moment, then turned to the other two Board members. 'Any further questions, gentlemen?' And when they both shook their heads, he smiled and got to his feet. 'Then that's all, Mr Steele.' He held out his hand. 'Thank you for coming here to give evidence.' He called to the petty officer waiting outside and ordered him to see me off the ship. Then, turning to me again, he said, 'I'm hoping to have a little party here on board before I leave. Perhaps you and your wife would care to come – a small return for the trouble we have caused you.' He looked round at his colleagues. 'Tomorrow evening, don't you think?' They nodded and he said to me, 'Tomorrow evening then, six o'clock say. The launch will pick you up shortly before.'

It cannot be every day that the Chairman of a Board of Enquiry gives a party on the afterdeck of the very ship whose grounding he has been enquiring into. But the circumstances were exceptional, and so was Julian Wheatcroft's behaviour. No sign of the distant severity he had shown as Chairman of the enquiry. Now all the well-educated charm of the man was back in place as he greeted his guests on the flight deck. The borrowed deck pumps had been temporarily stilled, the ship relatively quiet, and it was one of those really lovely Menorcan evenings, the air warm and not a breath of wind.

I watched him as he greeted Soo, a little bow and a warm smile, his eyes travelling quickly over her body and fastening on her face, alert, watchful, sexually aware. The same watchfulness was there as she and

Gareth greeted each other. It was obvious he was trying to make up his mind whether or not they had been lovers. She had assured me they had not, that it had been purely emotional. In retrospect, I see his problem. An emotional involvement did not concern him, only a physical one, particularly if the result were a child.

I had warned Soo that she would be virtually on show and that for Gareth's sake, if not for mine, she should be on her guard. In the event, she carried it off perfectly, greeting Gareth with an easy friendliness, offering him her cheek, smiling and happy-looking as she congratulated him on having survived such a difficult assignment. She did it with just the right touch of intimacy and warmth. I was proud of her, and watching Wheatcroft, I saw him relax, then turn away to say something to Lovelock, the commander from Plans, who had also been monitoring the meeting between Soo and Gareth. He nodded, the down-turned corners of his mouth twisting themselves into an unaccustomed smile. He, too, seemed suddenly relaxed.

It was a very small party, Gareth the only one of *Medusa*'s officers present, Soo and myself the only civilians. The other guests were the admiral commanding the Spanish fleet, his flag officer, and Fernando Perez from the Naval Base with his wife Ramona. Afterwards, when I talked it over with Soo, I found she had come to the same conclusion I had, that Wheatcroft's first objective in hosting such a very select little party was to take a look at her and check that it was safe for the Board to take the line it had virtually decided on.

His second objective was, of course, to make a short speech, largely for the benefit of the Spanish admiral and the commander of the Mahon Naval Base. For this he had arranged that Lieutenant Sykes should be waiting on deck so that the brief and very political speech he made was instantly translated into Spanish. And when he had finished, it was the Spanish admiral's turn to make a little speech.

Whether the admiral had been briefed or not I do not know, but at the end of his speech, when we were all applauding, he brought from his pocket an ornate little case, went across to Gareth, and taking out a bright ribbon with a decoration suspended from it, hung it round his neck.

Poor Gareth! He had clearly had no warning of this. He stood there for a moment, a flush on his face and his mouth opening and closing, no words coming. Finally, in desperation, he gave a naval salute and murmured one word, 'G-gracias.'

I thought that was the end of it. I think we all did. But then Julian Wheatcroft stepped forward again and said, 'There is something else I wish to say.' Victor Sykes was again translating the English into Spanish and I believe his continued presence to have been deliberate, ensuring as it did that the gist of everything that was being said would pass round the ship. 'Normally the findings of a Board of Enquiry are confidential and only revealed later when an announcement is made as to whether or not a court martial will result. However, the risks that Lieutenant Commander Lloyd Jones, his officers and men accepted and faced make the circumstances of *Medusa*'s grounding quite extra-ordinary.' He separated the words out so that they had the older, stronger meaning. 'And because I was very conscious that any recommendations I might make might be overturned, I've spent much of today in an exchange of signals with CINCFLEET and the Ministry of Defence. I may say that the Board was quite unanimous in its view that court martial proceedings were inappropriate in this case and I now have a directive – ' and here his voice became very formal and deliberate – 'from the Secretary of State for Defence, approved personally by the Prime Minister, that in the exceptional and unprecedented circumstances of the grounding it has been decided to rule out any question of a court martial.'

He paused there, then moved a step or two towards Gareth. 'I, too, have a gift for you. It is not, I'm afraid, as valuable or as beautiful as the decoration with which you have been honoured by the King of Spain. It was given to me just before I left London. It is from 10 Downing Street, a personal letter from the Prime Minister to you, and to all those serving on board HMS *Medusa*.' The long envelope in his hand, he stepped forward, handed it to Gareth, then took a step back and gave him a magnificent salute.

There was a long pause, Gareth staring down at it, Welsh emotion strangling any reply, actual tears in his eyes. It was a moment we all shared, but having been with him on various very crucial occasions, I could appreciate more than any of the others on the flight deck the depth of his feeling, the ordeal he had been through – not only facing the prospect of imminent death for himself and the men serving under him, but later in the loneliness of waiting for his career to be terminated in a court martial.

Poor ol' Byng! I remembered his words, slurred with drink, and now I saw him crying openly, the Spanish decoration catching the last of the sun as he pulled himself together and returned Captain Wheatcroft's salute.

THE DOOMED OASIS

To

*The Royal Air Force and the Officers
of the Trucial Oman Scouts*

With my admiration for the work they do in circumstances of difficulty, often of great hardship; and with my appreciation of their co-operation, without which this book could not have been written.

*

I would like to express my appreciation of the help I have received from Neil Innes during the actual writing of *The Doomed Oasis*. He was Minister of External Affairs to the Sultan of Muscat at the time I was journeying in Arabia; not only did he check the final typescript for me, but at various stages of the writing I benefited greatly from his knowledge. I should perhaps make it clear, however, that I have ignored his advice on the spelling of two Arab names, in particular believing that my own spelling of Makhmud would be more helpful in conveying the sound of that name than the correct Mahmud. Both the sheikhdom of Saraifa and the emirate of Hadd are, of course, entirely imaginary Arab States.

CONTENTS

Cold voices whisper and say—
'He is crazed with the spell of far Arabia,
They have stolen his wits away.'

WALTER DE LA MARE

PART ONE

THE COURT OF FIRST INSTANCE

Call Aubrey George Grant!
Aubrey George Grant!

The moment had come. My mouth felt suddenly dry. The Court was waiting and I knew the ordeal ahead of me was a long one. And at the back of my mind was the knowledge that in telling the truth, the whole truth, I might convict an innocent man. I felt the touch of her hand on mine, the quick pressure of her fingers, and I rose to my feet, the sweat sticking the shirt to my back as I followed the attendant. The doors of the courtroom stood open. I checked, a moment's hesitation in the entrance; the place was packed, the atmosphere tense with expectancy.

Quickly I walked down through the Court, the setting familiar to me, a part of my working life; only my role had changed. It was the first time I had entered Court as a witness. I kept my eyes on the Judge, on the pale London face above the tropical suit. He had

3

been specially appointed to try this unusual case and he looked tired after the long flight, shrunken almost, the suit too large; without the scarlet robes he seemed less awe-inspiring and the Law robbed of some of its majesty. Counsel, too, looked ordinary without wig and gown, and the courtroom itself – all open shirts or pale, loose-fitting jackets, a scattering of Bahrainis in flowing Arab robes. The Code of Criminal Procedure in this Court was based on the Indian Penal Code, yet in essence it was the same Law, and as I moved towards the witness box, the Judge leaned slightly forward, peering at me short-sightedly, his hands clasped together.

Once in the box I faced the crowded courtroom; no longer a mass of unidentifiable humanity, but a sea of faces all lifted to stare in silent expectation, waiting for the full story which they now knew I alone could give.

I had been called as a witness, not for the Defence, but for the Prosecution. Every word I uttered would be taken down and rushed out of Bahrain by telephone and radio; and thousands of miles away the metal drums of the presses would pour the story out to waiting millions. Representatives of almost every London newspaper were here and half the world's press, packed so tight in this improvised courtroom that they could hardly breathe. And outside in the broiling, humid heat were the photographers and the newsreel men and the television recording units, and at the airfield across the water on the island of Muharraq, special planes waited to fly the pictures that would be flashed on the screens of television sets in the homes of countless people.

Here and there in that sea of faces below me were people I recognized, people who had taken part in the events I was going to have to describe. There was Sir Philip Gorde, director of Gulfoman Oilfields Development, looking old and battered, his heavy-lidded eyes half-closed; and beside him, Erkhard, very neat and cool. Colonel George was there and Captain Berry, easily distinguishable, smart in their uniform of short-sleeved khaki shirts and well-creased khaki longs. Sue had followed me in, and it came as something of a shock to me to see that she had seated herself next to that strange, half-Arab, half-French girl who called herself Tessa. Captain Griffiths, too, his beard neat and pointed – a reminder of Cardiff and the visit that had started it all.

Raise your right hand.

I did so and my gaze shifted involuntarily to the prisoner in the dock. He was watching me and for a moment our eyes met. I thought he smiled, but I couldn't be sure. I had a sense of surprise, almost of shock. Perhaps it was the tropical suit, the neatly brushed hair; he looked a different man. There was only the arm still in a sling to remind me that this was the man whose singleness of purpose had captured the world's imagination. The Book thrust into my hand disrupted my thoughts.

Repeat after me. My lips were dry. I had turned away from him, but I knew he was still watching me. *I swear by Almighty God.*

5

'I swear by Almighty God—'

That the evidence I shall give the Court.

'That the evidence I shall give the Court—' And as I said it I was wondering how the public at home would react to what I was going to have to tell the Court. Until to-day they would have had quite a different picture of the prisoner = a mental picture culled from garbled versions of his exploits heard over radio and seen on television, read in newspapers and periodicals, a colourful, larger-than-life picture entirely at odds with the neat figure standing alone there in the dock accused of murder.

Shall be the truth.

'Shall be the truth—' They should never have brought the case. He was a national hero and whatever the verdict of the Court, the public's reaction would be a violent one. But would they be for him or against him?

The whole truth.

'The whole truth—'

And nothing but the truth.

'And nothing but the truth.'

Your full name please?

'Aubrey George Grant.'

And then Counsel for the Crown, on his feet and facing me: 'You are a solicitor by profession I believe?'

'Yes.'

'Were you called upon to act for the prisoner on his arrest?'

'Yes.'

'When did you cease to act for him?'

'As soon as I realized I was being regarded as a material witness for the Prosecution.'

'You have acted for the prisoner before, I think?'

'Yes.'

'When was that?'

'Just over four years ago.'

The Judge's voice suddenly interjected: 'How long ago?' His hand was cupped to his ear.

'Four years, my Lord.'

The Prosecution moved a step nearer, hands hung in the lapels of his jacket, the skin of the face cool as parchment in the humid heat. 'I will ask the witness to take his mind back now to the afternoon of March twenty-first four years ago. On that afternoon you received a telephone call from a Mrs Thomas of Seventeen, Everdale Road, Cardiff. And as a result of that telephone call you went to that address.'

'Yes.'

'Perhaps you will now tell the Court in your own words what happened—'

PART TWO

THE WHOLE TRUTH

ESCAPE TO SARAIFA

Everdale Road was in the Grangetown district of Cardiff. It was one of those terrace streets of grim Victorian brick, roofs hunched against the wet west wind, windowed eyes peering blindly for the view of river and sea that was blocked by other similar houses. Two streets away and you could look across the Taff to the litter of cranes, the glimpse of funnels that marked the Bute Docks. It always depressed me, this area of Cardiff; it lacked the squalid colour of Tiger Bay, the bridge across the Taff seeming to cut it off from the toughness and sense of purpose that gave a lift to the real dock area. The street was deserted except for one car, a small black saloon. It stood outside number seventeen, and as I drew in to the curb behind it, I glanced quickly at the house. There was nothing to distinguish it from the others, except the number. A light was on in one of the downstairs rooms. Neat lace curtains were looped back from the windows.

I got out and rang the bell, wondering what I was going to find inside. Trouble of some sort; nobody ever called me to this district unless they were in trouble. And the voice over the phone – it had been a woman's voice, low and urgent, near to panic. I glanced at my watch. Four-thirty. The light was already going out of the cloud-filled sky. A slight drizzle gave a black shine to the surface of the street.

Across the road a curtain moved; hidden eyes watching, something to gossip about. I knew the black saloon parked at the curb. It was Dr Harvey's. But if there was death in the house then the curtains would have been drawn. My hand was reaching out to the bell-push again when the latch of the door clicked and voices sounded: ' . . . nothing else I could have done, Mrs Thomas. A case for the police . . . you understand, I hope. And the ambulance will be here any minute now.' The door was flung open and Dr Harvey bustled out, almost cannoning into me. 'Oh, it's you, Grant.' He checked in mid-flight, black bag gripped in his hand, no overcoat as usual, a young, fair-haired, very serious man in a perpetual hurry. 'Well, I suppose you'll be able to make some sort of a case out of it in court. The boy's certainly going to need legal advice.' There was no love lost between us. We'd tangled over medical evidence before. 'Got to deliver a baby now. Can't do anything more for that chap.' And he almost ran out to his car.

'Mr Grant?' The woman was staring at me uncertainly.

I nodded. 'Of Evans, Jones & Evans, solicitors. You telephoned me a little while back.'

'Yes, of course.' She held the door open for me, a small neat-looking person of between forty and fifty with deep-set, shadowed eyes. Her hair was greying, swept straight back from the forehead, the face dead white against the dark background of the passage. 'Will you come in, please.' She shut the door behind me. 'Dafydd didn't want me to call you. But I thought you wouldn't mind as your firm it is that handled that little allowance for me.'

It was the first I knew we acted for her in any way. I thought she'd phoned me because I'm willing in certain circumstances to take a case without a fee. 'What's the trouble, Mrs Thomas?' I asked her, for she was standing motionless as though unwilling to let me go further into the house.

She hesitated, and then almost in a whisper, 'Well, it's Dafydd really, you see. He came back – and then . . . Oh dear, it's all so difficult to explain.' Now that she had shut the street door, I could see no more than the outline of her face, but her voice, trembling to a stop, told me she was having to fight to keep control of herself. She was frightened, too. 'I don't know what he'll do,' she whispered. 'And Sue not here. Sue could always manage him when I couldn't.'

'Sue is your daughter, is she?' I knew it would steady her if I asked questions.

'Yes, that's right. She works at the Infirmary, but I didn't phone her because she'd never get back here in time.'

'And David – that's your husband?'

'No, Dafydd's my son. He and Sue are twins. She understands him somehow.'

'I see, and he's in some sort of trouble?'

'Yes.' And then she added hastily, 'He's not a bad boy, not really.' She drew in her breath quickly as though gathering herself together. 'If I hadn't written to him like I did, it wouldn't have happened. But I'd had about all I could stand, you see, and then he came home and there was a bit of a row and Mr Thomas, he said things, you see, that he shouldn't have done, and suddenly they were hitting out at each other. It wasn't Dafydd's fault. He'd had a terrible shock, poor boy. And Mr Thomas, he'd had a few beers, and then—' She sucked in her breath again as though gulping for air. 'Well, then he had this stroke, you see, and I called Dr Harvey right away and then I tele-phoned you because I knew it meant trouble for Dafydd.' It had all come out in a rush as though she couldn't contain it any longer. 'My husband looked so bad, you see,' she added lamely, 'and I didn't know what would happen. I just didn't know what to do Mr Grant – not for the best, as you might say. And then Dr Harvey came and he said there wasn't much hope for him and he phoned the police so it's glad I am that I called you now. You'll know what to do and what Dafydd should say to them. He's not a bad boy,' she repeated in a voice that was suddenly on the defensive. 'Just a bit wild you know.' And she added quickly, 'Mr Thomas hit me you see.'

'There was a family row, in other words?'

'Yes. Yes, you could call it that. But I wouldn't like you to think that because Mr Thomas was a bit of a drinker there was anything wrong between us. He's good at heart, you know.'

'And he's had a stroke you say?'

'Yes, that's right. That's what Dr Harvey called it.' She seemed to have got a grip of herself. 'Come in now won't you, Mr Grant. He's lying on the couch in the parlour. And Dafydd's there too. I expect you'd like a word with him. But don't try and rush him, please,' she added in a whisper, and I got the impression she was afraid of her son. 'He needs a bit of handling, you see. And he's had a shock as I say – a dreadful shock.' She pushed open the door and stood back for me to enter. 'This is Mr Grant, Dafydd – Mr Grant the lawyer.'

The room was lit from the ceiling, a stark, glaring light without compromise. It showed me a couch with the body of a man lying on it. He was in his shirt sleeves, the brass gleam of a stud showing where his shirtband had been loosened. His eyes were closed and he was breathing with difficulty, his rather heavy, florid features fallen away so that the bone showed through the flesh. The nose had the veined look of a heavy drinker. Close against the gas fire, one elbow on the mantelpiece, leaned a youth of about twenty. He was rather over-dressed in a jacket with a lot of elaborate pockets and tucks and a pair of tight-fitting trousers. His face was as white as his mother's; the same features, too, except that the nose was more beaky, the jaw stronger. He didn't shift his position as I entered the room, didn't even look up. He was staring down at the gas fire and his immobility was oddly disconcerting.

Close by his feet was a litter of broken glass from the smashed front of one of those over-pretentious china cupboards. The mahogany beading as well as the glass had been broken in the struggle and the bric-à-brac with which the cabinet had been filled, mostly white china souvenirs from seaside towns, lay in confusion on the worn carpet. A vase, too, lay where it had fallen from the table by the window. It was unbroken, and beside it lay a much-thumbed photograph album spilling press-cuttings. There was something a little macabre about the whole room; nothing cleared up after the struggle and the father lying there half-dead on the couch with a blanket tucked round him; and the mother and son standing, facing each other, absolutely still.

I could feel the tension between them. It wasn't hate, but it was something just as strong, an emotion so violent that the man on the couch, myself, the state of the room didn't exist for them.

'Well, now.' I addressed the boy, my tone as matter-of-fact as I could make it in that sort of atmosphere. 'Suppose you tell me what happened.' But it was like talking to a brick wall. He had a sullen, withdrawn look.

'I've told you what happened,' his mother said in a whisper.

'Quite so, Mrs Thomas, but I'd like to hear it from your son.' She looked deathly tired. I turned to the boy again. 'You've had a shock,' I said gently. 'It's natural you should be a bit dazed by what's happened. . . .' But even as I said it I knew the boy wasn't dazed. The knuckles of the hand that gripped the mantelpiece were white with pressure and there was a muscle working at the back of the jaw. He was holding himself in like a boiler under pressure and I wasn't sure how best to handle him. His gaze had shifted now and he was staring at his mother. I felt sorry for the woman. 'Listen to me, young man,' I said. 'I understand Dr Harvey has called the police. They'll be here any minute now. If you want me to act for you, then you'd better start talking now, before they arrive.'

A slight movement of the shoulder, that was all the answer he made. It wasn't a shrug, more a muscular twitch as though he was impatient for me to go. 'Mr Grant is only trying to help, Dafydd.'

'*Dammo di*! What the hell good is a lawyer man now? It's done! and arguing about it won't alter anything.' His voice trembled. And then he turned on me, a flash of pale amber eyes, and told me to get out, the words violent, laced with obscenities.

'Dafydd!'

But she was frightened; she had no control over him. 'All right,' I said, and I moved towards the desk where I'd left my hat. 'I hope for your sake,' I added, 'that your father's condition isn't serious.'

'He's not my father.' The words flashed out from between clenched teeth. 'I'd have killed him if he'd been my father.' I turned to find his pale eyes fixed on his mother. 'I mean that, Ma. I swear I'll kill the swine – if I can ever find him.' The words had a violence and a bitterness that appalled me.

'He's not himself,' his mother murmured. 'He doesn't know what he's saying.' Her hands were plucking at the apron round her middle and her brown, doe-like eyes were wide with fear. She knew he'd meant it.

'You'd better get control of yourself,' I said. 'You've done enough damage for one day without threatening more and frightening your mother.'

But now the pressure inside him couldn't contain itself any more. 'You get out of here.' He said it quietly and because of that his words had force. 'What's happened here is nothing to do with you or anyone else. It's between my mother and me.' He spoke through clenched teeth as though he were still trying to keep some control over what he was saying. And then suddenly he lashed out wildly, all control gone: 'When you're suddenly told you're illegitimate, and your sister's illegitimate, too, you want to know a little more about it, don't you? You want to talk it over with your mother – ask her a few questions, find out who and what the hell you really are.'

He flung out an arm, pointing dramatically at the album on the floor. 'See that? Uncle Charles's scrap book. She subscribed to a press-cutting agency. Every story the newspapers published about him – it's all there, pasted in with loving care. My own mother clinging to the worn-out bed of an old love. Jesus Christ! It makes you want to weep. And me and Sue coming up the wrong side of the bloody blanket, and being fooled into calling that poor drunken sot Dada.' He stared at me balefully. 'Eight years old I was when I first stole a peek at the contents of that book. A relation, that's what she said, an uncle of mine. Started me getting interested in Arabia, it did. I thought he was a bloody hero. Instead, he's just a low-down, dirty heel who left my mother flat. Well, what do you say to that, eh? You're a lawyer. Maybe you can tell me what I ought to do about it?' And he glared at me as though I were in some way responsible.

And then he suddenly moved, a quick step forward that brought him face-to-face with me. 'Now you just get the hell out of here and let me talk to my mother alone, see.' His eyes had a wild look, the sort of look I'd only seen once before on a boy's face, but that had been in the midst of battle.

I'd known how to deal with it then. But this kid was different. It wasn't only that he looked tough; I had a feeling he was tough. Well, I'm not exactly soft, but I don't walk into things with my eyes open. But then I glanced at Mrs Thomas, saw how scared she was of him, and after that there was nothing for it but to stand my ground, not knowing what exactly he'd do, for I could feel the tension building up inside of him again. He was like a spring coiled too tight.

And then the ring of the ambulance bell sounded down the street and the violence suddenly died out of him. It drew up outside the house and a moment later two hospital attendants came in with a stretcher.

The attention of the three of us was focused then

on the man on the couch. He murmured as they shifted him, an inarticulate sound, and Mrs Thomas, fussing over him now, spoke his name. The tone of her voice had a quality that is only possible between people who have shared their lives together, and it seemed to reach him, for his eyes flicked briefly open and he murmured her name. 'Sarah.' It came thickly from his twisted lips, obscured by the effort of moving half-paralyzed muscles. 'Sarah – I'm sorry.' That was all. The eyes closed, the face became clay again, and they took him out.

Mrs Thomas followed them, sobbing uncontrollably. The door swung to of its own accord and the room was still. 'I shouldn't have hit him. It wasn't his fault.' The boy had turned away and his shoulders were moving. I realized suddenly that he was crying. 'Oh God!' he sobbed. 'I should have known. If I'd had any sense, I should have known.'

'You couldn't have known he'd have a stroke,' I told him.

He turned on me then. 'You don't understand.' The tears were standing in his eyes. 'He and I – we hated each other's guts. I can see why now. But at least he stood by us, poor sod.' And he added viciously, 'He was a damn' sight better than my real father. If I can ever lay my hands on that bastard—' He checked there and gave an odd little laugh. 'Bastard! That's funny, isn't it, me calling him a bastard.' He turned away then, brushing the back of his hand across his eyes. 'I wish I hadn't hit him,' he said quietly.

'He'll be all right.'

'You think so?' But then he shook his head. 'No, he's going to die. That's what the doctor said. He was the only father Sue and I ever knew,' he added, 'and now I've killed him.'

'Don't talk nonsense. It's not as dramatic as that. He's had a stroke – and anyway you're entitled to defend your mother when a man hits her.'

He looked at me. 'Did she say that?' And then he laughed, a little wildly. And after a moment he said, 'Yes, that's right – he hit her.' And he added, 'Christ! What a bloody mess!' The door of the ambulance banged in the street outside and he turned to stare out of the window. The engine started and it drove off. As though its departure had started an entirely new train of thought, he swung round on me. 'You're Whitaker's lawyer, aren't you?'

The name meant nothing to me, but then no doubt Mrs Thomas's allowance had been arranged by Evans years ago and it would be handled by my clerk as a matter of routine. 'Whitaker is the name of your father, is it – your natural father?'

'That's right. My *natural* father.' He spoke the word slowly, savouring it for the first time. And then he said, 'I want his address.'

'Why?'

'Why the hell do you think?' He was back at the window again. 'A bloke's got a right to know where his father lives, hasn't he?'

'Maybe,' I said. 'But I'm afraid I don't know his address.'

'That's a lie.' He came back to me, his eyes

searching my face. 'Well, you've got it on your files, haven't you? You could look it up.'

'If he's a client of mine, then I'm not at liberty to disclose—'

'Not even to his son?'

'No, not even to his son.' I hesitated. The boy's temper would cool and after all he'd a right to know where his father was. 'If I've got his address,' I said, 'then I'll write to him if you like and get his permission—'

'Oh, don't give me that crap. You know bloody well where he is.' He caught hold of my arm. 'Come on. Arabia, it is – somewhere in Arabia. Tell me, for Christ's sake.' He saw it was no good then and began to plead: 'Please, I haven't much time and I got to know. Do you hear? I got to know.' There was a desperate urgency in his voice. And then the grip on my arm tightened. 'Let's have it.' I thought he was going to hit out at me and my muscles tensed, ready for him.

'Dafydd!'

Mrs Thomas was standing in the doorway, her hands plucking again at the apron. 'I can't stand any more.' There was an edge to her voice that seemed to get through to him and he relaxed slowly and stepped back from me. 'I'll come for that address,' he muttered. 'Sooner or later I'll come to your office and get it out of you.' He was back at the window again, looking out. 'I'd like to talk to my mother now.' He stared at me, waiting for me to go.

I hesitated, glancing at Mrs Thomas. She was still

as stone, and her eyes, as they stared at her son, were wide and scared-looking. I heard the slow intake of her breath. 'I'll go and make some tea,' she said slowly, and I knew she wanted to escape into her kitchen. 'You'd like a cup of tea, wouldn't you now, Mr Grant?'

But before I could reply and give her the excuse she needed, her son had crossed over to her. 'Please, Ma.' His voice was urgent. 'There isn't much time, you see, and I got to talk to you.' He was pleading with her – a small boy now pleading with his mother, and I saw her weaken at once. I got my hat from the roll-top desk where I'd left it. 'It's all right, Mrs Thomas,' I said. 'I'll leave you now.' There was a phone on the desk, an old-fashioned hook-up instrument standing amongst a litter of books on greyhounds and racing form. 'You can always phone my office if you want me.'

She nodded dumbly. She was trembling slightly and I could see she was dreading the moment when she'd be left alone with him. But there was no point in my staying. This was something that lay between the two of them, alone. 'Take my advice,' I told him. 'When the police arrive, be a little more co-operative with them than you have been with me if you want to avoid trouble. And stick to your mother's story.'

He didn't say anything. The sullen look was back in his face. Mrs Thomas showed me to the door. 'I'm sorry,' she said. 'He's upset.'

'It's not unnatural.' I was remembering how I'd felt when I learned that my parents were divorced. I'd heard it first from a boy at school and I'd called

him a liar and half murdered the little swine. And then
when I discovered it was true, I'd wanted to kill my
father and had had to content myself with a letter,
which for sheer brutality had been inexcusable. 'It's a
pity you didn't tell him before.'

'I always meant to,' she said. 'But somehow – ' She
shrugged, a gesture of hopelessness, and as I went out
to my car I was wishing I could have done more to
help her.

As I turned out of Everdale Road a squad car
passed me. There were four of them in it, including
Sergeant Mathieson of the Cardiff CID. It seemed an
unnecessarily large force to answer Dr Harvey's call,
but I didn't go back. It was past five already and
Andrews would be waiting to clear the day's business.

Andrews was my clerk. He was also secretary,
switch-board operator, office boy. Poor devil, he had
come to me with the furniture and the two-roomed,
dingy office, all that remained of my uncle's once-
prosperous business, which he had left to me in a fit
of misplaced optimism, for though I'd passed my law
exams, I'd never practised. There'd been the war and
then I had drifted to Tanganyika and tea-planting, a
venture which had turned out badly, leaving me virtually broke at the time of his death, so that the legacy
of that miserable place seemed like the smile of
fortune.

'Know anything about a Mrs Thomas?' I asked
Andrews as he helped me off with my coat. He had
drawn the curtains and with the coal fire burning
brightly in the grate, the place looked almost snug,

despite the dust and the piles of documents and the black deed boxes littering the floor by the open strong room door. 'It's a matter of a small allowance she claims we handle for her.'

'Mrs Thomas is it?' I had seated myself at the desk and he stood over me, tall and slightly stooped, the skin stretched taut as vellum across the bones of his long face. 'You know, Mr Grant, almost half our clients are named Thomas.' It was part of the game that he must always make the simplest thing appear difficult.

'It's one of your old clients,' I said. 'Something I have apparently quite unwittingly inherited from the old man.'

'From Mister Evans, you mean.' That, too, was part of the game, and because his position was privileged I had to humour him. 'All right, Andrews. From old Mr Evans.' The firelight flickered on the lined, hang-dog face bent obsequiously over me. He'd been with my uncle since before he was articled and had stayed with him right through his long illness until he had died two years ago. God knows how old he was; his scrawny neck, covered by a hard stubble, stuck up out of the soiled stiff collar like the flesh of a plucked fowl. 'Well, what about it?' I said impatiently. 'I inherited so little in the way of business that it rather narrows the field. Does the name Whitaker ring a bell?'

'Whitaker?' His Adam's apple moved convulsively. 'Ah yes, of course. Colonel Whitaker. A little matter of a settlement. It used to come to us quarterly from

Bahrain in the form of a banker's draft, which we cashed and forwarded to an address in Grangetown.'

I asked him to get the file. But of course there wasn't any file. However, whilst I was signing the letters, he managed to dig up some record of the arrangement. It was written on the firm's notepaper in my uncle's sloped writing and went back to before the war. In it Charles Stanley Whitaker undertook to pay to *Sarah Davies the sum of twenty-five pounds quarterly for a period of fifteen years*, or in the event of his death, *a lump sum from the estate equivalent to the balance ALWAYS providing that such sum* . . . The clue to what it was all about was contained in the final paragraph, which read: *THIS settlement to be binding on my heirs and assigns and to be accepted by the said Sarah Davies in full settlement of any claims real or imagined*. The signature at the bottom was a barely decipherable scrawl, and below it Sarah Davies had signed her name in a clear, schoolgirl hand.

'If you ask me, Mr Grant, the Colonel got this young lady into trouble.'

The dry snigger with which Andrews accompanied this appraisal of the situation annoyed me. 'The young lady, as you call her, is now an unhappy and rather frightened woman of middle age,' I told him sharply. 'The son, according to this, is nineteen and he's only just discovered that he's illegitimate. There's a twin sister, too. Not a very amusing situation.' And Whitaker – was he still in Arabia, I wondered? 'Do you think the man has any idea he's a son and daughter here in Cardiff?'

'I couldn't say, sir.'

'Have we got his address?'

'The bank in Bahrain. That was the only address we ever had.'

And Bahrain was in the Persian Gulf. But it was over three years since the last payment had come through. He might be anywhere now – back in England, retired, probably. 'A pity we haven't got his address,' I said. I was thinking that the son must take after his father: the beaky nose and strong jaw were both physical characteristics that didn't suit his circumstances. 'This is all we've got on Whitaker, is it?'

Andrews nodded.

'Then how the devil do you know he's a colonel? There's no mention of colonel in this settlement.'

Apparently Andrews had seen his rank given in some newspaper story. 'Something to do with oil concessions, I think. There was a picture, too, with some sheikhs in flowing robes and Colonel Whitaker in the centre dressed in khaki shorts and a military cap.'

'How did you know it was the same man?'

'Well, I couldn't be sure. But I don't think there could be two of them out in that area.'

He was probably right there. 'I'll ask Captain Griffiths about him.' A man who spent his life taking his ship in and out of Arabian ports should know, and he was due in the office at five-thirty. 'Is the conveyance on that property of his ready now?'

Andrews produced it from the bottom of the pile, a bulky package that looked as though it contained enough deeds to cover a twenty thousand acre estate instead of a little cottage on the Gower Peninsula. 'There's still a map to be inserted in the conveyance. Otherwise it's all there, title deeds, searches, everything.'

I told him to get on to the man who was doing the map right away. 'Griffiths wants all the documents before he sails to-night.' The phone rang. It was Mrs Thomas and I knew by the tone of her voice that something had happened. 'They came just after you left and I'm so worried, Mr Grant, I don't know what to do. And now Sue has got back and she said to ring you. I'm very sorry to trouble you when you were so kind and came out here all for nothing, but you did say to telephone you if I needed any help and so I thought perhaps—'

'Just tell me what's happened, Mrs Thomas,' I said.

'Well, you see, they've taken Dafydd away and—' Her voice broke down then. 'I'm so terribly worried about him, Mr Grant. I don't know what's going to happen. So determined he is, you see. Once he's got an idea into his head . . . always been like that he has ever since he was little, you know. Nothing would ever make him change his mind once he had made it up.'

'Never mind about what's in your son's mind. What happened when the police arrived?'

'They just said he was to go with them.'

'To the police station?'

'I don't know.'

'For questioning, was it?'

'They didn't say. I asked them why they were arresting him, but they wouldn't tell me. Been in trouble he has, you know, and them behaving as though—'

'Did Sergeant Mathieson say he was arresting him?'

'No, he didn't say that exactly. He just said he was to come along with them. But it's the same thing, Mr Grant, isn't it?'

'Did he charge him?'

'No. No, I don't think so. He just said he was to come along, and he went. He didn't try to resist or anything. They just took him and now I don't know what is going to happen to him.'

'Mrs Thomas,' I said. 'There's something I want to ask you. Can you tell me where Colonel Whitaker is now?'

The quick gasp of her breath and then a long pause. 'No. No, I don't know. But somewhere in Arabia it will be.'

'He's still alive then?'

'Oh yes.'

'You've heard from him?'

Again the pause. 'No. No, I never heard from him. Never.' And she added quickly. 'Only the allowance. Very good he was about the allowance.' She sighed. 'Never a penny I took for myself, but spent it on Dafydd. Clever he is, you know – a quick brain and good with his hands. I thought perhaps he would become an engineer.' Her quick tongue ran on, about the books she'd bought him and how she'd sent him to night school, and I let her talk because it seemed to help her. 'He couldn't understand it when the money ceased. It was then he began to run wild, you see; down in the docks all the time and his heart set on getting to Arabia. Speaks Arabic you know.' She said it with pride, and in the same breath added, 'I tried to discourage him, but it was no good. He had books, you see, and all those Arabs down in the Tiger Bay district. In the blood it is, I suppose – in the blood and in their stars. And that book of cuttings. I should never have let him see it.' And then she added, 'A pity you weren't here when they came for him. I know it would never have happened if you'd been here.'

'Well, don't worry about it any more,' I said. 'I'll phone them and find out what it's all about. Have you heard how your husband is?' But she'd received no word from the hospital. 'Well, that's good,' I said. 'They'd have been in touch with you if they were worried about his condition. I'll phone you if I've any news about your son.' I put the phone down. 'First thing to-morrow, Andrews,' I said, 'get on to the news-papers and see if they've anything on their files about Whitaker. What that boy needs right now is a father, the sort of father he can look up to.'

I hurried through the rest of the business and as soon as Andrews had gone, I phoned Dr Harvey's surgery. 'George Grant here,' I said when he came on the line. 'Any news of Thomas?'

'Yes,' he said, 'and it's bad, I'm afraid. I've just had a call from the matron. He died in the ambulance on the way to hospital.'

'I see.'

'Did the police pick that boy up?'

'Yes.' It could well mean a charge of manslaughter. 'Has anybody thought of notifying Mrs Thomas that her husband is dead?'

'The matron is telephoning her right away.'

'About time, too,' I said. Incredible how soulless an institution can be. But, in fact, it was the boy I was worrying about more than the mother. 'They've taken David Thomas into custody,' I said.

'Good.'

His comment angered me. 'Why did you consider it your duty to notify the police? Did you know the man was going to die?'

'I thought it likely.' And then, after a pause, he added, 'He was a bookie, you know. Greyhounds mostly. Heavy drinker, heavy smoker, immoderate in everything, if you get me. That type goes quick. But I couldn't be certain, of course.' And he added, 'Frankly, I wouldn't have expected the boy to stay there till the police arrived. I'd have thought he'd clear out. Probably would have done if you hadn't been there.'

'I wasn't there,' I told him. 'I'd left before they arrived.'

'Oh well, doesn't make any odds. He's no good, that boy.'

'What makes you think that?'

'Oddly enough,' he said on a note of asperity, 'I don't hold with boys hitting their fathers. Far too much licence allowed this new generation. He's a street arab, that boy – dock arab rather.' He gave a quick, awkward laugh. 'It's the war, of course, but that doesn't excuse them entirely.'

I asked him then to tell me what he knew about the boy. But he couldn't tell me much. The Thomases had only been going to him since the start of the National Health Service, and he hadn't set eyes on the boy more than once or twice. He'd grown up with the dock gangs, he said, mixing too much with the Arabs, had been in and out of a number of jobs and had finally been sentenced for his part in the beating up of a rival gang leader. 'I imagine he's only just been released from Borstal,' he said. 'Dockside toughs like that are the devil in my parish.'

'And that's why you called the police?'

'Well, he killed his father, didn't he?' His voice sounded on the defensive.

'You don't make much allowance for human nature,' I said.

'No. Not with boys like that. You try stitching a few flick-knife wounds and bicycle chain gashes; you'd soon see it my way.'

'All right,' I said, and left it at that. He didn't know Thomas wasn't the boy's father or what had caused the row between them. 'Life's not all as straightforward as you chaps see it in your clinics,' I said and put the phone down.

By then it was five-thirty and Captain Griffiths had arrived. He was a small man with a pointed beard and a high, cackling laugh, and he wore a tweed suit which was a little too large for him. This, and his scrawny, wrinkled skin gave him a shrivelled look. But though he was not an impressive figure, long years of command had given him the knack of making his displeasure felt. 'You promised me the documents before I sailed, man.' He thrust his beard at me accusingly.

'Don't worry,' I said. 'You'll get them. When are you sailing?'

'Nine-thirty on the tide.'

'I'll bring them down myself.'

That seemed to satisfy him and since he showed an inclination to chat, I asked him about Whitaker. 'Colonel Charles Stanley Whitaker,' I said. 'Do you know him by any chance?'

'Yes, indeed. The Bedouin, that's what they call him out there. Or the Bloody Bedouin in the case of those that hate his guts and all his Arab affectations. That's the whites, you know. The Arabs call him *Al Arif* – the Wise One – or *Haji*. Yes, I know Colonel Whitaker. You can't trade in and out of the Gulf ports without meeting him periodically.'

'He's still out there then?'

'Oh lord, yes. A man like that would never be happy retiring to a cottage in the Gower.' His small blue eyes creased with silent laughter. 'He's a Moslem, you know. He's been on the *Haj* to Mecca, and they say he keeps a harem, and when it isn't a harem, there's talk of boys . . . But there.' He shook his head. 'It's just gossip. If I took account of all the gossip I heard on my ship there wouldn't be anyone with a shred of reputation left. Too much time, you see. Everybody's got too much time, and the damned humidity . . .' He gave that high-pitched cackling laugh. 'But dear me,' he went on, 'there's a real character for you. You don't

33

find men like Whitaker back here in Britain – not any more. One-eyed and a patch, and a great beak of a nose that makes him look like a bloody bird of prey.'

'And you've met him?'

'Yes, indeed. I've had him on board my ship, too – often. I've had him on board in all his flowing Bedouin robes with the silver of his great curved *khanjar* knife gleaming at his girdle and the black *agal* of Arabia round the *kaffyah* that covered his head; yes, and holding court on my own boat deck with the prayer mats out and his bodyguard all round him, armed to the teeth.'

'A sort of Lawrence?' I suggested.

'Well . . .' He sounded doubtful. 'He hasn't quite that standing with the political crowd. Too much of an Arab. Changing his religion like that, it made a difference, you see. But the oil boys all treat him like God, of course – or used to. But for him the Gulfoman Oilfields Development Company wouldn't have had a single concession out there. And then there was his theory – the Whitaker Theory, they called it. He believed that the proved oil-bearing country that runs down from Iraq through Kuwait, Dahran, Bahrain and Qattar would be found to continue, swinging southeast along the line of the Jebel mountains, through Buraimi and into the independent sheikhdom of Saraifa. Well, there's no knowing whether a man's right about a thing like that, except by prospecting and drilling. And there was Holmes, you see – he'd had the same sort of bee-in-his-bonnet about Bahrain and he'd been proved right.'

'And Whitaker wasn't?' I prompted, for he had paused, his mind engrossed in the past.

'No. It cost the Company a lot of money and nothing but dry wells for their trouble. And now things are changing out there.' He shook his head sadly. 'There's a new type of man coming to the top of these Middle East oil companies, technical men who understand oil, but not the Arab. Whitaker and the world he represents – it's doomed, you know; finished. You can't lord it in the deserts of Arabia, not now, with the oil flowing and half the world trying to grab a stake in it. And he's the manner of a ruling prince, you know. He might have been descended from the Prophet himself the way he behaved at times.'

It was an extraordinary picture that Griffiths had drawn for me. When he left to go back to his ship I felt that my drab office was the brighter for the colour his musical tongue had brought into it. I put some more coal on the fire and settled down to finish the day's work.

It was about half an hour later that I was interrupted by the sound of the street door bell. It startled me, for I very seldom have a caller after office hours except by appointment and a glance at my diary confirmed that I'd no appointment for that evening.

My visitor proved to be a girl, and as she stood there in the driving sleet, clutching her bicycle, she seemed vaguely familiar. She had the sort of face that comes together around the nose and mouth, a face that was attractive, rather than pretty, its composition based on the essential of bone formation. She smiled, a little nervously, a flash of white teeth, the bright gleam of pale eyes. I remember that it was her eyes that attracted me at the time. She was just a kid and she was brimming over with health and vitality. 'Mr Grant? I'm Susan Thomas. Can I speak to you a moment, please?' The words came in a quick rush, breathless with hurrying.

'Of course.' I held the door open for her. 'Come in.'

'May I put my b-bike inside?' There was a natural hesitancy in her voice that was oddly attractive. 'I had one stolen a few weeks back.' She wheeled it in and as I took her through to my office, she said, 'I was so afraid you'd have left and I didn't know where you lived.'

In the hard glare of my office lighting I was able to see her clearly. The beaky nose, the strong jaw, they were both there, recognisable now. But in her these facial characteristics were softened to femininity. Unlike her brother, I could see no resemblance to the mother. 'It's about your brother, I suppose?'

She nodded, shaking the sleet from her blonde hair whilst her long, quick fingers loosened the old fawn coat she wore. 'I only just got back from the Infirmary. Mother's beside herself. I had great difficulty—' She hesitated, a moment of uncertainty as her clear wide eyes stared and she made up her mind about me. 'She – she's reached an odd age, if you know what I mean. This is just too much for her.'

Nineteen years old, and she knew everything about

life, all the hard, unpleasant facts. 'Are you a nurse?' I asked her.

'Training to be.' She said it with a touch of pride. And then: 'You've got to do something about him, Mr Grant . . . find him, stop him from trying to kill his – from killing somebody else.'

I stared at her, appalled. 'What are you talking about?' I said. She was over-dramatizing, of course. 'You've heard about your—' I stopped there, uncertain what to call him. 'About Mr Thomas?'

'Yes.' She nodded, her face as withdrawn as her brother's had been, set and white. 'Mother told me.'

'The hospital phoned her then?'

'About half an hour ago. He died in the ambulance they said.' There was no emotion in her voice, but then her lip trembled slightly. 'It's David I'm worried about.'

'I was just going down to the police station.' I said. 'It was an accident, of course, but there's always the chance that the police may view it differently.'

'He's got a bad record, you know. And they never got on together. Of course,' she added, 'I knew he wasn't my father – my real father, that is.'

'Your mother told you, did she?' I was thinking that it was odd she should have told her daughter and not her son. 'Oh no,' she said. 'She never told me. But it's something you know, by instinct, sort of.'

'Then why in heaven's name didn't your brother know?' I said.

'Oh well, boys are so slow, you know. And it's not something you can just blurt out, is it, Mr Grant? I mean, it's something you feel, deep inside, and it's sort of secret.' And then she said, 'What will he do, do you think? Was he serious when he said he'd kill him? I wasn't there, you see. But Mother is convinced he meant it.'

'Kill who?' I said.

'His – my father. Colonel Whitaker. He swore he'd kill him, didn't he? That's what Mother says. You were there. Did he say that?'

'Well, yes,' I nodded. 'But I didn't take it very seriously. It had all come as a bit of a shock to him. Besides,' I added, 'there's not much he can do about it at the moment, even if he were serious. And by the time he's released, he'll have had a chance to get used to the idea.'

She stared at me. 'You haven't heard then?'

'Heard what?'

'David's escaped.'

'Escaped?' So that was why she was here. The stupid, crazy young fool! 'How do you know he's escaped?'

'The police just phoned. They said he'd escaped from a police car and that it was our duty to inform them if he returned to the house. That's why I came to see you. Mother's almost out of her mind. You see, it isn't only David she's worrying about. It's this Colonel Whitaker – my f-father. I don't understand after the way he treated her, but I think she's still in love with him . . . always has been probably. And now she doesn't know what to do for the best.' She came closer to me then, touched my arm in a gesture of entreaty.

'Please, Mr Grant, you've got to do something. You've got to help us. I'm scared to death Mother will go to the police and tell them what David said. That's what she wanted to do, right away. She said it was her duty, but I knew it wasn't that. She's just about out of her mind as a result of what David's done already. And he does have a bad record, you know. So I said I'd come to you and she promised she wouldn't do anything until I got home.' And she stood back, drained, her large eyes staring at me expectantly.

I didn't know what to say. There was nothing I could do. No point in my going out and searching the city for him. A filthy night like this the whole police force would have their work cut out to track him down. 'Where was it he escaped?'

'Somewhere along the Cowbridge Road, they said.'

'And your father – have you any idea how I can get in touch with him?'

Her eyes brightened for a moment. 'Oh, if you could.' But then she shook her head. 'I've no idea where he is now. Mother doesn't know. Did she show you the book of press cuttings?'

'No.'

'No, of course not, it was still lying there on the floor. The place was an awful mess.' And then she said, 'I checked myself because I had the same idea. But the last cutting she got was three years ago. I don't know whether he's been in the papers since then. Dad found out, or maybe he knew all the time – anyway, he made her stop them. That last cutting was a picture taken in Basra. But he may have retired by now. He was getting on – over fifty. And if he's retired, then he'd probably be in England somewhere, wouldn't he? That's what all these people who've lived all their lives abroad do when they retire. Do you think perhaps David knows where he is?'

'No,' I said. 'He tried to get the address out of me.' No point in telling her that he might have the same idea that I had and try to check the newspaper files. 'In any case,' I told her, 'he'll have his work cut out to elude the police. I think you can set your mother's mind at rest. The police will pick him up and . . . and time will do the rest. Your mother can see him in prison, talk to him; in no time at all he'll have accepted the situation.'

She thought that over for a moment and then nodded. 'Yes. That makes sense.' And then she said, 'Do you think that's why he escaped . . . I mean, did he really want to kill Colonel Whitaker, do you think? His own father?'

'At the moment perhaps.' There was no telling what the boy had in his mind. He might simply have been jealous of his mother's affection for an old love. But I couldn't tell her that. 'In my opinion, it was the shock,' I said. 'A perfectly natural reaction. When he's had time to think it over, get used to the idea—'

'But why did he escape? He's never done that before. He's been arrested twice, you see, but he never tried to escape.' And when I didn't say anything, she gave a little shrug. 'Oh well, it'll all come out in the wash, I expect.' She smiled briefly, but the smile didn't extend to her eyes, which were sad and suddenly without lustre. 'It was silly of me to come really.' She started for the door, hugging her coat round her. 'I should have known there was nothing you could do. It's Mother I'm worried about. David's in enough trouble—' She moved her shoulders as though bracing herself. 'I think perhaps I'll go and see Dr Harvey. Maybe he'd give her a sedative, something to make her sleep so she doesn't keep going over it in her mind and getting silly ideas in her head.' She turned and held out her hand. 'Goodbye, Mr Grant. And thank you. I feel a bit better now anyway.'

I took her back through the empty office to the street door and as she wheeled her bicycle out she asked me to telephone her if I had any news. 'During the day you can always get me at the Infirmary if it's important. I'd rather you didn't phone my mother. Promise?'

'Of course,' I said.

Shortly after she'd gone Andrews came in with the map. By the time I had dealt with the conveyance and finished my other work, it was almost seven-thirty. Time enough to call in at the police station on my way down to the docks. What the boy needed was to be given some purpose in life.

I was thinking about this as I pulled on my coat, wondering at the chance of birth, how some people are born to parents happily married, and others . . . my own childhood hadn't been all that happy. I shrugged my shoulders. Life was a battle anyway. Sex, money, happiness – it was all a struggle, like trying to build up this decrepit business. It took all the guts, all the energy you'd got sometimes just to make some sense out of life, and when things didn't work out . . . I set the guard carefully in front of the dying fire, feeling sorry for the boy, sorry for myself.

I suppose I was tired. It had been a frustrating week, and now it was Friday and the week-end stretching ahead. I was feeling the need of a drink. There was a pub I went to sometimes in the dock area, a rowdy place, but virile and full of masculinity and talk of far places, a seaman's pub that always gave me the illusion of islands just beyond the horizon. With a few Scotches, imagination could soar, leaping the tawdry problems of money and piddling lawyer's briefs.

I went out, closing the door of my office behind me, following the white beam of my torch through the empty outer office with its clumsy mahogany counter and frosted glass panels. I had reached the street door and my hand was on the latch when I remembered the package for Captain Griffiths. I had left it propped up on the mantelpiece so that I wouldn't forget it.

I went back to my office, my footsteps sounding hollow on the bare boards. He'd never forgive me if I let him sail without his dream of the future all set down in the mumbo-jumbo of legal phraseology. A man needed a dream, something to aim at. You couldn't go through life without a goal. For him it was retirement and that little whitewashed cottage looking out over the sweep of Rhosilli Bay; for me it was just a solicitor's office with new paint, new furniture and clients tumbling over each other for my services. My hand reached out for the handle of the door, and then, suddenly, there was the tinkle of glass falling. The sound came from beyond the door, startlingly loud in the empty stillness.

I switched off my torch and eased the door open a fraction, every nerve in my body tensed and expectant. I heard the scrape of the window latch, the scrabble of boots on the still, the rustle of the curtains as they were pushed aside. A burglar? But nobody but a fool would expect to find cash lying around loose in a solicitor's office. Perhaps he was after some particular document? But I could think of nothing I was handling at the moment sufficiently important to warrant breaking and entering. I heard him stumble against my chair and then I could hear his heavy breathing coming nearer as he crossed the room to the door. I guessed he'd be making for the light switch, and I flung the door wide and at the same time switched on my torch again.

David Thomas stood there, checked in the white beam of it. His fair hair was plastered down by the rain. His face was streaked with blood from a gash on his forehead, the left cheek bruised and filthy with mud. There was mud on his clothes, too; black, wet patches of it that clung to the sodden cloth. His jacket was ripped at the shoulder and one trouser leg was torn so badly that the flesh of his leg showed through the rent. He was breathing heavily as though he'd been running.

'What the hell are you doing here?' I said and

switched on the light. His face was ghastly white, his eyes unnaturally wide. He looked scared out of his wits. 'Well, I don't expect they'll think of looking for you in my office.' I closed the door and walked past him and put the curtain straight. Then I took the guard from the fire and put some more coal on, poking it till a flame showed. And all the time I was conscious of him standing there, watching me in silence, too surprised, too scared probably, to move. I pushed the old armchair reserved for clients close to the hearth. 'All right,' I said. 'Take your jacket off and come and sit by the fire and dry yourself out.' He did as I told him, too startled to have any initiative of his own left. 'Now,' I said, 'just tell me what in God's name made you do such a damn-fool thing?'

For a moment I thought he was going to close up on me the way that sort of kid does when things go wrong and people start asking questions. The sullen tough-boy look had come back into his face. 'Take your time,' I said. 'There's no hurry. You've got all evening if you want it.' I thought I'd try flattery then. 'Not many chaps manage to get away from the police so soon after being taken in charge. How did you do it?'

The tight lips relaxed slightly, a ghost of a smile. 'Luck,' he said. He was shivering and I poked the fire again, coaxing it into a blaze. 'They'd got a car to take me to one of their bloody jails. Said I'd feel more at home in the nick.' His tone was a sneer.

'And you made a break for it.'

'Yeah. That's right. There was only one of them in

the back with me and I made a dive for it when they were driving down the Cowbridge Road. I hit the pavement and just about knocked myself out. They nearly had me then. But there was a pub I knew and I dived in there and got away out the back.' And he added, 'I said I'd see you in your office.' There was a touch of bravado in the way he said it.

'Your sister was here a little while back,' I told him.

'Sue? What did she want?' He was on the defensive immediately.

'Wanted me to help you.'

'Help me?' He gave a derisive laugh. 'The only way you can help me is by giving me that address. That's what I came for.'

'Your mother's worried sick,' I told him.

'So what?'

I lost patience with him then. 'Can't you get it into your thick head that your actions affect other people? Stop being so damned irresponsible. The police phoned your mother that you'd escaped and now she's half out of her mind—'

But he wasn't interested in the heartbreak he was causing other people. 'She should have thought of that before she wrote me that letter,' he said. 'She was half out of her mind then. Did Sue tell you I'd two more months to do in a Borstal Institute?'

'No.'

'Well, I had. Two more months and I'd have been out and in the clear. And then I got this letter threatening she's going to commit suicide. Your Da's driving me to it, she said, and I can't stand it any more. And then to come home and find she's been holding out on me all the time, kidding me I was that drunken old fool's son. Christ! And you talk about being irresponsible.'

'It isn't an easy thing for a woman to tell her son.'

'She's had nineteen years. In nineteen years she ought to have been able to screw up her courage. Instead, she drives the old man to fling it in my face.' He stared at the fire, his shoulders hunched, his face bitter. 'Does Sue know?' he asked at length. 'Does she know she's illegitimate?'

'Yes.'

'And what does she feel about it?'

'She said she'd known for a long time – deep down.'

'Then why the hell didn't she tell me?'

'I said – deep down. Her mother didn't tell her. She just knew.'

He looked sulky then. 'We never kept anything from each other before.'

'It's not the sort of thing you want to share with anybody else,' I said.

'Too right, it isn't.' He suddenly beat his fist against the arm of the chair. 'Christ! If I'd only known before.'

'It wouldn't have helped you,' I told him.

He thought about that for a moment and then he nodded. 'No, I guess you're right.' And he added, 'I always wondered why the old man hated my guts.' He leaned suddenly forward, picked up the poker and jabbed at the fire. 'Guess I hated his guts, too,' he said viciously.

'Well, he's dead now,' I said. 'Did you know that?'

He nodded and let go of the poker so that it clattered into the grate. 'Yep. They told me that. Croaked on the way to hospital, blast him.'

His attitude to the man's death shocked me. 'For God's sake!' I said. 'Haven't you any compassion for the man who was a father to you?'

'He wasn't my father,' he cried. 'I told you that before.'

'He was your father in the eyes of the law.'

'Then the law ought to be changed, oughtn't it? You can't make chalk cheese by a legal declaration.'

'He supported you all the time you were growing up,' I reminded him.

'All right, he supported me. But he hated me all the same. I always knew that. When he took a strap to me, he enjoyed it. He hasn't been able to do that for a long time now. But he'd other ways of getting at me, jeering at me because I read a lot, and at my Arab friends. Do you know what he'd done whilst I'd been in Borstal? I went up to my old room after you'd left. All my books on Arabia, every damn' one of them, he'd pulled out and torn to pieces. The only books he hadn't destroyed were the technical ones. I'd a lot of them on oil – geology, seismology, geophysics. He left me those because he didn't think I cared about them.' He stared at me. 'Now he's dead, and I'm glad. Glad, do you hear?' His voice had risen and suddenly the tears were welling up into his eyes and he began to cry. 'I didn't mean to kill him,' he sobbed. 'Honest. I didn't mean to.' He broke down completely then, sobbing like a child, and I went over to him and gripped his shoulder. 'It was an accident,' I said, trying to steady him.

'They don't believe it.'

'Did they prefer a charge?'

'No, but they think I killed him. I know they do.' And he burst out, 'I haven't a chance with them.'

'You certainly haven't made it any better by making a break for it like that.' I was wondering whether I could persuade him to come back with me to the police station and give himself up. I hesitated and then walked over to the phone, but he was on his feet immediately. 'What are you going to do? Ring the police?' There was panic in his voice.

'No,' I said. 'I'm going to ring your home – get your mother down here, your sister, too.'

'What for? What good'll that do?'

'If your mother makes a statement, explaining exactly how it happened—'

'It's no good,' he said. 'She wouldn't do it. She'd rather have me hanged—'

'Oh, don't be childish,' I said.

'It's true,' he cried. 'She told me so herself – after you'd gone.' He followed me to the desk and his voice was intense, very serious: 'She thinks I'm going to kill Whitaker if I ever lay my hands on him. And she loves him. After all these years, she still loves the man. I don't understand it, but that's how it is. You'd think after the swine had treated her like that, after he'd left her flat—' He pulled a blood-stained handkerchief from his pocket and blew his nose. 'When I got back this afternoon the old man was giving her hell. I could hear it out in the street. He was calling her all sorts of names. I suppose he was drunker than usual. He had that book of press-cuttings in his hand, and when I told him to shut his mouth, he taunted me with being a bastard, said he'd had all he could stand of another man's whelps. And then he turned on my mother and added, 'And all I can stand of another man's whore. After all I've done to cover up for you,' he said, 'you creep off as soon as I'm out of the house to mope over your lover's pictures.' And he flung the book at her. That's when I went for him.' He paused, staring at me, his eyes over-bright. 'That book was full of press-cuttings of him, pictures some of them. I've grown up with that book, grown up with the man himself. I know him, know his way of life, everything about him. It's like I told you – he was a sort of God to me. I wanted to be like him, tough, independent, an adventurer in far places. I tried to get a job as a seaman on ships going out that way from Cardiff docks, but at first I was too young, and then there was the Union. I even tried to stow away once. And now I find he's no more than a rotten, dirty little sham who'd leave a woman to bear her twins alone. I told Ma I'd kill him if I ever laid hands on him. Remember? You were there when I said it.'

I nodded.

'Well, she believed me. She's convinced I really will kill him if I ever catch up with him.'

'And you didn't mean what you said – is that what you're trying to tell me?'

He walked back to the fire and stood staring at it for a moment. Then he slumped down in the chair again, his body limp. 'I don't know,' he murmured. 'Honest, I don't know. All I do know is that I have to find him.'

'And that's why you came here, to search my office for his address?'

He nodded. 'I knew you'd have it somewhere in your files.'

'Well, I haven't.' I hesitated. But after all the boy had a right to know where his father was. 'Will you promise me something? Will you promise me that if you find him, you'll remember that he's your father and that blood is something you just can't rub out with violence.'

He looked at me and was silent a long time. At length he said, 'I can't promise anything. I don't know how I'd act.' He was being honest at least. 'But I'll try to remember what you've just said.' And then on a sudden, urgent note: 'I've got to find him. I've just got to find him. Please, please try to understand.'

The need of that kid . . . It was the thing that had been lacking for him all his life. It was his mother's need reflected and enlarged. The sins of the fathers . . . why in God's name should a sense of insecurity lead to violence, in people and in races? 'All right,' I said. 'I accept that.' And I passed on to him what Griffiths had told me. 'But then you know the sort of man your father is. Anyway, there it is, he's still out there. And if you want to contact him, I imagine a letter to the Gulfoman Oilfields Development Company—'

'A letter's no good. I wrote him already – twice. He never answered.' He looked up at me. 'This Captain Griffiths, is his ship the *Emerald Isle*? She sails regularly to the Persian Gulf.' And when I nodded, he said, 'That was the ship I tried to stow away on. I was fourteen then, and a year later I tried to sign on. She's in port now, is she?'

'Yes.'

'When is she sailing?'

'Tonight.'

'Tonight?' He looked up at me, suddenly eager like a dog being offered a walk. 'Tonight. When? What time?' He had jumped to his feet, all the tiredness falling from him. 'For Christsake, what time?'

I hesitated. It was no part of a lawyer's job to get involved in a criminal case. My duty was plain. 'The sensible thing would be for you to give yourself up to the police.'

He didn't hear me. His eyes had fastened on the envelope I had left propped up on the mantelpiece. 'Were you taking this down to the ship tonight?'

I nodded and his hand reached out for the envelope, clutched at it. 'I'll deliver it for you.' He held it as though it were a talisman, his eyes bright with the chance it represented. 'That's all I need. The excuse to go on board. And they wouldn't catch me this time, not till we were at sea.' He glanced at the window, balanced on the balls of his feet, as though about to take off the way he had come. But then I supposed he realized I should only phone the police. 'Will you let me take it?' His voice was urgent, his eyes pleading. 'Once on board the *Emerald Isle* . . . Please, sir.'

That 'sir' was a measure of his desperation.

'Please,' he said again. 'It's the only hope I got.'

He was probably right at that. And if I didn't let him take it, what other chance would he ever get in life? He'd escaped from Borstal. He'd escaped from the police. With that sort of record he'd be lucky to get away with three years for manslaughter. After that he'd be case-hardened, a criminal for life. And there was the sister, too. A nice girl, that. I sighed. 'I'm supposed to be a lawyer,' I reminded him . . . or maybe I was reminding myself. 'Not a travel agency for boys who've escaped from the police.'

'But you'll let me deliver it, won't you?'

What the hell can you do when faced with youth in all its shining innocence and eagerness? 'All right,' I said. 'You can try it, if you like. But God knows what Griffiths will do.'

'All I want is the chance to meet up with my father.'

I realized then that his mind had leap-frogged all the obstacles; he was already mentally sailing the coast of Arabia in search of his father. 'All I'm giving you,' I warned him, 'is the excuse to get on board that ship. She sails at nine-thirty. And those documents have got to be delivered into Captain Griffith's hands, understand?'

'I'll give them to him. I promise.'

'You know your way about the ship?'

'I knew every corner of her once. It'll come back to me as soon as I get on board.'

'Well, kindly remember that I'm a solicitor. When you're caught, as you will be eventually, don't implicate me. Shall we say you walked into my office to get legal advice, saw the envelope I had forgotten and took it on the spur of the moment. Is that understood?'

'Yes, sir.'

'I'll take you down to Bute East Dock now,' I said. 'After that you're on your own.' I hesitated. It wasn't much of a chance I was giving him. He'd no clothes other than what he stood up in, no money probably, nothing, not even a passport. But at least I'd have done what I could for him – what I'd have hoped somebody would do for a son of mine if he'd got himself into a mess like this. But then I hadn't a son; I hadn't anybody. 'Better clean the blood off your face,' I said and showed him where the wash place was. 'And you'll need something to hide your torn clothes.'

I left him in the lavatory and went through the office to the cupboard under the stairs. There was an old overcoat that had been there ever since I'd taken over the place, a black hat, too. He tried them on when he'd finished cleaning himself up. The coat wasn't too bad a fit and with the sweatband padded with strips from an old conveyance the hat was passable. I wondered what my uncle would have said if he knew to what use these sartorial relics of his were being put. And because I wanted him to realize how slender his chances were, I said, 'If you're caught before the ship sails, don't try and bluff it out with Captain Griffiths.

Tell him the truth and say you want to give yourself up to the police.'

He nodded, his face bloodless, his pale eyes almost fever bright with the nervous tension that was building up in him. The dark coat and the black hat accentuated his pallor, accentuated, too, his beaky nose and the strong jaw. In the old lawyer's cast-off clothes he looked much older than his nineteen years.

There was a back way out of the office and I took him out by that. It was still sleeting and there was nobody in the street where I parked my car. We drove in silence down Park Place and across Castle Street, and then we crossed the railway and were in a maze of little streets that edge the docks. I slowed in a dark gap between street lights and told him to climb into the back and lie on the floor with the rug I kept for my dog pulled over him.

It was fortunate that I took this precaution, for the police at the dock entrance had been alerted and there was a constable there who recognized me; a fortnight before he had given evidence in a case I'd defended. I told him my business and he let me through. I hadn't expected the police to be watching the docks already and my hands were sweating as I drove on across the slippery steel of the railway tracks.

The *Emerald Isle* was at the far end of the Bute East Dock, close to the lock. She had completed loading and she had steam up, smoke trailing from her single stack. The cranes along the quay were still, their gaunt steel fingers pointed at the night. I stopped in the shadow of one of the sheds. The sleet had turned to snow and it was beginning to lie, so that the dock looked ghostly white in the ship's lights. 'Well, there you are,' I said. 'That's the ship.'

He scrambled out from under the rug. 'Couldn't you come with me?' he asked, suddenly scared now that the moment had arrived. 'If you were to have a word with Captain Griffiths—'

I didn't reply to that, but simply handed him the package. I knew he knew it was out of the question, for he didn't ask me again. A moment later the rear door opened and I heard him get out. 'I – I'd like to thank you,' he stammered. 'Whatever happens – I won't let you down.'

'Good luck!' I said.

'Thanks.' And then he was walking across the dock, not hesitantly, but with a firm, purposeful tread. I watched him mount the gangway, saw him pause and speak to one of the crew, an Arab; and then he disappeared from sight through a door in the bridge deck.

I lit a cigarette and sat there, wondering what would happen now. I didn't think he'd much of a chance, but you never know; he was a resourceful kid.

I finished my cigarette and lit another. I was thinking about the constable on the gate. I ought to have realized that that would have been one of the first things they'd do following his escape. And the man had recognized me. I tried to analyse my motives in doing such a crazy thing, but I couldn't sort it out. The cold crept into the car as I waited and still nothing happened, except that the snow thickened and the dock turned dazzling white. A tug hooted out in the river, a lost, owl sound in the winter night. It was twenty minutes past nine.

Ten minutes later a whistle sounded from somewhere high up on the *Emerald Isle* and two men came quickly out of a hut at the end of the dock. They manhandled the gangway ashore and then stood by the warps. Another whistle and the for'ard warp went slack, fell with a splash into the dock. Black smoke belched from the funnel, and as the stern warp was let go, a gap opened up between the ship's side and the quay. I switched the engine on then, turned the heater up and sat there smoking as the *Emerald Isle* locked out into the River Taff. And when her lights had finally disappeared behind the whitened shoulders of the loading sheds, I drove back to the solitude of my flat, hoping to God I'd done the right thing.

The story of what happened to him after that I got partly from Captain Griffiths on his return and partly from a letter David wrote me. When he left me on the dock there and went on board the *Emerald Isle* there was no clear-cut plan in his mind. He knew the layout, of course. She was the only ship trading regularly out of Cardiff to Arabian ports, and she had exercised a fatal fascination for him since he was old enough to wander in the docks. It was the Somali steward and not a deck hand who met him at the top of the gangway and on the spur of the moment, almost without thinking, he inquired whether the passenger accommodation was fully booked. The steward told him No; there were six cabins and only three were occupied. Feeling suddenly more confident, he asked to see the Captain.

Captain Griffiths was in his cabin on the port side of the bridge deck housing and when David was shown in he was seated at his desk checking the Mate's trim figures. He took the packet, glanced at it and then looked up at David. 'You work for Mr Grant, do you?'

'I – I run errands for him.'

'Office boy, eh? Well, you're only just in time. We sail in quarter of an hour.' Griffiths peered up at him from under his bushy brows. 'What's the matter with your face, boy? Been in a fight?'

'No. No, sir. I – I had a fall.'

'Must have been a bad one. You're as white as a sheet.' He bent down, pulled open a drawer of his desk and came up with a bottle of whisky. 'I'll give you a drink for your pains.' He gave that high-pitched cackling laugh, filled the glasses half full and handed one of them to David. 'Well, young fellow, you can wish me luck, for it's a Welsh land-owner I am now.' And he slapped the packet of documents with unconcealed pride. 'There's times, you know,' he confided as he swallowed his drink, 'when I feel like the Wandering Jew himself, doomed to ply from one silt-laden port to another, right through to Eternity. This,' and his hand touched the packet again, 'this may help me to preserve my sanity when the temperature's in the hundreds and the humidity's so thick your lungs feel as though they're stuffed full of wet cotton wool and

57

will never breathe clean air again; when conditions are like that, then I'll take these documents out and read them through just to convince myself that I really do have a little place on the Gower Peninsula where rain washes the air clean of dust and heat and the damned, Godforsaken, everlasting flies.'

'That's the Persian Gulf you'll be referring to, isn't it? Then maybe you'll know where Colonel Whitaker lives now?' He hadn't intended to ask that question, but the unaccustomed liquor had overlaid his nervousness.

Griffiths glanced up at him quickly. 'Funny thing,' he murmured. 'Grant asked me that same question only this afternoon. Is Colonel Whitaker one of the firm's clients?'

'I – I don't know, sir.'

'Then what made you ask about him?'

David hesitated. But if he were to succeed in stowing away on board, there was no harm in telling Captain Griffiths the truth right now. 'He's my father.'

'Your father!' The blue eyes stared. 'Good God! Didn't know the Bedouin was married.'

'My natural father, sir.'

Griffiths's eyes suddenly crinkled at the corners. 'Natural father, you say? Well, by God, that's a good one.' And he lay back in his swivel chair, pointed his beard at the steel deck above and cackled with laughter. And then he stopped suddenly. 'I'm sorry, boy. You're sensitive about it, I can see. Have you ever met your father?'

'No, sir.'

'Well, if you had, you'd know why I laughed. Bedouin sons – and daughters. There's gossip enough about him, but never a whisper of a son in Wales, you see. I'll tell him, next time he's aboard – I'll say to him casually—' But David was spared the rest, for the bridge communicator buzzed and a voice said, 'Tug coming alongside now, sir.'

'Very good, Mr Evans.' Griffiths got to his feet. 'I'm needed on the bridge.' He paused in front of David, staring up at his face. 'Yes. I can see the likeness now. Any messages you want to give him?' And when David shook his head dumbly, he patted him on the arm. 'Well, I'll tell him I saw you when next he comes aboard. And now you'd better get off the ship quick or you'll find yourself in Arabia with a deal of explaining to do.' And he went off, cackling with laughter, to the bridge above.

David found himself standing alone outside the Captain's cabin. An alleyway ran athwartships. Numbered mahogany doors led off it on either side. He listened, every nerve taut. He could hear voices on the bridge and down below in the saloon, but the deck on which he stood seemed utterly deserted. Treading softly, he walked the length of the alleyway to the starb'd side, as far away from the Captain's cabin as possible. The first door he tried was locked, the second opened to a glimpse of heavily-labelled baggage and the startled face of a man lying prone on his bunk with a book. A tug blared so close alongside that he jumped. Cabin Number Four was empty and he slipped inside and locked the door. And after that he stood for a long time, quite still and breathing heavily, listening to the sounds of the ship, waiting, tense, for the sudden outcry that would inevitably follow the discovery that he had not gone ashore.

That period of waiting, ten minutes at the most, seemed the longest he had ever known. And then a whistle sounded. It was so like the shrill of a police whistle that he reached for the handle of the door, instinctively seeking escape in movement. But then the engine-room telegraph rang from the bridge overhead and the ship suddenly came to life, a gentle throbbing against the soles of his shoes. He knelt on the unmade bunk then and cautiously pulled back the curtain that covered the porthole. He could see the deck rail and beyond it a flat expanse of water with the snow driving across it. And then the water was swirling to the bite of the screws and he knew the ship was moving.

He took off his hat and coat then and lay down on the bunk under a ship's blanket, listening with his ears attuned to every sound. A gong sounded for the evening meal and there was movement in the next cabin, the gush of a tap, the bang of a suitcase. The shrill of the whistle on the bridge was answered a moment later by the tug's farewell blast on her siren. The beat of the engines increased, and later, after they had slowed to drop the pilot, the ship began to roll.

He slept during the night, rolled from side to side of the narrow bunk. But when daylight came, he lay awake, tense and hungry. Footsteps sounded in the alleyway, cabin doors slammed, somewhere a loose porthole cover rattled back and forth. The hours of daylight seemed endless, but nobody came, nobody even tried the handle of the cabin door. It was as though he didn't exist and perversely he felt deserted, lost, forgotten in this strange world he'd been thrust into by events. He had no watch so that he'd no idea of the time. The sky was grey with a low wrack of cloud, no sun. The violence of the movement was exhausting and towards nightfall he was sick, retching emptily into the washbasin. Nobody seemed to hear the sound of his misery, nobody seemed to care. The seas, thudding against the bows of the ship, made her tremble, so that everything rattled, and each time she buried her bows the noise of the impact was followed by a long, shuddering movement that seemed to run through his tired body as though he were himself being exposed to the onslaught of the gale.

Night followed the day at last and he slept; and then it was day again. Darkness and light succeeding each other. He lost count of the days, and when the sun came out and the sea subsided, he knew he was too weak to hold out alone in that cabin any longer. The moment had come to face the future.

Just above his head, within easy reach of his left hand, was a bell push. He lay half a day, staring at the yellow bone button imbedded in its wooden orifice, before he could summon the courage to press it, and when the steward came he told the startled Somali to take him to the Captain.

Griffiths was seated at his desk so that to David's bemused mind it seemed like that first time he'd met him, except that now the cabin was full of sunlight and they were off the coast of Portugal. The Somali was explaining excitedly and Griffiths's small blue eyes were staring up at him. The Captain silenced the man with a movement of his hand. 'All right, Ishmail. You can leave us now.' And as the steward turned to go, his eyes rolling in his head, Griffiths added, 'And see you don't talk about this. The passengers are not to know that a stowaway has been hiding in their accommodation.' And when the door closed and they were alone, he turned to David. 'Now young man, perhaps you'd explain why the devil you stowed away on my ship?'

David hesitated. It was difficult to know where to begin, though he'd had four days of solitude to think about it. He was scared, too. The little man in the worn blue jacket with the gold braid on the sleeves was more frightening to him than either of the judges who had sentenced him, for his future was in his hands. 'Well, come on, man, come on.' The beard waggled impatiently, the blue eyes bored into him.

I would like to think that he remembered my advice then, but more probably he was too weak and confused to invent a satisfactory story. At any rate, he told it straight, from the receipt of his mother's hysterical letter and his escape from Borstal, right through to the tragedy of his return to the house in Everdale Road. And Griffiths listened without comment, except that halfway through he took pity on David's weakness, for he was leaning on the edge of the desk to support himself, and told him to pull up a chair and sit down. And when finally he was asked to account for his possession of the documents that had been his excuse for boarding the ship, he stuck to the explanation we'd agreed.

But Griffiths was much too sharp for him. 'So you took the packet from Mr Grant's office and decided to deliver it yourself?'

'Yes, sir.'

'You say you found the door of Mr Grant's office open. That means he'd only gone out for a moment. When he came back and found the packet gone, the natural thing would be for him to come down to the ship and give me some explanation. You're lying, you see.'

There was nothing he could do then but tell Captain Griffiths the truth, and the blue eyes, staring into his, began to crease at the corners. By the time he had finished, Griffiths was leaning back in the swivel chair and roaring with laughter, his mouth so wide open that David could see the movement of his uvula in the red hollow of his gullet. 'Well I'll be damned!' Griffiths said, wiping his eyes. 'And Grant an accessory – ' And then he started in on a cross-examination that seemed to go on and on.

Finally he got up and stood for a long time staring out of the porthole at the sunlight dancing on the waves made by ship's passage through the water, whilst David sat there, numbed and hopeless. 'Well, I believe you,' Griffiths said, still staring out to the sea. 'You could never have made all that up.' There was a long silence. 'You got Grant to help you – and how you did that I don't know, considering he'd never met your father. He was risking his reputation, everything. You've no passport, of course? That means you can't land in the normal way. And you've never had word from your father, which means he doesn't care to acknowledge your existence – right?'

And when David didn't say anything, Griffiths swung round from the porthole, his beard thrust aggressively forward. 'And you stow away on my ship, expecting me to get you into Arabia. How the devil do you think I'm going to do that, eh?'

'I don't know, sir.'

'Perhaps Grant suggested something?' But David shook his head unhappily and Griffiths snapped, 'A lawyer – he should have had more sense.' And he stumped across the cabin and stood peering down at David's face. 'Is your father going to acknowledge you now, do you think? How old are you?'

'Nineteen.'

'And do you think Colonel Whitaker's going to be pleased to have a bastard he sired nineteen, twenty years ago, suddenly turn up with no passport, nothing – and a jailbird at that?'

David got to his feet then. 'I'm sorry, Captain Griffiths,' he said stiffly. 'I didn't realize—' The words didn't come easily and his mouth felt dry and caked. 'I've always dreamed of this, you see – of getting out to Arabia. I suppose it's in my – bastard blood.' He said it with bitterness, for he was convinced now that the world was against him, as it always had been – as it always would be. 'I'll work my passage,' he added wearily, 'and when we get to Aden you can hand me over to the authorities.'

Griffiths nodded. 'That's the first sensible suggestion you've made. And it's exactly what I ought to do.' He had turned away and stood for a moment lost in thought. 'Your father did me a good turn once. I owe him something for that, but the question is would I be doing him a good turn—' He gave a quick shrug and subsided into his chair, chuckling to himself. 'It has its humorous side, you know.' And David watched, fascinated and with a sudden feeling of intense excitement, as Griffiths's hand reached out to the bridge communicator. 'Mr Evans. Come down to my cabin for a moment, will you?' And then, looking at David: 'Well, now, for the sake of Mr Grant, whom I wouldn't have suspected of such lawlessness, and for the sake of your father, who's going to get the shock of his life, I'm going to sign you on as a deck hand. But understand this,' he added, 'any trouble at Aden and I hand you over to the authorities.'

David was too relieved, too dazed to speak. The Mate came in and Griffiths said, 'Stowaway for you, Mr Evans. Have the galley give him some food and then put him to work. I'm signing him on. And see the passengers, at any rate, don't know how he came aboard. His name is – Whitaker.' David caught the glint of humour in the blue eyes.

'Thank you, sir,' he mumbled, but as he turned away all he could think about was that name, spoken aloud for the first time. Whitaker. Somehow it seemed to fit, as though it had always belonged to him; it was a symbol, too, a declaration that the past was gone, the future ahead.

All down the Mediterranean and through the Suez Canal, the life of the ship, the sun's increasing warmth, the sight of places all dreamed about and now suddenly come to life, absorbed him completely, each day bringing the promise of Arabia twenty-four steaming hours nearer. But when they entered the Red Sea, with the water flat like a mirror and the desert hills of the Hejaz shimmering to port, he knew they were getting close to Aden. And at Aden the police might be waiting for him.

It was night when the anchor was let go off Steamer Point, and as he stood on the foredeck directing a stream of water on to the hawsehole, he could see the lights of Crater and the black shape of the volcanic hills behind towering against the stars. His first Arabian port. It touched his nostrils with a breath of sun-hot oil waste. But instead of exitement, all he felt was fear.

Customs and Immigration came aboard. He stood by the rail, in the shadow of one of the boats, and watched them climb the side from a launch. His work was done and he'd nothing to think about now but the possibility of arrest. A subdued murmur came to him from the town, strange Arab cries, drifting across the water. Another launch glided to the ship's side. The agent this time. And later two of the passengers were climbing down into it, followed by their baggage. The officials were leaving, too, and he watched the launches curve away from the ship, two ghostly arrow-tips puttering into the night. He breathed gently again, savouring the warm, strange-scented air . . . and then the steward called his name. 'Captain want you in cabin.'

Slowly he went for'ard to the bridge deck housing. Captain Griffiths was seated in the leather armchair, his face a little flushed, his eyes bright, a tumbler of whisky at his elbow. 'Well, young fellow, it appears that you're in the clear. Nobody is in the least bit interested in you here.' And he added, 'Doubtless you have Mr Grant to thank for that. I'm sorry I can't send him a message; the man must be half out of his mind considering the chance he took.'

'I'll write to him as soon as I can,' David murmured.

The Captain nodded. 'Time enough for that when you're safely ashore. But it's only fair to tell you that if I fail to contact your father, then you'll complete the voyage and be paid off at Cardiff.' And having delivered this warning, he went on, 'I'll be going ashore in the morning and I'll cable Colonel Whitaker care of GODCO – that's the Gulfoman Oilfields Development Company. It may reach him, it may not. Depends where your father is, you see; he's not an easy man to contact. Meantime, I am instructing Mr Evans to give you work that will keep you out of sight of the passengers. We have two oil men with us on the voyage up the coast, also an official from the PRPG's office – that's the Political Resident Persian Gulf. See to it that you keep out of their way. If you do get ashore, then I don't want anybody saying afterwards that they saw you on board my ship.' And with that David found himself dismissed.

He saw Captain Griffiths go ashore next morning in the agent's launch. All day they were working cargo, the winches clattering as they unloaded No. 1 hold into the lighter dhows alongside and filled it again with a fresh cargo. In the evening four passengers came aboard, all white, and a dhow-load of Arabs bound for Mukalla who strewed themselves and their belongings about the deck. And then the anchor was hauled up and they shifted to the bunkering wharf. The *Emerald Isle* sailed at midnight, steaming east-north-east along the southern coast of Arabia, the coast of myrrh and frankincense, of Mocha coffee and Sheba's queen.

It was a voyage to thrill the heart of any youngster, but David saw little of it, for he was confined to the bowels of the ship, chipping and painting, and all he saw of Mukalla, that gateway to the Hadhramaut, was a glimpse through a scuttle – a huddle of terraced Arab houses, so white in the sunlight that it looked like an ivory chess set laid out at the foot of the arid mountains. Only at night was he allowed on deck, and he spent hours, motionless in the bows of the ship, drinking in the beauty and the mystery of the Arabian Sea, for the water was alive with phosphorescence. From his vantage point he could look down at the bow wave, at the water rushing away from the ship in two great swathes as bright as moonlight, and ahead, in the inky blackness of the sea, great whorls of light like nebulei were shattered into a thousand phosphorescent fragments as the ship's passage broke up the shoals of fish – and like outriders the sharks flashed torpedo-tracks of light as they ploughed their voracious way through the depths. And every now and then a tanker passed them, decks almost awash, with oil from Kuwait, Bahrain and Dahran.

They passed inside the Kuria Muria islands at night, and to get a better view of them he ignored his orders and crept up to the boat deck. He was standing there close beside one of the boats when the door of the passenger accommodation opened and two figures emerged, momentarily outlined against the yellow light. They came aft, two voices talking earnestly, as he shrank into the shadow of the boat, bending down as though to adjust the falls.

' . . . the last time I was at the Bahrain office. But even in Abu Dhabi, we've heard rumours.' The accent was North Country.

'Well, that's the situation. Thought I'd warn you. Wouldn't like you to back the wrong horse and find yourself out on your ear just because you didn't know what was going on.'

'Aye; well, thanks. But the Great Gorde. . . . It takes a bit of getting used to, you must admit. He's been the Company out here for so long.'

'I wouldn't know about that, old man. I'm new out here and as far as I'm concerned Erkhard is the man.'

The voices were no more than a whisper in the night. The two oil men were leaning over the rail at the other end of the boat and David was just going to creep away when he heard the name of his father mentioned. 'Is it true Colonel Whitaker's the cause of the trouble? That's the rumour.' He froze into immobility, listening fascinated as the other man gave a short laugh. 'Well, yes, in a way; the Bloody Bedouin's got too big for his boots. And that theory of his, a lot of damned nonsense. He's not thinking of the Company, only of his Arab friends.'

'Oh, I don't know. The Company owes him a lot.'

'Concessions, yes – and a string of dry wells. The man's a dangerous amateur. I'm warning you, Entwhistle – you talk like that when Erkhard visits you at Abu Dhabi and you'll be out so damn' quick—'

'It's Gorde I deal with.'

'Okay. But you can take my word for it that it'll be Erkhard who does the next tour of inspection of the development sites. And unless you've got something to show him—'

The voices faded as the two men moved away, walking slowly and in step back towards the deck housing. David moved quickly, slipping down the ladder to the main deck, back to his position in the bows. He wanted to be alone, for that brief overheard conversation had given him a strange glimpse of the world on which he had set his heart.

The ship stopped at Nasira Island with stores for the RAF and then on again, rounding Ras al Hadd at night and ploughing north-west into the Gulf of Oman.

On the afternoon of the seventh day out from Aden she anchored at Muscat, in a cove so narrow and rocky that David could scarcely believe his eyes; it might have been the Pembrokeshire coast of Wales except that it was a white, sun-drenched Arab town that stood close by the water's edge at the head of the inlet. On either side the rocks bore the names of visiting ships with dates going back to the 1800's, all painted in foot-high letters. Long, double-ended boats of palm wood, their broad planks sewn together with thongs, swarmed round the ship, paddled by Arabs whose faces shone black in the sun.

They were there twenty-four hours and in the night David thought more than once of diving over the side. The shore was so near. But once ashore, what hope had he? There was nowhere for him to go. In a halting conversation with one of the crew, a coast Arab from a fishing village to the north called Khor al Fakhan, he learned that Muscat was backed by volcanic mountains of indescribable brutality. They were almost fifty miles deep with every route through guarded by watch towers; and beyond the mountains was the desert of the Rub al Khali – the Empty Quarter. He knew it was hopeless, and so he stayed on board, and the next afternoon they sailed.

He was having his evening meal when he was told to report to the bridge. Captain Griffiths was there, seated on his wooden stool, staring out over the bows to the starlit sea ahead. The only other man on the bridge was the Arab helmsman standing immobile, his eyes fixed on the lit compass card in its binnacles, only his hands moving as he made small adjustments to the wheel. 'Ah, there you are.' Griffiths had turned his head. 'When I went ashore at Muscat last night there was a slave from Saraifa waiting for me with a message from your father. You'll doubtless be relieved to know that he's willing to take you off my hands.' And as David mumbled his thanks, the lips smiled behind the beard. 'I may say I'm just as relieved as you are.' And he added, brusquely, 'There's an Arab *sambuq* waiting now off Ras al-Khaima to pick you up. Tonight we shall pass through the Straits of Hormuz into the Persian Gulf. With luck we should sight the *sambuq* about an hour after dawn. Now, you speak Arabic I'm told.'

'A little,' David admitted. 'But it's not easy to make myself understood – it's the different dialects, I think.'

'Well, do you think you can pass yourself off as an Arab?' And without waiting for a reply, Griffiths added, 'It's the passengers, you see. They'll talk if they see a white member of my crew being put aboard a dhow.' A few words of briefing and then the Captain's hand gripped his arm. 'Good luck now, man. And a word of advice before you go – tread warily. It's no ordinary man you've got for a father, indeed it isn't. He's the devil of a temper when he's roused. So go easy and watch your step.' And with that he dismissed him and turned again in his seat to stare through the glass at the lights of a ship coming up over the dark horizon.

David left the bridge, dazed and almost reluctant, for now the future was upon him – unknown, a little frightening. At dawn he would leave the ship and the companionship of the men he'd lived with for the past few weeks, and that last link with the home he'd known all his life would steam away, leaving him alone in a strange country, amongst strange people. It surprised him that he felt no excitement, no exhilaration – only loneliness and a sense of desolation. He didn't know it then, but it was in this moment that he said goodbye to his boyhood.

The Mate found him sitting on his bunk, staring vacantly into space. 'Here you are, Whitaker.' And he tossed a bundle of clothing down beside him. 'Ali Mahommed sold them to me – *kaffyah*, *agal*, robe, sandals, the lot, even to an old brass *khanjar* knife. Three pounds ten, and I've deducted it from your pay.' He placed some East African notes and some silver on top of the clothes. 'The Old Man told you what to do, did he? Okay, so long as you greet the *naukhuda* with a *salaam alaikum* and a few more words of Arabic. And get along to the paintshop and put some stain on your face and hands. Your face is about as pink as a white baby's bottom.'

Dressing up as an Arab for the first time in his life helped to pass the time, but still the long hours of the night stretched ahead. He lay awake a long time thinking about what the morrow would bring and about the man he hadn't known was his father till that tragic day. And then suddenly it was light and almost immediately, it seemed, one of the Arab crew came down to tell him the *sambuq* had been sighted. He listened then, waiting, tense and expectant. And then the pulse of the engines slowed and finally died away. This was it – the moment of irrevocable departure. His hand touched the brass hilt of the great curved, flat-bladed knife at his girdle. He checked the *kaffyah*, made certain that the black *agal* was in its place, circling his head. He went quickly up to the after well-deck and waited in the shelter of the main deck ladder. The rope ladder was over the side opposite No. 3 hatch, one of the crew waiting there to help him over. The faint chug of a diesel sounded in the still morning air, coming slowly nearer. He heard the bump of the dhow as it came alongside, the guttural cry of Arab voices, and then the man by the ladder was beckoning him.

He went out quickly with his head down, hidden by his *kaffyah*. A dark-skinned hand caught his arm, steadied him as he went over the bulwarks. Glancing quickly up, he caught a glimpse of the Captain leaning with his elbows on the rail of the bridge wing and below, on the boat deck, a short, tubby man in a pale dressing-gown standing watching. And after that he could see nothing but the ship's rusty side.

Hands reached up, caught him as he jumped to the worn wood deck of the dhow. He called out a greeting in Arabic as he had been told and at the same moment he heard the distant clang of the engine-room telegraph. The beat of the *Emerald Isle's* engines increased and the hull plates began to slide past, a gap opening between himself and the ship. He turned away to hide his face and found himself on a long-prowed craft built of battered wood, worn smooth by the years and bleached almost white by the torrid heat of the Persian Gulf. A single patched sail curved above it like the dirty wing of a goose hanging dead in the airless morning. The sea around was still as a mirror and white like molten glass, and then the swirl of the ship's screws shattered it.

There were three men on the *sambuq* and only the *naukhuda*, or captain, wore a turban as well as a loin cloth. He was an old man with a wisp of a grey moustache and a few grey hairs on his chin which he stroked constantly. The crew was composed of a smooth-faced boy with a withered arm and a big, barrel-chested man, black as a negro, with a satin skin that rippled with every movement. The *naukhuda* took his hand in his and held it for a long time, whilst the other two crowded close, staring at his face, feeling his clothes – six brown eyes gazing at him full of curiosity. A flood of questions, the old man using the deferential *sahib*, legacy of India. Whenever he said anything, all three listened respectfully. But it was no good. He couldn't seem to make himself understood.

At length he gave it up and judging that it would be safe now to turn his head to take a last look at the *Emerald Isle*, he was appalled to find that she had vanished utterly, swallowed in the humid haze of the day's beginning. For a time he could still hear the beat of her engines, but finally even that was gone and he was alone with his three Arabs in a flat calm sea that had an oily shimmer to its hard, unbroken surface.

He felt abandoned then, more alone than he'd ever been in his life before. But it was a mood that didn't last, for in less than an hour the haze thinned and away to port the vague outline of a mass of mountains emerged. A few minutes later and the sky was clear, a blue bowl reflected in the sea, and the mountains stood out magnificently, tumbling down from the sky in sheer red cliffs to disappear in a mirage effect at the water's edge. Ahead, a long dhow stood with limp sail suspended in the air, and beyond it the world seemed to vanish – no mountains, nothing, only the endless sky. For the first time he understood why men talked of the desert as a sea.

Twice the *sambuq's* aged engine petered out. Each time it was the boy who got it going. The *naukhuda* sat dreamily at the helm, steering with the toes of his right foot curled round the smooth wood of the rudder bar. A charcoal fire had been burning on the low poop ever since he'd come on board and the big cooking pot above it eventually produced a mess of rice and mutton which they ate in their fingers. A small wind stirred the surface of the sea, increased until it filled the sail and the engine was switched off. In the sudden quiet, the sound of the water sliding past the hull seemed almost loud. The mainsheet was eased out and the *sambuq* took wing. 'Ras al-Khaima.' The *naukhuda* pointed across the port bow. At the very foot of the mountains and low on the horizon, he made out the dun-coloured shape of houses, the tufts of palms. And shortly after that the coast ahead showed up, low and flat, a shimmering line of dunes.

The sun was barely halfway up the sky when they closed that dune coast. A line of camels marched sedately along the sand of the foreshore and close under the low cliffs a Land Rover stood parked, a lone figure in Arab clothes standing beside it. He thought then that this was his father and braced himself for that first meeting, wondering what he would be like. But when the *naukhuda* paddled him ashore in the *sambuq's* dugout, it was an Arab who waded into the shallow water to meet them.

Again the difficulty of trying to make himself understood. The Arab's name was Yousif and he spoke a little English. 'Coll-onell Sahib not here. You come Saraifa now.' The word Saraifa was shouted at him several times as though he were deaf.

'How far is Saraifa?' The man stared at him as though he were mad. He was a very dirty-looking individual, his greasy turban trailing one end over his shoulders, a torn and very filthy European jacket worn over his Arab robes. His dark face was smudged with oil; this and the little black moustache below the curved nose gave him a sinister appearance. David tried again: 'Saraifa . . . ten miles, twenty?' He held up his fingers.

'Saraifa no far in machine of Coll-onell Sahib.' The gap-toothed smile was clearly meant to placate. 'Me driver to Coll-onell Sahib. Drive very quick.' That seemed to exhaust his fund of English, for he turned to the *naukhuda* and launched into a guttural flood of conversation. At length the *naukhuda* stepped forward, kissed his hand and touched it to his heart with a little bow. David gave him one of the notes the Mate had handed him and found his hand held in the other's horny palm whilst the old man made him a long farewell speech.

Then at last he was in the Land Rover and they

were roaring along the sand of the foreshore, the driver bent over the wheel like a rider urging on his horse, with the stray end of his filthy turban streaming out behind him. A mile or two further on they left the sea's edge by a camel track that climbed the shallow cliffs. Looking back, David got a last glimpse of the dhow that had brought him to the Arabian shore, and then they were bouncing past the Bedouin caravan he had seen moving along the sands. The camels stared with supercilious gaze, padding effortlessly through the sand under their mountainous loads. The men, wild and bearded, raised their hands unsmilingly in desert salutation. The silver mountings of their old-fashioned guns winked in the hot sun, and David caught the wicked gleam of *khanjar* knives and the brass of cartridge belts. He was seeing for the first time the desert world that was to be his home.

ENQUIRIES OF AN EXECUTOR

The account of his actual arrival in Arabia was contained in the letter he dispatched to me almost immediately after he had reached Saraifa. For that reason, I suppose, it told me little about the actual meeting between himself and his father. Scribbled in pencil on scraps of paper, it had been written mostly on board the *Emerald Isle*. Except for the final page it had been completed at a water-hole somewhere in the desert where he and Yousif had spent the night. The final page was nothing more than a hastily-written postscript: *Saraifa at last, but I arrived at a bad time – my father was with the Sheikh and an oil director and his pilot, and he leaves with them in the morning for Bahrain. He seemed angry at first, but it's all right now, I think. The Sheikh's son, Khalid, is to look after me whilst he is away and I am to go on a hunting expedition with him to get to know desert ways. My father is a great man here with a bodyguard and a mud fort or palace where I am writing now. He has* *only one eye and a black patch over the other, which makes him a bit terrifying at first and everybody seems afraid of him. Men keep coming into this room for one reason and another, but really to stare at me. It is all very strange – but exciting. Thank you again, David.*

At the end of the year he sent me a Christmas card. It was a Gulfoman Oilfields Development Company card and was postmarked Basra. He was at an oil school studying geology and seemed happy. That was the last I heard of him until I received the news, three years later, that he was missing in the Rub al Khali desert, the Empty Quarter.

By then I was involved in his father's affairs. It was a strange business and one that was causing me considerable concern – though at the outset it had seemed straightforward enough. In fact, I wasn't in the least surprised when he asked me to act for him. A lawyer's business is a very personal one and tends to grow through personal contact. *What my son has told me about you, and the fact that your firm acted for me for many years in the matter of the settlement to his mother, leads me to place complete confidence in your discretion and in your ability to use your own initiative when required.* He wanted to consolidate his financial affairs, he said, and he sent me Power of Attorney and gave me authority to collect all monies, meet any accounts that became due and generally manage his business interests. There was nothing particularly unusual about this, except that I was on no account to attempt to communicate with him in any way once the arrangement was working.

My correspondence with him lasted over several months. His letters were all hand-written and the only address he gave was his bank in Bahrain. Shortly after it was all agreed, money began to flow in from all over the Middle East, from Arab merchants and bankers, from traders, from a firm of stockbrokers in Cairo and a large sum from the cashier of the London Office of the Gulfoman Oilfields Development Company. This went on for about a year. Some of it was in kind – pearls from a dealer in Bahrain, even a box full of Maria Theresa dollars and another full of silver, presumably gifts from the local sheikhs.

Finally the flow had dried up and, presuming that the operation was against his retirement, I invested the money for him, mostly in local industry of which I had personal knowledge. The market, of course, was a restricted one, but it never occurred to me that he would almost immediately want large sums in cash. And then in May of the following year accounts began to come through for settlement – for stores, equipment, vehicles; the largest single item almost £5,000 for a second-hand seismological truck, complete with geophones and all the necessary equipment for a geophysical survey, and there had been a shipping agent's account for freighting it down from Basra to Muscat on the *Emerald Isle*.

It was clear that he was embarking on a programme of oil exploration on his own, expecting it to be financed by the nominee account, and it worried me, for I'd no means of knowing where it was going to end. I ignored my instructions then and wrote him several times, care of his bank, but received no reply. And in the New Year I received another batch of accounts, this time for fuel and stores and drilling pipe. I was by then thoroughly alarmed about the whole situation. He obviously didn't realize that there were restrictions on bank lending in force and I was reluctant to sell securities on a weak market. I was able to meet the immediate accounts, but I had to know what his future plans were. On March 5 I received an account for the hire of a complete drilling rig. I phoned an oil man I knew in Milford Haven, and he gave me figures for the probable cost of drilling, even with a hired rig, that staggered me. I wrote to Whitaker then stating that unless he sent me a statement of his plans and the probable cost by return, I should have no alternative but to fly out at his expense to discuss the whole situation.

That was the position on the morning of March 24 when I came into the office and found an airmail letter with a Bahrain stamp amongst my post. I thought it was the reply I was expecting, but when I opened it I found it was from Susan Thomas. Apparently she was now working as a nurse at a hospital in Dubai. She enclosed a copy of a cable she had received from the offices of the Gulfoman Oilfields Development Company in Bahrain. I read it through twice before my mind was able to take in and accept what the words meant, so great was my sense of shock.

Nurse Susan Thomas the Hospital Dubai from Godco – March 18: Regret inform you your brother David Whitaker missing desert Rub al Khali since February twenty-eight stop Truck now discovered abandoned some fifty miles west north west of Saraifa Oasis stop Extensive ground search with air co-operation RAF in difficult dune country has revealed no trace also unreported Nomad tribesmen stop Now reluctantly called off must be presumed dead stop Company offers deepest sympathy you and your mother – Erkhard.

Presumed dead! It was hard to believe. Dealing as I had been for the last two years with his father's affairs I had often thought about him, wondered how he was getting on, what he was doing. I had even thought of writing to him to ask about his father's plans. And now this. My own sense of disbelief was echoed by Susan's letter – a purely intuitive reaction. *We were twins, as you know, yet all this time, whilst they have been searching, I knew nothing, felt nothing. If David is dead, then surely I would have known.* And then, a little further on in the letter: *Early last month he came to see me, very late at night. He was in some sort of trouble. But what it was he wouldn't say. He seemed withdrawn and he had a rather wild look. I felt he was in danger, but I still cannot believe he is dead.* And then the words: *He told me then that if anything were to happen to him I was to write to you at once.* In the final paragraph she apologised for being a nuisance and added: *But please, please contact the London Office of the Company and try to persuade them to have the search resumed.* The letter was signed simply *Susan* as though I were an old friend.

I was due in court at 10 o'clock and still had the rest of my post to go through; I put the letter aside and didn't get back to it until late that afternoon when I rang the London Office of the Gulfoman Oilfields Development Company. But of course they knew nothing. A thin, cultured voice informed me that all local administration was dealt with by the Bahrain office. 'The cable is signed Erkhard, you say? Then I think you may take it that everything possible has already been done and the facts are as stated. Mr Erkhard is our General Manager out there and in charge of all developments.' However, he took my name and address and promised to pass on my observations to Bahrain.

I cleared my desk and then got my car and drove down to Grangetown to break the news to Mrs Thomas; not a very pleasant task, but one that I couldn't very well avoid, since Susan had written: *This is something I cannot bring myself to do in a letter. It would be so much kinder if you would do it – more personal, and you can explain the circumstances better. Tell her I will write later.*

Mrs Thomas had aged, of course; but more so than I would have expected. Her hair was completely grey now, no longer drawn back tightly from her forehead, but hanging untidily in wisps. The dress she wore was none too clean and the eyes looked almost furtive as they flickered from one thing to another, never at rest and never looking directly at me. At the same time, the lines of strain had gone; her face seemed to have filled out, become smoother.

She invited me into the parlour where the couch was still in the same place, the roll-top desk still littered with books on racing form. She was nervous and she was talking all the time as we stood there, almost in the same positions, like actors cued to their places, talking about David, about Sue, about her life and how lonely it was now. 'But Dafydd is a great comfort to me. He was never much of a letter writer, but since he went to Arabia—' Her eyes flicked to my face. 'Is it about Dafydd you've come, Mr Grant?' But then they had fled to another part of the room and she was saying, 'I'm expecting a letter from him soon. He doesn't write regularly, of course. He's in such strange places. But such a picture he gives me, I can almost see it, you know . . . the Bedouin men and the camels and the heat; like a dream it is and me twenty again and waiting for letters.' She gave a little hurried laugh, almost a titter. 'I get confused sometimes. Over two years it is now since Sue went out there. I've been alone ever since, you see, and the mind plays tricks—'

'When did you last hear from David?' I asked her.

'Oh, recently. Quite recently. And I'll have another letter from him soon. Any day now, I expect—' And then, sheering away from the subject, she said, 'You've never seen his room, have you? All his books. I'd like you to see his room.' And without waiting for a reply, she bustled out of the room as though anxious to escape from me. 'I've kept it just as it was, you know.'

She led me up the ill-lit stairs to a little room at the end of a short landing. The place smelt musty and had the chill of long abandonment. A flick-knife lay on the painted top of a chest of drawers like a warrior's trophy from some forgotten war and above the bed was a shelf of books. 'He was a great one for reading,' she said. 'Anything about Arabia. I did my best to get him interested in other things, but there ... I knew he'd go there sooner or later. It was in the blood as you might say.'

There were about fifty books there, most of them books on Arabia, including expensive volumes like Doughty's *Arabia Deserta* – all damaged, but stuck together with loving care. It was a strange glimpse of a young man's yearning. 'I believe Colonel Whitaker once wrote a book about Arabia,' I said. 'I tried to get a copy, but it was out of print.'

She nodded. 'It's a long time since anybody could get a copy. It wasn't very successful, you see. But there is one here somewhere.' She leaned her weight against the bed and ran a work-coarsened finger along the bookshelf. And then she took down a book and handed it to me. The title was *Wanderings by Camel through the Empty Quarter*. 'Signed it is, you see,' she said proudly. 'He gave it to me before he left.' And she added wistfully, 'It was the only present he ever gave me.'

The book, of course, brought back memories to her. She smiled at me shyly – almost coyly. 'You know it was whilst he was home writing that and getting it published that I came to know him. I was in service then at Llanfihangel Hall. That was his family's place.' She hesitated. 'I suppose he was bored really.' The coy little smile had spread to her eyes so that her whole face was strangely transfigured. 'But we enjoyed our-selves.' She said it with a happy little sigh, and then she added, 'Ah well, you only live once, Mr Grant. That's what I tell myself whenever I'm feeling lonely. You've had your fun, Sarah, I say. You've had your fun and you've paid the price. Are you married, Mr Grant?'

'No.'

'And no illegitimate children?' She gave a queer laugh as I shook my head. 'Well, there you are. People like you miss a great deal in life.' And she added with surprising perception: 'You shouldn't always live at second hand, you know. Rummaging about in other people's lives—'

'We do our best to help,' I murmured uncomfort-ably. And then I asked her if I could borrow Whitaker's book for a few days. I thought it might help me to understand the sort of man he was. She looked at me in surprise. 'No,' she said quickly, her eyes darting to the book. 'No, I don't think I'd like anyone to borrow that.' And she took it from me and put it quickly back in its place. 'I'll make you some tea if you like,' she said as she took me back down the stairs.

At the bottom, under the light, there was a faded photograph of a pretty girl in a high-necked frock. 'That was taken just about the time I met the Major,' she said as she saw me looking at it. 'He was a major then, you see – from the Kaiser's War. You didn't recognise it as me, I suppose?' She smiled. 'I was considered very pretty then, you know – though I didn't look so pretty when he'd finished with me and I was bearing twins; more like a balloon, you know. Now won't you stay and have a cup of tea, Mr Grant, and you can tell me how you managed to get Dafydd out to his father. I should have thanked you for doing that, shouldn't I, but at the time I thought it might—' She hesitated. 'You see, I've always been afraid of what would happen when they met. And then Dafydd started to go wrong – all those Arab friends of his—' We had reached the parlour again and she said, 'I shall never forget that afternoon. Mr Thomas lying there on the couch, and Dafydd—' She pointed towards the spot where he had stood. 'And Dafydd standing there and swearing he'd kill his own Da. But there—' She gave me a weak uneasy smile. 'They're together now. And nothing has happened, has it? It was silly of me to take a young boy so seriously.' And she added almost violently, 'But it scared me at the time. It scared me silly.'

'You say they're together *now*?'

'Oh, yes – in a place called Saraifa. That's an oasis—'

'What was the date of that last letter you had?'

'I – I don't remember.' Her mouth was suddenly trembling. 'It was quite recent, Mr Grant.'

'Could I see it please?'

She hesitated, her eyes wandering round the room.

And then finally she went to the roll-top desk and took a single sheet of paper from the top of a neat little pile of similar sheets. 'August it was,' she said almost in a whisper. 'August the twenty-third.'

Seven months ago. 'And you haven't heard from him since?'

She shook her head, her hand trembling as she stared down at the letter.

'And he was at Saraifa; does he say what he was doing there?'

'He'd been on a gazelle hunt with Sheikh Makhmud and his son—'

'What sort of work, I mean?'

'No, he doesn't mention work. But it would be something to do with oil. He's a geologist, you see, and works for one of the oil companies.' She was reading the letter to herself again, her lips forming the words which I was certain she knew by heart. 'He writes beautiful letters, you know – all about the country and the people he meets. He writes so I can almost imagine I'm out there with him.' She put the letter back on the pile. 'That was my dream once, that I'd go out there to live.' She stood there smiling to herself and staring out at the dingy street. 'Just a dream,' she repeated. 'But with the books and the maps I can see it all from his letters. I'm a Welsh woman, you see. I have the gift of imagination.' And then with a sudden edge of bitterness to her voice: 'You need imagination sometimes in a hole like this.'

How could I tell her the boy was dead? 'Have you heard from his father at all?'

She shook her head. 'No, I've never heard from the Major – not once in all these years.' There was a catch in her voice and she moved quickly away towards the door. 'I'll make you some tea.'

'Please don't bother,' I said. 'I have to go now.'

But she was between me and the door, her hands fumbling at her dress, her eyes searching my face. She had finally screwed herself up to the pitch of facing the implication of my visit. 'What's happened, Mr Grant?' she asked. 'What's happened between them? As soon as I saw you standing there on the doorstep—'

'Nothing has happened between them. According to my information—'

But she didn't let me finish, wasn't even listening. 'I knew they should never have met,' she cried. 'They're alike, you see. They've the same nature – obstinate, very obstinate.' She was almost sobbing for breath. 'I knew what it would mean. It's in their stars. They're both Sagittarius, you see. And he was such a fine man when I knew him. Such a fine man – and lusty, so full of fire and vitality.' She was wringing her hands and a sound came from her lips like the sound of keening. 'Known it I have, always. Oh God!' she whispered. And then, staring straight at me: 'How did it happen? Do you know how it happened?'

There was nothing for it then but to let her know the facts, such as they were. And because it was easier I handed her the copy of the cable her daughter had sent me. She read it through slowly, her eyes widening as the shock of it went home until they became fixed, almost vacant. 'Dafydd!' she murmured his name.

'He's reported missing, that's all,' I said, trying to comfort her, to offer her some hope.

But she didn't seem to take that in. 'Dead,' she whispered. And then she repeated his name. 'Dafydd?' And her tone was one of shocked surprise. 'I never thought it would be Dafydd. That's not right at all.' The fixed stare was almost trance-like. 'It was never Dafydd that was going to die.' And a shiver ran through her.

'I'll write to your daughter. No doubt she'll let you have any further information direct.' She didn't say anything and her eyes still had that fixed, trance-like look as I took the copy of the cable from her nerveless hand. Her behaviour was so odd I didn't like to leave it with her. 'Don't worry too much. There's still a chance—'

'No.' The word seemed to explode out of her mouth. 'No, better it is like this, God rest his poor soul.'

Appalled, I hurried past her, out into the fresh evening air. The stars – what a thing to be believing in at a time like this. Poor woman!

But as I drove away, it was the father I was thinking about, a sense of uneasiness growing in my mind, fostered by the violence of her strange reaction. Going back to that house, to that poor woman driven half out of her senses by an old love she couldn't discard; it was all suddenly fresh in my memory – her fears and the way he'd sworn to kill his father. What had happened between those two in the intervening years? Or was this just an accident – one of those things that can happen to any young man prospecting out there in the remote deserts of Arabia?

Back at the office I got out the Whitaker file and read that postscript to David's letter again. But there was nothing in it to give me a clue as to how his father had reacted. The words might have been written by any youngster plunged into new and strange surroundings, except that he had described his father as though he were looking at him with the eyes of a complete stranger. But then that was what he was. Right at the bottom of the file was the dossier Andrews had produced from press-cuttings in the library of the Welsh edition of a popular daily and I read it through again:

Charles Stanley Whitaker, born Llanfihangel Hall near Usk 1899. Joined the cavalry as a trooper in 1915, served with Allenby in the offensive against the Turks and rose to the rank of major. After the war, he stayed on in the Middle East. Policeman, trader, dhow-owner; he adopted the Moslem religion, made the pilgrimage to Mecca, has lived with the Bedouin. His book on his crossing of the Rub al Khali desert was published in 1936. By then he had already become something of a legend. Following publication of his book, he went back to the Middle East, and after three years with Gulfoman Oilfields Development, he joined Wavell's staff on the outbreak of war with the rank of colonel. Awarded the V.C. for gallantry, wounded twice, served with Wingate and later with Wilson. Was still a colonel at the end of the war. He then rejoined Gulfoman Oilfields Development as political representative.

There was a picture pinned to the dossier which showed him in Arab dress standing beside a Land Rover on a desert airstrip. The black patch over the right eye was plainly visible; so, too, was the prominent, beak-like nose. He was slightly stooped, as though conscious of his height; he was a head taller than the other two men in the picture. This and the beard and the black patch over the eye, gave him a very formidable appearance, and though the picture wasn't a very clear one, looking at it again, I couldn't help feeling that he was a man capable of anything, and I could appreciate the impression he had made on a Welsh servant girl all those years ago. He would have been thirty-six then, a good deal younger, and I suppose he had taken her the way he would have taken a slave girl in a Bedouin encampment; but for her it had been something different, an experience so out of the ordinary that she had thought of nothing else for the last twenty-five years.

I wondered whether she still possessed that album full of press-cuttings. I would like to have looked through it and also through the letters from her son, but I couldn't face the thought of going back to the house. I returned the file to its place and wrote to Susan advising her to make the journey to Bahrain and see Erkhard. *Nothing can be done, it appears, at this*

end, I told her. *Erkhard seems to be the only man who
has the authority to order the search to be resumed.*

Two days later the news of David's death was in
The Times, a rather guarded account it seemed to me.
It was clearly based on a Company handout, but it
did include a brief description by one of the RAF pilots
who had flown the search.

> Flight-Lieutenant Hill described the truck as
> similar to those used by oil companies for seis-
> mological work, though no company markings
> showed on either bonnet or sides. It was
> halfway up the side of a big sand dune as
> though it had stalled or bogged down in an
> effort to surmount this obstacle. It was hardly
> surprising, he said, that he had flown several
> times over the area without seeing it; high
> winds – the local *shamal* – had piled the sand
> up on one side of it. He had only sighted the
> truck because the sun was low and it was
> casting a shadow.

It was less a news story than a short article and most
of it was about Colonel Whitaker – *that strange, half-
Arab figure, so prominent in the search for Gulf oil
during the past twenty years.* It was 'From Our Own
Correspondent,' and I had a vague sense as I read it
that there was something behind the piece, something that he was not in a position to reveal but that
was nevertheless there for those who could read
between the lines. Such phrases as: *The fascination of*

this man who has maintained his theory about oil in the face of persistent failure; and Whether he is another Holmes or not, whether the oil company he served for so long will live to regret his departure, only time will tell. Finally there was this: *It appears there is some foundation for the rumour that his son, though employed by GODCO, was on loan to him for some private purpose, presumably connected with prospecting for oil.*

The suggestion that David had been on loan to his father at the time of his disappearance did nothing to allay the uneasiness that had resulted from my visit to Mrs Thomas. And then the following morning Captain Griffiths walked into my office and I knew for certain that there was something more to the boy's death than the Company had so far revealed.

Griffiths had docked at first light and was still in uniform, having come straight from his ship. 'I promised to deliver this personally into your hands.' He put a fat envelope down on the desk in front of me. 'Personally, you understand. He wouldn't risk it through the post.'

'Who's it from?' I asked. But the address was handwritten, the writing familiar. I knew it was from David before he answered my question. 'Young Whitaker,' he said and sat himself down in the chair opposite my desk.

I was too startled to say anything for a moment, for the boy had been alive when he'd handed this to Griffiths. I picked it up, staring at the address as though that would give me some clue as to what was inside. 'When did he give you this?'

'Well now—' He frowned. 'It was Sharjah and we were anchored about a mile off—'

'Yes, but what was the date?'

'It's the date I'm trying to remember, man.' His little beard bristled. 'Without my log I can't be sure. But we left Basra on January twenty-third and we called at Kuwait, Bahrain, Doha, Abu Dhabi and Dubai before we anchored off Sharjah; it would be about the middle of the first week in February.'

And David had been reported missing on February 28. Griffiths must have been one of the last people he saw before he went out into the desert – perhaps one of the last of his own race to see him alive. 'Still the same offices, I see.' Griffiths had pulled his pipe out and was busy filling it. He didn't know the boy was dead.

'The trouble is the clients don't pay their bills,' I said and slit the packet open. The old rogue had never settled my account, though he'd admitted that Whitaker had made him a present of fifty quid for getting the boy out to Arabia. Inside was a handwritten letter folded around another envelope that had GODCO, BAHRAIN, printed on the flap. Across the front of it he had typed: DAVID WHITAKER – TO BE OPENED ONLY IN THE EVENT OF MY DEATH.

Those words – they came as a shock. I stared at them, wondering how he could possibly have known he was going to die. Or was it just a coincidence?

'What's the matter?' Griffiths asked. 'What's he been up to?'

I suppose he thought he was in some sort of legal trouble. 'You haven't seen *The Times* then?'

'Of course not. I only got in this morning. Why?'

'David Whitaker is dead,' I said. And I told him about the truck they'd found abandoned and the description of it given in *The Times*. 'You must have been one of the last people to see him alive.'

'I see.' His acceptance of it might have surprised me, except that my mind was still on that envelope. 'It's almost uncanny,' I murmured.

'What is?'

'Your coming here, with this.' I turned the envelope round so that he could see what was typed across it. 'He must have had some sort of a premonition—'

Griffiths nodded his head slowly. 'That explains it.' And he added, 'May his soul rest in peace, the poor devil.' He said it quietly, with reverence, as though he were on the deck of his ship and consigning the boy's body to the deep.

'Explains what?' I asked him.

'The circumstances—' He hesitated. 'Very strange they were.' And then he looked at me, his gaze very direct. 'I don't think you quite understand, Mr Grant. That boy risked his life on a filthy night with a *shamal* blowing to get that packet to me without anyone knowing.'

'Risked his life?' I was reading through the covering letter, only half listening to him.

'Yes indeed, for he came off in one of those

fisherman's dugouts and just an Arab boy with him. It was a damned foolhardy thing to do. There was a wicked sea running. He needed a lawyer, he said, somebody he could trust.'

'Why? Did he say why he needed a lawyer?'

'No.' Griffiths shook his head. 'No, he didn't say why, and it's something I've been asking myself ever since I put that envelope away in the ship's safe. What would a young geophysicist want with a lawyer out there in the middle of Arabia?'

I finished reading the letter and then I put it down on the desk. Griffiths was lighting his pipe, his head cocked on one side. 'Well, he's dead now, you say.' He was eyeing the unopened envelope the way a thrush eyes a worm.

'Perhaps you'd tell me just what happened?' I suggested.

'Well—' He hesitated, his eyes still on the envelope. 'It was night, you see. We had finished unloading and the deck lights had been switched off about an hour when one of my Arab crew reports a dugout alongside and a white man in it called Thomas asking for me. Well, I couldn't recall his name, how should I? I have so many passengers; they come and go along the coast – oil men, Locust Control, Levy officers, Air Force personnel, Government officials. How should I remember his name, even if he was another Welshman? It was four years since he'd used it anyway. And then he came stumbling into my cabin and I recognised him at once of course.'

I thought he was going to stop there, but after a

moment's silence he went on: 'Only the previous voyage I'd had him on board as a passenger, from Bahrain down to Dubai. He'd changed a great deal in those six months; all the vitality of youth seemed to have been whipped out of him, his skin burned almost black by the sun and the hard, angular bones of the face showing through. But it was the eyes, man. They weren't the eyes of a youngster any more; they were the eyes of a man who'd looked the world in the face and been badly frightened by it.'

'Who was he afraid of?' I was thinking of the father then.

'I didn't say he was afraid of anybody.'

'Did he talk to you at all – about himself?'

'Oh yes, indeed. He was talking all the time. To be honest, Mr Grant, I thought he might be going round the bend. Some of them do that you know . . . the heat and the sand, and if it's lonely work—'

'Yes, but what did he say?'

'Nothing very much. Nothing that I can remember, that is. He was talking very fast, you see, the words tumbling over themselves – about his job and where he'd been.'

'And where had he been? Had he been to Saraifa?'

But Griffiths shook his head. 'I can't remember,' he said. 'I don't think he mentioned Saraifa. It was talk for the sake of talking, you know – for the sake of hearing the sound of his own voice and having somebody listen to it. He'd been in some wild places, I think, and mostly on his own, with nobody with him but Arabs.'

I asked about the packet then. 'Did he talk about that at all?'

'No. He sat at my desk and wrote that covering letter. And when he'd finished it, he borrowed an envelope from me, sealed the whole thing up and asked me to put it in my safe and deliver it to you personally the moment I docked.'

'Didn't you ask him why it was so urgent?'

'Of course I did. I was damned curious about the whole thing. But his manner was so odd—'

'He didn't say anything about it being political dynamite then?'

'Political dynamite?' Griffiths's bushy eyebrows lifted. 'No, he didn't say anything like that.' A wary look had come into his eyes. 'Is that what he says in that letter?'

I nodded. 'Where's Colonel Whitaker now? Can you tell me that?'

But he didn't know for certain. 'Probably in Saraifa,' he said. 'Why?' His tone was suddenly cautious as though he were a witness under cross-examination, and since I had no intention of telling him the reason for my interest in Whitaker, I asked him about the previous voyage when he'd had David on board as a passenger. 'Was he going to join his father, do you know?'

But he couldn't even tell me that. 'All he said was that he was going down into the Rub al Khali.' He took out his watch and glanced at it. 'It was a hell of a time to be going down into the Empty Quarter,' he added as though glad to escape into generalities. 'That time of the year the sand is hot enough to burn the tyres off a truck and the soles off your boots.'

'It was summer?'

He nodded. 'Early July it would have been.'

And that was the month I'd received the shipping agent's account. 'Did you have a seismological truck on board?'

'Yes.' He stared at me curiously, surprised that I should know about it. 'It was deck cargo and we shipped it down to Muscat. I remember that because we had a devil of a job getting it ashore; had to lash four of the local boats together and bridge them with planks.'

'You don't think it could be the same truck – the one that was found abandoned?'

But of course he couldn't tell me that.

'Did you know he was on loan to his father? Did he say anything about that?'

He shook his head and got to his feet.

'Did he talk about his father at all?'

'No, he didn't mention him.' He said it flatly as though to discourage any further questions. 'I must be going now, Mr Grant. Just docked – a lot of things to see to, you know'

I was reluctant to let him go. 'One more question, Captain Griffiths.' I was standing facing him then. 'You said once that you heard all the gossip out there. Have you heard any rumours about Saraifa?'

'Rumours?'

'That Colonel Whitaker is prospecting for oil there.'

He started to say something, but then he seemed to think better of it and shook his head. 'A man like that, you never know what's true and what isn't. And Saraifa is a long way from the coast. A trouble spot, too.' He glanced uneasily at his watch again.

I read him *The Times* Correspondent's report, the paragraph about David being on loan to his father. But all he said was, 'The Whitaker Theory. It crops up whenever anybody writes about that man.' And then he was moving towards the door. 'Well, I've done what I promised, and that's that.' He held out his hand. 'Sad about David Whitaker, very sad. Good boy – lots of character.' He shook my hand briefly, cast a quick glance at the envelope still lying unopened on my desk and then went to the door. His last words to me as I saw him out were: 'It's a tricky business – oil. Lot of money involved; politics, too. And if he was operating anywhere near the Hadd-Saraifa border ... Well, you'd understand if you'd ever been out there.' He said it in a fatherly way as though he were giving me some sound advice.

I was reluctant to let him go. That little Welsh sea captain was stuffed full of all the gossip of the Gulf if I could only have wrung it out of him. But I don't think he wanted to talk and anyway I was anxious to find out what that envelope contained. The covering letter had given me no real indication.

You helped me once long ago. Now I'm asking you to help me again. He mentioned the envelope then and asked me to put it in a safe place and only open it in the event of his death. *You're the only man I feel I can trust with a thing like this.* And he added, *I should warn you that it's political dynamite, and if anybody knew it was in your possession it might lead to trouble.* He concluded with apologies for bothering me with his affairs, and then these words: *Thank you again for helping me to a life that has suited me and that I have enjoyed.* It was signed: *Yours gratefully – David.*

I read it through again standing at my desk, and there was no escaping the significance of those final words. For some reason he had believed he was going to die. Had he been ill, suffering from some terrible disease? But that didn't fit Griffiths's description of him. Nervous, wrought up, even frightened – yes; but not ill. And why the secrecy anyway?

I picked up the envelope and slit it open. Inside was a typewritten letter, his Will, and two envelopes – one addressed to Sir Philip Gorde at the London Office of GODCO, the other marked: LOCATION AND SKETCH MAP. Location of what? But it wasn't difficult to guess, for what else but the discovery of oil could be described as political dynamite in the deserts of Arabia?

The letter didn't say so in so many words, but it made it pretty clear. And because it gives some indication of his frame of mind – and also because it formed the basis of my subsequent actions – I give it here in full. It was dated December 29 of the previous year and above the date he had typed – *Somewhere in the Sheikhdom of Saraifa*:

Dear Mr Grant,
The time has come to put my affairs into the hands of somebody I know and can trust. I am working here on an old survey. It was carried out a long time ago and the man who did it is dead now. If my own results confirm his report – and I shall know very shortly – I shall try and catch Captain Griffiths at Sharjah when the *Emerald Isle* stops there about the end of next month. I cannot explain to you why it is necessary. All I can say is that this is a forbidden zone and that I am working against time and without authority. Everything is against me – almost like it was when I came to you last. I've always been a bit of a rebel at heart. But outside of the pack, you're on your own. And whatever happens to me, I'm determined that Saraifa shall have the benefit of my efforts. The oasis fights a losing battle with the desert. Without money it is doomed. And I spent six of the happiest months of my life there.

When you read this I shall be dead. Please then take the following action: Contact Sir Philip Gorde, who is on the board of directors of GODCO, and give him the envelope I have addressed to him. It contains a document which is correctly-phrased and is a copy of other concession agreements. It will also contain my survey report, but without the locations. The locations will be contained in a separate envelope, together with additional copies of my survey report. This envelope is only to be handed over after Sir Philip Gorde has signed the concession agreement and legally bound the Company, to your satisfaction, to drill *four* test wells at the locations indicated. (The *four* had been written in ink, presumably later.)

In the event that Sir Philip Gorde refuses to sign, then you will please take whatever action you think best in the interests of Saraifa. Khalid, the Sheikh's son, knows what I am doing and you will find he fully understands what is at stake so far as the oasis is concerned. It is essential that somehow you get the concession taken up. Saraifa needs oil desperately and if you succeed you will not find Khalid lacking in appreciation, or Sheikh Makhmud for that matter. You may, of course, make what use you can of the circumstances of my death, my parentage and my past to achieve publicity and so attract the interest of other oil companies.

Enclosed also is my Will. I have appointed you my Executor and after making the necessary arrangements with my bank in Bahrain, you will please draw on the account for fees and expenses. Please understand that I would not again involve you in my affairs if I were not desperate. In the event of my death I have instructed my sister to contact you immediately.

David Whitaker

It was an unusual communication for a solicitor to receive, most unusual; and reading it through again I was struck by the fact that he made no mention of his father. In the whole of that document there wasn't one reference to Colonel Whitaker. *Everything is against me.* There were other phrases, too. I was greatly disturbed about the whole thing, particularly as I knew that Whitaker was engaged in an operation that must run counter to the interests of the company he had served and which David was serving at the time of his death.

However, there was no point in speculating. His instructions were clear and I picked up the phone and rang the London Office of GODCO. And whilst I was waiting for the call to come through I had a look at the Will. He had typed it himself, but it was a perfectly legal document even though the witnesses to his signature were two Arabs. It appointed me Executor and his sister, Susan, sole legatee with instructions to take care of their mother. Again no reference to his father.

This and the letter and the fact that he had made such careful provision against the possibility of death, gave a strange quality of isolation to his activities, as though he were operating alone in a hostile world. I think it was then that I seriously began to consider the possibility that his disappearance was no accident.

My call to GODCO came through and I was put on to the same thin, cultured voice. No, Sir Philip was not available, would not be for some time. He was on a tour of the Company's Middle East properties and not expected back for at least a month. I could contact him through the Bahrain Office if the matter were important.

I put the phone down and sat there for a long time, considering. But I don't think there was ever any real doubt in my mind. I hadn't heard from Whitaker and, quite apart from his son's death, the necessity for a meeting with him was urgent. It was just that the Persian Gulf was a long way away and I had got out of the habit of travelling. Fortunately I now had an arrangement with another firm of solicitors which enabled me to get away when necessary and in the end I put a call through to a local travel agency. BOAC flights direct to Bahrain were weekly, leaving on Thursdays at 1000 hours and arriving 0305 hours Friday. That just gave me the time to make all my arrangements, get visas and clear my desk of the more urgent matters. I told them to book me out on the next flight, locked the contents of the envelope in the safe and went out for a drink. I needed to think, for I was beginning to realize what it was he'd landed on my desk. *Political dynamite!* If he was a good geophysicist, then what I'd locked away in my safe might well be the location of a new oilfield.

Three days later I flew out of London Airport in a storm of rain and wind. March going out like a lion; but at Rome it was hot and all down the Mediterranean we had bright sunshine. And I sat in my seat with an empty feeling inside me, for the day before I'd left Cardiff a man had come to see me, a tired-looking, hard-faced man with a skin like leather who'd refused to give Andrews his name or state his business.

Even when he was alone with me in my office he went about it in such a tortuous way that it only gradually dawned on me what he was after. It was cleverly done – a hint here, a hint there, and the abyss gradually opening up at my feet. He knew David had boarded the *Emerald Isle* off Sharjah, knew, too, that Griffiths had delivered that packet to me. He'd been down to see him at his cottage in the Gower. He'd been to the police, too; had talked with Sergeant Mathieson and had checked the files. He knew the boy's real name, his whole background, everything, and what he wanted from me was that packet.

He smiled when I told him I couldn't discuss my client's affairs. 'Professional etiquette? Your professional etiquette, Mr Grant, is somewhat elastic, if you follow me.' It was a cat-and-mouse game, for he knew I'd helped the boy to get out of the country. 'There are several charges outstanding and a warrant.'

'The boy is dead,' I reminded him.

But it made no difference. He had his instructions, he said. These were to take possession of the packet. 'You can hand it to me or forward it to the Company – one or the other.' I asked him what authority he had for making such an outrageous proposal, but all he'd say was that it was in the country's interests. One knows, of course, that there are men like that employed by Government and by large companies, but one doesn't expect to come across them. They belong to a half-world that lies outside the experience of ordinary citizens.

'In your own interests I suggest you hand it to me. Nobody need know anything then.'

It was blackmail and by then I was sweating, for I was beginning to realize what I was up against. Politics and oil – the Middle East: the scope of a provincial lawyer doesn't cover that sort of world . . . I just hadn't the right sort of pull, the contacts, the friends in high places.

'You can go to the devil,' I told him.

He got to his feet then. 'I had hoped for your co-operation.' And he added, 'Think it over, Mr Grant. The police have an interest in this and if they begin an investigation . . . It could be very unpleasant for you. A man in your position, a lawyer – ' He left it at that and picked up his hat.

I wondered then whether he knew I was leaving for Bahrain in two days' time. The Foreign Office had my passport. They could still refuse to grant me the necessary visas. 'All right,' I said. 'I'll think it over.'

And the next day, in London, I found I had been granted a visa for Bahrain, but not for either Dubai or Saraifa. A note pinned to my passport stated that for *any further visas you should apply to the office of the Political Resident Persian Gulf in Bahrain.*

Darkness fell, the port light showing red. I woke to the touch of the air hostess's hand on my shoulder and the sighing sound of the flaps going down. The sliver of a new moon had risen, reflected with the stars in the still surface of the sea coming up to meet us, a steel mirror suddenly patterned with the arrowheads of fish traps as we skimmed the shallows. A moment later we touched down in Bahrain. And at three-thirty in the morning the air was still heavy with the day's heat. It came at us as soon as the door was opened, suffocating in its humidity.

The squat, white-fronted coral houses of Muharraq were without life as the airport bus drove us across the long causeway to the main island and the town of Manama. A solitary dhow was putting to sea, the curve of its sail a thing of ghostly beauty against the blackness of the water; all the others lay dormant in the mud or bare-poled against the coral hards with sails furled.

Only the BOAC hotel showed any sign of life at that hour. It was down an empty side street, the airline's bluebird insignia standing out against the drab of concrete; lights were burning against our coming. I was given a room with a balcony that was full of the sounds of a late-night party, laughter and the clink of glasses. There was a lot of coming and going in the passage outside and I went to sleep to the sound of a girl's voice, harsh and loud and slightly drunk.

Sunlight woke me four hours later, the hard sunlight of a hot country. An Arab boy brought me tea and I drank it, lying naked on the bed, a stale feeling at the back of the eye-balls and my body hot and without energy. Getting up, shaving, having breakfast – it was all an effort. And this was only April. I wondered what it must be like in mid-summer.

When I enquired at the desk for the offices of the Gulfoman Oilfields Development Company I was told that they were several miles out of town on the Awali road. A fat man in a tropical suit of powder blue was asking about a taxi he'd booked for Awali. He was an Italian who had joined the flight at Rome and I asked him whether he would give me a lift. '*Si, si, signore.* Of course.'

His name was Ruffini and he was a journalist. 'You are in oil? he asked as we drove past the Customs Quay crowded with dhows. And when I said No he looked surprised. 'But you 'ave an appointment at GODCO, no?'

'A matter of an estate,' I told him. 'A client of mine has died.'

'So!' He sighed. 'A lawyer's business – always to concern itself with death. Is depressing for you, no?' He offered me an American cigarette. 'Who do you see at this Company? Is none of my business,' he added quickly, seeing my hesitation. 'But though I am never in Bahrain before, I 'ave contacts, introductions you say. If I can 'elp you – ' He left it at that, reaching into his breast pocket for a pair of dark glasses. And because he was being helpful I told him who it was I'd come to see.

'You know anything about this Sir Philip Gorde?' he asked.

'He's a director of the Company in London.'

'But not the most important man out here, I think.' And he leaned forward and asked the driver, a pock-marked Bahraini with a lot of gold teeth, 'Who is the big man at GODCO?'

'Is Meester Erkhard.'

Ruffini nodded. 'Alexander Erkhard. *Bene*. That is also my information.'

'Many years,' the driver added, turning to face us. 'Many years it is Sir Gorde. Not now.' The car touched the road verge, sending up a cloud of dust. 'Ten years now I have taxi and am driving down the Awali road, sir, with men from BAPCO, GODCO, ARAMCO. I speak not well Eenglish, but understand plenty, get me? I look after the boys good, very bloody good. They all friends of Mahommed Ali. That my name, sir.' He was looking over his shoulder again. 'You want something, you find my car outside BOAC Hotel.'

'When did Mr Erkhard come out to Bahrain?' I asked.

'Five, six years ago, sir. Before I get this Buick.'

'And Sir Philip Gorde was the big man then?'

'That's right, sir. He is here before Awali, before I am born – a friend of the Ruler, of all Arabs. Very great man, Sir Gorde. But then he is sick and this Mr Erkhard, he come to Bahrain. Everything different then. Not friend of Ruler, not friend to Arabs.' And he spat out of the open window. 'Here is GODCO office now.'

We turned left with a screech of tyres. The dusty date gardens were left behind and a white building stood at the end of a tree-lined road. Beyond it lay the sea, a blue line shimmering on the horizon. '*Ecco!*' Ruffini gripped my arm, pointing away to the right, to a litter of small mounds. 'Tumuli. *E molto interessante*.

There is a Danish man who dig in those tumuli. The oldest burial ground in Arabia per'aps.'

The brakes slammed on and the car stopped with a jerk. I got out. 'I will see you at the 'otel. Per'aps we 'ave a drink together, eh?' I thanked him for the lift and he waved a pudgy hand. '*Ciao!*' The taxi swung away and I went in through the double glass doors. It was like walking into a refrigerator, for the place was air-conditioned to the temperature of a London office. Glass and tiled walls, steel furniture and the girl at the reception desk cool and immaculate. But when I asked for Sir Philip Gorde she frowned. 'I don't think Sir Philip is back yet. Have you an appointment?'

'No,' I said. 'But I've flown out from England specially to see him.'

She asked me my name and then got on the phone. A white-faced electric clock ticked the seconds away on the wall above her head. Finally she shook her head. 'I'm sorry. It's as I thought. Sir Philip is still in Abu Dhabi.'

'When will he be back?' I asked. Abu Dhabi was the first of the Trucial sheikhdoms and at least a hundred and fifty miles from Bahrain.

She started talking on the phone again and I lit a cigarette and waited. At length she said, 'Could you tell me the nature of your business with Sir Philip please?'

'If he's in Abu Dhabi,' I said, 'there's not much point, is there?'

She cupped her hand over the mouthpiece. 'If it's

urgent, then I think they'd contact him for you. I told them you'd come out from England specially.'

I hesitated. But there was no point in concealing what I'd come about. 'It concerns David Whitaker,' I said. 'I'm a lawyer.'

'David Whitaker.' She repeated it automatically, and then the name suddenly registered and her eyes widened. 'Yes,' she said quickly. 'Of course. I'll see what I can do.'

I leaned on the desk and waited, watching her as she talked into the phone. There was a long pause while she just stood there, holding it, and occasionally glancing at me with an expression of curiosity she couldn't conceal. And then I heard her say, 'Yes, of course, sir. I'll send him up right away.' She put the phone down and came back to the desk. 'Mr Erkhard will see you himself.' She said it on a note of surprise. 'If you'll go up to the first floor his secretary will be waiting for you.'

I thanked her and went up the stairs. Erkhard's secretary proved to be a man, neat and immaculate with a copy-book smile of greeting. 'Mr Grant? Will you come this way please.' He took me along a cool corridor and into an office that looked out across the tumuli. 'Mr Erkhard's very busy and you've come unexpectedly without an appointment. If you'd keep it as short as possible.'

'I didn't ask to see Mr Erkhard,' I said, and that seemed to upset him. 'No, no, of course. I understand.' He paused at the communicating door on the far side, a discreet little pause that gave emphasis and importance to the moment. Then he opened the door. 'Mr Grant, sir.'

The room was dove-grey, the furniture black steel. The big window looking out across the tumuli was a single sheet of flawless glass fitted with plastic Venetian blinds. The desk at which Erkhard was seated filled most of the far side of the room, and all the wall behind him was taken up with a relief map of Arabia dotted with flags. He didn't rise to greet me, but simply waved me to the chair opposite his desk. 'You're a lawyer, I understand?'

I nodded and sat down.

'And you're out here on account of young Whitaker's death?'

'I'm his Executor.'

'Ah, yes.' There was a peculiar softness about his manner, a smoothness almost. It was something to do with the roundness of his face and the way the lips were moulded into the suggestion of a smile. He was sitting perfectly still, watching me – waiting, I felt. It was disconcerting and I found him a difficult man to place, probably because he wasn't a type I had met before. In a weaker man that half-smile might have appeared ingratiating. But there was nothing weak about Erkhard. And the eyes were cold as they stared at me unblinkingly. 'Have you seen the young man's family?' There was an accent, but so slight it was barely noticeable.

'The mother,' I told him. 'I haven't seen the sister yet.'

'She's out here in Dubai – a nurse.'

I nodded. 'You cabled her the news. She sent me a copy.'

'Yes. A very unfortunate business. It's not often we have a casualty.' There was a long pause, and then he said, 'Why are you here, Mr Grant? Are you hoping to persuade us to resume the search? I had a message, something to that effect from London Office.' And he added, 'I assure you it would be quite useless.'

'Perhaps if I had a full account of the circumstances,' I suggested.

'Of course. There is a report of the search. I'll see that you're given a copy before you leave.' Another long pause. 'You were asking for Sir Philip Gorde, I understand. Why?' And when I didn't answer, he added, 'I signed that cable to Nurse Thomas and you've been in touch with London. You knew perfectly well that I gave the order for the search to be abandoned.' He stared at me. 'Perhaps you would care to explain?'

'There's nothing to explain,' I said. 'It happens that I have to see Sir Philip on a private matter.'

'Connected with Whitaker?'

'Yes.'

He got suddenly to his feet. 'I'm the General Manager in Arabia, Mr Grant. Whitaker was employed by me. His death is my responsibility, not Sir Philip Gorde's.'

'I appreciate that.'

'Then your correct approach was surely to ask for an interview with me?'

It seemed to worry him and I wondered why. He

was staring down at me, waiting for an answer. Finally he turned away and stood looking out of the window at the brown, dried-up landscape. His light tropical suit was obviously tailored in London and the silk shirt was monogrammed with his initials. 'Sir Philip is in Abu Dhabi.' He said it quietly as though he were speaking to himself. 'Tomorrow, or perhaps the day after, he will be going on to Sharjah. That's another of the Trucial sheikhdoms, further to the east. He will not be back here for at least a week, perhaps a fortnight.' He turned then and looked directly at me again. 'How do you propose to contact him? Have you thought of that?'

'I only got in this morning,' I said.

'Have you visas for the Trucial sheikhdoms?'

'No. I have to apply to the Political Resident's office—'

'Mr Grant.' He was smiling again. 'I don't think you understand. It isn't easy to get visas for the Trucial Oman. The PRPG is very naturally extremely reluctant—' He gave a little shrug. 'This is Arabia, you know, not Europe. The political situation is far from stable and there is a great deal at stake; enormous sums of capital have been sunk in this area.' He paused there to give me time to consider. 'Of course, we could help you. Not only in the matter of your application for a visa, but in transport, too. We have flights going east along the coast to our various development projects. In fact, I think there is one going to Abu Dhabi tomorrow. But,' he added, 'in order to help you we should have to know the exact purpose of your visit.'

He was taking a lot of trouble over this. 'I'm sorry,' I said. 'Beyond saying that my business with Sir Philip concerns the Estate – a matter of a signature – I cannot disclose—'

'You have a document for him to sign?' He sounded puzzled, and when I refused to be drawn, he gave a little shrug and returned to his desk. 'Since it is a private matter and not the concern of the Company, I'm afraid I can't help you, Mr Grant. I'll send Gorde a personal note, of course, to tell him you're here.' A fractional hesitation and then with that little smile that never remotely touched his eyes: 'And if you'd care to communicate with him direct, then I've no doubt we could arrange for a letter to be delivered to him by tomorrow's plane.' His hand reached out to the onyx bell-push on the desk.

'One moment,' I said. I wasn't sure how to handle it, but I knew that once I was out of that office, the opportunity to question him would be gone for ever. 'I wonder . . . perhaps you would be good enough to clear up one or two points for me?' I said it tentatively. 'Whilst I'm here,' I added.

There was a momentary hesitation whilst his hand still hovered on the bell-push.

'I'm a little puzzled about certain aspects of the boy's death,' I murmured.

The hand moved back from the bell-push, reluctantly. And then he smiled and leaned back in his chair. 'Of course.'

'You say he was employed by you at the time of his death?'

'He was employed by the Company, yes.'

I hesitated. The devil of it was I didn't know what I was after. Something . . . but what? The map, towering behind him, caught my eye. 'Could you show me exactly where it was his truck was found?'

He got up at once, almost with relief, I felt. The position he indicated was well to the south-west of Buraimi Oasis, a position where three dotted lines met. Peering over his shoulder I saw that these marked the boundaries of Saudi Arabia, the Sheikhdom of Saraifa and the emirate of Hadd. His finger rested on a point inside the Saudi Arabian border. The whole area was shaded with little dots. 'The sands of the Rub al Khali,' he explained. 'Dune country. It's called the Empty Quarter.'

'You've no concessions in Saudi Arabia, have you?'

'No.'

'Then what was he doing there?'

'That's something we should like to know, Mr Grant.'

'He was there without your authority then?'

'Of course.' His nod was very emphatic.

'If he was carrying out a survey, then presumably he had a survey crew. What happened to them?'

He hesitated and the quick glance he gave me suggested that this was something he didn't want to go into. But in the end he said, 'He had an Arab crew. They were picked up by Askari of the Emir of Hadd. However, the men have been interviewed. It appears they became nervous. Hardly surprising in that area.

Anyway, they downed tools, took the Land Rover and left Whitaker there on his own.'

'In Saudi Arabia?'

'No, no.'

'Where then?'

He glanced at me quickly again, his eyes narrowing. 'They wouldn't say. At least . . . they couldn't give the exact location.'

'Was it somewhere on the Hadd border?' I asked, remembering what Griffiths had said.

He ignored that. 'Doubtless they could have led us to the place, but the Emir refused to allow them outside the Wadi Hadd al-Akhbar.' He gave a little shrug. 'The Emir is very difficult.' And he added, 'But of course this is hardly a matter that concerns you.'

'On the contrary,' I said sharply, 'it's important that I know exactly where the boy was supposed to be operating at the time of his death. Until I know that—'

But he shook his head. 'Best leave it at that, Mr Grant.'

'Because of the political aspect?' I was convinced now that the locations in my briefcase would show that David had been operating somewhere along the Hadd-Saraifa border.

'Politics come into it, yes. They always do in Arabia.'

'And particularly where oil is concerned?'

He nodded agreement, and I asked him then whether he thought there was oil in that area. He looked at me very tight-lipped and said:

'We've no reason to imagine so.'

'Then what's the political problem?'

He hesitated, and then half turned to the map again. 'Those borders,' he said. 'They're all three in dispute. Particularly the border between Hadd and Saraifa.'

'Would you describe that as 'political dynamite'?' His eyes narrowed and I pushed it further: 'If oil were discovered there?'

'Yes,' he said, and turned back to his desk. 'I think, Mr Grant, we are getting a long way from the purpose of your visit.'

'I don't think so.' He wanted to terminate the interview. Equally I wanted to continue it. 'Did David Whitaker submit a survey report to you at any time during, say, the two months before his death?'

'No.'

I stared at him, wondering whether that was the truth. And then I decided to play the thing I'd been holding in reserve. 'Suppose I told you that I have in my possession the location he was working on at the time of his death?'

He affected disbelief. But it lacked something, the quickness of spontaneity, the sharpness of genuine surprise. And suddenly my mind clicked. 'Four days ago,' I murmured, 'in my office in Cardiff . . . I was visited by a gentleman who attempted by threats to get those locations from me.' He didn't say anything and I let the silence drag out. 'He didn't get them, of course,' I said quietly. I was staring at him, but he kept his eyes on the desk.

'I don't think this concerns me.' The silence had forced it out of him. His hand reached for the bell-push.

I waited, and he hesitated. Curiosity had won. He turned to me and said harshly, 'David Whitaker was employed by us. We should know the locations he was surveying. We have a right.'

'Have you?' I asked.

'Yes. And I'll add this: I find it very difficult to understand why you should have been given this information whilst the Company has been left in the dark.'

He was facing me, and after what seemed a long time his eyes fell away to the desk again. He was puzzled. A little frightened, too. I thought he'd every reason to be both. 'David Whitaker knew he was going to die.' I said it slowly and with emphasis. And before he had time to recover from the shock of what I'd said, I shifted my ground. 'Does Colonel Whitaker know his son's dead?'

'I really cannot say.' He was still considering the implication of what I'd told him, and I was convinced it was something he hadn't known before.

'We regarded the sister as the most suitable person to inform.' And he added, 'The boy was illegitimate, you know.' It was a mistake, for it confirmed something I had come to suspect – that David's background was known to the Company. But he didn't seem conscious of it. Nor did he seem conscious of the drift of my questions. 'I think you will agree, when you've read the report of the search, that everything possible was done.'

'But they didn't find his body?'

'No. And if you knew the sort of country it is there, that wouldn't surprise you.' He seemed anxious to reassure me on this point. 'It's a big dune country and the sand is moving all the time. It obliterates everything. Even his truck was half-buried when they located it.'

'It was a seismological truck, I believe?'

He nodded.

'One of yours?'

He didn't answer immediately and there was a sudden stillness in the room. And when he spoke he chose his words carefully. 'I've already told you he was employed by the Company at the time of his death.'

'Oil company trucks are usually marked with the name of the company, aren't they?'

'What are you implying?'

'There were no markings on this particular truck.'

'How do you know?'

'There was a report of the search in *The Times*.'

'Oh, so you've seen that.' He hesitated. 'Not every truck, you know, is marked with the Company's name.'

'That doesn't answer my question,' I said. 'Was that truck a Company truck or not?'

I thought he was going to evade the question. But then he said, 'No. No, it wasn't one of our trucks.'

'Whose truck was it then?'

But he'd had enough. 'I'm not prepared to discuss the Company's affairs. The truck has no bearing on the boy's death.'

'I think it has,' I said, as his hand reached for the bell-push again. And I added, 'One final question. Can you tell me where I'll find Colonel Whitaker?'

'Whitaker? I thought it was Gorde you'd come to see?'

'Whitaker, too,' I told him. 'David may have been employed by you, but he was on loan to his father at the time of his death.'

'Quite untrue. *The Times* is in error.' And he pressed the bell. The interview was at an end.

As though he had been waiting for his cue, the secretary came in immediately. 'See that Mr Grant has a copy of the report on the Whitaker search, will you, Firweather. He can take it away with him.' Erkhard turned to me. 'Have you a taxi waiting?' And when I shook my head, he told his secretary to arrange for a Company car to drive me back to Manama.

'You haven't told me where I'll find Colonel Whitaker?' I said as I got to my feet.

He couldn't very well refuse to answer me in front of his secretary. 'In Saraifa, I imagine.' And he added, 'But if you're thinking of going there, I should remind you that you will not be granted a visa.'

Did that mean he'd use his influence to prevent me getting one? I hesitated, glancing up at the map. The flags had names on them and because it might be the only opportunity I'd have, I went across to it and had a close look at them. There were only two anywhere near the Saraifa-Hadd border and the names on them were Ogden and Entwhistle. 'That map is confidential,

Mr Grant.' It was the secretary, at my side now and quite agitated.

'You needn't worry,' I said. 'I know nothing about oil, so it doesn't tell me anything. Who did the ground search?' I asked Erkhard.

'Entwhistle,' he answered without looking up.

'I'll give you that report now,' the secretary said.

Erkhard didn't look up as I left, determined to give me no excuse for further questions. In the outer office I asked if I could write a note to Sir Philip Gorde. The secretary gave me a sheet of Company notepaper and I wrote it at his desk with him more or less standing over me. I marked the envelope *Personal*, but I was careful to say nothing in it that Erkhard didn't know already. The secretary promised to see that it went out by the next plane. 'If there is a reply, I'll send it down to your hotel.' He gave me a duplicated copy of the report of the search and showed me out.

I read that report in the car driving back to Manama. It told me very little that I didn't already know. The truck had been discovered by nomads of the Rashid tribe who had passed the news on to some Harasis going down to the Gulf of Masira. The *naukhuda* of a dhow had brought the news across to Masira Island and the RAF Station there had radioed it on to RAF HQ Aden. A Valetta, landing at Masira on the milk-run up from Kormaksar, had begun the aerial search on March 11, and the abandoned truck had been located after a three-day search. Erkhard had then ordered Entwhistle, who was operating about seventy miles away, to break off his seismological survey work and proceed at speed to the area.

Due to a broken spring Entwhistle had not reached the abandoned truck until three days later. He had then carried out a systematic search, but had found no trace of David and the few nomads he encountered knew nothing about him. After four days lack of supplies had forced him to retire. Meantime, the Valetta supported by a plane chartered by GODCO, had carried out an intensive air search. This had been abandoned on March 16. Everything had then depended on the ground search, but the rough going had put Entwhistle's radio out of action and it was not until he joined up with Ogden's outfit on March 24 that he was able to report his failure to find even the body.

It was obvious that no blame attached to the Company. As Erkhard had said, everything possible had been done. I put the report away in my briefcase. The only man who could tell me anything more was Entwhistle, and remembering the position of his flag on Erkhard's operations map, I knew there wasn't much chance of my having a talk with him.

We were approaching the town now, the twin minarets of the Suq al-Khamis Mosque standing slender against the sky, and I told the driver to take me to the Political Resident's office. 'The PRPG, sir?' He slowed the car. 'Is not in Manama. Is out at Jufair by the Naval Base.' He hesitated. He was a very superior-looking Bahraini. 'You wish me to drive you there?'

'Please.'

He turned right and we reached the Jufair road by

the National Cinema. 'Have you a pass, sir? Everybody need a pass to enter Jufair Naval Base.' But the native sentry on the gate knew the car and he let us through without question. We were close to the sea then with a frigate lying white as a swan on the oily-calm water. The road curved amongst the trees, the Government blocks standing discreetly back in semblance of a country estate. It was all manifestly English, and so, too, was the Passport Control Office with its forms. Purpose of visit . . . what did I put for that? I handed my passport to the clerk, together with my application for visas. 'Abu Dhabi, Dubai, Sharjah and Saraifa. That's quite a tour.' He shook his head doubtfully, turning over the pages of my passport. 'The first three, they're Trucial sheikhdoms – they may be possible. But Saraifa; that's quite out of the question.'

'Isn't that for the Ruler to decide?' I asked. 'I understand it's an independent sheikhdom.'

The suggestion seemed to strike him as a novel one. 'We decide who goes to Saraifa,' he said stiffly. And he added, 'If you'll come back later—'

'This afternoon? I want to leave for Abu Dhabi tomorrow.'

'This afternoon?' He sounded doubtful. 'Well, perhaps—'

I drove to the BOAC office then, only to discover that if I wanted to fly to Abu Dhabi I should have to charter a plane. Gulf Airways ran a service to Sharjah, but not to Abu Dhabi. It was my first experience of the difficulties of communication in the country. Back at the hotel in time for lunch I was hailed by Ruffini, sitting alone like a pale blue toad in front of a tall glass. 'You like a beer?'

He had seen one of the chief executives of BAPCO – the Bahrain Petroleum Company – out at the oil town of Awali, and then had an interview with Erkhard. 'This afternoon I go to Jufair, but I do not think they tell me anything.' He leaned towards me across the table. 'You puzzle me, Signor Grant,' he said. 'A lawyer, always with your briefcase. You say you are not interested in oil, yet your business is with two of the most important oil men in the Gulf.'

The boy brought my drink. '*Salute!*' Ruffini raised his glass. 'That girl at the reception desk – she is new to GODCO and she talk. This morning, when you ask for Sir Philip Gorde and he is not there, Erkhard immediately sees you 'imself. Why?' His eyes were fixed on my face, full of curiosity. 'Why are you so important? What is in that briefcase of yours, *signore*?' He shook his head and gave a mock sigh. 'You will not tell me, of course. Not yet.' His face creased in a smile and he gulped down the rest of his drink. 'Let's go and eat.'

Over lunch he told me why he was in Bahrain. He worked for a newspaper group in Milan and he'd had a tip-off from one of Italy's leading oil men. 'I think he is right,' he said. 'There is trouble. But where?' He had been up since six, talking in the bazaars, to Indians chiefly. A squadron of bren-gun carriers of the RAF Regiment was rumoured to have been sent to Sharjah and two RAF reconnaissance planes had been fitted with long-range tanks. There was talk, too, of additional transport allocated to the Trucial Oman Scouts and the GOC Persian Gulf was known to be on a tour of inspection. 'If there is trouble 'ere,' he said, 'then it mean only one thing – oil.' And suddenly, without warning, he said, 'What about this David Whitaker, eh?' He smiled at me. 'Now you are surprised. But that little girl knew him and you told her your business is about this boy who is missing.' He stared at me. 'But you don't want to talk about it, eh?'

'There's nothing to talk about,' I said. 'I'm his Executor, that's all.'

'An' you 'ave to see Sir Philip Gorde, who is four years ago one of the most important men in the Gulf, but not any more – who is also the life-long friend of Colonel Whitaker, the boy's father. An' you 'ave nothing to tell me, eh?' He shook his head sadly. 'Per'aps, you do not know it, my friend – but I think maybe you are sitting on the story I want.' He stared at me a moment, and then very seriously: 'You will think I am being very stupid now, but walk with care. I like you. I like men who 'ave a sense of duty. That is why I am warning you.'

'You sound very serious.' I wanted to laugh it off. But he said, 'I am very serious. Oil is big money. And in a country like this it is also political dynamite.' Probably he misread the shock his choice of words gave me, for he added quickly, 'You don't believe that, eh? Well, I will take a bet with you. You will not get to Abu Dhabi or to Sharjah. Saraifa is closed anyway. You will, in fact, not be allowed out of Bahrain. And you will be got out of 'ere somehow before Sir Philip Gorde returns. Have you got your visas yet?'

'I have to go back to Jufair this afternoon.'

'Okay,' he said. 'You can come with me. But you will not get any visa.'

He was right there. They were very apologetic about it down at Jufair but the only man who could deal with my application had unfortunately been called away on urgent business. Perhaps if I came back to-morrow. There was no point in arguing. The brick wall of officialdom can't be battered down unless you have the right contacts, and I'd no contacts at all. I went for a walk along the naval jetty. There was a wind blowing off the anchorage, but it was a hot wind and did nothing to refresh me. Half an hour later Ruffini joined me. 'Do you get your visas?' He gave me a wicked smile. He knew I hadn't got them.

'Did you get the low-down on the political situation?' I asked him.

He gave a fat chuckle and shook his head. 'The same thing. Nobody is saying anything. What is more,' he added, 'you and me, we are in the same boat. No visas for Ruffini also. He is to stay 'ere and mind his bloody business.' He hoisted himself on to the sea wall. 'Officials can be very stupid. If I have to stay on in Bahrain and write my story from 'ere, then I have to guess at what goes on, and maybe I guess wrong.' He was staring out across the anchorage, his eyes screwed up against the dazzle of the water. 'That gunboat for instance—' He nodded towards the frigate, which was slowly fetching up to her anchor, the clatter of her winch coming to us very clear across the water. 'An exercise, they tell me. Routine. Maybe that is all it is and they are speaking the truth. But 'ow do I know?'

We stayed and watched her steam out of the anchorage and then Ruffini heaved himself down off the wall. 'Do you ever 'ear of the Emir of Hadd?' he asked as we walked back to the taxi. 'The Emir Abdul-Zaid bin Sultan? Well, no matter.' He wiped the perspiration from his face. 'But try shooting that name at the political people 'ere and see 'ow their faces go blank. I tell you,' he added, 'this country is worse than a Sicilian village, full of old vendettas and not a clear boundary anywhere to mark the finish of one sheikh's piece of sand and the beginning of the next.'

He took me back to the hotel and I lay and sweated on my bed till dinner time, wondering how I was to contact Gorde and thinking about Ruffini. Was there really trouble brewing? But it all seemed remote – as remote as Colonel Whitaker out there in Saraifa and utterly inaccessible. And next day, after a full morning's work, I was no nearer either of my objectives.

I rang the Passport Office, but nothing had been decided. And when I checked on transportation I found that even if I were willing to charter a plane, there was none available with sufficient range to fly direct to Saraifa, and in any case flights there were prohibited. I went to the bank then and settled David's affairs as far as I was able. It was the same bank that his father dealt with and the manager was helpful. He confirmed that Colonel Whitaker was living in Saraifa, this contrary to his very strict instructions. But he could tell me little else and I went back to the hotel and had a drink with two RAF officers and a civilian pilot, a Canadian named Otto Smith. After lunch we all went down to the Sailing Club for a bathe.

Half the English colony was there, for it was Saturday, and amongst them was the girl from the GODCO reception desk sprawled half naked on the cement of the old seaplane jetty. 'So you're off to Sharjah, Mr Grant?' And when I told her I was having visa trouble, she smiled and said, 'I think you'll find it's all right.'

'How do you know?'

'Oh, I know everything.' She laughed. 'No, I happened to see your name on the flight list for tomorrow's plane.'

She was perfectly right. When I got back to the hotel that evening I found my passport waiting for me, stamped with visas for Sharjah and Dubai. There was also a message, signed by Erkhard's secretary, informing me that 'owing to the Company's desire to help you in every possible way' free passage was being granted to me in a Company plane leaving for Sharjah at 1030 hours the following morning, Sunday. The message added that accommodation would be available at the Fort and it was not anticipated that I should have to wait long before Sir Philip arrived from Abu Dhabi.

There was no doubt in my mind that Erkhard had intervened to get me the necessary visas. But why? The day before he had made it clear that he didn't intend to help me. And after the way I had cross-examined him I hadn't expected it. And yet here he was giving me a free ride on a Company plane. I sat on my bed and smoked a cigarette whilst the hot evening breeze blew in through the open window, and the only conclusion I came to was that they had sent my note to Gorde and he had given the necessary instructions. Whatever the reasons, it was a great relief to me and I got up and started to pack.

I had just closed the larger of my two suitcases when there was a knock at the door. It was one of the house-boys to say there was a young Arab asking for me at the desk. 'It is a boy from the bazaar, sir. From the al-Menza Club.' And he grinned at me.

I had a wash and then dressed. The boy was still there when I got down quarter of an hour later. He was little more than an urchin and none too clean, and when he realized I didn't speak Arabic, he seized hold of my wrist, pulling at me and hissing the words 'al-Menza' and 'girl-want'. 'Girl-want' seemed to be the sum total of his English and I told him to go to hell. He understood that for he grinned and shook his head. 'Girl-spik. Spik, sahib.'

I got hold of the house-boy and then he said the boy had been sent by one of the girls at the al-Menza Club. 'She wishes to speak with you, sir.' This time he didn't grin. And he added with a puzzled frown. 'It is a personal request. This boy is from the house where she lives.'

I didn't like it. 'Tell him No,' I said and I went over to an empty table and ordered a beer. It took two house-boys and a lot of argument to get rid of the boy. I drank my beer and then went in to dinner, a solitary, dreary meal. I had just finished when the waiter came to tell me a taxi-driver was waiting outside for me. It was Mahommed Ali. 'There is a boy in my taxi,' he said. 'Is wishing you to go to the al-Menza to meet a girl.'

'I've already told him I'm not interested.'

'You should go, sir. She 'as something to tell you.'

I hesitated. But after all the man was a taxi-driver attached to the hotel. 'You'll drive me there, will you?'

'OK, sir.'

It wasn't far to the bazaar area and we finished up in a side street that was barely wide enough for the car. The al-Menza was sandwiched between a cobbler's shop and a narrow alley, the door guarded by a turbanned Sudanese. I told the driver to wait and the boy took me by the hand and hurried me down the alley and through the black gap of a doorway into a dark passage. He left me there and a moment later footsteps sounded, high-heeled and sharp, and then a girl's voice, low, with a peculiarly resonant quality, almost husky. 'Monsieur.' She took my hand, her fingers hard, not caressing. 'Through 'ere, pleez.'

A door was pushed open and there were soft lights and the faint beat of Western music, a jive record playing somewhere in the building. A beaded curtain rattled back and we were in a little room no bigger than a cell. The floor was bare earth with a rug and a few cushions. A naked light bulb dangling from the ceiling showed me my companion.

I don't know quite how to describe that girl. She certainly wasn't beautiful, though I suppose that is a matter of taste, for she was obviously Arab; Arab mixed with something else – European, I thought, with a touch of the real African. She stood very straight with a lithe, almost animal grace. She was the sort of girl you could picture at the well drawing water and striding across the sand with a pitcher on her head. She was that, and she was the other sort, too – the husky voice; dropped a shade it would be totally erotic, a vicious invitation. No point in dramatizing; she was just a Middle Eastern tart, but I'd never met one before and it made an impression.

We sat cross-legged on the cushions, facing each other. She wore a queer sort of dress and I had a feeling that at the touch of a secret button she'd come gliding out of it like a butterfly out of a chrysalis. Her hands were pressed tight together and she leaned forward, her eyes, her lips devoid of invitation, hard almost and urgent. 'You know why I ask you to come 'ere?'

I shook my head.

'You do not guess?' There was the ghost of a smile on her half-open lips. But when I said, 'No,' she snapped them shut. 'If you are not the man,' she blazed; 'if you 'ave come 'ere because it is the sort of place—' At that moment she didn't look at all nice. 'All right,' she said, biting on her teeth. 'You tell me now – is it because of David you come to Bahrain or not?'

David! I stared at her, beginning to understand. 'Did David come here then?'

'Of course. He was an oil man and this place is for oil men. They 'ave the same devil in them as other men where the sun is 'ot – but David was nice, a vair nice boy.' She smiled then and the hardness went out of her face leaving it for a moment like a picture of Madonna-with-child, despite the slightly flattened nose, the thickened lips. It was a queer face, change-able as a child's. 'How did you know I was here on account of David Whitaker?' I asked her. 'It is David Whitaker you're talking about?'

She nodded. 'One of the men from the GODCO Office is 'ere las' night. He tol' me about you.' She didn't say anything after that, but sat staring at me with her big, dark eyes as though trying to make up her mind about me. 'You like some coffee?' she asked at length.

'Please.' I needed time, and I think she'd guessed that. She was gone only a few moments, but it gave me a chance to collect myself and to realize that she was perhaps the one person in Bahrain who could tell me what sort of a man David had become in the four years since I'd seen him. She put the coffee down between us, two small cups, black and sweet. I gave her a cigarette and sat smoking and drinking my coffee, waiting for her to start talking. I had that much sense. If I'd rushed her she'd have closed up on me.

'Have you seen his sister?' she asked finally.

'Not yet.' It wasn't the question I'd expected.

'But you 'ave 'eard from her, no? Does she think he is dead?'

I sat there, quite still, staring at her. 'What else could she think?' I said quietly.

'And you? Do you think he is dead?'

I hesitated, wondering what it was leading up to. 'His truck was found abandoned in the desert. There was a ground and air search.' I left it at that.

'I ask you whether you think he is dead?'

'What else am I supposed to think?'

'I don't know.' She shook her head. 'I jus' don' know. He is not the sort of boy to die. He believes too much, want too much of life.'

'What, for instance?'

She shook her head slowly. 'I don' know what he want. Is a vair strange boy, David. He have moods; sometimes he sit for hours without saying nothing, without moving even. At such times he have a great sense of – of *tranquillité*. You understand? I have known him sit all night, cross-legged and in silence without moving almost a muscle. At other times he talk and the words pour out of him and his eyes shine like there is a fever in him.'

'What did he talk about?'

She shrugged her shoulders. 'So many words. I don' understand half of what he say. About the desert mostly, and the Bedou. Water, too; he loved water – much more than oil, I think. And the *falajes*; he often talk about the *falajes* and about Saraifa – how the desert is moving into the oasis.'

I asked her what the word *falaj* meant, but she

couldn't explain it. 'Is something to do with water; tunnels I think under the ground because he say it is vair hot there, like in a Turkish bath, an' there are fishes. And when you look up you can see the stars.' She frowned. 'I don't know what it is, but he say once it is like the wind-towers at Dubai – something brought from Persia. But I have never seen the wind-towers at Dubai,' she added.

'And this was in Saraifa?' I asked.

'*Oui.* Saraifa. With David it is always Saraifa. He has a – a *folie* for that place.' She said it almost sadly, and she added, 'He wish to prove something there, but what I do not know – 'imself per'aps.' For a while she sat quite still and silent, and then she said very softly: 'He was a man with a dream.' She looked up at me suddenly. 'And dreams don' die, do they? Or are men's dreams like the seed in a place like this – all barren?'

I didn't know what to answer. 'You loved him, did you?' I asked gently.

'Loved?' She shrugged. 'You want everything black and white. What is love between man and woman – and in a place like this?' Her shoulders moved again, slight and impatient. 'Per'aps. But sometimes he could be cruel. He had a vein of cruelty in him – like the Arabs. At other times—' She smiled. 'He showed me a glimpse of what life could be. And when he talked about his dreams, then he is near to God. You see,' she added, her voice suddenly tense, 'he is important to me. The most important thing in my whole life. That is why I cannot believe he is dead.'

I asked her when she had last seen him and she

laughed in my face. 'You don' see a man when he is lying in your arms. You feel – feel . . . if you are a woman.' She stared at me and then she giggled like a girl. 'You look so shocked. Have you never been with a woman like me before? But no, of course, you are English. I forget. You see, I am Algerienne, from Afrique Nord. All my life I am accustomed to Frenchmen – and Arabs.' She spat the word 'Arabs' out as though she hated them. 'I should have been still in Algerie, but when the Indo-China war is on, they send us out to Saigon, a whole plane full of women like me. We come down at Sharjah because of engine trouble and we are there in the Fort for two weeks. There I met a merchant from Bahrain, so I don' go to Saigon, but come 'ere to Bahrain, and later I am put into the al-Menza Club as hostess. That is 'ow I come to meet David.'

'Yes, but when did you last see him?' I asked again.

'In July of las' year. And it was not 'ere, but at the place where I live.'

'That was just before he sailed for Dubai?'

'*Oui.*' Her eyes were searching my face. 'He was – how you say?' She hesitated, searching for a word. But then she shrugged. 'Vair sad I think. He say that there is only one man in the 'ole world that 'e can really trust and that this friend is in England.'

'Didn't he trust his father?' I asked.

'Le Colonel?' She moved her shoulders, an expressive shrug that seemed to indicate doubt. 'When I see him that las' time he trust nobody out here – only this friend in England. You are from England and yesterday you are at the Company's offices enquiring about David.' She leaned forward so that the deep line between her full breasts was a black shadow. 'Tell me now, are you this friend?'

'Didn't he tell you his friend's name?'

'No, he don' say his name – or if he do, I 'ave forgot.'

'Well, I'm his lawyer. Does that help?'

'A man of business?'

'Yes. His Executor, in fact. That means that I carry out his instructions when he is dead.'

'And now you carry them out? That is why you are 'ere in Bahrain?'

'Yes.'

'Are you never his friend – before?'

'Once,' I said. 'Four years ago.' And I told her how I'd helped him to get away in the *Emerald Isle*. Evidently she knew this story, for she nodded her head several times and her eyes were bright with the memory of his telling of it. 'Yes,' she said when I had finished. 'Now I know you are the man.' And then she leaned forward and gripped hold of my hand. 'Where you go now – after Bahrain?' she asked. 'You go to find him, yes?' And she added, 'You will give him a message pleez? It is important.'

I stared at her. Her dark face was so intense, her belief in his immunity from death so tragic.

'Pleez.' Her voice was urgent, pleading. 'It is vair important.'

'He's dead,' I reminded her gently.

She dropped my hand as though she had hold of

a snake. 'His truck is found abandoned in the desert. That is all.' She glared at me as though challenging me to destroy her belief. 'That is all, you 'ear me? Pleez.' She touched my hand again, a gesture of supplication. 'Find 'im for me, monsieur. There is trouble coming in the desert and he is in danger. Warn him pleez.'

There was no point in telling her again that he was dead. 'What sort of trouble?' I asked.

She shrugged. 'War. Fighting. What other trouble do men make?' And when I asked her where the fighting was going to break out, she said, 'In Saraifa, I think. That is the rumour in the bazaar. And that boy who bring you 'ere, Akhmed; he is the son of a famous pearl-diver. He knows the *naukhudas* of all the dhows and there is talk of *sambuqs* with arms coming across the sea from Persia. I don' know whether it is true or not, but that is the talk. And 'ere in Bahrain we hear all the talk. That is why I ask to see you, to tell you that you must warn him. He is in great danger because of 'is father.'

'What's Colonel Whitaker got to do with it?' I asked.

'He is drilling an oil well in Saraifa. Oh,' she said angrily, 'the greed of you men. Money, money, money – you think of nothing else and you must cut each other's throats to get more and more. But with David it is different. He don' want money. He want something... I don' know. I don' know what he want. But not money. He don' care about money.'

It was extraordinary; this girl telling me what

Colonel Whitaker was doing, confirming what I had
already guessed. 'How do you know Colonel Whitaker
is drilling for oil?' I asked.

'How? I tell you, this place is for oil men. They
'ave their intelligence and because they are 'omesick
and half dead with ennui, they talk.' She gave a little
laugh. 'There is so much talk in this 'ouse that I can
almost tell you what each oil man eat for breakfast
from Doha right down the Gulf to Ras al-Khaima.'

I sat for a moment thinking about the rumours
she'd heard, remembering what Ruffini had said out
there on the Jufair jetty.

'You will tell him what I say. You will warn him?'

'Of course.' What else could I say?

'Do you go to Saraifa? If you go there, pleez you
should talk with Khalid. He is the sheikh's eldest son.
He and David hunted together when he is first in the
desert. They are like brothers he always say.'

I gave a little shrug. How would Khalid know?
How would anybody know what had happened? The
boy was dead. 'I'll see his father,' I said. 'If I can.'

'*Non, non.*' There was urgency, a sense almost of
fear in her voice.

I stared at her hard. 'Why not?' But if she knew
anything, she wasn't saying. And because I didn't like
the way my thoughts were running, I asked her where
David had been going that last time she had seen him.

'To Dubhai,' she answered. 'By ship.'

'The *Emerald Isle*?'

She nodded.

'And after that – after Dubhai?'

Again that slight, impatient movement of the shoulders.

'He don' say. He don' tell me where he go.'

'Was it Saraifa?'

'Perhaps. I don' know.'

'There's some suggestion that he was on loan to his father, that he was doing a survey for Colonel—'

'*Non, non.*' Again the urgency, the leap of something stark in the wide dark eyes. '*C'est impossible.*' She shook head emphatically.

'Why is it impossible?'

'Because—' She shook her head again. 'He cannot go to work with him. I know that now.' And she added under her breath: '*Que le bon Dieu le protège!*' I felt I had to know the reason, but when I pressed her for it, she shied away from the subject. 'I must go now.' She got to her feet in one easy, balanced motion. It was as though my questions had started an ugly train of thought – as though to admit that he'd gone to Saraifa to join his father was to admit the fact of his death. And as I stood up I was remembering again the nagging suspicion that had been in my mind that day Griffiths had come to see me in Cardiff.

'*Au revoir.*' She held out her hand and I was conscious again of the steel grip of those thin fingers. 'You are his friend. I know that now. And when you find him you will warn him?' I nodded, not saying anything. 'And you can give him my love also,' she said with a sudden flash of gaiety. And then serious again: 'The boy Akhmed will be waiting each morning for you at the 'otel. I have arranged it. He knows many people and he can help you if you wish. And remember please,' she added, 'this is an island very close to the great deserts of Arabia – much closer than Algerie is to the Sahara. And the desert is Arab. Your Eenglish officials and the oil men, they know only what 'appen on the surface. They can see the bees swarm, but they do not know when the old queen die. You understand?' And with that she pulled back the bead curtain and I was out in the passage again where the dance music sounded faintly. She took me as far as the alleyway where the boy was waiting and then with a final touch of those fingers, a flash of white teeth, she was gone.

It was only after I was back in the car that I realized I didn't know her name. I got it from the boy – Tessa; a very European name for a girl of her mixed parentage. Later I learned that it was a shortened form of Tebessa, the town on the Algerian-Tunisian border where she had been born.

I lay awake a long time that night wondering about David, about what had really happened. Three women – his mother, his sister, and now this girl Tessa – all convinced he was alive. And the picture she had sketched of him, the warning of trouble brewing. I went to sleep with the unpleasant feeling that I was being caught up in the march of events. And in the morning Mahommed Ali drove me to the airport.

THE EMPTY QUARTER

We took off shortly after ten, skimming low over sand flats that ran out into the shallows where fish stakes stood in broad arrows. The white coral buildings of Muharraq vanished behind us and after that the waters of the Gulf stretched away on either side, a flat sea mirror shimmering in the heat, and the colours were all pastel shades.

The plane was piloted by the Canadian I had swum with the previous day – Otto Smith. He had joined me on the apron just before take-off and realising that I'd never seen what he called 'this Godforsaken country' before, he had offered to make it a low-level flight. We flew, in fact, at less than a thousand feet. A white-winged dhow swam like a child's toy on the sheet steel surface below, and where the water shallowed to islands banked with sand it was translucent green, the sand banks sugar white.

We crossed the Qattar Peninsula; a glimpse of an oil camp, the airstrip marked out with oil drums, the camp a wheel of concentric buildings and the rig a single lonely tower. A sheikh's palace standing on an empty beach, square like a military fort, the mud of its walls barely discernible against desert sand. The palm frond shacks of a *barasti* fishing village, and then the sea again, until the white of gypsum appeared on the starboard side and miniature buttes of sand standing out of the water marked the mainland coast of Arabia.

The plane was full of equipment and stores bound for an oil camp along the coast towards Ras al-Khaimai, beyond Sharjah. There were only three passengers besides myself – an officer of the Trucial Oman Scouts and two oil men who were straight out from England and could tell me nothing. I sat in silence, in a mood of strange elation, for the sight of the desert so close below the plane gave me the illusion at least that Saraifa was within my reach.

We followed the coast all the way. Shallow sand dunes replaced the glare of gypsum flats, the coast became dotted with palms and here and there a pattern of nets spread out on the shore to dry marked a fishing village. About an hour and a half out Otto Smith called me for'ard to look at Dubai. 'The Venice of Arabia,' he shouted to me above the roar of the engines. A broad estuary dog-legged through the sandbanks, dwindling amongst the town's buildings which crowded down to the waterfront, capped by innumerable towers, slender like campanili – the wind-towers that Tessa had talked of, a simple system of air-conditioning brought from Persia by the pirates and smugglers of the past.

Ten minutes later we reached Sharjah; another estuary, but smaller and with a sand bar across the entrance, and the mud town crumbling to ruin. We came in low over a camel train headed south into the desert, the glint of silver on guns, the flash of white teeth in dark faces, and a woman, black like a crow, with a black mask covering her face, riding the last camel. Watch towers stood lone sentinels against the dunes, and far away to the east and south-east the mountains of the Jebel were a hazy, dust-red wall. We came to rest close by the white glare of the Fort, and behind it lay the camp of the Trucial Oman Scouts.

Sharjah Fort was like any desert fort, only now it was an airlines transit hotel. Two rusty iron cannon lay in the sand on either side of the arched entrance and all the interior was an open rectangular space with rooms built against the walls. Otto took me to the lounge and bought me a beer. The room was large, the walls enlivened with maps and coloured posters; the tiled floor gritty with blown sand. 'How long are you going to stay here?' he asked me. And when I said I was waiting for Gorde he looked surprised. 'Well, you're going to have a darn long wait,' he said.

'How do you mean?'

'Didn't they tell you? He sent a radio message through yesterday to say he'd changed his plans. He's being flown back to Bahrain to-morrow.'

So that was it . . . that was why Erkhard had changed his mind. A free ride in a Company plane and

I'd be in Sharjah by the time Gorde got back to Bahrain. 'Thank God you told me in time,' I said.

'In time? Oh, you mean you want to ride back with me.' He shook his head. 'Sorry, fellow. I got a full load from Ras al-Khaima. And not to Bahrain either – to one of the off-shore islands.' And he added, 'It's too bad. They should have told you.'

I sat, staring at my beer, momentarily at a loss. 'Is there any way I can get to Abu Dhabi from here?'

'Today?' He shook his head. 'Anyway, you haven't a visa, have you?'

That was no good then. 'When's the next flight back to Bahrain, do you know?'

'Civil? Oh, there'll be one through in a day or two. The manager will have the flight schedules.'

I asked him then who would be flying Gorde back to Bahrain, but he didn't know. 'Might be Bill Adams, might be me.' He took a long pull at his beer. 'Probably me, I guess. He likes to have me fly him. Reminds him of the old days when he was boss out here and we flew everywhere together.' And he began telling me about an old Walrus they'd flown in the early days just before the war. 'One of those push-prop amphibians. Boy! We had fun with that old kite. And Gorde didn't give a damn; he'd let me slam it down any old place.'

'Could you give him a message?' I asked, for I was quite certain now that the note I'd left with Erkhard's secretary would never be delivered.

'Sure, what is it?'

I hesitated. 'Perhaps I'd better write it.'

'Okay. You write it. Then whoever picks him up tomorrow can give it to him.' His freckled face crinkled in a grin. 'You might've been waiting here for weeks. Not that there aren't worse places than Sharjah to be marooned in. This time of year the bathing is wizard. Know what I think? I think that in a few years' time this coast will be one of the world's great winter playgrounds.' I finished my note whilst he was extolling the tourist attractions of the Persian Gulf, and then he began talking about the strange places he had landed in. 'Have you ever been to Saraifa Oasis?' I asked him.

'Saraifa? Sure I have. We had a concession there once.'

I asked him how far it was to Saraifa and he said something over two hundred miles. A long way across the desert, but less than two hours' flying by plane. 'Has it got an airfield?'

'Sure. You don't think I walked, do you? But that was four years ago,' he added. 'I'm told the sand has moved in since then. Funny thing.' He glanced at me quickly. 'You're out here on account of young Whitaker; his lawyer – that right?'

I nodded.

'Well, that last time I flew Gorde in to Saraifa, it was the day David Whitaker arrived there. It was about the last thing Gorde did before he handed over to Erkhard and went home on sick leave. We flew in to Saraifa to break it to the Sheikh Makhmud that the Company wasn't going to renew the concession. They were arguing about it all evening with that one-eyed devil, *Haj* Whitaker, sitting there like an Arab and swearing by the Koran that he'd get even with Erkhard. Has anybody mentioned the Whitaker Theory to you?'

I nodded.

'Oh well, you'll know what it meant to the old Bedouin then. Saraifa was his baby. He'd negotiated the concession and if it hadn't been for Erkhard they might have been drilling there now. But Erkhard was the new broom and if Whitaker could have got at him that night I swear he'd have killed him with his bare hands. It was as elemental as that. Now, of course,' he added, 'it's a different story. Erkhard's under pressure and *Haj* Whitaker—' His navigator called him from the doorway. 'Okay, Eddie. Be right with you.' He swallowed the rest of his beer and got to his feet.

'You were saying you were there in Saraifa when David Whitaker arrived?' I said.

'Oh, yes. Well . . . I was just there, that's all. He was dressed in Bedouin clothes; he was very young and he looked scared stiff. Couldn't blame the poor kid. He'd never been in Arabia before, never met his father before, and that black-hearted bastard just stared at him as though he wished the floor would open up and swallow him. He even introduced the boy to us as David Thomas. It seemed like he didn't want to acknowledge him as his own son, which wasn't very clever of him, for the boy had the same cast of features – the nose, the jaw, the heavy eyebrows. Well, I must go now.' He held out his hand for the envelope. 'Don't worry. I'll see Gorde gets it. And I'll come and rescue you sometime during the week if you haven't flown out by Gulf Airways.' A wave of the hand and he was gone, out through the screen door. I was alone then with the posters and the lazy circling flies and the old magazines.

It was siesta time and after the departure of the plane the Fort went back to sleep. I was allotted a room and after I'd had a shower, I went up on to the terrace that ran like a broad firing step round the inside of the walls and sat there in a pair of shorts and sunglasses staring at the shimmering line of the mountains. Down there to the south, where the high volcanic peaks disappeared below the sand horizon, lay Saraifa. Two hundred odd miles, Otto had said. I remembered Griffiths's description of conditions in summer – *hot enough to burn the tyres off a truck and the soles off your boots*. The heat came up at me with a furnace fierceness and the flat expanse of the airfield lay in mirage-pools of water.

But if I'd been manœuvred clear of Gorde, and Whitaker was inaccessible, there was at least one person available to me here. And as the sun sank and the breeze came up, damp off the sea, I dressed and made enquiries about getting to Dubai. A lieutenant of the Trucial Oman Scouts, who was in the lounge having a drink, offered to take me in after the evening meal.

It was just over twelve miles to Dubai, out past the sheikh's palace with its string of fairy lights and the hum of its generator, and along a winding road beaten out of the *sabkhat*. The road was as black and hard as macadam and all to the right of us were salt flats running out into the sea – a thin, baked crust, treacherously overlaying a slough of mud that was as lifeless as the surface of the moon. To the left the desert sand was humped like the waves of a petrified sea, and far in the distance the mountains of the Jebel, purple and remote, stood sharp-etched on the earth's rim.

As we drove through this empty world I asked the lieutenant whether his outfit was expecting trouble in the interior. He laughed. 'We're always ready for trouble. That's what we're for.' And when I mentioned the rumours circulating in the bazaars of Bahrain, he said, 'Oh, you don't want to worry about them. Bahrain's always buzzing with rumours.' He had a soldier's contempt for civilians and I think he thought I was scared.

The hospital was a mile or two outside Dubai, a solitary building sprawled over a sand hill. The last glow of the sun had gone, the sky fading to darkness, and the building stood black against the sand. Night was falling fast. 'Give Doc Logan my salaams and tell him I'll come over to-morrow and help him drink his Scotch,' my lieutenant said and roared off in his Land Rover towards the distant wind-towers of Dubai.

The hospital was a ramshackle building, part mud, part wood; a strange place to meet a girl I hadn't seen for four years. She came to the little waiting-room dressed in apron and cap, and at the sight of me she stopped and stared in surprise, for nobody had bothered to enquire my name. 'Mr Grant! I – I can't believe it.' She came forward and shook my hand.

'Well, you're not the only one,' I said. 'I can hardly believe it myself.'

Her hand was smooth and dry and firm. Her face looked thinner and the fat of youth had been worked out of her body; her blonde hair was bleached almost white by the sun, her skin tanned. She looked fit and the shine of youth was still in her eyes. It was a strange meeting, and for me – and I think also for her – it brought a feeling of relief, for there was that bond between us and from that moment neither of us could feel entirely alone any more. It was also to have the effect of making me determined, somehow, to get to Saraifa.

'We can't talk here,' she said. 'I'll be b-back in a minute.' Still that slight attractive hesitation in her speech.

When she returned she had removed her cap and apron and wore a light coat. We left the hospital and strolled north whilst the sand turned from brown to silver and the stars came out. I held her arm because I felt her need and mine for the touch of companionship, and the wind was warm on my face.

She had received my letter, but she hadn't been to Bahrain, hadn't even written to Erkhard. 'What was the use?' She seemed at first to have accepted the fact of her brother's death and she was quite willing to talk about him. And as she talked, the picture that emerged was of a man I had only just begun to guess at.

She had come to Dubai two years ago, not so much

to be near him – she had had the sense to realize that she would very rarely see him – but because of his fascination for Arabia, which he had somehow managed to convey to her. 'I was here almost three months before I saw him, and then he came, without warning. He was straight out of the desert, from a survey down by the Liwa Oases, and I didn't recognise him at first. He was dressed as an Arab, you see. But it wasn't that,' she added. 'And he hadn't changed, not really.'

She paused there, as though collecting the details of that meeting from the recesses of her memory. 'I can't explain it,' she said finally. 'He was just different, that's all. He had become a man and there was a remoteness about him. Do you read the Bible, Mr Grant? Those descriptions of the prophets. There was something of that about him. He always had enthusiasm, a sort of inner fire, but now it seemed to have depth and purpose.'

She had only seen him four times in the two years she had been out there, but each time her reaction had been the same. 'It was as though he had become dedicated.'

'Dedicated to what?' I asked. But she couldn't tell me, not in so many words.

'To a way of life,' she said, and went on to talk about the influence his father had had on him. The relationship hadn't been at all easy at first. 'They started off on the wrong foot, you see. When David arrived at Saraifa Sir Philip Gorde was there with his pilot. The driver should have taken David to his father's house; instead he was brought straight to Sheikh Makhmud's palace. It meant, of course, that his arrival was immediately known to two Europeans. It complicated the whole thing, particularly as David was virtually smuggled into Arabia. His father thought it due to wilful disobedience and he was furious.' She smiled at me. 'I think they hated each other at first. They were too much alike, you see.'

I asked her whether she'd met Colonel Whitaker, and she nodded. 'Once, just over a year ago.' He'd come to the hospital to see her. 'It was just curiosity,' she said. 'There's no feeling between us – not like there is between him and David. David's got much more of his father in him than I have. And anyway,' she added, 'after being so long in Arabia he has the native attitude to girls; necessary for the procreation of the race, but useless otherwise. Being a nurse, I know. They'll go to any lengths to get a sick boy to the hospital, but a girl child – she can die or not, just as she pleases.'

I asked her then what impression she had got of her father and she gave a slight shrug. 'There's no love lost between us, if that's what you mean.'

'Yes, but what's he like?' And I explained that I was looking after his financial affairs and had come out partly in the hope of meeting him.

She didn't answer for a moment, as though she had to think about it. 'It's odd,' she said at length. 'He's my own father. I know that. I think we could both feel that in our bones. But it meant nothing.' She hesitated. Finally she said, 'My only impression is one of hardness, almost of cruelty. It's the desert, I think;

the desert and the Moslem faith and the Arabs he's lived with so long. He's a little terrifying – tall, one-eyed, imperious. He's like an Arab, but the sheikhs I've met are much softer, gentler men, more guileful. He has a strange quality of command, the sort of quality I imagine some of our kings once had when they believed implicitly in the Divine Right. You could never be easy in his company, His whole personality, it radiates—' She paused, at a loss for words. 'I can't explain it, but he frightens me.'

'What about David?' I asked. 'Did he feel the same way?'

'At first. Later he came under his spell so that he looked upon him as something akin to God.' He had been, she said, under the spell of his father when he had first come to see her. He had had six months at Saraifa, living the life of an Arab, and a year at an oil school learning to become a geophysicist. He had come to her straight from his first experience of field work and was then going on leave to Saraifa. 'He talked a lot about Saraifa – about the way the desert was moving in on the oasis, slowly obliterating the date gardens. He could be very emotional about it.' She smiled gently. 'He was like a woman at times, the way he wanted to defend Saraifa.'

'Defend it?' I thought for a moment she was referring to the rumours of trouble.

'From the Rub al Khali,' she said. 'From the sand. He dreamed of taking a seismological outfit there and proving his father's theory. Oil, he said, was the only hope. If he could prove there was oil there, then the concession would be renewed and there would be money to rebuild the *falajes*.'

That word again. I asked her what it meant, but all she said was, 'It's some system for bringing water to Saraifa and it has largely been destroyed.' She sighed and sat down on the sand, her hands clasped about her knees. I gave her a cigarette and she sat there smoking, remembering I suppose the last time they had been together.

'Did he ever take a seismological truck into Saraifa?' I asked her.

She looked at me quickly, her eyes big and round in the starlight. I think she had forgotten for the moment that I was there. 'I don't know,' she said. And after a long silence she added softly, 'I know so little about him really. I don't know what he was doing, or why he was so depressed; and the truck abandoned like that. I know so little.' And then she looked at me again and said with great emphasis: 'But I know he was a man – a real man; and also that he would endeavour to the limit for something he believed in.'

'Saraifa?'

She nodded. 'Perhaps – for Saraifa.'

'Because of his father?'

She didn't answer for a while. At length, she said, 'No. Not because of his father.'

'What then?'

'The people, his friend Khalid – the sand killing the place. I don't know. The sand probably. That was something physical. He was always fascinated by physical things. He liked action.'

'But he was a dreamer, too?'

She nodded. 'Yes, he was a dreamer, too. He was always a rebel in the world he knew. When we were kids . . . he'd escape into a world of his own. A m-mental world, you see. It was always much larger than life. He'd invent games – just for the two of us. And then, later – well, the gang life attracted him for the same reason. It was a form of escape.'

'And you think his father's world – Saraifa – was an escape?'

She shrugged. 'Escape or reality – what does it matter? It was real to him. I remember the second time he came to see me. He took me to dinner at the Fort at Sharjah and he was full of plans, bubbling over with them. He was going to take over from a man called Entwhistle who was sick. And after that he was going on a month's leave – to Saraifa. A busman's holiday; he was going to run a survey for his father. He was so full of it,' she said a little sadly. 'And so bloody opti-mistic,' she added, almost savagely.

'Where exactly in Saraifa was he going to try for oil?'

'I don't know. What does it matter?'

'Was this in July of last year?'

She nodded, a glance of surprise. 'He had his own ideas; something he'd unearthed in some old geological report. I couldn't follow it all. When he's excited he talks nineteen-to-the-dozen and I'm never certain what is fact and what he's made up. He seemed to think he could do in a month what GODCO had failed to do the whole time they'd had the concession. He was always like that. He could build a whole kingdom in five minutes – in his mind.' She gave a little laugh. 'Once, you know, he ran a tramp shipping line out of Cardiff. It got so big that every ship that came into the docks belonged to him. That was the first time he got into trouble. He beat up a night watchman for telling him to get off the bridge of an old laid-up Victory ship.' She sighed. 'That was the sort of boy he was.'

'And after he'd been to Saraifa?' I asked. 'Did he come and see you?'

'No, he flew straight back to Bahrain. I didn't see him until December.'

She didn't seem to want to talk about it, for I had to drag it out of her. Yes, he had been going to Saraifa again. She admitted it reluctantly. He'd been loaned to his father.

'Are you sure?' I asked.

'I can't be sure about anything, but that's what I understood.'

So the *Times* Correspondent had been right. And I remembered how Erkhard had skated round the question.

'It was all so strange,' she murmured. 'I thought it was what he'd been wanting all along. Instead he seemed – I don't know how to put it – almost appalled at the prospect. He was in a most extraordinary state of nervous tension—'

'Had he seen Erkhard?' I asked. 'Was it Erkhard who had loaned him to his father?'

'I don't know. He wouldn't talk about it. He just

came to tell me where he was going and what he was doing. He didn't stay long. In fact,' she added, 'it was a rather awkward meeting and I had the feeling he'd only come because he'd felt it was his duty.'

But I was barely listening to her, my mind on Erkhard and this extraordinary arrangement. If it was true, then it could only mean one thing – that Erkhard and Whitaker had some sort of an arrangement . . . an improbable combination if Otto was to be believed. 'And this was in December?'

She nodded.

'You said you'd seen him four times,' I said. 'When was the fourth?'

'The fourth?' She stared at me and her face looked very pale. 'It was in February.' She couldn't remember the date, but it was early in February. I knew then that he'd come to her after he had boarded the *Emerald Isle*, probably that same night, because she said she was called out well after midnight by an Arab boy and had found him sitting alone on the sand. 'Somewhere near here,' she said, looking about her.

'Did he talk about his father?'

'No,' she said. 'Though—' She hesitated. 'I think they'd had a row. I can't be sure. It wasn't anything he said.' And she added, 'He wasn't very communicative, you see.'

I asked her how he'd behaved. 'Was he scared at all? Did he behave as though he was in fear of his life?'

She looked at me quickly, her eyes searching my face. 'No,' she said slowly. 'No, I don't think he was scared. More—' She shook her head. 'I can't explain. He just behaved strangely, that's all – very strangely.' In fact, most of the time he'd been with her he'd sat in absolute silence. 'David could do that. As a kid I got used to those silences. But . . . I don't know. This seemed deeper, somehow, as though—' But she couldn't put it into words. 'He didn't talk much,' she reiterated. 'There was a moon and I remember his eyes riveted on my face. It was as though he couldn't look at me enough. I felt . . . it was as though he wanted to capture an impression, take a sort of mental picture with him. It was a very strange, uncomfortable feeling – and he looked so like his father in the Arab clothes he was wearing.'

'Did he tell you what he was doing?'

'No. He wouldn't tell me anything, but I had the feeling that it was dangerous. He was terribly thin, nothing but skin and bone, and his eyes, staring at me, looked enormous and very pale in the moonlight. When he left he kissed me, not with warmth, but as though he were kissing a priestess who held the key to the future in her hands. And just before he left me, he said a strange thing. He said, 'Whatever you hear of me, Sue, don't believe it.' And he added that if anything happened to him, I was to write to you. And then he left me, walking quickly across the sand without looking back.'

We were sitting on a little rise and the sand fell away from us, sloping gently to a *barasti* settlement, the dark shapes of the palm-frond huts barely visible, for the moon was new and only just risen. Nothing stirred and the only sound was the bleat of a goat. 'I can't believe he's dead,' she said. 'I won't believe it.'

And because it was what she wanted to believe I told her about the girl in Bahrain and about her mother's reaction.

'Yes,' she said. 'Mum did everything she could to discourage his interest in Arabia. But too late. When we were small she shared her thoughts with us, and her thoughts were of the man she called our 'Uncle Charles.' That album of press-cuttings – they were almost the first pictures I ever remember looking at. And now here we are, the two of us, in Arabia.'

'And your father?' I asked. 'Did he talk to you about Saraifa?'

'To me?' She smiled and shook her head. 'I'm only a girl. He wouldn't talk to me about what he was doing.'

'You say David was loaned to him by GODCO,' I prompted.

She nodded and when I pressed her for the reason, she said almost sharply, 'Oh, his father is doing what he's always done out here – dabbling in oil.' And then almost gently: 'It's rather sad really. One by one the concessions he negotiated for GODCO have been abandoned. He was once a great figure out here – a sort of Lawrence.' She had pity for him, even if she had no love.

'And now?' I asked.

'Now?' She shook her head. 'I don't know. David wouldn't talk about him, not that last time. But there are all these rumours. He had this theory, you know.

Some say it's crazy, but I've met others who believed he was right.'

I asked her whether she'd met Entwhistle. I thought perhaps he might have been to see her. But she shook her head.

'What about these rumours?' I said.

'They're just rumours.' She shrugged. 'I don't know whether they're true or not. Nobody I've met has ever been to Saraifa. With the border in dispute nobody is allowed to go there. It's just . . . well, the desert is like the sea used to be, you know – exaggerated stories are passed on by word of mouth.'

I pressed her then to tell me what the stories were and she said, 'He's supposed to be drilling on his own account – with an old broken-down rig operated entirely by Bedouin. The oil boys I've talked to all say that's nonsense, that uneducated desert Arabs couldn't possibly operate an oil rig. But I don't know. Though I'm scared of him and have no feeling for him. I know he's a remarkable man, and you've only got to talk to the officers here to realize that the Bedouin are very quick to pick up a working knowledge of machinery.'

She threw the stub of her cigarette away and got to her feet. 'I wish to God I knew what had happened.' Her voice trembled; she was very near to tears. There was a lot more I suppose she could have told me about him, but I didn't press her. I thought there was plenty of time and that I'd see her again. For her sake I steered the talk to other things. We passed a watch tower, standing like a lonely border keep, and she told me they were still manned, the guard climbing in through the hole halfway up the tower's side every night and pulling the ladder up after him.

'It looks so peaceful here,' I said.

She laughed. 'It is – on the surface. But who knows what is going on underneath? Certainly not our people. Some of these young English boys who are sent out here to advise—' She shook her head. 'Sometimes I wonder. What must the sheikhs think? This desert way of life, it goes right back to Hagar and Ishmael, racially and culturally hardly changed. They know human nature the way these youngsters out from England will never know it. They're full of guile and intrigue; the Pax Britannica, even the oil, is just an incident in time. It's only a few years back, you know, that the Sheikh of Dubai fell upon an Abu Dhabi raiding force, killing over fifty of them. It wasn't very far from here.'

Back at the hospital she asked me whether I had arranged transport to get me back to Sharjah. 'I can walk,' I said. But she wouldn't hear of it. 'You'd lose your way in the dark. You'd either wander into the desert or else into the *sabkhat*. Step through the crust of that and nobody would ever see you again.' She insisted that I stayed at the hospital.

They had a small guest room and I spent the night there, and in the morning she arranged a lift for me in a TOS truck going back to Sharjah. She looked cool and very matter-of-fact as she said goodbye to me. 'Come and see me again before you leave. And if you have any news—' She left it at that, and I sat and watched her from the back of the truck as we drove away, a solitary figure in white standing motionless outside the hospital. She hadn't moved when I lost sight of her behind a shoulder of sand.

It was that lack of movement; I became suddenly intinctively aware of a loneliness that matched my own, and my heart went out to her. And as the truck roared along the packed mud surface of the Sharjah track it wasn't of the girl who had walked with me in the moonlight on my first night on the edge of the Arabian desert that I was thinking, but of that other girl – the girl who had come to my shabby office in Cardiff to plead for help for her brother. She was a woman now and though she might not like her father, I felt he had given her something of himself that made her, like him, an unusual person. She had courage, loyalty and a strange aura of calm, an acceptance of life as it was. They were qualities both restful and disturbing, and remembering every detail of that walk in the sands, the watch tower and her perceptive comments on the desert world, I knew I didn't want to lose her, knew that somehow I must discover what had happened to David and set her mind at rest. I was half in love with her. I knew that before ever the truck reached Sharjah, and all that morning I walked, filled with a restlessness that was the restlessness of frustration. But you could walk for a day and still have no sense of progress in the merciless emptiness of the sea of sand that stretched away to the south.

I had my lunch in the company of a German commercial traveller and two American tourists staying the night on their way to India. The German could talk of nothing but the fact that his product had been copied in Karachi and was on sale in almost the identical wrapping in the bazaars of Dubai. The Americans were from Detroit, plaintive and unable to see any attraction in the untamed beauty of the desert, faintly disturbed by the condition of the Arabs, nostalgic for a hotel that would give them the built-in sense of security of a Statler.

The sound of aircraft coming in low interrupted the desultory conversation. Ten minutes later the screen door was flung open and Otto came in with his navigator. 'Hi!' He waved his hand and came over to me. 'Fairy godfather, that's me. Anything you want, Otto produces it. The Old Man's in the manager's office right now.'

'Gorde?'

He nodded. 'But watch out. He's hopping mad about something.'

'Thanks,' I said, and went across to my room and got my briefcase.

The manager's office was by the arched entrance and seated opposite him in one of the big leather armchairs was a much older man with a yellowish face that was shrivelled like a nut. He had a tall glass in his hand and on the floor at his side lay a rubber-ferruled stick. Small bloodshot eyes stared at me over deep pouches as I introduced myself. He didn't say anything but just sat there summing me up.

I was conscious at once that this was a very different man to Erkhard. He looked as though he belonged in the desert, a man who had had all the red blood baked out of him by the heat. He wore an old pair of desert boots, khaki trousers and a freshly-laundered cream shirt with a silk square knotted round his throat like a sweat rag. A battered brown trilby, the band stained black by the perspiration of years, was tipped to the back of his grizzled head.

'You got my message,' I said.

He nodded. 'Yes. I got your message. But that wasn't what brought me.' His voice was dry, rasping, the words staccato as though life were too short for conversation. 'Should be in Bahrain now.' He gave the manager a brusque nod of dismissal and when we were alone he said, 'There's a newspaper on the desk there. That's why I'm here. Read it. I've marked the passage.'

It was the airmail edition of a leading London daily. The marked passage was on the foreign news page. It was headed: NEW OIL DISCOVERY IN ARABIA? – Desert Death of Ex-Borstal Boy Starts Rumours. It was written 'by a Special Correspondent' and besides giving a full and graphic account of David Whitaker's disappearance and the search that had followed, it included his background; everything was there, everything that I knew about the boy myself – his escape from the police in Cardiff, the fact that he was Colonel Whitaker's son, even the details of how he'd been smuggled into Arabia on a native dhow. The story ran to almost a column with a double-column head, and about the only thing it didn't give was the location he'd been surveying immediately prior to his death.

'Well?' Gorde rasped. 'Are you responsible for that?'

'No.'

'Then who is?'

That was what I was wondering. Whoever had written it had access to all the information that I had. 'I don't know,' I said.

'You're David Whitaker's solicitor. His Executor, in fact, Otto tells me.'

'Yes.'

'And just over two days ago you were in London.'

'Nevertheless, I'm not responsible for it.'

'A young kid just out of oil school and operating in an area he'd no business in . . . a criminal to boot.' He glared at me, his fingers drumming at the leather arm of the chair. 'The Political Resident had that paper specially flown down to me at Abu Dhabi. The Foreign Office has teleprinted him that half the London press have taken the story up. He's furious.'

'The facts are correct,' I said.

'The facts!' But he wasn't thinking of the boy's background. 'You know where his truck was found abandoned? Inside the borders of Saudi Arabia,' he almost snarled. 'A story like that – it could spark off another Buraimi; only worse, much worse.' He paused then, staring at me curiously. 'Your note said you wanted to see me. You said it was urgent, something about this boy – a communication.'

I didn't answer at once, for I'd read through to the end of the newspaper story, to the editorial footnote that had been added at the bottom: *The London Office of the Gulfoman Oilfields Development Company issued a statement yesterday denying that there was any truth in rumours that the Company had made an important new oil strike. Asked whether David Whitaker had made a confidential report prior to his death, an official of the Company stated categorically that nothing was known in London about any such report. Despite the Company's denials, GODCO shares went ahead yesterday in active dealings on the London Stock Exchange.*

'Well?'

'Suppose there's something in it?'

'Suppose pigs had wings,' he snarled. 'Well, come on, man. What was it you wanted to see me about?'

For answer I opened my briefcase and handed over the envelope David had addressed to him. 'Have you seen Colonel Whitaker since you've been out here?' I asked.

'What's that got to do with it?' He was staring down at the envelope, and when I started to explain, he cut me short. 'Oh I've heard the talk if that's what you mean. But it's nothing to do with the Company. If Charles Whitaker likes to waste his money trying to prove a theory—' He grunted. 'It's just damned awkward, that's all. The boy's death makes a colourful story and coming on top of his father's activities—' He gave a little shrug and slit open the flap of the envelope with his finger. 'Erkhard was trying to keep it quiet – and rightly. Saraifa is a trouble-spot. Always has been. And the political chaps are touchy about it.'

'That doesn't explain why he should try to prevent me seeing you.'

He had taken out a letter and two wads of

foolscap. 'What's that? What are you talking about?' He reached into his pocket for his glasses.

I told him then how I'd been given facilities for Sharjah as soon as it was known that he had changed his plans and was flying back to Bahrain.

'What are you suggesting?' he demanded.

'That Erkhard didn't intend us to meet.'

'Nonsense. What difference could it make to him?' He put on his glasses and after that he didn't talk as he read steadily through the contents. Finally he said, 'Do you know what this is, Mr Grant?' He tapped one of the foolscap sheets. 'Do you know what he's trying to get me to do?'

'Sign some sort of undertaking, but I don't know exactly—'

'Undertaking!' he rasped. 'If I sign this—' He waved the sheet of paper at me. 'It would commit the Company to drilling four test wells at locations to be supplied by you.' He took his glasses off and stared at me. 'Is that right? You hold the locations?'

'Yes,' I said. 'They're in a separate envelope. If you sign that document, then I'm instructed to hand it across to you.'

'But not otherwise?'

'No.'

'And you've got it with you?'

I nodded. 'It's here in my briefcase.'

'And if I don't sign . . . What do you do then?'

'In that case I imagine my actions wouldn't concern you.'

'No?' He laughed. And then he was looking down

at the document again. 'I see here that you will be acting as agent for Sheikh Makhmud and his son Khalid in this matter. Have you ever met Sheikh Makhmud?'

I shook my head.

'And you know nothing about the Middle East.' He was staring at me and his eyes had the suggestion of a twinkle. 'It has its humorous side, you know. The boy must have thought you a most remarkable lawyer.' He went back to the document again. 'Further, it commits the Company to the payment of an advance of a hundred thousand pounds in respect of oil royalties of 50 per cent, provided always that Sheikh Makhmud and his son agree to grant to the Company the sole concession from date of signature to the year 2000. Well,' he said, 'there's your undertaking. The boy must have had a touch of the sun when he typed that.' And he tossed it across to me. 'Read it yourself and tell me what you think of it – as a lawyer.'

I glanced through it quickly, wondering what he expected me to see in it. 'It looks perfectly legal,' I said.

'Exactly. That's what makes it so damned odd. He'd taken the trouble to look up all the legal jargon for that sort of a document.' He leaned suddenly forward. 'He couldn't have got that in the desert, could he? It means he looked it up before ever he went out there, before he'd even run his survey.'

'What are you suggesting?'

'That his report's a phoney. I'm not a fool, Grant. That boy's been got at, and I can guess who's got at

him. Here. Take a look at the survey report.' He thrust
it at me. 'He used his own typewriter for that. The
other's different, probably an office machine. He typed
that document and then went out into the desert—'

'David lost his life as a result of that survey,' I
reminded him.

'Did he? How do you know what caused his
death?' He glared at me. 'You don't, and nor do I.
Nobody knows – or even what's happened to him.
Has anyone mentioned the Whitaker Theory to you?'

'I know about it,' I said. 'Is that why you think
he's been got at?'

He nodded. 'Way back in the thirties Charles Whitaker began claiming that we'd find the oilfields
continuing down from the Gulf here between the sand
seas of the Empty Quarter and the Coastal mountain
ranges to the east. It seemed a possibility, and remembering how Holmes's theory had finally been proved
right in Bahrain, I took a chance on it and moved
some of my development teams in from the coast. It
was an expensive business and Buraimi was about the
limit from the practical point of view. I was operating
partly in the Sharjah sheikhdom and partly in Muscat
territory, and after I'd burned my fingers, even the big
companies like Shell and ARAMCO wouldn't look at
his theory.'

'That was a long time ago now,' I said.

'Yes, before the war.'

'What about Saraifa? Did you do any development
work there?'

'No, it was too far from the coast. I sent a geological party in in 1939, but the initial reports weren't very encouraging and then the war came and the chap in charge of the survey was killed. We didn't try again, though Charles was always pressing us to do so. He had a political appointment for a short time after the end of the war, but when he rejoined the Company in 1949 he was still just as convinced that he'd be proved right in the end.' He shook his head. 'Poor fellow! It had become an obsession – Saraifa in particular; he wanted us to try again there. The wartime development of desert transport made it a practical proposition, but the political situation between Saraifa and Hadd was worsening, and anyway I'd lost faith in his theory by then.' He stared at the foolscap sheets in my hand. 'If that survey report had been turned in by one of our most experienced geophysicists I wouldn't touch it.'

'Because of the political factor?'

'No. Not just because of the political factor.'

'What then?'

He hesitated. 'Because it doesn't fit in with the reasons I'm out in the Gulf area.' He stared at me then, his eyes narrowed above the tired pouches of flesh. 'The fact is,' he said, 'the Company's been spending too much money out here and getting too little in return. Nobody is supposed to know this yet – not even Erkhard, though I think he's guessed. My instructions are to carry out a thorough investigation of all our development projects in the Gulf with a view to cutting down our commitments. It amounts to a reassessment of the value of each project and those that show no real promise of yielding results are to be abandoned. So you see—' He gave a little shrug, his hands spread out. 'This is hardly the moment for me or anybody else to involve the Company in new commitments.'

'I see.' There was really nothing more to be said and I folded the papers and put them in my briefcase.

'It's a funny thing.' He was leaning back in his chair, his eyes half-closed, chuckling to himself. 'The Company did this once before. They sent Alex Erkhard out and because I was sick and hadn't the energy to fight him, he got my job. And now, four years later, I'm back with the same powers he had and the knowledge that he's made more mistakes than I did and lost the Company a lot of friends.' Again that dry, rasping chuckle, and then his eyelids flicked back. 'What I've told you is in the strictest confidence, you understand. You've been put to a lot of trouble to contact me. I thought it only fair to explain the situation to you. If it's any satisfaction to you, I'd add that a report like that isn't conclusive. Seismology never is; it's simply an indication. The only way to be sure you're sitting on an oilfield is to drill down and find out.'

'And suppose Whitaker's doing just that?'

'Hmm. To know the answer to that we'd have to know the locations the boy was surveying and where his father's drilling.' He stared at me. 'Well, there it is. You've got your instructions—'

I nodded. There was no point in continuing the discussion. 'You're going back to Bahrain, I take it, Sir Philip?'

'Bahrain? Oh, you'd like a lift in my plane, is that it?'

I nodded. 'Please.'

He seemed to hesitate. But then he said, 'All right.' He picked up his drink. 'You know my pilot – Otto Smith? Perhaps you'd be good enough to get him for me.' He tapped his leg. 'Can't move about like I used to.'

'I'll get him,' I said. And I went out and left him there, leaning back in the chair with his eyes half-closed as though exhausted.

I had some difficulty in finding Otto, but eventually I ran him to earth in the showers, sitting naked, smoking a cigarette and gossiping with the navigator. I waited whilst he dressed and then went back with him to the manager's office.

Gorde was in the same position, but now he had my briefcase open on his lap and he was peering down at a sheet of paper he held in his hand.

I can't remember what I said to him – I was too angry. I think I called him some pretty unpleasant names, but all he said was, 'What did you expect me to do?' His tone was mild. Almost he seemed amused. 'If I'd asked you to let me see the locations you'd have refused. Quite rightly.' And he added, 'I just wanted to check them against the position where his truck was found.'

'But you've no right—'

'Of course I'd no right,' he said. 'But yelling at me and getting yourself into a muck sweat won't alter the fact that I now have them. Do you know where they are?' he asked, peering up at me.

'No,' I said. 'I haven't had an opportunity—'

'On the Saraifa-Hadd border. Right bang on the bloody border.' He glared at me. 'I suppose you'll tell me you didn't know that the border was in dispute?' The way he said it implied that I'd tried to put something over on him. Angrily I told him that I didn't have the advantage of his lack of scruples. 'I kept strictly to my instructions and refrained from opening the envelope until I'd seen you.'

'All right,' he said. 'We'll talk about it in a moment.' He levered himself round in his chair. 'Is the plane refuelled yet, Otto?'

'I don't know, sir. I'll check if you like. Are you wanting to leave right away?'

'Yes, right away. But first I want you to check that your tanks are full. A personal check please. You've got to have enough fuel on board to fly to the Saraifa border and back.'

'I'm afraid we have to have authority to fly to Saraifa, Sir Philip.'

'Since when?'

Otto hesitated. 'I don't know exactly. Since the trouble there, I guess. It was just after you left; a border clash between Saraifa and Hadd. They had to send the Trucial Oman Scouts in and since then nobody has been allowed to go to Saraifa.'

Gorde gave a little sigh. 'Let's not argue about it, Otto. I intend to have a quick look at these locations.

Now then, how do we go about it without some little clerk reporting my movements to the PRPG, eh?'

Otto thought for a moment. 'I think the best thing would be to say we're doing a recce of certain areas, taking a look at a seismological outfit we've got operating at the foot of the Jebel, possibly landing at Ras al-Khaima if we've time, otherwise returning here. If we make it vague like that, I guess it'll be all right. That is so long as you don't want to land at Saraifa.'

'I don't know what I want to do,' Gorde grumbled. 'Haven't had time to think about it yet.' He poked around in my briefcase until he found a sheet of plain paper. 'Communications here still functions for civilian messages, doesn't it?' And when the other nodded, he pulled a gold pencil from his pocket and began to write. I watched him as he signed his name and read it through. I was more curious than angry now; he'd taken matters out of my hands and for the moment my only concern was to get on this flight.

'Have Communications send that off right away.' He held out the message. 'Then check your fuel. Oh, and Otto,' he added as the pilot was leaving. 'We'll be flying on to Bahrain tonight.' The door closed and he turned to me. 'I suppose you think I owe you an apology, hm?' He handed me back my briefcase. 'Well, maybe I do. But I spent a lot of my time in Saraifa, and anyway I'm an oil man. We've no built-in moral code like you boys when it comes to things like locations.' He folded the foolscap sheet and put it back in its envelope and sat there tapping it against his thumbnail, lost in thought. 'It's just possible, I suppose—' He said it softly, speaking to himself.

'That Colonel Whitaker's drilling in one of these locations?'

But he shook his head. 'In that area? He wouldn't be such a fool.' Silence again, and the rhythmic tapping of that envelope. 'However—' The small, bloodshot eyes peered at me curiously, and then he began to chuckle. 'A provincial lawyer – and it's just possible you might have got hold of the thing the Company has been searching the Gulf for during almost thirty years.' The rasp of that chuckle seemed to threaten to choke him. 'You and Charles Whitaker. God Almighty!' he gasped. 'And that boy . . . he'd never have dared operate on that border on his own.'

'You think they were together then?'

'How the hell do I know?' He handed me the envelope. 'I don't know where Charles is drilling any more than you do. I'm not even certain he is drilling. It's just rumours.' He reached for his stick and dragged himself to his feet. 'But I mean to find out,' he said. 'If Charles is drilling on these locations—' He let it go at that and since he seemed to take it for granted that I was going with him, I stuffed the envelope into my pocket, picked up my briefcase and followed him to the door. As he pulled it open he said to me over his shoulder, 'Prove Whitaker's theory correct, and on that border, and you'll be in politics so deep, my friend, that you'll wish you'd never been born. But I can't believe it,' he added, limping out into the bright sunshine. 'Pig-headed, proud, revengeful . . . He still couldn't be such a bloody fool.' And he stumped off across the courtyard, shaking his head and muttering to himself.

We took off ten minutes later and by then I'd had an opportunity to glance at the contents of that envelope. There were several foolscap sheets headed: REPORT OF SURVEYS CARRIED OUT ON SARAIFA TERRITORY; and it was sub-headed: Basis on which an Immediate Programme of Test Drilling is Recommended at Points A, B, C & D. Pinned to it were four sheets of graph paper, covered with figures and diagrams. There was also a sketch map giving his survey points, a whole series of them, each with the position pinpointed in latitude and longitude. A number of Arab names were given, but none that I could recall from my brief examination of the map in Erkhard's office. Points A, B, C & D were marked in red ink; they were very close to each other, in a little huddle at the eastern end of the line of his survey. There was no covering letter. Just the report and the sketch map.

I read the report through carefully as we flew south into the desert. It was typewritten, highly technical – quite beyond my comprehension. For this reason I do not intend to give the details. But there were several references to the 'Whitaker Theory,' and right at the beginning there was a paragraph that read: *It should not be imagined that I stumbled on this by accident. If anything comes of it, the credit must go to Henry Farr. He surveyed the area in the very early days of the war. The Saraifa Concession was fairly new then and Farr's outfit was the only survey team in the area. Moreover he made his report at a time of crisis in the Middle East; it was pigeon-holed away in the Company's headquarters and shortly afterwards he died fighting in Abyssinia. I was fortunate enough to come upon this report when searching old surveys for anything that had a bearing on Saraifa—*

I leaned back in my seat, thinking about the war and how that old report had got lost in the files. Colonel Whitaker had fought in Eritrea. The same area. I wondered whether he and Farr had ever met. I was thinking about that when Gorde leaned across to me. 'Well?' he said. 'What are you going to do about that report when you get back to Bahrain?' He was smiling, tight-lipped. 'The boy's like his father,' he grunted. 'A dreamer. The same dream, too.'

'The dreams of youth sometimes come true,' I said. I was remembering how Sue had talked of him.

His eyes clouded and he looked away from me, staring out of his window towards the mountains. 'Ah yes, the dreams of youth.' He gave a little sigh. 'But the boy's dead and Charles isn't a young man any more.'

'And what about Farr?' I asked.

He shrugged. 'He's dead, too.'

'You don't think they could be right?'

'The Whitaker Theory?' He gave a snort. 'Charles had a nose for oil, a sort of instinct for it, like Holmes. But he didn't know a damn' thing about geology. That nose of his cost the Company a lot of money. We struck oil, but never in large enough quantities. I should know,' he almost snarled. 'I backed him and it cost me my job out here. And I loved it,' he added quietly. 'I love this country. Look at it.'

He leaned across, pointing to the desert that lay below the wing-tip, a corrugated dune sea stretching to the mountains that lay all along the horizon. 'Clean and hard and cruel. I had twenty years of it. I know it better than I know my own country and it calls to me the way the sea calls to a sailor – and I'm stuck in a damned office in London; I haven't been out here for almost four years.' And he relapsed into silence, staring out of his window.

But a moment later he touched my arm and pointed downwards. A great sweep of dunes thrust eastwards, narrowing like a finger till the tip of the yellow sand touched the red rock wall of the mountains. Right below us a black line wound like a thread across the dunes – a camel caravan going south and leaving a faded snail-like smudge behind it in the sand. 'The Ramlah Anej,' he said in my ear. 'We're crossing the eastern edge of the Rub al Khali.' And he added with a sort of boyish delight, 'I'm one of the very few men who've crossed the Empty Quarter by camel. Charles and I did it together. We said we were looking for oil, but that was just an excuse.' He was smiling and his eyes were alight with the memory of it, so that through age and illness I got a glimpse of the young man he'd once been.

After that he fell silent and left me alone with my thoughts as the aircraft roared steadily south, the mountains always away to the left, always marching with us, a moon-mad landscape of volcanic peaks, sometimes near, sometimes receding to the lip of the earth's surface. And below us, the sun marked the desert floor with the imprint of our plane, a minute shadow dogging our course.

It was just after four when the navigator came aft and woke Gorde, who had fallen asleep with the curtain drawn across his window and his battered hat tipped to shade his eyes. 'Jebel al-Akhbar coming up now, sir. Otto wants to know whether you'd like to fly over Hadd or make a detour?'

'May as well have a look at the Emir's hide-out,' Gorde murmured, rubbing the sleep out of his eyes. 'Long time since I last saw it.' He got to his feet and motioned me to follow him.

The view from the flight deck was a blinding glare made bearable only by the green shade above the pilot's head. All away to the right of us was sand as far as the eye could strain, a petrified sea corrugated by the action of the wind. But from the left mountains were closing in, bare, black, lava-ash mountains marked by patches of a livid, chemical green. They swept round ahead of us in a long curve, terminating abruptly at the sand sea's edge in a bold headland topped by a pinnacle of bare rock. 'Jebel al-Akhbar,' Gorde said, nodding towards it over the pilot's head. 'There's an old stone fort on the top of it and the town of Hadd is right underneath. Remarkable place. There's a saying amongst the Arabs of this part – Who holds al-Akhbar, holds Hadd. You'll see in a minute.'

Otto was pushing the control column forward and

as we lost height the headland began to come up fast. 'See the fort?' Gorde's hand gripped my arm. 'I got a gazelle there once. The Emir invited us hunting and a saluki bitch named Adilla cornered it for me right under the walls there. My first visit to Saraifa,' he added. 'The time we signed the original concession.'

I could see the fort clearly now, a biggish place, crumbling into ruin, with an outer ring of mud and rock walls and in the centre a single watch tower perched high on a pinnacle of rock. We skimmed it with about a hundred feet to spare and on the farther side the hill dropped sheer to a valley shaped like a crescent moon and half-ringed with mountains.

The valley floor was flat, a patchwork quilt of cultivation; date palms, grey with dust, stood thick as Indian corn in mud-walled enclosures, and there were fields of millet green with new growth. In the further reaches of the valley, where cultivation dwindled into grey, volcanic ash, a solitary sand-devil swirled a spiral of dust high into the air.

'Hadd.' Gorde stabbed downwards with his thumb, and peering over his shoulder I caught a glimpse of a mud town that seemed built into the rock below the fort. Right below us a mêlée of men and goats and camels stood transfixed beside a well. Mud walls towered above them, and looking back I saw the town of Hadd climbing into its rocky cleft with a great fortified palace built on many levels facing towards the desert. A green flag fluttered from a flagpole. 'Always reminds me of the Hadhramaut,' Gorde shouted in my ear. 'They build like that in the Wadi Duan. Well-sited, isn't it?' He might have been a soldier, his interest was so professional.

Otto half-turned in his seat. 'I'm setting course now for the position given in the search report, that OK?' And when Gorde nodded he banked the plane so that I had a last glimpse of the Wadi Hadd al-Akhbar, a little oasis of green set against a nightmare back-drop of volcanic rock. And then it was gone and the arid, lifeless desert stretched out ahead of us.

Gorde produced the slip of paper he'd used for making notes and handed it to the navigator. 'Those are the fixes for the Saraifa-Hadd border locations. Plot them now. We'll be flying over them as soon as we've had a look at the spot where he abandoned his truck.'

We flew on in silence then and gradually the gravel plain gave place to sand, the dunes getting higher, their shadows longer until they were towering crescent-shaped downlands stretching into infinity. The navigator passed Otto an alteration of course and the shadow of the plane came ahead of us, growing imperceptibly bigger, as we lost height. 'Have we crossed the border?'

The navigator nodded. 'Just crossing it now.'

Gorde's hand gripped my elbow. 'That's the trouble with this damned country,' he said. 'The borders are nothing but map references. Nobody cared so long as it was just a waste of desert sand. But you try explaining map references to an Arab sheikh once he's dazzled by the prospect of oil.'

The navigator leaned across and made a circling

movement with his hand. Otto tipped the plane over on the port wing-tip and we searched the glaring dunes below us. We circled like that, slowly, for several minutes, and then suddenly we straightened out, swooping down towards the humped back of a dune, and there, halfway up it, was the truck, almost obliterated by sand. I never saw such a desperately lonely-looking object in my life, a piece of dead machinery lying there like a wrecked boat in the midst of an ocean of sand.

We slid down on to it like a hawk stooping to its prey. It was a big closed-in truck, old and battered-looking and patched with rust. There were no markings on it and as it rushed away beneath us Gorde echoed my own thoughts: 'What was the fool doing, driving that truck alone into these dunes?' he demanded. 'Do you know?' He was glaring at me, and when I shook my head, he grunted as though he didn't believe me. 'A good twenty miles west of the survey locations,' he growled. 'He must have had some reason.'

Otto banked steeply so that the truck was there, just beyond the port wing for us to stare at. But looking at it couldn't explain its presence on the slope of that dune, and in the end Gorde gave instructions for us to proceed to the locations David had surveyed and motioned me to follow him back into the relative quiet of the passenger cabin.

'Well,' he said, dropping into his seat, 'what do you make of it, eh?' But I could see he didn't expect an answer. He was slumped in his seat, an old man lost in thought. 'Doesn't make sense, does it?' he grumbled. 'The boy dead somewhere down there below us and his father not caring a damn and busy drilling a well—' He turned to me. 'How did they get on, those two, do you know? What were their relations just prior to the boy's death?' And when I didn't say anything, he snapped, 'Come on, man. You must know something. You've come all the way out from England; you wouldn't have done that unless you knew a little more than you've told me.' He stared at me angrily. 'Have you seen his sister?'

I nodded.

'Well, what does she say about it? He must have talked to her.'

'She'd like to think he's still alive.'

'What, in this country – and the truck lying there on that dune for almost two months?'

'She's never been into the desert.'

'No, of course not.' He asked me again what she had said about him, and whilst I was telling him the desert below gradually changed, the dunes altering shape until they were long ridges like waves with gravel flats in the troughs.

I was just telling him about the last visit David had made to his sister when the plane gave a lurch, the port wing tipped down and over Gorde's shoulder I caught a glimpse of tyre marks running straight like the line of a railway along the length of a flat stretch between two dunes. A pile of rusted tins, the black trace of a fire, the remains of a dug latrine; they were there for an instant and then the plane straightened up and we flew on, following the tyre marks that had scored a straight line wherever the sand was soft.

Gorde got up then and I followed him forward. Indications of another camp came up at us, swept by beneath the plane. We were flying very low, the line of the dunes on either side closing us in. And then, straight ahead, the black shadow of a truck. It was stationary and we came up on it fast, belly to the gravel flat, roaring over it so close that I could read the black lettering on its side – G-O-D-C-O – and could see the drill at its rear turning.

It was the same sort of truck as the one we had seen abandoned a short while back, and as we turned and came down on it again, a figure in khaki shorts and an Australian bush hat waved to us. There were Arabs moving about by the drill and close by the truck was a Land Rover with G-O-D-C-O painted across its bonnet.

Gorde swung round on me. 'What the devil's a seismological truck doing here? Did you know it was here?'

'Of course not.' For one wild moment I thought those three women might be right and I almost tore the glasses from Gorde's hand. But the khaki figure was broad and thick-set, the round, brick-red face covered with ginger hair.

Gorde tapped Otto on the shoulder. 'Can you land here?' he demanded. 'I want to talk to that man. Who is it? Do you know?'

'Looks like Jack Entwhistle,' Otto answered, and he swung the plane over again, circling back with the wing-tip almost scraping the top of the dunes. He was flying with his eyes glued to his side window, searching the ground. 'Looks okay,' he said. 'No big stones, no wadis that I can see. I guess I can get down. Don't know how it will be taking off again.'

Gorde didn't even hesitate. 'Then put her down,' he said. His face had gone a sickly yellow. He was furious.

'Hold tight then.' The plane banked again, came in level over the flat gravel pan and I felt the drag as the flaps and under-carriage went down. He flew about half a mile with the ground so close that we might have been in a car, then he gave her full throttle, lifted her up and round in a turn that left my stomach behind me. We came back on to the line of the gravel, slow and dropping this time with the truck standing bang in our path. The wheels touched, bounced once on a rough patch, and next time we stayed down, bumping heavily over the rough surface, stones rattling against the outside of the fuselage, until the brakes came on and we slowed to a halt.

We were about three hundred yards from the truck and the man who had waved to us was already in the Land Rover coming towards us. By the time the navigator had got the fuselage door open the Land Rover was drawing up alongside. The air that came in through the open door was hot with the glare of sun on sand. There was no wind and the heat seemed trapped between the dunes. Gorde moved awkwardly down the fuselage, supporting himself with his hands on the backs of the seats. He looked tired and old and very grim as he faced the man who came in from the desert. 'Entwhistle, isn't it?'

'That's raight, Sir Philip.' The man was North Country, square and stocky, the eyes grey in the red, dust-filmed face. He looked pleased. 'It's grand to see you out here again, sir. How are you?' He wiped his hand on the seat of his shorts and held it out.

Gorde ignored the hand, ignored the warmth and friendliness of the other's tone. 'Who gave you orders to run a survey here?'

Entwhistle hesitated, dropped his hand. He looked momentarily off-balance, uncertain of himself.

'Was it Erkhard?'

'No, sir. To be honest, Sir Philip, nobody gave me orders.'

'Then what the hell are you doing here? You're a hundred miles from your survey area.'

'Aye, I know that.' He ran his hand a little nervously over his face. 'It isn't easy to explain. You see—' He hesitated. 'I was the chap who carried out the ground search for David Whitaker. You know about that, do you?'

Gorde nodded. 'Go on,' he said, his voice flat. 'And make it short. I haven't any time to waste.'

But Entwhistle wasn't the sort of man to be browbeaten. 'If it comes to that, Sir Philip, I don't have any time to waste myself. I want to run this survey and get the hell out of here as fast as I can.' His tone was obstinate. 'This isn't what you'd call a healthy place. I got here two days ago and we hadn't been camped twenty-four hours before we had a visit from a bunch of Bedou. They didn't behave like nomads; more like the Emir's men. Though we're still in Saraifa here.'

'The Saraifa concession was abandoned four years ago,' Gorde said sharply. 'You've no right here. None whatever.'

'I'm well aware of that, Sir Philip.'

'Then why are you here?'

Entwhistle hesitated, rubbing gently at a desert sore that showed red and ugly beneath the sweat stain of his right armpit. 'You never met David Whitaker, did you, sir?'

'What's that got to do with it?'

'Oh, well—' He hesitated, and then, unable apparently to put it into words, he sought refuge in facts: 'I couldn't exactly say it in my report of the search. It would have put the Company on the spot, if you see what I mean. But there was something fishy about that truck there on a sand dune across the border into Saudi. There was nought wrong with it mechanically, you know. It was just out of fuel as though he'd driven it straight into the Empty Quarter until he'd no more petrol. And if you'd known David—' Again the hesitation, and then a quick shrug. 'He knew the desert – knew it a damn' sight better than I'll ever know it. What was he doing there, that's what I'd like to know? If he'd been scared out of here by the Emir's men, why didn't he head for Saraifa?'

'Come to the point,' Gorde said impatiently. 'I want to know why you're here.'

'Aye. Well, I went over every inch of that truck. I thought if there'd been foul play or anything like that, he'd have left some clue, something that a chap like myself, a fellow geophysicist, would understand. The only thing I found was an old attaché case full of correspondence and copies of survey reports. One of those reports concerned this area.'

'I don't seem to remember reading that in the account you sent to Erkhard.'

'No.'

'You thought you'd keep it to yourself, eh? Thought you'd check on his findings on the quiet?'

Entwhistle scratched uncomfortably at the sore. 'He was on loan to his father, you see. It didn't concern the Company exactly. And he seemed so sure he'd—'

'It never occurred to you, I suppose, that there's a political factor?'

Entwhistle's grey eyes stared at Gorde without flinching. 'David Whitaker was a good bloke. I don't know whether he sent a copy of that survey report to the Bahrain Office or not; and I don't care. Nobody had done anything about it. Not even his father. He was out on his own and he thought he was on to something. I spent the better part of a week searching the desert for his body, and it seemed to me if I couldn't give him a headstone, I might at least see if he was right and we could name an oilfield after him. Maybe it sounds a little crazy to you, Sir Philip,' he added almost belligerently, 'but I just felt it was up to me to do something. I don't like to see a good chap's life thrown away for nothing. And if Erkhard kicks me off the Company's payroll as a result, I shan't cry my eyes out.'

Gorde didn't say anything for a moment. He seemed lost in thought. 'How far have you got with the check?' he asked at length.

'There are four locations given as probable anticlines in the report. I've done a check on the most south-easterly – Location D, he called it. Now I've just begun drilling the first shot-hole on Location C. If you care to come to the truck I can show you David Whitaker's report. Or has Mr Erkhard already shown it to you?'

'No, he hasn't. Nevertheless,' Gorde added, 'I've seen a copy. Grant here was kind enough to show it to me.' This on a note of irony, and he introduced me then. 'A lawyer. Like you, he wants to know what young Whitaker was doing across the border into Saudi.' He turned to me. 'I don't suppose you've ever seen a seismological truck, have you?' And when I shook my head, he said, 'Well, if you want to see the sort of work David Whitaker was engaged on, I'm sure Entwhistle would show you over his vehicle.' He turned back to Entwhistle. 'No point in stopping you in the middle of drilling a shot-hole. You can finish the check on your Location C. Then you're to pull out. Understand?'

'Yes, sir.' Relief and something akin to affection showed for an instant in Entwhistle's face.

'Results to be sent direct to me. And now take Grant to your truck and show him how it works. Meanwhile, I'll write a letter for you to Sheikh Makhmud, just in case. I don't doubt he knows you're here.' He stood back from the door. 'Ten minutes,' he said to me. 'All right? And then I want to find Charles Whitaker's rig; find out why he isn't drilling here if his son was so damn' sure.'

I nodded. I didn't even hesitate. I was being given the opportunity of ten minutes alone with Entwhistle. I jumped out of the plane and it was like jumping into the full glare of an open-hearth furnace. Entwhistle remained a moment talking to Gorde, and when he joined me in the Land Rover he glanced at me curiously so that I wondered what Gorde had told him about me. Stones rattled against the rusted mudguards as we batted over the gravel towards the truck which seemed to be standing in a pool of water. The mirage only lifted when we were within a hundred yards of it.

I was more interested in Entwhistle than in the mechanics of his seismological equipment, and as soon as we were in the shade of the truck's interior, I asked him what he thought had happened to David. 'I suppose there's no chance that he's still alive?'

It didn't seem to surprise him that I'd made the suggestion. 'Did you see my personal report to Erkhard, or was it some sort of a composite thing rehashed by the Bahrain Office?' he asked.

'It was a general report,' I told him.

'Aye, I thought so. They'll be letting the dust collect on mine in some pigeon-hole. Can't blame them. I made it pretty plain what I thought.' He hesitated, rubbing his hand across the ginger stubble on his chin. 'A rum do, and no mistake. There was that truck half-buried in sand and about forty miles from the nearest waterhole. And nothing wrong with the damned thing but lack of petrol. Even the spare jerry-cans were empty.'

'What are you suggesting?' I asked.

He hesitated. 'I don't rightly know,' he muttered, eyeing me cautiously. 'But I know this,' he added with sudden violence; 'a chap like David doesn't drive into waterless desert with empty fuel cans. And to run out of juice just there . . . except for the centre of the Empty Quarter he couldn't have picked a spot that was much farther from water.' He stared at me and I think we were both thinking the same thing, for he said, 'I'd like to know what his father thinks about it. In fact, when I've finished here I intend to drive over to Saraifa and see if the old Bedou knows—' He stopped and cocked his head on one side, listening. Faint through the noise of the drill came the distant sound of an engine. I didn't understand at first, but then it grew louder, over-topping the noise of the drill, and in a sudden panic of realisation, I dived for the door, just in time to see the plane become airborne.

It passed so low over the top of the truck that I instinctively ducked, and as I straightened up I was cursing myself for a fool. I should have known. I should have realized Gorde might want to get me out of the way. I turned furiously on Entwhistle, who was standing in the doorway of the truck looking slightly uncomfortable. 'You knew about this?'

'Aye, he told me.' He smiled a little doubtfully. 'He asked me to give you his apologies for any inconvenience.'

'God rot the old man!' I muttered savagely. To be

caught like that, to be fooled into thinking he was just trying to be helpful, and all the time—

I stared at the plane, which was rapidly dwindling to a speck, feeling suddenly helpless, isolated out here in an oven-hot world that I didn't understand. 'A day or two, he said,' Entwhistle murmured apologetically. 'That's all. I'll try and make it as pleasant as possible.'

The plane had altered course. I saw it circle once and then it was heading back towards us and for a wild moment I thought perhaps he'd changed his mind. It came in low, flying slowly with the flaps down. But the under-carriage remained up. As it bumbled close over our heads something white fluttered down from the pilot's window. And then it turned and disappeared low over the dunes, and the sound of it was lost again in the noise of the drill.

Entwhistle was already running to retrieve the object they had dropped to us. He came back with a cigarette packet and a crumpled sheet of paper. 'All right. You can stop drilling,' he shouted. He repeated the order in Arabic and as the drill slowed to an abrupt silence, he handed me the paper. On it was written in pencil: *Stop drilling and proceed at once to Saraifa. Concentration of armed tribesmen camped in the dunes two miles north of you. Warn Sheikh Makhmud and give him my salaams. Philip Gorde.* A chill feeling crept up my spine as I read that message, and Entwhistle's comment did nothing to restore my morale. 'Bit of luck, the Old Man flying down here.' He flipped the coin that Otto had used to weight the packet. 'Mightn't have seen the sun rise tomorrow otherwise.'

It came as a shock to me to realize that he was perfectly serious. 'They would have attacked you?' I asked.

'Slit our throats, probably.' He sounded quite cheerful.

'But—' I looked about me, at the dunes asleep in the heat of the day, the furnace-hot world of the desert all around me, quiet and peaceful. It was hard to believe. 'But you're still on Saraifa territory,' I said.

He shrugged. 'The Emir would dispute that. And the political boys, all those bloody old Etonians – they don't want any trouble. My name's going to be mud.' He stared down at the coin in his hand. And then he put it in his pocket and set about organizing the packing up of the outfit, leaving me standing there, feeling slightly lost, a stranger in a strange world.

THE DOOMED
OASIS

His crew were all Arab and they went about the business of breaking camp noisily but efficiently. They had done it many times. In fact, it seemed a natural process out there amongst the dunes. They were mostly young men, a colourful mixture of race and dress, their teeth flashing white in their dark faces as they fooled around, making light of the work. They were fit and full of life and laughter; they had a football which they kicked at each other periodically, the guttural Arab tongue coming in staccato bursts from their lips.

There was nothing for me to do and I sat perched on the Land Rover's mudguard, watching them and looking around me at the surrounding country. There was a dune, I remember, that ran away into the distance like the Prescelly hills north of St David's. I was looking at it, thinking of holidays I had spent in that part of Wales, and suddenly my eyes became riveted on a dark speck that showed for an instant on its back.

It vanished almost immediately so that I thought my eyes had played me a trick. In that shimmering heat it was difficult to be sure. And then it showed again, nearer this time. I could have sworn it was a man moving below the crest of the dune. I was just on the point of telling Entwhistle that he had a visitor when I was jolted off my seat; the clang of metal against metal was followed instantly by the crack of a rifle, and I was looking down at a hole the size of my fist in the side of the Land Rover's bonnet.

For an instant everything was still. There was no sound, no movement; Entwhistle and his Arabs just stood there, shocked into immobility, staring at that hole in the side of the Land Rover. Then Entwhistle shouted something. Rifles cracked from the top of the dune, little spurts of sand were kicked up round us. A bullet ricocheted off the truck's drill and went whining past my head. Entwhistle flung himself at the Land Rover. 'Jump in!' he shouted. His crew were running for the truck. Another bullet smacked into the Land Rover, so close that the wind of it fanned my trouser legs, and then I heard shouts, saw men running towards us from the line of the dunes. The engines burst into life, drowning all other sounds. I dived for the seat beside Entwhistle as he slammed the Land Rover into gear. Two Arabs landed almost on top of me as the vehicle jerked forward. Behind us the truck was moving, too, and beyond its lumbering shape I caught a glimpse of long-haired tribesmen dropping on to their knees, aiming their rifles. But I never heard the shots. All I could hear was the revving of the engine as Entwhistle ran through the gears.

A moment later and we were clear, out of their range. The two Arabs sorted themselves out and I turned to Entwhistle. His foot was hard down on the accelerator and his lips were moving. 'The bastards!' he was saying. 'The bloody bastards!' And then he looked at me. 'Dum-dum bullets.' His face was white under the sunburn. 'They cut them across to make them soft nosed. Blow a hole in you the size of a barn door.' It was this rather than the attack that seemed to outrage him.

'Who were they?' I asked, and was shocked to find that I hadn't proper control over my voice.

'The Emir's men. They must have seen the plane turn back and realized we were being warned of their presence.' He turned to make certain that the truck was following. 'Fine introduction you've had to desert life.' He grinned, but not very certainly. He shouted something in Arabic to the two men perched on the baggage behind and they answered him with a flood of words. Shortly afterwards he pulled up. The truck drew up beside us, its engine throbbing, excited Arab faces looking down at us, all talking at once.

He got out then and spoke to the driver, walked all round the truck and then came back and lifted the bonnet of the Land Rover. 'Look at that,' he said. I got out and my legs felt weak as I stared at the hole that first bullet had made. Little bits of lead were spattered all over the engine. 'Bastards!' he said and slammed the bonnet shut. 'Well, it might have been worse, I suppose. Nobody's hurt and the vehicles are all right.'

It was only after we'd got moving again that I realized the windscreen in front of me was shattered. Little bits of glass were falling into my lap. I kept my eyes half-closed until I had picked out all the bits. 'How far is it to Saraifa?' I asked him.

'Not much more than forty miles by air.' I gathered it was a good deal more the way we'd have to go, for the dunes ran south-east and we had to get east. 'Might make it shortly after dark if we don't get bogged down too often.'

It was just after four-thirty then. We kept to the gravel flats between the dunes, travelling at almost thirty miles an hour. The air that came rushing in through the shattered windscreen was a hot, searing blast that scorched the face. The ground was hard as iron, criss-crossed with innumerable ridges over which the Land Rover rattled in an endless series of back-breaking jolts.

In these circumstances conversation wasn't easy; the wind of our movement, the noise of the engine, the rattle of stones – we had to shout to make ourselves heard. And Entwhistle wasn't a talkative man. He'd lived on his own too much. Besides, he had a North Countryman's lack of imagination. He even used the word 'humdrum' when I asked him about his job. And yet I got the impression that he loved it. But it was the job, not Arabia he loved. He'd no feeling for the country or its people. More than once he used the contemptuous term 'wogs' when speaking of the Arabs.

But though he wouldn't talk about himself much, he was quite prepared to talk about David.

He had met him three times in all; once in Bahrain and then later when he was sick and David had relieved him. 'Queer chap,' he said. 'Fact is I didn't like him much when he came out to take over my outfit. But then,' he added, 'you don't like anybody very much when you're suffering from jaundice.'

'But you felt differently about him later?' I prompted.

'Aye. Got to know him a bit better then. We were two days together whilst we moved to a new location. Then he went off to Saraifa. He'd got some leave due and he was going to spend it mucking around with an old seismological truck his father had got hold of.' I asked him what had made him change his mind about David, and he said, 'Oh, the way he talked. He was a great talker. Mind you,' he added, 'he was still too chummy with the wogs for my liking, but you couldn't help admiring the chap. Wanted to make the desert blossom and all that.'

'Water?' I asked.

He nodded. 'That's it. He'd got a bee-in-his-bonnet about it. Talked about Saraifa being doomed. Well, of course, it is. I've only been there once, but – well, you'll see for yourself. A few more years—' He didn't talk for a while after that, for we had come to soft sand; he took it fast, his foot pressed hard down on the accelerator, and we bucketed through it like a small boat in a seaway.

We came off the sand on to a hard gravel pan that

scintillated with a myriad diamond gleams. 'Mica,' he shouted. The glare of it was dazzling. 'You interested in geology?'

I shook my head.

'Pity.' He seemed genuinely sorry. 'Damned interesting country.' For him there was nothing else of interest in Arabia. We bucked another stretch of sand, ridged into shallow waves, and then he told me what had decided him to check David's survey report. Amongst the papers in that attaché case he had found Farr's report. 'Didn't tell the Old Man. Thought I'd keep it in reserve. God knows where David dug it up. It was twenty years old, the paper all faded; the typing too. Could hardly read the damned thing.'

'Have you got it with you?' I asked.

'Aye.' He nodded. 'I wasn't going to leave that behind. I'll show it to you later. Can't think why the Company didn't do something about it.'

'There was a war on,' I said. 'And Farr was killed in Abyssinia.'

'You know about it then?' He seemed surprised.

'David referred to it in his report.'

'Oh yes, of course.'

We hit another patch of sand, a solid vista of it that stretched interminably ahead of us. We didn't talk much after that. It was soft sand and the going was tough. Twice the seismological truck got bogged down and we had to lay sand mats. The sun sank slowly down into the desert behind us as we ploughed on, engines roaring, radiators steaming. We were in big dune country that was like a huge, petrified sea, the waves coming up one after the other, yet never moving, always motionless, and the shadows lengthening behind them. It had an eerie, still quality; and it left me with a sense of awe, for it had a certain majesty, a cruel, lost quality that was unnerving. Once I shouted, 'Is it like this all the way to Saraifa?'

'Christ! I hope not,' he yelled back.

'But don't you know?' I asked.

'How the hell should I? Never been here before.'

The sun set, a brick-red ball of fire, hazed it seemed with dust. Here and there we came upon the derelict remains of trees, gnarled and twisted in a life-long struggle against crippling odds. Dusk descended swiftly and the light faded out of the dunes. Behind us they stood like downlands etched sharp against the sky's last light. Above us the stars suddenly appeared. Again the truck behind us became bogged and we dug the sand mats down in front of the wheels and pushed and strained to gain a few yards. And when at last we got it moving there was no light left and it was dark.

'Will you be able to find Saraifa in the dark?' I asked Entwhistle.

'*Inshallah*,' he said, and we pushed on.

How he did it I don't know, but about an hour later the dunes became smaller, the stunted tree-growth more noticeable, and then suddenly we ran out on to hard gravel again. And shortly after that the headlights picked up the first of the date gardens, a sad relic of a once fertile place, the walls no longer visible, just the starved tops of the palms sticking up out of the sand.

We passed between two of these ruined gardens and then we joined a well-worn track where the sand had been ground to a fine powder; there were the marks of tyres, the droppings of camels. The headlights picked out the round bulk of a watch tower with men running from it, their guns gleaming with silver furnishings. Entwhistle slowed as they stood, barring our path. They wore turbans and long white robes and strapped across their shoulders was a sort of harness of leather studded with the brass of cartridges; stuffed into their belts were the broad, curved-bladed *khanjar* knives, the hilts of silver glinting wickedly. As we stopped they came swarming over us, enveloping us with their harsh guttural speech, all talking at once, white teeth flashing in villainous dark faces.

'What do they want?' A black-bearded ruffian had the muzzle of his gun jammed against the side of my neck, and though I tried to keep my voice under control I don't think I was very successful.

'All right, all right,' Entwhistle was shouting at them. 'One at a time for God's sake.' He didn't seem in the least bit scared. Finally, after a long conversation with my bearded friend, he said, 'It looks like trouble. We're more or less under arrest.' He spoke to the bearded Arab again and then he was ordering men on to the Land Rover and others to the truck behind. 'It seems,' he said as we moved off, 'that Sheikh Makhmud sent a party out in two Land Rovers this afternoon to arrest my outfit and bring me back to Saraifa for questioning.' And he added, 'This could be the sort of thing David came up against. They're scared stiff of the Emir and frightened to death of any activity on the Hadd border.'

'Didn't you know that before you decided to run a survey there?' I asked.

'Of course I did. But I was reckoning to run the survey and get out before anyone discovered I was there.' He crashed the gears savagely. 'I took a chance and it didn't come off, that's all.'

We skirted the crumbling wall of a date garden. The palms were green here, the gardens uninvaded by the desert sand. And then suddenly we were in the open, driving on hard gravel, and straight ahead of us, a black bulk against the stars, was the shadowy shape of the Sheikh's palace standing like a fortress on its hill. The wooden gate of the arched entrance was closed, but it opened to the cries of our guards, and then we were inside, in a great courtyard packed with men and camels and lit by the flames of cooking fires. In an instant we were surrounded, lapped round by a tide of men, all shouting and brandishing their weapons.

A big, portly man appeared, his face black as a Sudanese. 'The Sheikh's secretary,' Entwhistle said to me. He looked like a eunuch, fat and soft, his manner almost feminine. He gave orders for the care of the men and then escorted us into the palace, along dark corridors sparsely lit by smoking lamps made out of old cans, to a small room that looked out on to a central courtyard. Here the earthen floor was carpeted with rugs, the walls lined with cushions; an Arab rose to greet us. He was a compact, stocky man with almost black eyes and a proudly curved nose. The *khanjar* knife stuck in the girdle of his finely-woven robe was a beautiful example of the silversmith's craft. 'Sheikh Makhmud,' Entwhistle whispered.

I found my hand held in a firm grip. 'You are welcome to Saraifa,' the Sheikh said in halting English. 'My house is your house.' He had an air of command, yet his voice was gentle. But the thing that surprised me most was the fact that he wore glasses. They were silver-rimmed glasses and they drew attention to the blackness of his eyes. His clean-shaven face was long and tired-looking. He was a man of about Gorde's age, I suppose. The other occupant of the room had also risen, a thin man with a greying moustache and a little pointed beard, his eyes heavily made up with *kohl*. He was Makhmud's brother, Sultan.

We sat cross-legged on the cushions and there was nothing in the Sheikh's manner to indicate that we were anything but honoured guests. Polite conversation was made, partly in the Arab language, partly in English. Slaves came with a silver jug and a silver ewer. We washed our hands and then they brought in a simple dish of rice and mutton. 'You eat with your right hand,' Entwhistle whispered to me, and I tried to copy his practised movements.

I was hungry enough not to care that the meat was stringy and over-fat. We ate almost in silence and when we had finished, the hand-washing was repeated and then coffee was served in little handleless cups, poured by a slave from a silver pot of intricate native design. And with the coffee came the questions. Sheikh

Makhmud's voice was no longer gentle. It had a harsh, imperious quality, and Entwhistle was soon in difficulties with the language, lapsing periodically into English as he tried to explain his presence on the Saraifa-Hadd border. In the end he passed Sheikh Makhmud the note Gorde had written.

Entwhistle had just launched into an account of the attack that had been made on us when a young man entered. He was short, well-built, and beneath his brown cloak he wore an old tweed jacket. But it was the features that caught the eye; they were delicate, almost classic features, the nose straight, the eyes set wide apart, with high cheek-bones and the full lips framed by a neatly trimmed moustache that flowed round the corners and down into a little pointed beard. He looked as though he had just come in from the desert and I knew instinctively that this was Khalid, the Sheikh's son; he had an air about him that showed he was born to command.

He greeted his father and his uncle, waved us to remain seated and folded himself up on a cushion against the wall. The brass of cartridge belt, the silver of *khanjar* knife gleamed beneath the jacket. He sat in silence, listening intently, his body so still that I was given the impression of great muscular control – a hard-sinewed body below the Arab robes.

There was a long silence when Entwhistle had finished. And then Sheikh Makhmud made what sounded like a pronouncement, and Entwhistle exclaimed: 'Good God! I'm not going to do that.' He turned to me. 'He wants us to go to the Emir and explain that we were on the border without authority.'

'You go freely,' Sheikh Makhmud said in English. 'Or you go with escort. Which you prefer?'

Entwhistle didn't say anything. His face was set and pale.

'Is very difficult this situation,' the Sheikh said almost apologetically. 'Very dangerous also. You must make the Emir understand please.'

'Very dangerous for us, too,' Entwhistle muttered angrily.

'I don't want any trouble.'

'You want oil, don't you?'

'Colonel Whitaker is already drilling for oil.'

'Then what was his son doing on the Hadd border?' Entwhistle demanded. 'He ran a survey there. He wrote a report. And then he vanished.' There was no answer. 'Khalid. You were his friend. What happened to him?'

But Khalid was staring out into the courtyard.

In the silence I heard myself say, 'He got a letter through to me just before he disappeared. He knew he was going to die.' I felt then stiffen, the silence suddenly intense. I looked at Khalid. 'Did he die a natural death?' His eyes met mine for a moment and then fell away. 'Somebody here must know how he died – and why.'

Nobody answered and the stillness of those three Arabs scared me. It was the stillness of unease. 'Where's Colonel Whitaker?' I asked.

The Sheikh stirred uncomfortably. 'You are full of questions. Who are you?'

Briefly I explained. I was still explaining when there was a sudden uproar in the passage outside and a man burst into the room, followed closely by the Sheikh's secretary. A staccato burst of Arabic and they were all suddenly on their feet. I heard the word *falaj* run from mouth to mouth, saw Khalid rush out, quick as a cat on his feet. His father followed more slowly, the others crowding behind him.

'What is it?' I asked Entwhistle. 'What's happened?'

'One of the *falajes*, I don't know exactly but for some reason the water has stopped.'

We were alone now. Everybody had forgotten about us. It was as though that word had some sort of magic in it. 'What exactly is a *falaj*?' He didn't seem to hear me and I repeated the question.

'*Falaj*?' He seemed to drag his mind back. 'Oh, it's the water system on which the date gardens depend. The water comes from the mountains of the Jebel anything up to thirty miles away and it's piped into Saraifa by underground channels.'

'And the underground channels are the *falajes*?'

'Yes, that's it. They're centuries old – a Persian irrigation system. In fact, they're the same as the Persian *quantas*.' He went to the passage and stood listening. 'Bit of luck,' he said, dropping his voice to a whisper. 'If we can get hold of the Land Rover—' He grabbed hold of my arm. 'Come on.'

I followed him down the dimly lit mud corridors

and out into the courtyard. The cooking fires still smoked. The camels still crouched in a shapeless, belching huddle under the walls. But in the whole courtyard there wasn't a single Arab to be seen. 'Look! Even the guard on the gate has gone.'

'But why?' I asked. 'Why should that word—?'

'Water. Don't you understand?' He sounded impatient. 'Water is life here in the desert.'

'But they can't depend on one channel. There must be many to irrigate a place like this.'

'Five or six, that's all.' He was searching the courtyard. 'There used to be more than a hundred once. But tribal wars—' He gripped my arm. 'There's the Land Rover. Over by the wall there.' He pointed. 'Come on! There's just a chance—'

'What's the idea?' I asked.

'Get out whilst the going's good. Hurry, man!' His voice was high-pitched, urgent. 'I'm not risking my neck on a mission of explanation to that bloody Emir.' He had seized hold of my arm again. 'Quick!'

I started to follow him, but then I stopped. 'I'm staying,' I said.

'Christ, man! Do you want to get killed?'

'No, but I want to find out why that boy was killed.'

He stared at me. 'You think it was like that – that he was murdered?'

'I don't know,' I said. I didn't know anything for certain. 'But I'm not leaving here until I've seen Colonel Whitaker.'

He hesitated. But then he shrugged his shoulders.

'Okay. It's your funeral, as you might say. But watch your step,' he added. 'He's a tricky bastard by all accounts. And if what you're suggesting is true and David was murdered, then your life wouldn't be worth much, would it?'

'I'll be all right,' I said.

'Aye, I hope so. But just remember you're right on the edge of Saudi Arabia here and the British Raj is worn a bit thin in these parts.' He hesitated, looking at me, and then he started towards the Land Rover.

I stood and watched him, certain I was being a fool, but equally certain that I wasn't leaving. I saw him jump into the driving seat, heard the whine of the starter, the roar of the engine. And then the Land Rover was moving and he swung it round and came tearing towards me. 'Jump in, Grant,' he shouted, as he pulled up beside me. 'Hurry, man! Hurry!'

'No,' I said. 'I'm not leaving.' My voice was like the voice of a stranger to me. 'You get out whilst you can. I'll be all right.' And I added, 'I'll make your excuses to the Sheikh for you.' I meant it to be a jocular, carefree remark, but my voice sounded hollow. He was still hesitating and I said quickly, 'Good luck to you!'

He stared at me hard and then he gave a little nod. 'Okay. I expect you'll be all right. I'll notify the authorities, of course.' And he slammed in the gear and went roaring across the courtyard and out through the empty gateway. The cloud of dust he'd raised gradually settled and I walked to the gate and stood there watching his headlights threading a luminous trail through the date gardens. And when they finally disappeared in the open desert beyond, I went slowly down the hill, heading for the murmur of voices, the glimmer of lights amongst the palms beyond the village.

I was alone then – more alone than I'd ever been in my life before.

The moon was just risen and with the stars the village was lit by a soft translucence. The mud buildings were pale and empty, the open square deserted save for the hens nested in the dust and a solitary sad-looking donkey. Beyond the village I followed the crumbling wall of a date garden until I came out into the open again. All Saraifa seemed gathered there, the men bunched together like a crowd at a cock-fight, the women dark bundles flitting on the edge of the crowd or squatting like hens in the sand. Everybody was talking at once, a thick hubbub of sound that seemed to lose itself instantly in the great solitude of the desert that stretched away to the east, to the dimly-seen line of the mountains.

Nobody took any notice of me as I skirted the crowd. It was thickest close by the date garden. Out towards the desert it thinned, and here I found a raised water channel built of rock and spanning a hollow Roman aqueduct. It was my first sight of a *falaj*; and it was empty. I leaned over it, touched the inside with my fingers. It was still damp and in a little puddle of water at the bottom tiny fish flashed silver in the starlight as they gasped for breath. Clearly the water had only recently ceased to flow, turned off as though by a tap.

Fascinated, I crossed the hollow to the far side. For perhaps twenty yards the *falaj* was open, a neat, vertical-sided trench running a black shadow line across the sand. It was about two feet across and the same deep. I walked along it to the point where it was roofed over. For a hundred yards or so I could trace the outline of it, but after that the sand swallowed it up entirely. From a slight rise I looked towards the mountains. Anything up to thirty miles, Entwhistle had said, and they were the source of the water.

I walked slowly back along the line of the *falaj*, to the point where it broke surface, and at the sight of the empty trough with the little fish gasping out their lives, I could understand the calamity of it, the sense of disaster that had seized upon the people of this channel-fed oasis. A dry *falaj* meant a ruined date garden, the beginnings of famine. Only five or six left out of more than a hundred, tribal wars . . . The place was as vulnerable as an oil refinery fed by a desert pipeline. Cut the *falaj* and Saraifa ceased to exist.

The sound of male voices died away, leaving only the high-pitched chatter of the women; there was a stillness of decision as I approached the crowd gathered about the *falaj* channel where it entered the date garden. In the centre stood Sheikh Makhmud and his brother Sultan. Khalid was facing them, arguing fiercely. His features had no trace of effeminacy in them now. From the skirts of the crowd I saw Sheikh Makhmud turn impatiently away from his son. He called a man forth by name – Mahommed bin Rashid; a fierce, hawk-faced man with a black beard, the one who had stopped us as we entered Saraifa. He gave him an order and a long *A-a-agh* of satisfaction issued from the throats of the crowd. Instantly all was confusion. Men brandished their weapons, calling on Allah, as a dozen or more of them were singled out and went hurrying back to the palace. Sheikh Makhmud turned and with his brother and his secretary followed them slowly.

It was the signal for the crowd to break up, and as they straggled away from the empty *falaj*, Khalid was left standing there alone. A few men only remained, a little, compact group of silent followers ranged behind him. They were different from the rest in that their arms were without any silver trappings; they carried British service-pattern rifles.

He stood for a long time without moving, staring after his father and the crowd that followed him, noisy now with the excitement of action. And when they had disappeared from sight he turned to his men with a gesture of dismissal and they, too, moved away, but still silent, still in a compact group. He was completely alone then, staring down at the empty water channel, lost in his own thoughts. Even when I approached him he didn't stir. I don't think he knew I was there, for when I asked him whether he spoke English, he turned to me with a start of surprise.

'A little English – yess.' His speech was slightly sibilant, his features marred when he opened his mouth by long, widely-spaced teeth. 'I am at Bombay

University, my education.' He was staring up the hill towards the palace, his mind still on what had happened. 'They think they are being brave and that I am afraid. They don't understand.' His tone was bitter and angry. 'Their guns are very much old and the men of Hadd will be waiting for them.'

I asked whether it was Hadd who had stopped the water supply and he said, 'Yess. They perpetrate it once before. Then the British help us. Your people send soldiers with automatic guns and mortars. But not now. This time we are alone.'

He turned and I saw his dark eyes, sad in the starlight. 'The *falajes* you understand, sir, are very much vulnerable.' He had acquired the Indian penchant for long words. And he added with great determination, speaking slowly as though stating something to himself, 'We must fight for them now. But not like this. This way is to die.' He began to walk slowly towards the palace.

There were many things I wanted to ask him, but this didn't seem the moment and I walked beside him in silence, conscious of his preoccupation. His head was bent and he moved slowly, his sandals dragging in the sand. He was only two years older than David. I learned that later. Yet his manner was that of a man upon whom the whole responsibility for this desert community rested. 'Do you know Arabia much, sir?' he asked suddenly. And when I told him this was my first visit and that I'd only arrived a few days ago, he nodded and said, 'You are from a town called Cardiff, yess? David speak of you sometimes.'

That mention of Cardiff, the knowledge that this young Arab knew who I was . . . Saraifa seemed suddenly less remote, my position here less solitary. 'When David first come here, he is like you; he speak Arabic a little, but he don't understand our customs or the way we live here in the desert. The *falajes* mean nothing to him and he has never seen the big dunes when the *shamal* is blowing.' He had stopped and he was smiling at me. Despite the wide-spaced, fang-like teeth it was a gentle smile. 'I am glad you come now.' He offered me his hand and I found my wrist gripped and held in a strong clasp. 'You are David's friend and I will see that no harm come to you.'

I thanked him, conscious that he had given me the opening I needed. But already I was becoming vaguely aware of the subtlety of the Arab mind and this time I was determined not to make the mistake of asking direct questions. Sue's words came unconsciously into my mind. 'David wanted to defend Saraifa, too.' I saw his face soften as he nodded and I asked, 'What was it about this place that so captured his imagination? His sister said he could be very emotional about it.'

'His sister?' He smiled. 'I have seen his sister once, when I am taking a plane at Sharjah. She is with the doctor and I do not speak. A very fine person I think.'

I knew then that David had spoken of Sue to Khalid. 'What is there about Saraifa,' I said, 'that he fell in love with it the way other men do with a woman?'

He shrugged. 'He came here for refuge and we

made him welcome. Also his father live here. It became his home.'

But that didn't explain it entirely. 'It was something more than that,' I said.

'Yess.' He nodded. 'Is a very strange chap. A *Nasrani* – a Christian. He live very much by your Book, the Bible.' That surprised me, but before I could make any comment, he added, 'I should hate him because he is an infidel. Instead, I love him like my own brother.' He shook his head with a puzzled frown. 'Perhaps it is because I have to teach him everything. When he first come here, he knows nothing – he has never hunted, never owned a hawk; he does not know how to ride a camel or how to make a camp in the desert. For six months we are living together, here in Saraifa, in the desert hunting, up in the mountains shooting wild hare and gazelle. But he is very good with machines and later, when he is on leave from the Oil Company and we are working for the reconstruction of one of the old *falajes*, then he spend all his time down in the underground channels with the family who specialize in that work. You see, sir, this oasis is one time very much bigger with very many *falajes* bringing water to the date gardens. Then Saraifa is rich. Richer than Buraimi to the north. Richer perhaps even than the Wadi Hadhramaut to the south. It is, I think, the richest place in all Arabia. But nobody can remember that time. Now it is—' He stopped abruptly, his head on one side listening.

And then I heard it, too – the soft pad-pad of camels' feet on gravel. Down the slope towards us came a bunch of camels moving with that awkward, lumbering gait. A dozen dark shapes swayed past us, the riders kneeling in the saddles, their robes flying, their rifles held in their hands. For an instant they were like paper cut-outs painted black against the stars, beautiful, balanced silhouettes. Then they were gone and the pad of their camels' feet faded away into the sand as they headed towards the mountains.

'*Wallahi, qalilet-el-mukh!*' Khalid muttered as he stared after them. And then to me: 'That man, Mahommed bin Rashid. You heard him when my father give the order. *Inshallah*, he said, we will kill every harlot's son of them. But he is more like to die himself, I think.' And he turned away, adding as he strode angrily up the hill, 'Allah give him more brain in the world hereafter.'

The sight of that handful of men riding east into the desert along the line of the *falaj*, had changed his mood. He was preoccupied, and though I tried to resume our conversation, he didn't speak to me again until we reached the gates of the palace. Abruptly he asked me what sleeping quarters I had been allotted. And when I told him none, he said, 'Then I arrange it. Excuse my father please. He is very much occupied.' He asked about Entwhistle. 'Good,' he said when I told him he'd gone. 'He is not a fool, that man. He knows when it is dangerous.' And he added, 'It would have been better perhaps if you had gone with him.'

'I'm not leaving here,' I said, 'until I know what happened to David.'

There was a moment then when he hesitated as

though about to tell me something. But all he said was, 'Is best you talk to his father – *Haj* Whitaker.'

'I intend to,' I said. And when I asked him whether Colonel Whitaker was in Saraifa, he replied, 'I don't know. He has his house here, but is most times at the place of drilling.'

'And where's that?'

'To the south of 'ere, about ten miles towards Sheikh Hassa's village of Dhaid.'

We had entered the great courtyard. A man sidled up to us, made his salaams to Khalid. He was dark and toothy with a ragged wisp of a turban on his head, and his eyes watched me curiously as they talked together. My name was mentioned and finally Khalid turned to me. 'Now all is arranged. Yousif speak a little English. He will show you where you sleep.' His hand gripped my arm. 'Ask *Haj* Whitaker why he goes to see the Emir of Hadd almost two moons past. Ask him that, Meester Grant.' It was whispered to me, his lips close against my ear and a hard, angry glint in his eyes.

But before I could question him he had drawn back. He said something to Yousif and with a quick *Salaam alaikum* he left me, moving quickly through the camp fires, the only man in all that throng who wore a European jacket.

'Come!' Yousif seized hold of my hand. Heads were turned now in my direction and here and there a man got up from the fireside and began to move towards us. I had no desire to stay there, an object of curiosity. Yousif guided me through dark passages and up to a turret room by a winding staircase where the plaster steps were worn smooth as polished marble by the tread of many feet. The floor was bare earth, the roof beamed with palm tree boles. A slit of a window no bigger than a firing embrasure looked out on to the flat, beaten expanses of the village square. I was in one of the mud towers of the outer wall and here he left me with no light but the glimmer of moonlight filtering in through the embrasure.

Strange, disembodied sounds drifted up to me on the warm night air; the murmur of Arab voices, the grunt of camels, a child crying – and in the distance the weird chuckle of a hyena. I knelt on the firing step, peering down. Beyond the mud houses I could see the darker mass of the palms. Bare feet sounded on the turret stairs and the yellow light of a hurricane-lamp appeared: the room was suddenly full of armed men bearing bedding, which they laid on the floor – a carpet, some blankets, an oryx skin and a silken cushion. 'May Allah guard you,' Yousif said, 'and may your sleep be as the sleep of a little child.'

He was halfway through the door before I realized what that long speech in English must mean. 'You're Colonel Whitaker's man, aren't you?'

He checked and turned. 'Yes, sahib. Me driver for Coll-onel.' He was staring at me, his eyes very wide so that the whites showed yellow in the lamplight. 'I tell Coll-onel you are here in Sheikh's palace.' He was gone then.

There was no doubt in my mind that he'd been sent to find me. Whitaker was in Saraifa and Khalid had known it as soon as Yousif had sidled up to us. I sat down on the silken cushion, staring blindly at that cell-like room. There was nothing to do now but wait. I felt tired; dirty, too. But I'd no water with which to wash. No soap, no clothes – nothing but what I was wearing. Yousif had left me the hurricane lamp and its light reached dimly to the palm wood rafters. A large desert spider moved among them with deliberation. I watched it for a long time as it went about its unpleasant business, and finally I killed it, overcome with a fellow-feeling for the flies caught in its web. And then I put out the lamp and rolled myself up in a blanket.

It was hot, but I must have fallen asleep for I didn't hear Yousif return; he was suddenly there, his torch stabbing the darkness, almost blinding me. 'Coll-onel say you come.'

I sat up, glancing at my watch. It was past eleven-thirty.

'Now?'

'Yes, now.'

Down in the courtyard the fires were almost out, the Sheikh's retainers lying like corpses wrapped in their robes. A few stirred as we crossed to the gate, now barred and guarded; a brief argument and then I was in a battered Land Rover being driven at reckless speed across the deserted village square, down into the date gardens. Behind us the palace fort stood bone-white in the moonlight, and then the palms closed round us.

Whitaker's house was an old mud fort on the far

side of the oasis. Most of it seemed to be in ruins, the courtyard empty, the mud walls cracked and crumbling. There was sand everywhere as we hurried through a maze of passages and empty rooms. The place seemed dead and I wondered that a man could live alone like this and retain his sanity, for he seemed to have no servants but Yousif and to live in spartan simplicity in one corner of this vast, rambling building.

We came at last to a room where old portemanteaux and tin boxes stood ranged against the walls, and then I was out on a rooftop that looked out upon the desert. He was standing against the parapet, a tall, robed figure in silhouette, for there was no light there, only the moon and the stars. Yousif coughed and announced my presence.

Whitaker turned then and came towards me. His face was in shadow, but I could see the black patch over the eye. No word of greeting, no attempt to shake my hand. 'Sit down,' he said and waved imperiously to a carpet and some cushions spread on the floor. 'Yousif. *Gahwa*.' His servant disappeared and as I sat down I was conscious of the stillness all about us – no sound of Arab voices, none of the tumult of the Sheikh's palace, no murmur of the village below the walls. The place was as isolated, as deserted as though we were the only people in the whole oasis.

He folded himself up, cross-legged on the carpet facing me, and I could see his face then, the beard thinning and grey, the cheeks hollowed and lined by the desert years, that single imperious eye deep-sunken above the great nose. 'You had a good journey, I trust.'

His voice was oddly-pitched, hard but unusually high, and he spoke the words slowly as though English were no longer a familiar language.

'It was interesting,' I said.

'No doubt. But quite unnecessary. It was clearly understood between us that you would make no attempt to contact me direct. And though I admit the financial situation must have seemed—'

'I came about your son,' I said.

'My son?' He looked surprised. 'Your letter merely said you were worried about the amount of money I was spending.'

'Your son appointed me his Executor.'

He moved his head slightly, the eye glinting in the moonlight, bright and watchful. He didn't say anything. Behind him the low parapet hid the desert so that all I could see was the great vault of the night studded with stars. The air was deathly still, impregnated with the day's heat.

'I'm not convinced your son died a natural death.' I hadn't meant to put it like that. It was his stillness, the overpowering silence that had forced it out of me.

He made no comment and I knew that this was going to be more difficult than my interview with Erkhard, more difficult even than my meeting with Gorde, and some sixth sense warned me that this man was much more unpredictable. The clatter of cups came as a distinct relief. Yousif moved silently as a shadow on to the rooftop and poured us coffee from a battered silver pot. The cups were handleless, the Mocha coffee black and bitter. 'Does his mother know he's dead?' It surprised me that he should think of her; and when I told him that I'd broken the news to her myself, he asked, 'How did she take it?'

'She didn't believe it at first.' And because I had an overwhelming desire to break through his strange aura of calm, I added, 'In fact she seemed to think it was your own death I was reporting.'

'Why? Why did she think I was dead?'

'The stars,' I said. 'She believes in astrology.'

He sighed. 'Yes, I remember now. I used to talk to her about the stars.' And he added, 'It's a long time ago. A long time.'

'Do you believe in astrology then?' I asked.

He shrugged, sipping noisily at his coffee. 'Here in the desert we live a great deal by the stars. It is very difficult not to believe that they have some influence.' And then, abruptly changing the conversation: 'How did you get here? It's not easy to get to Saraifa.' I started to tell him, but as soon as I mentioned Gorde, he said, 'Philip Gorde? I didn't know he was out here.' It seemed to upset him. 'Did he tell you why he was here?' He mistook my silence. 'No, of course not. He'd hardly tell you that.' He shook his cup at Yousif to indicate that he'd had enough, and when I did the same the man departed as silently as he had come, leaving a dish of some sticky sweetmeat between us. '*Halwa*. Do you like it?' Whitaker made a vague gesture of invitation.

'I've never tried it.'

We were alone again now and the silence between us hung heavy as the thick night air, a blanket through which each tried to gauge the other. I let it drag out, and it was Whitaker who finally broke it. 'You were telling me about your journey.' He stared at me, waiting for me to continue. I broke off a piece of the *halwa*. It was cloying on the tongue and it had a sickly-sweet taste. 'You arrived here with Entwhistle, one of the Company's geologists. What was he doing on the Hadd border, do you know? The fellow had no business there.'

'He was checking your son's survey,' I said.

There was a sudden stillness. 'I see.' He said it quietly. And then, in a voice that was suddenly trembling with anger: 'On whose orders? Not Philip Gorde's surely?'

'No.'

'Erkhard?'

'You seem very worried about this?'

'Worried!' The word seemed forced out of him. 'Don't you understand what's happened here to-night? The thing I've been dreading. . . . The thing I've been trying to avoid ever since I knew—' He checked himself. And then in a quieter voice: 'No, you're new out here. You wouldn't understand. One of the *falajes* has been stopped. And all because of this blundering fool Entwhistle running a survey on the Hadd border.' His voice had risen again, trembling with anger.

'He was doing what David was doing at the time he disappeared,' I said quietly.

But it didn't seem to register. He had withdrawn into his own thoughts. 'Twenty years—' His voice sounded tired. And then his eye was staring at me again. 'How would you feel if the thing you'd worked for over a period of twenty years was in danger of being ruined by young fools too impatient to understand the politics of the desert?' He turned his head and stared for a moment into the night. 'The air is heavy. There'll be a storm soon.' He gathered his robes about him and rose to his feet, crossing to the parapet and leaning against it, staring out into the desert like some Biblical figure from the distant past. 'Come here, Grant.' And when I joined him, he stretched out his arm. 'Look, do you see those dunes?' He gripped my arm, pointing west into the desert.

Standing on that rooftop was like standing on the bridge of a ship lying anchored off a low-lying island. To the left lay the dark-treed expanse of the oasis, and beyond the date gardens I could see the village and the squat bulk of the Sheikh's palace standing on its gravel rise. But to the right, where his arm pointed, was nothing but desert. Dim in the moonlight the dunes stretched away into infinity, a ridged sea of sand, pale as milk. 'When you've seen a storm here you'll understand. Then all the desert seems in motion, like the sea beating against the shore of the oasis, flooding into the date gardens. The dunes smoke. They stream with sand. They're like waves breaking; the whole great desert of the Empty Quarter thundering in, the sand flowing like water.' He turned to me and his grip on my arm tightened. 'The only thing that stands between Saraifa and destruction is the camel thorn. Out there – do you see? Those trees. They're like a breakwater holding the sand sea back, and they're dying for lack of water.'

'The *falajes*?' I asked, and he nodded. 'Entwhistle said there used to be around a hundred of them.'

'Yes. We've traced them from aerial photographs.'

'Your son was very much concerned about—'

'Oh yes, concerned. . . . But he lacked patience. He was like a young bull. No subtlety. No subtlety at all.' And he added, 'What's been done to-night can be quickly repaired. There's an open well every mile or so along the length of the underground channel of the *falaj*. They've blocked one of these wells with sand and stone. It can be unblocked almost as quickly. But the old *falajes*—' He shook his head. 'The wells are fallen in, the underground channels collapsed. Restoring them is a lengthy and costly business. Sheikh Makhmud has managed to restore just one in the four-teen years he's been Sheikh of Saraifa. It took two years and cost more than twenty thousand pounds. If Saraifa is to survive—' He gave a little shrug. 'We need a dozen new *falajes*, not one.'

'And only oil will pay for them?'

He nodded. 'Yes.'

'David took the same view,' I said. 'That's why he was prospecting on the Hadd border.' And I added, 'What happened, Colonel Whitaker? What happened to your son?'

He turned and looked at me. 'You think I should know?'

'I've come a long way,' I said, 'in the certainty that you must know.'

His eyebrows lifted, the single eye stared at me, not blinking. 'The certainty?'

'Yes,' I said. 'The certainty.' And I added, 'He was on loan to you at the time he disappeared. It was the seismological truck you purchased in Basra last June that he left abandoned on the side of a dune twenty miles inside the borders of Saudi Arabia. And just before he disappeared, you visited the Emir of Hadd. You must know what happened.'

'Well, I don't.' He said it flatly and it was difficult not to accept it.

'Then why did you visit Hadd?'

'Who else could do it?' And he added, 'David was on the Hadd border against my orders, against Sheikh Makhmud's orders, too. Somebody had to try and convince the Emir there wasn't any oil there.'

'Because the border's in dispute?'

'Yes. There's been trouble there ever since the Company was first granted a concession to prospect in Saraifa. As you probably know, Saraifa is an independent sheikhdom. Unlike the Trucial States, it's not even in treaty relation with the British Crown, though it's generally considered to be a part of the British sphere of influence. Hadd is different again. It's independent in theory and in fact, and during the last few years it has strengthened its ties with Arab countries. Some years back we were finally driven to sending troops in, to keep the peace, and they occupied the fort of Jebel al-Akhbar overlooking the town of Hadd. But we couldn't do that now. It would be much too dangerous.' He hesitated, and then he added, 'The risk would only be justified if vital interests of our own were involved.'

'What sort of vital interests?' I asked. But I knew the answer before he gave it.

'Oil,' he said. 'From a Western point of view – as you'd know if you'd been out here any length of time – everything in Arabia comes back to oil.'

'Your son's death, too?' I asked. He looked at me, but didn't say anything. 'When did you first hear he was missing?'

'Towards the end of February.'

'Could you give me a date?'

He frowned and for a moment I thought he wasn't going to answer that. But then he said, 'I can't be certain. Your calendar doesn't mean very much to us out here in the desert. But by the moon it would be about the beginning of the last week in February.'

Almost a week before the abandoned truck had been found by the Bedouin, more than three weeks before his disappearance had been reported to the Company. 'You didn't notify Erkhard.'

'No.'

'Why not? David was in the Company's employ, even if he was on loan to you.'

He didn't say anything. He seemed suddenly to have withdrawn inside himself. I think perhaps he was waiting for my next question, knowing it was coming. 'The truck was discovered abandoned on February twenty-eight,' I said. 'Yet you say you knew he was missing almost a week before that. How did you know?'

There was a long pause. At length he said, 'Some askari were despatched from Saraifa. When they reached his camp they found it deserted, not a soul there; the truck and the Land Rover had gone, too.'

'Askari?'

'Yes. Members of Sheikh Makhmud's bodyguard. Their orders were to arrest him and bring him back to Saraifa.'

'Alive?'

'Of course.' He stared at me angrily. 'What other instructions do you imagine they would be given? They were dispatched by Sheikh Makhmud – at my request. That was immediately after my return from Hadd.' And he added. 'It was done for his own good – and because it was necessary. The Emir was in a very dangerous mood.'

So that was how it had been. 'And you didn't want Erkhard to know that he'd been operating on the Hadd border?'

'I didn't want Erkhard to know and I didn't want the political boys to know. As I've said, David was there against my express orders. God Almighty!' he breathed. 'The impatience of youth. They want the moon for breakfast and the sun for lunch.' He leaned on the parapet, staring down to the white sand below. 'I blame myself,' he said quietly. 'I should have packed him off back to Cardiff. Instead, I let him stay. More, I tried to think of him as my son, as God's gift from my loins, a prodigal given back into my hands.' He shook his head. 'I should have known it wouldn't work.'

He paused there and I didn't say anything for I felt his isolation here might trap him into some self-revelation if I didn't try to force it. He looked at me again, the desert lines deep-etched by the moon, a long, sad, solitary face. 'As you know, I'm a Moslem. I wanted him to become a Mahommedan, too. I wanted him to make the desert his home and to carry on where I left off in due course.' He sighed softly. 'I forgot the boy was already nineteen, and only half mine . . . and that half as obstinate as the devil.' He smiled. In that harsh face it was a smile of extra-ordinary tenderness. 'I turned him into a Christian instead.' He said it with bitterness, adding, 'In the end I think he came to hate me.'

'Why?'

The question was out before I could stop myself and I saw him freeze and close up on me. 'People get at cross-purposes, you know.' His tone was casual now. 'It's one of the sad things about human relation-ships. But there . . . No point in talking about it now. The boy's dead, and that's that.'

'You can't be sure of that,' I said.

He stared at me, his eye blazing in the darkness. 'What do you mean? I had all the chaps I could spare out looking for him. Khalid was searching too, and Makhmud had men hunting for him all over Saraifa. The only place we never thought of searching was west into the Empty Quarter.' And he said, with gentleness, softly to himself: 'The desert is like the sea. No man can disappear into it for two months and come out alive.'

'All right,' I said. 'He's dead. But if you haven't discovered what happened to him, what do you think happened to him?'

His eye looked into mine. 'Have you ever been frightened?'

'Yes, once,' I said. 'In Tanganyika.'

He nodded. 'Then you'll understand me when I say no man knows how he'll react to fear until he's faced with it. Especially when he's alone. And David was alone. His Arab crew had deserted him. We found that out later They panicked.'

'And you think David did the same?'

He shrugged. 'It's a cruel place, the desert. And solitary as hell. Empty too. Even in company the Bedou sing to keep their spirits up.' It was much what Griffiths had said and it seemed plausible enough. He took my arm and led me back to the carpet. 'You were telling me about your journey—'

I told him as much as I thought he'd a right to know – about the package Griffiths had brought me and my meeting with Erkhard. But it was Gorde he was really interested in – Gorde and Entwhistle and the fact that the two of them had been together at the locations David had been surveying. It seemed to worry him and he questioned me closely about Gorde's reactions – what had he said, where was he going when he'd left me there with Entwhistle? And then he asked me what it was that had decided Entwhistle to check David's survey. 'He must have known he was risking his life there on that border. What made him think it was so important?'

I hesitated. He was sitting there, watching me, very still, very tense, and I knew suddenly that this was what the whole interview had been leading up to and that he was deeply concerned. 'When Entwhistle searched the abandoned truck,' I said, 'he found all David's papers. They included his own survey report and also the report of a much older survey run just before the war. I think it was that report—'

'Whose report?' The question was shot at me out of the dark. 'Was it Henry Farr's report?'

I stared at him. 'You know about that?'

'Of course. Henry sent me a copy of it. He was well aware of my interest in the area. Later we had a talk about it – just before he went into Abyssinia.'

'But if you knew about it—' It seemed so incredible. 'In his letter to me David said he found it in the Company's files. You never told him about it?'

'No.'

'Why ever not? You must have known how he felt about Saraifa, his desperate urge to—'

'He was employed by the Company – by Erkhard.' His voice was taut and hard, a note almost of hostility.

'But . . . I don't understand,' I said. 'All these years . . . And Khalid says you're drilling to the south of the oasis. That's at least forty miles from David's locations.'

'Exactly. Just about as far from the Hadd border as it's possible to get and still be in Saraifa.' He got to his feet and began pacing up and down, seeking relief in movement from the nervous tension that I now realized had existed inside him from the first moment of our meeting. 'It's not easy to explain. You don't understand the situation.' He stopped suddenly and faced me. 'For twenty years I've had to sit on this, convinced that my theory was right, that the oil-bearing strata continued from the Gulf down into Saraifa, between the Empty Quarter and the mountains you can see there to the east.' His voice was sharp and bitter with frustration. 'I had to find some way—' He paused, standing there over me, and he was silent a long time as though reaching for a decision. Finally he said, 'You know so much . . . You may as well know the rest. Erkhard's coming here tomorrow, flying down from Sharjah. He's under pressure as I think you'll have guessed from your conversation with Philip Gorde. With God's help I'll get him to sign the concession, and once the Company's involved—' He turned and resumed his pacing. 'There was no other way. No company would sign a concession with Saraifa if they knew it involved drilling on the Hadd-Saraifa border. No company would dare. But once they're committed . . .' He beat his fist against the palm of his hand. 'I've seen it happen before. The technical men come in. They're not concerned with politics. They ride roughshod over everything and in the end the Government is forced to support them.'

'So there isn't any oil where you're drilling?'

'No, not as far as I know.'

It was a strange business. He'd spent all that money, almost a year of desperate effort to lure the Company into becoming involved again in Saraifa. It was clever, but . . . 'And you think Erkhard will sign the concession agreement?'

'I think so, yes. In the four years he's been General Manager he hasn't been very successful. His position isn't as strong as it was when he came out here.'

'But why didn't you tell David what you were doing?'

'How could I? He was Erkhard's man.' And he added, 'I still have contacts in the Bahrain Office. According to them, he was under orders to report on everything I was doing.'

'And he agreed?'

'They knew his background. After that, of course, I couldn't trust him.'

'Then why was he on loan to you?'

'Erkhard offered him to me. I'd had him here before; I couldn't very well refuse.' And then sadly: 'I didn't dare tell him. Besides, he lacked patience. He always approached things head-on, wanting to force the issue. If I'd thought he'd have been guided by me—' He shrugged. 'Well, it can't be helped now.'

He turned to me, his manner suddenly matter-of-fact. 'You must be tired, and I've a long day ahead of me. You're fixed up all right, I take it, at the Sheikh's palace?'

I nodded and got to my feet. 'But I still don't understand why you did nothing about the Farr report – after the war when the Company had the concession?'

'Various reasons,' he answered. 'Most of them political. All the time the Company had the concession there was spasmodic fighting on the border. The Emir, you see, was determined to grab any oil there was for himself. And when we finally sent in troops to keep the peace, it was too late for me to do anything about it. The concession had lapsed, Philip Gorde had gone home sick and Erkhard had taken over. Erkhard would have dealt with the Emir or anybody else. He'd no feeling for Saraifa the way Philip had.' He turned abruptly and shouted for Yousif. And then, looking at me very hard, he said, 'You've come at a strange moment, Grant, and I've told you things I've told no other man. I've had to, or you'd have caused more trouble. By the mere fact of coming out here . . .' He hesitated and I knew he was thinking of Gorde. 'What did Philip say, was he surprised when he discovered where I was drilling?'

'I don't think he knows,' I said. 'He wasn't even sure you were drilling.'

'Oh, he knows. A plane passed over the rig this afternoon. I thought for a moment it must be Erkhard arriving a day early, but when it circled and turned away I began to wonder.' He was looking out into the desert again and his face showed the strain he was under. 'I could have wished it had been anyone but Philip Gorde. He's the only man in the whole Company who knows enough to guess what I'm up to. But there's nothing I can do about it now.' Yousif had appeared and he held out his hand to me. 'You're a lawyer, Grant. You've been involved in our affairs for a long time. I rely on you not to talk.' He held my hand gripped in his. 'We have two enemies here in Saraifa

– the Emir and the Sands.' He gestured towards the white expanse of the dunes and added softly, 'Tomorrow, with God's help, I'll lay the foundation of victory over them both.' It was said with great intensity, his eyes fixed on my face.

I left him then, standing alone as I had found him on that rooftop, a strange, almost fanatical figure against the backcloth of endless desert. Even when I got back to my turret room, the memory of him was so clear in my mind that I felt he was still with me. But I was too exhausted to think clearly about that extraordinary meeting. I fell asleep and dreamed instead of women crying over children dead of thirst.

I woke in the small hours to the reality of their cries, a queer, keening sound coming up from the square below. The palace, too, was alive with voices, and though they were muffled by distance and the thickness of the walls, I caught the vibrant note of disaster.

It was quite chilly as I flung off my blanket and went to the embrasure. The village square was ghostly pale in moonlight, empty save for a little group immediately below me, a dozen women and some children huddled like rags around the dead body of a man. He had been shot in the face and he wasn't a pretty sight there in the moonlight. Nearby a camel lay in a pool of blood.

It was just after four by my watch and already the sky was paling in the east. I put on my shoes and went down into the courtyard. The place was in an uproar, fires smoking and men standing in little groups, all talking at once. The nearest fell silent as they saw me and the word *Nasrani* passed from mouth to mouth, a whisper of fear, perhaps of hate. I beat a hasty retreat to the seclusion of my turret cell.

Sleep was impossible after that and I sat huddled in my blanket and watched the dawn break over the Jebel mountains, the grey light of it creeping across the palm tops, heralded by the brazen sound of an ass braying. The keening ceased and when I went to the window embrasure there was no sign of the dead man and the camel's carcase had gone. It might have been a bad dream, for as daylight flooded the square it was full of the sound of children and their carefree laughter.

There was a *shireeya*, or open waterhole, a short distance from the tower and young Arab girls were driving goats towards it. There were boys there, too, with their asses, filling goat-skin bags and dripping a dark trail of the precious fluid as they took it to houses in the village. Skinny, undersized fowl pecked in the dirt; a shapeless bundle of womanhood passed, her face hideously concealed by the black mask of the *burqa*. And when the sun lifted its glaring face above the distant line of the mountains, the palms, the sand, the mud houses were all miraculously suffused with colour, as though I were looking at the scene through rose-tinted glasses. Exhausted, I lay down again and was instantly asleep.

I woke to the cry of '*Gahwa*' and a barefoot attendant pouring coffee for me, his gun slung across his back, the brass of his cartridge belt gleaming in the light from the embrasure. It was eight-thirty and the flies crawled over the dates he left for my breakfast.

I ate the dates slowly, for time hung heavy on my hands and I didn't dare venture out alone after what had happened. My eyes felt tired, my body lethargic. My mind wandered in weary circles as the heat of the desert grew in intensity, invading the room. It was almost eleven when Khalid came for me. A brief salaam, a polite hope that I'd slept well, and then he said, 'My father holds a *majlis*. He desires your presence, sir.' His face looked grave and the eyes, deepsunk and shadowed, spoke of a sleepless night. 'The Emir of Hadd has sent one of his sheikhs to make demand for a new border.' His voice sounded weary, too.

'What happened last night?' I asked. 'There were women crying and a dead body in the square.'

'They waited in ambush by the fourteenth well. Mahommed bin Rashid is dead and two of his men also. Three are wounded. Come! My father waits for you.'

I asked him if I could wash first, but he said there was no time. 'You must explain now please to the Emir's representative why you and Meester Entwhistle are on the border.' And then urgently: 'Tell Sheikh Abdullah there is no oil there.'

'I'm not a geologist.'

'He don't know that. He thinks you work for the Oil Company.'

'Well, I don't.' I spoke sharply, irritable with lack

of sleep. 'I'm a lawyer, and all I'm interested in is what happened to David Whitaker.'

His dark eyes stared at me hard. 'Is better you don't talk about David at this meeting,' he said quietly.

'Why?' Angry and tired, I didn't stop to think what I was saying. 'Because your father sent some of his bodyguard to arrest him?'

'You saw *Haj* Whitaker last night. You know why they were sent. He was on the Hadd border against my father's orders.'

'Against Whitaker's orders, too, I gather.'

'Yess. If he had been a Muslim instead of a *Nasrani*—' He gave a little shrug. 'The Prophet has taught us that the word of the father is as a law and that the son must obey.' And he added, 'My father is wishing to avoid trouble. He does not believe that a few miles of desert sand is worth fighting for.'

'And you do?'

Again the little shrug. 'My father is an old man and he has known *Haj* Whitaker many years now. He is guided by him in these matters. And I – I also am not a geologist.'

'Who did your father send with the soldiers?' I asked. 'Was it you?'

'No. Mahommed bin Rashid.' He turned abruptly. 'Come, please. My father is waiting.' And as I followed him down the turret stairs, he said over his shoulder, 'Please. You will not speak of David.' He said it fiercely, with great urgency.

He led me through passages that were cool in semi-darkness and up to a rooftop by another staircase. The *majlis,* or audience, was being held in an open room with arches that looked out across the rooftops to the oasis. Sheikh Makhmud didn't rise to greet me. His face looked tired and strained, sullen with anger. He was also, I think, a little frightened. Beside him sat the representative of Hadd, a bearded, sly-eyed, power-fully-built man with an elaborately embroidered cloak and a head-dress that was like a turban of many colours.

Sheikh Makhmud motioned me to sit facing him. I was thus in the position of the accused facing a court, for all the notables were there, seated cross-legged and grave on silken cushions ranged round the inner walls of that airy room. On a carpet in the centre were bowls of camel milk and tinned pears. Nobody touched them except the flies. The atmosphere was tense, almost electric.

The situation was distinctly unpleasant for it was obvious as soon as Sheikh Makhmud began to ques-tion me in halting English that he regarded me as responsible for the situation that had developed. Entwhistle's absence didn't help and though I answered the questions truthfully, I could see from Sheikh Abdul-lah's manner that he didn't believe me. He listened to the translation with a lack of interest that he didn't bother to conceal.

In the end I lost my temper with him. I scrambled to my feet and standing over the man, delivered myself of the sort of broadside I occasionally indulged in in the courts. My action might have been dictated by expediency, for attack was undoubtedly the best method of defence. But, in fact, my nerves were on edge. 'Your men attacked us without warning and without cause,' I shouted at him. And I described how the soft-nosed bullet had slammed into the bonnet of the Land Rover, how the fusillade of shots had raised spurts of sand all around us. He looked suddenly uncomfortable. 'Only a few years ago,' I said, 'my country had to send troops here to keep the peace. Now you break it again. Why? What explanation do you wish me to give when I return to Bahrain?'

My words translated, the crafty eyes slid from my face to the assembled men and he licked his lips as though suddenly uncertain of himself. 'You have no answer,' I said, and with that I gave Sheikh Makhmud a quick bow and made my exit. I couldn't go far, for armed retainers barred the staircase leading down from the roof. But I had made my point and felt better for it, even though I was now forced to remain out in the full glare of the sun. I sat myself down on the oven-lid heat of the mud parapet and pretended to be absorbed in watching a camel caravan being loaded at a huddle of *barastis* close by the date gardens. Behind me I could hear the guttural sound of their talk as they continued to deliberate.

Coffee was served and Khalid came over and joined me. 'Is no good,' he said. 'The Emir listens to Cairo Radio and he believes he has powerful friends. It has made him bold. Also he has many new rifles. They have come up from the Yemen, I think. From the coast also.' And he added, 'Only if we have oil here in

Saraifa will your people give us their full support. We know that.'

'Mr Erkhard is seeing Colonel Whitaker today,' I said.

He nodded. 'My father will not make a decision until he hears from *Haj* Whitaker. He is full of hope.'

'And you?' I asked, for the way he said it suggested he didn't share his father's optimism.

He shrugged. 'I also hope, but *Haj* Whitaker is old, and he is tired and sick.'

'Sick?'

'Sick here.' And he touched his heart.

I asked him then what exactly Sheikh Abdullah was demanding. 'A new border,' he said and drew it for me in the sand of the rooftop floor with the toe of his sandalled foot. It meant that all the area David had surveyed would belong to Hadd.

'And if your father refuses?'

Again that fatalistic shrug. 'Then Sheikh Abdullah say they will destroy another *falaj*, and another and another, until we have no water for the dates, no water for our beasts, none for ourselves even. We die then of thirst and starvation.' He was staring out across the oasis. 'I am young yet. I had thought to rebuild the *falajes*, one by one, until Saraifa is like a garden again and the desert at bay. That is my dream.'

'And David's, too.'

'Yes, it is the dream we share since we first hunt the gazelle together.' His eyes had a far-away look, his voice sad with the loss of that dream. His father called to him and he finished his coffee and went back to his place. The conference was resumed, and looking at the faces of the men gathered in that room, I knew he was right. They were in no mood to fight and if Whitaker didn't save them then they would accept it as the will of Allah and agree to the Emir's demands.

The camel caravan down by the palm-tree fringe finished loading. I watched the heavily-laden beasts move off through the date gardens, headed north into the desert. The whole oasis shimmered in the heat, and beyond it stretched the sands, a golden sea thrusting yellow drifts amongst the palms. The sun climbed the sky. The heat became unbearable, the talk spasmodic, and Sheikh Abdullah sat there, his heavy eyelids drooping, not saying anything, just waiting.

I was half asleep when I saw the dust trail of the vehicle. It was coming through the date gardens from the south, driven fast, and when it emerged into the open I saw it was a Land Rover packed with Arabs, all shouting and waving their guns in a frenzy of excitement. And as it reached the outskirts of the village they began firing into the air.

A few minutes later Yousif burst through the retainers standing at the head of the stairs. He went straight up to Sheikh Makhmud, interrupting the deliberations with that extraordinary lack of respect that seems a contradiction almost of the feudalism of the Bedou world. He was excited and Arabic words poured from him in a flood as he handed the Sheikh a folded slip of paper.

As soon as Sheikh Makhmud had read it his whole manner changed. His eyes lit up. He became revitalized, a man suddenly in command of the situation. He said a few words, speaking softly and with great control. The name of Allah was repeatedly mentioned, presumably in praise. And then he rose to his feet. The effect was remarkable. The place was suddenly in an uproar, everybody on their feet and all talking at once. There was a general movement towards the stairs and Sheikh Makhmud swept out ahead of his elders, moving fast and with a light, soundless tread, so that he seemed to flow like water from the rooftop.

Khalid followed him, the others crowding after them, and in a moment there was only myself and the Emir's representative left. He looked unhappy, his arrogance undermined by this development which had clearly affected his embassy. I smiled at him, waving him to the staircase ahead of me, and was amused at the childish way he turned his back on me in a huff.

From the rooftop I could see men running. The news seemed to have spread round the oasis in a flash. And south, beyond the palms, another dust trail moved across the desert. By the time I had found my way down to the great courtyard the whole male population of Saraifa seemed gathered there. And when the Land Rover, driven by Colonel Whitaker himself, turned slowly through the gateway, forcing a passage through the crush to where Sheikh Makhmud stood waiting, a great shout went up: *Haji! Haji!* In the passenger seat beside Whitaker sat Erkhard, as cool and neat and spotless as when I had seen him last.

The greetings over, the Company's General Manager was taken into the palace. I had a glimpse of

Whitaker's face as he walked beside Sheikh Makhmud, towering over him and all the Arabs round him. He wasn't smiling and yet it expressed his elation; a secret, almost violent emotion. Twenty years was a long time, and this the culmination of his life, the moment of victory. It seemed a pity David couldn't be here to share it.

Nobody took any notice of me now. I walked out through the main gate, down into the shade of the palms, and sat by the steaming waters of the *shireeya*. Gorde, Whitaker, Erkhard, Entwhistle – those three women; my brain reeled with the heat. Unable to fix any pattern to my thoughts, I returned finally to my turret room. It was cooler there, the shadowed interior peaceful, and I took my siesta to the lazy buzzing of flies, the distant murmur of people wild with joy.

I must have slept heavily for when I woke the sun was low and there was a little pile of freshly-laundered clothes beside me – a tropical suit, shirt, tie, pants, socks. There was also a note from Whitaker: *The concession is signed and there is a feast to celebrate. I thought you might like a change of clothes. Yousif will call for you at sunset.*

As soon as I started to put them on I knew the clothes weren't his, for he was much taller and these fitted me reasonably well. They were obviously David's and it seemed to me strange that I should be attending this feast in his clothes.

The acrid smell of wood smoke permeated the room and the hubbub of sound from the village square drew me to the embrasure. The whole beaten expanse was full of people and cooking fires. The carcases of sheep and goats hung by their hind legs, their slashed throats dripping blood into bowls. Chickens were being prepared and blackened pots of rice simmered over the fires. Half Saraifa was in the square and there was a great coming and going of the Sheikh's armed retainers who carried the cooked dishes into the palace. The sun sank and the sky blazed red for an instant and then died to purple and light greens.

'You come now, sir, please.'

Yousif stood at the head of the stairway almost unrecognizable in clean clothes and spotless turban, a curved *khanjar* knife gleaming silver at his waist. He took me down to a central courtyard that I hadn't seen before. It was packed with retainers, the silver and brass of guns and cartridges gleaming in the shadows. The Sheikh and his guests were already gathered in the long, colonnaded room on the far side, and dishes lay in lines in the dust.

Khalid came forward to greet me. He was beautifully clad in long robes of finest cashmere, a brown cloak gold-embroidered, and his eyes, newly made-up with *kohl*, looking enormous, his beard shining and silky with some scented lotion. Whitaker was seated on one side of Sheikh Makhmud, Erkhard on the other. And next to Whitaker sat Sheikh Abdullah of Hadd. 'You sit with me,' Khalid said.

As I passed Erkhard, he looked up. 'Grant!' I couldn't help being amused at his surprise. 'They told me in Sharjah that you'd left with Gorde, but I didn't expect to see you here.' He frowned. 'Where is Gorde, do you know?'

'I think he flew back to Bahrain.'

He nodded. 'Good.'

As I took my place beside Khalid, retainers were already moving among the guests with ewers of water. We rinsed our hands and the first great platters were moved forward on to the rugs. The occasion was very formal. Nobody talked unless the Sheikh himself was talking. The result was that conversation went in disconcerting leaps – one moment bedlam, the next a silence in which the only sound was the coming and going of the retainers in the courtyard.

The feast was a monstrous, gargantuan affair – mutton, goat's flesh, young camel, chicken, gazelle. The platters came on and on and kept on coming, the meat nestled on piled-up heaps of rice, eggs floating in a spiced gravy like little yellow balls, omelettes piled in tiers, flat and leathery like girdle cakes, flat discs of bread, liquid butter and cheese. Half the dishes never got beyond the colonnades, but remained outside in the dust, enough to feed an army. Like all Bedouin feasts it was intended as a meal for the Sheikh's bodyguard who were waiting on us, for all the palace retainers, and finally for the people of Saraifa themselves so that they should all feel that they had shared in the event.

The cooking was rough desert cooking, the meat overdone and swimming in fat, the dishes lukewarm at best. But I was so damned hungry I scarcely thought about what I was eating. Khalid kept plying me with

delicacies – the tongue of gazelle I remember and something that I popped into my mouth and swallowed
whole, hoping it wasn't what I thought it was. An old
man sat in a corner playing intermittently on what I
can only describe as a lute. The palace poet, I was
told. Later he would unburden himself of a poem in
praise of the guests and of the occasion. 'It will be a
long poem,' Khalid said and his eyes smiled whilst his
face remained quite serious. There was a sudden
silence and into it the man next to me tossed a belch
of impressive loudness. There was a great deal of
belching. It was a mark of appreciation and before we
were halfway through the meal I found myself doing
the same, so quickly and easily does one fall into other
people's conventions. Also my stomach was by then
very full.

Outside in the courtyard Sheikh Makhmud's fal-
coners paraded their birds. He was very proud of his
falcons, and seeing them, talons gripped around
wooden perches spiked into the sand or around the
leather-gauntleted arms of their keepers, I found myself
glancing at Whitaker, noticing the same quick, preda-
tory look, the same sharp, beaky features. Our eyes
met for a moment and it seemed to me that the mood
of exhilaration had drained out of him as though
success had a sour taste; or perhaps it was the clothes
I was wearing, reminding him of his son.

The main dishes had all been removed now. Lights
were brought, for the sun had set and it was growing
dark. They were modern, chromium-plated pressure
lamps and they were hung on nails in the walls, where

they hissed and glared and had to be constantly pumped to maintain the pressure. And with the lamps came dishes of every sort of tinned fruit. There was *hadwa*, too. Coffee followed, and at a sign from Sheikh Makhmud the poet moved into the centre. He sat facing the guests and began plucking at his lute, chanting a ballad – the story, Khalid said, of Saraifa's need of water and *Haj* Whitaker's long search for oil. It had the effect of intensifying the mood of excitement that gripped all the Arabs . . . all except Sheikh Abdullah, who sat staring stonily into space.

And then suddenly the stillness was shattered by the noise of an aircraft flying low. The ballad-singer faltered, the sound of the lute ceased; the story came abruptly to a halt, unfinished.

The sound swept in a roar over the palms. I thought I caught a glimpse of a dark shape against the stars, and then the engine died. It was coming in to land and Sheikh Makhmud called to his secretary and a guard was despatched to escort the visitors. Everybody was talking at once and Erkhard leaned across to me and hissed, 'Who is it? Do you know?'

I didn't answer, but I think he must have guessed, for his eyes were coldly bleak and there was a tightness about his mouth. I looked past him to where Whitaker sat. His face was expressionless, but his body had a stillness that was without repose.

After what seemed a very long wait Gorde and Otto were escorted into the courtyard.

It was a strange moment, for Gorde walked straight in on the feast, limping and leaning on his stick, the sweat-stained trilby jammed firmly on his grizzled head, his battered features set in grim lines. He didn't greet Sheikh Makhmud. He didn't greet anyone. He stopped in the middle of the centre archway and stared in silence at the gathering, my briefcase tucked under his arm. It was an effective entrance, and I knew by his aggressive manner that he had intended it to be. Impressive, too, for he was dressed exactly as I had last seen him, and behind him crowded the bodyguard, all armed to the teeth. It was impressive because of the contrast; the man so small, so completely at the mercy of the armed men behind him, and yet so dynamic, so completely in command of the situation.

He ignored Sheikh Makhmud's greeting. 'What's the feast for?' That harsh voice seemed to cut through the room.

Nobody moved. Nobody spoke. Even Sheikh Makhmud seemed stunned into silence.

'Mister Erkhard.' The 'Mister' was a calculated slap in the face. 'I take it you've signed a concession agreement? There's nothing else for Saraifa to celebrate at this moment.' And then, without giving Erkhard a chance to reply, he turned to Sheikh Makhmud. 'I hope you're not a party to this – that you signed in ignorance of the true situation.'

'I don't understand.' Sheikh Makhmud's hands fluttered in a way that suggested dark moths endeavouring to cope with the intrusion of unwelcome thoughts. Slipping into Arabic he began a speech of welcome.

Rudely Gorde cut him short. 'Have you got the concession agreement on you? I'd like to see it please.' He held out his hand and such was the driving force of the man's personality, the absolute conviction that men would obey him, that Sheikh Makhmud slipped his hand into the folds of his robe and brought out the document. Meekly he handed it over. 'I think you find everything is all right.' The soft words, the gentle voice gave no sign of doubt or tension.

Gorde called to one of the bodyguard to bring him a light. A stillness hung over the scene as he unfolded the document and glanced quickly through it. Then he raised his head and looked directly at Erkhard. 'And you signed this on behalf of the Company.'

The note of censure brought an immediate reaction from Erkhard. 'As General Manager I'm entitled to sign concession agreements.' His voice was thin, a little venomous as he added, 'You should know that. You signed enough of them in your day.'

'But never one like this.' And slapping the document with his hand, he added, 'This isn't our normal agreement. Our normal form of agreement simply gives the Company the right to prospect. This makes it a legal charge upon the Company to do so. Moreover—' And his gaze fastened on Whitaker – 'it doesn't limit it to the area south of here where your rig is. It covers the whole of Saraifa, including the area in dispute on the Hadd border.'

'Philip.' Whitaker had risen to his feet. 'I'd like a word with you.'

'And I'd like a word with you,' Gorde said sharply.

'In private.'

'No. We'll settle this thing here and now. I just want a straight answer to a straight question. Is there or is there not oil where you're drilling?'

'We're only down to three thousand odd feet.'

'That doesn't answer my question.' Gorde stared at him coldly. 'There isn't any oil, is there? There never was any oil there, and there never will be.'

'I don't believe it.' Erkhard, too, was on his feet.

'It doesn't matter whether you believe it or not, Alex,' Gorde rapped back. 'It's the truth.'

'But he's drilling with his own money. He's invested every penny he's got. Ask Grant. He handles his financial affairs and Whitaker admits he's out here partly because his money is almost exhausted. A man doesn't put all his savings first into a thorough seismological survey and then into a drilling programme—'

'Bait.' The tone of Gorde's voice brought Erkhard up short. 'He was baiting the trap.'

'I don't understand.'

'Of course you don't. You'd never in a thousand years understand a man like Charles Whitaker. You ride him out of the Company and it never occurs to you that he'll get his own back some day. If you hadn't been so intent on trying at the last minute to rectify your position . . . And you thought you were getting an oilfield on the cheap, for the price of his development cost plus 50 per cent on royalties. Well, you ask him. You just ask him whether there's any oil there.'

But it wasn't necessary. One glance at Whitaker's face told Erkhard all he needed to know. It was drawn and haggard, the colour of putty, and though the mouth moved, no words came. Erkhard crossed to Gorde, took the document from his hand and tore it across and across and dropped the pieces in the dust.

There was a deathly hush. All eyes were turned on Sheikh Makhmud, waiting for his reaction. His face was the colour of clay, a shocked, almost old-womanish face, and his hands were trembling in the wide sleeves of his robe. 'Sir Philip.' He had some difficulty in controlling his voice. 'Your Company has signed an agreement. To tear up the paper is not to say the agreement does not exist.'

'You can take us to court,' Erkhard said. 'But if Gorde's right, you'll lose your case.'

Sheikh Makhmud waved his hands to signify that he had no intention of taking the Company to court. He ignored Erkhard, addressing himself to Gorde. 'I have always trusted the British. And you also; you have been my friend.'

'I am still your friend,' Gorde said.

'Then please you will honour the agreement.'

'There is no agreement.' His voice held a note of pity now. 'Mr Erkhard has done the only thing possible in the circumstances.' He turned to Whitaker. 'For God's sake, Charles; did you have to raise their hopes like this?' It was clear from his words that he didn't like the role he was being forced to play. 'The truth was bound to come out in the end.'

'What is the truth?' The pale eye was fastened on Gorde in an aloof stare. 'Do you know it? Are you so sure there's no oil in Saraifa? For twenty years now I have searched—'

'To hell with your theory,' Gorde snapped. 'Just answer me this; a simple Yes or No. Is there oil where you're drilling?'

'I've told you, we're only down to just over three thousand feet. Erkhard could have waited—'

'You know damn' well he couldn't wait. You're not such a fool that you haven't guessed why I'm out here risking my health on another tour of the Gulf.'

'You thought my theory sound enough at one time. Remember?'

'And I backed you,' Gorde rasped. 'I backed you because you'd got faith in yourself. But now I wonder. Now I think you've lost that faith. I don't think you believe in your theory any more.'

'What makes you say that?' Whitaker's voice was sharp, unnaturally high, and his face looked shocked.

Gorde leaned his squat body forward. 'Because,' he said, 'if you'd any faith in your theory, you'd have backed your son. Instead, you left him to die out there on his own – alone, deserted.' Each word punched home in that rasping voice. It was a terrible indictment. And he added, 'Didn't you understand that he was attempting to do what you'd no longer the guts to even try and do – to find oil, real oil. Not this sham, this clever, crooked dodge to trap us into signing—'

'Philip!' It came from Whitaker's mouth as a strangled cry. 'I want to talk to you – alone.'

It was an appeal, the call of past friendship. But Gorde ignored it. 'I've nothing to say to you, Charles.'

The words came bleak and cold. 'Except perhaps this: if there is any oil in Saraifa, then my guess is that it's right there on the border where your son was prospecting. But,' he added, turning to Sheikh Makhmud, 'I have to tell you that there's absolutely no question of our Company – or any other company, for that matter – undertaking exploratory work there at the present time. I was with the Political Resident for two hours this morning. He made the Government's attitude very clear. And now that I know what happened here last night, simply because one of our geologists was inadvertently on that border, I think he's right.'

There was silence then and for a moment Colonel Whitaker continued to stand there as though shocked into immobility. Knowing what I did, I felt sorry for him. Gorde had misinterpreted his motives, but there was nothing he could do about it at that moment. Whitaker knew that. Abruptly he gathered his dark, embroidered cloak about him. 'I'm sorry you had to come when you did, Philip.' His tone was bitter; his manner arrogant, unbending, aloof. 'You'll live, I hope, to regret the words you've said and your hasty judgment. I did what I thought best for Saraifa, and Makhmud knows it.' He walked past Gorde then, his one eye staring straight ahead of him as though on parade; a beaten, proud old man. The ranks of the bodyguard parted and he walked through them, magnificent and solitary.

With his departure the whole place became a babel of sound. It was as though Whitaker alone had held down the safety-valve of the crowd's temper. Violence quivered on the sultry air and I got up quickly and went over to Gorde. 'I think you ought to see Whitaker,' I said. 'As soon as possible. Tonight.'

'Why?'

But the place had suddenly become quiet. Sheikh Makhmud was on his feet making a speech, presumably of explanation. 'I can't tell you here. But I think it's important you should see him.'

'It's true, is it – you look after his financial affairs?' He stared at me, his face tired now, leaning heavily on his stick. 'Where's Entwhistle?' I told him and he nodded. 'Sensible fellow. This is no place to be just now.' He glanced at the sea of faces that packed the courtyard beyond. 'It all looks very feudal, doesn't it? But there's an element of democracy in these desert states. The sheikhs rule by consent, not by right. Just bear that in mind.' He was turning away, but then he checked. 'Here's your briefcase.' He handed it to me. 'You'll find all the papers there.'

Again I pressed him to see Whitaker, but he shook his head. 'It wouldn't serve any purpose after what I've said. And anyway I don't intend to. He's the pride of the devil, has Charles.'

'Go and see him,' I said. 'And take these papers with you.' I held the briefcase out to him.

He looked at the case and then at me. 'I took them along with me when I went to see the PRPG this morning. I thought I might persuade him—' He gave that little shrug of his. 'If he could have given us the All Clear politically I think I might have taken a chance on that boy's survey and backed Erkhard. But he didn't. More, he gave me a direct order that the Company was to keep clear of the area.'

It was final, and as though to emphasize the point, he said, 'I'll be leaving tomorrow morning as soon as it's light. No doubt Charles will take care of you, but if you want a lift out . . .' Sheikh Makhmud stopped talking and the courtyard was in an uproar again. Gorde's hand gripped my arm. 'Hope turned to despair makes men dangerous,' he said, his small, bloodshot eyes looking into mine. 'There's going to be trouble here and these people are in an ugly mood.'

He turned abruptly away from me and in the midst of the noise and confusion I heard him say casually to Sheikh Makhmud, 'Mind if we have something to eat? I'm damned hungry.'

Immediately, Sheikh Makhmud was the solicitous host, courteous and hospitable. '*Faddal! Faddal!*' He waved Gorde to the place vacated by Whitaker, found room for Otto, called for food to be brought. Khalid was in the courtyard now, pacifying the tribesmen, shepherding them out. He was quick, decisive, a born leader, but they went sullenly.

I returned to my place, feeling nervous and ill-at-ease. I didn't need to be told that they were in an ugly mood. I could feel it all around me. It was like an electric charge. And the uproar had spread from the feasting place into the great courtyard beyond and out into the village of Saraifa. The sound of their voices murmured on the night air, a continual angry buzzing as the whole population swarmed about the palace.

Men came in and out to stand and stare, and it seemed to me that their eyes in the lamplight blazed with a wild, fanatical hate. Erkhard felt it, too, for he leaned across to me and said, 'It's all very well for Gorde to say he'll leave at daybreak. He's got his plane here. Mine is ten miles away beside that rig.' And he added, 'Damn the man! A Moslem. I should have guessed he'd be up to every sort of trickery.'

'Did you have to turn him against his son?' I said angrily.

But it didn't register with him. 'Greed,' he said. 'It's an Arab failing.'

I thought that was good, coming from an oil man with his reputation. But I didn't have a chance to reply, for Yousif was suddenly bending over me. 'Coll-onel want you come,' he hissed. 'Very important, sahib.'

I hesitated, unwilling to leave the protection of Sheikh Makhmud's presence or to lose contact with Gorde and his promise of a lift out. But I couldn't very well refuse. 'All right,' I said and got to my feet. Courtesy demanded that I pay my respects to Sheikh Makhmud before leaving. He didn't rise and his eyes regarded me coldly from behind their glasses. No doubt he held me partly responsible for what had happened. His face looked haggard, the line of his mouth bitter. I turned to Gorde. 'I'm going to see Whitaker now,' I said. 'But I'd like to accept your offer of a lift.'

He had just taken a piece of meat from the dish in front of him and he looked up, licking the grease from his fingers. 'First light,' he said. 'And watch it, Grant.

Charles has lost face and anything can happen to a man that's been hit as hard as he has.'

Yousif's hand was on my arm and as I turned I saw Sheikh Abdullah's dark eyes fixed on me. The men in the courtyard fell back from me, suddenly silent, as we made our way out. Their eyes followed me, gleaming in the lamplight, and once again I caught the whisper of that word – *Nasrani*. There was no mistaking the significance of it this time. They were hating us all that night.

THE QUICKSANDS OF UMM AL SAMIM

Whitaker was waiting for me on that same rooftop overlooking the desert, but this time he was pacing up and down it. His movements were caged and restless. He checked only momentarily as I entered. 'Will Philip Gorde come and see me, do you think?' he asked, and when I told him No, he resumed his pacing. 'After all these years, to talk to me like that!'

It was too dark for me to see his face, but I could tell from the stooped outline of his shoulders, the lowered head, above all the nervous quickness of his movements, the way he spoke, that his mood was one of desperation. 'All my life I've had to use subtlety. It's been part of my job out here. Always the need to find my way through the maze of Arab politics. Never a straight course. Always the devious approach. These oil men out from England – stupid men like Erkhard who don't understand the Arab mentality – they don't realize the problems of these Bedou sheikhs, the feuds, the vague boundaries that didn't matter so long as it was desert sand and nothing more. History, culture, race – they go back three thousand years and more, virtually without change, untouched by Western civilization. It's a culture in which the individual is still dominant, personality and human emotions the overriding factor governing men's actions. And over all this are the outside factors – international politics, the Foreign Office. Even Philip doesn't really know the Arab – though he likes to think he does.'

It was the fact of having somebody with him of his own race. The words came out of him in a pent-up torrent. But what he said was said for his own benefit, not for mine; an attempt to justify his actions. But when he'd said it all, he turned and faced me, suddenly almost humble: 'Suppose I go to Philip myself?'

There was no point in raising his hopes. 'I don't think it would do any good.' And I told him about Gorde's visit to the PRPG.

His head came up. 'In other words, I was right. The Company's not allowed to enter into any agreement involving the Hadd border.' There was relief in his voice, but it was overlaid by the bitterness of frustration. And he added acidly, 'Nice of the Political Resident to confirm my own assessment of the situation so exactly.' His shoulders sagged; he turned his face towards the desert. 'Then I've no alternative now . . .' He said it to himself, not to me, standing very still, looking out to where the stars met the hard line of the sands. 'Over thirty years I've been out here,

Grant. I'm practically a Bedou. I think like them, act like them ... I'm over sixty now and I know more about the Arab and Arabia ...' He stopped there and in the stillness I could hear the breeze rattling the palms. He turned slowly and stared at me. 'All these years out here and a boy of twenty-four sees it clearer than I do.' His voice was harsh, his face grim, the lines cut by sand and sun so deep they might have been scored by a knife.

'It's a pity you didn't reach that conclusion earlier,' I said.

He took a step forward, his eye bulging, his body taut, gripped in a sudden blaze of anger. But all he said was, 'Yes, it's a pity.' He turned and resumed his pacing, the shoulders stooped again. 'Heredity is a strange thing,' he murmured. 'If we'd been less alike ...' He shrugged and added, 'In that case I don't suppose he'd have gone back to the locations against my orders.' He fell silent again then. The breeze was from the east and it brought with it the murmur of Saraifa like the beat of the surf on a distant shore.

'You wanted to see me,' I reminded him. The sound of that distant crowd made me anxious to get back to Gorde.

'Yes, about finances.' He kicked a cushion towards me and told me to sit down. 'Just what have I got left?' he demanded, folding himself up on the floor beside me.

I was glad Gorde had returned my briefcase then. I could have told him the position more or less from memory, but all the papers were there and it made it easier. He shouted for Yousif to bring a light and for the next ten minutes I went over the figures with him. He hadn't much left. But there were some shares I hadn't sold and they'd appreciated quite considerably, and after repaying bank loans, I thought he'd have just enough if he lived quietly. I thought he'd decided to go home, you see, to leave Arabia and retire. It seemed reasonable for a man of his age. 'I'm sorry it's not more,' I said, putting the papers back in their folder.

He nodded. 'I'll have to borrow then.'

'It would be better,' I said, returning the file to my briefcase, 'if you could arrange to live within your means.'

He stared at me, and then he burst out laughing. But the laughter was without humour. 'So you think I'm beaten, do you? You think I'm turning tail and heading for home like a village cur...' The fury building up in him seemed to get hold of his throat so that the words became blurred. 'That's what they'll all be thinking, I don't doubt – Gorde, Makhmud, that man Erkhard.' And then in a voice that was suddenly matter-of-fact: 'I take it you'll be going back in one of the Company planes?'

'Gorde has offered me a lift.'

'Good. I'll have letters for you to various merchants in Bahrain. A list of things to order, too. Would you like to wait here whilst I write them or shall I send Yousif up with them later? When it Philip leaving, by the way?'

'First light.' And because I wanted to make certain

I didn't miss the flight I asked him to have the letters sent after me.

He nodded. 'That gives me the night in which to think this thing over.' He summoned Yousif and gave him instructions to take me back to the palace. 'By the way,' he said, as I got to my feet, 'you mentioned a package Griffiths had brought you, something David took to him on board the *Emerald Isle*. Was that his survey report?'

I nodded.

'Based on Henry Farr's old report?'

'Yes.'

'I take it Entwhistle was running a check on David's locations? You don't know with what result, I suppose?'

'No. He didn't say.'

He had risen to his feet and standing close to me, he seemed to tower over me. 'I'd like to see my son's survey report. Have you got it with you in your briefcase?'

I realized then why he'd considered his finances inadequate. 'Good God!' I said. 'You're surely not going to start drilling operations on that border . . .' I was staring at him, remembering what Gorde had said. But there was nothing wild-eyed about him. He was bitter, yes. He'd been humiliated, deeply shocked, by the behaviour of a man he'd always regarded as his friend, but the eye that met mine was level and unflinching and I knew that he hadn't yet crossed the borderline into madness. 'You haven't a hope of succeeding now,' I said. 'The Emir will be watching that border and the instant you start drilling . . .'

He smiled thinly. 'I'm not afraid of death, you know. Being a Muslim makes one fatalistic.' He turned away leaning his body on the parapet and staring out across the dunes, grey now with the first light of the risen moon. 'I don't know what I'm going to do yet. I haven't made up my mind.' He hesitated and then turned to me. 'But if I should decide to go ahead then I'd like to have David's report. He gives the locations, I take it?' And when I nodded, he said, 'Do they coincide with Henry Farr's?'

'I don't know.'

'No, of course not. I ran a check survey myself, you know. That was a long time ago now when I had a bodyguard of more than a dozen men, all on the Company's payroll, and the use of the Company's equipment. In those days – quite soon after the war – I reckoned my chaps could hold the Emir off if it came to a showdown long enough for me to pull out with my equipment. But it never came to that. I got away with it without the Emir knowing. But I knew I couldn't do that with a drilling rig.'

'Then how do you expect to get away with it now?' I demanded.

He shrugged. 'I don't know that I can.' He was smiling softly to himself. 'But I've been out here a long time, Grant. I know that little Emir inside out. I've had spies in Hadd sending me back reports and I think I know enough now . . .' He gave a little shrug and the smile was no longer soft; it was hard, almost cruel.

'I'm outside the Company now. It makes a difference. And it's just possible that I could get away with it where the Company couldn't.' He straightened up. 'Well, what about it? Are you going to let me have David's report?'

It wasn't ethical, of course. He hadn't been mentioned in his son's Will. But then I'd failed with Gorde and I could now regard myself as free to take what action I liked. Also I thought that had David known what I now knew, he would have wanted his father to have the locations. I gave him a copy of the survey report and after writing the location fixes out on a slip of paper, I gave him that, too.

He glanced at it and then slipped it into the folds of his cloak. 'Thank you.' He held out his hand. 'You've come a long journey. I'm sorry it didn't have a pleasanter ending. I'll send Yousif with the letters in a few hours.'

I hesitated. But I knew he wasn't a man to take advice. 'In that case you'd better let me know what I'm to tell Gorde.'

'Nothing,' he said. 'Nothing at all.'

I left him then, standing alone on that rooftop with the desert clean and white behind him, and followed Yousif out to the battered Land Rover. It was cooler now and I felt almost relaxed. In a few hours I should be able to have a bath and a change and sit back with a long, cool drink. And yet, riding down the palm-shadowed track between the date gardens, I found myself filled with a strange nostalgia for the place. It had an appeal I found difficult to define, a sort of poetry, and the dim-remembered lines of a poem came into my mind, something about being 'crazed with the spell of far Arabia' and stealing his wits away.

I was beginning to understand what this place had meant to David, to a boy who'd never had a real home before and who was wide open to the strange beauty of it and as impressionable as any Celt.

I was still thinking about this when we ran out from the shadow of the palms and saw the square, black with the mass of men standing there. The roar of their voices came to us in a wall of sound. Yousif eased his foot off the accelerator, hesitating, uncertain whether to drive straight to the main gate or not. And then three figures rose from beside the *shireeya* and stood blocking our path.

'Sheikh Khalid's men,' Yousif said and there was relief in his voice as he braked to a stop. They clambered on to the mudguards, talking urgently in the hard, guttural tongue that is always associated in my mind with flies and sand. 'We go a different way. Is much better.' Yousif swung the Land Rover round, circling the gravel rise and approaching the palace from the rear through a litter of *barastis*, all apparently deserted. We stopped finally at a small door with an iron-barred grille set in an otherwise blank wall.

Khalid's three men closed round me as I got out, and when I told Yousif I wanted to be taken straight to Gorde, he said, 'You go with them now, sahib, Sheikh Khalid's orders.' And he drove off, leaving me there.

Eyes peered at us through the grille. The door

opened and I was hustled through the dark passages of the palace and up to my turret room. There my three guards left me, and standing at the embrasure I looked down on what was obviously a very explosive situation. The crowd was being harangued by a man on a rooftop opposite, and another was shouting to them from the back of a camel. The whole square was packed solid. Every man and boy in the oasis must have been gathered there, and many of them were armed.

Camels were being brought into the square and men were mounting on the outskirts of the crowd. And all the time the agitators shouting and the crowd roaring and the tension mounting. The air was thick with mcnace, and then somebody fired a rifle.

The bullet smacked into the mud wall not far from my embrasure. It was all that was needed to set that crowd alight. Other guns were fired, little sparks of flame, a noise like fire-crackers, and a great shout; the crowd became fluid, flowing like water, moving with the sudden purpose of a river in spate. Men leaped to their camels, mounting on the arch of their lowered necks, driving them with the flood tide down the slope to the dark fringe of the date gardens.

In a moment the square was deserted, and with the murmur of the crowd dying to silence, the dark walls of my room closed in on me. I had a sudden, over-whelming need then to find Gorde and the others, and I picked up my briefcase and felt my way down the black curve of the stairs. A light showed faint in the passage at the bottom. A figure stirred in the shadows. Thick Arabic words and the thrust of a gun muzzle in my stomach halted me. It was one of Khalid's men, and he was nervous, his finger on the trigger.

There was nothing for it but to retreat to my room again. In the mood prevailing in the oasis it was some comfort to know that I had a guard. I lay down and tried to get some rest. The sound of the crowd was still faintly audible. It came to me through the embrasure, soft as a breeze whispering through the palm trees. And then it died and there was an unnatural quiet.

It didn't last long, for the shouting started again. Shots, too. It was a long way away. I got up and went to the embrasure, peering out at the empty square and the dark line of the palms shadowed by the moon. A glow lit the night sky to the east. It grew and blossomed. Then suddenly an explosion, a great waft of flame and smoke beyond the date gardens. And after that silence, the flame abruptly gone and the palms a dark shadow-line again in the moon's light.

Voices called within the palace, the sound muffled by the thickness of mud walls, and then for a while it was quiet. But soon the crowd was ebbing back into the square, flowing into it in little groups, silent now and strangely subdued. I was sure that it was Gorde's plane I'd seen go up in smoke and flame, and I stayed by the embrasure, watching the tide of humanity as it filled the square, wondering what they'd do now – hoping to God their passions were spent.

Bare feet sounded on the stairs. I turned, uncertain what to expect, my mouth suddenly dry. The beam of a torch probed the room, blinding me as it fastened on my face. But it was only my three guards back again, jabbering Arabic at me and gesturing for me to accompany them. I was hurried along dark passages, past gaping doorways where men sat huddled in dim-lit rooms, arguing fiercely. The whole palace was in a ferment.

We came finally to a low-ceilinged room lit by a pressure lamp, and in its harsh glare I saw Khalid sitting surrounded by robed figures. They were mostly young men and they had their guns resting across their knees or leaning close at hand against the walls. He rose to greet me, his face unsmiling, the bones sharp-etched in the lamplight. 'I am sorry, sir, for the disturbance you have been given.' A gesture of dismissal and the room quietly emptied, the conference broken up. 'Please to sit.' He waved me to a cushion on the carpeted floor and sat down opposite me, his legs folding neatly under him with the ease of a man who has never known a chair.

'What happened?' I asked. 'Did they set fire to Gorde's plane?'

'Is a mistake. They are angry and they fire some bullets into it.' He was very tense, coiled up like a spring too tightly wound. Somewhere a child was crying, and I heard women's voices, soft and comforting. 'You 'ave been to see *Haj* Whitaker, is not so?' And when I nodded, he said, 'I understand you are concerned in the management of his affairs?'

'His financial affairs.' I didn't want him to think I was responsible for anything that had happened out here. His manner, his whole bearing had changed, the surface layer of a university education gone entirely. I glanced over my shoulder. My three guards were still there, squatting in the open doorway.

Khalid was staring at me out of his dark eyes. The *kohl* had worn off. Lacking that artificial lustre, his eyes looked sad and sombre. 'I have spoken with my father. I understand now what it is *Haj* Whitaker try to do for Saraifa. Unfortunately I am not before to-night in my father's confidence.' And he added with a trace of bitterness, 'Better if he had told me. Better also if *Haj* Whitaker explain to David what he is doing.' He paused there and I was conscious again of the strain he was under, of the tension building up in him. He leaned forward suddenly. 'What will he do now?' he asked me. 'Now that Meester Erk-hard don't honour the concession he sign. What will *Haj* Whitaker do?'

'That's his affair,' I said. I didn't want to become involved in this.

'Please, Meester Grant. I must know.'

'I don't think he's made up his mind yet.'

He stared at me. 'Do you think he may leave Saraifa?' And when I didn't answer, his eyes clouded and he seemed to sag. 'We have very much need of him now,' he said quietly. 'He has the ear of many sheikhs, of some of his own people also.' And he added, 'Since ever I am a small boy I have known about this great man *Haj* Whitaker. I can remember the feast to celebrate the original concession. He was young then and full of fire. But always, always people here – my father and myself also – we have looked to *Haj* Whitaker. He is known from the Persian Gulf to the Hadhramaut, from Muscat on the Indian Sea to the waterholes of the Rub al Khali and the Liwa Oasis as a great man and the friend of all the Bedou. Particularly he is known as the friend of Sheikh Makhmud. If he desert us now . . .'

'I'm sure he's no intention of deserting you.'

But he didn't seem to hear me. 'There must be some reconciliation. It is altogether vital.' He stared at me hard. 'Meester Grant. There is something I must know. It is if I can trust you?'

'That's up to you,' I said, wondering what was coming. And I added, 'I've been virtually a prisoner since I returned from seeing Colonel Whitaker.'

He gave a quick, impatient shrug. 'Is for your own safety.'

But I wondered. 'Where's Sir Philip Gorde?' I didn't want to be involved in this any further. 'I'd like to be taken to him now.'

'First you will listen please to what I have to tell you.'

He seemed to consider, his dark eyes fixed on me, searching my face. 'I think you are a friend to David before you work for his father, is not so?'

'It was because I befriended David that Colonel Whitaker asked me to look after his financial affairs.'

'Yess. Yess, I believe that.' But his eyes still searched my face as though he wasn't sure.

'What is it you want to tell me?' I wanted to get this over. Presumably Gorde and Otto would be leaving with Erkhard and I wanted to be on that plane, away from the dark feuds of this desert world.

He didn't answer at once. But then he suddenly seemed to make up his mind. He leaned forward. 'David is alive,' he said.

I stared at him, too astounded for the moment to utter a word. 'Alive?' Those three women . . . but remembering their attitude, I remembered Whitaker's too. 'What do you mean?' I was suddenly extremely angry with Khalid. 'How can he be alive?' And when he didn't say anything, I added, 'It's more than six weeks since your father sent an armed guard to arrest him, and they found his camp deserted.'

'I know. But is alive.' He said it very seriously.

'Where is he then?' I still didn't believe him. I thought it was a damned stupid lie he'd thought up to try and keep Whitaker in Saraifa. As if Whitaker, with all his experience of the desert, would believe it. 'You tell me where he is and . . .'

'No.' His voice was flat and decisive. 'No, I don't tell you — not yet. But is alive. That I promise, Meester Grant.' I suppose he realized that just stating it wouldn't convince me, for he went on quickly: 'When *Haj* Whitaker is gone to visit the Emir, I am much disturbed for David's life. He is already on that border almost two moons with the truck that was brought by his father across the Jebel mountains from Muscat. He is altogether alone and his father I believe to be hating him for things he has said.'

'What sort of things?'

He shrugged. 'He don't tell me. But he is very much

unhappy, I know that. He come here to this room to see me before he leave and he warn me there is no oil where *Haj* Whitaker is drilling, that the only place there is any probability of oil is on that border. He says also that his father is an old man now and has lost faith in himself and that he is drilling to cheat the Company, for revenge against this Meester Erk-hard and nothing more.'

'And you believed him?'

'He is as my brother. He don't lie to me.' And then he told me how he'd taken two of his men and a spare camel and had ridden to the border as soon as he knew David was to be arrested. He'd found David alone, deserted by his crew. After emptying the spare cans from the seismological truck, David had driven it into the Rub al Khali desert until it had run out of petrol on the side of that dune. 'Then he leaves the truck and rides on with us. It is all as we arrange it together.'

'You mean you planned it in advance?'

'Yess. It is all arranged between us because I am afraid for this emergency.'

The details fitted. They fitted so well that I was forced to accept what he'd told me as the truth. But he wouldn't reveal where David was hidden. 'He is with my two men – Hamid and a boy called Ali. They are of the Wahiba and altogether to be trusted.'

'Why have you told me this?' I asked.

'Because everything is gone wrong, everything David planned – and now I need your help. You are David's friend and also you work for his father. I think per'aps only you can bring reconciliation between them. And without reconciliation . . .' But he seemed reluctant to put his fears into words. 'What do you think now, sir?' he asked abruptly. 'Is reconciliation possible? How will *Haj* Whitaker act when he finds David is alive?'

'How would you react if you thought your son were dead?' But I realized I'd no idea what Whitaker's reaction would be. I didn't know enough about their relationship, how he'd come to regard his son in those last months. If Sue were right and they really had been close at one time . . . 'It'll come as a hell of a shock to him.'

'Yess, but is it possible – a reconciliation?'

'Of course. Particularly now that Colonel Whitaker . . .' I hesitated, wondering whether I ought to tell him what was in Whitaker's mind. But I thought he'd a right to know that he was considering drilling on his son's locations. After all, it was what David had wanted. They'd be able to work on it together now.

With this thought in mind, I was quite unprepared for the violence of Khalid's reaction when I told him. 'Is imbecility!' he cried, jumping to his feet. 'He cannot do that now. Is altogether too late.' He was pacing up and down, very agitated and waving his arms about. 'Sheikh Abdullah has already left to return to Hadd. He will report to the Emir all that has occurred here. If then *Haj* Whitaker remove his oil rig to the border . . .' He turned to me, still in great agitation, and said, 'It will mean war between us and Hadd. War, do you understand? For my father is guided by *Haj* Whitaker. The Emir knows that. And if *Haj*

Whitaker himself is on that border, then the Emir will know there is oil there and that my father will concede no revision of the boundaries between Hadd and Saraifa. You understand? You will help me?' He didn't give me time to answer, but summoned my escort. 'We leave at once, for there is little time. Excuse please. I go to my father now.'

He left then and I was alone with my three Arab guards. The child had stopped crying. There was no sound of women's voices. The palace slept, and sitting there, thinking about David, convinced now that he was still alive, I gradually became resigned to the fact that I wasn't going to get away in the plane that morning.

Khalid was gone about ten minutes. When he came back his face was pale, his manner subdued. 'I tell my father I am going to Dhaid to gather more men.'

'Did you tell him about Whitaker?'

'No, I don't tell him. And I don't tell him about David either – not yet. Is very much disturbed already. Come!'

'Is David at Dhaid?' I asked.

'No. But Sheikh Hassa holds that village for us. He will give us camels, and perhaps Salim bin Gharuf is there. I don't know. We have to hurry.' He gave an order to my escort and I was hustled out of the palace into the great courtyard where his Land Rover stood. The escort piled in behind us and as we drove down into the date gardens it was difficult to believe that the people of this peaceful place were threatened with extinction; that they had been so roused that night that they'd set fire to an oil company plane. The breeze had died and the whole world was still. Nothing moved. And when we ran out into the desert beyond the palms, it was into a dead, white world, for the moon was high now. We headed south, Khalid driving the Land Rover flat out, bucking the soft sand patches, eating up the flat gravel stretches at a tearing speed.

We were held up for a time by a choked petrol feed and the first grey light of dawn was taking the brightness from the moon when a needle-tip of latticed steel showed above the grey whale-back of a dune. It was Whitaker's oil rig, a mobile outfit – the sort they call an 'A' rig, truck and drill combined. It stood up out of the desert floor like a steel spear planted in the sand as a challenge to the vast wastes of emptiness that surrounded it. Beside it was a *barasti*, two Bedou tents and some tattered wisps of black cloth that acted as windbreaks.

As we neared it we heard the sound of the diesel, could see the Arab drilling crew busy drawing pipe. Other Arabs were loading a second truck with lengths of pipe. Early though it was the place was humming with activity, and when Khalid stopped and questioned them, he learned that Yousif had arrived just over an hour before with orders for them to prepare to move.

Whitaker had made his decision. He was moving his rig to the Hadd border and up in my empty turret room there were doubtless letters waiting for me to take to Bahrain. 'Is crazy!' Khalid cried, jumping back into the driving seat. 'Why does he do this now? He should do it before or not at all.' He drove on then, passing close below the derrick. It looked old and battered, the metal bare of paint and burnished bright in places by the drifting sands. The derrick man was up aloft stacking pipe, his loin cloth smeared with oil, his turbanned head a bundle of cloth against the paling sky.

Dawn was coming swiftly now and beyond the shallow slope of a dune I saw the tinsel-gleam of Erkhard's aircraft. It stood at the far end of a cleared stretch of gravel and the sight of it brought back to me my urge to escape from the desert. But when I demanded to be taken to it, Khalid took no notice except to give an order to the Arabs in the back. I reached for the ignition key. A brown hand seized my arm, another gripped my shoulders and I was held pinned to my seat while we plunged at more than thirty miles an hour into a world of small dunes, and the plane vanished beyond my reach.

After that the going was very bad for mile after weary mile. And when finally we came out of the little dune country, it was on to a gravel plain ribbed by crumbling limestone outcrops. A few dried-up herbs, brittle as dead twigs, bore witness to the fact that it had rained there once, many years ago. The land was dry and dead, flat as a pan, and as dawn broke and the sun came up, I lost all sense of horizon, for the whitish surface reflected the glare in an endless mirage.

All the way from the rig the going was bad. We had more trouble with the petrol feed and it was past midday before we caught sight of the low hill on which Dhaid stood. It throbbed in the heat haze, looking like the back of a stranded whale surrounded by pools of water. The crumbling mud walls of the village were merged in colour and substance with the crumbling rock on which they were built, so that it wasn't until we stopped at the foot of a well-worn camel track that I could make out the shape of the buildings. There was a single arched gateway, and we had barely started up the track on foot when the villagers poured out of it and rushed upon us, leaping from rock to rock, shouting and brandishing their weapons.

Khalid showed no alarm, walking steadily forward, his gait, his whole bearing suddenly full of dignity. And then they were upon us, engulfing us; a wild, ragamuffin lot, teeth and eyes flashing, dark sinewy hands stretched out to us in the clasp of friendship. They were dirty, dusty-looking men, some with no more than a loin cloth, and they looked dangerous with their black hair and bearded faces and their animal exuberance; and yet the warmth of that unexpected welcome was such after that empty, gruelling drive that I greeted them like brothers, their horny, calloused hands gripped around my wrists. It was the beginning of my acceptance of desert life.

Sheikh Hassa followed behind the rest of the village, picking his way sedately over the rock, his gun-bearer just ahead of him carrying his new BSA rifle which was his pride and joy. He was a short, tough-looking man with a shaggy black beard that gave him an almost piratical appearance. He greeted Khalid with deference, touching his hand with his fingers, carrying them to his lips and to his heart. 'Faddal.' And we went up the track and through the gateway into the village. A crowded square pulsating in the heat, a cool, darkened room spread with a rug, camel milk in bowls still warm from the beast's udder, and talk – endless, endless talk. I leaned back on the cushions, my eyelids falling, my head nodding. The buzz of flies. The buzz of talk. Not even coffee could keep me awake.

And then Khalid called to me and introduced me to a sinewy old man who stood half-naked in the gloom, a filthy loin cloth round his waist and his headcloth wound in a great pile above his greying locks so that he looked top-heavy. This was Salim bin Gharuf. 'He is of the Duru,' Khalid said, 'and he knows the place.' I asked him what place, but he ignored that. 'Is better now that you wear these please.' He produced a bundle of Bedou clothing, holding them out to me.

They were cast-off clothes and none too clean. 'Is this really necessary?' I demanded.

He nodded emphatically. 'Is better you look like one of us now.'

'Why? Where are we going?'

'I tell you later. Not here. You will change please.' He helped me off with my European clothes and wound the loin cloth round my waist; the long, dusty robe, the length of cloth twisted about my head, sandals, too, and an old brass-hilted knife for my belt. Sheikh Hassa watched me critically. I think the clothes were his. Men came and peered and the crowded room resounded with their mirth. Khalid sensed my annoyance. 'They don't mean any disrespect, sir. And you are going where no *faranji* has been before – save David.'

It was meant to mollify, but all it did was rouse my curiosity again. 'Well, if you won't tell me where he is,' I said, 'at least tell me how long it will take us to reach him.'

'A day and then half a day if we travel fast. Perhaps two days. I don't know. There is possibility of a storm.'

I think perhaps he might have told me more, but at that moment a man burst into the room shouting something, and instantly all was confusion. The room emptied with a rush that carried me with it out on to the white glare of a rooftop. Below us a single camel climbed wearily up the track, urged on by its rider. Khalid pushed past me. 'Is one of my father's racing camels,' he said.

Five minutes later he returned with the rider, a thick-set man with long hair twisted up in his head-cloth. Khalid talked for a moment with Sheikh Hassa and then with Salim. Finally he came to me. 'The oil men have left and at dawn this morning several large raiding parties from Hadd crossed our borders. My father orders me to return.'

My surprise was occasioned less by the news than by the realization that the camel must have made the journey in less time than we had taken in the Land Rover. But Khalid's next words jolted me into awareness of what it meant to me personally. 'You go now with Salim.'

'But . . .'

'Please, Meester Grant.' His face looked old now beyond his years, haggard after the long drive, the sleepless night. His eyes, staring at me, burned with an inner fire. 'Is altogether important now. Tell David what has happened, that his plan has failed and that there is no hope now of the oil concession. He must go to his father immediately.'

But my mind was on the practicalities. 'That's all very well,' I said, glancing uneasily at the old man. 'But Salim doesn't speak any English. And I don't know the country.' I looked about me quickly. Khalid's bodyguard was behind him, Sheikh Hassa right beside me. There was no escape. 'Where am I supposed to go anyway? Where is David?'

'You go to Umm al Samim.'

Sheikh Hassa leaned his black beard forward, and his harsh voice repeated the words 'Umm al Samim' on a note of surprise. And then he looked at me and rolled his eyes up into his head and laughed and made a strangling sound.

'What's he mean by that?' I demanded. 'What's he trying to tell me?'

Khalid's hand gripped my arm. 'The Umm al Samim is quicksands. But there is a way,' he added quickly, and I glanced at Hassa and knew that he'd been telling me that I was going to my death. 'I tell you there is a way,' Khalid said fiercely. 'Salim knows it as far as the first good ground. He will guide you as he guided us when we make original exploration two seasons past.'

'And what about the rest?'

'You will find by testing with a stick. Perhaps when you call, David or the Wahiba will hear you.' His grip on my arm tightened. 'You will go?'

'Suppose I refuse?'

'Then I take you with me back to Saraifa.' He was looking me straight in the face. 'This is what you want, isn't it correct – to find David? Now you find him.' And he added, staring at me hard, 'Are you afraid to go?'

'No, I'm not afraid.' I saw him smile. He knew after that I'd hardly refuse. 'All right, Khalid,' I said. 'I'll go. But what do you want me to do? A boy hiding out in some quicksands isn't going to help you now.'

'He must help us – he and his father. We are at point of desperation now, and it is his fault.' He said it without rancour, a statement of fact, and he added, 'It was a good plan, the way he visualize it – to go into hiding and by making appearance he is dead to draw attention to his survey. He think you will succeed to obtain the signature of Sir Gorde to a concession and that then per'aps we have oil, at least the support of the Company and so of your people. But instead all is turned to disaster. Because he is working on that border the raiders of Hadd are in our territory and the concession *Haj* Whitaker arrange is torn up. We have no Arab friends like the Emir has. We are alone and everything is in conspiracy now to destroy us.'

His words, the intensity with which he spoke, showed me the tragedy of it – father and son working for the same ends, but against each other. 'Yes, but what can he do?'

'He must ride to a meeting with his father. Salim has good camels. You and David together – you must persuade *Haj* Whitaker to stop drilling on the Hadd border and to go to Bahrain, to the Political Resident. If they don't send soldiers, then please to send us modern weapons and automatic guns so that we can fight.'

'Very well,' I said. 'I'll do what you say. I only hope it works out.'

'Tell David also . . .' He hesitated. 'Tell him it is possible I do not see him again. And if that is happening, then say to him that he is my brother, and the Emir Abdul-Zaid bin Sultan – my enemy into death.'

'What do you mean?' I asked.

'He will understand.'

'But you're not going to your death.'

'*Inshallah*! I do not know that.' His tone was fatalistic. 'This is an old feud, Meester Grant. As old as Saraifa is old, or Hadd. It goes back many centuries to the days when all the *falajes* are running with water, a hundred channels making irrigation for the palms. Then Saraifa is a great garden extending many miles and the dates go by camel north, to the sea and to India, across the mountains to the Batina coast, and south to the Hadhramaut – even, some say, to Mukalla and the olden port of Cana to be carried by dhow to the far places of the world. But we are always too much occupied with our gardens and the people of Hadd are very much envying us for our riches. They are men of the hills, cruel and hard and altogether without goodness. So.' He gave a helpless little shrug.

'So it is that we are always fighting for our date gardens and one after another the *falaj* channels are being destroyed until Saraifa is as you see it now, open to the desert and soon to die if the *falajes* are not rebuilt. Do you know, Meester Grant, there is not one man who can tell me, even when I am a little boy – even by the hearsay of others, his father or his grandfather – what it is like when there are more than six *falajes* working. Always wars . . . always, until the British come a hundred years ago. And now' – he spread his hands in a little gesture of helplessness – 'Now another war perhaps, and if we do not have a victory, then it is finish and in a few months the *shamal* will have blown the sands of the Rub al Khali over our walls and our houses and we shall be like those old lost cities in India . . . There will be nothing to show that we ever exist in this place.' He stopped there, a little breathless because he had put so much of himself and his emotions into foreign words. 'You tell him that please.' He turned then and spoke rapidly to Salim. The tattered figure moved towards me. 'You go now,' Khalid said. '*Fi aman allah!* In the peace of God.'

'And you also,' I said. The skinny hand of my guide was on my arm, a steel grip propelling me down mud steps out into the shadowed cool of an alley. In a little open space beyond there were camels crouched and at his cries three tall beasts lumbered to their feet. They had provisions already loaded and dark skin bags bulging with water. A boy brought two more camels and Salim chattered a gap-toothed protest as he realized that I didn't even know how to mount my beast. They brought it to its knees and put me on it and at a word it hoisted me violently into the air. The old man put his foot on the lowered neck of the other and stepped lightly into the saddle, tucking his legs behind him.

We left Dhaid by a small gateway facing south, just the two of us and the three pack beasts tied nose-to-tail. The boy ran beside us as far as the base of the limestone hill and then we were out on the gravel flat and travelling fast, a peculiar, swaying gait. It required all my concentration just to remain in the saddle. Perhaps it was as well, for it left me no time to consider my predicament. Our shadows lumbered beside us, for the sun was slanting towards the west, and Salim began to sing a high-pitched, monotonous song. It was a small sound in the solitude that surrounded us, but though I couldn't understand the words, I found it comforting.

The sun vanished before it reached the horizon, hazed and purple as a mulberry. We camped at dusk where the dusty green of new vegetation spattered the sand between ribs of limestone. The camels were let graze and Salim built a fire of furze and cooked a mess of rice and meat. One of the pack beasts was in milk and we drank it warm from the same bowl. And when he'd looked at his ancient rifle, oiling it carefully, we mounted and went on again.

We travelled all that night without a break. The moon turned the desert to a bleak, bone white, and in the early hours a mist came up and it was cold. By then I was too tired to care where I was going and only the pain of the saddle chafing the inside of my thighs, the ache of unaccustomed muscles kept me awake. The dawn brought a searing wind that whipped the mist aside and flung a moving cloud of sand in our faces. Lightning flashed in the gloom behind us, but no rain fell – just the wind and the driving sand particles.

We stopped again for food, lukewarm and gritty with sand, and then on again until the heat and the moving sand drove us into camp. I laid my head on my briefcase, covering my face with my headcloth, and slept like the dead, only to be woken again and told to mount. My nose and mouth were dry with sand and we went on and on at a walking pace that was relentless in the demands it made on my endurance. Dawn broke and the sun lipped the mountains that poked their rugged tops above the horizon to the east. Salim didn't sing that day and as the wind died and the sand became still, the heat increased until my head reeled and dark specks swam before my eyes.

By midday we were walking our camels along the edge of a dead, flat world that stretched away into the west, to disappear without horizon in a blur of haze. There was no dune nor any outcrop of rock, no tree, no bush, nothing to break the flat monotony of it. Salim turned in his saddle. 'Umm al Samim,' he said with a sweep of his hand, the palm held downward and quivering. I remembered the strangled sound Sheikh Hassa had made at the mention of that name, and yet it looked quite innocent; only that unnatural flatness and the dark discolouration of water seepage revealed the quagmire that lay concealed below the crust of wind-blown sand.

We followed the shore of the sands for about an hour whilst the sun beat down on us and the dull expanse shimmered with humidity. And then, by the gnarled remains of some camel thorn, we dismounted and started into the quicksands, leading our camels.

Close in-shore there were patches of solid ground, but farther out there was nothing that seemed to have any substance, the ground and air both quivering as we struggled forward. I can't remember any sense of fear. Fear is a luxury requiring energy, and I had none to spare. I can, however, remember every physical detail.

It was a *sabhkat* on the grand scale, and beneath the hard-baked crust my feet touched slime. At times it was difficult to stand at all, at others I broke through to the black filth below, and at every step I could feel the quiver of the mud. The camels slithered, bellowing in their fear, in constant danger of losing their legs and falling straddled. We had to drag the wretched beasts, even beat them, to keep them moving. This and the need to be ready to give them some support when they slipped did much to keep my mind from the filthy death that threatened at every step. And whenever I had a moment to look ahead, there was the Umm al Samim stretched out pulsating in the humid glare, innocent-seeming under its crust of sand, yet deadly-looking because it was so flat and level – as level as a lake.

And it seemed to have no end. It was like the sea when visibility is cut by haze. But here there were no buoys, no markers that I could see, nothing from which Salim could get his bearings. Yet once I saw the old tracks of camels, the round holes half filled with sand, and whenever I broke through to the mud below, my feet found solid ground before I was in farther than my knees; in some way that was not apparent to me Salim was following a rib of rock hidden below the surface of the sand.

Time had no meaning in the pitiless heat and the sweat rolled dripping down my back. I had a moment of panic when I would have turned and run if it had been possible. But then a camel slipped and a moment later Salim seized my arm and pointed ahead with his rifle. Little tufts of withered herbs lay limp in isolated clumps, and on the edge of visibility a gnarled thorn tree shimmered like a witch, its gaunt arms crooked and beckoning.

With the first of the withered herbs I felt the ground under my feet. It was hard and firm, and when I set my foot down nothing quaked, there was no gurgling sound, no sound of imminent break-up of the crust. Where the camel thorn stood there was naked rock and I flung myself down, revelling in the scorched hardness of it.

We were on a little island, raised imperceptibly above the flat level of the quicksands, and it was as far as Salim had ever penetrated. I watched him as he searched for Khalid's tracks, stopping every now and then to call, a high-pitched, carrying sound made with his hands cupped round his mouth. But the steaming heat absorbed his cries like a damp blanket and there was no answer.

In the end he gave it up and began prodding with his camel stick along the edge of the sands. Twice I had to pull him out, but finally he found firm ground beneath the crust and leaving the camels we started forward again, moving a step at a time, watching the quiver of the crust and prodding with the stick.

Behind us our tracks vanished into nothing. The rock island vanished, too, the white glare swallowing even the bulk of our camels. We were alone then, just the old man and myself in a little circle of flat sand that quaked and gurgled and sucked at our feet.

I don't know how long we were feeling our way like that. Once we saw the faint outline of a camel's pad, but only once. And then suddenly thorn trees throbbed in the haze ahead, looking huge, but dwindling as we approached the firm ground on which they stood. They were no more than waist-height and standing beside them, Salim cupped his hands and called again.

This time his cry was answered, a human voice calling to us, away to our left where the sands ran flat. I thought it was imagination, perhaps an unnatural echo of Salim's voice, for there was nothing there; an empty void throbbing in the heat, and the air so intensely pale it hurt the eyes.

And then suddenly the void was no longer empty. A man had materialized like a genie out of the heart of a furnace, his face burned black by the pitiless heat, his lips cracked, his ragged beard bleached by the sun, his hair, too, under the filthy headcloth.

He came forward and then stopped, suddenly suspicious, reaching for the gun slung at his shoulder. 'Salim!' Recognition brought a quick flash of teeth, white in the burnt dark face. *'Wellah! Salaam alaikum.'* He came forward and gripped Salim's wrist in a Bedou handclasp, whilst the old man talked, his words coming fast and high-pitched with excitement. And then the man turned to stare at me, pale eyes widening in startled disbelief. It was only when he finally spoke my name that I realized this strange nomadic-looking figure was David Whitaker. 'It's a long time,' I said. 'I didn't recognize you.'

He laughed and said, 'Yes, a hell of a long time.' He reached out his hand and his grip was hard on mine. Not content with that he took hold of both my shoulders and held them as though overwhelmed by the need for physical human contact. 'I can't believe it,' he said. And again, 'I can't believe it.'

I could hardly believe it myself. He was greatly changed. As Sue had said, he'd become a man. But even in that first glimpse of him I recognized again the quality of eagerness that had first attracted me to him. 'So you really are alive.' I don't think I'd fully accepted the fact until that moment.

'Yes, I'm alive – just.' His dark face was cracked in a boyish grin. 'Christ!' he said. 'It never occurred to me you'd come out here to look for me. Hell of a bloody journey. How did you know where I was?' But I suppose he saw I was exhausted, for he added quickly,

'Come up to the camp. You can stretch out and I'll have Ali brew some coffee.' He called to two men who had materialized out of the weird glare and were hovering on the edge of visibility. 'My companions,' he said.

They came forward warily, like dogs suspicious of a new scent, and they both had service rifles gripped in their hands. The elder he introduced as Hamid; a big man with long hair to his shoulders, bearded and impressive like a prophet. The other was little more than a boy, his face full-lipped and smooth, almost a girl's face, and he moved with the same natural grace. His name was Ali bin Maktum.

'Now let's have coffee and we'll talk.' David took my arm and led me to where the ground was higher and tattered pieces of black Bedou cloth had been erected as windbreaks, stretched on the bleached wood of camel thorn over holes they had scraped in the soft limestone. '*Faddal!*' It was said with Bedou courtesy, but with an ironical little smile touching the corners of his mouth.

He sent Hamid off to look to our camels, and whilst the boy Ali brewed coffee over a desert fire of sand and petrol, he sat beside me talking hard about the heat and the humidity and the loneliness he had been suffering in this godforsaken place. I let him run on, for I was tired and he needed to talk. He was desperate for the company of his own kind. He'd been there six weeks and in that time Khalid had made the journey twice to bring them food and water. 'I wouldn't trust anyone else. They might have talked.'

He was tracing patterns in the sand then, his head bent, shadowed by the headcloth. Flies buzzed in the sudden silence. 'Why are you here?' His voice came taut with the anxiety of a question too long delayed. 'Who told you where to find me – Khalid?'

'Yes,' I said. 'Khalid.' And I added, 'There's a lot to tell you.'

He misunderstood me, for his head came up, his eyes bright with sudden excitement. 'It's all right then, is it? You saw Sir Philip Gorde and he signed that concession agreement I typed out?' The words came breathless, his eyes alight with hope. But the hope faded as he saw my face. 'You did see Sir Philip, didn't you?'

'Yes,' I said. 'I gave him the envelope.'

'Well then . . .'

'He didn't sign the agreement.'

The effect of my words was to knock all the youth right out of him. His face looked suddenly old and strained, lines showed so that he seemed more like his father, and his shoulders sagged. 'So it didn't work.' He said it flatly as though he hadn't the spirit left for any display of emotion, and I realized that all the weeks he'd been waiting here alone he'd been buoyed up by this one hope. 'I thought if I disappeared completely, so completely that everyone thought I was dead . . . They did think I was dead, didn't they?'

'Yes,' I said. 'Everyone, including your father, presumed you were dead.' And I added, a little irritably because I was so tired, 'You've caused a lot of people a great deal of trouble; and your mother and sister a lot of needless grief.'

I thought for a moment he hadn't heard me. But then he said, 'Yes, indeed, I realize that. But Sue at least would understand.' His face softened. 'How is she? Did you see her?'

'Yes,' I said. 'I saw her.' And that, too, seemed a long time ago now. 'I don't think she ever quite accepted the idea that you were dead. Nor did your mother or that girl in Bahrain.'

'Tessa?' The lines of strain were momentarily smoothed out. 'You saw her, too?' He seemed surprised, and he added, 'I'm sorry, I'm afraid I've put you to a great deal of trouble.' He was staring down at the sand patterns between his feet. Abruptly he rubbed them out. 'I was so convinced it was the only way. I had to get past Erkhard somehow. I thought if I could get my report to Sir Philip Gorde. He was the one man . . .' His voice faded. And then, still talking to himself: 'But I couldn't just send it to him. It had to be done in some way that would enable him to override the political objections. I thought all the publicity connected with my disappearance . . . I'd planned it all very carefully. I had a lucky break, too. That night I visited Captain Griffiths on the *Emerald Isle*, there was an agency correspondent in transit to India stopping the night at the Fort in Sharjah. I saw him, told him the whole story – my background, how I'd escaped from Borstal and got myself out to Arabia, everything. I thought a story like that . . .' He darted a quick glance at me. 'Didn't he print it?'

'After you were reported missing, when the search had failed and you were presumed dead.'

'Yes, I made him promise he wouldn't use it unless something happened to me. But didn't it have any effect?'

'It seemed to cause quite a stir in the Foreign Office.'

'But what about the Company?'

'It put the shares up,' I said, trying to lighten it for him.

'Hell! is that all?' He gave a bitter little laugh. 'And I've been sitting here . . . waiting, hoping . . .' His shoulders had sagged again and he stared out into the throbbing glare, his eyes narrowed angrily. 'All these weeks, wasted – utterly wasted.' His voice was bleak. He looked weary – weary and depressed beyond words. 'I suppose you think now I've behaved like a fool – disappearing like that, pretending I was dead? But please try and understand.' He was leaning towards me, his face young and defenceless, his voice urgent now. 'I was on my own and I knew there wasn't any oil where my father was drilling. I ran a check survey without his knowledge; it was an anticline all right, but badly faulted. It couldn't hold any oil.' His voice had dropped to weariness again. He'd been over all this many times in his mind. 'I don't know whether he was kidding himself or trying to cheat the Company or just doing it to get his own back on Erkhard. But I wanted the Company to drill on my locations, not his. I wanted oil. I wanted it for Saraifa and I wanted it to be the real thing.'

'Your father wanted it, too,' I said gently. 'And he, too, was convinced there was oil where you did your survey.'

'That's not true. He refused to believe me. Told me I was inexperienced, that I'd no business to be on that border and forbade me ever to go near it again.'

'I think,' I said, 'you'd better listen to what I have to tell you.'

The coffee was ready then and I waited until Ali had poured it for us from the battered silver pot. It was Mocha coffee, bitter and wonderfully refreshing, and as I sipped the scalding liquid I told him the whole story of my journey and all that had happened. Once whilst I was telling it, he said, 'I'm sorry. I didn't realize.' And later, when I came to the point where Gorde had left me with Entwhistle and we'd been fired on, he apologized again. 'I'm afraid you've had a hell of a time, sir, and all my fault.' That 'sir' took me back, for it still didn't come easily from him.

But it was my account of that first interview with his father that really shook him. When I had explained to him what his father had been trying to do, he was appalled. 'But Christ! Why didn't he tell me? I'd no idea. None at all. And when Khalid told me he'd been to see the Emir of Hadd . . .' He stared at me, his face fine-drawn, his voice trembling as he repeated, 'Why the hell didn't he tell me what he was trying to do?'

'I think you know why,' I said. 'You were employed by the Company, and the Company to him meant Erkhard.' And I added, 'Erkhard knew your background, didn't he? He used that as a lever to get you to spy on your father.'

It was a shot in the dark, but it went home. 'He tried to.' His tone was almost sullen; he looked uncomfortable.

'And you agreed?' I'd no wish to conduct a cross-examination, but I thought it essential he should see it from his father's point of view if I were to succeed in bringing them together again.

'I hadn't any choice,' he said, stung to anger by my question. 'Erkhard threatened to turn me over to the Cardiff police.'

'And your father knew about that?'

'It didn't mean I was going to do what Erkhard wanted.'

'But you'd agreed to do it,' I insisted, 'and your father knew you'd agreed.'

'I suppose so.' He admitted it reluctantly. 'He's still got his friends inside the Company.'

So there it was at last, the basic cause of the rift between them – the thing that girl Tessa had hinted at, that Sue had felt but hadn't been able to explain.

'Christ!' he said. 'What a bloody stupid mess! And all because we didn't trust each other like we should have done. How could I guess what he was up to? Though it's just the sort of twisted, devious approach . . .' His voice faded and once more he was staring out into the void. 'I got very close to him at one time, but even then I was always conscious of a gulf, of something hidden that I couldn't fathom. He's very unpredictable, you know, Mr Grant. More Arab than the Arabs, if you see what I mean.' He was very much on the defensive then. 'After four years I can't say I really understood him. Switching races like that, and his religion, too – it left a sort of gulf that couldn't be bridged. And when Khalid told me he'd been to see the Emir, it made me wonder . . .' He hesitated. 'Well, as I say, he's unpredictable, so I decided it was time I put my plan into action and disappeared. Khalid thought so, too. He'd brought Hamid and Ali, two of his most trusted men, and a spare camel. So . . .' He shrugged. 'I knew it was hard on Sue. Hard on Tessa, too – and on my mother. But I was alone, you see. I'd nobody to turn to, except Khalid. He was the only man in the world who had faith in me. And I couldn't look to the Company for help. Erkhard had made that very plain. And anyway, oil companies are in business for themselves, not for the Arabs. They've been known to sit on an oilfield for years for political or commercial reasons . . .' The sweat was pouring off him and he wiped his hand across his brow. 'Well, go on,' he said. 'What happened when Erkhard came to Saraifa – did my father succeed in getting a concession signed?'

But I think he'd guessed that I shouldn't have come here alone if it were all settled. He listened, silent, not saying a word, as I told him the rest of my story. Once his eyes came alight with sudden excitement; that was when I told him of my second talk with Whitaker and how Khalid and I had seen the drilling rig being dismantled for the move up to the Hadd border. The thought that his father was at last doing what he'd been wanting him to do for so long gave him a momentary sense of hope. But it was only momentary, for I went straight on to tell him of the scene at Dhaid and how the lone rider had brought the news that Gorde and Erkhard had left and Hadd forces had crossed the border into Saraifa. 'So it's come to that, has it? Open war between Hadd and Saraifa.' His body was suddenly trembling as though with fever and his voice was bitter. 'And Khalid sent you to me. What did he say before you left? What message did he give you?'

'He said he thought this time Saraifa had reached the point of desperation.' And I gave him the gist of what Khalid had said to me. When I had finished he didn't say anything for a long time, sitting there lost in thought, staring out across the flat misery of the Umm al Samim. 'The only home I ever had,' he whispered. 'Did you see it when the *shamal* was blowing, with the Rub al Khali like a sea, the dunes all smoking and the sands pouring into the date gardens? It's like a flood then.' His father's words – his father's voice almost. 'The oasis is doomed, you see. Doomed to extinction by the desert. But that's a natural process; something to be fought with the natural resources of the country. Khalid and I, we were going to rebuild the old *falaj* channels with the money from oil royalties. That was our dream. But this . . .' He stared at me hard, his eyes wide. 'You're sure it's war, are you? It's not just a border raid?'

I gave him Khalid's speech then, as near as I could remember it word for word.

'So it's my fault, is it?' He said it with deep bitterness and after that he was silent for a long time. Finally, he looked at me. 'Unto death, you said. Khalid used those exact words, did he?' And when I nodded, 'So it's not just a raid – it's the real thing this time.' He was almost in tears, he was so deeply moved. And then sadly: 'My father's fault, too – he's made his decision too late.' And he began cursing softly to himself. 'Those dung-eating bastards from Hadd, they'll smash down the last of the *falaj* channels. What would have taken twenty years by natural means will take less than that number of months. The desert will roll in. Christ Almighty! The bastards!' It was a cry from the heart and I was conscious of desperation here, too – a desperation that matched Khalid's. 'They can't fight a war against Hadd. They've nothing to fight it with – only antiquated guns.'

He began questioning me then, pressing me for details, many of which I couldn't give him, for he wasn't interested in his father now, or Gorde or the Company; his attention was fixed on Hadd and the way Sheikh Abdullah, the Emir's representative, had behaved, and what had passed between him and Sheikh Makhmud that morning before Whitaker and Erkhard had arrived. The sun sank in a blood-red haze and the air became dank. My head nodded, my body suddenly drained of warmth and shivering with fatigue. 'You'd better get some rest now,' he said finally. 'We'll be leaving as soon as the moon's up and it's light enough to see our way through the quick-sands.' He seemed to have reached some decision, for his voice was firmer, his manner less depressed. He brought me a tattered blanket musty with sand. 'I've kept you talking when you should have been getting some sleep.'

'What do you plan to do?' I asked him. 'You'll go to your father, I take it?'

'Yes. He's still got a few of his bodyguard left. A dozen men and I could create a diversion that would keep the Emir busy until my father has time to make his influence felt in Bahrain. Khalid's right. We must work together now – my father and I.' The mention of Khalid's name seemed to bring his mind back to his friend. 'He said he was my brother, didn't he? Unto death?'

'Your brother, yes,' I said. 'But as I remember it, he used the words 'into death' in connection with the Emir – 'my enemy into death'.'

'Well, pray God it doesn't come to that.' There were tears in his eyes and standing there, staring straight into the flaming sunset, he quoted from the Bible: *'The Lord be between me and thee, and between my seed and thy seed for ever.'*

Dimly I recognized the quotation as the oath sworn by his namesake; I didn't realize it then, but this was the covenant, sworn in the midst of the quicksands of the Umm al Samim, that was to take him to that fort on top of Jebel al-Akhbar and to the terrible final tragedy.

I saw the sun set and the quicksands turn to blood, and then the sky faded to the palest pastel green and the stars came out. Lying there, it was like being stranded on a coral reef in the midst of a flat lagoon.

Sometime in the small hours the wind woke me, blowing a drift of sand in my face. The moon was up, but its face was hidden in a cloud of moving sand. There was no question of our leaving and I lay till dawn, unable to sleep, my eye-balls gritty, my nose and mouth clogged with sand, and when the sun rose all it showed was a sepia haze. We ate in extreme discomfort, the sand whistling like driven spume across the flat surface of the Umm al Samim.

The storm lasted until almost midday, and then it ceased as abruptly as it had started. We cooked a meal of rice and dried meat, and then we started back, collecting our camels on the way and struggling through the quicksands to the solid desert shore. We mounted them and keeping the Umm al Samim on our left, rode till dusk, when we camped. A meal and a short two-hour rest and then on again with Salim arguing sullenly. 'The old fool thinks the beasts will founder.' David's face was grim. He was in a hurry and he had no sympathy for men or beasts. 'Like all the Bedou he loves his camels more than he loves himself.'

We marched all night and there were times when I hoped the camels would founder. My muscles were stiff and aching, and where the wooden saddle chafed my legs, I was in agony. The starlight faded, swamped by the brighter light of the risen moon, and in the grey of dawning day we reached the big well at Ain. Salim went forward alone to water the camels, for early as it was there were others at the well before us. 'Men of the Duru tribe, I expect,' David said as we sat on the ground with the loads stacked round us, brewing coffee. 'Salim will bring us the news.'

I dozed and woke to the sound of the old man's voice. 'What's happened?' I asked, for his face was lit by the excitement of some great event. 'What's he saying?'

'He's talked with some men of the Rashid, back from selling camels at Saraifa.' David's face was grey in the dawn. 'They say there's been fighting already – a battle.'

'Between Hadd and Saraifa?'

'It's hearsay, that's all. They don't know anything.' He didn't want to believe it, but his voice was urgent as he gave the order to mount.

We loaded the camels in a hurry, and as we started out again, I saw that our direction had changed. I asked him where we were going and he said, 'Dhaid. We'll get the news there.' And after that he didn't talk. His mood was sullen and withdrawn, his temper short, and he answered Salim angrily whenever the old man protested at the pace of our march.

We rode all day and far into the night, and in the morning the camels were almost done, their pace painfully slow. We reached Dhaid a little after midday. Nobody came out to meet us. Camels dotted the limestone slopes of the hill and men lay listless under the walls of the village. Inside the arched entrance, the little open place was packed with people; whole families with their beasts and chattels were crowded there in the oven heat that beat back from the walls.

They were all from Saraifa – refugees; the atmosphere was heavy with disaster, the news bad. Two more *falajes*, they said, had been destroyed and a battle fought, out by one of the wells. Khalid was reported dead, his father's soldiers routed. 'Old-fashioned rifles against automatic weapons.' David's tone was bitter. 'For months the Emir has been receiving a steady trickle of arms. And we've done nothing about it. Nothing at all.'

'They're independent states,' I reminded him.

'That's what the political boys said when I told them arms were being smuggled in dhows to the Batina coast and brought by camel across the mountains. A perfect excuse for doing nothing. And now, if Khalid is dead . . .' His voice shook. His face looked ghastly, the skin burned black, yet deathly pale. 'Sheikh Makhmud's an old man. He can't fight this sort of a war. And the Emir has only to block two more *falajes* and his men can just sit and wait for the end.'

We left Salim with the camels and fought our way through the crowds to Sheikh Hassa's house. We found him in the room where I had left Khalid a few days before. He was sitting surrounded by a crush of men all talking at once. The new rifle lay forgotten on the floor. Beside him sat a young man with long features that were tense and pale. 'Mahommed,' David whispered. 'Khalid's half-brother.' He'd fled from the battlefield, but he'd seen enough to confirm the rumours we'd heard in the market place. The battle had been fought by the ninth well out along the line of the Mahdah *falaj* and the casualties had been heavy. Sheikh Makhmud himself had been wounded and the latest reports of survivors indicated that he had retired to the oasis with the remnant of his forces and was shut up in his palace and preparing to surrender.

David talked to the two of them for about ten minutes, and then we left. 'Sheikh Hassa's scared,' he said as we pushed our way out into the shade of the alleyway. 'All these frightened people flooding into his village . . . It's knocked the fight right out of him. And Mahommed's only a boy. Hassa will hand over Dhaid without firing a shot.' He said it angrily, with deep bitterness. And he added, 'Fifty resolute men could defend this place for a month – long enough to preserve its independence from Hadd.'

'What about Khalid?' I asked. 'Did his brother say what had happened to him?'

'No. He doesn't know.' His face was grey and haggard. 'All this killing and destroying – it's so bloody futile, a lust for oil. Can't they understand the oil won't last? It's just a phase, and when it's past they'll be faced with the desert again; and the only thing that will matter then is what they've built with the oil against the future.' And he added angrily, 'The Emir didn't care a damn about that border until my father got Gorde to sign a concession. It was just sand and nothing grew there. And then to cancel it . . . I can almost see the look on Sheikh Makhmud's face that night. God!' he exclaimed. 'The callousness of men like Erkhard – Gorde, too. They don't care. These people are human beings and they're being mucked around by hard-faced men who think only in terms of commerce and money.'

We were out of the alley, back in the glare of the crowded market place. He spoke to Salim and gave him money, a handful of Maria Theresa silver dollars poured from a leather bag, and then we settled ourselves in the dust by the entrance gate, leaning our backs against the crumbling mud walls amongst a crowd of listless refugees who watched us curiously. 'I've sent Salim to buy fresh camels,' David said. 'We'll leave as soon as he returns.'

'How long will it take us to reach the Hadd border?' I was feeling very tired.

But his mind was on Khalid. 'I must find out what's happened to him.' He was silent a long time then, tracing patterns in the sand with his camel stick. And then abruptly he rubbed them out with the flat of his palm. 'If he's dead . . .' His emotions seemed to grip him by the throat so that the sentence was cut off abruptly. And then, his voice suddenly practical, 'In that case, there are his men. He had more than a score of them, a paid personal bodyguard. Wahiba mostly and some Rashid; all good fighters.' He was staring hungrily out into the burning distance of the desert. 'I need men,' he whispered, his teeth clenched. 'Men who'll fight. Not these—' He gestured with contempt at the listless figures around us. 'A score of men properly armed and I could put the fear of God into that bloody little Emir.'

I didn't bother to ask him how, for I thought it was just wishful thinking and all in his imagination. My eyes were closing with the heat and the weariness of my aching muscles. I heard him say something about getting me to Sharjah as soon as he could and then I was asleep.

I woke to the voices of Salim and the two Wahiba; they were arguing loudly whilst David sat listening, a tattered Bible propped on the rifle across his knees. Two camels stood disdainfully in front of us. 'They've become infected with the mood of this place, blast them!' David closed the Book and got to his feet. A crowd was beginning to collect. He said something to Hamid and the man looked suddenly like a dog that's been beaten. And then David took his rifle from him and handed it to me. 'Come on!' he said. 'Let's get going.' He spoke angrily to the two Wahiba and then we mounted.

The camels were thoroughbred Oman racing camels. I could feel the difference immediately. The crowd parted, letting us through, and we picked our way daintily down the rocks. Out on the flat gravel of the desert below, we moved into an ungainly canter, circling the hill on which Dhaid rested and heading north-east again.

'These people,' David said, 'they're so damned uncertain; full of guts one minute, craven the next. Salim I didn't expect to come. But Hamid and Ali . . .' He sounded depressed. 'My father now, he can handle them the way I'll never be able to.' There was admiration, a note of envy in his voice. 'They'd never have left him in the lurch.' We rode in silence then and at a gruelling pace, the heat very great so that I was thankful for the water we had got at Dhaid.

We camped at dusk and David had just lit a fire

when he turned suddenly and grabbed his rifle. I heard the pad of camels' feet and then the riders emerged out of the gathering darkness. There were three of them and David relaxed. 'Salim, too,' he whispered. He didn't give them any greeting and they slunk to the fire like dogs. I gave Hamid back his rifle. He took it as though it were a gift and made me a long speech of thanks. 'They're like children,' David said. His voice sounded happy.

We had a handful of dates each and some coffee, that was all. And then we rode on.

In the early hours of the morning, with the moon high and a white miasma of mist lying over the desert, we approached the ninth well of the Mahdah *falaj*. Hamid and Ali were scouting ahead on either flank. David and Salim rode close together, their rifles ready-to-hand across their knees. The tension had been mounting all through that night ride, for we'd no idea what we were going to find at the end of it.

For the first time I rode my camel without conscious thought of what I was doing, my whole being concentrated in my eyes, searching the mist ahead. The desert was very still and, half-concealed under that white veil, it had a strange, almost eerie quality. From far ahead came a weird banshee howl. It rose to a high note and then dropped to an ugly cough. 'Hyena,' David said and there was loathing in his voice. The sound, repeated much nearer and to our flank, checked my camel in its stride. It was an eerie, disgusting sound. A little later Salim stopped to stare at some camel tracks. Their droppings, too, and he dismounted, sifted them through his fingers, smelt them, and then delivered his verdict – men of the Bait Kathir and they had come south the night before with two camels belonging to Saraifa.

'Loot,' David said, and we rode on in silence until about ten minutes later Hamid signalled to us. He had sighted the first corpse. It had been stripped of its clothes and there wasn't much meat left on the bones, which stared white through the torn flesh. The teeth, bared in the remains of a beard, had fastened in agony upon a tuft of dried-up herb.

It wasn't a pretty sight with the sand all trampled round about and stained black with blood, and after that the bodies lay thick. They had been caught in ambush and slaughtered as they rushed a small gravel rise where the enemy had lain in wait. There were camels, too, their carcases bared to the bones and white and brittle-looking like the withered remains of dwarf trees dead of drought. The whole place smelt of death and things moved on the edge of visibility. Two men slunk away like ghouls, mounted their camels and disappeared into the mist.

We let them go for David's only interest was to discover whether Khalid had been killed. Methodically he and Salim checked every corpse, while the two Wahiba scouted the edges of the battlefield. David could put a name to most of the bodies, despite decomposition and the mutilations of scavengers, and one I recognized myself: the leader of Khalid's escort. He lay face down in the tyre marks of a Land Rover, and close beside were the bodies of three more of Khalid's men, stripped of their clothes and arms.

We hadn't far to go after that. The tyre marks lipped a rise and a little beyond, the burned-out remains of the Land Rover itself loomed out of the mist. They had sought cover behind it and their bodies had been ripped to pieces by a murderous fire. Khalid lay with eyeless sockets and half his face torn away. The near-naked body was already disintegrating and where the stomach had been torn open the rotten flesh crawled with maggots and the blood was dry and black like powder. Four of his men lay near him in much the same state of putrefaction.

'The waste!' David breathed. He was standing, staring down at the remains of his friend and there were tears in his eyes. 'The bloody, senseless waste!' There was a shovel still clipped to the Land Rover, its handle burned away. He seized hold of it and attacked the ground with violent energy, digging a shallow grave. And when we'd laid what was left of Khalid to rest and covered it with sand, David stood back with bowed head. 'He might have saved Saraifa. He was the only one of them who had the vision and the drive and energy to do it.' He wiped his face with his headcloth. 'May he rest in peace, and may Allah guide him to the world beyond.' He turned his back abruptly on the grave and strode blindly off across the sand towards the gravel rise that had been the scene of the ambush.

Along the back of it ran a ridge of bare rock. Behind it the ground was scattered with the brass of empty cartridges. 'War surplus.' He tossed one of them to me. 'Governments sell that stuff. They never think of the loss of life their bloody auctions will ultimately cause. A pity the little bureaucrat . . .' But he let it go at that, wandering on along the ridge. At four places we came upon the empty magazines of automatic guns; in each case they lay beside the tyre marks of vehicles. 'They hadn't a chance,' he said bitterly and started back to where Salim waited with the camels.

Before we reached them, Ali came hurrying back. He had been scouting to the east, along the line of the *falaj*, and had almost stumbled into a small Hadd force camped by the next well. He said the walls of the well had been thrown down, the whole thing filled with sand and rock. We waited for Hamid. He was a long time coming and when he did arrive his manner was strange, his eyes rolling in his head as words poured out of him. 'He's just buried his father,' David said. 'The old man's body had a dozen bullets in it.' Grimly he gave the order to mount.

I was glad to go. Dawn was breaking and a hot wind beginning to blow from the north-west. I was sick of the sight of so much death. So was David. This, after the lonely weeks he'd spent in that filthy area of quicksands . . . I didn't need the set, withdrawn look of his face, the occasional mumbling of the lips, to tell me that he was mentally very near the end of his tether. 'Where are we going?' I asked as we rode towards the next well, the wall of which was just visible on the horizon, a little rock turret above the drifting, moving sands.

'Saraifa,' he said. 'I'll know the worst then.' I think he could already picture the misery that awaited us.

Halfway there we met with a family of the Junuba heading towards the mountains with a long string of camels loaded with dates for the coast. They gave us the news. The last *falaj* had ceased to flow that morning. Sheikh Makhmud was said to have died during the night. His brother, Sheikh Sultan, ruled in his place. We purchased some dates from them – we had been unable to buy any supplies in Dhaid – and hurried on.

All the way to Saraifa the traces of disaster were with us, the carcase of a camel, a body sprawled in the sand, discarded arms. But according to the Junuba, the Emir's men were not in the oasis. 'They don't need to attack now,' David said. 'They can sit on the *falajes* they've destroyed and just wait for the end, like vultures waiting for a man to die.' And he added, 'Sheikh Sultan will make peace. He's a gutless, effeminate old man, and they know it.'

The wind increased in force until it was blowing a strong *shamal* and we never saw Saraifa until the crumbling walls of a date garden appeared abruptly out of the miasma clouds of wind-blown sand. The palms thrashed in the blinding air as they closed around us.

We passed a patch of cultivation, the green crop already wilted and turning sear. And when we reached the first *shireeya*, we found it dry, the mud bottom hard as concrete, split with innumerable cracks. The *falaj* channel that supplied it was empty. The skeletal shape of little fish lay in the sand at the bottom of it.

Only when we came to the outskirts of Saraifa itself was there any sign of human activity. Camels were being loaded, household possessions picked over. But most of the *barastis* were already empty, the human life gone from them. Men stopped to talk to us, but only momentarily. They were bent on flight.

It was the same when we reached the mud buildings in the centre of Saraifa. Everywhere there were beasts being loaded. But it was the tail-end of the exodus, most of the houses already deserted. And in the great square under the palace walls, the watering place no longer delivered its precious fluid to a noisy crowd of boys with their asses; the ground round it was caked hard and the only person there was an old man with a child of about two.

We circled the walls and came to the main gate. The great wooden portals were closed. No retainers stood guard on the bastions above. The palace had the look of a place shut against the plague and given over to despair. David sat for a moment on his camel, looking down on the date gardens half-hidden beneath the weight of driven sand, and tears were streaming down his face. He turned to me suddenly and swore an oath, demanding that the Almighty should be his witness – and the oath was the destruction of Hadd. 'Khalid is dead,' he added, and his eyes burned in their sockets. 'Now I must do what he'd have done, and I'll not rest till the *falajes* are running again – not only the five they've destroyed, but the others, too. That

I swear, before Almighty God, or my life is worth nothing.'

We rode out of Saraifa then, leaving behind us the pitiful sight of a people driven from their homes by thirst, heading into the desert, our heads bent against the wind, our mouths covered. Once David paused, his arm flung out, pointing. 'Now you see it. Now you see the Rub al Khali rolling in like the sea.' And indeed it did look like the sea, for through gaps in the flying curtain of sand I could see the dunes smoking like waves in the gusts, the sand blowing off their tops in streamers. 'That's what Khalid was fighting. Like water, isn't it? Like water flooding in over a low-lying land.' And riding on, he said, 'With the people gone, the wells all dry . . . this place won't last long.' His words came in snatches on the wind. 'How long will they survive, do you think – those families hurrying to go? They're not nomads. They can't live in the Sands. They'll die by slow degrees, turned away by sheikh after sheikh who fears they and their beasts will drink his own people out of water. And what can they live on when their camels are gone?'

He was riding close beside me then. 'Sometimes I hate the human race . . . hate myself, too, for being human and as cruel as the rest.' And then quietly, his teeth clenched, his eyes blazing: 'There'll be men die in Hadd for what I've seen today.'

It was the strange choice of words, the way he was trembling and the violence of his manner; I thought he'd been driven half out of his mind by Khalid's death and the tragic things we'd seen. 'All I need is a few men,' he whispered to me. 'Khalid's are all dead. Half a dozen men, that's all I need.'

The sun's heat increased and the wind gradually died. I suffered badly from thirst for we hadn't much water left and we were riding fast. Towards midday, in a flat gravel pan between high dunes, we came upon the tracks of heavy vehicles. We followed them and shortly afterwards heard the roar of diesels. It was the drilling rig, both trucks floundering in a patch of soft sand. The big eight-wheeler was out in front, the rig folded down across its back, and it was winching the second truck, loaded with pipe and fuel drums, across the soft patch.

They were working with furious energy, for they'd had refugees from Saraifa through their camp just before they'd pulled out, and they were scared. We stopped with them long enough to brew coffee and give our beasts a rest, and when we rode on David said to me, 'Why's he want to bring that rig here now? What good will it do?' He was haggard-eyed, his face pale under its tan. 'They told me he'd requisitioned Entwhistle's seismological outfit – the men as well as the truck. He did that just after the battle, when he knew what had happened. I don't understand it. He must realize it's too late now . . .'

The shadows of the dunes were lengthening, their crests sharp-etched against the flaming sky. We were working our way across them then and as the sun finally sank, we came to the top of a dune, out of the shadow into the lurid light of the blood-red sunset, and in the gravel flat below we saw the tracks of vehicles and the blackened circles of camp fires. 'Location B,' David said and we rode down into shadow again.

The camp had been abandoned that morning. So much Salim was able to tell us from the ashes of the camp fires, and after that we kept just below the dune crests, riding cautiously with Ali scouting ahead.

We'd only just lost sight of the abandoned camp when the thud of an explosion shook the ground, and the sands on the steep face of a dune opposite slid into motion with a peculiar thrumming, singing sound. Our camels stood halted, their bodies trembling, and the singing sound of the sands went on for a long time. There was no further explosion. But almost as soon as we started forwards again. Ali called to us and at the same moment there was the crack of a rifle and a bullet sang uncomfortably close.

I don't remember dismounting. I was suddenly stretched on the sand with Salim pulling my camel down beside me. David and Hamid were crawling forward to the dune crest, their guns ready. I thought for a moment we had been ambushed. But then Ali shouted a greeting. He had dropped his rifle and was standing up, throwing sand into the air. It was the Bedou sign that we came in friendship, and in a moment we were dragging our camels down the steep face of the dune and three Arabs were running to meet us, brandishing their weapons and shouting.

We had reached Colonel Whitaker's camp at Location C. The tents were huddled against the base of a dune, black shapes in the fading light, and out on the gravel flat. Entwhistle's seismological truck stood lit by the glow of cooking fires. There were perhaps fifteen men in that camp and they flitted towards us like bats in the dusk. As they crowded round us, one of them recognized David. All was confusion then, a babel of tongues asking questions, demanding news.

David didn't greet them. I doubt whether he even saw them. His eyes were fixed on his father, who had come out of one of the tents and was standing, waiting for us, a dark, robed figure in silhouette against the light of a pressure lamp. David handed his camel to Salim and went blindly forward. I think he still held his father in some awe, but as I followed him I began to realize how much the day had changed him. He had purpose now, a driving, over-riding purpose that showed in the way he strode forward.

There wasn't enough light for me to see the expression on Colonel Whitaker's face when he realized who it was. And he didn't speak, even when David stood directly in front of him. Neither of them spoke. They just stood there, staring at each other. I was close enough then to see Whitaker's face. It was without expression. No surprise, no sign of any feeling.

'It's your son,' I said. 'He's alive.'

'So I see.' The voice was harsh, the single eye fixed on David. 'You've decided to return from the dead. Why?'

'Khalid asked me to come here and talk to you. He wanted us to . . .'

'Khalid's dead.'

'I know that. I buried his body this morning.'

David's voice trembled with the effort to keep himself under control. 'He died because his father hadn't the sense to avoid a pitched battle.' And he added, 'We passed that rig of yours a few miles back. It's too late now to start drilling on my locations.'

'On your locations?'

'On Farr's then – as checked by me.'

'And by me,' Whitaker snapped. 'Since you've got Grant with you, I presume you now have some idea what I was trying to do. If you hadn't disappeared like that . . .'

'Don't for God's sake let's have another row.' David's voice was strangely quiet. 'And don't let's start raking over the past. It's too late for that now. Khalid was right. We've got to work together. I came because I need men.'

'Men?' Colonel Whitaker stared at him with a puzzled frown. 'What do you need men for?'

'I'll tell you in a moment. But first I'd like to know what you're planning to do with that rig? You can't surely intend to drill here – not now, after what's happened?'

'Why not?'

'But it's crazy. It'll take you months . . .'

'You call it crazy now, do you?' Whitaker's voice was hard and pitched suddenly very high. 'Last time I saw you, you were raising hell because I wouldn't drill here. Well, now I'm going to try it your way.'

'But don't you realize what's happened in Saraifa?'

'Of course I do. Sheikh Makhmud is dead and I've lost an old friend. His brother, Sultan, is Ruler in his place, and you know what that means. Saraifa is finished.'

David stared at him in disbelief. 'You mean you're going to do a deal with the Emir?' His tone was shocked.

Whitaker's face was without expression. 'I've seen him, yes. We've reached a tentative agreement.' And then as he saw the look of contempt on David's face, he exclaimed, '*Allah akhbar!* When are you going to grow up, boy?'

'You don't have to worry on that score, sir. I've grown up fast enough these past few months.' David's voice was calmer, much quieter. He seemed suddenly sure of himself. 'But there's no point in discussing what's gone. It's the future I'm concerned with – the future of Saraifa. Can I rely on you for support or not?'

Whitaker frowned. 'Support for what?'

'For an attack on Hadd. I've worked it all out in my mind.' David's voice came alive then, full of sudden enthusiasm. 'For centuries they've been destroying other people's wells. They've never known what it is to be short of water themselves. I'm going to give them a taste of their own medicine. I'm going to destroy the wells in Hadd.'

'Are you out of your mind?' Whitaker glared at him. 'Even if you did blow up a well, what good would it do? In a day or at most two they would have repaired it.'

'I don't think so,' David said quietly. 'Just let me have a few men.'

'Men? You won't get men out of me for a crack-brained scheme like this.' And then in a gentler voice, 'See here, David. I realize you've probably been through a lot during the past two months. And if you've been out to the battlefield on the Mahdah *falaj*, as I rather suspect from your attitude, I don't imagine it was a pleasant sight.'

'It wasn't a pleasant sight riding through Saraifa and seeing the people there without water and fleeing from the oasis,' David answered hotly.

'No. But . . .' Colonel Whitaker hesitated. He'd seen the obstinate look on David's face. No doubt he sensed his mood, too, which was desperately determined. 'Come into the tent,' he said. 'I refuse to continue this discussion out here.' He glanced at me. 'If you'll excuse us, Grant. I'd like to talk to my son alone for a moment.' He pulled back the flap of the tent. '*Faddal*.' It was said quite automatically. A carpet showed red in the glare of the lamplight, some cushions, a tin box, and the two of them were inside the tent and the flap fell.

The outline of the dunes, smooth and flowing like downlands, faded into darkness as I sat alone on the sand, a centre of curiosity for the whole camp. The sky was clouded over so that there were no stars and it was very dark.

It was about half an hour later that David suddenly emerged out of the night and sat down beside me. 'What happened?' I asked him.

'Nothing,' he replied tersely. And after that he sat for a long time without saying a word, without moving. Finally he turned to me of his own accord. 'I don't understand him,' he said. 'It was like talking to a complete stranger.' And he added, 'I don't think Saraifa means anything to him any more.' The bitterness of his voice was overlaid with frustration. 'It's tragic,' he whispered. 'Half a dozen men. That's all I asked him for. But he thinks it's all a dream, that I don't know what I'm doing.'

'You told him about Khalid – what he'd said to me?'

'Of course.'

'And it made no difference?'

'None.'

'What did you talk about then?'

He laughed a little wildly. 'About locations, geological formations, a drilling programme. He wasn't interested in anything else.' And then speaking more to himself than to me: 'I couldn't get through to him. I just couldn't seem to get through.' He beat his fist against the ground. 'What do you do when a man's like that?' He stared at me angrily. 'I don't understand him. Do you know what he said? He said I was forgiven. He said everything was to be just as it was between us in the early days when I first worked with him. I'm to stay here and help him drill a well. He and I – together; we're going to drill the most important well in Arabia.' Again that slightly wild laugh. 'And when I mentioned Hadd, he said Hadd or Saraifa, what did it matter now? He'll treat with the Emir, with the Devil himself, so long as he's left in peace to drill his well and prove his bloody theory to the damnation of Philip Gorde and all the rest of the oil boys. God! I wonder I didn't kill him.' And he added, 'The man's mad. He must be mad.'

'Obsessed perhaps . . .' I murmured.

'Mad.' He glared at me. 'How else do you explain his attitude, his fantastic assumption that I'd be content to sit here drilling a well after what's happened? For Khalid's sake I'd have agreed to anything. I'd have played the dutiful bastard sitting at the feet of the Great Bedouin. But when I asked him for men . . .' He shook his head. 'He wouldn't give them to me. He wouldn't do a damned thing to help. Said I was crazy even to think of it. Me? And all he could talk about, with Makhmud dead and men he'd known for years lying by that well with their guts half eaten out – all be could talk about was his damned theory and how he'd known all along he was right. I tell you the man's mad.' His voice was sharp with frustration. 'I wish to God,' he said bitterly, 'I'd never come out here, never set eyes on him. And to think I worshipped the man. Yes, worshipped him. I thought he was the greatest man living.'

The bitterness in his voice . . . 'What are you going to do?' I asked him.

'Take what men I can and get the hell out of here. Do what I planned to do – without his help.' His voice had a bite to it and he slid to his feet. 'There's nothing else left for me to do – nothing that means anything, nothing useful.' He left me then and hurried down to the dark shapes sitting around the cook fires, calling to them in their own tongue, gathering them about him. And then he began to harangue them.

A little wind had sprung up and it chilled the sweat on my body. But it wasn't the drop in temperature that made me shiver. I was caught up in a situation that was beyond my control, isolated here in the desert with two men equally obsessed – the one with oil, the other with an oasis. And then Whitaker's voice close behind me: 'Grant. You've got to talk him out of it.'

I got to my feet. He was standing there, a dark silhouette against the dunes, staring down at where his son stood amongst the smoke of the fires. 'His plan is madness.'

But I'd been with David too long not to feel sympathy for him. 'He's fighting for something he believes in,' I said. 'Why don't you help him?'

'By giving him men?' His harsh, beaked face was set and stony. 'I've few enough for my purpose as it is.' And then in a softer voice: 'I had my loyalties, too. But now, with Makhmud dead, I'm free to do what perhaps I should have done in the first place. I've seen the Emir. I've sent Yousif to Sharjah with those letters to merchants there. I'm re-checking the earlier surveys. In a few days we'll spud in and start to drill. And when I've brought in the first discovery well, then all this trouble between Hadd and Saraifa will be seen in perspective, a small matter compared with the vast changes an oilfield will bring to the desert here.'

'And your son?' I asked.

He shrugged. 'As I told you before, when I thought he was dead, I'd hoped he'd follow me, a second Whitaker to carry on where I left off. Instead, I find myself cursed with an obstinate, stupid youth who's no respect for my judgment and opposes me at every turn.' He put his hand on my arm and in a surprisingly gentle voice, he said, 'Talk to him, Grant. Try and do for me what I know I can't do myself. His plan is suicidal.'

He was looking straight at me and I was shocked to see there were tears running down his cheeks – not only from the one good eye, but welling out from beneath the black patch that concealed the other. 'Do what you can,' he said softly. And then he turned quickly away and went back to his tent.

Ten minutes later David was back at my side, looking tired and drained. 'One man,' he said in a bleak voice. 'One man will come with me. That's all. Hamid's brother, bin Suleiman. And he's coming, not because he understands my plan, but simply because with him, as with Hamid, it's a blood feud now.' He gave a shrug and a quick laugh. 'Well, the fewer the better perhaps. They'll drink less water, and water is going to be our trouble.' He called to Hamid and gave the order to load the camels. 'We'll leave as soon as I've got the things I need out of Entwhistle's truck.'

I started to try and talk him out of it, but he brushed my words aside. 'My mind's made up. Talking won't change it.' And then he said, 'What about you? Are you staying here or will you come with me?' He stared at me, a long, speculative look. 'If you should decide to come with me, then I can promise to get you away to the coast with Salim as your guide.' And he added, 'If you don't come, then I think I may be throwing my life away for nothing. You're my only hope of contact with the outside world, and if the world doesn't know what I'm doing, then it's all wasted.'

I asked him what exactly he planned to do, but he wouldn't tell me the details. 'You'd have to know the ground or you might agree with my father and think it crazy. But I assure you,' he added with great conviction, 'that with any luck at all it will work. It's the last thing the Emir will be expecting, and the fact that we'll be a very small party . . .' He smiled. 'It makes it easier really – the first part at any rate. And I promise you you'll not be involved in the rest. Think it over, will you, sir? I need your help in this – desperately.' He left it like that and disappeared abruptly into the night.

I lay on the hard ground, listening to the movement of the camels, the sounds of preparation for another journey. A little wind came in puffs, sifting the sand, and it was dark. A stillness had enveloped the camp. I don't think I'm any more of a coward than the next man, but to seek out death, deliberately and in cold blood . . . You see, it never occurred to me he could succeed. I thought his father was right and that he was throwing away his life in a futile gesture. I remembered Gorde's description of Whitaker – an old man tilting at windmills. David was very like his father in some ways. I closed my eyes, thinking of Tanganyika and the hard life I'd led there, and then I felt a hand on my shoulder. 'Well?' David asked, and when I nodded almost without thinking, he passed me a rifle. 'I take it you know how to use it?' He had another which he handed to bin Suleiman and a revolver with holster and belt which he strapped to his own waist.

The stark reality of what I was doing came with the feel of the well-oiled breech under my hand. It took me back to days I thought I'd forgotten – to the deadly slopes of Monte Cassino, to Anzio and the Gothic Line. I rose quietly to my feet. Salim and Ali were loading cartons of explosive cartridges on to one of the camels. Hamid and his brother, a squat, hairy man with wild eyes and a low-browed head, were packing coils of fine wire and a contact plunger with its batteries into the saddle bags of another beast.

The camels staggered to their feet, bulking suddenly large against the overcast sky, and we were on our way.

A lone figure standing by one of the tents watched us go. It was Colonel Whitaker. He made no move to stop us, nor did he call out. We left the camp in silence and though they knew we were going, no man stirred from the camp fires. It was as though they feared to have any contact with us; it was as though we had already passed beyond the shadows of death.

Clear of the camp we turned east, working our way silently up the face of a dune in short zigzags. At the crest we stopped to mount, and then we were riding, the dark desert all around us and the swaying shapes of our camels the only movement in the stillness of night.

The clouds thinned and gradually cleared, leaving

us exposed in bright moonlight. But if the Emir had men watching Whitaker's camp, we never saw them. Dawn found us camped among sparse camel thorn on a flat gravel plain. Sharp-etched against the break of day stood the jagged tops of the mountains. Dates and coffee, and then sleep. 'We start at dusk,' David said and buried his face in his headcloth.

The withered camel thorn gave little shelter and as the sun climbed the burning vault of the sky, it became very hot. Flies worried us, clinging to the sweat of exposed flesh, and we suffered from thirst for our water bags were empty and all we had was the contents of two water bottles. We took it in turns to keep watch, but the shimmering expanse of gravel that surrounded us remained empty of life.

As the sun sank we lit a fire and had a huge meal of rice and dried meat. A bowl of warm camel's milk passed from mouth to mouth. Our four Arabs talked excitedly amongst themselves and the meal finished, they began to oil their guns, cleaning them with loving care. In contrast David and I sat silent, doing nothing. The sun set and in an instant the sky had paled. The visibility was fantastic in the dry air, everything sharp and clear, as though magnified. 'You'd better tell me what you plan to do,' I said, and my voice reflected the tension that had been growing in me all through that long, inactive day.

David was staring at the distant line of the mountains and for a moment I thought he hadn't heard my question. But then he said, 'It isn't easy to explain to somebody who has never been to Hadd.'

'I've flown over it,' I said.

He looked at me then, a sudden quickening of interest. 'Did you see the fort of Jebel al-Akhbar? Did you see how the town is backed right into the rock?' And when I explained how I'd passed close over it in Gorde's plane, he said, 'Then you know the situation. That fort is the key to Hadd. Who holds that fort holds the people of Hadd in the hollow of his hand. It's as simple as that.' He was suddenly excited, his eyes bright with the vision of what he planned to do. 'When there was trouble here before, the Trucial Oman Scouts moved into the fort and that was the end of it.'

'We're not the Trucial Oman Scouts.' I thought it was time he faced up to the facts. 'There are six of us, that's all. We're armed with rifles and nothing else. And our ammunition is limited.'

'There's ammunition for us in the fort,' he said. 'Two boxes of it and a box of grenades.' Apparently he and Khalid had found them left there by the TOS and half buried under a pile of rubble. They were out hunting as the Emir's guests and had taken refuge in the fort during a sandstorm. 'It's a long time ago now,' he added, 'but I think we'll find the boxes still there. We buried them pretty deep. As for numbers . . .' He gave a little shrug. 'One man, well armed and determined, could hold that tower for as long as his water held out.' He smiled grimly. 'Water. It always comes back to water in the desert, doesn't it?' And he slid to his feet and gave the order to move.

As we rode he pointed out the fort to me, small as

a pinhead on top of a hill that miraculously detached itself from the line of the mountains, standing clear in the last of the daylight and much nearer than I had expected. 'Dawn tomorrow,' he said, 'that's where we'll be.' He looked very much like his father as he stared at me, his youthful features set in the grimmer mould of an older man. 'God willing!' he breathed. 'And when we're there you'll understand.' He rode on then with his four Wahiba, talking with them urgently in their own tongue and leaving me to ride alone, prey to my own forebodings.

Dusk fell and merged imperceptibly into night. The stars lit our way and in no time at all it seemed, there was the Jebel al-Akhbar, a black hat of a hill bulked against the night sky. We rode slowly in a tight little bunch. The time was a little after ten. 'We'll water our camels at the well on the outskirts, fill our water bags . . .' David's voice was taut.

'And if there's a guard?' I whispered.

'We're travellers from Buraimi on our way to the coast. Bin Suleiman will explain. He's known here.'

'And after we've filled our water bags?'

'Ssh!' The camels had stopped at a signal from Hamid. We sat still as death, listening. There were rock outcrops ahead and the dim shapes of buildings. A solitary light showed high up on the slope of the hill, which now towered above us, a dark mass against the stars. Somewhere a goat bleated. There was no other sound.

A whispered word from David and we moved forward again. The well-head appeared, a simple wooden structure topping a crumbling wall of mud and stone. We dismounted and the leathern bucket was dropped into the depths. The wooden roller creaked as it was drawn up. One by one the camels were watered; one by one the skin bags filled. And all the time the wood creaked and we stood with our guns ready. But nobody came. The solitary light vanished from the slope of the hill, leaving the whole town dark as though it were a deserted ruin. Salim and Ali left with the camels and David went to work with cartridges of explosive and detonators. And when he'd mined the well, we went forward on foot, running the thin line of the wire out behind us.

The second well was close under the walls and there were camels couched near it. We could hear them stirring uneasily, could even see some of them, dark shapes against the lighter stone. A man coughed and sat up, dislodging a stone. The sound of it was magnified by the silence. And then I saw his figure coming towards us. Hamid and bin Suleiman moved to intercept. They talked together in whispers whilst David went on working and I helped him, glancing every now and then over my shoulder, expecting every moment to hear the man cry out and raise the alarm.

But nothing happened. The camels quietened down, the man went back to his interrupted sleep and David was left to complete his work in peace. He worked fast and with absolute sureness, but it all took time. It was past midnight before he had finished and a paler light above the mountains warned that the moon was rising.

As we trailed our wire towards a gap in the crumbling walls, two shots sounded far out in the desert behind us. We checked, standing there motionless and sweating. But there were no more shots. 'Somebody out hunting gazelle,' David whispered. 'They do it at night by the lights of their Land Rovers.' And we went on through the gap which led to a narrow alley. There were no doors to the buildings on either side, only window openings high up. The alley led into the market place. More camels, some goats and figures asleep against the walls of the houses. The well was on the far side. There was a baby camel there and a small boy lay curled up beside it. The camel, its coat fluffy as a kitten's, rose on straddling, spindly legs and gazed at us in amazed silence. The boy stirred, but didn't wake. A dog began to bark. I caught hold of David's arm. 'You've done enough surely,' I whispered.

'Scared?' He grinned in the darkness and shrugged me off. 'We can't climb to the fort till the moon's up.' And he squatted down in the dust and went to work. The boy suddenly sat up, staring at us round-eyed. I thought, My God! If he kills that child . . . But David said something and the boy got slowly to his feet and came hesitantly forward, gazing in fascination. David gave him the wire to hold. A man moved in the shadows by an archway. The boy's father. As he came forward, other figures stirred. A little knot of men gathered round us. But the boy sitting there in the dust beside David, helping him, made it all seem innocent. They stood and watched for a while, talking with

Hamid and bin Suleiman, and then they drifted back to their sleep.

The moon rose. The mud walls of the houses on the far side of the open place stood suddenly white, and moment by moment the dark shadow-line retreated until it touched the base of the buildings and began to creep across the ground towards us. At last David tied his mine to the well rope and lowered it down. We left then, and the boy came with us, trailing the baby camel behind him. Other figures followed us, curious but not hostile. 'They don't belong to Hadd,' David whispered. 'They're Bedou in from the desert to sell camels. Otherwise we'd never have got out of there alive.'

'What did they think we were doing?'

'I said we were testing the wells before installing pumping equipment. They know all about pumps. They've seen them in Buraimi and also in Saraifa.' By the second well we picked up the line of our wire, clipped on another coil and trailed it to the limit up the hill just outside the walls. There David fastened it to the terminals of the plunger, and then he handed it to the boy and told him what to do. 'He'll tell the story of this moment till the end of his days.' He patted the boy on the shoulder, smiling almost cheerfully as he turned and left him.

We climbed quickly, came out from the shadow of the wall on to the moonlit slope of the hill and on a rock, well above the rooftops of the highest houses, we halted. The boy was squatting there beside the detonator, his face turned towards us. David raised his hand above his head and then let it fall. The boy turned away and his shoulders hunched as he thrust down on the plunger.

The silence ceased abruptly, the stillness of the night rent by three deep, rumbling explosions that were instantly muffled and snuffed out by the collapse of the earth walls of the wells. The sound nevertheless went on, travelling back through the mountains, reverberating from face after face and gradually fading.

The boy still hadn't moved when all sound had ceased. The baby camel stood beside him. It was as though the shattering effect of the explosion had turned them both to stone. Then suddenly he was jerked to life. For an instant his face was turned towards us, white and startled in the moonlight, and then he fled screaming down the hillside, the camel breaking away in ungainly puppet strides.

FORT JEBEL AL-AKHBAR

We turned then and followed a zig-zag track that climbed by crumbling outcrops, and below us the town came to life, the sound of voices, the glimmer of lights. A shot stabbed the night, but it wasn't directed at anything in particular and we were close under the fort before the pursuit got under way. We could see them clear on the moonlit slope below us, zig-zagging up the path by which we had come. There were about a dozen of them, climbing in single file and moving fast with the agility of mountain goats.

The fort tower hung on the lip of the cliff above us, a white stone keep crumbling to decay, and where the track doubled back through a narrow defile in the rocks, David posted Hamid to guard our rear. 'I hope to God we find Salim there,' he panted. The path had steepened so that we climbed with our hands as well as our feet, rocks slipping away from under us. And then we reached the walls and the track led through a narrow opening.

We were inside the outer defences then, an open space of half an acre or more that occupied all the top of the hill. The walls had originally been about twenty feet high with a firing step round the inside, but they were now in a bad state of repair and there were few places where they were higher than ten feet. They were horse-shoe shaped, the two ends finishing abruptly at the cliff edge, the tower between them. There was no sign of the camels.

'Damn the old fool! He should have been here by now.' David's sudden uneasiness made me wonder whether perhaps Salim had taken the opportunity to desert us. But when I suggested this, he shook his head. 'Why do you think I sent Ali with him? That boy knew what these camels meant to us. No, something has happened to them.'

A shot ripped the silence apart. Hamid had opened fire on our pursuers and the sound of it echoed back from the naked rock faces that surrounded us. A scatter of shots sounded from lower down the slope and a bullet hit the wall close by us with a soft thud.

'Wait for me here. I'm going to see what's happened.' David ran quickly across the open courtyard of the fort and out through the main gate on the north side, and when he was gone, I climbed to the broken top of the wall and threw myself down beside bin Suleiman. From this vantage point we commanded the final approach to the fort.

Perched high on the edge of the sheer cliff face, I could see right down into the town of Hadd. The market square, where we'd mined the third well, was clearly visible, a white rectangle with people moving about or standing in little groups. It was not more than a thousand feet away, an easy rifle shot. And the wells outside the walls; I could see them, too. I began to understand then why David had been so sure these damaged wells would stay out of action.

Immediately below was the defile. I could see Hamid stretched out on top of one of the rock shoulders. His rifle gleamed as he raised it to his shoulder. A stab of flame, the crack of the shot, and then silence again. On the slope beyond there was now no sign of pursuit. The men who had started to follow us were pinned down amongst the rocks. It was an incredible position, impossible to take from that side so long as it was defended by men who knew how to shoot.

A bullet whined low over my head and I ducked automatically, poking my rifle forward and searching the steep slope beyond the defile. But there was nothing to fire at. The night was still and without movement.

We remained in that position for two solid hours whilst the stars moved sedately round the sky and all away to our right the desert stretched its white expanse. The sense of isolation, of a long wait for ultimate death, gradually took hold of me. It had a strange effect, a throw-back, I think, to the mood that had filled me as we lay pinned down like rats on the slopes of Monte Cassino . . . a mood compounded of fear and the desire to survive that expressed itself in the need to kill, so that when a figure moved on the slope below me, my whole being was concentrated in my trigger finger, and as he stumbled and fell my only feeling was one of elation, a deep, trembling satisfaction.

A little after three the first glimmer of dawn brought the mountains into sharp relief. A small wind whispered among the stones and it was quite chill. It was the time of night when the body is at the lowest ebb and I began to worry about David, and about our rear. By now men from the village below could surely have circled Jebel al-Akhbar to climb by the camel track to the main gate. I called to bin Suleiman and made a motion with my hand to indicate what I was going to do, and then I abandoned my position and started on a tour of the walls.

The result was encouraging. They were built on sheer rock slopes. Only on the north side was there any means of reaching the fort. There the camel track climbed steeply from the desert below to enter by the only gateway. Old palm tree timbers sagged from rusted iron hinges. This was the way attack must come if it were to succeed. Bastion towers flanked the gate on either side and from the top of one of them I could see down the whole length of the track. It was empty. So, too, were the slopes of the hill. There was no cover and nowhere could I see any sign of David or the camels.

I was turning away when my eye caught a movement on the white floor of the desert below; four shapes moving slowly, their shadows more sharply defined than the shapes themselves. They were camels moving towards the bottom of the track, and as they turned to start the climb, I made out the figure of a solitary rider on the leading camel.

I lay down then on the broken stone top of the bastion and pushed the safety catch of my rifle forward. Our camels had numbered six and with David there should have been three riders. They came on very slowly whilst the grey of dawn overlaid the moonlight and the whiteness faded out of the desert.

As the light improved and they came nearer, I saw the body of a man lying slumped over the saddle of the second camel. Skin bags bulging with water confirmed that the beasts were ours and soon after that I was able to recognize David. I met him as he rode in through the broken gateway. He didn't say anything as he dismounted, but his face looked grey. 'What happened?' I asked.

'Those shots we heard . . . They rode straight into a party of the Emir's men camped outside the town.' He asked me then whether they'd tried to rush us yet.

'No,' I said. 'They're still pinned down less than a third of the way up the slope.'

'Good. Give me a hand, will you?' He led the second camel to the foot of the tower and got it couched. The body tied with cord across its back was Ali's. 'He's badly hurt.' We laid him gently on the ground. He moaned softly, barely conscious. He'd a ghastly wound in the chest. I'd seen the effect of a soft-nosed Bedouin bullet on the metal of a Land Rover; now I was seeing its effect on human flesh and the sight appalled me. He'd a knife wound in the shoulder, too, and he'd lost a lot of blood; the dark, broad-lipped, girlish face had taken on a sickly pallor.

David stood for a moment, staring down at him. 'Poor kid,' he murmured. 'I found him lying in a pool of blood by the ashes of their camp fire. I suppose they thought he was dead. Salim's body was close beside him. They'd slit his throat.' His voice shook. 'The murdering, dung-eating bastards! Why did they have to do it? There were at least twenty of them there, twenty of them against an old man and a boy.' Apparently he'd found the camp deserted, our four camels wandering loose. 'They must have been disturbed by the sound of the explosions,' he said. 'Otherwise they wouldn't have left the camels. They only took one. It was the other that led me to their camp; it was wandering around on three legs, bellowing with pain. I had to finish it off.' He gave a quick, angry shrug as though wanting to dismiss the whole thing from his mind. 'Well, let's get him up into the tower. He can't lie here.'

He got the camel to its feet and stood it close by the wall of the tower. Standing on its back he was just able to reach the hole halfway up the tower's side. He scrambled in and from the dark interior produced a crude ladder made of palm wood. We dragged the boy up and laid him on the dirt floor and David plugged and bound the wounds again, using his headcloth which he tore in strips. 'A bloody lousy piece of luck,' he said. 'I'd planned to get you away before daylight. With Salim to guide you, you'd have been in Buraimi tomorrow, in Sharjah by the next day. I'd got it all planned. Now . . .' He shrugged. 'We'll have to do some fresh thinking.'

It was daylight now. It came filtering into the interior of the tower through the entrance hole and through four narrow slits in the thick walls. They were firing embrasures and they reminded me of the turret room I'd occupied in Saraifa. But the view was vastly different. Two of them looked out east and west, each covering an arm of the walls. The other two, close together, faced south; they looked straight down on to Hadd itself.

'Well, that's all I can do for him.' David got to his feet. 'You stay here. I must have a word with Hamid and bin Suleiman. And then we must deal with the camels.'

He left me sitting by one of the embrasures and I had time to think then. The excitement of the action that had sustained me so far was gone now. The future stared me in the face and I began to be afraid of it. However impregnable the fort's position, there were still only four of us, and right there below me was that Arab town teeming with life and utterly hostile. I could see men clustered thick in the open square and some of them were armed. It could only be a matter of time.

They had already started work on the well inside the walls. Men were being lowered into it and every now and then a bundle of stones and rubble was handed up. The sun was rising behind the mountains. The sky was crimson and all the desert flushed the colour of a rose. It looked very beautiful, so serene in the clear morning air, and the mountains standing like cut-outs painted purple.

It was just after the sun had lipped the mountain tops that David climbed back into the tower. 'They've started work on that well in the square, haven't they?'

I nodded. The little square was teeming like an ant-hill.

'What are they – townspeople or the Emir's body-guard?' He had his rifle with him and he came straight over to where I was squatting on the floor beside the embrasure.

'Both,' I said. The men working on the well were mostly stripped to the waist. But standing about, watching them, were a number of armed men, their bodies strapped about with cartridges, a band of brass that glinted in the sun; their rifles, untrammelled with silver, had the dull gleam of modern weapons.

He pushed past me, kneeling in the embrasure, steadying himself with his elbows on the sill as he brought the rifle to his shoulder and fired. The sound of the shot was very loud in that dim, confined place. 'That's one of them that won't go murdering old men and boys again.' He was trembling slightly as he sat back on his heels.

The crowd in the square was scattering. A little knot gathered in one corner, and then that, too, melted away and the square was suddenly empty. 'An occasional shot like that and they'll learn to leave it alone. In a day or two, they'll begin to understand what it's like to have the sources of water cut off, the wells dry.' He got up and set his gun against the wall.

'Not that they'll die of thirst. They're better off than the people we saw in Saraifa.' He went back down the ladder and left me staring at the empty rectangle of the sun-drenched square, littered with the baulks of timber they'd brought in to shore up the inner walls of the well. Behind me the wounded boy moaned restlessly, muttering words I couldn't understand, and when I went to him, I found his dark eyes wide open and staring, his skin dry and parched. I gave him some water and then David called to me.

He and Hamid had started unloading the camels. Bin Suleiman kept watch from the eastern wall. We worked fast, but the sun was high above the mountains before we'd humped all the stores and the last of the water skins up into the tower. 'What about the camels?' I asked as we lifted the saddles from their backs. It was already blisteringly hot, the bare rock acting as a fire-brick and throwing back the sun's heat. There was no vestige of vegetation inside the fort for them to feed on.

'I'll keep one for you. The other three will have to be slaughtered.'

They were fine beasts in the prime of life and in beautiful condition. But when I started to remonstrate, he cut me short. 'What did you imagine we were going to do with them? We've no other meat.' He stared at me angrily. 'Even the Bedou, who love camels a damn' sight more than I do, don't hesitate to kill them when they're short of food. And we're going to be short of everything before we're through.'

I stood and stared at him. Without camels, he'd have no means of retreat. He'd be trapped here . . .

'Do you reckon you could get through to Buraimi on your own?'

I hesitated. But I knew now there was no alternative for me – only death here on this pitiless hilltop. 'I could try.'

'Good. We'll keep the one you've been riding then and get you away tonight as soon as it's dark.'

Immediately after we'd breakfasted, bin Suleiman butchered the three camels, slitting their throats and letting the blood drain into a tin bowl. The carcases were then disembowelled and the meat cut into strips and hung to dry in the sun. Flies buzzed and the place smelt of blood, and yet it didn't seem unnatural. Sand and rock and the blazing sky, that boy lying in the dim interior of the tower, his breath gurgling in his throat and blood seeping on to the floor, and below us an Arab town ruled by a man consumed by a murderous greed. Death didn't seem so hateful when life itself was so cruel.

Action followed hard upon my thoughts. Hamid, from his lookout post on the very top of the tower, called down to us; men were circling the hill to the north. From the walls we watched them climb by the camel track. They were well spaced out, their guns ready in their hands. Others were coming up by the zig-zag path direct from Hadd. Lying prone on the blistering stones, we waited, holding our fire. The stillness seemed to break their nerve, for they began shooting at a range of almost three hundred yards.

The attack when it came was a senseless, ill-directed affair, men clawing their way up the last steep rock ascent to the walls without any supporting fire. We caught them in the open, unprotected, and the attack petered out almost before it had begun. They went back down the sides of the hill, taking their wounded with them and not leaving even a single sniper to harass us from the shelter of the rocks. 'It won't be as easy as that next time they come.' David's eyes had a cold, dead look, untouched by the light of battle that I'd glimpsed for a moment on bin Suleiman's broad animal face.

We had used, I suppose, no more than two or three dozen rounds, but it was sufficient to make David anxious about his ammunition. Whilst the two Wahiba kept watch, David and I lowered the ladder through a hole in the mud floor of the tower and climbed down into the black rubble-filled pit below. It was slow work, searching in the dark, for we'd nothing but our hands to dig with and after so long David wasn't at all certain where he had buried the boxes. We must have been down there at least an hour, and all the time we were scrabbling at the rubble with our hands, Ali lay delirious on the floor above. Twice Hamid's rifle cracked as he carried out David's orders and kept the wells in Hadd clear of people. Those sounds and the darkness and the feeling that at any moment we might be overwhelmed through lack of ammunition gave a sense of desperate urgency to our work.

Finally we found the boxes and hauled them through the hole to the floor above – more than a thousand rounds of ammunition and two dozen grenades. We'd barely got the boxes open when Hamid reported a Land Rover leaving the palace. We watched it from the embrasures, blaring its horn as it snaked through Hadd's crooked alleys and out through the main gates of the town. It headed south toward Saraifa and David let it go, not firing a shot. 'The sooner Sheikh Abdullah is informed of the situation here,' he said, 'the sooner his raiding force will leave Saraifa in peace.' His eyes were shining now, for this was what he'd intended. That little puff of dust trailing across the desert was the visual proof of the success of his plan.

'But what happens,' I said, 'when Sheikh Abdullah attacks us here with all his forces?'

He smiled, a flash of white teeth in the dark, lean face. 'We're not short of ammunition now.'

'But we're short of men. There are only four of us. How many do you think Sheikh Abdullah musters?' I thought it was time he faced up to the situation.

'It's not numbers that count,' he answered tersely. 'Not up here. Whoever built this fort designed it to be held by a handful of men.' And he added, 'We're bloody good shots, you see. Hamid and bin Suleiman, they're like all Bedou; they've had guns in their hands since they were kids. And me, I learned to shoot out hunting with Khalid.' He was almost grinning then. 'I tell you, man, I can hit a gazelle running with a rifle bullet – and a gazelle's a bloody sight smaller than a man. Anyway,' he added, 'no call for you to worry.

With any luck we'll get you away under cover of darkness to-night.'

'And what about you?' I asked. 'You've no camels now.'

'No.' He stared at me, a strange, sad look in his eyes. And then he gave a little shrug. 'There comes a moment in every man's life, I suppose, when his destiny catches up with him.'

Again I was conscious of his strange choice of words, the sense of fatalism. 'If you don't get out . . . if you stay here until Sheikh Abdullah's men have surrounded you . . .' What could I say to make him see sense? 'You'll die here,' I told him bluntly.

'Probably.'

We stood there, staring at each other, and I knew there was nothing I could say that would make him change his mind. He didn't care. He was filled with a burning sense of mission. It showed in his eyes and I was reminded of the word Sue had used to describe his mood – the word 'dedicated.' All the misdirected energy that had involved him in gang warfare in Cardiff docks; now it had found an outlet, a purpose, something he believed in. Death meant nothing. 'What about Hamid and bin Suleiman?' I asked. 'Will they fight with you to the end?'

'Yes,' he said. 'They've a blood feud on their hands and they want to kill.'

There was nothing more to be said then. 'If I reach Buraimi and get through to the coast, I'll inform the authorities of the situation at once.'

'Of course.' He said it with a bitter little smile so

that I was afraid he'd read my thoughts and knew I was thinking that help would arrive too late. But then he said, 'It's no good talking to the authorities, you know. They won't do anything. Much better give the story to the newspapers. I wouldn't like to die without anybody knowing what I'd tried to do.' Again that bitter little smile, and then he turned away. 'Better get some sleep now. You've a long journey and you'll need to be fresh for it.'

But sleep wasn't easy. The only place where there was any shade was the tower, and there Ali's agony of mind and body was a thin thread of sound piercing each moment of unconsciousness so that I dreamed I was listening to David's death throes, at times to my own. He died as the sun sank – a brief rattle in the throat and silence. And at that same moment David scrambled in by the entrance hole to announce that there were vehicles coming from the direction of Saraifa.

'I think Ali is dead,' I said.

He bent over the boy and then nodded. 'I should have put him out of his misery,' he said. 'Without a doctor, he hadn't a hope, poor kid.'

From the embrasures we watched a trailer of dust moving in from the desert . . . three open Land Rovers packed with men, a machine-gun mounted in the back of each vehicle. David called down to Hamid who was cooking rice over a fire and he grabbed his gun and climbed the outer wall to lie prone beside bin Suleiman. David motioned me to the other embrasure. 'Don't fire till I do. And remember, every man you hit is one less for us to deal with later.' He had dropped to his knees, his rifle ready in the slit of the embrasure.

The three Land Rovers reached the main gates and there they halted, stopped by the crowd of people who swarmed round them, all pointing and gesticulating towards us. An Arab askari in the leading Land Rover swung his machine-gun and a long burst ripped the sunset stillness. Bullets splattered against the base of the tower. The guns of the other two Land Rovers followed suit – a sound like ripping calico. Several rifles were let off.

It was a demonstration designed to restore morale. My hand trembled as I set the sights of my rifle to 500. And then David fired and I was conscious of nothing but my finger on the trigger and the third Land Rover fastened like a toy to the V of my sights. The smell of cordite singed my nostrils. Fire blossomed like a yellow flower against the dun of desert sand. Men scattered. Some fell. And in a moment there was nothing to shoot at.

One Land Rover in flames, the other two deserted; some bodies lying in the dust. Tracer bullets exploded like fireworks from the back of the burning vehicles, and almost immediately a second Land Rover caught fire as the petrol tank went up. 'I'm afraid they won't give us an opportunity like that again.' David sat back on his haunches and cleared his gun. 'It will be night attacks from now on.'

Hadd was deserted now. Not a soul to be seen anywhere, the alleyways and the square empty. The Emir's green flag hung limp above the palace; nothing stirred. Hamid went back to his cooking. The sun set and the excitement of the action ebbed away, leaving a sense of nervous exhaustion. 'You'd better leave as soon as it's dark,' David said. Dusk had fallen and we were feeding in relays. He began to brief me on the route to follow, and listening to his instructions, the lonely desolate miles of desert stretched out ahead. The embers of the fire were warm. The dark shapes of the surrounding walls gave a sense of security. I was loath to go, and yet I knew the security of those walls false, the embers probably the last fire for which they would have fuel.

He gave me dates and a bottle filled with water, sufficient to take me to the first well, and then began to saddle the camel. 'You'll be seeing Sue?'

I nodded.

'Give her my love; tell her I'll be thinking of her and of a day we spent on the Gower. She'll know what I mean.'

'She thinks you're dead,' I reminded him.

'Well, tell her I'm not – not yet, anyway.' And he laughed and slung the heavy blanket over the wooden saddle.

Ten minutes and I'd have been away. Just ten minutes, that was all I needed. But then the sound of a rifle cut the stillness of the night and a man screamed and went on screaming – a thin, high-pitched sound that had in it all that anyone could ever know of pain. Bin Suleiman shouted a warning from the east-facing wall and David let go the camel and raced to meet the attack. 'Get out now,' he called to me over his shoulder.

'Get out before it's too late.' He called something to Hamid who was posted on the far side of the fort by the main entrance gate and then the darkness had swallowed him. A stab of flame showed high up on the wall and the echo of the shot cut through the man's screams as though it had severed his vocal cords. A sudden silence followed, an unnatural stillness.

The camel, startled by the noise, had fled into the night. I found him close under the wall of the tower. Bewildered and obstinate, the wretched beast refused to move, and by the time I had coaxed him to the main gate it was too late. Firing had broken out all round us. A figure appeared at my side, gripped my arm and shouted something in Arabic. It was Hamid and he gestured towards the tower. Rocks thundered against the wooden timbers of the gate we had barricaded that afternoon. Hamid fired, working the bolt of his rifle furiously, the noise of his shots beating against my ear drums.

And then he was gone, running for the tower. I let the camel go and followed him, my gun clutched in my hands. Bin Suleiman was at the ladder ahead of me. David followed close behind as I flung myself through the hole and into the darkness beyond. As soon as we were all inside, we drew the ladder up. Bullets splattered the wall – the soft, dull thud of lead, the whine of ricochets. 'Didn't expect them to attack so soon,' David panted.

We heard the wood splinter as they broke down the gate. They were inside the walls then, vague shadows in the starlight, and we fired down on them from the embrasures. The shouts, the screams, the din of firing . . . it went on for about ten minutes, and then suddenly they were gone and the inside of the fort was empty save for half a dozen robed figures lying still or dragging themselves laboriously towards the shelter of the walls.

From the top of those walls our attackers kept up a steady fire. Bullets whistled in through the entrance hole so often that the slap of lead on the opposite wall became commonplace. They caused us no inconvenience for they struck one particular spot only and the convex curve of the wall prevented them from ricocheting. We kept a watch at one of the embrasures, but did not bother to return their fire. 'Let them waste their ammunition,' David said. 'Our turn will come when the moon rises.'

Once they misinterpreted our silence and left their positions along the outer walls. We waited until they were in the open, and as they hesitated, considering how to reach the entrance hole, we caught them in a withering fire. Our eyes, accustomed to the darkness of the tower's interior, picked them out with ease in the starlight. Very few got back to the safety of the walls or out through the gateway. And when the moon rose about an hour later, we climbed the ladder to the very top of the tower and from there we were able to pick them off as they lay exposed along the tops of the walls.

Below us Hadd lay white and clearly visible. There was great activity round all the wells. David fired one shot. That was all. The people scattered, activity ceased and in an instant the whole town appeared deserted again.

We took it in turns to sleep then, but there was no further attack and sunrise found us in command of the whole area of the fort. With no cover from which they could command our position, the Hadd forces had retired. We took the guns and ammunition from the dead and dragged the bodies outside the walls. Nobody fired on us. The hilltop was ours and the sun beat down and the rockwalls became too hot to touch. We buried Ali and retired to the shade of the tower. The camel that was to have carried me to Buraimi had disappeared. There was nothing for me to do but resign myself to the inevitable.

'How long do you think you can hold out here?' I asked.

'Until our water's gone,' David answered. 'Or until we run out of ammunition.'

'And Hadd?' I asked. 'How desperate will they become?'

He shrugged. 'There's a well in the Emir's palace, and they can always evacuate the town and camp out in the date gardens. There's plenty of water there. It's more a question of the Emir's pride. He can't afford to sit on his arse and do nothing.'

And each night we'd be a little wearier, the hours of vigilance more deadly. I closed my eyes. The heat was suffocating, the floor on which we lay as hard as iron. Sleep was impossible. The flies crawled over my face and my eyeballs felt gritty against the closed lids.

The hours dragged slowly by. We'd nothing to do but lie there and keep watch in turns.

Shortly after midday a cloud of dust moved in from the desert – men on camels riding towards Hadd from the south. It was Sheikh Abdullah's main force. They halted well beyond range of our rifles and the smoke of their cooking fires plumed up into the still air. There were more than a hundred of them, and at dusk they broke up into small groups and moved off to encircle our hill. They seemed well organized and under a central command.

It was that and the fact that they were mounted on camels that decided me. I went to where David was standing by one of the embrasures. 'I'm going to try and get out to-night,' I told him. 'Whilst it's dark, I'll get out on to the hillside and lie up and wait for a chance to take one of their camels.' And I added, 'Why don't you do the same? A quick sortie. It's better than dying here like a rat in a trap.'

'No.' The words came sharp and hard and violent. His eyes burned in their shadowed sockets, staring at me angrily as though I'd tried to tempt him. 'To be caught running away – that isn't what I want. And they'd give me a cruel death. This way . . .' Again I was conscious of that sense of mission blazing in his eyes. 'This way I'll write a page of desert history that old men will tell their sons, and I'll teach the people of Hadd a lesson they'll never forget.' And then in a quieter, less dramatic voice: 'Think you can make it, on your own?'

'I don't know,' I said. 'But it's dark and there's

bound to be a certain amount of chaos when they put in their attack.'

He nodded. 'Okay, it's worth trying. But they're Bedou. They've eyes like cats and they know the desert. And remember, the moon rises in four hours' time. If you're not away by then . . .' He left it at that and stood for a moment, watching me, as I gathered together the few things I needed – a canvas bandolier of ammunition, my rifle, the water bottle, a twist of rag containing a few dates and some pieces of dried meat. My matches and my last packet of cigarettes I left with him and also something I'd become very attached to – a little silver medallion of St. Christopher given me by a mission boy in Tanganyika after I'd saved his life. 'You're travelling a longer road than I am,' I said.

Ten minutes later I was saying goodbye to him by the splintered timbers of the main gate. When I told him I'd get help to him somehow, he laughed. It was a quiet, carefree, strangely assured sound. 'Don't worry about me. Think about yourself.' He gripped my hand. 'Good luck, sir! And thank you. You've been a very big factor in my life – a man I could always trust.' For a moment I saw his eyes, pale in the starlight, and bright now with the nervous tension that comes before a battle. And then with a quick last pressure of the hand, a muttered 'God be with you,' he pushed me gently out on to the camel track.

Behind me the timbers creaked as he closed the gate. I heard the two palm trunks with which we'd shored it up from the inside thud into position.

I started down the track then and in an instant the walls had vanished, merged with the dark shapes of the surrounding rocks. Black night engulfed me and I left the track, feeling my way down the slope, my feet stumbling amongst loose scree and broken rocks.

High overhead a thin film of cirrus cloud hid the stars. It was this that saved me, for I was lying out in the open not two hundred paces from them as they climbed to take up their positions on the north side of the fort. I kept my face down and my body glued tight to the rock against which I lay. My rifle, clutched ready in my hand, was covered by my cloak so that no gleam of metal showed, and the two grenades David had given me dug into my groin as I waited, tense and expectant, for the moment of discovery.

And then they were past and the scuff of their sandalled feet faded on the slope above me.

I lifted my head then, but all I could see was the dark hillside in my immediate vicinity. No sign of the men who had passed, no shadows moving on the edge of the darkness. I slid to my feet, found the track and went quickly down the hill. And at the bottom I walked straight into a camel. I don't know which of us was the more surprised. It had been left to graze and it stood with a tuft of withered herb hanging from its rubbery lips, staring at me in astonishment.

There were other camels; they seemed to be all round me, humped shapes in the dark, champing and belching. I seized the head rope of the one facing me, forced it down, and stepping on to its neck the way the Arabs did, I found myself sprawled across its back as it started into motion with a bellow of fear and rage. There was a guttural Arab cry. A shot rang out, the bullet whining close over my head. But the only thing I cared about at that moment was whether I could hang on, for the brute had gone straight into a gallop.

If it hadn't still been saddled I should undoubtedly have come off, but the saddle gave me something to hold on to, and after a while the crazy motion slowed and I was able to get my feet astride and by means of the head rope obtain some control. And when I finally brought the animal to a halt, there was no sound of pursuit. There was no sound of any sort. That wild, swaying gallop seemed to have carried me right out into a void.

And then, behind me, the sound of shots, carrying clear and hard on the still night air. The rip and blatter of a machine-gun. Twisting round in my saddle I saw the fire-fly flicker of the attackers' guns high up on the black bulk of Jebel al-Akhbar. Distant shouts and cries came to me faintly. More firing, and the sharper crack of small explosions. Three of them. Grenades by the sound of it. The cries faded, the fire slackened. Suddenly there was no longer any sound and I was alone again, riding across an endless dark plain, haunted by the thought of David, wondering what had happened.

The silence and the sense of space were overwhelming now; particularly when the curtain of cirrus moved away and the stars were uncovered. Then I could see the desert stretching away from me in every direction and I felt as lost as any solitary mariner floating alone in an empty sea. Far behind me the Jebel al-Akhbar lifted its dark shape above the desert's rim, for all the world like an island, and all around me were small petrified waves, an undulating dunescape that seemed to disappear into infinity.

In the darkness, without any stars to guide me, I had trusted to luck and let the camel have its head. Now I saw it had carried me westward – towards the big dunes of the Empty Quarter and Whitaker's lonely camp. I kept going, not changing my direction. It was a dangerous decision. I knew that. I'd only the one bottle of water and there were no wells where I was heading, no caravan routes to guide me, nothing but empty desert. My decision was based on the fact that Whitaker's camp was much nearer than Buraimi – and after all he was the boy's father.

I had two chances – that was all – our own camel tracks and the tracks of Whitaker's trucks. If I missed both of these, or if they had become obliterated by windblown sand, then I knew I'd never get out of the desert alive. I rode through the night without a stop, guiding myself as best I could by the stars, and when the dawn came, I turned so that the rising sun was behind my right shoulder. If my navigation was right, then I had placed myself to the south of the line between Jebel al-Akhbar and Whitaker's camp. Some time during the morning my new course should intersect the tracks made by our camels three nights back.

It was the first time I had ridden in the desert alone. The solitude was immense, the emptiness over-powering. The heat, too – it came at me in waves, so that time had no meaning. It seared my eyes and beat against the membranes of my brain. I drank sparingly from the water bottle, rinsing the tepid liquid round my mouth. A wind sprang up and small grains of sand were lifted from the gravel floor and flung in my face, a fine-ground dust that clogged nose and throat and made the simple act of swallowing an agony without any saliva. To look the desert in the face, searching for our old tracks, was like pricking needles into my eyes.

By midday I'd finished the water and still no sign of our tracks. I was trembling then, but not with the heat. I had reached the Sands and the dunes were growing bigger like an ocean's swell building up against the continental shelf. Dune followed dune and the sense of space, the feeling that this petrified world of sand went on and on without end appalled me.

A dirty scum formed in my mouth as I rode and my tongue became a swollen, leathery mass. The camel's pace was slow and reluctant. We had passed no vegetation, no sign of anything growing, and as the sun slanted to the west fear took hold of me, for I knew I was headed into a desert that was four hundred miles across. Memory plagued me with the vision of a stream I knew in the Black Mountains of Wales where the water ran over rocks brown with peat and fell tinkling to a cool translucent pool. The sun sank into a purple haze, and the sense of space, with the dark, shadowed dune crests stretched out in endless ridges ahead of me, was more terrifying than the close confinement that produces claustrophobia.

And then a chance turn of the head, a sudden glance, and there it was; a diagonal line ruled faintly across the back of a dune away to my left. I stared at it through slitted, grit-swollen eyes, afraid I was imagining it. But it was real enough – a single, scuffed-up thread scored by the feet of camels and half-obliterated by sand. In the hard gravel at the foot of the dune I counted the tracks of six camels. I had actually crossed the line of our three day old march without knowing it. If the sun had been higher I should never have seen that faint shadow line. I should have ridden on to certain death. I realized then why David had insisted on my making for Buraimi. I had been very fortunate indeed.

I headed into the sunset then, following the tracks, knowing they would lead me to Whitaker's camp. The camel seemed to know it, too, for its pace quickened.

The sun set and darkness came. I camped at the foot of a dune, not daring to go on for fear of losing the faint, intermittent line of those tracks. The desert lost its warmth immediately. I ate a few dates, but my mouth was too dry and sore to chew on the meat. Tired though I was, I couldn't sleep. The moon rose just before the dawn and I went on. The tracks became more difficult to follow; at times I lost them and had to cast about until I came upon them again. A wind was blowing and the sifting sand was covering them moment by moment. The sun rose and it was suddenly very hot.

Long before I reached Whitaker's camp, the sound of the drilling rig was borne to me on the wind. The steady hum of machinery was utterly incongruous in that empty, desolate world. One of his Bedouin guards brought me into the camp and as I slid exhausted from my camel, I saw Whitaker himself coming towards me from the rig.

I must have passed out then, for the next I knew I was lying in his tent and he was bending over me, holding a mug of water to my cracked lips. The water was warm, but its wetness cleaned my mouth, eased the swollen dryness of my tongue, and as I began to swallow, I suddenly wanted to go on drinking and drinking for my body was all dried up. But he took the mug away. 'Are you alone?' he asked. And when I nodded, he said, 'What happened? Is he dead?'

I sat up, staring at him. Something in the way he'd said it . . . But his face was in shadow and I thought I must have imagined it. 'He was alive when I left him.'

'I see. So he's still up there.' And he added, 'He'd made his gesture. He'd carried out a successful attack on the wells. Why couldn't he leave it at that?'

I started to explain about David's determination to keep the wells from being repaired, but he cut me short. 'I know all about that. I got the news from Hadd yesterday. My chap said the streets of Hadd were deserted and no man dared venture out of his house for fear of being fired at. He also said that the inhabitants had made a daylight attack on the fort and had been driven off by heavy fire.'

'There were just the four of us,' I said. And I told him how Salim had been killed at the outset and Ali fatally wounded.

'And he's alone up there now with just Hamid and his brother, bin Suleiman?' He was silent for a moment, and then he said, 'I gather the Emir sent to Saraifa for Sheikh Abdullah. Had his forces arrived before you left?' And when I nodded, he said, 'What happened? Were you there when they attacked the fort?'

'No.' And I explained how I'd got out just before the attack started. 'I don't know what happened. But if David did manage to beat off that attack, there'll be others, or else they'll just snipe at him from the rocks until they've worn him down or his water runs out.'

'So he's got himself trapped.' And then almost irritably: 'What's wrong with the boy? Does he want to die?'

'He will,' I said angrily, 'if you don't get help to him somehow.'

'I've done what I can. Yousif was just back from Sharjah and I sent him straight off with letters to Colonel George who commands the Trucial Oman Scouts and to Gorde. It's up to the authorities now. Fortunately, I don't think the Emir has any idea yet who it is holding that fort.'

It was something at least that he'd notified the authorities, and I lay back exhausted. He gave me some more water and then left me, saying he'd arrange for some food to be brought. When it came, it was a half-cold dish of rice and camel meat. I ate it slowly, feeling my strength beginning to return, and then I slept. I hadn't intended to sleep, but the food and the heat in the tent . . . I couldn't keep my eyes open.

I woke to the sound of voices speaking in English. It was almost three in the afternoon. The camp was strangely quiet. The drilling rig had stopped. I peered out of the tent. An Army officer in khaki shirt and shorts and a peaked cap was standing talking to Whitaker. There was an RAF officer there, too, and resting on the gravel beside the silent rig was a helicopter.

Whitaker saw me as I came out of the tent and called me over. 'This is Colonel George of the TOS.' He was a short, thick-set man, bouncing with energy, of a type that a Frenchman in Zanzibar had once described to me as a typical officer of the *bled*.

Small, protruding eyes stared at me curiously from beneath the peaked cap. 'I was in Buraimi when I got Whitaker's message. The RAF had loaned me a helicopter so I thought I'd fly down and see what it was all about.' His words were sharp and crisp. 'Understand young Whitaker's alive and that he's playing merry hell with our aggressive little Emir. Correct?'

I didn't answer, for I was staring past him to a strange figure walking towards us from the rig – a short, fat figure in a powder blue tropical suit that was now crumpled and dirty and sweat-stained. 'Ruffini!' I called.

He came almost running. 'Mister Grant!' He seized hold of my hand. I think he would have liked to embrace me, he seemed so pathetically glad to see somebody he knew. ''Ow are you? I 'ave been so concerned for you. When you don't return with Gorde, I am asking questions, making a damn' nuisance of myself, and nobody tell me nothing.'

'What are you doing here?' I asked.

'What is a newspaper man ever doing? Looking for a story. I go to Buraimi, by invitation of the sheikh and an Italian oil man who is there also. Then this gentleman is sent by the British authorities to remove me. They don't wish for Ruffini to be in Buraimi or anywhere else in the desert. So I am under arrest.'

'No question of arrest,' Colonel George snapped. 'I've explained to you . . .'

But Ruffini wasn't listening. 'I tell you once before, signore,' he said to me, still holding on to my hand, 'I think you are sitting on the story I want. Now I talk to some of the Bedouin 'ere and I know it is true. What is this boy doing? They say you are with him in that fort, that you come from Hadd this morning.'

I could have wished it had been a British journalist. But that wasn't so important as the fact that chance had put me in touch with the outside world. Ruffini might be prevented from filing his copy immediately, but the knowledge that sooner or later David's story would become known might stir the authorities to action.

But when I suggested this to Colonel George, he shook his head. 'I don't think you quite understand the official view.' We were back in the tent then and I'd been talking and answering questions for more than an hour. The TOS, he said, had been reinforced with Regular Army units some time back and had been standing by for more than a month, ready to move at short notice. The attack on Saraifa and the battle at the Mahdah *falaj* was just the sort of trouble their Intelligence had expected and as soon as he'd received the news he'd given the order to prepare to move. It was two nights ago. We'd everything lined up, the convoy spread out round the perimeter of Sharjah airfield and everybody ready to go. And then the Foreign Office clamped down, the Political Resident called the whole thing off.

'But why?' I asked.

'Why? Because of Cairo, Saudi, the Americans, the United Nations, world opinion.' Cairo Radio, he said, had first referred to the Hadd-Saraifa border dispute two weeks back. There were reports from Riyadh that Saudi intended to raise the matter at the next meeting of UNO.

The Political Resident came under the Foreign Office, and to the Foreign Office this wasn't just a local problem, but a small facet in the pattern of world diplomacy. Until that moment I had seen the attack upon Saraifa as it appeared to David, a personal matter; now I was being forced to stand back mentally and look at the situation as a whole, from the viewpoint of authority.

'Twenty-four hours,' Colonel George said. 'That's all we needed. In twenty-four hours we could have put paid to the Emir's little game and saved a hell of a lot of lives. I know we've no treaty obligation so far as Saraifa is concerned, but it lies within the British sphere of influence and we've certainly a moral obligation to protect them against this sort of thing.' He shrugged. 'Well, there it is. I'm just a soldier, not a politician.' He glanced at his watch and then at the RAF pilot officer. 'Time we were moving, eh?' Outside the tent, he turned to Whitaker. 'That boy of yours. He's going to get himself killed if somebody doesn't do something.' The protruding eyeballs stared. 'You've been out here a long time, Colonel. Couldn't you see the Emir; talk to your son? You must have considerable influence still.'

'A little. But not with my son it seems.' Whitaker was clearly disconcerted. 'He's acting contrary to my advice – contrary to my express orders, in fact.' He hesitated. 'Of course, if the Political Resident authorized me to negotiate a settlement of the Hadd-Saraifa border dispute, I have some influence with the Emir. But,' he added, 'a just settlement for Saraifa would almost certainly require the backing of British military forces.'

'That's out of the question at the moment.'

'Then . . .' Whitaker gave an awkward little shrug.

Colonel George grunted, a small, peremptory sound.

'Pity! That boy's got a lot of guts and he's going to die.' He started towards the helicopter, but then he stopped and faced Whitaker again. 'I've heard stories about you . . . And if half of what I've heard is true, your son's doing just the sort of thing you'd have done yourself in your younger days, eh?' He paused, and then in a harder voice: 'I'll tell you something, Whitaker; if that boy holds out for a week, he'll go down in desert history, his name remembered long after yours is forgotten.' He stared at him hard for a moment and then marched off across the gravel towards the helicopter. 'Sorry I can't give you a lift out, Grant. No room. We've got to deliver this wop journalist to Sharjah. But I've got one of my Company commanders with a wireless truck up at Buraimi. I propose to send him down to patrol Hadd's northern border and keep tabs on the situation. I'll tell him to pick you up if you like. Name's Berry. Sound chap. Understands the Bedou. That do you?'

I nodded, and behind me Whitaker said, 'You might tell him to keep an eye out for my two vehicles. My fuel tanker and the supply truck should have been in two days ago.'

The rotor blade of the helicopter began to turn. Ruffini gripped my hand. '*A rivederla*. I see the story of this David Whitaker reaches London. Don't worry. We have an arrangement with one of your newspapers.' He was sweating already as he ducked into the oven-heat of the fuselage.

Colonel George paused in the open door. 'Want to give me a message for his sister? I could send it straight down to the hospital. She'd get it this evening.'

I hesitated. 'Just tell her he's alive. That's all she needs to know at the moment.'

'I should have thought something more personal was called for.' He stared at me, playfully tapping my arm. 'Probably you don't realize it, but she's been raising hell on your account. As soon as she knew you were missing, she came straight down to Sharjah. She caught that oil chap, Gorde, just as he was boarding his plane and the story is she tore him off such a strip for abandoning you that he dropped his stick and took off without it. Since then she's been badgering the life out of me. I'll be damn' glad to be able to tell her you're safe. Well?' He cocked his eyebrow at me and grinned. 'I'll give her your love – will that do?' And without waiting for a reply he got into the helicopter and slammed the door.

Whitaker and I watched it take off, a mechanical dragonfly whirring in the clean, bright air. I turned then, conscious of the quickened beat of my pulse, the sudden desire to be alone. It was strangely heart-warming to know that somebody had been concerned about whether I got back safely or not. I walked to the steep, shadowed edge of the dunes and lay there, longing for a cigarette. The drill, so useless now without its fuel, stood like a toy, dwarfed by the dunes, the Arab crew lying about, listless with nothing to do. Whitaker had gone to his tent. The shadows lengthened and I wondered what was happening on that hilltop forty miles to the east. Was David still alive?

The answer came next day, just after Whitaker's two trucks had pulled in and the noise of their arrival had woken me from the first long, uninterrupted sleep I had enjoyed in well over a week. Everything was confusion, stores being unloaded, the rig started up, when a bullet-scarred Land Rover appeared, flying the Emir's green flag. Out of it stepped a big, portly man with very black features under a large turban. 'The Emir's secretary,' Whitaker said and went forward to greet him. A bodyguard of four askari sat silent in the back of the vehicle; wild-eyed men with greasy locks hanging to their shoulders, who fingered their weapons nervously.

Whitaker took the secretary to his tent and they remained there over an hour, talking over tinned fruit and coffee. Finally the man left, but before getting into the Land Rover, he made a long, angry speech, a harangue that was clearly intended for the whole camp.

'What did he want?' I asked as the dust of his departure finally settled and the men returned to their jobs.

'If I don't go at once to Hadd and get David out of that fort, the Emir will hold me responsible.' Whitaker's face was very pale, his whole body trembling. '*Allah akhbar!*' he muttered. 'Why did the idiot have to choose this moment, when I'd talked the Emir into agreement and had obtained the financial backing I needed? Why now?'

'He's still alive then?'

He turned his eye on me, a fixed, glassy look. 'Yes,' he said. 'He's alive. The night you left him, he beat back the attack, captured a prisoner and sent him to the Emir next day with a message. It announced who he was and the terms in which he'd vacate the fort and leave them free to repair the wells.' The terms required the Emir to declare publicly that he accepted the present borders between Hadd and Saraifa for all time, and this declaration was to be supported by a signed document to the same effect, lodged with the United Nations. David also demanded an escort of the Trucial Oman Scouts to see him and his men safely out of Hadd territory.'

But it wasn't the terms that upset Whitaker. It was the fact that David had disclosed his identity. 'Did he have to involve me?' he demanded angrily, staring towards the rig.

'I don't suppose he meant to involve you,' I said. 'You're involved by the simple fact that you're his father.'

'His father!' He turned on me. 'I took a servant girl,' he said harshly. 'A moment in time, a passing need – but that was all. It ended there and I made provision for her.'

'You can't buy immunity from your actions.'

He ignored that. 'Twenty years, and the moment catches up with me and I'm faced with the brat; a raw, undisciplined boy with a vicious background.' He glared at me. 'And you sent him out here.'

'He'd have come in any case,' I said. 'Once he knew you were his father.' I was angry myself then. 'I don't think you realize what a shock it was to him to learn that he was illegitimate – to discover that his mother had been deserted in childbirth.'

'She'd no claim on me,' he said quickly. 'And even if she had, it doesn't justify his coming out here with some idea at the back of his mind that he was going to kill me. Did you know about that? I had it all out of him shortly after he arrived – that and his criminal background and how he was wanted by the police for causing the death of that man Thomas.' And he added, 'I should have sent him packing. I should have realized the boy was bent on destroying me, on ruining all my plans.'

'You know that's not true,' I said.

'Then why did he pretend he was dead when he wasn't? And now, when the truth of my theory is within my grasp, when the thing I've been searching for all my life is here, he gets me involved in this stupid, useless demonstration of his.' He was sweating and there were little flecks of white at the corners of his mouth.

'What he's doing,' I said, 'he's doing because he's accepted the things you believed in; he made your world his own, Saraifa his home. And the background you complain of is the reason he's doing it so success-fully. He's got the Emir to withdraw his forces from Saraifa. Now is the time surely when your influence . . .'

'My influence? What influence do you think I have now? Men have been killed and that's something only blood can wipe out.' And he added, staring into the distance, 'If I'd gone with the Emir's secretary, I'd have been held hostage for David's submission – his life or mine. And when next the Emir sends an emissary, he'll come in force. That was made very plain.'

He put his hand up to his head, covering his eye as though to shut out the desert and concentrate on what was in his mind. 'It's madness,' he breathed. 'Madness. He can't achieve anything . . .'

'How do you know?' I demanded angrily. 'Ruffini has the whole story now and . . .'

'That Italian?' He let his hand fall, staring at me

in surprise. 'How can he affect the situation? The authorities are not going to take any notice of him.' He said it as though to convince himself, and then in a voice so hoarse it seemed to be torn out of him: 'He'll die up there and that'll be the end of it.' The look on his face was quite frightening. He turned and walked slowly to his tent. I didn't see him again that evening, and the next day his manner was still very strange. We hardly exchanged a word and I was glad when Captain Berry arrived.

Looking back on it, I suppose I should have tried to understand his predicament. He hadn't enough men to get David out by force and he was probably right in saying the situation had gone beyond the reach of his influence with the Emir. What I didn't realize was that I was seeing a man in the grip of events, forced to a re-assessment of his whole life and the values by which he had lived – and being driven half out of his mind in the process.

It was late afternoon when Berry got in. A lean, bony-looking Scot with fair hair and a face that was almost brick-red in the slanting sun, he brought a breath of sanity into that sultry camp, for he was from outside and not emotionally involved in what was happening forty miles to the east. He had a message for me from Colonel George picked up on his radio that morning. 'I'm to tell you that your Italian friend got his story out in time and that you're not to worry. Everything possible is being done. The Colonel has been ordered to Bahrain to report to the Political Resident in person. Oh, and he said a Nurse Thomas sent you her love and is glad to know you're safe. Okay?'

I nodded, not trusting myself to speak. For the moment I could think of nothing but that message from Sue. Captain Berry was speaking to Whitaker, something about his son showing what one determined and resolute man could achieve. He was one of those soldiers that believe action is the solution to everything. 'You must be very proud of him, sir.' Colonel Whitaker's face was without expression, but a nerve flickered along the line of his jaw and he turned away.

Berry watched him for a moment, a puzzled look on his face. 'That's a man I've always wanted to meet,' he said. 'But I'm surprised he left this to his son. After what's happened in Saraifa, I should have thought he'd have been busy raising the desert tribes. It would have solved our difficulty if he had. We might be allowed to support a desert rising against the Emir.'

'I take it,' I said, 'you'll be leaving at once.' It wasn't only that I wanted to know what had happened since I'd left Jebel al-Akhbar. I wanted to get away from that camp.

But he told me it was out of the question. They'd been driving for over twenty hours. Both the wireless truck and the Land Rover had to be serviced, the men needed sleep. He had a wireless operator with him and five levies of the TOS under a corporal. 'Leave at first light. Makes no difference, I'm afraid,' he added, seeing my impatience. 'I can't help Colonel Whitaker's son. Mine's only a watching brief. Anyway, it's no good bashing these dunes in the dark.'

He'd brought spare kit for me so that I had the luxury of a camp bed that night. And in the morning I was able to discard my Arab clothes, which by then were very filthy, and put on a clean khaki shirt and shorts. We breakfasted on bully-beef and tinned peaches, washed down with a brew of strong tea, and then we left.

Colonel Whitaker was there to see us go and as he said goodbye to me he gave me instructions that were to have considerable significance later: 'If anything happens to me, Grant, I leave you to look after my affairs. I think you know enough about me now to understand what I want done if they find oil here.' We drove off then and I remember thinking he looked a very lonely figure standing there with the clutter of the rig behind him. We went north, taking the shortest route across Hadd territory and driving fast. Keeping to the flat gravel stretches between the dunes, we were clear of Hadd's northern border by ten-thirty. We turned east then, and the going became much slower, for we were crossing the lines of the dunes.

At set times we stopped to make radio contact with TOS HQ. The only news of any importance was that Colonel George, before he left for Bahrain and therefore presumably acting on his own initiative, had ordered Berry's Company south into the desert for exercises.

Shortly after midday the dunes began to get smaller and in an area where it had rained quite recently we came upon the black tents of a Bedouin encampment, and there were camels browsing on untidy bushes of *abal*. Berry stopped and spoke with some of the men. 'Well, your chap was alive yesterday,' he said as we drove on. 'I thought they were Al Bu Shamis, but they were of the Awamir and they came up past Jebel al-Akhbar yesterday. They say they heard intermittent firing. They also told me that the people of Saraifa are beginning to return to the oasis, that two *falajes* are running again and Khalid's half-brother, Mahommed, is calling men to arms.'

It was the first indication I had that what David had done had not been done in vain.

Soon after that we became bogged down for several hours in an area of small dunes so confused that it looked like a petrified tidal race. As a result we didn't sight Jebel al-Akhbar until late afternoon. We stopped at sunset. The hill looked deceptively close in the clear still air, the colours of the rock almost mauve, the sky behind quite green. 'It's about six miles away,' Berry said, handing me his glasses. I could see the fort quite distinctly then, the tower in silhouette against the fantastic sky. Nothing moved there. No sign of life.

I was tired after the long drive and I felt depressed. Darkness fell. We had our food and after the meal Berry disappeared into the back of the truck. He wanted to hear the BBC News. It kept him in touch, he said; but what he meant was that it brought home nearer and made the desert seem less remote.

Nature's needs took me into the desert and when he called to me I didn't hear what it was he shouted, but only caught the excitement in his voice. Back at the truck I found him seated with the earphones pressed tight against his head. 'It was in the summary,' he said. And then after a while, 'Your chap's made the headlines apparently. A big story in one of the papers this morning.' He removed the earphones and switched off. 'They even got his name right and the name of the fort . . . And the Foreign Secretary is to be asked a question about it in the House tonight.' He rolled his long body over the tailboard and stood beside me. 'Funny thing,' he said. 'If it had been a soldier up there on the Jebel al-Akhbar, they'd have taken it for granted, or more probably somebody would have raised hell because the fellow had disobeyed orders. But because he's a civilian . . .' He gave a quick, derisive laugh. 'Not that it makes any difference. One newspaper story and a question in the House won't change my orders. We'll be left to sit here and watch him die. That is if he isn't dead already.'

We'd heard no sound since we'd gone into camp. The night was deathly still, not a breath of air. And Berry made it plain to me that he couldn't go any nearer. His orders were to stay in Trucial territory and in front of us stretched the invisible barrier of the Hadd border. 'You can be certain we're under observation. If I cross that border the political repercussions would be endless. As it is my Colonel's sticking his neck out sending me down here on his own authority.'

We stayed up late to listen to the last news summary from home. The item we were waiting for came towards the end. *Questioned in the House this evening about reports that a British civilian, David Whitaker, with two Arabs, was holding the fort of*

Jebel al-Akhbar in the Arabian Emirate of Hadd, the
Foreign Secretary said that the newspaper report ema-
nated from a foreign source and was almost certainly
without foundation. He added that he was having
enquiries made . . . Cairo Radio this evening accused
Britain of concentrating a large force on the Hadd
border, including armoured cars and artillery . . .

'Armoured cars and artillery!' Berry snapped the
receiver off. 'Why the hell do they repeat that sort of
nonsense?' Like most soldiers who know what the
situation is on the spot it made him contemptuous of
the organs of publicity. 'And you heard what the
Foreign Secretary said. It's all going to be hushed up.
Oil and politics; it's always the same out here in the
Middle East. For the sake of peace and quiet a petty
tyrant is going to be allowed to get away with murder.'
He jumped out of the truck and stood staring a
moment towards the Jebel al-Akhbar. Finally he gave
a little shrug. 'Care for a drink? I've got a little Scotch
left.'

I shook my head. I was wondering whether any of
the other papers would take the story up, and if so,
whether they'd make enough of it to stir up public
opinion. Only public opinion could force the Government to accept its responsibility for Saraifa and take
action; and without that David's sacrifice became
pointless. 'I think I'll turn in now,' I said. 'I'm still
very tired.'

I slept like the dead that night and in the morning
it wasn't the sun that woke me, but Berry shaking my
arm. 'Somebody's still in the fort. I heard shots just

after dawn – very faint, but definitely rifle fire. I've reported it to HQ.'

I scrambled up, sweaty from lying in my sleeping bag in the blazing sun, but even through the glasses there was nothing to be seen, just the Jebel al-Akhbar shimmering in a heat haze. Berry glanced at his watch. 'You might like to listen to what the newspapers are saying back home.'

We went into the back of the truck and switched on the radio. It was an overseas service of the BBC with a round-up of news and opinions from the national press. I don't know what I expected – what Berry expected. A few references, perhaps a leader. Instead, every newspaper had taken up the story. For almost ten minutes the thin voice of the announcer came to me through the earphones, speaking as though from another world, and giving variations on the theme of the story I had told Ruffini. David was head-line news. One I particularly remember: BORSTAL BOY HOLDS FORT FOR FOREIGN OFFICE. And another popular paper was quoted as attacking the Foreign Secretary for trying to hoodwink the public.

But the press reaction seemed to have made no impression on the official attitude. The only indication of increased interest was that radio contact with TOS HQ was every hour now on the hour. Colonel George, we learned, was back in Sharjah. Ruffini was still there. Berry's Company was in a position ten miles west of Buraimi and about a hundred miles to the north of us. The day dragged on. The sun rose until the sky was a burnished bowl, a throbbing ache to the eyes, and the

desert sand beneath our feet as hot as the lid of a
stove. Several times we heard the distant sound of
shots, but though we took it in turns to keep watch
through the glasses, we saw no movement.

We dozed between watches, ate snacks out of tins,
and waited. Water was rationed and we became thirsty.
Boredom set in. We listened to the BBC, but David
was no longer in the news. Time was running out for
him and my presence here seemed to serve no purpose.
Those occasional, intermittent shots didn't tell me
whether he was alive or dead; they only indicated that
the fort was still held. Repeatedly I tried to persuade
Berry to move forward and recce under cover of darkness. But he was absolutely adamant. 'I cross that
border with British military vehicles and God knows
where it would end.'

By the end of the day we were beginning to get on
each other's nerves. The truth was that nothing would
have pleased Berry more than to be allowed to call up
his Company and go in and settle the whole business.
In his quiet Scots way he was so tensed-up over the
situation that the battle would have been a welcome
relief. Instead of which he was tied down within sight
of the Emir's stronghold in the company of a man who
was becoming more and more irritable at the delay.

It wasn't that I didn't understand his difficulty. If
he acted on his own initiative he might plunge the
whole of Arabia into war, involve his own country and
certainly ruin his career. It was a diplomatic tightrope
that I couldn't possibly expect him to walk. But understanding his difficulty didn't help me to bear the

inaction. To have to sit there, doing nothing, whilst six miles away that boy was dying by inches . . . The heat and frustration, it nearly drove me mad.

I suppose it was the strain of the past fortnight. Berry gave me salt tablets, a large whisky and sent me to bed at dusk. At midnight he woke me to say we'd be moving at first light. 'The Colonel's finally got Bahrain to agree to my making an attempt to get him out alive. I'm to try and arrange an audience with the Emir in the morning.'

'And suppose he refuses to see you?' I asked.

'He won't. What's more he'll accept my offer to mediate.'

'You seem very confident.'

'I am. I'm offering him a way out that'll save his face. If we do what the men of his bodyguard have failed to do and get young Whitaker out of the fort, then the Emir at least gets credit for being cunning. That's something to set against the laughter of the Bedou round their desert camp fires. I take it you'd like to come with me?'

'Of course.'

He hesitated. 'I think I'd better make it clear that I could be wrong about the Emir. He hasn't a particularly savoury reputation and if he did decide to turn nasty . . .' He gave a little shrug. 'So long as you understand the position.'

Six hours later we were on the move, motoring across the flat, stony plain with the Jebel al-Akhbar growing bigger every minute until it towered above us, a grey, sugar-loaf mass against the rising sun. A

Union Jack fluttered from the Land Rover's bonnet. There were just the two of us and Berry's driver, Ismail, a tall, dark-skinned man, very neat in his khaki uniform and coloured TOS headcloth. No sound reached us above the noise of the engine. I could see no sign of movement on the hill above us.

We rounded the shoulder of Jebel al Akhbar by a dusty track and there suddenly was Hadd, yellow now in the sunshine with the Emir's green flag hanging limp above the palace and the town silent and strangely empty with the tower I had known so well perched above it on the lip of the limestone cliffs. We passed a camp of the Emir's men. Smoke spiralled blue from their cooking fires in the still morning air and they watched us curiously, wild, lank-haired men, their bodies strapped around with cartridges, their rifles slung across their shoulders. Several were wounded, the blood caked black on their bandages.

The well outside the town was as we had left it that night, the wall destroyed by the explosion and nothing done to repair it. We entered Hadd by the main gate. The streets were empty, the little square deserted. Baulks of palm timber still lay where they had been thrown down in panic beside the damaged well. 'Looks as though the population has moved out into the date gardens,' Berry said. 'Three men and they've stopped the life of this whole town dead. It's incredible.'

But looking up it wasn't quite so incredible. That tower hung right over the town. All the way to the gates of the palace we could see it perched there above us. The narrowness of the streets was no protection; it looked right down into them.

Berry's appreciation of the Emir's situation proved correct. After keeping us waiting for over an hour, he received us in a small room off one of the palace rooftops. There were armchairs in the Western style and a table on which stood an expensive German camera and some models of tanks and armoured cars. The walls were hung with finely silvered guns and pictures of the Emir driving through Hadd in a glossy American car.

The man himself was small and wiry, with a face that somehow managed to combine craftiness with great dignity; it was a long, rather cruel face, its length emphasised by the big nose and the little pointed beard glistening black with oil. His eyes were heavily made-up with *kohl*. Sheikh Abdullah was there and several other notables, including the Emir's secretary, and though I couldn't follow what was said, I was conscious of the atmosphere, which was distinctly hostile.

The audience lasted a long time, with the Emir insisting at first that Berry storm the fort with his own troops, take David prisoner, and have him shot. When he refused, the Emir launched into a harangue that was so violent that the spittle actually flew from his lips.

'I thought for a moment,' Berry said afterwards, 'that we were for it.' Threatening us, however, didn't solve the Emir's problem, which was that he was being made to look a fool before his own people and all the desert world. After a long argument he finally agreed that if we were able to persuade the defenders to evacuate the fort they would be allowed to go unmolested.

We waited whilst Sheikh Abdullah gave one of his men orders to climb the slopes of Jebel al-Akhbar under a white flag and announce a ceasefire. Berry had guessed that there were snipers posted among the rocks below the fort walls and he was taking no chances. 'The extraordinary thing is,' he said as we hurried out of the palace, 'that they're convinced there are at least a dozen men up there in the fort.'

We drove back through the silent town, out past the deserted wells and the askari encampment, and took the dusty track that led round the shoulder of the hill. We left the Land Rover at the foot of the camel track on the north side and started up on foot. The sun was high now and the heat throbbed back from the bare, scorched rock, beating up through the soles of our shoes. For a time the fort was lost behind ridges, but as we climbed higher the walls gradually came into view. There was no sign of Sheikh Abdullah's snipers, no movement on the hilltop. The air was very still, the silence and the heat appalling. It was just over five days since I had come down this very track in the dark. Five days – just over one hundred and thirty hours to be exact, and under constant attack ... It didn't seem possible that David, or any of them could still be alive. And yet Hadd was deserted and the Emir had agreed to Berry's terms. We climbed fast, hoping for the best – fearing the worst. They must be out of water by now, wounded probably, perhaps only one of them left alive.

The timbers of the main gate sagged open, splintered by the rocks that lay at the foot of the two crumbling bastions. As we climbed the last steep rise, the tower appeared, framed in the gateway, pale yellow in the sun with the shadowed opening halfway up yawning like a mouth agape. No sign of life. No sound. I called out. 'David! It's George Grant!' The rocks echoed back his name and nothing stirred. 'David!'

And then unbelievably, he answered – a hollow, croaking sound from the interior of the tower. 'I have Captain Berry of the Trucial Oman Scouts with me.' My throat was parched, my voice hoarse. 'The Emir offers you a safe conduct.' Even as I said it I wondered, the stillness and the heat beating at my nerves. Concealed amongst the rocks below us were men with rifles. How did we know they wouldn't open fire on us? The hairs at the back of my neck crawled; treachery seemed to hang in the hot air and even as David told us to come in through the open gateway, I knew we shouldn't have trusted the Emir.

The open expanse of the fort's interior was a shambles. There were the remains of fires, the tattered remnants of camels' carcases – those things I remembered. But now there were bodies of Arabs, too, lying where they had fallen, unburied and rotting, buzzing with flies. I counted nine of them; the place smelt of death, was littered with the débris of attacks beaten back. And the sun – the cauterising, sterilising sun – blazed down.

Something moved in the black mouth of the tower and the rickety ladder was thrust out of it. It fell the last few feet to the ground and David appeared, climbing stiffly and very slowly down it. At the bottom he paused as though to gather his strength together, and then he turned and faced us, standing very stiffly erect, a blood-stained strip of cloth round his right forearm and blood showing in a black patch below his left shoulder.

Berry took a tentative step forward. 'We've just seen the Emir. If you leave with us now, he's agreed to allow you to cross the border into Trucial territory unmolested.'

'And you believed him?' David started to move towards us, but then he stopped. He was swaying slightly, too weak to walk.

'He's ordered a cease-fire.'

He nodded slowly. 'That's true. I heard the order given. A man came up by the path from Hadd a little while back. He carried a white flag. But then he disappeared; went to earth amongst the rocks.' His voice was thin and very weak. 'I don't trust the bastards,' he added, coming towards us very slowly.

Close-to he looked ghastly. His eyes had gone quite yellow, the skin of his face yellow, too, and all the flesh fined away so that the cheeks were sunken, the bones staring. His body seemed smaller, dried up and shrivelled. He looked about half his normal size, completely desiccated. The death's head face, the yellow, burning eyes, the croaking voice . . . I thought he couldn't last much longer and I pleaded with him to take his chance. But he was like a man in a trance. 'Have the authorities decided to act? Will they support Saraifa?' And when we told him No, all he said was, 'They will. They will. If I hold out long enough, they'll be forced to act.' The eyes fastened on me. 'Why didn't you go to Sharjah? Why come here? This isn't what I wanted.' His voice sounded desperately tired, utterly dispirited. 'Didn't you understand? I wanted the world to know. If people at home don't know what I'm trying to do . . .'

'The people at home do know,' I said, and I told him about Ruffini and how the story had been taken up by the national press and a question asked in the House. His eyes lit up, his whole bearing suddenly changed. 'Wonderful!' he breathed. 'Wonderful!' He was standing erect now, his head up, his voice much stronger. 'Time,' he said. 'Time and a little luck. That's all I need now.'

'Time is against you,' Berry said. 'This is your last chance to get out of here alive.'

'Is it?' The dry, cracked lips produced a twisted smile. 'Do you really believe the Emir would let us get out of here alive – particularly when they see how few we are? He'd lose too much face. Anyway I'm not going. I'll stay here till I die unless the Emir agrees to my terms or the authorities make some move to safeguard Saraifa.'

'Surely to God you've done enough,' I said, and gave him the rumour we'd heard about the two *falajes* running again at Saraifa and the people returning to the oasis. Berry, more practical, said, 'How much water have you got left?'

'Not much. But it's cooler inside the tower. We're drinking very little.'

'And your two men?' Berry asked. 'Are they alive?'

'Yes, they're still alive. Hamid's very weak – a bullet through the shoulder and a splinter of rock from a ricochet in the back. Bin Suleiman's leg is smashed. But they'll both last as long as the water.'

'So you won't leave with us?'

'No.'

Berry nodded, accepting his decision as final. He seemed to understand David's attitude and he didn't attempt to reason with him. Instead, he unstrapped his web belt, slipping his water bottle from it. 'It's not much,' he said, holding it out. 'But one day could make the difference. I'll report your decision by radio to HQ as soon as I get back to my wireless truck.'

David took the water bottle and though there couldn't possibly be any moisture left in that emaciated, dried-up hull of a body, his eyes glistened for a moment. 'Thanks,' he whispered. 'I'll remember.' His thin hands were gripped tight round the bottle. 'One more day,' he breathed. 'You'll have that – I promise.' He wasn't looking at Berry or at me. He was looking upwards, to the burning vault of the sky . . . a pact with God. And on this barren, burned-rock hilltop where the air was heavy with the stink of rotting bodies, it would be an Old Testament God. 'One more day,' he whispered again in that croaking voice, and at that moment a rifle cracked.

The thud of the bullet, the scream of pain, the clatter of a gun barrel on rock – it was all on the instant and I turned to see the body of an Arab writhing on the eastern wall. It reached the edge, paused and then fell, and as it pitched, screaming, on its face, a second shot rang out.

The screams thinned to silence. The body on the ground arched, a series of violent jerks; something sounded in the throat and after that it lay still. I glanced at Berry. He hadn't moved. Nor had David. The click of metal on stone drew my eye to the top of the tower. The glint of a rifle, a thin wisp of smoke. Everything was still again; it was difficult to believe that in that instant a man had died.

'You see! That's all the treacherous bastard's safe-conduct is worth.' David gave a dry little laugh. 'You'd better get out of here whilst you still can.'

Berry hesitated, and then he nodded. He reached into his pocket and produced some field dressings and a small first-aid kit. 'Had an idea these might be required.' He handed them over and then drew himself up and gave David a formal, parade-ground salute. 'Good luck!' he said, and turned quickly.

David looked at the first-aid tin and the dressings, his eyes quite blank, his face suddenly fallen-in, the flesh tight on the bones of the skull. I could only guess what he was thinking. A few more days and if he hadn't been killed by a bullet, he'd be dead of thirst. He looked up. 'This is goodbye, sir.' He held out his hand. 'Tell my father, will you, that I hope it's a bloody good well . . . but if he lets the Emir get his hands on one penny of the royalties I'll haunt him to the grave and beyond.'

His skin was dry, the bones of the hand like an old man's bones. I stared at him, not knowing what to say, for I was sure I wouldn't see him again. He was so damned young to die – and like this, in cold blood with his eyes open, trading life for the sake of a gesture. And yet, like Berry, I didn't try and argue with him. 'Goodbye,' I said, and turned quickly before my eyes betrayed me.

At the gateway I paused and looked back. He hadn't moved. He was still standing there, quite alone and swaying slightly, all his muscles slack with weariness. We stared at each other for a second and then I went out through the gateway, and I knew if the Emir attacked again that night, it would be the end. 'What a waste!' I said to Berry, stumbling almost blindly down the track.

He looked at me. 'I don't agree.' His voice was hard and there was a ring to it as though I'd struck a chord deep down. 'If there weren't men like David Whitaker . . .' He shrugged. 'It's a big question, isn't it? Why we're born; what we do with our lives.' And he added after a pause, 'I'd like to think, given his circumstances, that I'd behave the same way.' He had loosened his pistol holster and his eyes searched the rocks as we hurried back down the track. But we saw nobody and the only sound was the heat throbbing at our temples. The Land Rover was still there with Ismail standing beside it. Treachery had gone back to its lair and high up over the fort the black speck of some carrion bird planed on the still air.

Berry had seen it, too, and as we drove off, he said, 'I give him four days. In four days I reckon he'll be dead of thirst.'

'He's weak,' I said. 'They've only got to make a determined attack now.'

But Berry shook his head. 'So long as there's one man left in that tower capable of firing a rifle or tossing a grenade they'll never take it, and Sheikh Abdullah knows it now. Only artillery or mortars could blast them out. I couldn't understand, even from your description, how three men could hold a fort against a hundred tribesmen, but now that I've seen the place . . .' He was staring back at it over his shoulder. 'I am only surprised that a civilian should have appreciated the military possibilities of it.'

'He was a gang leader in Cardiff docks before he came out to join his father in Saraifa,' I said.

He laughed. 'Well, I suppose that's as good a training as any.' And after that we drove in silence.

When we got back to the wireless truck, Berry found a message ordering him to return to Sharjah immediately. 'But why?' I said. 'You're not on Hadd territory.'

'They've got cold feet over the situation by the sound of it. My Company's been ordered back, too.' He stood staring towards Jebel al-Akhbar and there was an obstinate look on his face. 'I've given orders that we move at dawn and I've notified HQ that I'm held here the night with a damaged spring on the wireless truck. Twelve hours isn't much, but you never know. The situation could alter.'

By this simple stratagem we were still there on the border when the slanting sun showed a cloud of dust moving across the desert from the direction of Hadd. Through the glasses we counted thirty-two camels, and the riders were all armed. Berry ordered his corporal to issue additional ammunition and personally sited both the Bren guns on a low ridge. But the raiding force kept to Hadd territory, heading due west towards the Sands. 'Their objective must be Whitaker's camp,' Berry said. 'There's nothing else out there.' But he made no move to follow them. 'Colonel Whitaker will have to look after himself.'

I thought of the lone figure we'd left standing with the clutter of that drilling rig behind him. This was what he had feared, the emissary returning in force. Whitaker would go with them this time. He'd have no alternative. I wondered what would happen when he met the Emir. Would he agree to go up to the fort? And if he did, how would David react?

But that was all in the future. I watched the dust cloud until it disappeared below the rim of the horizon and then I fetched my briefcase and settled down to write a report. It was finished by the time the sun had set and darkness closing in. I gave it to Berry and he agreed to have his wireless operator transmit it to Sharjah at the next contact with HQ. The report was a long one, for it covered David's situation, our visit to the fort and the treacherous attempt on his life, and I addressed it to Ruffini. We were both civilians and I thought there was just a chance that it might be passed across to him before anyone in authority stopped it.

'If he's still there,' Berry said. The thing was sent now and we were sitting in the truck waiting for the BBC News. More questions in the House, and the Opposition had attacked the Government for refusing to grant newspaper correspondents visas for any Arabian territory except Bahrain. They were accused of trying to hush up an ugly situation.

And then, in the morning, when we picked up the BBC newspaper round-up I was staggered to find that virtually the whole national press had carried a story obviously based on the report I had sent to Ruffini. Somehow he had got it through uncensored and the result was a fantastic perversion of the facts, so colourful, so written up as to be almost unrecognizable from the sad spectacle we had witnessed; and yet it was all there, the heroic quality of David's stand magnified a thousand-fold to give jaded townspeople the best breakfast-table reading for weeks. And the story had spread from the front pages right through to the leader columns, an angry, outraged demand for Government action.

And when the last editorial flag had been waved by the BBC announcer and the last exhortation of the Government to act immediately had been read, Berry and I looked at each other in astonishment. I think we were both of us quite dazed by the violence of the reaction at home. It was only twelve hours since Berry's wireless operator had laboriously tapped out in morse my long report and in that short time David's situation had been put before the highest tribunal in the land – the British public. Moreover, something had obviously roused the press to anger – the secretive attitude of Whitehall presumably. As one paper put it: *Up to a late hour last night, despite a barrage of phone calls, nobody in authority appeared to be in a position to confirm or positively deny the story. The only comment was: 'We regard the source as highly unreliable.' This is either stupendous arrogance, or stupendous ignorance. We suspect both and we demand that the Foreign Secretary take immediate action. The country is deeply disturbed.*

On the strength of that Berry cancelled his orders to move, and within half an hour his action was confirmed. Colonel George, acting on a hunch that political decisions would now have to be reversed, and entirely on his own initiative I gathered later, had already turned Berry's Company round and ordered it to drive with all possible speed to the Hadd border. 'I'm to wait here until they arrive,' Berry said. 'By then the Colonel hopes to be here himself to take command.'

'How long before they get here?' I asked.

'If they keep going without being stopped in the dunes they'll arrive sometime after midnight, I imagine.' He started to go back to the wireless truck, but then he stopped. 'It might interest you to know that Signor Ruffini was appointed Reuters Correspondent with the full knowledge of the Political Resident yesterday afternoon. But for that very odd appointment I imagine your report would have been passed to Bahrain. In which case I've no doubt it would now be rotting in some pigeon-hole in the Residency instead of making the world's headlines.'

The official attitude was obvious. By agreeing to Reuters' request – perhaps even instigating it – they could justify their refusal to grant visas to correspondents by saying that the press already had coverage from an accredited agency correspondent, and that the very man from whom the story had originated. No doubt they took the view that as a foreigner Ruffini would be more amenable to control than a British correspondent and therefore unlikely to cause them further embarrassment. It was a little ironical that in their hurry to appoint him they had given me almost direct and immediate access to the whole of the British press.

'I am to tell you,' Berry added with a thin smile, 'that no further messages for Ruffini will be accepted through military channels. A matter of bolting the door after the horse has gone.'

'What about that raiding party headed for Whitaker's camp?' I said. I hadn't mentioned it in my report to Ruffini the previous night. 'Somebody ought to be told.'

'Already done,' he said. 'It won't be passed on to Ruffini, but the PRPG will be notified and so will Sir Philip Gorde. He's in Sharjah now.'

So that was that, and nothing to do now but wait. The day passed slowly. No sound from the direction of Jebel al-Akhbar. Not a single shot all day. The hill seemed suddenly dead. The heat was very bad. The wireless operator was on constant watch on the head-quarters waveband. We switched only once to the BBC News. A Foreign Office spokesman had stated that whilst there was no official news, there was reason to believe that press reports were substantially correct and that a young Englishman had instigated some sort of guerilla activity against the Emir of Hadd. The whole matter was under urgent review. There were rumours of reinforcements standing by in readiness to be flown to Bahrain and two destroyers had left Aden, steaming north along the Arabian coast. Cairo Radio had stepped up its propaganda offensive.

Late in the afternoon I was woken from a stifling sleep in the shadow of the W / T truck with the news that the Hadd raiding force was returning. 'And there's been no sound from the fort at all.' Berry passed me the glasses as I stood with slitted eyes gazing at a dust cloud right in the path of the sun. 'Thirty-three of them now,' he said. The dust made it difficult, but as they passed to the south of us and I could see them more distinctly, I confirmed his count. 'They must have been travelling all night and moving very fast.' The figures flickered indistinctly in the heat. 'The Emir will have picked up the Arab news,' he added. 'He'll know he hasn't much time. Had Whitaker a radio, do you know?'

'I don't think so.'

'Then he probably doesn't know what's happening at home – that the Government's being forced to take action. Oh well,' he added, 'if he goes up to the fort and his son's still alive, Colonel Whitaker will learn from him what we were able to tell him yesterday. It might make some difference.'

I thought of that scene; father and son facing each other in the shambles of that fort. Watching the Emir's force move past us, men and camels all lifted bodily off the ground by a mirage and turned into strange, distorted shapes by the heat rising from that sea of sand, I felt once again the cruelty of this desert world. It was so hard, so empty, so casual of human life – a crucible to transmute the flesh to skin and bone, the mind to something as distorted as those shapes dancing in a mirage. I had a premonition of disaster then; but not, I think, of tragedy – certainly not a tragedy quite so grim.

I watched them until they disappeared beyond the shoulder of Jebel al-Akhbar, and shortly afterwards the sun set. One more night. But there was still no news, no certainty of action. 'Better turn in and get some sleep,' Berry suggested. 'I haven't even got an ETA from the Colonel yet.'

'Will we move in the morning, do you think? David can't last out much longer.' And in the morning he might be faced with his father's desperate situation. 'For God's sake! It's got to be to-morrow.'

'You'd better pray then,' he snapped back irritably. 'For only God and the Foreign Office know what action will be taken and when.' And he added angrily, 'I don't even know whether the Colonel's order to my Company has been officially confirmed.'

I took his advice then and went to my camp bed.

But sleep was out of the question. The night was hot and very still, the stars bright. Time dragged and I dozed, to be jerked awake by the distant sound of engines. It was 0155 hours and Berry's Company was motoring in, dark shapes moving in convoy across the desert without lights. An officer reported all present and correct, but warned that the only orders he'd received were to wait for the Colonel and not to cross the border.

Orders whispered in the night, the dark trucks spewing men out on to the sand; the area of our camp was suddenly full of movement, an ant-heap settling to sleep, and a voice at my elbow said, ''Ullo Mister Grant. Is Ruffini.' His pudgy hand gripped my arm, patted my shoulder, words tumbled out of him. They had rushed him up to this Company to get him out of the way. He'd been made fabulous offers by several newspapers. 'I am lucky, eh – lucky to be a journalist and out 'ere at this minute?' But I think he was a little scared. He was certainly lonely. His knowledge of the Arabs was based on Mussolini's short-lived empire.

A bare two hours' sleep and then the dawn breaking . . . Another day, and the ant-heap stirred and came to life, little groups of men forming and re-forming, an ever-changing pattern against the blistering yellow of sand and gravel. And standing there on the rim of the desert to the south-east, the Jebel al-Akhbar – black at first against the rising sun, but soon dun-coloured and bare. No sound, no move-ment to be seen through the glasses. And the desert all around us, that was empty and silent, too.

And then that solitary shot. We were sitting under a canvas awning, rigged from the side of the headquarters truck, and drinking tea. We all heard it, a sharp, faint sound from the direction of Jebel al-Akhbar. But when we looked through the glasses, there was nothing to see, and there was no further sound; just that one isolated shot. The time was 1034.

We had no reason to regard it as any different from the other shots we had heard, though afterwards we realized the sound had been slighter. We settled down again and finished our tea, an island of men camped in a void, waiting whilst the sun climbed the brassy sky and the oven-lid of the day's heat clamped down on us, stifling all talk.

Only Ruffini was active, trotting sweating from one to the other of us, tirelessly questioning, endlessly scribbling, staring through creased-up eyes at the Jebel al-Akhbar, and then finally badgering Berry until he had given orders for his copy to be transmitted over the radio to Sharjah.

And then, just before midday, the dead stillness of the desert torn apart by the buzz-saw sound of a helicopter. It came sidling in from the north, a strange aerial insect painted for desert war, and in the instant of its settling the whole camp was suddenly changed to a single organism full of purpose. With Ruffini I stood apart on the edge of this ordered turmoil and watched the man responsible for it, surrounded by his officers, standing with his legs straddled, head thrown back – a man conscious of the dramatic quality of the moment.

Ruffini noticed it, too. 'El Colonello – 'e is going to war.'

But my attention had shifted from Colonel George. Coming towards me from the helicopter was the squat, battered figure of Philip Gorde. 'Grant.' He was leaning heavily on his stick as he faced me. 'Where's Charles Whitaker? What's happened to him?' And when I told him what we feared, he said, 'Christ Almighty man, couldn't you do something?' But then he shrugged. 'No, of course not. Bloody politicians!' he growled. 'Always too late making up their minds. Hope we're in time, that's all.' He was staring at me out of his bloodshot eyes. 'I gather he'd moved his rig up to the border. He'd started to drill, had he?'

'Yes.'

'I wish I'd known that earlier.' He looked tired, his face liverish. 'Not that I could have done anything to help him,' he added heavily. 'It's a hell of a situation. And that boy of his a bloody little hero. Doesn't he realize what he's doing to his father – or doesn't he care? God!' He was jabbing at the ground with his stick. 'Well, we'll just have to hope we get there in time,' he said again and he stumped off to talk to Colonel George.

The cluster of officers was breaking up now; voices shouting orders, men running, the whirr of starter motors, the roar of engines, a Land Rover disappearing in a cloud of dust.

'Ah, there you are, Grant.' The Colonel, neat and dapper, cool almost in the torrid heat, came towards me. 'The boy's still alive, I gather.'

'There was a shot fired . . .'

'So Berry tells me. We'll just have to hope for the best. I'm sending a small force up to take over the fort. The rest of the outfit will move direct on Hadd. Berry's gone ahead to make contact with the Emir. You and Ruffini can ride in the headquarters truck.'

The column was lining up now and ten minutes later we were on the move. 'If he is still alive, it is a great story, eh?' Ruffini said. 'You think he is still alive?'

'How the hell do I know?' But Berry had given him four days. I was pinning my hopes to that.

'Well, it don't matter – alive or dead he is a hero. And this is the biggest story I am ever writing.'

That was all Ruffini saw in it – a newspaper story, nothing more. And Gorde hating David because I hadn't had time to explain his motives. I felt suddenly sad, depressed by the thought that David's action would be misunderstood. How could you explain to men like Gorde what Khalid's death had meant to him, how he'd felt when he'd seen the people of Saraifa forced to leave the oasis?

Half an hour later the column halted. We were close under the Jebel al-Akhbar. Time passed and nothing happened. The wait seemed endless. And then suddenly the Colonel's Land Rover came roaring down the column. He had Gorde in the seat beside him. 'Jump in,' he called to me. 'Ruffini, too. The Emir has agreed to meet me at the first well.' He was in a mood of boyish elation, a reaction from nervous tension. The column was moving again now and several vehicles had swung away and were headed for the camel track on the north side of Jebel al-Akhbar.

We reached the head of the column just as it breasted the shoulder of the Jebel. There once more was Hadd, jammed against the limestone cliffs, with the Emir's palace flying the limp green flag and the fort stark against the sky above it. 'Hell!' Colonel George signalled his driver to stop and Berry's Land Rover drew up alongside. The column ground to a halt behind us. 'I don't like it,' the Colonel said. 'Too quiet.'

Between us and the crumbling walls of Hadd there wasn't a living soul; no sign of Sheikh Abdullah's askari, no vestige of the camp we'd seen two days before. Even up by the date gardens nothing moved. All the Wadi Hadd al-Akhbar, as far as the eye could strain through the glare and the mirages, was empty of human life.

'The blighter's up to something. What do you think, Berry?'

'I think we'd better be prepared for trouble, sir. I told you I didn't like the speed with which he saw me, the crafty look in his eye.'

The Colonel nodded. 'Go ahead then.'

The orders were signalled and the column fanned out across the level gravel plain, whilst we drove straight to the first well. Behind us the Bedouin Scouts leapt from their trucks and spread out over the sand – mortars and machine-guns, ammunition. And not a shot fired at us. We sat in the Land Rover, roasting by the shattered parapet of the well, and the tension mounted with the uncanny silence. Nothing stirred anywhere.

A full hour the Emir kept us waiting there in the blazing sun. He judged it nicely. A little longer and Colonel George's patience would have been exhausted. And then at last life stirred in the mud-dun town, a scattering of figures moving towards us across the flat, shelved expanse of gravel that lay between the well and the walls; old men and children – not an armed man amongst them. 'He's going to play the injured innocent,' Gorde whispered in my ear.

The old men and the children had closed around us. Some had empty drinking bowls, others goats' skins; they whined and begged for water as they had been told to do. 'My heart bleeds,' Gorde snorted with contempt. 'Ah, here he comes.'

Through the arched entrance to the town came a figure riding a white camel, riding absolutely alone – not a single retainer. 'He's clever,' the Colonel muttered. 'There isn't a desert ruler who wouldn't have regarded this as an occasion to parade his full power. And to ride a camel when he's got an almost brand new Cadillac . . .' His eyes were fixed with a puzzled frown on the solitary figure, on the slow, stately gait of that lone camel. He turned abruptly to Gorde. 'What's he got up his sleeve? Something. That Cadillac was a present from Saudi. He'd surely want to flaunt that in our faces.'

Gorde didn't say anything and we sat and waited. The crowd fell back, the clamouring ceased. The Emir rode his camel through them and sitting there in the

Land Rover I realized suddenly why he hadn't used his Cadillac. With set face and without any gesture of greeting, he rode his beast right up to us, and when he finally halted it, the supercilious head was right over us, the rubbery lips white with foam, dripping saliva on the Colonel's beret. The Emir himself towered above us, godlike against the burning sky.

It was extraordinarily effective. The man was simply dressed in spotless robes and looked much bigger, the features more impressive, the curve of the nose more marked.

He waited in silence for Colonel George to greet him. Instead the Colonel barked an order and his driver backed the Land Rover, turning it so that the bonnet faced the Emir. But it was no good. Patiently, without expression, the camel moved, resumed the same dominating position.

And then the Emir began to speak. It was an address that lasted almost a quarter of an hour. The manner of delivery was cold and restrained, but underlying the restraint was the hate that filled the man. It was there in the thin, vibrant tone of his voice, in the black gaze of his eyes, in every gesture – a bitter fury of hatred. And that bloody camel, slavering over my head, seemed the very embodiment of his master's mood.

Gorde whispered the gist of the Emir's speech to me. It followed a familiar pattern. It ignored entirely the unprovoked attack on Saraifa, the cruel intention behind the blocking of the *falajes*, the murderous slaughter of men driven to desperate action to save life and home. Instead, it dwelt at length on Hadd's territorial claims. These the Emir based on a particular period in Hadd's history, a period that went back more than five hundred years. He conveniently brushed aside all that had happened in the area since that time. He attacked the oil companies for sucking Arabia's life blood. The spittle flew from his mouth as he called them '*Nasrani* thieves, jackals of the West, Imperialist bloodsuckers.' He ignored the fact that without the companies the oil would have remained beneath the sands, that the wealth of Arabia depended on them, that the very arms he'd been given had been bought with the royalties they paid. And in attacking the oil companies, he also attacked Britain and America. 'Imperialist murderers!' he called us.

'He's coming to the point now,' Gorde muttered. The camel belched, a deep rumbling sound, that blew a fleck of froth from its lips into my lap. The Emir leaned forward, the dark, cruel face bending down towards us. '*Murderers!*' he screamed. I thought he was going to spit in our faces.

'Start the engine,' Colonel George ordered his driver. 'I'm not standing for any more of this.' He said something to the Emir. The man smiled. That smile – it was curiously excited. *I call you murderers because you come here armed to protect a murderer.* He gestured with his hands, pointing towards the fort. And when Colonel George tried to explain David's motives, the rough justice of his action in depriving the Hadd of water, the Emir silenced him. *You do not think it is murder when an Arab man is killed. What do you say if he is the murderer of a white man – one of yourselves?*

He turned, raising his body in the saddle, shouting and signalling with his hand. A closed Land Rover emerged from Hadd. The crowd, which had drawn in a tight circle round us, scattered before it, and as it roared past us a figure in Arab clothes was thrust out of the back of it, a limp rag of a figure, battered and covered in blood.

It hit the sand beside us, rolled over once and then lay sprawled face upwards in an undignified heap; and as the cloud of dust settled, I saw what it was that lay there . . . The dead body of Colonel Whitaker.

He had been shot in the face and his head was badly battered, his arms broken. His clothes were black with blood. Flies settled in a swarm and I felt suddenly sick.

You know this man? the Emir demanded. And when Colonel George nodded, the Emir explained that *Haj* Whitaker had that morning agreed to go up to the fort and reason with his son. What had happened up there he did not say. He merely gestured to the body. *This man's son has murdered my people. You say it is not murder. Look now at that which lies before you and tell me – is that murder?*

Colonel George sat there, his eyes hard, his face set. He had no answer. 'His own father!' His voice was shocked and he made no attempt to challenge the Emir's version of what had happened.

'You can't be sure,' I said.

It was Gorde who answered. 'Do you think it

would have occurred to him to have the body flung at our feet like that if Charles had been killed by one of his men?' He was staring down at the bloody figure lying in the dust, his hands clenched. Then he looked up at the Emir and demanded to know where the body had been found, and when the Emir replied that his men had picked it up at the foot of the cliffs directly below the tower, he nodded his head slowly. As far as he was concerned that settled it.

It was very hot there in the sun, yet a cold shiver ran through me. I was remembering the solitary shot we'd heard that morning, and into my mind came Mrs Thomas's words – *It was never Dafydd that was going to die.*

Colonel George was the first to recover. Ignoring the body, he dealt with the terms on which the fort would be evacuated and his forces withdrawn. And when the Emir finally agreed, he made the pre-arranged signal to his troops waiting on the Jebel al-Akhbar and withdrew his force into the desert, taking Whitaker's body with him.

Back at our old encampment we found the helicopter gone and one of the trucks belonging to the Jebel al-Akhbar detachment already returned. After interviewing the driver, Colonel George announced, 'David Whitaker is apparently still alive. The helicopter's gone up to bring him out.' He said it flatly, and behind me I heard Gorde murmur, 'God help him! He'd have been better dead.'

The helicopter took off from the fort, and when it landed they carried David to the shade of the headquarters truck awning. When I saw him, I thought for a moment it was all over. His face was relaxed, the eyes closed; the flesh, tight-drawn, was bloodless. It was a death's head, all skull and bone, and the skin like parchment. But then the eyes flicked open and he saw me. The cracked lips smiled and he tried to say something, but no words came. He was too dried-up to speak. The eyes closed again and he went into a coma.

The helicopter had also brought bin Suleiman out. He was badly wounded and very weak but he was alive. Only Hamid was dead. They brought his body down and buried it beside Colonel Whitaker's within sight of the Jebel al-Akhbar. Gorde stood with bared head and hard, frozen eyes as they laid his old friend to rest in his shallow desert grave, and Ruffini was there, sitting on the ground, his pencil moving steadily across the pages of the notebook held against his knee.

The burial over, I went to talk to him. I wanted to try and persuade him to soft-pedal the fatal news. I was thinking of Sue rather than David. The boy was a hero and the newspapers avid for news. And now the world was going to be told that he'd killed his father. I was probably the only person who could justify it, who understood the provocation. The public's reaction would be one of revulsion. Sue would be torn to bits, her life made a hell. I touched Ruffini on the shoulder. 'About Colonel Whitaker,' I said.

He paused, his face creased against the sun's glare as he glanced up at me. 'We talk about him later,' he said. And he added, 'It is fantastic, the most fantastic story I ever write. There is this boy David, who by 'imself has forced the British Government to take action. And now this man they 'ave just buried – his father who is a great figure in the desert, a sort of . . .' He clicked his fingers, searching for a name. 'It doesn't matter. What matter is that he is dead, killed by a stupid tyrant, a sort of Arabian *condottiere*, in a lousy little mud town in the desert.'

'You mean you think the Emir . . .' I checked, staring down at him.

'And for what?' he demanded, his mind concentrated on assembling the English phrases he wanted. 'He kill him to blacken his son's name, a ridiculous attempt to destroy this heroic young man. It is a tragedy, a great tragedy. And with the death of Colonel Whitaker, it is the end of an epoch in the desert, the last great Englishman in Arabia . . .' He bent his head, his pencil flying again.

I stared at him in astonishment. He'd been there. He'd understood what the Emir had said. And he didn't believe him. His story would accuse the Emir of Colonel Whitaker's murder, and because he was the only journalist here, the press would carry his version. I could only hope that the authorities would leave it at that.

Colonel George took that story with him when he left shortly afterwards in the helicopter. He also took David, and because of that Gorde was left to travel by Land Rover. I was standing beside him as the helicopter took off. He turned to me and I can still remember the rasp in his voice as he said, 'If that little bastard of Whitaker's lives, you'll have a lot to answer for.'

'How do you mean?' My mouth felt suddenly dry.

'You sent him out here, knowing he'd killed a man, knowing he was a self-dramatizing little gangster. Fellows like that don't change, and patricide is something every society abominates. He's a hero now. But when the public learns the truth . . .' He stared at me, his eyes cold and hard. 'Charles Whitaker was a man in a thousand, probably the greatest Englishman who ever made the desert his home. I've known him since I first came out to Arabia, and you can rest assured I'll see to it that the truth is known.' He turned abruptly, without giving me a chance to say anything, and I watched him as he limped across to where Berry was organising his convoy.

Colonel George had placed a Land Rover at Gorde's disposal and he left immediately, so that I had no opportunity to talk to him. And when I finally reached Sharjah, he was on his way back to England and it was already too late. David had been placed under arrest and an official statement had been issued to the press.

PART THREE

THE COURT STANDS ADJOURNED

It was the third day of the trial and David Whitaker had gone into the witness box immediately after the lunchtime recess. Counsel for the Defence had taken him through the salient points arising from my evidence with the object of showing his relationship with his father in the best possible light. Now, late in the afternoon, he had arrived at the crucial point – Colonel Whitaker's visit to Fort Jebel al-Akhbar. The packed Court was very still, every eye on the fair-haired boy standing, neat and tidy, in the box, his arm in a sling and the sun-burned face looking almost black in contrast with his light tropical suit.

'I would like the Court to have a clear picture of your situation on that particular morning.' Counsel glanced down at his papers, his hands resting lightly on the desk in front of him. 'By then you had been on the Jebel al-Akhbar seven days. Is that right?'

'Yes.'

'And there were only two of you left. Salim, Ali

and Hamid were dead; Grant had gone. There was just yourself and bin Suleiman, and you were both wounded.'

'Yes.'

'Had you been attacked during the night?'

'No, it was some days since they'd made any attempt to take the fort.'

'But you were under fire?'

'They'd got men lying out in the rocks all round the fort, but we were all right as long as we remained in the tower. They'd fire a few shots once in a while just to remind us they were there, and at night they'd move up to the walls. But they didn't bother us much. We were pretty used to them by then, you see.' Just the trace of a Welsh accent to remind the Court that this was the same boy who had run wild in Cardiff docks.

The reporters were scribbling furiously. This was the big moment and when the Court adjourned there would be a rush for the telephone to catch the daily papers before they went to press.

'On the morning in question, were there any shots fired – other than the shot that killed your father?'

'No, none.'

'Did that strike you as unusual?'

'I can't remember that I thought about it. It was some time since any shots had been fired. They were lying quiet, you see, hoping we'd think there was nobody there and get careless. But we knew the bastards were there, waiting for us.'

'So you remained inside the tower?'

'Of course. I hadn't been out of the tower since Mr Grant came up to talk to me. There wasn't any point. It was cooler there and the walls were good protection.'

'Was there any other reason you didn't leave it?'

'I tell you, man, they were lying out there waiting for us. I wasn't risking being shot at when there wasn't any point.'

'Quite so. But what I'm getting at is this: wasn't it a fact that you were too weak by then to attempt a descent from the tower?'

'Well, yes, I suppose so. Anyway, there wasn't any reason for us to be wasting what little strength we had left to no purpose.'

'Were you weak because of lack of water or lack of food – or was it because you were wounded that you hadn't the strength to leave the tower?'

'I tell you, there wasn't any point.' His tone was irritable; he didn't seem to understand what his Counsel was trying to establish.

'When had you last had any food?'

'I can't remember. We'd some dried camel meat left, but it wasn't any use to us. We couldn't swallow it. We did try and chew it, but it was very painful and in the end we didn't bother.'

'You couldn't chew because of lack of water?'

'Yes. We'd no saliva and our tongues were swollen and quite black. Our mouths were absolutely dry.'

'Had you any water left?'

'Captain Berry had given me a water bottle. We'd

finished our own supplies and now that bottle was half empty.'

'Your situation then was quite desperate.'

'Pretty desperate.'

'I want the Court to be absolutely clear about this.' Counsel paused, glancing from the Judge to the crowded press desks. 'In your opinion, how much longer do you think you could have held out? In other words' – and here he spoke slowly and with great emphasis – 'how long before you were dead of thirst?'

David shook his head. 'I can't be certain. We'd have finished the water bottle that day. If we'd been left alone we might have stayed alive a few days more.'

'You heard the evidence of Doctor Logan who saw you when you arrived in Sharjah. He said you were in such a weak condition that he didn't believe you could have lasted more than another twenty-four hours.'

David's head went up. 'That all depends on how urgently you want to stay alive, doesn't it? I'd have lasted longer than that. But not if they'd attacked us.'

Counsel seized on this. 'You say, not if they'd attacked you. Do you mean you were too weak by then to defend yourselves?'

'That's about it.'

'Could you stand?'

'I don't know. I didn't try.'

'Could you have lifted a rifle to your shoulder and fired it?'

'If they'd attacked us I expect I'd have managed somehow.'

'But you were so weak that it would have required

the urgency of an attack to give you the strength to lift even a rifle to your shoulder?'

David hesitated. 'I suppose so,' he murmured. And then in a clearer voice, 'It's difficult to explain to you people here. But everything was an effort by then. Everything,' he repeated.

'Quite so. And if you couldn't lift a rifle to your shoulder except in a moment of great urgency, then you'd hardly have had the strength to descend from the tower by that ladder and then climb back up again and pull the ladder . . .'

'Objection!' Counsel for the Prosecution was on his feet facing the Judge. 'The Defence is putting words into the witness's mouth.'

But Counsel for the Defence had made his point. 'I will re-phrase the question then.' And turning to the witness box again, he asked, 'Did you at any time on the morning in question, and before the Trucial Oman Scouts arrived to take over the fort, leave the tower for any purpose whatsoever?'

'No, sir.'

'Did you at any time attempt to lower the ladder?'

'No.'

The Court breathed an audible sigh. 'One more question before we come to the moment of the meeting with your father: Did you know that the Trucial Oman Scouts would move into the Emirate of Hadd that day? In other words, had you any reason to suppose that your ordeal was nearing its end?'

'None at all.'

'We have the evidence of Mr Grant that from their

position six miles away beyond the Hadd border they could see the fort quite clearly through field glasses. Could you see them? In other words, could you see that over a dozen vehicles had materialized at that position during the night?'

'No.'

'As far as you were concerned, nothing had altered that morning – your situation remained as desperate?'

'Yes.'

'All you knew of what was going on in the world outside was what Mr Grant had told you two days before.'

'That's right.'

Counsel paused, again consulting his papers. 'Now we come to the moment of your father's arrival at the fort. You'd no reason to expect him?'

'How could I?'

'Quite so. I suppose you've no idea what time it was when he arrived?'

David shook his head. 'My watch had stopped. I'd forgotten to wind it a few days back. All I know is the sun had been up some time.'

'Had you any warning that you were going to receive a visitor?'

'There was some shouting; an order in Arabic not to fire. It was given by a man holding a white flag. The last time that had happened was when Mr Grant came with Captain Berry.'

'That was the occasion on which a treacherous attempt had been made on your life?' And when David nodded, Counsel added, 'And on that occasion you had taken the precaution of sending bin Suleiman to the top of the tower, just in case. Did you take the same precaution this time?'

'No.'

'Why not?'

'He was unconscious.'

'And you hadn't the strength to climb up there yourself?'

'No.'

'Would you tell the Court please what happened when your father arrived.'

'Well . . .' David hesitated, his eyes glancing quickly round the courtroom. Finally he turned towards the Judge. 'I thought it was an Arab at first – one of the Emir's men. He came in by the main gate, and he was dressed in Arab clothes, you see. I didn't recognize him – my eyes weren't too good. But then he stopped just inside the gate and called me by name and said who he was.'

'Were you surprised to see him?'

David shrugged. 'He was there. That was all there was to it.' And he added, 'No, I don't think I was surprised. When you're in the state I was, you just don't register anything.'

'What happened then?'

'Well, he came to the foot of the tower and we talked.'

'What about?'

'I don't remember.'

'He wanted you to abandon the fort, didn't he?'

'At first.'

'He changed his mind then?'

'Yes.'

'What made him change his mind?'

An obstinate look had come into David's face. 'He just changed it, that's all.'

'Was that after you'd told your father that your defence of the fort had made headline news back home?'

'I don't remember.'

'You did tell him that, didn't you? You did pass on to him this information which you had obtained from Mr Grant?'

'I don't know. I expect so.'

'Was your father surprised?' And when David didn't answer, Counsel went on, 'What I want the Court to know is whether or not Colonel Whitaker knew about the newspaper stories of your exploits and the fact that there had been questions in the House. The evidence at the moment points to the fact that he couldn't have known before you told him. Would you agree?'

'I really can't say.'

'But he must have made some comment, shown some reaction?'

'I tell you, I don't remember. I wasn't in a fit state to remember details.'

'You were talking to him from one of the embrasures of the tower or from the entrance hole?'

'From the embrasure. I should have been an easier target if I'd dragged myself to the entrance hole and I was afraid of getting sniped at.'

'And the whole interview was carried on with you in that same position. You didn't move at all?'

'No.'

'Where was Colonel Whitaker?'

'Standing right below me.'

'Could you see him?'

'Yes.'

'And when the interview was ended; where did he go then?'

'I think he moved nearer to the tower, away to my right. I can't be sure, but I lost sight of him.'

'Towards the cliff-top?'

'Yes.'

'And what happened then?'

'Well, a little time passed, and then . . . then there was a shot.'

'A rifle shot or a pistol shot?'

'It was a rifle shot.'

'You're certain of that?'

'Yes.'

'And after the shot, was there any other sound?'

'Yes, a sound of falling stones. That's when I knew he'd gone over the cliff.'

'What did you do then?'

'I dragged myself to the southern embrasure, but I couldn't see directly down the cliff face so I didn't know what had happened. I tried to call out to him, but I don't think my voice made any real sound.'

Counsel leaned forward, his voice pitched low. 'You've heard a ballistics expert give it as his opinion that your father was killed by a bullet from a pistol, not a rifle.'

'It was a rifle.'

Counsel stared at him and the whole Court could see the quandary he was in. But the evidence that had gone before had to be disposed of. 'You have also heard Dr Logan's evidence. He has said that post-mortem examination strongly suggests that the shot that killed your father was fired at close range. He, too, thinks it was a pistol shot.'

'How do they know?' David said almost belligerently. 'They didn't find the bullet, did they? And they weren't there. I was, and I'm telling you it was a rifle shot.'

The Judge leaned forward. 'I would like to get this quite clear. You have said that your condition was such that you cannot remember what passed between you. You have, in fact, left the Court with the impression that your powers of perception at that time were at a very low ebb. Yet on this point of the shot, you are quite categorical. You say it was a rifle shot?'

'Yes, sir.'

'Had you a rifle in your hand?'

'No, sir. I didn't fire the shot. It was fired by one of those treacherous—'

But the Judge stopped him. 'You will kindly confine yourself to answering the questions put to you. Am I to take it that you're absolutely clear in your mind that the fatal shot was fired from a rifle and not from a pistol?'

'Yes.'

The murmur of a sigh filled the courtroom. They didn't like it. The Judge sat back, nodding to Counsel to continue. I glanced at Sue. Her face was white. She, too, felt the change of mood in the room. It was obvious that David was withholding vital evidence about what had passed between his father and himself, and he'd been altogether too determined to put the blame for his father's death on the Emir's men. I heard the man next to me whisper to his companion, 'He hasn't a hope if he goes on like this.'

Counsel stood for a moment staring down at his papers, undecided whether to pursue the matter further. Finally he lifted his head and faced the witness box again. 'Suppose we consider for a moment that you were in no fit state to be certain on this point and that it was, in fact, a pistol shot that killed your father. Had you a pistol?'

David stared at him, sullen and white-faced. 'You know I had. That ballistic chap's already given evidence that he examined it.'

'Quite. A six-chambered revolver with two rounds still left in the chambers. And you had some spare rounds loose in a leather bag. Exactly how many rounds had you fired with that weapon?'

'Just the four. I didn't use any of the spare rounds.'

'Why?'

'A rifle was more useful. I only used the revolver once. That was on the night Mr Grant left. They got pretty close then and when I'd emptied the magazine of my rifle, I used the revolver.'

'And you fired four rounds with it that night?'

'Yes.'

'I see.' Counsel paused. And then, speaking very slowly, he said, 'If we accept the medical evidence, based on Dr Logan's post-mortem following the exhumation of your father's body, and the evidence of the ballistics expert, then the possibility of your father having been killed by one of the Emir's men is ruled out entirely.' He leaned forward, staring at David. 'I want you to be quite clear on this point. There remain then only two possibilities. Either you killed your father or he killed himself.' A long pause this time. And then the question, put bluntly, 'Did Colonel Whitaker kill himself?'

'He hadn't got a rifle. He wasn't armed.'

'Are you sure? He might have had a pistol concealed under his robes.' And then Counsel put the question again, trying for the way out, pressing the issue in an attempt to give David the one chance that might save him. 'Did Colonel Whitaker shoot himself or did he not?'

David stared at him, his eyes unnaturally big in his dark face. And then his mouth opening slowly and the courtroom hushed, some sixth sense warning us all that he was about to close the door on this one hope of acquittal. And finally the words: 'I've told you before – he was killed by a rifle shot fired by one of the Emir's men.' And then turning from Counsel towards the Court, he added in a firm, clear voice, 'Does anyone imagine my father was the sort of man who'd kill himself?'

That, more than anything else, settled it in the minds of the Court, for he was voicing what everyone there felt. And after that there was nothing Counsel could really do to help him. 'The Defence rests.' He sat down abruptly and the stillness in the courtroom was absolute.

The Judge spoke then, his thin, tired voice sounding remote and detached. 'It is almost five-thirty.' He was leaning slightly forward. 'And I gather there are certain gentlemen here who have deadlines to catch.' The dry humour produced an easing of tension, a little whisper of relieved laughter. 'I intend to adjourn now until tomorrow. But before I do so I think it is my duty to address a word to the prisoner. Your Counsel has advised you to go into the witness box and you have elected so to do – rightly in my view since otherwise the Court would have no means of knowing what happened on the morning of your father's death.' The voice was warmer now, almost fatherly. 'Today you have been answering questions put to you by your own Counsel. When the Court resumes tomorrow, however, it will be the Prosecution's turn to cross-examine you, and I must warn you that he is likely to question you most closely on what passed between you and your father. The witness, Aubrey George Grant, has shown in his evidence that there was a great deal of misunderstanding, not to say friction, between the two of you. I feel it my duty to warn you, therefore, that it will greatly prejudice your case if you refuse to tell the Court what passed between you, and I would ask you to take advantage of the adjournment to consider very carefully your attitude here. Justice is dependent on the evidence of witnesses. You are now a witness. You would be wise not to withhold, from whatever motive, vital evidence.' For a moment he remained, leaning forward, staring at the prisoner. Then he picked up his gavel and rapped. 'The Court stands adjourned until ten o'clock tomorrow morning.'

The Court rose, the Judge bowed, and the rush for the doors began. Still standing in the box, David glanced slowly round the courtroom. He was sweating and he looked tired. For a brief moment his gaze rested on his sister and he gave her an uncertain, almost apologetic smile; then police guards closed round him and he was lost to view beyond the milling heads of the crowd. 'I suppose the Judge meant it kindly.' Sue's hand was on my arm and I could feel her trembling slightly. 'But David won't change his mind, and tomorrow the Prosecution will make a strong case out of his silence, won't they?' She sounded nervously exhausted, her voice tired.

'It won't look good,' I said.

'And it was a mistake, wasn't it – trying to blame it on one of the Emir's men?'

'Yes.' No point in pretending it wasn't a mistake. 'The medical evidence is against it; the ballistics expert, too . . .' We passed out into the sunlight and the humid heat of Bahrain engulfed us like a steam bath. The street was crowded with cars, packed with people, a solid mass of Bahrainis. Gorde was waiting beside his car and he called to me. 'A word with you, Grant.'

He took me aside. 'That boy's going to be convicted if somebody doesn't persuade him to talk.'

'I thought you were behind this witch-hunt,' I said angrily.

'I made a statement; but I hadn't all the facts, had I?' He stared at me accusingly as though I were to blame for that. 'Now that I've heard your evidence, seen the way he's behaving in the witness box . . .' He hesitated and then turned abruptly towards the car. 'Get in, Grant. You, too, Miss Thomas. I want to talk to you.' And as the driver nosed the car through the crowds, he turned to Sue and said, 'I think I could arrange for you to see your brother tonight.'

She gave a hopeless little shrug. 'It wouldn't do any good. I think he'd rather be convicted, you see, than have the world know that Colonel Whitaker, that legendary figure of the desert, committed suicide.' She was very near to tears and she added with a hint of wildness in her voice, 'Just because his father's dead, all David's feeling for him, the hero-worship my mother fed him when he was a kid, has returned, magnified a thousand times by the friction there was between them when he was alive. Nothing that I can say will make him change his mind. I know that.'

'I see.' Gorde didn't seem surprised. 'Then we must think of something else. Nobody's happy about the situation, least of all the authorities.' He put his hand out and his gnarled fingers rested for a moment on Sue's arm. 'Miss Thomas. Your father was a strange man. And he'd been a long time in the desert. A hell of a long time, and alone.' He spoke with surprising gentleness. 'He was a great man in his way. You should be proud of him.'

She stared at him, dry-eyed, her face white. 'Well, I'm not. I don't care about him. To me it doesn't matter a damn whether he killed himself or was killed by somebody else. He's dead. All I care about is David.'

Gorde sighed. 'Would it help you to understand him if I told you that he tried to join David in that tower – that David either couldn't or wouldn't lower the ladder to him. He actually got as far as the entrance hole but couldn't pull himself in.'

'How do you know?'

'Bin Suleiman. After he left hospital, he disappeared. I've had men scouring the desert for him ever since. They brought him in two days ago. Your brother says he was unconscious. So he was, most of the time.'

'You mean he regained consciousness?' I asked. And when Gorde nodded I thought he'd found the witness who could save David. 'Why didn't you notify David's Counsel then?'

'Because it wouldn't help. Bin Suleiman heard them talking, but he didn't know who it was David was talking to and he didn't know what they were saying. They were talking in English. And the fact that Charles climbed up to the entrance hole, which is the only material fact he can add to the evidence, would only operate against David. Bin Suleiman thought it was one of the Emir's men trying to get in and he reached for his rifle. The effort, or more probably the pain of movement, caused him to lose consciousness again so that he knows nothing of what happened after that.'

'But it's sufficient to cause you to change your mind about David's guilt,' I said. 'Why?'

'Oh, it's not that. That's only a fragment of the picture that's been building up in my mind. One of the first things I did was to send Entwhistle down to take over at Charles's camp on the Hadd border. He reported the rig gutted, the seismological truck burned out, the place deserted. He had the sense to go on to Saraifa where he had a talk with some of Charles's men. That raiding party you saw heading into the desert towards the rig attacked the camp at dawn. They came in firing their guns and when they'd got hold of Charles, the Emir's secretary had him bound to a camel and made him sit there whilst they set fire to everything. When they started back towards Hadd there wasn't a thing left that they hadn't destroyed.'

Visualizing the scene, I began to understand how desperate Whitaker's mood must have been. 'He said he had some sort of hold over the Emir,' I murmured. 'I can even remember his words; he said, 'I know that little Emir inside out'.'

'Probably he did – certainly well enough to know that the man was in a vicious mood and prepared to go to any lengths. I sent a couple of the best Bedouins we've got on the pay-roll into Hadd a month ago. They reported that when he reached Hadd the Emir gave Charles the choice – either he brought his son down from the fort, alive or dead, or he'd be taken out into the Empty Quarter and left there to die.'

'Didn't it occur to him that Whitaker might throw in his lot with his son?' I asked.

'Oh, it was more subtle than that. The Emir also thought he knew his man. That was why he ordered the destruction of the rig. He offered to finance Charles's drilling operations once his son was out of the way and the Jebel al-Akhbar in his hands. That's the story anyway.'

'But surely the Defence had a right to know—'

'Rumours,' Gorde growled. 'It wasn't evidence. Besides, how could I be sure what had happened till I knew the facts? I wanted your evidence and David Whitaker's evidence . . .' He shrugged. 'Even now I can't be sure.'

'But you think you know what happened?' Sue was leaning forward, staring at him.

'Yes, I think I know now. I think Charles realized, after talking to his son, that what he'd regarded as a useless demonstration had, in fact, a chance of succeeding. He wanted to join David then, but probably he hadn't told his son what the alternative was and David refused to lower the ladder. Charles tried to get into the tower and failed, and then he stood on the edge of the cliff looking down on to Hadd, knowing that if he went back to the Emir he'd be going to his death. It's a slow death to die of thirst, and it would serve no purpose. Whereas to die quickly, by a bullet . . . I suppose he'd been allowed to carry a pistol with him and I've no doubt he thought that a dramatic end like that—' He sighed. 'He'd nothing to live for any more – the rig destroyed, his son doing what he might have done himself. But he could still do something. He could still die. And like that, tumbling down from that cliff top, the news of his death would be spread by camel men from waterhole to waterhole. He still had a great reputation amongst the Bedou and his death would be attributed to the Emir's treachery. I suppose he thought it might provoke a desert rising against the tyrant.' He hesitated, and then he gave a little shrug. 'I'm just guessing, that's all. I knew Charles very well, and that I think was what was in his mind.' He looked at Sue then. 'That's why, Miss Thomas, I think you should be proud of your father. And he was right in a way. His death did influence the situation. If he hadn't died like that the Emir might not have agreed to Colonel George's terms. There might have been fighting and God knows where it would have ended.'

'You must tell this to the Court,' Sue said.

But he shook his head. 'It's no good, Miss Thomas. The Judge trying this case has been brought out from England. He couldn't begin to understand the sort of man Charles was – the sweep of his vision, the almost Arab subtlety of his mind. And the only absolute proof – the pistol with one bullet fired – I don't possess. My men searched the ground where his body was picked up, but they couldn't find that or anything else that has a bearing on the case. Doubtless the Emir had it destroyed since he wanted to show Charles as a defenceless man murdered by his son. No,' he said quietly. 'This is a matter for action now.' He turned and ordered the driver to head for my hotel. 'We'll drop Grant and then you'll come on with me, Miss Thomas. I'll arrange for you to see your brother to-night. When you do, give him this.' He pulled his wallet out of his pocket and removed a thick wad of East African notes. 'There'll be a message, too.' He handed the notes to Sue.

She stared at him, too startled for a moment to say anything. And then she burst out: 'I don't know what you're planning to do, Sir Philip. But whatever it is, you're not doing it for David. You're doing it because you want him back in Saraifa. You're signing a con-cession and you want to be sure you'll be drilling . . .'

'How do you know we're signing a concession?' Gorde barked in that peculiar rasping voice of his. 'Alex Erkhard knows. A few other executives, but that's all. How the devil has it got to your ears?'

'It's true then.' She turned to me, her voice tired. 'In Court, when you were giving evidence – I sat next to that girlfriend of David's. She told me. She'd got it from one of the oil men at the al-Menza Club and she said she was telling me because, if things went badly for David, I might be able to make use of it.' She glanced at Gorde and there was suddenly a glint of that irrepressible Celtic humour in her eyes. 'She thought you'd need David – alive and free.'

Gorde caught the glint and the hard, battered fea-tures relaxed in a smile. 'She sounds a clever girl. What's her name?'

'Tessa,' I said.

'And she's a hostess at the al-Menza?' He nodded. 'I'll remember that. But please understand this, Miss Thomas: Free, your brother could be very useful to us. I admit that. Arabs respect force, particularly the force of a strong and fearless personality. The Emir is afraid of him and in Saraifa he'd be worth more to us than a hundred armed men. We don't want any more trouble on that border. But I promise you this: anything I can do will be done for one reason only – because I'm satisfied now that he's innocent.'

'Of course, Sir Philip.' Sue's voice, the little smile on her lips, were tinged with irony. But I noticed also that her eyes were alight with excitement.

The car slid to a stop. We had reached my hotel. 'You get out here, Grant. I'm taking Miss Thomas on with me.' Gorde's hand gripped my arm. 'Don't try and get in touch with her tonight, and don't talk to anybody. What we've said here is between ourselves. Understand?'

I nodded and got out. The car drove off then and I went into the hotel. It was full of newspaper men; they crowded round me as soon as I entered. What did I think of David Whitaker's chances? Was he going to talk? I told them I'd no comment to make and escaped to my room. I had my dinner brought up to me, read the papers, which were full of the trial, and went to bed early.

To this day I don't know what part Gorde played in the events of that night. Sue saw David shortly after ten o'clock. She was allowed to see him alone and she said afterwards that he looked tired at first, though he was quite cheerful. She gave him the money and also Gorde's message, and after that the tiredness seemed to drop from him. The message was simply: *Bin Suleiman is in Bahrain. He and another Bedouin will be waiting by the side entrance all night.* He asked her a lot of questions then, about Gorde's attitude to him and what he thought had happened up there in the fort. And when she had answered them all, he seemed anxious for her to go, his eyes very bright, his manner tense, almost nervous.

It was hot in my room and I didn't sleep very well. My nerves were on edge and I kept worrying about Sue. And then just as it was beginning to get light I heard footsteps in the corridor outside and the door of the next room was flung open; muffled conversation and the movements of a man dressing in a hurry. I looked at my watch. It was just after four. I got dressed and went down. By then the hotel was in a ferment, reporters and camera men trying to telephone for cars, the word 'escape' on everybody's lips. Within half an hour the hotel was deserted.

I got one of the house-boys to bring me some coffee and sat over it smoking endless cigarettes, waiting, and wondering what had happened. In less than an hour the first of the newspaper men were drifting back and it was official – David had escaped. I never got the details absolutely clear. I doubt whether anyone did, for the thing was hushed up and there was no enquiry of any sort. There was a lot of talk about a force of Bedou from the desert, but that was clearly a story invented by his guards to cover themselves. The only

Arab definitely implicated was bin Suleiman, and then only because a strolling reporter happened to recognise him loitering outside the walls. FAITHFUL COMPANION RESCUES AL-AKHBAR HERO ran the headlines of that particular newspaper. But it was more subtly managed than that, though whether David bribed his guards to unlock the doors or whether it was all arranged by some outside agency I don't know. The fact is that David was able to walk out of the place and from that point it must have been very carefully organised, for when his guards raised the alarm at 0335 hours he had completely disappeared. There were rumours that he was being hidden in a rich merchant's house, that he was lying up, disguised as an Arab, in a house on Muharraq, that he had been got away in a dhow. The whole of Bahrain seethed with rumours, but nobody knew anything definite and neither Sue nor I dared go and see Tessa, who was the one person we both thought might know where he'd been taken.

The newspaper men stayed another twenty-four hours and then they were suddenly gone, like a cloud of locusts moving on, the story dead. And all Gorde would say when I went to see him was, 'I don't know anything, and I wouldn't tell you if I did. But this way it's a lot easier for everybody.' The heavy-lidded eyes stared at me. 'Tell his sister not to worry. I expect she'll hear from him in due course.'

We were married in a registry office in Cardiff four months later and when we got back from our honeymoon there was a letter waiting for us. It came in a parcel containing a silver coffee pot, very intricately worked. The letter was headed Saraifa: –

A mutual friend of ours in GODCO has sent me word that you two are getting married. Congratulations! I thought you'd both like something from Arabia as a wedding present. It should have been native work from Saraifa. But I came to the conclusion that only the best would do. The coffee pot comes from Riyadh, by courtesy of GODCO, and is as good as any Arab potentate possesses. Remember me sometimes when you use it.

The situation here has settled down. I have a small force under my command, composed mainly of men of the Wahiba and the Rashid, and the money for its upkeep is provided. All five falaj channels are running with water and we hope within about a month to have the first of the old channels back in use. The Concession agreement has provided the funds and we are running the channel right through the oasis to irrigate the camel thorn we'll be planting as a break against the sands of the Empty Quarter.

As soon as you have time, I want you both to come out here for a holiday. I think I can promise you more comfort than you had last time, and there'll be plenty for you to see. Come next winter. The weather is perfect at that time of the year. We'll have struck oil by then. And if it's all that we hope, it will be called the Whitaker Oilfield.

Not much news except that the Emir has invited Sheikh Mahommed and myself to go hawking. We shall go in force, exchange presents, and I hope live in peace thereafter. God bless you both!

> *Affectionately,*
> *'The Brother of Sheikh Khalid'*
> *(By which title I am now known)*